EMMA BLAIR OMNIBUS

Where No Man Cries
When Dreams Come True

D1188660

EMMA BLAIR OMNIBUS

Where No Man Cries
When Dreams Come True

EMMA BLAIR

A *Time Warner* Paperback

This omnibus edition first published in Great Britain by
Time Warner Paperbacks in 2002
Emma Blair Omnibus Copyright © Emma Blair 2002

Previously published separately:
Where No Man Cries first published in Great Britain in 1982 by Arrow Books
Published by Warner Books in 1997
Reprinted 1997, 1998, 2000
Copyright © Emma Blair 1982

When Dreams Come True first published in Great Britain in 1987
by Michael Joseph
Published by Sphere Books Ltd 1988
Reprinted 1990, 1991
Published by Warner Books in 1993
Reprinted 1994, 1995, 1996, 1998, 1999, 2000
Copyright © Emma Blair 1987

The moral right of the author has been asserted.

*All characters in this publication are fictitious and any
resemblance to real persons, living or dead, is purely coincidental.*

All rights reserved.
No part of this publication may be reproduced, stored in a retrieval system,
or transmitted, in any form or by any means, without the prior permission in
writing of the publisher, nor be otherwise circulated in any form of binding or
cover other than that in which it is published and without a similar condition
including this condition being imposed on the subsequent purchaser.

A CIP catalogue record for this book is available from the British Library.

ISBN 0 7515 3301 7

Printed and bound in Great Britain by
Mackays of Chatham plc, Chatham, Kent

Time Warner Paperbacks
An imprint of
Time Warner Books UK
Brettenham House
Lancaster Place
London WC2E 7EN

www.TimeWarnerBooks.co.uk

Where No Man Cries

For Ina

Part I

The Dear Green Place
1921–22

1

With a final rub of the cloth Carrie McBain finished work on the grate. Sighing with contentment she sat back on her haunches and studied her handiwork. Black-leading the fireplace had always been one of her jobs until she got married and moved out of the house. Occasionally when she was back visiting, she still did it for her mother.

The windows were open and a strong shaft of warm August sunlight was beaming into the room. There were dust motes in the air which was filled with the sweet smell of grass and the perfume given off by the wild plants growing down by the river.

Carrie ran a hand over her distended stomach. It wouldn't be long now till the baby came – a fortnight, according to the doctor.

Carefully she wiped her hands on a rag before laboriously climbing to her feet. She had a pain in her back that had been with her for several months now, but it only really gripped her if she moved suddenly.

Crossing to a window she stared out at a man fishing in the River Cart. The man's long rod flicked lazily as he waded in close to the bank.

The river had once been well known for its salmon fishing, but that had been in the days before Armstrong's had been built. Now, in 1921, the ever-growing amount of effluence pouring out from the engineering firm was slowly but inexorably choking the life out of the river.

The salmon that survived were few.

Still, Carrie thought grimly, rather a poisoned river and families with food in their bellies than fat fish and starving folk.

She sighed and massaged her stomach. The wean was kicking again. There were times when it kicked so hard a limb would protrude quite plainly.

'Are you all right in there?' Winnie, a bustling, stout woman shouted from the kitchen.

'Aye, I'm fine, Ma!' Carrie called back. It wouldn't be long now till they stopped for a cup of tea. She was looking forward to that.

Carrie was always pleased to be back in the house in Tallon Street where she'd been brought up. Not that it was a house in the proper sense, being a three-bedroomed flat three-flights up. The word 'house' was a euphemism. In Glasgow everyone lives in a house whether it's a mansion in Kelvinside or a rat-infested single end in the Gorbals.

There had been a time when the Chisholms were tenement dwellers, but Big Donald, Carrie's father, was an industrious man with an eye always open to bettering the family lot. Thanks to his efforts they had been one of the first to move into Tallon Street, superior accommodation with every apartment boasting an inside toilet and bath, when it had been built by the Corporation.

Big Donald enjoyed his drink and tobacco. The difference between him and many of his workmates was that he knew when to call a halt. Never once had Winnie gone without money for the rent or food for the table because Donald's wages had been blown in the pub. That was something of which very few working-class women in Glasgow could boast. Donald Chisholm was a formidable man. A strict disciplinarian who believed that children should be seen and not heard.

When the children were young, God help any of them foolish enough to cheek Winnie in his hearing. Retribution, in the form of his leather belt across their backsides, was swift and painful.

Yet it was this same Donald who nearly always slipped his children sweeties and other goodies along with their Saturday pennies, for he dearly loved his wife and family although it would never have entered his head to actually say so to them. Amongst Glasgow folk that just wasn't the done thing. Any man foolish enough to do so, unless totally drunk and maudlin with it, would be considered soft and a jessie.

For Donald, love was a practical thing. Something to be practised rather than talked about. When Harriet, his eldest daughter, had had the croup as a baby he had thought it the natural thing to stay up night after night helping Winnie nurse her, while continuing to go to work each morning. He belonged to a hardy breed who believed in action rather than words.

Carrie's man, John, was another out of the same mould. In the Armstrong foundry, where he worked under Donald, he was well liked and had a name as a grafter.

Carrie thought of her husband now as she watched the fisherman wade amongst the rhubarb-type plants which grew in profusion along the river bank and in the shallows. They'd been married two years and this child was their first. She was desperately hoping for a boy, sure that a male child was what John wanted. But her husband wasn't to be drawn on the subject. He would only say that if the child was born healthy then he'd be pleased well enough.

Warmth flooded through Carrie as she thought of that. Like her mother she'd been lucky enough to find herself a good man. It was a fact she well appreciated.

She was about to turn and make for the bathroom to wash her hands when she heard a key scrape in the outside lock. When the front door closed it was done gently as though the person who'd entered was a stranger to the house.

Carrie frowned when she heard her father's voice speaking in low undertones. A swift glance at the clock on the mantelpiece confirmed that it was far too early for him to be home for his dinner. It was only ten thirty, a full hour and a half before the works' hooter was due to sound the break.

Besides, if it had been dinner time, then John and her younger brother, Hugh, would have been with him. John always came to the house in Tallon Street for his midday meal on the days when she was visiting.

Something was wrong. It had to be. Fear clutched her insides as she waddled to the door. It opened and Donald entered. Winnie, looking completely stunned, was behind him.

Carrie came up short when she saw her father's grim expression.

'There's been an accident at the foundry, lass,' he said.

'Hugh?'

'No, John.'

The breath caught in her throat and the baby fluttered in her belly. She'd automatically assumed that any accident must involve Hugh. He was such a daft lad at times, and at seventeen just at an age to do something silly and get himself hurt.

But John was always so careful. It had never entered her mind that something might happen to him. 'Is he bad?' she demanded.

For a moment Donald baulked at what he had to say. Then the words came, slowly, evenly and without emphasis. 'John's dead,' he said.

Carrie felt as though she'd been punched squarely on the forehead. She staggered back, her hands coming up to clutch at the life moving within her. It was some sort of horrible joke. It had to be.

'There, there lass,' said Donald coming quickly forward and taking her in his arms. His large, work-worn hands patted her hair.

'Dead?' The word slipped from her mouth to hang suspended in the air.

'Aye,' Donald replied softly.

Winnie sobbed and stuck a fist in her mouth. Her large

bosom heaved in sympathy.

'Oh, my God!' Carrie cried, her face crumpling into a concertina of pain and tears. Her whole body shook as she clung desperately to her father.

'Let it come. Just let it all come out,' Donald soothed, wishing he'd had the presence of mind to bring a drink home with him. If anyone ever needed one it was Carrie at this moment.

'I've got to go to him,' Carrie said suddenly. She wrenched herself from her father's embrace and staggered towards the door.

'Not yet! Not until they've had a chance to sort him out a wee bit,' Donald called after her.

Carrie whirled, her eyes filled with horror. 'What happened?' she demanded harshly.

Donald was suddenly reticent. 'Never you mind for the moment,' he replied. 'There's time enough to go into that.'

'I want to know! I want to know!' she screamed. Then she flew back to her father and thumped him on the chest. 'Tell me! Tell me!'

For once in his life Donald was at a complete loss. He glanced beseechingly across at his wife.

Winnie hurried over to take Carrie by the arm. 'Get a hold of yourself now!' she said sternly. 'This is no way to carry on.'

Carrie was hysterical as she continued pounding on her father's chest with her free hand. It seemed to her that a great chasm was threatening to engulf her.

'Tell me! Tell me! Tell me!' she screeched over and over again.

Donald knew his younger daughter only too well. Having worked herself up into this state only the truth would now suffice. 'John was crushed,' he said.

Carrie froze. 'Crushed?' Then the enormity of what that meant, in a foundry context, hit her. Her eyes rolled upwards and she dropped to the floor in a dead faint.

Winnie bent to attend to her daughter, at the same time telling Donald to hurry through to the kitchen and get some water. He left the room at a run, surprisingly nimble on his feet for such a big man.

Carrie's face was clammy to touch and there were large drops of sweat on her forehead. Her skin was a dirty white with a greenish tinge to it.

Winnie was using the hem of her dress to wipe away the sweat when Carrie's eyes blinked open. 'The pain!' she groaned.

Carrie's back arched and her body convulsed.

Winnie knew immediately what was happening. Taking a deep breath, she told herself to keep calm. When Donald returned, she took the cup from him and held it to Carrie's mouth. While Carrie drank she said, 'Go downstairs and see if Mrs Cooper is at home. If she is, then ask her to come up right away. When you've done that, run for the doctor. Tell him Carrie's started having her wean.'

Donald didn't bother asking his wife if she was sure. A man used to issuing orders, he also knew how to obey them. He rose at once from his kneeling position and tore from the room.

'Do you think you can make your bed?' Winnie asked.

Carrie gritted her teeth as another violent pain wracked her insides. Her breath came in pants as she waited for the pain to subside. When it was on the retreat she nodded.

One flight down, Big Donald was hammering on Mrs Cooper's door. She was a widow who lived directly below the Chisholms along with her teenage son, Robert. Although she had a name for sticking her nose into other people's affairs, she was also considered to be a reliable, trustworthy and good neighbour when needed.

When Mrs Cooper finally answered Donald, he hurriedly explained to her why she was wanted upstairs. Before he'd finished speaking she was undoing her pinny.

With a backward shout over his shoulder that he was off for the doctor, he clattered on his way. His heavy, tackety workboots struck sparks from the stone stairs as he ran.

By this time Winnie had managed to get Carrie into bed and stripped of some of her clothes. When Mrs Cooper arrived the two of them worked Carrie's dress up over her head and slipped it off that way.

Carrie stared up at the whitewashed ceiling. There was a far-away, glazed look in her eyes indicating she was in a state of shock.

Winnie and Mrs Cooper both knew from the frequency of the contractions that the birth was imminent and were praying the doctor would arrive in time. Still, if he didn't then they'd just have to deliver the baby themselves. It wouldn't be the first time either of them had done that.

'Poor lamb,' Mrs Cooper crooned, stroking the side of Carrie's cheek.

'Crushed,' Carrie said hollowly. Tears welled in her eyes and streamed down the sides of her face on to the pillow.

Mrs Cooper was left with Carrie while Winnie boiled some water and then ransacked her linen drawer for old sheets and towels.

Carrie threw back her head and screamed, not aware that her fingers, hooked like talons, were digging into Mrs Cooper's arm.

Between contractions Carrie mumbled her dead husband's name.

Mrs Cooper's heart went out to Carrie. She knew only too well what it was like to lose your man. It was six long, lonely years since she'd lost hers.

Donald burst into the surgery and demanded to see the doctor right away. The receptionist took one look at his frantic face and scurried off down a passageway to the consulting room.

Donald gulped in air. His chest was on fire, and he felt as though he'd swallowed a mouthful of molten metal. The thought of metal brought him back to the accident and those last few seconds before the five-ton casting crushed the life out of John McBain.

He'd been at the other end of the foundry and hadn't witnessed what had happened. What he did know was that the casting, being moved by crane, had veered and yawed out of control to slam into John who had been walking along a gantry.

Death had been instantaneous.

The question was why John was up in that particular gantry in the first place. The gantry had been declared unsafe the previous week and out of bounds until it was made secure.

Donald's thoughts were interrupted by the receptionist telling him to go through to the consulting room where the doctor would see him.

Donald was slightly in awe of Dr Robertson for no other reason than the fact the man spoke with a pronounced southern English accent.

Donald stood deferentially with cap in hand while he explained what had happened at the foundry and the effect the news of this had had on Carrie.

Before Donald had finished his story Robertson had already begun packing his black bag.

Hurrying through to the waiting room, Robertson issued a stream of instructions to the receptionist and then, with Donald hard behind him, he rushed out into the street to his car.

'Get in, man!' Robertson barked as Donald hesitated, unsure of whether or not he was to accompany the doctor.

Robertson cranked the car and it immediately burst into life. Seconds later they were chugging in the direction of Tallon Street.

In Carrie's old bedroom Winnie was holding one hand and Mrs Cooper the other while Carrie screamed, her legs jerking upwards and in towards her swollen torso. Dilation was already well advanced.

Winnie heard the rattle of a key in the outside lock and breathed a sigh of relief when, seconds later, she heard Robertson's cultured tones.

'It's yourself then, doctor,' Winnie said gratefully as

Robertson breezed into the room.

Behind Robertson's back, Winnie and Mrs Cooper exchanged glances. Although unspoken between them, they both knew something was wrong with Carrie's labour.

Donald had hung back in the hallway where he now lit a cigarette. This would be his station until it was all over. Here he would be on hand should they need him to do anything.

Robertson washed his hands in a steaming bowl of water provided for that purpose. Above the well-trimmed military moustache the keen, darting eyes were taking everything in. He had already noted that although trying to appear to the contrary, both Winnie and Mrs Cooper were uneasy about something.

'Now then, Carrie,' he said in his best bedside manner, 'let's just see what's what.' He sat on the edge of the bed and began to probe carefully with his fingers.

Carrie lay with her eyes closed. In her mind what she was seeing was a day not long before she and John had been married when he'd taken part in the all Glasgow tug-of-war championships. She'd been there cheering him on as his team, representing Armstrong's, had fought a valiant final contest with the City of Glasgow Police.

In the end the Armstrong team, amidst much shouting and general hullabalooing, had finally managed to pull their opponents over the line to win the match and championship.

The winners had received medals, silver inlaid with red and white enamel and topped by a scroll, which had later been inscribed with each of their names on the back.

John's medal was in the top drawer of the sideboard in McLellan Street: it was taken out every so often and polished. John was fond of saying it was the only thing he'd ever won. Now he'd never win anything else.

Carrie sobbed and a lump rose in her throat. Then the pain was back and there was no time to think of medals or anything else except the terrible, searing agony doing its damndest to split her in two.

Robertson was a worried man. His probing had confirmed that there were complications with the impending birth, a fact that had not been evident when he'd last examined Carrie a few weeks previously.

The baby's head, upon entering the pelvis, had failed to rotate through the required 180 degress, resulting in it now being in what was known as a persistent posterior position. He knew that if the birth went ahead this way he'd lose the baby for sure and probably Carrie as well.

As he wiped his hands on a towel, he was only too aware of the older women's eyes on him. He smiled and nodded reassuringly. Then, bending again over Carrie, he desperately cudgelled his brains for a way to remedy or at least help the situation.

Miracles do still happen, and that day one happened for Carrie McBain. Minutes before the baby started to emerge, its head suddenly rotated into the right position.

The first Robertson knew of his was when the head had appeared sufficiently for him to see that the forehead was facing downwards. He was suddenly bathed in warm, sticky sweat as he awaited further developments.

'Oh, Christ!' Carrie moaned. A trickle of bright red blood spilled from a corner of her mouth, the result of her having bitten her tongue during a particularly violent contraction.

'You're doing fine,' Winnie said.

'Just keep pushing,' Mrs Cooper added.

The baby's face slid fully into view and, as it did so, it turned sideways so that it was facing to the left.

Robertson heaved a sigh of relief. Everything was now normal.

The baby's face was a bright blue colour which, together with the black hair lying plastered to its head, was smeared with a white cheesy substance known as vernix. The face, screwed up in an angry grimace, also bore streaks of blood.

Carrie's body suddenly relaxed and she sucked in breath after breath. 'Is it over?' she asked in a thin, strained voice.

'Not quite,' Robertson replied. But you're half way there.'

The contractions started again almost immediately. Carrie's body seemed to explode from the inside as first one and then the other of the baby's shoulders emerged.

Her fingernails raked the bedsheet. The pain was now almost unbearable, and she felt that at any moment she was going to slip into the blessed relief of unconsciousness.

Not yet. Not yet, she told herself, over and over again. She wanted the baby fully born before she allowed herself the luxury of oblivion.

It crossed her mind then she might be dying. It seemed to her there was a warm blackness beckoning, and if she only allowed herself to be embraced by this all--enveloping calm she would never again waken in the world she knew. It would be so easy to slip over. John was waiting for her after all. They would be together again, this time for eternity.

The baby, a voice seemed to whisper in her ear, don't forget about the wee one. It'll need someone to look after it. Don't leave it all alone like John once was. He'd be furious to think you even contemplated the idea.

'Push Carrie! Push!' Robertson thundered.

Carrie grunted and did her best to obey, but the message being sent so urgently by her brain didn't seem to be getting through to her body.

Winnie wiped a fresh trickle of blood from the side of Carrie's mouth, while in her mind she relived the four births she'd undergone herself.

In the hallway Donald turned to face the outside door when it opened to admit Hugh. The boy's face was haggard underneath the dirt from the foundry. His brother-in-law was the first man he'd ever seen killed.

'Well?' Donald demanded quietly.

'The undertakers came and took him away. They want

to know whether he's to stay at their place or go up in a coffin to McLellan Street.'

Donald ran a hand over his face. This decision wasn't his to make. Only Carrie should decide what was to be done. That was her right.

Hugh jerked a thumb towards the bedroom. 'What's going on in there?'

In a low voice Donald told his son about the shock of John's death bringing on the baby. Hugh paled when a fresh bout of screaming rent the air.

Gratefully Hugh accepted a Willy Woodbine from his father and lit up. As he smoked he thought of the mangled mess which only that morning had been John McBain. In a macabre way it had fascinated him to discover the human body contained so much blood. The area round the gantry where the accident had taken place had been awash with the stuff. The body itself bore no resemblance to what it had once been.

The shock of seeing John's remains had been overwhelming, and for a few terrible minutes he'd thought he was going to throw up. Not that anyone would have blamed him if he had.

It amazed him to realize he was hungry. Death and birth might be all around him, but it certainly hadn't affected his stomach any. He wondered if he should sneak into the kitchen and make himself a jam piece. One thing was certain: there wasn't going to be any dinner that day.

'Do you think I should go and get Harriet?' he asked. His elder sister worked as a machinist in a clothing factory about half a mile away. Carrie had also worked there before having to leave because of her advancing pregnancy.

Big Donald shook his head. There was no point in taking the lassie away from her work when there were already enough people on hand. Besides, Harriet was naturally squeamish about certain things and would probably have ended up being more of a hindrance than a help.

In the bedroom Carrie gave a long drawn-out sigh as her body completed the ejection. The baby, large and raw-looking, slid neatly into Robertson's waiting hands.

Winnie craned forward. 'It's a wee boy!' she breathed.

'A wee boy,' Carrie repeated.

Mrs Cooper stuck her head round the door and called the news to Donald and Hugh.

Donald beamed and smacked his meaty hands together. 'That's rare!' he said.

Winnie and Mrs Cooper both laughed when the baby opened his mouth and gave a lusty cry.

'Is he . . . all right?' Carrie asked. It was the one question every newly delivered mother feels compelled to ask, and the one they dread to have answered in the negative.

Robertson thoroughly checked the baby's fingers, toes and external organs. 'He's a smasher,' he replied eventually. 'There's absolutely nothing wrong with him.'

Carrie nodded gratefully, the ghost of a smile hovering round her bloodless lips.

Robertson tied off the baby's umbilical cord and then handed him over to his grandmother.

Winnie swathed the baby, first in a torn-off piece of clean cotton sheet and then in a shawl that had been in the family for generations. Every one of her family had worn that shawl. It was part of Chisholm tradition.

Mrs Cooper washed Carrie down and then, with Robertson's help, changed the bedding. When Carrie had been made decent, Donald and Hugh were allowed into the room.

Donald stared in wonderment at the baby cradled in his wife's arms. The miracle of birth never ceased to amaze him.

The baby's eyelids flickered and jerked open. Eyes of the palest blue stared out at the world for the first time.

The mouth twisted and seemed to be preparing to cry again, so Winnie started humming a lullaby that had long been a great favourite of hers. The mouth immediately slackened and settled back into repose.

Carrie felt more tired than she'd ever done before in her life. It was as though every particle of energy in her body had been carefully and methodically drained away.

The blackness was behind her now. She no longer felt drawn to what it had to offer. Her time for dying hadn't come yet.

Hugh was bursting with pride. He would have liked to hold the baby but didn't think that the manly thing to do. Instead he stuck his chest out and nodded knowingly as though he'd been through this sort of thing many times before.

'Please?' Carrie asked, holding out her hands.

Staring down at her newborn son, it seemed to her that his blue eyes were drinking her in, studying her every feature for future reference. But of course she knew that to be pure imagination on her part.

'He's to be called Angus,' she said. 'That was the name John and I had agreed on.'

Donald and Winnie nodded their approval. They knew that Angus had been the name of John's father who'd died before John was born.

History tragically repeating itself, Donald thought, somehow managing to retain the smile on his face.

'Angus,' Carrie said again. Laying her head back on the pillow, she closed her eyes.

A few seconds later both mother and son were fast asleep.

Mrs Cooper tiptoed from the room to put the kettle on for a cup of tea.

2

The day of the funeral dawned a scorcher. From horizon to horizon the sky was unmarred by even the vaguest wisp of cloud. The sun hung heavy and fat, looking like the centre of a perfectly fried egg.

Head bowed and supported on either side by Donald and Hugh, Carrie stepped aboard the hired black carriage which would take them to the cemetery.

All the curtains and blinds in Tallon Street had been drawn as a mark of respect. A neighbour from across the way stood with his cap in his hand. He wouldn't move until the carriage had gone past him.

It was the first time Carrie had been out since Angus's birth, and she felt a little light-headed. Anxiously she gazed up at the Coopers' window, fancying she could hear the wee fellow crying. Mrs Cooper was looking after Angus while she was at the funeral.

Winnie squeezed Carrie's arm, knowing what was running through her daughter's mind. Carrie's anxiety subsided and she shot her mother the briefest of smiles. Mrs Cooper was a dab hand with children. Angus would be all right in her more than capable hands.

The carriage moved forward at a dignified pace as they made their way up Tallon Street. Carrie had decided John was to remain at the undertakers until the time of the funeral. They were headed there now to pick up the coffin.

Harriet Chisholm stared stonily out the carriage

window as they clip-clopped up the cobbled street. She hated funerals. In fact, she loathed them so much the very thought of having to go to one was enough to make her feel sick for days beforehand. Harriet was only too well aware that one day she, too, would die and the thought terrified her.

As a wee lassie she'd had terrible nightmares about dying. Nightmares that would bring her out of her sleep whimpering with terror. With small fist stuck in her mouth and a cold sweat literally dripping from her, she'd lie staring into the darkness. Her nightmares about death were always the same: flesh-eating worms slowly devouring her body, the claustrophobia of the grave; and the awful, awful loneliness which was undoubtedly the worst thing of all.

Loneliness was a word Harriet was well acquainted with. For as long as she could remember she had been alone, with the sort of loneliness that's there even when you're surrounded by others.

Perhaps things would have been different if she'd been born pretty, or at least attractive. But she hadn't been. There had been no magical transformation for this ugly duckling. The ugly duckling had grown up into just as ugly a duck.

With bitter shame she remembered it had been a great dare at one time amongst the boys of her class to corner and kiss her. For a long time she'd wondered why she was in such demand till at a birthday party that beautiful blonde bitch, Aileen Summers, had whispered the answer in her ear during a game of postie postie.

She'd fled the room and the house, running down the road with a face awash with hot tears and Aileen's words still ringing in her ears.

The boys had been kissing her as the worst dare they could think of to test their manhood. 'Kiss Harriet Chisholm and not be sick' was how they put it. Laughing and wiping their mouths afterwards, saying it wasn't as bad as all that, as long as you kept your eyes shut so you didn't see her face.

Tall, angular and bony she'd been at school. And despite her many prayers she'd grown up exactly the same – a fact that burned resentfully in her breast, causing her to view the world through a cold and jaundiced eye.

Harriet's gaze flickered sideways to where Carrie was sitting with Winnie. Although hardly a raving beauty, Carrie was none the less far more attractive than she was. And how she'd always envied Carrie that.

If only men could see inside her, she thought. If only they would take the trouble to see the real her inside this hated shell which housed her being. But in her experience men didn't have that sort of insight when it came to women. All they were interested in were the externals.

She glanced across again at Carrie. It saddened her to see her sister so obviously suffering, but there was a side of her that was jealous of Carrie even now.

Hadn't Carrie had a man of her own? A good, loving husband who'd worshipped the very ground she'd walked on. And didn't she now have a gorgeous baby as a legacy of that marriage?

It was certainly a lot more than Harriet was ever likely to get.

Her eyes glittered as she stared out at the passing scene. She would have given anything to have landed a man like John McBain. And as for Angus, she would have sold her soul for a wean like him.

What was to become of her? she wondered bitterly. Was her fate to end up a dry old spinster? She was sure it was. Angus and any other nephews and nieces she might have would pay a duty call to Aunty Harriet on those Sunday afternoons when their parents forced them to come and see her.

'You're looking well, Aunty Harriet. And how are you today?'

Bitterness welled up inside her as she imagined how pitifully grateful she'd probably be for the visits while knowing that to them she would undoubtedly be a figure of fun, someone they laughed and sniggered about when they were on their own.

Her hands twitched towards her bag and the cigarettes it contained. But she daren't light up, even though she was desperate for a smoke. Her father would have a fit had she tried. And even though she was a grown woman she was still as scared of him as she'd always been.

She recalled the leatherings and beltings he'd given them all when they were young. Hugh and Carrie had taken their punishments in silence. As indeed had Alex. She, on the other hand, had howled the place down at the very threat of his hand or belt.

A physical coward, Donald had called her. And he was right. She couldn't stand pain and was convinced her sensitivity to it was far greater than other people's.

But Donald didn't agree. He just said she was a big feartie. Always had been and always would be.

God how she hated herself. If only she'd been born beautiful, or at least attractive. If only she hadn't been so damned clever, which seemed to put off so many men.

If only. . . . If only. . . .

Big Donald eyed Carrie closely. The loss of John had been a terrible blow to her, as indeed it had to them all. She was taking it badly but that was only to be expected. The pair of them had been so much in love.

At least she had the bairn to keep her occupied and help take her mind off matters. The wee chap would be a big solace to her in the difficult times ahead.

When they arrived at the undertakers, Donald and Hugh got out of the carriage and went inside. The hearse was already in place. The four black horses, each with a magnificent black plume flowing backwards from its head, were hooked up and waiting patiently to go.

After the coffin had been loaded aboard, the wreaths that had arrived at the undertakers were strewn decorously around it.

When all was ready, Donald and Hugh climbed back aboard the carriage, and followed the hearse to the cemetery.

Carrie felt as though she was only the shell of what she'd been before. She was learning to cope with the days, but the nights were something again. It was the early morning hours that were hardest, when she was up giving Angus his feed. Then she was all alone and, while the baby suckled, her mind filled itself with memories.

She'd lie in bed with her thoughts whirling after Angus had gone back to sleep. Once or twice it had been so bad she'd woken Harriet and kept her sister talking until the dawn came creeping over the chimney tops. She knew that was grossly unfair of her as Harriet had her work to go to, but Harriet had never complained.

The pair of them would lie there talking about anything and everything. It didn't matter what they spoke about. The important thing was they did. To her credit, Harriet understood that.

Hugh was sweating and uncomfortable because of the rigid shirt collar jabbing into his throat. He was dressed in his one and only suit with a black armband stitched round the right sleeve. He felt lost and rather lonely sitting there amongst his family. He would be glad when all this was over.

It was hard to believe that a man as full of life as John McBain had been was now dead, and that within the hour they'd be burying him in the cold, dank earth.

Gooseflesh prickled on Hugh's neck as it came home to him for the first time that he, too, was only mortal.

On the way to the cemetery men doffed their hats and caps while the few they passed in uniform saluted.

During the drive, Winnie's mind was filled with thoughts of her son, Alex, who'd been killed just outside Sherman, Texas, in 1911. Alex had been sixteen when he left home, saying in the time-honoured way that he wanted to see the world and maybe find his fortune.

He'd been gone a little over six months when word arrived back to say he'd been hurt badly in an accident. Three days later, further word came saying he was dead.

The people in the American hospital had been

extremely kind. A doctor had written them a letter which had come in the parcel containing Alex's effects. Some months later the same doctor sent them a photo of the grave.

Winnie kept that photo in her handbag so she could have it with her at all times. Never a day went by that she didn't take it out and look at it.

Occasionally on the anniversary of Alex's death Donald would go down to the pub and drink a lot more than was good for him. Those were the only times Winnie ever saw her husband the worse for wear because of alcohol.

Robert Smith and his wife, Meg, were waiting for them at the cemetery gates. The Smiths were the nearest thing John had to a family as they had taken him in when he was a bare-arsed lad after his mother died. No formal adoption had ever taken place, so John had always maintained his own family name of McBain.

After being greeted by the Smiths, Carrie had a few words with the other pallbearers. Two of these were foundrymen who had been particular friends of John and the third was a chap called Archie Marjoribanks, an old school chum with whom John had run the streets as a boy and who had kept in touch ever since.

Donald, Hugh and old man Smith comprised one line of pallbearers, the two foundrymen and Marjoribanks the other.

Once the coffin was shouldered, the six men moved slowly forward while the women followed.

A large gang from Armstrong's stood grouped round the graveside, a few of whom were in their work clothes as they would be going straight on to weekend caretaking duties after the ceremony.

The Reverend Duncan Forbes stood at the top end of the grave with a large, well-thumbed Bible open in his hand. Looking rather like an Old Testament prophet with his longish white hair and hawk-like, yet ascetic, features, he was a gentle man who genuinely cared.

Friends and neighbours from Tallon Street and

McLellan Street had turned up as well as various relatives of the Chisholm family. Chief amongst the latter was Donald's brother, Sandy, who was a merchant seaman.

The coffin was carefully laid by the graveside and the ceremony began with a prayer.

Old man Smith was heartbroken as he stared down at the coffin. John had been everything to him and his wife, the focal point of their waning lives. They had never had any children themselves, a fact to which he and Meg had never become reconciled.

It had always upset them both that John had never wanted to follow them into the newsagent and confectioner's shop they owned, which was a good, well-established business with an ever-increasing turnover.

Robert Smith sighed. If John had come into the shop, this would never have happened.

He glanced across to where Carrie was standing. He'd not altogether approved of that marriage, albeit it was obvious to anyone with half an eye in his head that John and the lassie had been daft on one another.

What had worried him at the time was the fact that the Chisholms and the Smiths – and since taking John in he'd considered John a Smith – although both working-class families, occupied different rungs on the social ladder. The Smiths were *rough*, whereas the Chisholms had bettered themselves by escaping into a *good* area. Cathcart was a far cry from Scotland Street where the Smiths lived and where John had been brought up. The Smiths were considerably well off, while the Chisholms lived from week to week on what was brought into the house.

Robert Smith greatly admired Big Donald, although the man's overpowering masculinity both awed and frightened him a little. Robert was a shy, retiring person, who, outside of business, had very little to say for himself. However, people who mistook his shyness for weakness soon learned better. In his own quiet way Robert was as ruthless as any self-made tycoon who's fought his way to the top.

What worried him now was the fact that Angus had

been left without a father, and he knew the harsh economic realities, both now and in the future. He knew Carrie would do her best by the child, and furthermore he trusted Big Donald to play his part in supporting the wee fellow, but Carrie would certainly find a capital sum handy. That was why he'd brought £200 along with him today.

The money hadn't come from a bank, but out of the safe he had bolted to the kitchen floor at home. A lot of people would have been surprised to know what was in that safe. Certainly the tax man would.

The Reverend Forbes spoke about John and the terrible tragedy that had befallen the McBain family. Then he called for them all to join him in singing 'Abide with Me'.

Carrie watched, dry-eyed, as the coffin was lowered into the grave. At a signal from the minister she stepped forward to pick up a handful of earth which she threw on to the coffin lid. One by one the chief mourners came forward and followed suit.

When the ceremony was over Carrie spoke to the men from Armstrong's who'd come along to pay their last respects. Some she knew, others she didn't.

Donald stood staring at the great mound of wreaths and flowers piled high beside the grave.

'They did him proud,' Robert Smith said, coming up to Donald from behind.

'Aye, they did that,' Donald agreed, lifting his eyes and staring out over the rolling green countryside.

Donald loved being in the country. He found it soothing after the racket and clatter of the foundry. The sky was clear now, but on weekdays when the Glasgow smokestacks and chimneys were belching soot and fug into the air, it was a different matter entirely. Then the sky was stained with a great grey cloud which hung, lowering, over the city.

It always amused Donald to think that the word Glasgow came from the Gaelic meaning 'Dear Green Place'. What a joke when you considered the filthy industrial hell that 'Green Place' had now become.

Winnie and Harriet waited patiently while the Reverend Forbes quietly spoke to Carrie. Judging from the expression on her face she seemed to be finding some comfort in what he was saying.

Winnie finally caught Donald's attention and signalled to him that they really must be away if they were to get back in time to receive those who were coming to tea.

Carrie had one last look at the grave. As she turned away the gravediggers moved into position and soon their spades were flying rhythmically.

When they had all arrived back at Tallon Street, Carrie stopped off at Mrs Cooper's for Angus.

Bella Millar, who lived in one of the ground floor apartments, and Mrs McElvey from across the street, had laid out the tea while the Chisholms were at the funeral. Both of these women were close friends of Winnie and the girls.

A few people had already arrived, the Smiths amongst them, and these had been ushered into the big room where they now stood talking and trying to be at ease.

Winnie said hello and then fled to the kitchen, leaving Harriet to play hostess, a task she performed easily.

Drinks were dispensed and then shortly afterwards everyone was asked to go through to the front room where an assortment of borrowed tables and chairs had been arranged so that the entire company could sit down in one sitting.

After the meal Big Donald asked them all to go back through to the big room where there would be more drinks for those who wished them.

Winnie, Harriet and a few of the women – Meg Smith insisted on being one of them – stayed behind to clear things away and do the washing up. They would have their own blether while they were getting on with it, and then go back to the big room.

In the big room Archie Marjoribanks found himself standing close to Carrie who was talking to the young

Robert Cooper. Marjoribanks had already consumed a large number of whiskies, some of which had come from the half bottle he was carrying in his inside jacket pocket, enough to make him half cut and querulous. Accepting another large one from Donald, he literally threw it down his throat. Turning to Carrie he said, 'I only hope Armstrong's are going to pay you a fair bit of compensation. They must be liable, surely to God, as John was killed on the premises.'

A sudden feel of unease settled on the room at these words and those who worked at Amrstrong's glanced from one to the other.

'It's not quite as black and white as that,' Donald said. He then tried to change the subject but Marjoribanks would have none of it.

Marjoribanks was a man of medium height with a stocky build and auburn hair. He would have been reasonably handsome if it hadn't been for his eyes which gave him a foxy look.

'I don't understand,' Marjoribanks persisted, his attention now centred on Donald. 'John was killed in the foundry, therefore compensation must be due. Surely that's the way it is nowadays?'

'Sir Alan might not see it that way,' Donald replied softly.

'Sir Alan?'

'Him that owns the place. John was on a gantry that had been declared unsafe and put out of bounds when the accident occurred. You can bet Sir Alan's going to make an awful lot of that.'

'I see,' said Marjoribanks, frowning.

'The union will be meeting Sir Alan first thing Monday morning,' Donald continued. 'We should know what's what then.'

Wishing to put an end to the conversation, Donald moved to the bottles to pour out more drinks. He was furious with Marjoribanks, thinking the man crass and insensitive. Talk of compensation was completely out of order at a time like this.

Unaware of the offence he'd caused, Marjoribanks turned his attention back to Carrie. Although he'd met her several times in the past he'd never bothered to have a really good look at her. He saw now that she was a rather attractive woman and one very much to his taste.

Carrie decided to check up on Angus. She gave Marjoribanks a brief smile in passing because he was staring so intently at her.

Marjoribanks quickly returned the smile, convinced that Carrie had taken a shine to him. Later, the memory of that smile started him thinking.

Carrie was coming out of the bedroom where Angus was sleeping when she found Robert Smith waiting for her. She genuinely liked the old man, having always found him sympathetic. She didn't know about his early objection to her marriage as John had never seen fit to mention it to her.

Robert Smith pressed a buff-coloured envelope into her hand. 'A little something to help you and the wean out,' he said.

'Oh, but I couldn't!'

'Don't be daft, woman. Of course you can,' he said and folded her fingers round the envelope.

Carrie took a deep breath. This was most unexpected. 'Well, if you're sure . . . ?'

'Of course I'm sure. I wouldn't have given it to you otherwise.'

Carrie wondered whether the thing to do was to open the envelope there and then or wait till later. When she saw he was staring expectantly at her she presumed he wanted her to open it in front of him.

Using her finger she slit the envelope. She gasped when she saw the thickness of the wad of fivers that were inside.

Robert Smith wasn't a man who gave much away, but when he did he enjoyed the experience. The thunder-struck expression on Carrie's face delighted him. He would derive enormous pleasure in describing that expression to his wife, Meg, whose voice he could now hear coming from behind the closed kitchen door.

'We just ask that you bring the wee fellow to see us once in a while,' he said. Leaning across he kissed Carrie on the cheek. Then he was swiftly making his way back to the big room where he intended having a large glass of Donald's whisky.

Carrie slipped back into the bedroom where Angus was sleeping and stood with her back pressed hard against the door. Her hands were trembling as she slowly counted the wad of fivers.

'Two hundred pounds,' she breathed. Her heart was thudding and her legs felt weak at the knees. The hand holding the money was sticky and hot.

Closing her eyes, she offered up a silent prayer of gratitude. There was a halfpenny policy on John's life, but when that was realized it would hardly be enough to bury him, much less anything else.

The £200 windfall was a fortune to her and she swore there and then to put every farthing of it to good use. Now it wouldn't be necessary for her to find a job right away which was an enormous weight off her mind as jobs were so few and far between.

When she rejoined the assembled company she felt a sense of optimism for the future that she hadn't known before.

3

Early on the Monday evening Winnie was sitting at the big room window. From this vantage point she could see the bend beyond which lay the sombre-looking cluster of buildings comprising Armstrong's. The hooter had just blown and at any moment the men would come streaming round the bend, hurrying home for their tea.

Normally, Winnie would have been in the kitchen getting the evening meal ready, but that night they were having salad and the rest of the boiled ham left over from the funeral. Everything was already prepared and laid out on the front room table, waiting for Donald and Hugh to arrive.

Carrie was in the bedroom feeding the wee one while Harriet was talking to her.

Winnie gently massaged her left temple. She had a bit of a headache which had been brought on by the day's heat. It had been another scorcher. Every window in the house was wide open to any breeze that might be about to waft through.

Winnie had spoken to Carrie that afternoon about the house in McLellan Street, wanting to know what Carrie's plans were. The one thing Carrie was certain about was that she didn't want to go back there to live. The place held too many memories for her.

She had said they'd speak to Donald that night to see if he'd be agreeable to Carrie and Angus staying on permanently in Carrie's old room. As Harriet would have to share the room with the two of them, she too would have to be consulted.

The first of the men had started coming round the bend which meant that it would only be a matter of minutes before Donald and Hugh were home.

She often thought that Donald expected too much from Hugh, and consequently was far too hard on him. The trouble was that Donald couldn't seem to understand that Hugh was going through a stage he himself had never been allowed, for Donald's youth had ended abruptly when he was ten years old on the day he went to graft in the bakery.

According to Donald there had been fourteen of them, slaving away in a room little bigger than the one she was in now, and at least one-third of that space had been taken up by the two ovens.

On a number of occasions Donald had described to her what it had been like to walk into that room when the ovens were going full blast. Like being thrust into the very maw of hell itself, was one way he'd put it.

It hadn't been uncommon for grown men to suddenly keel over in a dead faint, and once a man called Barton had thrown himself to the floor where he'd cried and drummed his fists like a baby.

In those days Donald hadn't known what it was to own a pair of shoes, but he had known what hard work was. By Christ he had.

The Chisholms were a Highland family, as were her own, who'd made the long trek south to the big city because they'd been slowly starving to death on their croft outside a village called Invershuie.

Donald's father knew a lot about sheep and precious little else. But work was to be had in Glasgow, and not long after his arrival, he had landed himself a job as a labourer down at the Broomielaw, working for a well-to-do tobacco merchant called Gordon.

Alastair Chisholm was thirty-two years old the day he dropped down dead, so completely and utterly exhausted that his worn-out body had no other recourse but to up and quit on him. When he'd died, Donald had just turned ten and Sandy was thirteen. There was another brother, Willy, who was seven, and Nettie, the only girl in the family, who was three.

A week after his father died, Donald started at the bakery. Sandy had already been grafting for just over a year at a rope works.

The young Donald had worked his fingers to the bone helping to keep the family alive, and later when the chance of an apprenticeship came up in a city foundry he'd jumped at it.

By that time Willie was older and able to bring in some money, and Nettie wasn't such a tie on their mother who was able to get to do scrubbing and general housework.

By the time Donald was twelve, the hard, punishing

work he'd been forced to endure had long since knocked any vestiges of his youth clean out of him. He'd become a man in every sense of the word.

Winnie sighed and patted the greying hair piled up on her head in two side rolls. Before they went to sleep that night she'd have another quiet word with Donald, asking him to try and be more understanding with Hugh.

Winnie started, realizing she'd drifted off into a world of her own. Crowds of men were hurrying past now, while just up ahead she could make out Hugh's tall, slim figure.

Hugh looked up at the window and saw his mother's face peering down at him. He gave her a cheery wave before turning into their close and bounding up the stairs three at a time.

Winnie was waiting for him at the door.

'Papa's stayed behind to have a word with the union official. He said to tell you he won't be long .'

Winnie read Hugh's face correctly. 'The meeting didn't go well, then, I take it?'

Hugh pushed past her into the house, wanting for once to be the first at the sink. Normally that was Donald's privilege. 'No, it didn't,' he called back over his shoulder. 'But I think you'd better wait and hear the story from Papa. You know what he's like about that sort of thing.'

Harriet emerged from her bedroom to glance questioningly at Winnie who in a few terse sentences explained the situation. Harriet made a sort of harrumphing sound, a vocal mannerism of hers which could make her appear very formidable indeed, and disappeared back into the bedroom to relay the information to Carrie.

Carrie had been in a depressed state of mind ever since that morning when she'd been back to McLellan Street to pick up some more clothes for herself and the baby.

There had been the terrible moment when she'd come across some dirty clothes of John's which had been pushed into a corner. His own distinctive smell still clung to them and that had hit her like a body blow.

Then there had been his pipe; his spare collar studs lying on the mantelpiece above the fireplace, his favourite chair which he'd been threatening to repair for over a year, and the brass poker he'd made in the foundry when an apprentice.

The sight of each of these articles which she so closely associated with him had torn afresh at her still raw grief.

'Are you all right?' Harriet asked.

Carrie somehow managed a smile. 'Just thinking. Remembering.' Then suddenly, 'I saw that Archie Marjoribanks giving you the eye the other day. If you ask me, I think he took a fancy to you.'

Harriet snorted and looked away. 'Don't be soft. That sort of man wouldn't be interested in the likes of me.'

'Why not, for heaven's sake?'

Harriet smiled grimly and didn't reply. Instead she started buffing her nails. She would have liked to grow them long and talonlike, but of course that was impossible when she spent five and a half days every week knocking her pan out over an industrial sewing machine.

God, how she hated the factory! With her brain she should have been able to do a lot better for herself than that. The trouble was there were so few opportunities for women and virtually none where something more than hard physical slog or a beautiful body was demanded of one.

Harriet ground her teeth in frustration, thinking that the entire world had conspired to thwart her ambitions.

Well, one day the work situation would have to ease, and when it did she wouldn't be slow in putting herself forward. Unless, of course, there were other ways to skin this particular cat?

That sudden electrifying thought was something completely new, and she wondered why it hadn't occurred to her before.

Her eyes half closed and a look of muted excitement settled on her face as she began to brood on the idea of a possible alternative.

In the bathroom Hugh finished his wash and vigorously dried himself off. It had been a terrible day in the foundry with everyone being acutely aware that young John McBain, who'd been laughing and joking with them only a few days previously, was now dead and buried.

The entire work force had paused when the casting, still with traces of blood on its side, had been hauled away by a gang of labourers to be loaded on to a wagon and dispatched to the people who'd placed the order for it. Armstrong's wasn't the sort of firm to destroy a perfectly good casting just because some poor bugger had the misfortune to be killed by it.

Going through to the living room, Hugh threw himself into one of the fireside chairs. He was ravenously hungry but knew only too well that no one would be allowed to start on their tea until Big Donald arrived home and was ready to sit down. That was one of the house rules.

It was over an hour later when the front door clicked to announce Big Donald's return.

When he entered the living room he found Winnie, Carrie and Harriet waiting expectantly for him. Hugh, head fallen to one side, was fast asleep and snoring.

Donald wasn't a man who believed in mincing words so he came straight to the point. 'There's no hope for a penny piece of compensation, lass,' he said to Carrie. 'Sir Alan just won't entertain the idea.'

Carrie hadn't believed it would be much, but she had expected something. She'd thought that Armstrong would have felt obliged at least to make a token gesture. It seemed that wasn't to be the case. She thanked God yet again for Robert Smith's £200, without which she would have been destitute.

'The mean, miserable bastard!' Harriet hissed.

'Did you speak to Sir Alan yourself?' Winnie asked.

'I did,' Donald replied. 'The trouble is that John was up on that gantry without authority. Sir Alan argues that it doesn't matter that the casting was out of control. If

John hadn't been where he was he wouldn't have been killed. Sir Alan says that as John's death was John's own fault, he daren't make even an *ex gratia* payment to Carrie in case it sets a precedent.'

'What do you think, Papa?' Carrie asked in a tight voice.

Donald's face contorted into a mask of suppressed fury. He clenched and unclenched his massive fists. A terrible injustice had been done that day and what angered him was that he'd been totally powerless to do anything about it.

'I did think of telling Armstrong what to do with my job.'

Winnie paled, and a vein in her neck began to throb.

'But, of course, there wouldn't have been any sense in that. There isn't a snowball's hope in hell of me or anyone else in the works getting another job in Glasgow at the moment, and that's why that man can treat us any way he bloody well pleases.'

'You did right, Papa,' Carrie said. 'John wouldn't have expected you to do otherwise.'

Harriet said, 'I was talking to a girl at work the other day whose husband was recently out at the Gareloch. According to him, it's chock-a-block with laid-up ships.'

'She told the truth,' Donald growled. 'That's why there are no orders on the books. There's a glut of merchant tonnage left over from the war, far more than is now needed. If things go on the way they are I can see at least half the men on Clydeside being idle before the year's out.'

'Oh, don't say that!' Winnie exclaimed, her eyes wide with fear.

Donald stalked to the sideboard where he knew there to be some whisky left over from the funeral. He poured himself a large one and gulped it down. Then he poured himself another.

He was worried sick that he might end up in the position of not being able to provide for his family. To Donald that was a horrifying prospect, and the worst sin a man like him could commit. The entire strength of his male ego was centred round two things: his virility, and his ability to be the family bread-winner.

Crossing to the open window, he gazed down on to the back green. His overriding fear was that they'd lose this house and be forced to move back to the slums from which he and Winnie had struggled so hard and so long to escape.

Winnie sighed and ran a hand wearily over her hair. The possibility of Donald being made idle was something she was going to have to face. Somehow she was going to have to find a way of cutting back so that she could put a wee bit by against that black day, should it ever arrive. Still, looking on the bright side, no matter how bad things got, there was bound to come a time when they'd get better again. That thought lightened her heart and, combined with the love she had for her family and they for her, gave her the courage to face whatever the future held in store for them.

Thinking of the slums had led to Donald remembering his mother. She'd been a beauty in her day, with long, flowing, lustrous hair and a peerless complexion. But her looks had soon withered as a result of producing four children and then struggling to cope when Alastair died. When she was thirty-five her face was heavily lined and she had grey hair which turned snow white a decade later.

Many's the time they'd all huddled together for warmth in the one bed while she regaled them with tales of Invershuie. She'd speak of her young days and the adventures she'd had in the wild glens and mountains surrounding the village.

Once she'd confided to them that she'd known their father all her life and there had never been anyone else whom she'd ever wanted to marry. Young Nettie had cried at that, saying she hated Glasgow and wanted her daddy back. Fiona Chisholm had held her only daughter tight then and in a cracked voice confessed that she too wanted their daddy back.

Donald finally emerged from his dream to remember that he still had John's last wage packet in his trouser pocket.

Crossing to Carrie, he laid the small brown envelope in her lap. 'That was what John had coming,' he said, unable to keep the bitterness out of his voice.

Winnie startled everyone by rising and declaring, 'I hope that man Armstrong rots in hell for what he did today.'

She stared defiantly round the room: it was almost unknown for her to swear.

'Amen to that,' said Donald, agreeing with his wife's sentiments. 'Now let's eat before our stomachs begin to think our throats have been cut.'

Hugh needed no further telling. He was the first one to sit at the table.

4

Summer gave way to autumn and that, in turn, to winter. Early one Saturday evening in February, Hugh answered a knock on the front door to find Archie Marjoribanks standing there with a bunch of flowers in one hand and a brown paper bag full of clinking bottles in the other.

For a moment Hugh was taken aback. Then, grinning, he ushered Marjoribanks through to the living room where the family was assembled.

When Carrie heard Marjoribanks's voice in the hallway, she shot Harriet a look which clearly said, 'See I was right. He *is* interested in you!'

Harriet frowned, an action she normally tried to avoid as it caused a deep cleft of unattractive flesh to appear above her nose.

As Marjoribanks entered the room, Donald carefully folded his evening paper and laid it by the side of his chair. Rising slowly and ponderously, he shook Marjoribanks by the hand.

The flowers were for Winnie. They were terribly expensive at this time of year, but although she protested, she was obviously delighted and touched.

The bottles were beer and lemonade.

Hugh hurried to the sideboard where the glasses were kept while Marjoribanks was urged to sit down.

Marjoribanks cleared his throat and said he hoped they didn't mind him visiting, but being an old china of John's he was naturally concerned as to how Carrie and the baby were managing.

He was hastily assured by Winnie that mother and son were doing just fine. Carrie smiled and confirmed that this was so.

Hugh poured the beers and shandies while Carrie handed them round. He hesitated over whether or not to pour himself one. Empty glass in hand, he turned to gaze inquiringly at Donald, who after only the briefest of hestitations gave him the nod to go ahead.

For a while Donald and Marjoribanks discussed the state of the country which they both agreed had deteriorated since the previous summer. Then they talked about the pay-offs which had taken place at Armstrong's just before Christmas when 180 men had been sent home at the end of the week with the words ringing in their ears that they weren't to bother reporting back the following Monday.

Amrstrong's was a marine engineering firm, manufacturing and servicing pumps for the ships built on Clydeside. It had taken time but now the general slump in the yards was feeding back to the ancillary firms depending on them of which Armstrong's was one.

Normally a person of definite opinion, Donald now

found himself in the unusual position of not being sure what he thought of Marjoribanks. The man *had* spoken out of line at the funeral tea, but perhaps that wasn't such a bad thing after all. He had been concerned for Carrie's rights. But there was something elusive about the man, some aspect of his personality which defied Donald's analysis.

He had a great deal of charm, there was no denying that. He smiled a lot. Maybe too much. And he certainly knew how to flatter, as had been demonstrated in the little speech he'd made to Winnie when handing her the flowers.

Perhaps it was the flattery which had triggered his unease, Donald thought. He distrusted people who used flattery to their own advantage.

The conversation veered on to Marjoribanks's job, and much to Hugh's delight it transpired that he worked on the railways.

Hugh was something of a railway buff, having become mad keen on them when he was only a tiny lad. He now spoke eagerly with Marjoribanks about the far-reaching changes taking place at that time amongst the many railway companies up and down the length and breadth of Britain.

Marjoribanks was a shunter with the Caledonian Railway which was soon to integrate with a new company to form what was to be known as the London, Midland and Scottish Railway, LMS for short.

A light came into Marjoribanks's eyes as he talked about the engines currently in use with Caledonian, such as the old Dugald Drummonds whose designer was renowned for experimenting with 200lb pressure – a fearsome figure at the time.

Hugh wanted to know about the new Cardean Class 4-6-0 and the Pickersgill's two cylinder 4-6-0 express due to go into general service later that year.

Donald's unease melted as Hugh and Marjoribanks delved deeper into the facts and figures of the Caledonian and its rolling stock.

It was soon apparent from Marjoribanks's enthusiastic comments that he both loved and was good at his job. This put him several notches higher in Big Donald's estimation.

After more discussion Marjoribanks extended Hugh an invitation to come along to the Central Station one weekend, promising to show him around and, if possible, give him a short ride in an engine cab.

Needless to say, Hugh was ecstatic and immediately asked if the following Saturday would be suitable. The date was fixed, and to the accompaniment of a delighted laugh from Hugh they shook hands on it.

After that Winnie rose to say she was going to make a cup of tea. She had just baked some fresh scones that afternoon and wanted to impress Marjoribanks with them. Both Carrie and Harriet offered to help, but she told them to sit down again as she could manage on her own.

Winnie had guessed correctly that there was more to Marjoribanks's visit than a mere social call. What was yet unclear to her was which of her two daughters he was interested in. Carrie with Angus to look after needed another man, of course, but in a way she rather hoped it was Harriet he had his eye on.

Harriet worried her at times. She was too introspective and given to brooding for her own good. The real trouble with Harriet was that she was extremely intelligent and refused to hide the fact. Obvious intelligence tended to put men off as she'd once tried explaining to her, but Harriet had merely glowered and thrust her chin forward.

Look at her now! Winnie thought. Sitting there staring daggers at poor Mr Marjoribanks, who so far hadn't spoken one word out of place and had, in fact, been civility itself. No wonder she couldn't land herself a man if that was the way she treated them!

Harriet was surprised by her reaction towards Archie Marjoribanks. Coldly dissecting that reaction, she came to the conclusion he both attracted and repelled her at the same time.

He was a smoothie, all right – glib and surprisingly articulate. But his accent was dreadfully common. Far more so than John's had been, who had been brought up in the same district as he.

She wondered if it was the way his eyes bent in towards one another that put her off. To her mind they made him look like a crook.

Harriet had just lit her umpteenth cigarette since Marjoribanks's arrival when she suddenly became aware that he was staring at her. Her gaze flickered towards him and their eyes locked.

The embarrassed burning sensation started in the pit of her stomach and then swiftly radiated outwards. She wanted to squirm under that gaze, knowing he was mentally stripping her with a clinical objectivity that was both exciting and disgusting. There was a wealth of sexual knowledge in those eyes so dispassionately viewing her. That and a glint of humour as though he was inwardly laughing at the pitiful object she saw herself to be.

Fury exploded within her. How dare he look at her as if she were some common tart parading on the street corner! She wanted to pick something up and throw it at him. She wanted to grind her cigarette into his leering face. She wanted Donald to thrash him within an inch of his life and then throw him down the stairs. She wanted . . .

When the full realization of what she really *did* want burst in her, she was filled with both horror and shame.

Marjoribanks's mocking eyes once more trapped hers, this time for only the briefest of seconds – just long enough for him to let her know he was aware of what was running through her mind. Then he deliberately turned his back on her and struck up a new line of conversation with Donald who at that moment had just stopped speaking.

Harriet had an overwhelming urge to leap to her feet and flee the room, but she fought it down. This is ridiculous, she told herself. She was a mature woman of twenty-eight and not some silly wee lassie to be reduced to a jelly just because a man had looked at her *that* way. Of course it wasn't the look that was really bothering her, but rather what it sparked off within her. For the first time in her life she found herself scared of a man, not merely because he was bigger and stronger than she was, but due to something that went far deeper and whose roots were lodged in the very essence of her femininity.

A few minutes later Winnie bustled in, pushing a trolley loaded down with goodies. Carrie broke off speaking to help her mother by handing out the plates while Winnie poured the tea.

Marjoribanks was highly amused at Harriet's reaction to him. It was a long long time since he'd come across a girl at that age whom he could immediately sense was a virgin. In a way she reminded him of his dead wife, Libby, who'd also had that supercilious quality which he'd found so attractive.

For a moment or two he considered changing his mind about which sister to go after, but in the end decided it had to be Carrie. At least he wouldn't mind waking up in the morning and seeing her face next to his, which was a lot more than he could say for Harriet. Jesus, she was plain! But there *was* sex there. A vast untapped reservoir desperate to burst its banks. He could have relished being the one to do the bursting.

Sipping his tea he turned his attention to Carrie. Her pins were good which was important. He appreciated good legs. The backside, belly and breasts were overweight, but that would be because she was still feeding. She had an excellent profile, and her facial skin was flawless, unlike Harriet's which was marked from childhood spots.

But what was most in Carrie's favour was that she had an extremely pleasant personality as well as being easy to get on with and always eager to please. He knew all this for fact as John had mentioned it to him more than once.

The conversation died abruptly when they heard Angus yelling in his bedroom. Carrie hurried away to attend to him. She returned minutes later to report that the wee fellow must have been having a nightmare which luckily hadn't woken him.

At first Marjoribanks had viewed Angus as a liability, but thinking the matter through he'd come to realize how the child could be used to his advantage. If he did get married to Carrie, then Angus would be an enormous lever he'd have over her.

Half an hour later he decided it was time to go. Having reconfirmed Hugh's visit to the Central Station on the following Saturday – that had been a stroke of luck as it gave him the perfect opportunity to wangle another social call – he said his good-byes.

'Well, well, well,' said Donald after Marjoribanks had gone. Thoughtfully he rubbed his chin.

'I'll do the washing up,' said Harriet and started to gather the dirty dishes together. The trolley rattled as she vigorously pushed it from the room.

Hugh excused himself and went through to the big room where he slept on a bed settee. He wanted to go over his books on railways and dream about the coming Saturday.

Carrie had another look at Angus before taking herself through to the kitchen to help Harriet. 'What do you make of that, then?' she queried.

Harriet harrumphed. 'Make of what?' she snapped in reply.

Carrie was well used to her sister's moods and rudeness. Harriet just wouldn't have been Harriet without the tartness and caustic replies. Both in looks and temperament, they were as different as the proverbial chalk and cheese.

'I'm talking about Archie Marjoribanks paying a call,' Carrie said drily.

Harriet shrugged.

'You must have made some impression!'

'If you really want to know, I think he's got an awful

big tip for himself. He's arrogant, conceited and probably in the long run a bore to boot.'

Carrie turned her back to hide the smile which crept across her face. 'I can see he impressed you,' she said, her voice crackling at the edges with laughter.

Harriet glowered into the sink. The emotions Marjoribanks had aroused frightened her. There had been a few terrible moments back there in the living room when she'd fantasized about him using her. Degrading her. Even now the thought made her shiver.

'Are you all right? You've gone all pale suddenly,' Carrie said anxiously.

Harriet shrugged dismissively. 'I'm fine. Just tired, I think. We've been busy at the factory.'

'Well, that's something to be thankful for. Being busy, I mean. There are plenty who'd give their eye teeth to be in your shoes.'

'I'm only too aware of that,' Harriet said wearily.

'He was married, you know.'

'Who?

'Archie Marjoribanks. His wife died of cancer. I remember John telling me. He knew her, of course, but I never met the woman. I hardly know him, come to that.' She paused to stare thoughtfully before adding, 'I'm pretty sure there's a daughter, but I can't remember what her name is.'

Harriet sighed. 'For the last time, I'm not interested in him nor he in me,' she lied.

'Then why did he bother visiting?'

This was another of those times when Harriet wasn't sure whether Carrie was being naïvely ingenuous or downright dense. 'Well, there *are* two eligible females in this house now you know.'

'What?'

Harriet dried her hands on a spare tea towel before taking herself through to the living room for a last cigarette before bed. She left a stunned Carrie staring after her.

Carrie's thoughts were whirling. It had just never

entered her head that she might be the one who interested Marjoribanks.

Her first impulse was to dismiss the notion of a relationship out of hand as John was only six months dead
and still very much in her heart.

Taking a deep breath, she told herself to hold on a
minute and give the matter some thought. If what Harriet
said was true, then this wasn't an opportunity to be lightly
tossed aside.

For the moment, anyway, she had no feelings for
Archie Marjoribanks, but he seemed personable
enough and had a good sense of humour – an important
point for Carrie.

Although still only twenty-one, she was well aware of
how difficult it was going to be for her to land another
husband with Angus in tow. She appreciated only too
well the reluctance of Glasgow men to take on someone
else's family. But Marjoribanks was a widower with a
wee lassie of his own which rather put him in the same
boat she herself was in.

Of course no one could replace John. There was no
question of that. What she had to do was consider the
practicality of this possible new situation.

She could go on living here in Tallon Street – Donald
had told her she and the baby were welcome as long as
they wanted to stay – but with things as bad as they were
and steadily getting worse it would certainly be helpful
to the family if she was to get out and re-establish a home
of her own.

She still had most of the £200 Robert Smith had given
her, which meant she was economically independent for
some time yet. But that money wouldn't last forever,
and when it finally did run out, where was she going to
get a job when there were virtually none to be had?
She'd already been back several times to the factory
trying for her old place and each time had been turned
down flat.

Biting her lip, she wondered if John would have
approved of her remarrying. Of course he would, she

told herself. John had been a practical man who would have appreciated that life had to go on. He wouldn't have expected her to remain static. Especially not when an opportunity like this presented itself. John and Archie had been close friends when they were running the streets together. If she was going to remarry then it seemed the sensible thing to choose a man of whom John had so obviously been fond. Then there was the fact that Archie worked for the railways in a job that was known not only to be highly paid but also secure. Both these factors counted for an awful lot in these desperate times.

She decided her best policy for the moment was to go to bed and sleep on all this. If she could sleep, that is, with her mind in such a turmoil.

But Carrie did sleep and it was Harriet that the early hours of the morning found wide awake and staring at the ceiling. She was smoking a cigarette and thinking about Australia and the correspondence she'd had recently with the Australian authorities in London. It seemed her chances were high of being accepted for immigration; this was an alternative to her present life which attracted her. There was still an interview to come which meant she had to travel to London in about a month's time and, all being well with the outcome, there was no reason why she shouldn't set sail before the end of the year.

The thought of travelling to the other side of the world excited her immensely. The long sea voyage, the exotic sights, the new people she would meet. She'd already made up her mind to go to Sydney first because that seemed to be the centre of things down there.

It amazed her that she was so unafraid of leaving everyone and everything behind. Perhaps the fear and possible misgivings would come later when things were fixed and it was time for her to leave.

It was going to be so good to get away to a new life and the many things she would be experiencing for the first time. Not that her mother and father hadn't done their best by her, they had. It was just that she felt so confined and constricted by life in Glasgow. Also she felt ashamed that she was twenty-eight years old and still not married. Occasionally at work she'd catch girls looking at her in a funny way and she'd know they'd been talking about her. Pitying her.

Well, she didn't need anyone's pity. Not now or ever.

There would be a man in Australia for her. There just had to be!

She drew on the cigarette and gradually calmed down. What she was dreading most was telling Winnie and Donald she was going abroad. That was going to be sheer bloody murder.

Casting her mind back she remembered what it had been like when Alex left home. There had been an atmosphere in the house for weeks beforehand that you could've cut with a knife. Winnie's face had been continually tripping her while Donald had been like a rumbling volcano threatening to explode at any moment.

Alex had been fresh-faced and bright-eyed that morning he'd set off on his great adventure. Carrie, Hugh, Winnie and she had crowded the big room window as Alex and Donald, her father carrying Alex's suitcase, walked down the street to the tram stop.

Several of the neighbours had thrown their windows open and shouted good luck. Alex had responded with a cheery wave and in one instance with a kiss blown to an old wifey who'd been especially fond of him and he of her.

On reaching the top of the street, he'd turned and stood for a few seconds, drinking it all in: absorbing and memorizing every little detail to take with him on his journey.

Then he was gone and that was the last they ever saw of him.

Now she was going to have to tell her parents that she, too, was going to leave them by going overseas. It would break their hearts.

Sighing, she reached for yet another cigarette. The night had been a long one.

5

Nobody was surprised when Archie Marjoribanks turned up with Hugh after the lad's visit to the Central Station. The idea of being invited to tea had of course been craftily planted by Marjoribanks himself who'd accepted immediately Hugh made the proposal.

Arriving at the Chisholm house, Marjoribanks announced he'd just had a marvellous idea. He'd noticed a fish and chip shop round the corner and why didn't he take them all there for their tea, his treat? He beamed Carrie a winning smile which left no doubt that it was definitely Carrie he'd set his sights on.

Harriet said she was sorry but she had to wash her hair while Winnie came up with the excuse she was a wee bit chesty and going out in the cold might aggravate it. Donald said he would bide at home with his wife.

That left Hugh and Carrie with Hugh mad keen on the idea. Carrie swithered for a moment or two, saying that it wasn't all that long till Angus's feed. She finally agreed after Marjoribanks promised to get her there and back again within the hour.

As this was to be Carrie's first time out with Marjoribanks, Winnie didn't think it a bad thing at all for Hugh to be going along with them. That way things didn't look too obvious for either party and it would also take the pressure off a little bit.

The fish and chip shop was almost deserted, which meant they had no trouble getting seats at one of the marble-topped tables. Having helped Carrie sit down, Marjoribanks slipped Hugh a ten bob note and asked him to go up to the counter and do the ordering.

Carrie was suddenly shy and self-conscious as it had been a long time since she'd been out with a man other than John. She was grateful when Marjoribanks offered her a cigarette as it gave her hands something to do.

While Hugh waited patiently to be served Marjoribanks reminisced about the days when he and John had been youngsters together. Because he had a marvellous way with a story he soon had Carrie laughing so much she had to fumble in her handbag for a hanky with which to dab her streaming eyes.

Marjoribanks had enormous charm and he knew how to use it to best advantage. He now set to work on Carrie, breaking her down, reaching out to her with his personality, enveloping her with warmth and good feelings. By the time Hugh brought over their fish teas he'd sold himself to her lock, stock and winning smile.

While they ate Carrie inquired about his daughter. She nodded sympathetically when in hushed tones he told her how dreadfully the wee lass – who was six and called Sheena – was missing her mum. No matter how hard he tried to compensate for this loss, it just wasn't good enough by a long chalk.

Carrie commiserated about how difficult things must be for the pair of them and he, pulling a wry face, agreed.

Suddenly it dawned on Hugh that there was a lot more going on around this table than at first met the eye. Carefully he listened and watched till, with a shock, he realized Carrie and Marjoribanks were actually making up to one another.

Self-righteous anger blazed in him. John was hardly dead and buried and here was Carrie all set to get off with the man's supposed china!

But Hugh wasn't a fool and he had reached the stage

where he was learning to think twice about things before opening his mouth and making comment.

He recalled the funny look his mother had given his father just before they'd left the house and which he'd momentarily puzzled about at the time. Now the meaning of that look became clear to him. It had been one of connivance, which could only mean that not only were his parents aware of what was going on but that they actually approved!

Now he knew why Marjoribanks had wanted him to do the ordering. It was so these two could have time to chat on their own.

He was inordinately pleased with himself at having figured all this out and decided the best thing he could do would be to remove himself for a little while longer.

Hastily he finished what was left on his plate. Then with a cough he announced he was just going to pop out for an evening paper.

When Carrie said she needed some cigarettes it was Marjoribanks who insisted on handing him the money for them.

He rose and excused himself saying he wouldn't be long but already he'd made up his mind to spend a good fifteen or twenty minutes in the snooker room round the corner. When he strutted out into the drizzle that had started to fall he felt very grown up and wise in the ways of the world.

After Hugh had gone, Carrie told Marjoribanks about her trying to no avail to get her job back at Ballogie Clothing where she'd worked alongside Harriet before having to leave on account of her pregnancy.

This time it was Marjoribanks's turn to make sympathetic noises. When he asked her how she was managing, she told him about the money Robert Smith had given her.

'A good man, old Robert. One of the best,' Marjoribanks stated. His face suddenly creased into a dark scowl as he added, 'but you should have had some compensation from Armstrong's. It was criminal right enough that you didn't.'

There was black bitterness inside Carrie whenever she thought about Armstrong's and Sir Alan in particular. It wasn't an act of charity she was after. The very suggestion would have horrified her. But when a man had worked as hard and diligently as her John had done for Armstrong's then surely his life was worth something!

The flowers and wreaths at the funeral from Armstrong's had all been from John's mates. There hadn't been one solitary bloom from the management. And you would have thought that inquiries would have been made. A word to Donald or someone sent down to chap the door. But no. Nothing at all. Only silence. As far as Sir Alan Armstrong was concerned she and Angus might just as well never have existed.

Dragging herself back from her thoughts she discovered Marjoribanks was talking about where he lived.

His house was in Laidlaw Street which ran off Scotland Street where the Smiths had their shop. What he had was a room and kitchen one flight up. A good house, he assured her, with a range and cavity bed in the kitchen. This latter Sheena slept in while he was through in the front room.

'Tell me about your wife?' Carrie asked. 'I'd like to know.'

A sad, pained expression clouded Marjoribanks's face. She'd been a local girl whom he'd first met when he was Hugh's age. They'd taken an immediate liking to one another and started winching right away. A year after they'd met they got married and a few years later Sheena came along.

It had been a happy marriage. Although mind you they'd had their ups and downs, but then what couple didn't?

With a laugh Carrie agreed. She and John had been known to have had a few right old barneys in their time.

The laughter between them suddenly died as Marjoribanks's face became hard and his cheeks seemed to sink in upon themselves.

In a flat voice he said Sheena had been three when Libby's pain started. Excruciating pain that had caused her to shriek and scream in agony.

Various doctors had been consulted, all of whom agreed on the diagnosis and also on the fact there was nothing they could do for her other than try to alleviate the pain.

At twenty-two years of age Libby had advanced stomach cancer. Her torture had lasted just under a year until a few days before Sheena's fourth birthday when she'd passed away one night in her sleep. As far as he was concerned that final release was a blessing.

Carrie's heart went out to Marjoribanks and the wee lassie whom she hadn't yet met as she listened to all this. Finally after a long silence she said, 'I'd like to meet Sheena sometime.'

Marjoribanks immediately brightened and asked if she'd like to bring Angus over to Laidlaw Street the following Saturday when they could all have tea together?

Carrie replied she'd enjoy that. The arrangement was that she'd take the tram to Scotland Street where Marjoribanks would be waiting to meet her. He did offer to come to Tallon Street and collect her but she laughed that off saying she was perfectly capable of making the journey on her own.

Shortly after that her breasts began to ache and she felt the tell-tale wet which told it was time to feed the bairn. Luckily, Hugh arrived back with his paper and her cigarettes, having been gone almost a full half-hour.

Once outside, Marjoribanks took hold of her by the arm and together the three of them dashed down Tallon Street while above them the heavens opened and heavy rain fell in thundering sheets.

Later, when Carrie emerged from feeding Angus she found Marjoribanks had gone, having taken advantage of a break in the rain.

When she told Winnie and Donald about the arrangement that had been made in the fish and chip shop, Donald's reply was a non-committal grunt while

Winnie's only comment was that it wouldn't do her any harm to get out and about a wee bit more.

Sitting by the fire reading a book, Harriet looked up but didn't speak. She was convinced Carrie was making the biggest mistake of her life but refrained from saying so in case it was misinterpreted as jealousy on her part.

When the following Saturday arrived and it was time to embark on her visit, Carrie wrapped Angus up warmly and bound him to her by means of a tartan shawl. Donald himself saw her to the tramstop.

The journey was a familiar one for Carrie; she'd done it a number of times in the past with John but also on several occasions since the funeral when, true to her word, she'd taken Angus with her over to see the Smiths.

Marjoribanks was waiting for her as arranged and side by side they set off down Scotland Street.

With a new eye, Carrie viewed the area, for if things worked out between her and Marjoribanks this would be where she'd be coming to live.

She had to admit she didn't view the prospect with any great enthusiasm. The streets were manky and in parts choked with litter and refuse. The air smelled strongly of sewage and toilets. Many of the people they passed looked as though they hadn't seen a wash flannel in weeks, while others were so filthy they stank to high heaven.

Faces were pale and thin, features pinched, and although it was February nearly all the children were barefoot.

A couple of tough looking young boys clattered by propelling an iron hoop from a beer barrel by whacking it with a length of wooden stick.

A little girl sat with her feet dangling in the gutter and nursed a dolly made from rags. The doll was tattered and falling apart. She was singing a haunting lullaby about poverty and deprivation she'd learned at her mother's knee, and she sang it with feeling.

Carrie couldn't help comparing Scotland Street with

Tallon Street, something she hadn't actually consciously done before. And on this same conscious level she began to appreciate just how far her father's strivings had brought the Chisholm family.

She told herself that if Donald and John had been able to escape with squalor then so could she and Archie Marjoribanks. All it needed was incentive and determination and she had plenty of both.

Her heart plummeted when they turned into Laidlaw Street. Several of the houses were lying empty with their windows smashed in. They looked like eyeless and toothless monsters who'd succumbed to a combination of internal rot and old age.

Women sat by open windows chatting to their neighbours on either side and occasionally calling to one another across the street, even though it was raw and bitter out.

Carrie gulped as she turned into Marjoribanks's close. There was water running down the walls while from the back of the close came the distinctive stomach-churning smell of an overflowing outside lavatory.

'We're nearly there,' Marjoribanks said quickly ushering her up the stairs. 'I can't tell you how much Sheena is looking forward to meeting you.'

Pulling a large brass key from his pocket he opened the door to his first landing room and kitchen.

Expecting the worst by now Carrie was surprised to find the hallway immaculate, the linoleum on the floor dazzling in its brightness.

Sheena was waiting for them in the kitchen. She was standing in front of a blazing range on which a blackened kettle busily boiled its head off.

The first thing Carrie noted about the lassie was how scared she looked. No doubt it was at the prospect of meeting her. The second thing she saw were the scrapes and bruises on the girl's face.

Archie introduced them and very shyly Sheena extended her hand for it to be shaken. Although the room was warm the hand in Carrie's was as cold as ice. It was also limp as though Sheena wasn't used to shaking hands or else was frightened to put any expression into the gesture.

Carrie beamed Sheena a smile which seemed to put the girl at ease a little. Then Archie mentioned that the kettle was boiling and immediately Sheena scuttled to make some tea.

The kitchen gleamed just like the hallway and on mentioning this Carrie was informed by Archie that Sheena did all the cleaning round the house. Carrie was most impressed by this and said so. This earned her a grateful look from Sheena who was busy spooning tea from the caddy into the pot.

At the back of the range a soot-blackened crock hung on a hook and from this a tantalizing smell wafted forth. Carrie asked what was cooking. Sheen responded that it was an Irish stew.

Carrie was amazed at Sheena's capabilities. Not only was this chit of a girl running the entire household but she was making a damn good job ot if to boot!

Having been instructed to sit in what was obviously the best chair Carrie was then handed a cup of tea by Sheena. Before the girl could draw away Carrie clasped her chin and turned her head to one side. The scrapes and bruises were worse than Carrie had first thought; one bruise in particular was very angry and inflamed.

Prompted by Carrie the girl explained she'd missed her footing on the landing one night and tumbled down an entire flight of stairs.

Having said that, Sheena broke away from Carrie and hurried over to the range where she made herself busy.

Since their arrival the light had faded rapidly leaving the kitchen dark and filled with dancing shadows from the glow from the range.

Marjoribanks lit a spill which he used to light the two gas points jutting out above the brass rail running along the mantelpiece. The kitchen was instantly saturated with warm yellow light.

Carrie asked Sheena if she'd like to hold Angus and

wasn't at all surprised at the enthusiastic reply she received. After all, what little girl doesn't like to fuss with a baby.

Sheena very sensibly said she'd better sit down first before she held Angus. This she did in an old mothering chair which it seemed she'd long since claimed as her own.

Sheena had long, dark hair which fell rather limply in loose waves. Her eyes were two enormous blackcurrants far older and wiser than normal for girls of that age. Her nose had a slight droop at the end giving her something of a witchy appearance. Strangely sensual and provocative mulberry coloured lips added to the effect.

As though she'd been handling babies all her short life Sheena snuggled Angus deep into the crook of her arm and began to hum a popular tune of the day.

For a few seconds Angus showed concern at being deprived of his mother. Then his face burst into a smile and he frothed bubbles. He'd found a new friend.

Carrie rose and crossed to the sideboard on which stood a picture in a frame. As she'd guessed, it was of Archic and Libby's wedding.

Libby was small, dark and looked just like a grown up version of Sheena.

Carrie was suddenly aware of Marjoribanks standing beside her and that he to was gazing down at the picture. His lips were pursed and the sadness she'd seen in the fish and chip shop was back in his eyes.

'She looks nice,' Carrie said.

'I thought so and so did John. He always maintained I got the better bargain by far.'

Carrie couldn't think of a reply to that so she returned to her chair. Staring into the fire's flickering flames, she was aware of being closely studied by Sheena.

She liked the girl and was certain she was liked in return. All that was needed was a little time for the pair of them to get used to one another. If all went well it shouldn't be too long before they were great friends.

Carrie turned and indicated Angus. 'He's certainly

taken to you,' she said.

Sheena smiled, suddenly wide open and vulnerable. 'I like him too. I could sit here cuddling him all night.'

Angus cooed and stuck a chubby fist in the air. From the look on his face it was an idea he heartily approved of.

'Libby and I had hoped to have more children,' Marjoribanks said softly, then shrugged philosophically, 'But of course that wasn't to be.'

'Who knows how these things finally turn out?' Carried said enigmatically. A brief glance in his direction told her he'd got the point.

A little later she took Angus back to let Sheena get on with the business of setting out the meal. She thought the best thing to do was sit back and not interfere. Sheena might be young but for the time being, anyway, this kitchen was her preserve.

When everything was ready Carrie laid the now fast asleep Angus on his rug in front of the fire, close enough to benefit from the warmth but far enough away to escape any flying sparks.

She knew he wouldn't sleep too long as it was his feed time soon and he was notoriously prompt in his demands when it came to that.

The stew was excellent, certainly as good as anything she could have turned out and she didn't hesitate in saying so.

Besides the stew there were jacket potatoes and thick slices of bread and butter – navvies' doorstops, Winnie would have called the latter – all of which went down a treat.

It transpired that Libby had been teaching Sheena to cook ever since the lassie was old enough to take things in, which was just as well, Archie joked. His cooking was so abominable as to be completely inedible.

As soon as the meal was finished Sheena cleared the table and started the washing up.

Having asked Archie to remove himself to the front room Carrie lifted the now grizzling Angus and started feeding him.

While Angus sucked lustily Carrie sat watching Sheena working at the sink. With her sleeves drawn back, the girl was standing on a chair humming to herself as she attacked the pile of dirty dishes in front of her.

Carrie shook her head in wonderment. The girl was so grown up. It was hard to remember that Sheena was six and not sixty, for that was how she continually came across. A wee old wifey who'd seen and done it all and consequently would stand no nonsense from anyone.

Carrie winced as Angus nipped her nipple, his way of telling her that that breast was empty and would she please change him over. 'Beast!' she grinned.

For a while she tried to engage Sheena in conversation about school but the girl was vague and unforthcoming on the subject.

When Angus had been fed she called Marjoribanks back through and told him it was time she was going.

She changed the baby's nappy and then wrapped him up warmly. After shrugging herself into her coat Archie helped bind the baby to her by means of the tartan shawl.

When she was ready she solemnly thanked Sheena for the meal and said she hoped she would be seeing her again soon. Sheena seemed pleased by that prospect.

As they walked down the stairs Marjoribanks said the people on the ground floor had been on to the factor about the overflowing cludge and the factor had promised to have it seen to within the next few days. He didn't refer to the water running down the close walls.

Carrie had hoped to call in on the Smiths but there was no time for that now.

On the previous occasion she'd been up to see them, Robert had let drop several times that she'd be surprised if she knew what was in the black metal safe he kept bolted to the kitchen floor. There had been sly references to pearls and other extremely expensive items. When she'd obviously looked doubting he'd hurried from the room to return with a gorgeous piece of scrimshaw which she'd duly admired.

Thinking about it afterwards she'd come to the conclusion the fly old devil must be acting as a receiver for illegal merchandise brought in from abroad. The docks weren't all that far away and as a consequence the area was well frequented by merchant seamen.

She hoped old man Smith wasn't going to land himself in trouble, for his wife Meg's sake as much as his own.

When they reached the tramstop Archie asked to see her again and suggested the following Friday. He said he would like to take her dancing or if she wasn't up to that yet how about the pictures?

Carrie replied the pictures would be the best idea and a time was agreed when he would pick her up at Tallon Street.

Carrie immediately made a mental note that she was going to have to wean Angus onto a bottle so she wouldn't be as tied as she was now. She decided to buy the necessary paraphernalia first thing on Monday morning and try him on it.

During her journey home she thought about her meeting with Sheena. She'd been worried in case the girl turned out to be a problem but her fears had proved groundless. She and Sheena were going to be the very best of pals. She was sure of it.

As soon as Carrie let herself into the house she knew something had happened. Through the open doorway to the living room she saw her mother sitting at the table with a face like fizz.

She settled Angus in his bed before taking her coat off and going on through.

Donald sat hunched in his chair, pipe clamped between his teeth, glowering into the fire. Underneath the glower he looked angry and hurt.

Harriet was sitting on the pouffe by the window. Her face was pale, her expression one of defiance.

'Have you heard the latest?' Winnie demanded.

Carrie shook her head.

'Harriet is emigrating to Australia.'

It was a bombshell which left Carrie literally stunned. It was so unexpected, so completely out of the blue. 'When?' she finally managed to get out.

'I'll have to go to London in three weeks for an interview. If I'm successful I'll know sometime after that,' Harriet replied.

Winnie rose and, looking to be on the verge of tears, left the room.

After the door had closed behind her mother Harriet said, 'It's my life. Surely I'm allowed to decide what I want to do with it?'

Donald didn't reply but savagely poked the fire instead.

'Well?' The word cracked between Harriet and her father like a rifle shot. But there was no disrespect in her tone. Rather a plea to be understood.

'You're within your rights, lass,' Donald said reluctantly. Then as an afterthought, 'It's Alex, you see. She can't forget what happened to him.'

'I don't want to hurt anybody, Papa. I just want to do what I think is right for me.'

Carrie wasn't sure whether or not it was her imagination but it seemed to her that Donald had aged since she'd seen him last earlier in the day.

Donald took a deep breath and knocked out his pipe. He saw a lot of himself in Harriet. Good points as well as bad. Losing her this way would be like losing an arm. Of his children she was the one he'd always most closely identified with.

'I'd better see to your mother,' he said, adding, 'we won't stand in your way, lass. As you say, it's your life. Best do with it as you see fit. Tonight was . . . well, let's just say tonight was a wee bit of a shock, that's all. No doubt we'll have grown to accept it by the morning.'

'Thanks Papa.'

He followed Winnie through to their bedroom where, as he'd known he would, he found her lying crying in the dark.

'I knew it wasn't going to be easy and it wasn't,'

Harriet said.

'Want to talk about it?'

'No. Tomorrow maybe but not now.'

Carrie understood. She stayed long enough to smoke a last cigarette and then she left Harriet alone and gazing into the fire.

In times like these great comfort and solace could be found in a fire.

This would be first time Harriet had ever been out of Scotland and naturally enough she was excited at the prospect.

It was bitterly cold in the train compartment due to the heating not working so she was grateful for the woolly rug Winnie had insisted she bring with her, and for the flask of hot tea Carrie had made and packed.

It hadn't been easy getting time off from Ballogie Clothing but luckily she was chums with Jakey Sanderson, the supervisor. He'd managed to wangle it for her after she'd explained the position to him, having first of all sworn him to secrecy.

What Harriet didn't know was that Jakey had a cousin who'd been pestering him for months to get her a job which he'd promised to do the moment one of his girls left. That was why he'd been so obliging in helping Harriet get a few days off so she could travel to London.

As the train thundered through the night Harriet reflected that the days following her telling Winnie and Donald about her plans to emigrate hadn't been nearly so bad as she'd expected. There had been a weary, resigned quality about Winnie but there were no further words of either argument or recrimination. Regardless of hurt, acceptance had been total.

She'd gone into the big room one night to find Winnie sitting quietly by the window staring at the photo of Alex she always carried in her handbag. With guilt lying in her stomach like a lump of lead she'd turned and left the room.

Hugh's reactions to her news had been different to

anyone else's in the family. He'd been so excited you'd have thought it was him who was going rather than her.

The rhythmic clickety clack of the wheels finally lulled Harriet into a fitful sleep. When she woke the train was pulling into Euston Station.

Punctual to the minute, she presented herself at the address in the Strand where she'd been instructed to go.

For half an hour she sat on a hard wooden bench and then an official came out to see her. Gravely he told her the person she'd been due to see was off sick and could she possibly stay overnight at their expense and come back the following morning.

She was delighted as she'd been dreading the long return journey. Quickly she agreed and a taxi took her to a small hotel in Euston Square.

The room she was shown into was far grander than she could have afforded, so this little touch of luxury was an added bonus. She had a cup of tea and a token rest. Then she took herself out onto the streets of London.

Midday found her in Soho standing outside a little restaurant. Thinking herself terribly daring, she went inside and ordered something to eat.

Filled with all sorts of exquisite things and, as a consequence, feeling extraordinarily happy and alive, she strolled to Regent Street where she spent a long time window shopping.

Eventually, exhausted and foot sore she made her way back to the hotel in Euston Square where she slept for several hours like the proverbial log.

In the hotel the evening meal was called dinner and served a lot later than the tea she was used to.

At the appropriate time she made her way down to the dining room where she found a number of guests already gathered. Spying a small table set to one side she decided that was for her and sat down. She was unfolding her napkin when a deep voice said, 'Excuse me ma'am but I think you've made a mistake. This table is reserved for me.'

Harriet looked up, flushing as she did so. The man had

no sooner spoken than she'd seen the 'reserved' sign set out quite plainly in front of her. 'I'm terribly sorry,' she said and started to rise.

The man was short, paunchy and balding with a round, jovial face and laughing eyes. 'No please!' he said laying a restraining hand on her arm. 'Now that rights have been established it would be my pleasure if you would join me.'

Harriet was at a loss to know what to do. Her mind was made up for her when the man said, 'That's settled then,' and sat down facing her.

He was a lot older than she was. Nearly fifty she guessed. With a voice that came out as a lazy drawl and had a rather hypnotic quality about it.

'My name's Lou Dansie,' he said sticking out his hand.

'I'm Harriet Chisholm,' she replied as they shook.

'Scots?'

She nodded.

'Aaah! I thought so. Unmistakable, that brogue. I knew a lot of Jocks during the war.' He leaned across and whispered confidentially. 'I was sure as heck pleased those guys were on my side. Yes siree!'

She had to laugh. 'You must be an American.'

'From Los Angeles. And you?'

'Glasgow.'

'I've heard about there,' Dansie said. 'I think it would be too heavily industrial for my taste. Too dirty.'

Thinking that Dansie was being disparaging about her city, Harriet's temper flared. Then she realized from the look on his face that he'd merely been passing comment. Instantly she relaxed again, contrite at her hot-headedness.

'Aye well a place is *who* you know. If you're ever in Glasgow come and see my family and me. We'll try and see to it that you go away with a favourable impression.'

'I might just take you up on that,' Dansie replied, thinking that Harriet's spontaneous offer of hospitality was just like the Jocks he'd known in France. Those guys would share their last grain of food with you rather than let you go without.

Because he was easy to talk to Dansie soon had Harriet chattering on about her family and their life in Cathcart.

'Now, how about some claret?' he finally interrupted.

Harriet was taken aback. The fact of the matter was she'd never tasted wine in her life, it being viewed with the utmost suspicion north of the border.

Dansie saw her hesitation. 'Perhaps you'd prefer a burgundy or a beaujolais?' he asked.

Harriet decided frankness was always the best policy. She admitted that wine was totally unknown to her but as he seemed so keen on the idea she wasn't averse to trying some.

Dansie was aghast, declaring this to be a situation that would have to be remedied. He immediately summoned the wine waiter.

Harriet could hardly believe her ears when he ordered champagne. 'But that must be so expensive!' she gasped.

Dansie chuckled, enjoying the gesture he was making. The women he normally mixed with wouldn't have shown as much enthusiasm or delight had he been showering them with fistfuls of diamonds. 'Nothing less will do to mark the occasion!' he stated firmly and dispatched the wine waiter with a flourish.

Harriet had already decided she liked this little, stout man from America. Despite the differences in their ages and backgrounds there was an empathy between them.

Dansie was an expert at getting people to unburden themselves and this talent he now exercised on Harriet, who began to speak at length about her plans for emigration.

When the champagne came Dansie proposed a toast to Harriet wishing her success and happiness in her new life. Harriet declared she would drink to that and did so with a laugh.

She liked the champagne. It was light and tickly like cider only a lot more so. But it didn't seem to have a kick to it.

Dansie smiled enigmatically when she said that.

There was a bloom in Harriet's cheeks and a sparkle in her eyes that had nothing whatever to do with the wine. The dry spinster was being transformed into a desirable woman, desirable because she knew the man sitting opposite saw her as such.

After a while it dawned on Harriet she'd been doing all the talking. So telling Dansie it was his turn she shut up.

'Do you ever go to the motion pictures?' he asked.

The unexpectedness of the question and its seeming irrelevance caught her off guard. She nodded. She and Carrie often went, enjoying the sheer escapism the cinema had to offer.

With a smile Dansie informed her he was a contract writer with United Artists, the company formed two years previously by Mary Pickford, Douglas Fairbanks, Charlie Chaplin and D.W. Griffith.

Harriet was rocked. She was with someone who actually knew the fabled stars of the silver screen! Men and women who were like gods to her.

She listened eagerly to Dansie's account of life in Hollywood. The parties. The swimming pools. What a cut-throat business the movie industry was. The ambitions of the young hopefuls who flocked there. The bitter disappointment that lay in store for so many of them.

The razzle-dazzle of an opening night; what it was like to discover you'd been involved in a success, a failure.

Personalities who worked for Metro, Universal, Cosmopolitan, Vitagraph, First National, Paramount, Selznick. The names rolled off Dansie's tongue as naturally as Glasgow districts would have rolled off hers.

Films of the previous year he'd personally seen being made: 'The Four Horsemen of the Apocalypse', 'The Queen of Sheba', 'The Square Shooter', 'The Lotus Eater', 'Camille', 'A Virgin Paradise'.

Harriet was completely entranced by the spell of words that Dansie wove. She'd been transported to a world a million miles away from Tallon Street and

Ballogie Clothing. Here was glamour, excitement, all
the things she so desperately craved in life. Dansie went
on to describe how he'd been irresistibly drawn towards
movies having seen Florence Lawrence in 'The
Biograph Girl' and a one-reel version of Tolstoy's 'Re-
demption' in 1909.

To start with he'd worked as an actor, it seeming the
obvious way to get into the industry. But as time went by
he'd grown more and more frustrated by the actor's role
until one morning it had come to him like a bolt from the
blue that writing was his true vocation. He had realized
his destiny in life was to be a motion picture script writer.

He laid his right hand on the table and pointed to a
heavy gold ring he wore. 'Mary herself gave me that,' he
stated proudly.

'Pickford?'

He nodded.

Harriet gingerly reached out and touched the ring.
She might have been touching the Holy Grail so reverential was her gesture.

The courses came and went while Dansie explained
he'd been sent to Britain to gather background material
for a new picture he was to write for Fairbanks and
Pickford.

The previous year Fairbanks had starred in 'The
Three Musketeers' and the production had been so suc-
cessful that he was to star in another costume drama.
The subject chosen had been Bonnie Prince Charlie.
Fairbanks would play the Prince, of course, while
Pickford would be Flora McDonald.

So far Dansie had been in London for a fortnight and
during that time he'd been researching Charles Edward
Stuart at the British Museum. This would take him at
least another week and then he was travelling north by
motor car to Scotland where he would tour round all the
places known to be associated with the Young
Pretender's uprising.

Harriet put up no resistance when Dansie ordered
brandies. She'd have drunk turpentine by now had he

suggested it. Anything so long as this conversation continued.

Over coffee Dansie suggested they go on to a night club where they could talk further and perhaps dance. Harriet accepted instantly.

Sheena Marjoribanks lay in her cavity bed in the darkness listening to the sound of her father snoring through the wall. She shivered at the memory of the thrashing he'd given her a few nights previously with the thick leather belt he wore round his work trousers.

He'd been drinking. Not too much but still enough to spark off one of his terrible rages.

She could remember the many times he'd used that same belt on her mother and her mother screaming and pleading in the front room while she lay huddled here in her bed listening to it all.

'Oh, mummy!' she whispered stuffing her hand into her mouth. Tears burst from the corners of her eyes. Her mother's face danced before her. Those sad, forlorn features crammed full of misery and despair.

Some day she was going to escape from all this, she promised herself. As soon as she was old enough she was going to walk out through that front door and never come back.

In the meantime it would be good to have an ally about the place. She saw Carrie could be an ally and she would bring a baby to hug when the nights were long and cold and it was lonely to be on your own.

Thinking of Angus made her smile, and with him still in her thoughts, she drifted off to sleep.

Beside Harriet, Lou Dansie lay sleeping with his arm thrown over the top part of his face. His mouth puckered every time he exhaled, which he did often and noisily.

Harriet was glowing inside. The aftermath of love-making had left her for the first time in her life feeling fulfilled. She'd waited long enough for this moment but the wait had been worthwhile.

She ran her hands over her breasts and down her long, lean flanks, the flesh tingling to her touch. It might have been slumbering through the years until this small, paunchy American had come along and with a wave of his magic wand (she smiled at that) brought it ecstatically alive.

Dansie groaned and turned on to his side so that his back was towards her. She stared in fascination at the thick matting of black hair which started at the nape of his neck and grew downwards. Reaching out she stroked the hair on his shoulders, causing him to quiver.

'What are you thinking about?' he asked without turning round.

'You.'

'What about me?'

'You've told me nearly everything about yourself except the most important thing. Are you married?'

Dansie thought of his wife, Bess, and their daughter, Bonnie Sue who were 6000 miles away in Hollywood. It had been years since things were good between him and Bess but they'd stuck it out together because of the kid.

Hollywood was filled with children whose parents were divorced. Both he and Bess knew only too well what the majority of these kids turned out like. Lost souls. Neurotic messes. Bums. And in some extreme cases all three combined.

Neither he nor Bess could bear the thought of their daughter ending up like that, so they'd clung on to the few tattered remnants of their relationship.

'Well?' Harriet prompted.

'I'm married.'

He'd had to be, of course. It would have been too easy otherwise.

'Harriet?'

She drew him to her while placing a hand over his mouth. 'There are only a few hours left before you have to go back to your own room. Use them to love me,' she whispered.

6

Sitting by the window watching the men from Armstrong's trudge home from their work, Winnie's heart sank within her. The spring had gone out of their step, and without exception they walked with eyes downcast. Instead of the usual hum punctuated by the occasional laugh or piece of horse play, there was an air about them that was dark and sombre.

Winnie knew the signs. There had been a big lay-off. The only question remaining was how many had been made idle?

Closing her eyes and clasping her hands in her lap, she offered up a brief prayer. Luckily Donald was a gaffer and as such would be among the last to go. Hugh was still an apprentice which was an advantage at a time like this. Apprentices were always kept on to the end because they were cheap labour.

It was a strange night out, the sky peculiarly overcast and everything very still. The only sound to disturb the brooding silence was the tramp of the men's tackety boots on pavement and road.

There was Mrs McElvey's man, Bill, looking as though he'd lost a pound and found a tanner. Dazed and bewildered, he turned into his close and vanished from view.

Wee Tommy Taylor who always whistled to and from his work turned into Tallon Street. He wasn't whistling now.

Behind Tommy Taylor came Davey Beattie who

every Hogmanay came out onto the street directly after the bells to play his pipes. The expression on his face was the one he'd worn for weeks after receiving word that his two boys had fallen at Ypres.

Winnie rose and went through to the kitchen to make sure the tea was ready to go onto the table. That's where she was when the front door opened.

Wiping her hands on her pinny she hurried into the hall where she found Donald staring at the yellow distempered wall as though some profound truth was being unfolded to him there.

'Donald?'

When she got no reply or even a flicker of recognition she tried again. 'Donald?'

Coming out of the deep trance, he shook himself.

'How many?' Winnie asked, trepidation large within her. She'd never seen Donald in this sort of state before.

It took him a full minute, but finally he got that one terrible word out. 'Everyone,' he rasped.

She slumped and had to hold on to the wall for support. It was the nightmare come true. '*Everyone?*'

He nodded. 'Every last man jack of us laid off until further notice.'

Somehow she found the strength to stagger back to the kitchen where she sat on the edge of the opened coal bin.

Big Donald ran his wife a glass of water and then called through to Hugh that he wanted him.

Hugh was handed money by his father and told to run down the road and get a bottle of whisky.

'God knows but we all need a dram,' Donald said, adding, 'And if we don't get one the night who knows when we'll get the chance again?'

'This means we'll have to get by on Harriet's money and whatever Carrie can put into the kitty from what's left of old man Smith's two hundred,' Winnie said.

Donald and Winnie looked at one another, each with the same thought in mind. When Harriet went to Australia there wouldn't even be her money coming in.

Winnie buried her head in her hands, her mind numb at the prospect of what lay ahead of them.

Donald sat on the coal bunker beside his wife and, in a gesture that was both rough and gentle, put his arm round her shoulders. 'We'll get by somehow, lass. You just wait and see. After all, we've never died a winter yet!'

His voice was jocular and full of hope. Exactly the opposite to what he was feeling.

Sitting there, he noted that the linoleum under the sink was beginning to go. Well, it would be a long time now before that was replaced.

He clasped and unclasped his fist in frustration. There had to be work somewhere! And even as he was trying to reassure himself he knew in his heart of hearts the position was hopeless. There were tens of thousands out of work on Clydeside and now he and the rest of the men from Armstrong's had joined their ever swelling ranks.

Sneeringly he thought of Lloyd George and the coalition government. What a fiasco! What a shambles! It was long overdue for the working man to take power into his own hands in order to shape both his and his country's future. Only with the Labour Party in control would the ordinary man in the street get a fair crack of the whip. That was something Donald believed fervently and with total commitment.

Donald and Winnie were still sitting on the edge of the bunker when Hugh arrived back with the whisky. Carrie was with Hugh, having met up with him at the bottom of the stairs. She'd already heard the news on the street and had come straight home from her shopping.

Standing now just inside the kitchen door, Carrie watched Donald pour out four very large glasses of whisky.

Holding his glass, Hugh opened his mouth to make a flippant toast, but clamped it shut again when he saw the brooding volcanic expression on his father's face.

Sipping her whisky Carrie thought about Archie Marjoribanks. He'd already hinted at marriage, but she'd contrived to let him know that out of respect for John she wanted to wait a little while yet. Now it seemed she was going to have to think again due to this sudden alteration in circumstances.

She'd arranged to meet Archie in two nights' time when they planned to go to the jigging. She would sort it out with him then.

Hugh felt strangely lightheaded, a state which had nothing whatsoever to do with the drink but rather because it was gradually sinking into him that he'd been laid off and was now without a job.

Long, boring days stretched endlessly before him. The prospect was depressing. He'd seen what enforced idleness had done to other men, turning them into cabbages with no hope. No future. No nothing! It terrified him that he, too, in time would become like them.

He remembered then what Aly Paterson had said to him when he'd given up running with the milk to start in at Armstrong's. 'You're the best lad we've ever had and it breaks my heart to see you go,' Aly had said. Well, Aly still had the dairy up at Muirend and still did morning deliveries. It was certainly worth a try.

Harriet arrived home several hours later, having taken the midday train from Euston. Harriet thought it's an ill-wind which blows no one any good when she was told the calamitous news about Armstrong's. This was precisely the excuse she needed on which to hang her change of plans. She announced she had no intention of going to Australia now as it was essential she stayed at home and kept on her job at Ballogie Clothing.

Both Donald and Winnie were most humble at what they thought to be their daugher's enormous self-sacrifice.

What neither of them knew was that Harriet had already decided not to emigrate and hadn't even bothered to attend the interview for which she'd gone down to London especially.

Lou Dansie had paid the hotel bill. The arrangement between her and Dansie was that he would come to

Glasgow and see her before motoring through to Edinburgh where he intended making his base of operations while in Scotland.

She would be travelling through to stay with him at weekends.

Shortly after Harriet's return, Hugh slipped down to the wash-house where he kept his bike. He'd decided there was no time like the present to find out what the current situation was at Aly Paterson's dairy.

It was several miles from Tallon Street to Muirend and all of it uphill.

As Hugh strained at the pedals he recalled that a lot of the enjoyment of running with the milk had been the horses whom he'd liked enormously and who'd liked him in return.

There had been one which had been his favourite, an old black beast named Squinty whose eyes were so crossed as to almost disappear into one another.

He thought now of Squinty with affection and wondered whether the old horse was still going strong or if it had finally got past it and been put down.

He turned the bike off the hill and into Aly Paterson's driveway. The house situated at the end of the long run up was an imposing edifice of grey stone which Aly had built many years previously to replace the very old and tiny one already on the site.

In front and to one side of the house stood the dairy building; facing that across the yard were the stables.

Besides this small complex Aly also owned a farm on the road to East Kilbride from where he supplied the dairy with milk.

Aly himself answered Hugh's ring and after shaking hands and being pounded on the back Hugh was ushered straight into the parlour where several logs were crackling away cheerily in the large stone fireplace.

Aly's wife, Greta, greeted Hugh as a long lost son. Kissing him on the cheek, she announced she would away through and put the kettle on and see if she could find a nice wee bit of shortie.

Aly pooh-poohed this idea saying that as Hugh was a man now and doing a man's job – Hugh winced at that – he should be given a man's drink. The whisky decanter was then duly taken from the sideboard and a large one poured.

Acting on doctor's orders Aly didn't drink any more, what with a weak heart and high blood pressure. Thinking it unfair to indulge when her husband couldn't, Greta had also forsworn alcohol.

'To Stewart!' Hugh toasted bringing grins of delight to the Paterson's faces. Stewart was their only child and the apple of their eye.

Hugh had first met Stewart when he'd come to work at the dairy and the pair of them had taken an instant liking to one another. After a few weeks the two of them had become almost inseparable.

Now Stewart was at agricultural college in Dumfriesshire where he was learning the very latest in farming methods. On leaving college he would take over the farming side of the business.

Greta confided in Hugh that Stewart had met a lassie and it seemed an engagement was in the offing. But before Hugh could offer his congratulations, Greta went on to say in a sepulchral tone that, nice as the lassie was, she had one terrible drawback. She was, horror of horrors, *English!*'

Hugh was astounded by this disclosure. He wondered what had come over his old pal. Stewart married to an Englishwoman! It was unthinkable.

'Dear me,' he said, shaking his head.

Greta sniffed.

'It's enough to drive a man to drink,' said Aly, looking longingly at the decanter. But a sharp glance from Greta was enough to dispel the notion. When it came down to it he enjoyed living more than he did the booze.

Quickly changing the conversation Greta asked Hugh to what they owed the honour of his visit? In a few terse sentences he told them about the closure of Armstrong's which meant he was now out of a job.

Both the Patersons were shocked by this news and Greta immediately rose and refilled his glass.

'There have already been marches out in Rutherglen,' Aly said, grim faced. 'Thousands of men protesting that there's no work for them and demanding something be done about it. There's nearly two million unemployed in the country now, you know.'

'Two million?' Hugh repeated. He found the figure staggering.

'Thing are as bad as they've ever been,' said Aly. His own particular business hadn't yet felt the squeeze but if the present downward spiral continued then it was only a matter of time.

The white collar workers who comprised the majority of his customers had so far escaped the ravishes of being thrown out of work. But they were far from immune.

Hugh then bluntly asked if he could have his old job back and was told he could start first thing Monday morning. The going rate was three shillings a day which added up to twenty-one shillings a week. Only a shilling less than he'd been earning at Armstrong's!

Hugh was jubilant and profuse in his thanks, but Aly would have none of it, saying what were friends for if they couldn't do you a good turn when it was needed.

Hugh said his good-byes. Outside the house he whistled as he mounted his bike. He couldn't wait to get home and tell Donald and Winnie.

After Hugh had gone Greta said gently, 'You didn't really need another boy, did you?'

Aly shrugged and stuck his hands in his trouser pockets. 'What else could I do?'

Smiling, Greta crossed to her husband and hooked her arm round his. 'You're a big softie and I love you for it,' she said.

Clutching one another like teenagers they made their way upstairs.

Hugh arrived home just as Winnie was making a last cup

of tea before going to bed. Unable to contain himself he burst into the kitchen and blurted out his news to her.

Winnie's eyes were decidedly dewy as she folded him in her arms and hugged him tight. She then called out to Donald to come away through and hear what his big son had to tell him.

Donald listened in silence while Hugh reported the outcome of his visit to the Patersons. When Hugh had finished Donald cleared his throat and said gruffly they had a big son right enough.

Winnie knew how hard Donald was taking all this. It was going to tear him apart inside for the family to be dependent on what Hugh and Harriet brought in. But better that than them all slowly starving to death on the pittance the broo* would allot them, she thought grimly.

That night Harriet tossed and turned. Her newly awakened body was afire while her mind churned with thoughts about the man who'd started the blaze.

What had really changed her mind about emigration was finding out that as well as researching the Bonnie Prince Charlie film in Scotland, Lou intended remaining on there while he wrote the first drafts of the script – at least six months' work. That and the fact that his marriage was on the rocks.

A lot could happen in six months. And she would see that it did.

Early next morning Donald's eyes flickered open at their usual time. With the customary grunt at Winnie he climbed out of bed and stretched himself by the window. He was about to pull on his work trousers when Winnie quietly said, 'You've forgotten, Donald.'

It all came flooding back to him in a wash of resentment and sour bile. He was laid off. Useless.

His shoulders sagged and something of his masculinity seeped out of him. He was no longer the provider. Instead he would have to go down and join the dole

* Unemployment exchange.

queue, making himself in his own eyes no better than a common beggar. It was a galling thought and made him feel bitterly ashamed.

· He sat on the edge of the bed and started to speak. Out came many ideas and theories that had been percolating in his mind since the end of the war.

'They've got it all wrong,' he said slowly. Choosing his words with care. 'There are all these capitalists like Sir Alan Armstrong who've got the wind up and instead of spending their money they're hoarding it away in banks where it isn't doing anyone any good. If they keep on like that then the damn money will eventually become worthless. Not even worth the paper it's printed on. What they should be doing is spending and expanding trade. It's as obvious as the nose on your face but none of them has the sense to see it.

'Trade! If we don't do that then we stagnate, which is exactly what's happening to the country today. The capitalists are running scared and all they can think to do is hide away in their big houses assuring one another it'll all blow over. Well I've got news for them. This time things could get so bad that none of us will come out of it.'

With eyes blazing he continued, 'They must find the courage to take their money out of the banks and spend great chunks of it. It's the only way. Our only possible salvation!

'They have to recognize that for the truth before it's too late because if they don't it'll be the end of Britain as a country, far less a world power. God help us!'

Folding his pants, he laid them over the arm of the chair and then crawled back into bed where he lay with his arms by his side, staring at the ceiling.

Eventually he fell into a fitful sleep to dream of the first Labour government putting the country to rights and sorting out all social injustices.

Like everyone else who worked at Ballogie Clothing Jakey Sanderson had long since got used to the continual roar of more than 200 heavy industrial sewing machines clattering away flat out.

He strode down the back row of machines till he came to Harriet's where he stopped and waited till she realized he was there. When she looked up, he nodded in the direction of the cubicle that served him as an office. She gesticulated back she'd be right with him as soon as she'd finished off her present seam.

Jakey and Harriet were old pals, having known one another for many years, ever since Jakey had moved to Cathcart from Govan, in fact.

For a while they'd seen each other regularly at dances, and he had always come across and asked her up. The pair of them were excellent dancers and were rated highly amongst the Glasgow crowd. This was praise indeed as dancing was and always has been a sort of second religion in the city, the first of course being football.

As he let himself into his office, Jakey thought long-ingly of the cup of tea due to be served him soon. He had a terrible hangover from the night before, having run into his cousin Isa's man, Matt. It was to Isa that he'd promised the next available job.

The first thing Matt had asked about was the job, and it had been to Jakey's great delight that he'd been able to say one was coming up soon.

Matt had insisted they celebrate the news on him. Repairing to the nearest pub, pint after pint had been called for till they were both nearly awash. Then again at Matt's insistence they'd changed to big whiskies which had flowed in a seemingly never-ending stream.

Not once had Jakey been called on to put his hand in his pocket.

There was a knock on the cubicle door and Harriet entered to find Jakey sitting behind his desk beaming up at her.

'Well?' he demanded.

She couldn't think what he was talking about. 'Well, what?'

'How did the interview go?'

Of course he would want to know. He had gone to the trouble of arranging time off for her, after all. Normally she would have thought, but since meeting Lou Dansie her mind had become preoccupied with the American to the exclusion of all else.

'I'm afraid I got turned down,' she lied smoothly. Then with a wry smile, added, 'So it looks like you'll have to keep putting up with me.'

Jakey had to turn away so she didn't see the brief flash of combined anger and panic which contorted his face. This was terrible. More than that it was disastrous! He'd assured Matt the job was in the bag and as a consequence eagerly accepted all those drinks bought him by Isa's grateful husband. He'd committed himself, damn it to hell!

Things wouldn't have been quite so bad if it hadn't been Matt he'd promised, for Matt was a notorious hardman who carried a razor and had the reputation of breaking people's limbs just for fun. In local parlance Matt was a right heidcase.

He mopped sweat from his brow and then leaned back in his chair to stare up at Harriet. He liked the woman. Always had done. And she was a great partner at the jigging, unlike his wife who danced as though wearing clogs and two left ones at that. But now she'd landed him in a proper pickle and no mistake!

One way or another Isa was going to have to be found a job, and soon, because if she wasn't Matt would be round wanting his pound of flesh. And like Shylock, Matt had a nasty habit of putting a literal interpretation on things.

'Are you all right? You're looking awful funny,' Harriet asked.

Jakey forced a laugh and replied he was suffering from a wee touch of indigestion which he was sure would soon pass.

He then muttered a few words of sympathy to Harriet about not being accepted for emigration and she played along by pretending to be disappointed.

After she'd gone he hunched forward and stared morosely at his desk. There wasn't a hope that any of the other girls would hand in her notice in the near or even distant future. They would all be hanging on to their jobs like grim death. Even more so now that Armstrong's had closed down, throwing many of their relatives and boy-friends out of work.

But a solution to his dilemma would have to be found, and even now he knew what that solution was going to be.

Sighing, he reached for a cigarette and lit up. Much as he liked Harriet he feared Matt Walker even more.

At five am on the Monday morning Hugh presented himself at Paterson's dairy. As he was the first to arrive he went into the stables to have a look round for Squinty, and it was with a whoop of delight that he found his old friend munching away on some feed. A welcoming neigh told him he hadn't been forgotten.

He made a big thing of the horse, rubbing and scratch-ing its head while in response it nuzzled him under the armpit.

'Who the hell are you?' the voice demanded roughly.

Hugh turned to find himself staring at a squat, middle-aged man of less than normal height. Normally an easy-going, affable chap who rarely took exception to any-one, Hugh did so now. The moment he set eyes on Ronnie Sproat he knew he'd met an enemy.

He explained who he was and why he was there and then waited while Sproat considered this news.

What Hugh saw filled him with apprehension. Sproat was a walking powerhouse, his chest thick and burly, his thighs and biceps chunky with muscle. His face was concave, the nose no more than a button. His neck was short and sat atop his shoulders rather like a main branch sprouting from an oak. His eyes were dark and in this particular light like two empty holes punched on either side of his nose.

Hugh, on the other hand, was tall and willowy slim. It

would be a number of years yet before he came into his full strength.

Hugh knew that Sproat could beat the living daylights out of him without even half trying.

'I've heard of you,' Sproat sneered, showing badly decayed teeth, several of which were green with infection.

'Oh aye?' said Hugh, a little scared and not quite sure what was going to happen next. What he couldn't understand was why a discerning man like Aly Paterson had taken on a brute like this.

'You were a pal of Stewart's, were you no'?' Sproat demanded, picking his nose.

Hugh nodded, wary, waiting for anything to happen.

Sproat cogitated again and from the heavy frown on his face it was obvious his thinking processes were somewhat on the slow side.

Hugh found himself twitching and desperately wishing Sproat would say something. These long silences were unnerving.

'Did you know Stewart, then?' he asked finally, more to break the silence than because he was curious.

'I knew him all right,' Sproat replied, his eyes glittering ominously. 'I took over from him as head boy when he went away to college.'

Squinty snorted and tried to poke his nose back into Hugh's armpit.

Sproat's eyes narrowed as he watched this interchange between Squinty and Hugh, nodding to himself as though he found this of great significance. Then turning abruptly on his heel he strode from the stable.

Hugh breathed a sigh of relief and sank back against a wooden wall support. He didn't know what all that had been about, but one thing was sure – Stewart and Sproat were enemies and somehow the emnity between these two had reached out to include him. He just prayed Sproat wouldn't assign him to the lead cart which would, of course, be driven by Sproat personally.

He could hear Aly's voice now out in the yard so he

walked to the stable door. He saw that Aly was deep in conversation with Sproat.

Sproat was completely transformed from the brute who'd confronted him. The man's face was wreathed in smiles as he bowed and scraped obsequiously to Aly Paterson. Ronnie Sproat looked as though butter wouldn't melt in his mouth.

Glancing up, Aly caught sight of Hugh and beckoned him over. Hugh was introduced to Sproat who, with a grin, said they'd already met.

The other lads were arriving. Several of them had started to drag the gaudily painted carts from the back of the stables where they were kept. A shout went up from one of them to announce the arrival of the milk from the farm.

Hugh had just finished helping to load the last of the churns when he witnessed an incident which confirmed for him the sort of man Ronnie Sproat was.

A youngster of about twelve had arrived late, and Sproat, having manoeuvred him into a quiet corner, was now chiselling him about it.

Abruptly and savagely Sproat's hand swung to connect with the side of the boy's head, which knocked him off his feet and against a wall.

Just about to put the boot in, Sproat hesitated when he saw Hugh staring at him. Turning, he strolled slowly away, leaving the boy coughing and gasping on the ground.

Hugh ran forward and helped the boy to his feet. There was an angry weal on his face but no real damage had been done.

The lad thanked Hugh profusely, saying in a small scared voice that Sproat was a holy terror and God help anyone who crossed him.

It was obvious to Hugh that Aly Paterson couldn't know what was going on and the lad verified this by telling him Sproat had Aly eating out of his hand.

The lad then scampered off to his cart and climbed aboard. He and another young boy bent their heads together to discuss what had just taken place. They glanced fearfully across to the centre of the yard where Sproat stood with chest thrown out and thumbs hooked into his wide leather belt.

Judging from the expression on Sproat's face he thought himself the cock of the walk.

With a flash of insight Hugh realized that Sproat was mentally unbalanced. The man was a nutter and as such to be feared all the more.

Minutes later Sproat shouted Hugh across. Pointing to the stables he told Hugh to go in and get Squinty plus another horse to make up a pair.

When Hugh had led the two beasts out Sproat told him to couple them up to the lead cart. Having done that Sproat gestured him to find a seat amongst the churns.

Hugh's heart sank as he swung himself up over the tailboard. He was wondering just what he'd let himself in for.

7

Once the decision was taken, Carrie and Archie didn't waste any time. He took out a special licence and arranged for the ceremony to take place that Saturday at the old registry office in the Candleriggs. A quiet affair was planned with only the immediate family plus a few select friends.

Big Donald offered to have everyone back to Tallon Street after the marriage had taken place but Archie discreetly suggested it might be better if the gathering was held at what would be his bride's new home. Big Donald was only too happy to comply as it meant he wouldn't have to pick up the tab.

Things were extremely tight in the Chisholm household, the budget being literally managed on halfpennies and farthings.

Early on the big day, Harriet casually announced to the rest of the family that a friend of hers from London would be dropping by and furthermore he was coming to Laidlaw Street with her. She had, of course, first spoken to Carrie about this to obtain Carrie's permission.

This shock announcement was further compounded when at a few minutes past ten o'clock a magnificent 1920 Sunbeam 16 Tourer drew up outside the close.

Children playing in the street abandoned their games to come and gawp while all around curtains twitched as the neighbours peeked out, trying to see what all the commotion was about.

Never a shy woman at the best of times, Mrs McElvey threw her window right up and leaned out across the sill so she could get the best possible view.

The Sunbeam was a dull silver colour with a hood that folded back. It was Lou Dansie's pride and joy and the only one of its kind in California.

He'd ordered the car originally as a bit of one-upmanship but had soon come to love it for itself. He had brought it to Britain – the land where it had been built – for the simple reason he hadn't been able to bear leaving it behind.

Dansie was still shaken from his drive through Glasgow. He'd seen slums in America but nothing to compare with what he'd just witnessed:

It was a relief to find the street Harriet lived in a paragon of working-class respectability. He wouldn't have to worry about getting his throat cut here.

Carrying various packages containing presents he mounted the stairs to the top landing where the Chisholms lived. Harriet met him at the door and kissed him on the cheek. Then she ushered him inside to where the family were waiting in the living room.

Hands were shaken all round and the packages handed over to Winnie, who was momentarily flummoxed: this was the last thing she'd been expecting.

Carrie excused herself saying she had a lot yet still to do and Dansie replied he fully understood.

When Winnie discovered one of the packages contained a bottle of best malt whisky she handed it to Donald who went to the sideboard for glasses.

It was customary for drink brought into a house to be at least started on, if not finished, in the presence of the giver.

Big Donald was stumped for a second when Dansie said two ounces of liquor would do for him but in the end resolved his quandary by pouring out a large one which seemed to meet with Dansie's approval.

In the kitchen Winnie was unpacking large bars of chocolate and all sorts of strange and exotic foods.

Besides the food there were three beautiful silk headsquares, one for each of the women.

Donald was naturally curious about how Dansie and Harriet had met in London. Bluntly he asked how the meeting had come about?

Dansie's reply was near enough the truth. He said he and Harriet had been staying at the same hotel and had been forced through circumstances to share a table at dinner. Learning he was coming north to Scotland, she had extended an invitation for him to come and meet her family, an invitation he had been delighted to accept.

For over an hour the two men talked about the terrible unemployment ravaging the western world until Winnie interrupted them by announcing it was time she, Harriet and the baby left for Laidlaw Street where a meal was waiting to be prepared and laid out.

Dansie said it would be his pleasure to run them over there providing someone navigated for him.

Winnie was thrilled at the prospect of riding in the Sunbeam. It would be her first time in a motor vehicle.

Dansie was delighted and promised her she would sit

up front with him.

With Angus wrapped up tight against the cold they trooped downstairs where Dansie made a bit of a fuss ensuring Harriet and her mother were seated comfortably.

The neighbours were back at their windows as the Sunbeam moved sedately off down the street with children running screaming behind it.

During the drive Winnie asked Dansie if he'd ever been to the town of Sherman in Texas? When he said he had, she sighed and sank further back into the car's ample upholstery. In a small voice she requested he tell her what sort of place it was and what its inhabitants were like?

The request puzzled Dansie who knew nothing about Alex. But it was obviously important to Winnie so he did his best to comply.

All the time he spoke of Sherman, Winnie listened intently, drinking in every word.

When he had finally exhausted his knowledge of the subject she thanked him courteously and for the remainder of the journey sat tight-lipped and introspective.

By the time they reached Laidlaw Street they'd passed through some of the worst slum areas and it was an extremely humble Lou Dansie who parked the Sunbeam outside Marjoribanks's close.

His own problems which had seemed so enormous were really of little consequence when compared to all this. For the first time he began to view his life and the job he did in perspective. It was a sobering thought.

After seeing the women and baby upstairs he returned to the Sunbeam, worried that the rough looking crowd surrounding it might damage it in some way. For a few minutes he dithered, not sure how to tackle the situation. Then he had a brainwave. Approaching two of the toughest looking men there he politely asked if they'd be willing to do a job for him.

Both men were gaunt from hunger. They glanced at each other and then one growled they might be interested providing Dansie made it worth their while.

In actual fact they were desperate for work and would have done nearly anything to earn a few bob but their pride demanded they didn't appear too eager, especially as it was a foreigner they were dealing with.

Dansie handed them five shillings each and told them to sit in his car and see no damage came to it. When it was time for him to leave he would give them a further ten shillings each providing the car was just as he'd left it.

The two men couldn't believe their luck. This was a Godsend. And money for old rope, to boot! They climbed into the Sunbeam from where the larger of the two announced in a very loud, gravelly voice that if any so and so as much as breathed on the gentleman's motor then he and his good friend Sammy here would personally mollicate the unfortunate.

Dansie went back up the stairs with a lighter heart, convinced his car was in good hands, as indeed it was.

In the house he was introduced to Archie and Sheena who were both in a fluster trying to get dressed. He was grateful for the huge fire stoked up in the kitchen range. The Chisholm place had been terribly cold, he'd thought. And he'd no sooner seated himself close to the roaring flames than Winnie plonked Angus on his lap telling him to mind the wean.

He liked children so it was no hardship for him to entertain Angus while Winnie and Harriet got on with the business of preparing the meal.

As Archie and Sheena finally left for the registry office Archie called out that they shouldn't be too long and that there was drink in the sideboard. Everyone was to help themselves.

After Archie and Sheena had noisily clattered their way downstairs Harriet opened a screwtop of beer and handed it to Dansie. When their hands accidentally touched she smiled as did he.

In a surprisingly short time those who'd attended the ceremony were streaming in through the front door. Carrie and Archie were covered in confetti and laughing like excited children.

Dansie was introduced round while Archie got out the drink.

Big Donald and old man Smith found themselves together and for a few minutes chatted about Carrie and Archie. Then Robert brought up the subject of Donald having been laid off.

There was a hollowness where his belly should have been as Donald described what it was like signing on the dole. The queues that stretched seemingly for miles. The ranks of men shuffling forward inches at a time for the indignity of being given a few miserable shillings' charity.

The air of degradation and hopelessness that hung over these men like a pall. The lined faces twisted with worry and fear.

The collective sigh that seemed to go up from time to time as though the men had just realized anew that they were of no further use to society and had been discarded on the Corporation midden.

Donald threw whisky down his throat and followed that with the remains of his beer. He shuddered and exhaled slowly.

There was no self pity in him. He knew what he was and that he was as good at his job as the next man. Better probably. He had a reputation as a grafter and a perfectionist who took pride in his work which was why he'd been the youngest foreman Armstrong's had ever appointed.

Robert Smith wanted to express his sympathy with the situation but wasn't quite sure how to do so. Words seemed so inadequate. In the end he offered to get Donald another drink.

Standing by himself in a corner Hugh was already a little tiddly as he brooded about Ronnie Sproat. Life had been hell for him since he'd started back at the dairy, Sproat making him do the work of two, if not three. Every time there was a full churn to be moved or lifted Sproat saw to it that he did it on his own. On top of that he'd been forbidden to ride on the cart which meant he had to run alongside all the time.

He'd made a few discreet inquiries amongst the other lads but none of them knew what the trouble had been between Sproat and Stewart. Or if they did they were keeping stum.

He'd considered going to see Aly Paterson to tell him what was going on but that was before he'd realized how much Aly relied on the odious Sproat, who toadied up to Aly at every occasion.

Aly wasn't a well man. The trouble with his heart had slowed him down a lot and as a result he'd sloughed off more and more of the dairy's running onto Sproat's shoulders. Sproat was only too pleased to accept the additional responsibility as, apart from increasing his pay packet, it also gave him more power. And power was something Sproat liked very much.

Hugh knew now that, albeit he and the Patersons were close, should it come to a showdown, he was far more likely to be shown the door than Sproat. Aly had come to rely on his head boy.

There had been the incident at the stables just the other day when things had nearly flared into an all out confrontation. He'd been gathering some feed to place in Squinty's stall when suddenly a pitchfork had come plunging down from the hayloft to miss him by inches.

Sproat had been full of apologies, a combined sneer and half laugh in his voice as he spoke them. He'd said that his hands must be greasy for the pitchfork to have slipped out of them like that.

Completely drained by shock, Hugh had stood there for a few moments while anger alternated hot and cold within him. Pulling himself together, he bent down and picked up the pitchfork. Its prongs were bent at their tips from the impact with the stone floor.

Monkey-like Sproat leapt onto a dangling rope and descended. When he faced Hugh his eyes were mocking and full of malicious glee.

Hugh desperately wanted to lash out, to have a go at

this horrible man whom he detested so much. But somehow he managed to keep his fury under control, reminding himself that a blow up on his part was precisely what Sproat was after as it would merit Sproat giving him the sack.

Knowing Hugh was dying to hit him Sproat smiled and thought perhaps one more turn of the screw might do it.

Sproat was convinced Hugh was after his job as head boy. After all, wasn't Hugh a great china of the high and mighty Stewart? The same Stewart who'd once threatened him with dismissal should he ever be caught bullying any of the boys again.

Fear grabbed at Sproat's stomach as he thought of Hugh being made up to head boy: if that was ever to happen his little secret would be out with dire consequences for him.

Still smiling Sproat took the pitchfork from Hugh and on turning away pretended to slip. With a yell he fell over while bringing the pitchfork sharply down so that it cruelly raked Squinty's left flank.

Squinty squealed as blood spurted. Hunching his head, he frantically drummed his rear hooves and then lashed out with them.

Hugh was well aware that this had been a deliberate act on Sproat's part. The bastard had definitely had it in for Squinty ever since his first day back at the dairy when he'd said he and Squinty were old pals.

'Whooaa there boy!' Hugh shouted, running round to the side of the stall and clambering up its side so that Squinty could see him.

As soon as the horse's hooves had started flashing Sproat had rolled to safety. He frowned now as he lay on the floor. His plan wasn't going to work. Instead of coming at him Hugh had gone to the horse.

'It's all right! It's all right!' Hugh soothed, stroking the side of Squinty's head. The beast's eyes were rolling with fright and pain. Every few seconds a fresh wave of tremors rippled through its body.

Hugh looked at Sproat now standing well back from

the stall. 'It seems to be your day for accidents,' he said, not even bothering to hide the sarcasm and contempt in his voice.

Sproat didn't like that and for a moment it seemed he might made an issue of it. Instead, he shrugged and threw the pitchfork clattering onto the floor which caused Squinty to whinny and lash out again.

'That animal should have gone to the knacker's yard long before now,' Sproat said. 'It hardly does enough work to earn its keep.'

Hugh bit back the angry words crowding his mouth. Squinty might be old, but he grafted damned hard and what's more Sproat knew it. The thing was Aly would believe what Sproat told him and it could well be that out of sheer spite and maliciousness Sproat would arrange for the horse to be done away with.

As casually as he could Hugh said, 'I know a farmer who's on the lookout for an old cuddy. He'll pay reasonably for one too. Certainly more than the knacker's yard would. I'll mention it to Aly as it would mean a few more quid in his pocket should he decide to replace Squinty here.'

It was a complete fabrication which he'd made up on the spur of the moment and judging from the sour look on Sproat's face it would seem his bluff was going to work. Squinty was safe for a while yet.

After Sproat had left he washed Squinty's flank down and painted the wounds with antiseptic. Luckily for the horse they weren't nearly as bad as they looked. The scores were long but shallow, and, providing infection didn't set in, should heal quickly.

While Hugh continued to brood about Ronnie Sproat his uncle Sandy had at last managed to get Winnie on her own, something he'd been trying to do since they'd arrived back from the registry office.

Nodding in the direction of the hallway he whispered for her to follow him as he wanted a quiet word.

Out in the hallway he drew the living room door to

before turning to a puzzled Winnie. Slipping some crumpled white paper into her hand he said that was a wee something to help her and the family get by.

The crumpled white paper was two fivers which expanded from the ball they'd been crushed into when she unclenched her hand. 'Och Sandy,' she said gratefully. He and his wife Mary had their own family to keep which couldn't have left them with all that much to spare at the end of the week.

'I had some good overtime on my last voyage,' Sandy said, 'And I'm away again within the next fortnight so we'll be sitting pretty for a while at least.' Slightly embarrassed now he added. 'There's no need to say anything about this to that soft brother of mine. He'd probably make you hand it back.'

Winnie knew that Sandy was right. This was best kept quiet between her and her brother-in-law.

'It's just a loan, mind!' she insisted, coming to terms with accepting the money that way.

'Aye of course. If that's how you want it.'

'I do,' she replied, knowing in her heart of hearts there was a certain futility about her promise to pay it back as Donald could well be idle for years.

Standing on her tiptoes she pecked Sandy on the cheek. 'I won't forget you and Mary for this,' she said, a catch in her voice.

Poor Mary who was so fat that a trip down to her local shops and back again was the best she could manage. Hence the reason why Sandy had attended all the official family functions on his own for the past few years. 'Once round aunt Mary, twice round the block' had at one time been a saying that would always raise a laugh. But that had been in the days when a joke could still be made out of Mary's fatness.

Opening the front door Winnie rushed down the stairs to the toilet on the half landing. Having bolted herself in she stuffed the fivers down her bra. Then she sat down and had a right good bubble to herself.

*　　　*　　　*

Early the next afternoon Jakey Sanderson used his keys to let himself into Ballogie Clothing. There was nothing unusual in this as he often worked an hour or two on a Sunday in an effort to try and keep pace with the ever increasing amount of paperwork expected of him.

The machine room floor was a different place without the constant roar that filled it during the week. His footsteps echoed hollowly as he made his way to the back row where Harriet's machine stood.

Sitting, he thumbed the switch which caused the gun metal grey machine to surge with power.

There were three bundles of finished trousers lying beside the machine. Each tied with string and bearing Harriet's personal marker. Every machinist had her own personal marker so that it was always known who had done what and that way any item could be referred back to the person responsible for it.

Jakey untied the first bundle and lifting the top pair of trousers onto the machine set to work.

In a little under an hour he had altered various seams on half a dozen pairs of trousers in such a way as to make it look like faulty workmanship on Harriet's part.

When he was finished he switched off the machine and retied the bundles. Having checked that everything was just as he'd found it he left the factory and headed for home.

On the Monday afternoon Winnie was down on her hands and knees waxing the hallway linoleum when the front door opened and Harriet appeared.

'What brings you home at this time?' Winnie demanded, thinking Harriet must have been taken ill.

Harriet stood staring numbly down at her mother and looking as though the question hadn't got through to her. Her face was strained and there was a puzzled expression in her eyes.

Donald entered the hallway from the living room where he'd been idly carving Angus a wooden boat for when the lad was older.

'What's going on then?' he asked.

'I've been given the sack,' Harriet stated bluntly.

Winnie sucked in her breath and her hand came up to her mouth.

'What happened, lass?' Donald asked quietly, not betraying by the merest flicker just how shaken he was by this latest calamity.

They all went through to the living room. Harriet told them how Jakey Sanderson had come storming up to her with several bundles of trousers saying her work on these was a bloody disgrace.

The entire factory had come to a halt as hot words were bandied between herself and Jakey who'd proceeded to humiliate her by waving the offending articles in the air and shouting in a voice loud enough for everyone to hear that an apprentice could do better work than she could.

At that, her temper had boiled over – as Jakey had known it would – and she'd traded insult for insult till in the end he'd trumped her acid retorts by declaring she was fired.

Stunned, she'd collected her few things together and gone through to the accounts office where she'd had to wait half an hour while they made up her time.

Some of the girls had made a few voluble remarks about the sacking but they weren't in a position to do anything about it. Not one of them would stick her neck out in case she, too, lost her job.

After hearing all this Winnie groaned and sat back in her chair. Closing her eyes she gently massaged her forehead with workworn hands. With Harriet's money now gone it meant they were reduced to having to live off Donald's broo money and what Hugh brought in from the milk.

Harriet shook her head. She was at a complete loss to understand how she had turned out seams like the ones Jakey had confronted her with. And yet they were undeniably hers. The bundles they'd come from had all borne her personal marker.

Donald asked if there was any chance Jakey would change his mind. Harriet's reply was that he wouldn't.

If the sacking had been done in the privacy of his office then she would have gone back to him and pleaded for another chance. But as it had occurred with the entire factory listening on – and bearing in mind some of the things she'd called him which everyone had heard – there was no likelihood whatsoever of him reversing his decision. Too much face was involved.

'I'm sorry, Papa,' Harriet ended up saying.

Donald rose and crossed to her. He tried to smile but didn't quite manage to pull it off as he patted her on the shoulder.

He desperately wanted to be out of the house. He felt hemmed in. Claustrophobic. He would walk down to the river and watch the water swirl by. There was a certain therapeutic effect to be gained from watching running water, he'd always thought.

'It seems you've sacrificed the Australian idea for nothing,' Winnie said. Dejectedly she headed for the kitchen to put the kettle on.

Donald left Harriet sitting staring into space. As he made his way down to the front close he patted the one remaining Willy Woodbine in his pocket. All that remained of the five packet Carrie had slipped him earlier on in the week. He would smoke that as he watched the water. He had nothing better to do.

Harriet and Lou Dansie sat in the Bluebird Cafe. He listening while she recounted what had happened at Ballogie Clothing.

Dansie was secretly pleased at this turn of events. He'd managed to secure a rented house for himself in Edinburgh and all that week had been puzzling about how to get Harriet to come and share it with him. Now he knew.

When he put his suggestion to her she sat back and stared at him as though he'd just pulled a rabbit out of a hat, which, in a way, he had.

Naturally she didn't want Donald and Winnie to know they were living together. Dansie's reply to that was she would take digs, which he would pay for. And as far as anyone in Glasgow was concerned that would be where she was staying. In reality, however, she would be living with him in St Stephen's Place.

Harriet was a realist who was never slow to grasp an opportunity when it presented itself. Dansie's plan solved both her major problems in that it meant she would not only be working again but would also be with him.

After they'd finished their ice creams they walked to the nearby Queen's Park where they hammered out the details. Harriet was elated after the week's depression. Everything was going to be all right after all, thanks to Lou.

On an impulse she stopped and throwing her arms round him kissed him deeply. Several passers by stopped to stare but that didn't bother her. She was truly happy which was all that mattered.

When they arrived back at Tallon Street she announced straight off that Lou had engaged her as a researcher for his film about Bonnie Prince Charlie at the marvellous wage of three pounds ten shillings per week.

Winnie gasped when she heard. It was as much as Donald in a good week with lots of overtime had ever earned at Armstrong's.

Harriet hurried on to say she would also be taking typing lessons and when she was proficient would be helping Lou type out his script.

Of course all this meant she would have to stay in Edinburgh where the job was and she had decided that digs were the most suitable thing.

When Harriet mentioned she'd be sending home two pounds per week Winnie was so relieved she collapsed into a chair and for a moment it seemed she might even burst into tears.

Dansie then suggested Harriet return with him to

Edinburgh where he would put her up in a good hotel until she found suitable digs. He stressed the fact he was desperate for her to start as soon as possible.

Harriet hid the elation bursting within her. The idea of the hotel was merely a sop for her parents. That night she'd be ensconced in St Stephen's Place. In bed with Lou Dansie where she belonged.

With everything now neatly arranged Harriet hurried through to the bedroom to pack. While she was doing this Dansie reflected on the great changes wrought in his life since meeting her. The long stale years with Bess had been blown away, leaving him gloriously alive again. He and Harriet were no two ships passing in the night. He'd known that instinctively as had she. Theirs was a relationship with a long term stamp on it.

And hadn't Harriet pointed out to him that Bonnie Sue was now at an age where she wouldn't be nearly as affected by a divorce as she would've in the past?

That thought had certainly given him a lot to chew on, just as Harriet had intended.

8

It was early in the summer when things finally came to a head between Hugh and Ronnie Sproat. So far Hugh had been able to ride everything Sproat had thrown at him; in fact the more he'd done so, the more desperate Sproat had become.

Enormous changes had taken place in Hugh since he'd come back on the milk. His experiences with Sproat had toughened him both mentally and physically, transforming him from a boy/man into a fully fledged male.

He'd also broadened out a lot and the constant exercise of running miles per day plus hauling and humping heavy churns had increased his strength to the point where he thought he could at least give Sproat a good go of it should they ever square up to one another, a situation Sproat seemed determined to bring about.

Having just returned from the morning round Hugh led Squinty to his stall where he left him standing just in front of the opening into it. First he would rub Squinty down and then when that was done to his satisfaction he'd feed the old horse. Humming to himself, Hugh reached for the hand brush hanging from a beam.

Hidden in dense shadow Sproat stood at the back of the stables watching every move Hugh made. He had a brown feed sack clutched in one hand which every so often twitched as something stirred inside.

A few days before Sproat had noticed that Hugh was terrified of rats. He wasn't too keen on them himself, come to that, but they certainly didn't frighten him the way they did Hugh.

There are always rats around stables although there weren't many in this one thanks to the big ginger tom Aly kept who was a notorious and fearless ratter.

The previous evening Sproat had returned to the stables where it had taken him several hours of patient waiting in order to trap the long sleek beast now held prisoner in the sack.

Grinning in anticipation, he thought of the terror and blind panic Hugh would experience when the rat landed on him. He was going to enjoy this. He was going to enjoy it a lot.

He flexed the thick, corded muscles running the length of his shoulders and down his arms. If only Hugh would lose control and take a swing at him then his day would really be made. Given the slightest provocation he would beat Hugh to a pulp and relish every second of it.

But Hugh had to make the first move. That was a prerequisite. When the story came to be told to Aly Paterson he must be able to protest that he'd only been defending himself.

Stealthily he crept forward, watching out that he didn't tread on anything that would make a noise.

He froze when the rat squeaked and scratched its claws on the inside of the sack. But Hugh, completely engrossed in what he was doing, heard nothing.

Sproat continued his advance only to freeze a second time when he heard the voices of several of the lads outside. For a moment it seemed the lads would come into the stables, but having paused by the doorway they continued on past.

Sproat breathed relief. He would have been furious had the lads intruded to spoil his fun, the more so as he'd specifically detailed all of them to be working across at the dairy for the next half hour. It was no accident he and Hugh were the only ones in the stables.

Masking himself behind a partition belonging to one of the horse stalls, he felt for the thick leather glove tucked into his belt. Once the glove was on he laid the sack down on the floor in such a way that its opening was spread out in a taut line. Hurriedly he placed his feet so that most of the opening was blocked off, leaving only a narrow passage for the rat to get through.

Minutes later he was cursing inwardly. Although the rat was running around inside the sack it seemed too stupid to be able to work out what it had to do to escape.

'Come on, damn you!' he breathed. He was crouched over the sack, his gloved hand poised to swoop once the beast began to emerge.

Suddenly the rat found the passage and wriggled through so quickly he almost lost it. Three times he grabbed before he managed to get his fingers round its neck.

With vicious looking claws tearing the air the rat was hoisted up off the ground. Its black beady eyes glared malevolently as it looked for someone, something, on which to vent its fury.

Sweat was coursing down Sproat's face and back as he held the rat at arm's length. Raising himself up on his tiptoes he peered over the partition to see what position Hugh was in.

Hugh pulled the brush in long even strokes along Squinty's pelt. The horse was still steaming a little from its morning's exertions and the warm animal smell it gave off was one Hugh found extremely pleasant.

When Squinty snickered he didn't pay any attention thinking the old horse was telling him to hurry up so he could get his nose into the feed which was next on the agenda.

This time Squinty whinnied with a note which caused Hugh to pause in mid-stroke and look round.

The scream was torn from him when he saw the rat, claws extended and eyes ablaze, hurtling through the air straight towards him. His right hand with the brush still banded to it struck out and with good luck more than good judgement he connected with the rat, knocking it squealing to one side.

Sproat stood with hands on hips silently roaring with laughter. The look on Hugh's face as the rat had come hurtling towards him had been absolutely priceless.

The rat twisted in mid-air and as it dropped towards the floor its flailing claws managed to catch onto and sink into soft, warm flesh. Its teeth guillotined down to bury themselves in Squinty's leg.

Squinty reared up and shrieked, an almost human sound that raised the hair on the back of Hugh's neck.

Again and again the rat's claws cruelly raked Squinty's leg. Freeing its teeth it took its time about selecting a fresh target. This time when it bit a jet of darkly coloured blood shot out from a severed artery.

Numb with fright Hugh stood watching Squinty rear and plunge. He desperately wanted to help but the only thing he could think of was to grab hold of the rat and tear it free. But with the best will in the world there was just no way he could bring himself to do that.

Sproat's silent laughter stilled when he heard the distinct sound of Aly Paterson's voice at the stable door. It wouldn't do for him to be found standing by watching while one of their horses was in obvious trouble. With a shout he rushed forward to try and knock the rat off Squinty's leg with a piece of harness.

Eyes rolling and frothing at the mouth, Squinty thought this was some new enemy come to attack him. Wheeling suddenly round he lashed out with his rear hooves, catching Sproat full in the chest.

Surprise was written all over Sproat's face as he flew backwards to land with a sickening thud on the stone floor.

'What in the name of the wee man is going on here?' Aly demanded, Greta by his side.

The rat tore itself free and jumped to the floor where it went scampering away to disappear behind a bale of straw.

Hugh ran forward to try and grab hold of Squinty but the horse would have none of it. Iron hooves stamped savagely down, causing sparks to fly from the stone floor as it backed away.

Sproat saw his danger and tried to roll to safety but the excruciating pain tearing his chest apart forced him to stop and gasp for breath. As Squinty's flicking tail and backside reared over him he just had time to cover his face with his arm before the animal's hooves came pile-driving down.

Sproat yelled in agony as his legs broke under the impact. He fainted clean away when a sliver of white bone came jabbing through his trouser leg.

Squinty staggered and then sank to his knees in a pool of arterial blood. His eyes were already glazing in death when Hugh took hold of his head and began stroking it.

'There, there old boy,' Hugh whispered, letting Aly and Greta attend to the stricken Sproat.

'I'll send for the doctor!' Greta yelled to no one in particular as she ran from the stables.

'And a vet!' Hugh called after her, knowing full well

that long before a vet could arrive it would be all over for his old pal.

Sproat was still out cold, blood trickling from a corner of his mouth.

Squinty's exhaling breath rasped out causing his nose to flutter. His flanks heaved while all around him the pool of blood grew wider.

At the end of a mighty convulsion it was all over. What light was left in his dulled eyes winked out as death claimed him for her own.

'What happened?' Aly Paterson asked. He could see how moved Hugh was by the old horse's death.

Hugh shook his head, still shocked by the speed with which events had taken place.

Of one thing he was certain, however: Sproat was behind all this. The only trouble was he had no way of proving it.

In a voice husky with emotion he told Aly the literal truth of what had happened. Concluding his story, he was aware that Sproat had come to and was watching him from behind half closed lids.

Any lingering doubts about Sproat's involvement were blown away. The bastard was guilty as hell!

Greta returned to say one of the boys had been dispatched for the doctor.

Sproat was in terrible pain which, to give him his due, he bore remarkably well. Both his legs were broken and several of his ribs.

In a croaking voice he said he wasn't to be moved till after the doctor had examined him. He was scared that if he was, one of his broken ribs might puncture a lung.

A number of the lads came crowding round the stable door to see what had happened, a few of them not bothering to hide the triumphant glint in their eyes when they saw Sproat lying there in obvious agony.

Hugh pulled himself together and took command. He ordered two of the horses brought from their stalls and hitched to a delivery cart. When it was time for Sproat to be removed to hospital this would be as good a way as any to do it.

The boys accepted Hugh's commands willingly and set about their appointed tasks with a lightness in their step that hadn't been there before.

Sproat asked for a cigarette and got one. He coughed a little as he smoked and there was a strange, resigned look in his eyes. Occasionally he smiled in a lopsided, cynical way as though amused at some private joke.

The doctor arrived a quarter of an hour later and got on with his examination.

Greta was sent into the house for an old sheet which was torn into strips and used for bandages. After Sproat's chest had been strapped up rough splints were fashioned and bound tightly to his legs.

That done, all the available lads were called in to help as Sproat was manhandled onto a plank which was lifted and slid onto the waiting delivery cart. Two of the boys were designated to drive the cart to the hospital while the doctor followed on behind in his car.

There was nothing left for Hugh to do now but organize Squinty's burial. This he did in a piece of ground at the back of the dairy building which was nicely secluded with lupins and other wild flowers growing in profusion.

Insisting on digging the grave alone, he sweated over it for what seemed an eternity. When it was finally ready he got those boys still remaining to help him load the carcass onto a bogey which they trundled to the graveside.

When Squinty was deposited at the bottom of the grave he sent the lads away again while he filled it in.

When the burial was completed Aly Paterson brought him over a screwtop of beer and together they stood looking down at the mound of freshly turned earth.

It was then Aly asked him to take over as head boy. He immediately accepted. Both of them were aware it would be a long time before Sproat was fit to work again. Those legs alone would take months to heal. The job paid two pounds a week.

He was invited over to the house where he once more

went over his version of what had happened in the stables. As he spoke Greta tut-tutted and shook her head. She wasn't particularly partial to rats either.

On the first Friday after the incident Hugh did a money collection of all the rounds. It didn't take him long to work out that what he'd taken was in excess of Sproat's figures. Furthermore, no matter how hard he tried, he couldn't make this discrepancy resolve itself.

Armed with both money and books he went straight to Aly Paterson and the pair of them sat down to work out just what was what.

It became clear that Sproat had been on the fiddle to the tune of five pounds a week, a sum he'd gradually built up to and thereafter maintained.

Aly was shocked and heartbroken by this revelation, so much so he broke his rule and had a drink. Over their dram he sought Hugh's advice. Should he prosecute or merely cut his losses and let things go at that?

Hugh took his time in replying. He wasn't a vindictive person but not only was Sproat a bully and a thief, the villain was also responsible for Squinty's death and that was something he could neither forgive nor forget.

'Prosecute,' he advised.

When Ronnie Sproat finally did appear in court he was found guilty of embezzlement and sentenced to three years in Barlinne Prison. Hugh was there to hear sentence passed and it was with a grim smile that he watched Sproat being led away.

Squinty was revenged.

Harriet had never been happier in her life. She and Lou Dansie had long since settled into St Stephen's Place where they spent long hours working, he on his script which was coming along famously and she either researching or typing up his pages for him.

She'd discovered she had a natural aptitude for typing and had consequently picked it up easily and quickly. She was studying shorthand which she found more difficult to assimilate but was none the less becoming proficient at.

She adored the researching side of her job, taking great delight in visiting museums and other such places to pore over ancient and usually musty tomes, ferreting out snippets of information which she then fed to Dansie as though they were rare treats.

Nor was her research confined solely to the academic. Several times Dansie sent her off to various parts of the country where her brief was to quizz the locals and write down stories that had been handed down by word of mouth from generation to generation about the Prince and the Jacobite rebellion.

Harriet thrived on all this. Her new life seemed as far removed from Cathcart and Ballogie Clothing as St Stephen's Place was from the far side of the moon.

A bloom had appeared in her cheeks. The sort that love, happiness and a full sex life brings.

They often ate out, frequenting the best restaurants the capital had to offer. Other times they stayed cosily at home while Harriet cooked. She was a good cook who'd got a lot better since being encouraged to experiment, something Donald would have viewed with horror.

They drank a lot of wine. Dansie bought it by the case and had it delivered to the door.

They attended many concerts and plays – a whole new world for Harriet.

It was after just such an excursion to the theatre that they returned home one night to find a telegram lying on their front door mat.

Neither were particularly perturbed by this as telegrams were commonplace to their household, United Artists often cabling Dansie and he replying by the same method.

This one was different, however, as it came from Bess.

Dansie sat and read the telegram several times before looking up. When he did so it was obvious the wire contained bad news.

Crossing to the brandy decanter, he poured himself a stiff one.

With narrowed eyes Harriet sat patiently by waiting for the worst. She knew instinctively something momentous had occurred.

'It's Bonnie Sue,' Dansie said, his eyes filling with sudden tears. 'She's been taken into hospital. The doctors don't know what's wrong yet but whatever it is, it's serious.'

Harriet had never seen a grown man cry before and for a moment was quite mesmerized by it. Where she came from a man would rather die than be seen in such a state. Only women and weans cried. A man was above such a blatant show of emotion.

Finally she roused herself to ask if this mightn't be a ruse on Bess's part to lure him back to Los Angeles?

Dansie's brow creased as he considered this possibility. There was no reason why Bess should know about him and Harriet. Certainly he had never mentioned it in any of his letters home. But these things do have a way of leaking out and it wasn't impossible that news of their liaison had somehow travelled 6000 miles.

When he spoke it was to say Bess was capable of many things but not of using Bonnie Sue in that particular way. As far as he was concerned the telegram was genuine and he would treat it as such. Anyway he couldn't afford not to.

It was too late for him to do anything that night other than draft a reply. In the morning he would go straight to Waverley Station and catch a train for London from where he'd embark on the first available New York bound ship.

Harriet was shaking inwardly as she went upstairs to pack Lou's things, while he drank more brandy and pencilled out his reply.

There was to be no sleep for either of them that night. Instead they lay in bed and talked in whispers about what was to happen while he was away.

It was agreed between them that she would stay on at St Stephen's Place doing what research she thought might be beneficial and getting on with her shorthand studies.

He would give her a cheque before he left in the morning and once back in Los Angeles he would make the necessary arrangements for her and the house's up-keep through his bank.

The Sunbeam he would leave behind for his return.

They made love after that until it was time to rise and get ready to go to the station.

Harriet was desolate as she climbed into the cab Dansie had hailed in the street. Everything had happened so quickly she still couldn't believe that within the hour he would be on his way back to America.

There was an air of unreality encompassing her as she gazed through the cab's window at the cobbled streets and passing grey stone tenement buildings. She imagined this must be something like how Carrie had felt when told about John McBain's death.

Her left hand was opened and something cold slipped onto her wedding finger. When she looked down she saw she was now wearing Dansie's heavy gold ring, the one given him by Mary Pickford.

'Keep that for me till I get back,' he said, closing her hand into a fist again.

There was so much she wanted to say but the only words that would come seemed trite and meaningless. Looking into his eyes she could see it was the same with him so she snuggled close and they stayed that way till they arrived at the station.

It was cool inside the station with sudden gusts of wind that caused men to hold onto their hats and women to clutch at their skirts.

She went to purchase newspapers and a few magazines while he stood in line to buy his ticket. As they walked the length of the platform Harriet felt as though some-one was hacking at her insides with a blunt knife. She wanted to shout, scream, throw her arms round Lou.

Instead they kissed one last time and then he said he thought she should go, that way would be better for both of them.

For a few seconds more they remained clutched to one

another, and then tearing herself free she turned and walked back the way they'd come.

Time passed.

There was a letter from New York, another from Los Angeles, and after that silence.

The long weeks became a month and the month became two, then stretched to three. During this time Harriet busied herself as best she could and tried to delude herself that everything was all right.

Then one day while she was busy round the house and for once had neglected to go down to see what the mailman had delivered, the long awaited explanation came.

With trembling fingers she ripped open the envelope and sat down to read what Lou had to say.

Bonnie Sue had been stricken with a brain tumour which had come within an ace of killing her. A surgeon called Krantze had developed a brand new technique for dealing with this most horrible ailment and as a last resort had been instructed to operate.

The result had been only partially successful. Bonnie Sue's life had been saved but a terrible price had been paid. From now on the girl would be little better than a vegetable, her mind permanently that of a six-year-old.

An ice cold wind blew through Harriet when she read that. She knew then that Lou Dansie would never be coming back to her nor would she be going to him.

In that instant her whole life crumbled and fell apart. Her lips thinned to become a bloodless slash and her face sank in upon itself to become pinched and shrewish. She'd become the epitomy of an ageing spinster.

She continued reading: Bess knew nothing at all about their affair nor was he going to tell her now. There would be no divorce. As Bonnie Sue desperately needed both her parents from now on there was no way he could bring himself to break up his marriage, inflicting further pain and anguish on his mentally crippled daughter.

He was truly sorry. He still loved Harriet as much as

he had on the day they'd parted. But their affair was ended.

Harriet stopped reading to light a cigarette. She stared at her hands, wondering why she'd never noticed before how close her veins were to the surface? What a peculiar observation for a time like this, she thought.

Gazing round the room it seemed to her everything was just that little bit more so than it normally was. Colours more vivid. The ticking of the clock more resonant. Her senses of smell and touch more acute than usual.

It crossed her mind that she might be in a state of shock or on the verge of a nervous breakdown.

She returned again to the letter.

United Artists had cancelled the film about Bonnie Prince Charlie and a new project on the life and times of Robin Hood with Fairbanks again scheduled for the title role, was being set up.

This was a further blow to Lou who had invested a great deal of time and effort in his Bonnie Prince Charlie script.

He didn't elaborate on why the film had been cancelled but as he was working on a new assignment for United Artists she assumed it wasn't because of any fault on his part.

The latter pages of the letter consisted of instructions for winding up the let on the house and the disposal of the Sunbeam. She was to keep the money realized from the sale of the car. The various bits and pieces he'd bought she was to do with as she wished.

He ended the letter by repeating his love for her, adding that he wanted her to keep his Mary Pickford ring as a memento in the hope she would never forget him. He was never going to forget her till his dying day.

She laid the letter down and lit another cigarette from the butt of the first. Crossing to the whisky decanter she poured herself an extra large one.

Memories of the happy times they'd spent together came flooding back to her. Large, fat tears welled from the corners of her eyes to meander slowly down her cheeks. The dream was gone, the illusion burst. Hollywood and her love had somehow blown away, leaving only the reality of impending spinsterhood behind.

Finishing her drink she poured herself another. She wished Carrie had been there for her to talk to. Of all the people she knew her sister was the one most likely to understand just how she felt.

Picking up the letter and decanter she started for the bedroom. Tomorrow would be soon enough to begin what had to be done.

For the rest of the day she would lie womblike in the bed they'd shared together. She'd drink a lot and cry even more. Tears might be futile but they did bring some sort of relief.

The thick gold ring weighed down her wedding finger. Sometime soon she'd buy a gold chain on which to hang it round her neck. Bringing the ring to her lips she kissed it. 'Oh my darling!' she whispered.

Part II

Rosemary for Remembrance
1931–1938

Angus was ten years old when the Marjoribanks moved to Holmlea Road just round the corner from Tallon Street. The new house had three bedrooms, a kitchen, a living room, and an inside toilet cum bathroom. Carrie had never got used to either the stairhead closet or the zinc tub in front of the fire, so she appreciated the bathroom most of all.

Angus had a bedroom all to himself which he thought a grand thing, although at night he missed Sheena's heavy breathing, which had always been a great comfort to him, and the long whispering sessions they'd often secretly indulged in.

Now Sheena had left school and was employed as a conductress on the trams.

The work situation had eased over the past few years. Armstrong's had re-opened and one of the first people to be re-employed had been Donald, taken back in his old capacity as foreman moulder.

Although asked, Hugh hadn't returned to Armstrong's. He preferred staying on at Paterson's Dairy.

Aly was dead. His heart had finally given out and he'd passed away peacefully in his sleep three years previously. Stewart had married his English sweetheart and was now boss at Muirend and the farm just off the East Kilbride Road.

Hugh was still called head boy although he was really more of a manager as Stewart spent nearly all his time out at the farm where he and his wife lived.

Hugh had no regrets whatsoever about his decision. He enjoyed his work and loved being with the horses. The offer of a few pounds more per week wouldn't have enticed him back to the bedlam of the foundry.

On Angus's first day at Holmlea Primary he was taken along to a Mr Barr's class where he was told to sit beside a boy called Robin Kirkpatrick. The lesson at the time was spelling and during it the two boys stole surreptitious glances at one another, each trying to size the other up.

When the bell rang for playtime Angus followed the rest of the class downstairs and out into the playground where he found a quiet corner by some palings to eat the jelly pieces Carrie had packed for him.

He was in the middle of his second piece and watching some lassies playing peerie when Robin Kirkpatrick and several other boys came strolling across. Inside Angus was tense but, trying to appear nonchalant, he wiped jelly from his chin. He knew whatever happened next would decide whether or not he was accepted.

Robin Kirkpatrick was roughly the same height as Angus but a lot broader in the chest and shoulders. He had a rather ruddy face inclined towards pudginess. His hair was a deep auburn and hung limply in long and somewhat greasy strands.

Thinking it might be interpreted as a sign of weakness Angus decided not to speak first so he continued trying to look nonchalant as he switched his gaze from the peerie-playing lassies to a game of footer taking place further up the playground.

Robin Kirkpatrick noted Angus's interest in the footer and that gave him inspiration for his first question. 'Which team do you support?'

Angus turned to stare at Kirkpatrick, acting surprised at being addressed.

'What?'

The aggressiveness in Angus's voice threw Kirkpatrick a little. He was used to other boys being wary of his size.

'I said, who do you support?' This time he matched Angus's aggressive tone.

'The 'Gers are the boys,' Angus stated, as though it were Holy Catechism.

'Aye. That's right enough!' Kirkpatrick replied with grudging approval. Angus's answer had been the correct one.

By this time Angus had come to the conclusion that with the possible exception of Kirkpatrick none of the boys surrounding him were nearly as tough as some he'd known in his old school. There had been a number of real hardmen in his class there, all right.

'Where do you stay then?' Kirkpatrick continued doggedly.

When Angus replied he was living in Holmlea Road he was asked which number. It transpired he and Kirkpatrick were neighbours, living next close to one another.

The next question was what did his father do?

Angus replied that his father was dead – that caused several blank stares and shuffling of feet – but that his step-father was an engine driver. He added the last bit not out of deference to Archie but because flyly he knew the effect it would have.

Several of the boys gaped and even Kirkpatrick was taken aback. An engine driver! Probably the ambition of half the lads in that crowded playground.

'For LMS,' Angus threw in for good measure, smiling inwardly at the effect his words had produced.

'Gosh!' exclaimed one of the boys, his face full of awe.

Kirkpatrick broke the spell by stepping forward and slapping Angus on the back. He and the others were about to play a game of Cowies and Indians and would Angus care to join them?

Angus groped in his jacket pocket for the rubber dagger he had there and announced he would be only too happy to take part.

When it came to choosing up it seemed everyone

wanted to be on his side. Having an engine driver in the family did have its advantages.

After that Angus and Kitty – Robin hated the name but it was what everyone insisted on calling him – became the best of pals and through his new found friend Angus soon learned his way round Cathcart and all the best play places.

As summer gave way to autumn the pair were often down at the Cart, a place called Sandybank being their favourite spot, where they fished with string and jam jars for baggy minnows and the red bellied tiddlers known, for some obscure reason, as 'doctors' or 'docs'.

Snow came early that year and with it Hugh to Holmlea Road humping a present for Angus.

When Angus arrived home from school that day he found Hugh sitting in front of the fire chatting to Carrie. The present, wrapped in canvas bagging, took pride of place in the centre of the kitchen floor.

Hugh was extremely fond of his nephew and now that Carrie and Archie were living in the neighbourhood he was hoping to see a lot more of the lad than he'd done in the past. The present was by way of an overture to Angus who he hoped would soon find time to visit him at the dairy.

Angus ripped the canvas bagging away and whooped with delight at the newly made sledge, smartly painted in dark green with a red and black lightning flash running its entire length.

For Hugh, the beam on Angus's face was ample reward for the couple of hours it had taken him to make the sledge. He'd got the idea of knocking it together when he'd come across the runners stuck in a corner at the back of the hay loft. They'd been pretty rusty but with a bit of elbow grease he'd soon had them gleaming like new. The wood had come from an ancient cart in the process of being cannibalized.

Thanking Hugh profusely, Angus bolted down his tea, dying to get out in the snow and try out his new sledge. It was a brammer and far better than any the boys round about possessed.

He would call on Kitty and together they'd away up to the Queen's Park Reccy Ground, the most popular sledging site in the district.

After Angus had gone Hugh asked Carrie if everything was all right? She was dreadfully pale with dark heavy rings under her eyes. He'd also noticed some bruises on her arms and suspected Marjoribanks was knocking her about. This wasn't the first time he'd spotted black and blue marks on her.

Carrie knew precisely what her brother was driving at but shrugged it off, saying she wasn't sleeping too well with Archie working so many lates and nights.

When Hugh stared pointedly at the bruising she added casually she'd slipped the other day and banged her arm against the coal bunker. Having told the lie, she promptly changed the subject by putting a fresh kettle on for Sheena's tea and announcing the lassie would be arriving in from her work at any minute.

Carrie's attitude to Archie was complex. Over the years he'd worn her down to the point where she now dully accepted her lot.

It wasn't as though Archie was all bad, she'd often told herself. He did have his good points. He'd never been a day out of or off work since they'd got married and every Friday he came straight home and paid her the housekeeping money without fail.

He was also a generous man. All she had to do was ask and if it was possible he'd get it for her. Occasionally he would even surprise her by bringing home a gift which he'd hand over, saying gruffly it was a wee minding he thought she might like.

She'd long since come to the conclusion there was something wrong inside Archie's head. He could be pleasant and charming one minute, a raging animal the next, capable of almost anything.

Sexually there was a perverted side to him which he often indulged in. At such times all she could do was grit her teeth and pray the ordeal would soon be over.

Why she didn't leave Archie? In the beginning she had often considered it. But her options were strictly limited: getting a job – which still wasn't all that easy to come by – and finding a place where she and Angus could live together or, failing that, returning to Tallon Street.

There was no question of her finding another man. She wouldn't have wanted to even had it been possible.

What it boiled down to was she had reconciled herself to making the best of a bad job. Archie might be a sadistic bastard but he wasn't entirely unlivable with.

What she had made crystal clear to him was that if he ever beat up Angus the way he beat her up that would be the end of it. She would pack what few things she and the lad had and go.

Running a hand through greying hair she took a deep breath and wished she could find more energy. She was always so tired nowadays, drained to the point where she found it a terrible struggle just to get through the daily grind.

She had developed a permanent stoop and her skin had a washed out look about it.

At thirty-one she looked in her mid forties.

On arriving at Queen's Park Reccy Ground Angus and Kitty immediately joined in the fun, taking alternating shots to zoom over the hard packed snow, lying face down on the sledge or else sharing the same ride together by sitting one in front of the other.

It was Angus who first noticed the two lassies in trouble. The girls were about the same age as himself and Kitty, maybe just a little younger, and both dressed in extremely smart uniforms. They were surrounded by a gang of toughs intent on mischief.

'Yeh toffee-nosed Parkies!' one tough jeered, spitting at the taller of the two girls who recoiled in disgust as the gob landed on her coat.

Angus had never heard the expression 'Parkies' before. Kitty informed him Park School was up the town somewhere and catered for the daughters of the very rich.

Angus had no sympathy with rich girls. Or rich anyone come to that. But he did think it a bit thick that ten boys had ganged up on two puny lassies.

The tough who'd spat darted in and, catching the taller girl's scarf, yanked it from round her neck. The girl showed a lot of spunk in lashing out at him but missed and would have gone toppling over if it hadn't been for her companion catching and steadying her.

The second girl was close to tears which she was desperately trying to hold back. The taller girl stood proud and defiant with a look of utter contempt for their tormentors written across her face.

The tough with the scarf tied it round his waist and, wiggling his hips provocatively, taunted the taller girl by proposing she come and take the scarf back off him.

Hoots of strident laughter and obscene suggestions made both girls blush with embarrassment.

Angus knew the sensible thing would be to ignore what was happening but there was something about the taller girl which struck a sympathetic chord in him, making him want to go to her defence. When she caught his eye and silently pleaded with him he knew he was going to have to get involved.

At that moment one of the toughs ran at the taller girl and catching her by the shoulders sent her spinning to the ground. The tough immediately sat on her back and proceeded to rub her face with a handful of slush.

The girl spluttered and choked as the slush was driven into her mouth and up her nostrils. Her hat had been picked up by a tough who was now sporting it on his head.

'That's enough. Let her go now,' Angus said quietly, his fists balled by his side ready for action.

The tough sitting astride the taller girl stared incredulously up at Angus. 'What did you say, Jimmy?' he demanded.

'Let the lassie go,' Angus repeated.

Slowly the tough rose from his sitting position till he was fully upright on his rather bandy legs. With a nod to his mates he started moving in on Angus and Kitty who were now standing back to back. With a sudden roar all ten toughs simultaneously launched their attack.

For a few minutes Angus and Kitty held their own with hard blows given and taken by either side.

The beginning of the end came when Angus's feet were kicked from under him and with a strangled yell he went crashing to the ground. With no one to guard his back, Kitty was soon overpowered and when he fell, he landed heavily on Angus.

Kitty grunted with pain as a boot came thudding into his side. What he couldn't understand was why Angus had got them into this fight in the first place, over two lassies who undoubtedly had more money than sense. It was beyond him.

Angus and Kitty would have been onto a right doing but for the sudden intervention of Robert Cooper, Winnie's downstairs neighbour's son, who was now a houseman in the nearby Victoria Infirmary.

Robert and a few of his friends had been out for a breath of fresh air when they'd caught the sound of the fight. Seconds before he fell Angus had been recognized by Robert who immediately strode into action.

Tough after tough was hauled of the still struggling Kitty and Angus and thrown unceremoniously to one side. When the toughs realized they were facing new adversaries, and grown up ones at that, they lost heart and took to their heels.

The only injuries Angus and Kitty had were a few scratches plus a cut lip on Angus's part. They were both extremely lucky and knew it. The toughs could just as well have been carrying weapons which they wouldn't have hesitated in using.

A shaken Angus blurted out to Robert Cooper what had happened but when he came to look round for the Park School girls they'd both vanished. He was hurt, feeling the least the lassies could have done was to say thank you.

It was Kitty who pointed they'd probably run off when

they'd seen he and Angus were getting the worst of the punch up.

Robert and his pals insisted Angus and Kitty accompany them back to the hospital so that their cuts could be attended to. Despite protestations that they were both all right, the pair of them were taken back to the infirmary's casualty department to have iodine painted on their faces.

Several nurses came in to see the heroes – the nurses' words, not theirs – who'd been so gallant in going to the assistance of the put upon wee lassies. Angus and Kitty squirmed with embarrassment and couldn't wait to flee the building. But first they were taken along to a side room where tea and fancy cakes had been put out, a treat from these self same nurses whom Angus and Kitty now concluded weren't so bad after all.

Finally they did escape out into a night filled with swirling snow. Deciding it was getting late, they agreed to go home. As the pair of them trailed along the road Angus's mind was filled with images of the taller girl who'd had her face rubbed with slush. It was the queerest thing but in that moment when their eyes met and she had silently pleaded with him it was as though he'd known her all his life.

Arriving home he found Sheena sitting by the fire engrossed in a romantic novel. She looked up to tell him word had come for Carrie to go to Tallon Street as Winnie had taken ill.

Angus was immediately concerned as he was very fond of his granny. From what little Sheena knew he gathered Winnie had come down with a bad cold which had suddenly turned into something else.

Carrie's instructions were for him to go to bed when he got in and if she wasn't back by morning Sheena was to get the breakfast.

He then had to explain the iodine marks on his face. Not wanting to mention the Park School girls in case Sheena thought him soft he told a version of the story that excluded the two lassies.

Then he hurried through to his bedroom where he dried down the sledge before changing into his pyjamas.

Having changed and pulled the bedclothes back he decided on a last trip to the bathroom.

His feet pattered on the linoleum as he made his way along the hallway. The bathroom door swung open to his touch to reveal his step sister in all her naked glory.

Angus gawped. This was the first time he'd seen Sheena with no clothes on since she'd reached puberty. His eyes travelling from the generous swell of her breasts down to the furry clout protruding from between her legs. His mouth was suddenly dry and his heart palpitating fit to burst.

Sheena stared at Angus, as surprised as he was at his barging in on her. She was sure she'd locked the door! When she saw the transfixed expression on his face, her mouth slowly curved into a smile.

Angus wanted to turn and run but his feet were rooted to the spot. There was a terrible compulsion in him to reach out and touch his step-sister's naked flesh.

Sheena realized what was going through his mind and that excited her. 'Come here,' she said crooking a finger at him.

Like an automaton Angus moved towards her.

He stopped when he was only inches away, his eyes riveted on one of her nipples.

The hand that took his sweaty one was cool. 'Oh Sheena,' he mumbled as his fingers enclosed a breast.

At the back of his mind he was terrified the outside door would open to admit either Carrie or Archie. He daren't even think of what would happen should he and Sheena be found like this.

Sheena knew what she was doing was unforgivable but she couldn't help herself. There was a lot more of Archie in her than either he or she knew.

Angus started to tremble as his hand was guided down the length of his step-sister's body to come to rest on the woolly clout between her legs. The hair was a lot more wiry than he'd expected and it was damp which surprised him as he'd walked in on her before she'd had her uppey and downey.

The bathroom was warm. Heated by a small stove standing by the wc, the paraffin aroma mingled with the sweet and distinctive smell given off by Sheena's naked body.

'Are you scared?' she asked softly.

He lyingly shook his head.

Sheena's face was glistening with sweat and her lips parted in a way that made her look catlike. There was a burning sensation in her throat and between her legs where Angus's hand was. At that moment she would have given anything for him to have been a few years older.

Letting his hand go she said, 'You'd better run along to bed now and leave me to get washed.'

Angus nodded, not trusting himself to speak. His thoughts were whirling and confused, part of him wanting to run away from there as fast as his legs could carry him while another part wanted to stay.

It came to him consciously then that the Sheena he'd known these past ten years had changed beyond all recognition and in doing so had left him behind. She was no longer the same She-she who'd mothered him and held him tight in bed while strange things were happening between Archie and Carrie through the wall.

'Go Angus!' she commanded, turning her back on him and fumbling with the taps.

This time he wanted to reach out and touch her for quite different reasons than before. He couldn't bear the thought that the She-she he'd known was now lost to him. It was like losing an arm or leg.

'Go!' she repeated.

And he did.

When he was in his bed he hid under the covers and cried softly to himself, not because of what had happened but because he knew it marked the end of an era in his life.

That night he dreamt of the taller of the two Park School girls standing stark naked in the centre of the Reccy Ground.

Only it wasn't her own but rather Sheena's body she was flaunting beneath the falling snow.

Winnie was hot, sweaty and bordering on delirium. Although Carrie had changed the bedclothes not half an hour since, again they were saturated.

With hands clasped and shoulders hunched Donald sat by Winnie's bedside where he'd been since she'd taken a turn for the worse not long after he'd arrived in from his work.

He looked lost and very scared, for once not bothering to mask his emotions with manly indifference.

Dr Robertson had already been and gone and would return later. Solemn on arrival, he'd been downright grave on leaving.

Winnie blinked as globules of sweat rolled down her forehead and into her eyes. Instantly Carrie was there with a wrung out cloth to dab away the sweat and cool down her flushed cheeks.

Winnie turned her head to one side so she could look at Donald. She hadn't noticed before, probably because it had been a gradual thing. But she could see now just how much he'd aged during his six years of being idle.

There was skin hanging where his jowls had been and the neck below had gone thin and scrawny. Those magnificent broad shoulders which had been his pride and joy were now bent and bony, their muscles having withered with the onset of old age.

Closing her eyes she allowed herself to drift, seeing Donald as he'd been when they'd first met. He'd been tall and straight then and she the envy of every woman who saw them walking out together. She could remember thinking him a braw but serious young man whose one line of conversation consisted of what he was going to make of himself in life.

Whenever she could arrange to have a Sunday off he'd come and collect her and together they'd go walking down by the River Kelvin or in the Botanical Gardens, both of which were just across the way from the house in Bellhaven Terrace where she'd worked.

It wasn't long before they'd discovered they had a lot in common, coming from the same Highland stock: in her case from the clachan of Fanagmore on the banks of Loch Laxford in the wilds of Sutherlandshire.

For eighteen months Donald courted her. Then one summer's evening down by the Kelvin he'd asked her to marry him. She'd been so excited that for a full minute she hadn't been able to speak while he, poor man, died the death thinking she was going to turn him down.

But of course she hadn't, and the wedding, conducted by the young Reverend Duncan Forbes, had been one to remember.

Sandy Chisholm had been there with his wife Mary, as well as his other brother, Willy, his sister, Nettie and her man.

And Donald's mother, Fiona – looking grim and forbidding and every inch the Chisholm matriarch – had come, softening a little as the night wore on and more than just a few drams vanished down her throat.

From her own side two of her sisters had made the journey from Fanagmore. Her father and mother wouldn't dream of leaving the croft while the third sister didn't come because they only had enough money to send two.

Both Kathy and May had arrived looking prim and proper at the Orange Hall, intent on showing that anyone from Fanagmore was just as good, if indeed not better, than anyone from the heathenish Glasgow where it was well known all sorts of unspeakable things happened to a body if she wasn't careful. But time and whisky had loosened their reserve as well till in the end they'd been wheeching it up with the best of them.

Then it had been home for Donald and Winnie to their

own wee hoose in the Calton where after three years of marriage their firstborn came into the world. Alex had a wild look in his eye even as a baby. He grew up to be smaller than his father but just as broad-shouldered. Alex with the silvery laugh, which always made Winnie's insides jump just to hear it. And so clever with his hands he even won grudging praise from Donald. Grudging only inasmuch as Donald didn't want the lad to get swollen headed. Privately Donald was delighted, although he'd never dream of saying so to anyone other than her.

Winnie's eyes blinked open and she realized she must have fallen asleep and been dreaming. Everything had been so real – as though she'd somehow managed to step back in time.

'Oh Donald!' she husked, her throat parched from fever.

'I'm here lass. I'm here,' he said, taking her hands in his. Putting a strained smile on his face he told her to rest easy and she would soon be better.

He didn't believe that and neither did she. But they were both wrong.

For three days Winnie was at death's door and then, as suddenly as its onset, the fever broke and she started to mend.

During this time she'd been nursed by Carrie and Harriet taking it in shifts while Donald had remained steadfastly by her bedside only leaving the room when nature demanded it.

Learning that his mother wasn't going to die after all, Hugh was so relieved he decided to lash out and buy her something really special to cheer her up.

He took a tram into town where, because the capital outlay was beyond him for the moment, he bought her a wireless set on the newly introduced idea of hire purchase.

Winnie was delighted with the gift, though scandalized by its extravagance.

He left her listening avidly to a discussion about house

plants on the Home Service.

It was during tea that night that Harriet quizzed him about the wireless and he let slip he'd bought it on the never never.

The moment the words were out of his mouth he realized he'd made a terrible mistake. He should have known Donald would view with horror buying anything on hire purchase.

'What did you say?' Donald demanded, his voice tight with suppressed fury.

Hugh carefully laid his knife and fork on the plate before him. Taking a deep breath he sat back in his chair.

Before replying, he re-examined his motives for using the hire purchase agreement and came to the conclusion they were good ones.

He'd wanted to buy his mother a present and what he'd known she'd appreciate most had been for the moment outwith his pocket. The hire purchase scheme was merely a device allowing him to get round this temporary shortage of funds and enabling Winnie to have the set when she could most use it.

Speaking slowly and carefully he repeated his earlier statement.

The thick hairs protruding from Donald's nose quivered, the nostrils dilating and the nose itself flattening. He was appalled. What Hugh had done was unforgivable!

Fierce Highland pride welled up inside him. The creed was simple. If you couldn't afford to buy something then you went without until you could. The last thing you did was to enter into some sort of Shylock arrangement. Hands once renowned for their strength knotted into fists. He wanted to reach over and slap Hugh, to knock some sense into his son's head. Where was Hugh's pride? His self respect?

It didn't matter that Hugh's motives were laudable. If he hadn't been able to pay cash for the present then no present should have been made. Winnie could well do without. She'd survived fifty-seven years without a wireless so a wee while longer wasn't going to make all that much difference.

It was a matter of principle. He had his standards which were his father's and his father's father before him. He expected his family to live the same way. Donald's chair scraped back as he rose to his feet. Silently he strode from the room and a few seconds later the wireless playing by Winnie's bedside was switched off.

Hugh sighed and looked from Carrie to Harriet. What upset him most was that Winnie was going to lose her wee bit of comfort because he hadn't the sense to keep his mouth shut.

The living room door banged against the wall as Donald entered carrying the wireless. Crockery and cutlery jumped as the set was dumped on the table.

'Take the wireless back and we'll forget all about it. And you've your mother to thank for that. I was all for throwing you out of the house for doing such a damned stupid thing.'

Normally Donald wouldn't have over-reacted the way he was doing now but he was bone tired and not thinking straight. Nearly losing Winnie had exacted a terrible toll from him: it was affecting his judgement and sense of perspective.

'You would've thrown me out for that?' Hugh said, completely stunned.

'Oh Papa!' Carrie breathed.

All eyes turned as Angus entered the room. The happy expression on his face died as he realized something was going on. When Carrie beckoned him to her side he ran there to stand wide eyed and silent.

Driven by an inner demon Donald rattled on. Alex would never have passed up the chance of going back to Armstrong's. Alex would never have dreamt of playing milkie when there were men's jobs to be had. And most pertinent of all Alex would never have shamed his mother by buying her a present on hire purchase!

Harriet sucked in her breath.

Carrie bit her lip,

Awed and frightened by what was going on Angus clung tightly to Carrie's skirt. He didn't want his grandpa and Uncle Hugh to be like this. He wanted them to be friends.

Hugh had never realized how bitterly Donald had resented the fact he'd never resumed his job at the foundry. Nor had he realized his father had found him so much wanting compared to his dead brother.

'So there,' said Donald glowering. And coming forward he reached out with the intention of poking Hugh in the chest.

In the space of a few seconds Hugh's whole life had altered dramatically and would never be the same again. With a snarl he pushed his father's hand away and taking a step backwards said, 'Lay a finger on me and so help me God I'll flatten you.'

Donald laughed cruelly. 'Do you think you're man enough then?'

'Aye. I think I am,' Hugh retorted.

'This is ridiculous,' said Harriet. But before she could continue she was interrupted by a voice from the doorway.

'What's going on here?' Winnie said, the words little more than a whisper. She was in her nightdress with a shawl slung over her shoulders. She clung to the door frame for support.

'Winnie! You shouldn't be out of your bed, lass!' Donald exclaimed and hurried over to her.

'I could hear the shouting,' she said.

He ignored that and, turning her round, led her back towards their bedroom.

'You stay here,' Carrie instructed Angus before dashing after her parents and Harriet who'd gone ahead to straighten out the bed.

Suddenly Hugh was trembling and like a jelly inside. Not wanting Angus to see the emotions playing over his face he walked swiftly to the window and stared out over the backgreen and the River Cart beyond.

Donald had been right about one thing. The time had come for a break to be made. After what had been said it was impossible for him to remain in his father's house.

'Have you ever considered running with the milk in the mornings?' he asked.

Angus was taken aback at this coming straight out of the blue and for a moment or two was at a loss for words. It had been an ambition of his for some time now to go out with his Uncle Hugh on the milk rounds. Finding his voice again, he blurted this out, adding he had a pal who was just as keen as he was.

Pleased by the lad's reply, Hugh said that when Carrie pronounced Angus old enough he was to come out to the dairy where he and his china would be fixed up with jobs.

Going through to the big room Hugh packed his few possessions. He couldn't bring himself to walk out without saying goodbye to his mopther so tapping on her door he went in to tell her he was going.

'Oh son!' was all Winnie could say.

'Where will you stay?' Harriet asked.

Hugh shook his head. He hadn't got that far yet. With a lump in his throat he kissed his mother and turned to go.

'Don't forget to take the wireless with you,' Donald said uncompromisingly.

When Carrie let her brother out the front door he had his suitcase in one hand and the offending wireless on his shoulder. He walked up the street to the tramstop without once looking back.

Donald was a lot more shaken by what had happened than he let on. He hadn't meant to say some of those things to Hugh but somehow in the heat of the moment they'd come thundering out.

'I think I could sleep for a wee while,' Winnie lied. She wanted to be alone.

Harriet left the room to join Carrie and Angus through in the kitchen where the two women set about washing and drying the dishes while Angus sat watching.

Donald entered the kitchen carrying a bottle of whisky a little over half full plus two screwtops. 'Out,' he said, signing towards the door.

When Angus made to leave Donald restrained him. 'The men stay,' Donald growled, closing the door behind the bewildered females.

Donald poured two drams, one large, one small. The latter he topped up with water.

'Slainte!' man and boy chorused in unison.

The rawness of the alcohol caused Angus to scrunch up his face and cough. Donald chuckled. There were times when Angus reminded him of Alex as a boy. The eyes were the same, as was the way they both had in certain moods of thrusting out their lower lip.

But if Angus had Chisholm characteristics there was also a lot of John McBain in him. The same stubbornness. The same ability to withdraw into himself and view the world as though from a great distance. The same basic common sense which had made John McBain admired and respected by so many of his workmates and pals.

Donald poured himself another dram and added a beer as a chaser. He could see Angus was struggling with his drink but obviously determined to get it down.

'What do you want to be when you grow up?' he asked abruptly.

There was no hesitation about Angus's reply. He'd known the answer to that question for a long time. 'To start with I'd like to work at Armstrong's like my Da,' he said.

Donald grunted his approval, moved by the light shining in the boy's eyes, a light that was always there when Angus spoke of John McBain.

You could do a lot worse than Armstrong's,' Donald said. 'A lot of good men have learned their trade there.'

For a while both of them were silent, Angus imagining

what Armstrong's was like, Donald thinking of the reality.

'After I'm time served I'd like to go to sea. Do you think my Da would have approved?' Angus asked.

Donald considered that. 'I don't see why not,' he replied. 'It's a good life at sea if you enjoy that sort of thing and if you find it doesn't suit you or get tired of it there's nothing to stop you coming ashore again. There's lots hereabouts have done that.'

Angus stared into the pale amber of his drink and, as though it were a crystal ball, imagined some of the exciting and exotic places he would visit with the Merchant Navy. The prospect sent shivers up and down his spine and goose bumps on his arms.

'To Armstrong's and the sea, then!' Donald toasted.

'To Armstrong's and the sea!' Angus responded.

'What are you two up to in there?' Carrie demanded anxiously from behind the closed door.

'Men's talk!' Angus replied, at which he and Donald burst out laughing.

10

Angus had to wait until the following autumn before he was given permission by Carrie to run with the milk. In just under a year he'd grown nearly a foot which had changed him from a compact, chunky lad into a tall, gangling one.

Carrie knew it was just the age he was but nonetheless it worried her to see how drawn and haggard he'd become. It was only after a long talk with Hugh that she agreed for Angus to go to work for the dairy, the theory being fresh air and exercise couldn't help but do him good.

It was still dark that first morning when Angus dragged himself out of bed at four thirty to stand hopping on the cold linoleum floor while he struggled into his warmest clothing. He was bleary-eyed, with a sour, bilious feeling in the pit of his stomach as he made his way through to the kitchen where Carrie was waiting for him with a cup of tea and a hot bacon roll.

Spirits revived, he rushed downstairs and out to the backgreen where his bike was kept chained to a railing, the same bike that had once belonged to Hugh and which he'd fallen heir to when big enough to reach the pedals.

Kitty, sitting astride his machine, was waiting for him outside the front close and together they headed for Muirend.

Kitty had also grown during the past year but with him there had been none of the runaway stretching that had so elongated Angus's body. Whilst steadily inching upwards Kitty had managed to retain his powerful physique, which was, if anything, even more burly than before.

The friendship between the pair of them had gone from strength to strength till now it was hard to imagine them apart. They practically lived in one another's pockets.

When they arrived at the dairy Hugh was already busy about the yard. The day he'd left his father's house he'd taken himself to the dairy where he'd explained his plight to Greta Paterson. Greta's response had been immediate. He was to stay with her in the big house where she was fed up and sometimes a little scared of living on her own. He would be her lodger paying a nominal rent.

It hadn't taken him long to settle in and soon he'd come to regard the house as a home away from home.

The dairy with Hugh in charge boomed and before long he began to think of expanding.

After considering Hugh's plans – for if the outlet side of the business expanded then the production side would have to as well – Stewart Paterson came to the conclusion that what Hugh had in mind was viable and immediately set to work organizing his end of things.

The first thing Hugh did was to order four new delivery carts and a few weeks before taking delivery, he travelled down to a farm he knew of in Selkirkshire where he bought eight young horses to add to the dairy's complement.

New rounds meant more staff, which had made him think of the promise he'd made Angus the previous year. He and Carrie had talked the matter through and it was finally agreed Angus could make a start. They would see how the lad got on.

Apart from his health, Carrie's main worry was, at eleven, Angus was still a little young to run with the milk. After all, for five days a week he would still have a full day's schooling to get through after he'd done his round. But Hugh had been able to put her mind at rest with a few well chosen arguments, plus the promise that if Angus's schoolwork suffered in any way then the lad would be made to give the job up.

The first thing Hugh showed Angus and Kitty how to do was harness the horses and after that the correct procedure in loading churns and stacking the crates of bottles.

Hugh had timed the boys' start to coincide with the first day of the new rounds and, much to their delight, they discovered he would be in charge of the cart they were to be on.

When it was time to set off Hugh shouted to them to climb aboard and the moment they'd done so he flicked the reins and the cart jolted forward.

As they went, Hugh explained he'd already solicited the area they were to service and as a result they had a considerable number of orders to start off with.

Over a bridge across the River Cart they went, the air filled with the thunderous noise from a nearby weir, and then on towards the Old Castle Road.

This was new territory for both Angus and Kitty who gazed about with unbridled curiosity.

Although still dark, they could make out many large houses of the type favoured by the rich and well to do. There was a rural, village-like atmosphere about the place which they took to right away, it being such a contrast to Holmlea Road.

Soon they were sweating profusely as they raced from door to door filling the orders while Hugh moved the cart slowly along and kept an eye on them to see no mistakes were made.

Hugh was inordinately proud of Angus and secretly wished that Angus was his son.

During the past few years it had become a fetish with Hugh to have a son of his own but, try as he might, he just couldn't seem to find a woman whom he wanted to marry.

There were girl friends in plenty, and even a few affairs. But although he enjoyed the company of all these girls there wasn't one of them he was interested enough in to marry.

There were times when he was convinced he was destined never to meet a girl with whom he could fall in love and his fate was to remain a bachelor to the end of his days. When that mood was on him he would become depressed and take to the bottle, often sitting in his room drinking alone and sinking deeper and deeper into melancholia.

Dawn was breaking when they stopped at Young's Bakery, where Hugh treated Angus and Kitty to a bag of freshly baked rolls and a pint of milk each to wash them down. He had brought a flask of tea for himself which he now drank while smoking a cigarette.

It was Kitty who spotted the apple orchard behind a high stone wall completely encircling a house far bigger and grander than any of its neighbours. Nudging Angus he gestured towards the orchard, muttering in a low voice that the apples looked ripe and ready for plucking.

Casually the pair of them sauntered round to a better vantage point and after a whispered discussion came to the conclusion the wall wasn't as formidable as it had first appeared and that a couple of bright sparks like themselves shouldn't have too much difficulty in getting over it. They decided Saturday night would be the best time for a raid and that they would come back and try their luck then.

When the round was over they returned to the dairy, where Hugh showed them how to brush down and feed the horses. Having completed both these tasks to Hugh's satisfaction, they climbed onto their bikes and headed for home, where they would have a proper breakfast before going to school.

Carrie was waiting anxiously for Angus but her fears were allayed somewhat when she saw the sparkle in his eye and the colour the fresh morning air had brought to his cheeks. Nonetheless she would watch him closely for the next couple of weeks to make sure he wasn't over-taxing himself.

As the week passed Angus and Kitty came to know their milk round inside out. Every morning they'd stop at Young's the bakers for rolls and every morning they'd eye the apple orchard and discuss their plans for the forthcoming raid.

Finally Saturday arrived and after tea that evening they cycled over to the Old Castle Road and the tall imposing grey stone house with the orchard in its grounds.

It was that curious Scottish phenomenon, the gloaming, when they made their move.

Angus stood with his hands pressed against the wall while Kitty climbed onto his shoulders and from there leapt up to catch hold of the top of the wall. Once atop the wall Kitty lay along it and dangled an arm which Angus was able to grab hold of. Kitty then hauled Angus up beside him.

For the space of a few seconds they straddled the wall and then having made sure the coast was clear dropped down the other side to land in thick, luscious grass.

Angus's heart was thudding as he snaked towards the nearest tree, nearly jumping out of his skin when a large hoodie crow cawed shrilly overhead and went flapping past to disappear round the side of the house.

Reaching the tree, Angus grasped hold of the lowest branch and hauled himself up.

The trees, like most cultivated ones, were ridiculously easy to climb and soon the pair of them were pulling apples from the branches and stuffing them into their many and voluminous pockets, the garments they wore being chosen for this particular asset.

'You there! Boy! Come down this instant!'

The voice was female and rang with authority, its owner standing with hands on hips beneath Angus's tree, glowering furiously up into the foliage.

'If you don't come down right away I'll set the dogs loose in here while I ring for the police.'

Angus peered down but all he could see was a pair of legs beneath a crumpled skirt. Feeling sick, he decided the only thing to do was as he was bid. The thought of the police being called in terrified him for if they reported to Archie what he'd been up to then Archie would undoubtedly leather the backside off him.

'I'm coming missus!' he called out and started to descend, thinking he mustn't give Kitty away as, so far anyway, it seemed he was the only one to be spotted.

When he jumped from the lowest branch, he landed badly, causing him to topple over and go crashing to the ground. Ruefully he picked himself up and turned to face the female who'd caught him.

With a shock, he realized it wasn't a woman confronting him, but a girl, and furthermore one whose face was vaguely familiar.

'You!' the girl exclaimed and frowned.

Suddenly Angus placed her. The girl was the taller of the two from Park School whom he and Kitty had rescued from the toughs.

'I didn't know it was your house,' he mumbled and immediately felt a right fool as that seemed such a daft thing to say in the circumstances. Then accusingly, 'Why did you run off that night?'

Thrown onto the defensive, the girl sniffed, 'Well, if you must know, my friend and I could see you weren't going to win against those awful boys so we decided to run and fetch a policeman, only by the time we returned with one everyone had gone.'

'Oh!' said Angus, quite deflated.

'Were you badly hurt?'

Angus stuck out his thin, bony chest, an action which made him look ridiculous. He had one sock up and one down. His knees were covered in dirt and there was a jagged tear in his short grey pants from scrambling down the tree.

'We did win,' he tried to say casually, but instead it came out somewhat pompously.

The girl smiled and fractionally raised an eyebrow.

'We did!' Then in a smaller voice because he could see written all over her face she thought him a liar, 'A man I know and some of his friends happened by and they helped us out.'

Suddenly they were grinning at one another, he remembering how at their previous meeting he'd got the impression he'd known this girl all his life.

'My name's Rosemary,' she said, tilting her head to one side and studying him.

'Mine's Angus.'

'Angus,' she repeated, tasting the word as though it were something strange which had found its way into her mouth.

'And I'm Kitty and is it safe for me to come down now?' Kitty called from the tree in which he was hiding.

Rosemary thought that very funny and asked with a giggle if there were any more of them?

Kitty replied there weren't and dropped out of his tree, landing amidst an explosion of apples which seemed to burst from every part of his person.

Rosemary beckoned them into the shadow cast by the wall, explaining as they moved quickly through the grass that her father would be furious if he caught them and would certainly prosecute.

They left the orchard by the front gate, Rosemary having first checked they weren't being overlooked from the house. And once outside the three of them made their way to the bikes parked round the corner.

As they walked Rosemary questioned Angus about where he lived and how he and Kitty had come to know of her father's orchard.

Angus explained about his Uncle Hugh and the dairy and that he and Kitty came past her house every morning on their milk run. The fact that a milk run had been started up in the area interested her and she told Angus to call at the house next morning. She would see an order was waiting for him.

She said her mother had mentioned only a few weeks previously that the house could do with having its milk delivered so this was her opportunity to see her mother's wishes were carried out. At least so she told Angus.

Bidding Rosemary goodbye, Angus and Kitty slowly cycled in the direction of Holmlea Road, munching as they went.

They hadn't gone very far when Kitty started to tease Angus, saying Angus had a fancy for the Parkie girl and was she now to be regarded as Angus's girlfriend?

Angus's reply was a well aimed apple which caught the jeering Kitty on the side of the head causing him to momentarily lose control of his bike and very nearly come off.

The next morning Angus informed Hugh that the occupants of Arnprior House – the name of the mansion where Rosemary and her parents lived – wanted to place an order for a daily delivery.

Hugh was curious as to how Angus knew this but Angus just shrugged and said it was so.

With Angus in tow Hugh personally went up to

Arnprior House where at the rear entrance a servant girl answered their ring and placed a sizeable order.

Angus had been hoping for a glimpse of Rosemary but when he failed to see her he told himself it was ridiculous even to think she might be up and about at that time of morning.

When he got home after the round Carrie informed him she was going over to Scotland Street later in the day to see Robert and Meg Smith, and she wanted him to come with her. She'd never stopped being grateful to Robert for his generosity to her after John died.

Carrie knew the Smiths had fallen on hard times of late. Several business deals of Robert's had gone awry and he'd had to sell the shop to cover his losses.

That afternoon Carrie and Angus took a tram, getting of at the stop closest to the tenement where the Smiths lived. They hurried up the close to chap at the Smiths' door. It was opened by Meg looking a lot older than either of them remembered.

Meg was delighted to see them and ushered them straight through to the kitchen where Robert was sitting hunched in front of a mean fire.

If Carrie had been shocked by the change in Meg then she was positively stunned by Robert's transformation. Countless stitches laced one side of his face with the surrounding flesh yellowy purple and angry looking. The really big change in him, however, was in the eyes, which had a vacuous, glassy stare about them. When he tried to greet her and Angus all he could manage was to mutter incoherently in heavily impedimented speech.

Meg explained what had happened as she went about putting on the kettle for a cup of tea.

Robert had been over the Clyde on business when he'd run foul of a gang called the Conks currently terrorizing the Bridgeton area.

'The Norman Street Conquerors', to give them their full title, were a product of the times, a bunch of violent although not always stupid men who derived pleasure from terrorizing other people. Usually they'd gang up on their victim at night, invariably razoring him before getting him down on the ground where they would then either stab or kick him to death.

Robert had been lucky. Two patrolling policemen had whistled up reinforcements, forcing the Conks to give him the boot and flee.

He'd been taken to Duke Street Hospital where his slashes had been attended to. He'd then been examined by a consultant who'd confirmed the Casualty doctor's suspicion that brain damage had been sustained.

Meg tried to keep a brave face as she recounted this tale of woe but there was a catch in her voice and several times she had to turn away in order to restrain the tears threatening to engulf her.

No matter how hard she tried for it not to be, Carrie's gaze kept being drawn back to Robert, whose mouth hung slack and whose chin was covered in running streaks of spittle.

She noted the black safe had gone from its place on the floor, the safe Robert had been so fond of boasting about and around whose contents he'd always woven such a shroud of mystery.

Meg went on to tell Carrie that what little money she and Robert had left would soon be gone and then heaven alone knew what would become of them.

Carrie felt guilty thinking about the two hundred pounds Robert had given her but there was just no way she could return so large a gesture. Archie might well be in regular work but at the end of most weeks what he'd earned had gone.

Totting it up in her head she estimated she had just under fourteen pounds rainy day money hidden away at the bottom of an old tea caddy in her kitchen press, hardly a fortune but at least something to give Meg Smith.

Robert grunted and squirmed in his seat and a few seconds later a terrible smell began to permeate the room.

Meg sighed, a defeated almost at the end of her tether

look settling on her face. Smiling wryly at Carrie, she crossed to Robert and helped him to his feet.

Carrie offered to help but Meg said it wouldn't be necessary. The tea was now masked and if Carrie would pour herself and Angus out a cup she would take Robert through to the other room and do what had to be done.

Angus knew by hearsay a great deal about the Conks and over tea proceeded to tell his mother about the big battle they'd had recently with a rival gang called the 'Savoy Indians'.

Angus was still chuntering on about gang warfare when Meg arrived back to tell them Robert had started to doze off so she'd bundled him into bed where he'd stay for a good couple of hours at least.

Carrie, profoundly moved by the succession of tragedies that had befallen the old couple, commiserated with Meg.

In her anguish Meg let slip that the dealings Robert had been involved in for some years outside the shop and which had finally ruined him hadn't been entirely above board. This was, of course, what Carrie and her family had suspected for a long time. Well, Robert had more than repaid the penalty for his avarice and no man would ever reproach him now.

When it was time to go, Meg kissed Carrie on the cheek and then insisted on doing the same to Angus.

During the journey home both Carrie and Angus were silent. Once Angus shivered but his mother didn't notice. She was too wrapped up in her own thoughts about the old couple they'd left behind in Scotland Street.

Sir Alan Armstrong was a small, blunt-faced man with broad powerful shoulders and piercing blue eyes. He looked more like a man used to hard physical labour than the executive he was.

He sat now in his wood-panelled office overlooking the River Cart with a frown on his face and a cup of coffee in his hand.

His desk was neat and tidy, everything squared away

in its place. And that was the trouble! He would have preferred the desk to be littered with papers and plans: that would have meant there were orders coming in.

There were still a few orders waiting to be filled but once those were gone there none to take their place.

Sir Alan grunted with annoyance and swallowed the remains of his coffee. Laying down the cup and saucer he rose and strode to the window where he stood with feet slightly apart and hands clasped behind his back.

He was an angry man, but angry with himself more than anything else. Years ago he'd been advised to diversify his interests, to partially retool and turn out new products as a back up to the traditional Armstrong marine pumps.

There had been that desalination idea which he'd finally rejected because it meant investing a considerable amount of venture capital of which he'd had more than enough at the time, profits for the preceding few years having been exceptionally high.

Well, one thing was certain, he swore to himself. If he did somehow manage to survive this crisis then there would be no need to urge him to diversify in future. He'd learned his lesson and he'd learned it the hard way.

On a sudden impulse he strode through to his secretary's office and instructed her to book him on that night's London sleeper. Then he gave her the names of various London bankers and told her to make appointments with them for the following day.

He'd already been to London several times trying to secure a sizeable loan or second mortgage – his house already had a second mortgage on it – the buildings, plant and machinery that made up his firm. The trouble was that London banks had no confidence in Glasgow any more; to them the Clyde was dying a slow lingering death and any investments made by them would only prolong the agony.

Naturally this was a belief he contested and tomorrow he would once again try to argue them round to his way of thinking.

What was needed was for something cataclysmic to happen, not only to Glasgow but the country as a whole. It was a dreadful thought but he couldn't help thinking another war would be the answer.

He stood by the window watching the gulls fly overhead. The last war had been a terrible affair but how private enterprise had prospered while it lasted! The Clyde had never been so busy, every yard bustling like a beehive as ship after ship was built and launched.

He smiled grimly remembering what Armstrong's had been like in those days: everyone working as many hours as he was able and the order books filled to overflowing.

Sir Alan sighed. Great days! Great days! But would their like ever come again?

He and Cordelia had been married during the war and, my God, but they'd been in love! His heart swelled now just thinking about it. He'd taken her on honeymoon to Dunoon where they'd had the most glorious week before returning to the house he'd bought and had done throughout in the Old Castle Road.

Anxiety fluttered within him at the thought he might lose that house along with the firm. Virtually every ha'penny he owned plus a lot more he'd borrowed was sunk into making Armstrong's once more a viable proposition.

For the umpteenth time he told himself there had to be a way out of his present financial predicament. There just had to!

Taking out a clean white hanky he dabbed hands suddenly clammy with sweat. If the worst came to the worst he knew he wouldn't be able to face Cordelia and the girls. He would kill himself first.

That was why there was a small automatic pistol locked away in one of his desk drawers which he wouldn't hesitate to use if there was no other recourse left open.

He glanced sideways at the painting of his father hanging above the fireplace. That craggy, battle-scarred face had never know either defeat or failure. Or if it had, they'd been only little ones and nothing like the unholy mess he was now neck deep in.

His father would have known the right thing to do in the circumstances because his father had always known the right thing to do: that had been his father's particular genius.

He hadn't exactly liked his father but he had admired him. Sir William Armstrong had been a man you might hate. And plenty had. But at the end of the day you just had to admire him for the clever conniving double dealing devious bastard he'd been.

Still thinking about his father, Sir Alan strode from his office and down stairs that would take him to the yard below. It was a long-standing policy of his to try and make a surprise visit once a day to a part of the works and that day he decided on the foundry.

Big Donald wiped sweat from his brow as he watched white hot molten metal being poured in a sizzling, eye blinding stream into a mould that was the last of a batch of three. Beside him stood Gemmill, the chief pattern maker, who was waiting to discuss a mould that had been ordered and which Gemmill had run into difficulty with because of the peculiar dimensions involved.

Big Donald made a waving sign which was the signal for a foundryman to tap off the streaming metal. Sitting securely atop a brace of joined bogeys, the mould was then wheeled away by another two foundrymen who steered it by means of long iron poles with hooks on the end fitted into rings projecting from the mould's side.

'Now then,' shouted Gemmill – it being necesary to shout because of the constant roar that was part and parcel of foundry life – and immediately launched into a technical explanation of his problem.

As Donald listened his eyes were continually roving over every part of the foundry visible from where he stood; he kept a continual watch over his domain. Consequently he was the first one to see Sir Alan enter the foundry through a side door from a back part of the yard.

His eyes flicked again, rechecking that every man was

hard at work and everything was as it should be. Then he interrupted Gemmill to shout instructions to a crane operator working overhead.

'Morning Chisholm. Morning Gemmill,' Sir Alan said.

Gemmill jumped as though stung. He'd been totally unaware of Sir Alan's approach.

'How is everything going then, Chisholm?' Sir Alan demanded.

Donald said everything was fine and went on to explain the current stages of the various jobs in hand. While he was doing this, Gemmill shifted uneasily from foot to foot and every few seconds shot an ingratiating smile at Sir Alan.

Donald knew Gemmill to be a crawler and detested him for it, not that Gemmill was alone in his arse-licking attitude towards the management. There were many who were just as bad, if not worse, than him. With a few of them it was because that was the way they naturally were but with the vast majority it was because they were continually terrified of putting a foot wrong and losing their previous jobs.

Donald sympathized with these men but at the same time found it difficult to stomach what they did. The whining subservient tone they invariably adopted when talking to the management made him want to puke with disgust.

Gemmill was speaking now, taking up a point Donald had made and needlessly elaborating on it.

'You there!' Sir Alan shouted and strode away, leaving Gemmill in mid-sentence.

Donald quickly glanced round at the man Sir Alan had called out to and noted with relief that it wasn't a foundryman but one of the electricians who serviced the works. The electrician who'd been with Armstrong's for many years doffed his hooker doon as Sir Alan crossed to speak to him.

What Sir Alan wanted to know was why the electrician had put a sixty watt bulb in as a replacement for one that had blown in his private cloakroom when he had specifically asked for a hundred watt to be used?

The electrician bobbed his head in acknowledgement of Sir Alan's question. In a subservient voice he explained a hundred watts were too much for the tiny cloakroom and that sixty were more than sufficient.

To Sir Alan the electrician's reply was no less than sheer insolence. He had personally issued the instructions and no matter that the man may well be right he expected all his instructions to be carried out without question.

A frown furrowed Donald's brow as he listened to the exchange between Sir Alan and the leckie, who was cringing with a terrified expression stamped across his face.

'I beg your pardon, sir?' the electrician queried. Sure he'd heard incorrectly.

'You're fired,' Sir Alan repeated, adding with a snarl, 'Collect your time from the office and then get out.'

Donald opened his mouth to intervene. Then caution warned him if he wasn't careful he'd be the next to get his marching orders. He slowly shut it again, promising himself never to have the temerity to despise Gemmill and the like again for, by keeping quiet now, wasn't he just as bad as they?

Feeling sick, he turned away, unable to stand the sight of the grovelling electrician clutching at Sir Alan's trouser bottoms. He noted that Gemmill was watching with bulging eyes.

Sir Alan snorted and tore himself free from the leckie's frantic grasp, his eyes narrowing when he saw the way Gemmill was staring at him.

With a gulp Gemmill turned to Donald and started talking absolute nonsense about the job they'd been discussing before Sir Alan's arrival.

Donald knew the electrician vaguely. The man was married with a large family to support. Donald didn't envy the poor bugger having to tell his wife he'd been sacked and that from now on they were going to have to exist on the dole.

One thing was certain: having been sacked from one job it would be many a long day before the leckie found another, if indeed he ever would.

Crossing back to Donald and the chief pattern maker, Sir Alan said, 'Now then Gemmill. You were saying?'

Gemmill's voice quavered as he spoke but somehow he managed to pull himself together enough to make sense out of his reply.

No one looked at the electrician who, with head bowed, dragged himself from the foundry floor.

Angus was jolted from his sound sleep by a howl of anguish reverberating round the house. For several moments his mind remained fuzzy and then he snapped wide awake with the realization that it was his mother's voice he'd heard.

Carrie lay sprawled across the bed with Archie towering over her. She was sobbing and desperately trying to protect herself from the blows raining down.

She cried out in agony as a fist thudded deeply into her stomach. Half out of his mind with drink Archie grabbed hold of her nightdress and savagely jerked it down to expose her breasts. Laughing, he fell across her and began to suck.

Archie lifted his head as the door flew open and Angus burst into the room. 'Get out!' he slurred.

Angus was horrified at what he saw. Apart from the fact Carrie was near naked her face was horribly puffed and swollen, the flesh round one fast-closing eye rapidly assuming a greeny-purple colour.

'Angus!' Carrie croaked and thrusting Marjoribanks from her hastily yanked her nightdress back into place.

Angus started towards the bed but he'd only gone a few paces when arms restrained him and Sheena's voice whispered in his ear, 'Don't!'

Marjoribanks glowered at his daughter and stepson. 'Go back to bed!' he rumbled. Beside him, Carrie grimaced as his hand tightened on her thigh.

'You leave my Ma alone!' Angus screamed and

desperately tried to break away from Sheena who, luckily for him, was able to retain her hold.

Carrie swung her legs over the side of the bed and started to stand up only to be knocked back again by a sudden swipe from Archie who grunted she was to lie as she was.

Sheena stared in contempt at Archie. Her mind filled with memories of similar scenes from her early childhood when it had been *her* Ma he'd been abusing.

The breath caught in her throat and she drew back, dragging Angus with her, when she saw the look on Archie's face as he stared hard at her body. She, like Carrie, was clad only in a nightdress. It was the sort of look a girl should never experience from her father.

'You're obscene!' Sheena spat, drawing Angus even closer to her so he effectively covered her front.

For a man who'd consumed so much alcohol Marjoribanks moved astonishingly fast. One moment he was squatting atop his bed. The next he'd streaked across the room to backhand Sheena across the face.

Sheena screamed as she tumbled to the floor. Angus's anger gave way to fright as he was spun to one side where he stood gawking at Marjoribanks and wondering where all his courage had suddenly disappeared to.

Archie stood over his daughter staring down at her. 'You're a whore just like your mother was,' he breathed. 'I've seen it in you for years.'

'My Ma was no such thing. You're a fucking liar!' the girl retorted.

His hand flashed again to crack against her mouth, the force of the blow causing her head to bounce off the floor and her lower lip to split.

'Mind your tongue!' he roared.

Carrie slid from the bed. She had to get Angus and Sheena out of here. Better she take what he had to dish out than either of them. When he was in this sort of mood there was only one thing would calm him down. The sooner she got it over with the sooner he'd be snoring like a pig.

'Come away back to bed, Archie,' she pleaded, at the same time signalling to Angus to get out of the room.

'My Ma was not a whore,' Sheena insisted, her voice quiet and filled with dignity.

Marjoribanks stared hungrily at his daughter's voluptuous body lying spreadeagled before him and strove to remind himself that she was his own flesh and blood and as such untouchable. But by God she was beautiful!

His pulse quickened and there was a stirring in his groin which Sheena couldn't help but notice as he was stripped down to his long johns.

She averted her gaze and momentarily closed her eyes. There was a great pain inside her which had nothing to do with physical hurt. She felt lost. That and alone and terribly afraid.

Ignoring Carrie's signalling Angus ran to his mother and threw his arms round her waist, wishing fervently he was a grown man able to tackle Marjoribanks.

As he clung there an idea was born to him. He had to start making money, lots of it, so that one day he would be in a position to rescue Carrie from this brute she was married to.

Resolve hardened within him. He would buy her a nice wee house where the pair of them could live happily together. Sheena, too, if she wanted to join them.

Sheena slid herself away from Archie and cautiously stood up. Blood from her split lip dripped onto her nightdress.

'Run away through now. There's a good boy,' Carrie whispered to Angus.

'Everything is going to be all right, Ma. I'll see to it,' he whispered in reply.

Carrie frowned, realizing from his tone there was far more to his words than their apparent surface value.

Letting Carrie go, Angus crossed to his step-sister and took her by the hand. 'Goodnight Ma,' he said. Pulling Sheena so that she followed him, the pair of them left the room.

Less than a minute later Carrie was sprawled across

the bed with Archie heaving on top of her.

Big Donald was no fool and had known for a long time that Archie was beating Carrie. But according to the unwritten laws of the society they lived in it wasn't his place to interfere unless approached directly by her.

He was so angry the night Carrie appeared with a black eye and badly bruised face he had to go for a walk down by the river in order to bring under control the fury boiling within him.

During that walk Donald decided that although it wasn't his place to interfere, there was nothing to stop him conniving to find out just how bad the situation was. He would do this by arranging for one of the women to sound Carrie out on the subject.

After much cogitation he came to the conclusion Harriet was best suited for the task as Carrie was far more likely to open up to her sister than she would be to Winnie.

It was well known in the family that Marjoribanks invariably worked late on a Wednesday so Harriet chose that night to present herself at the house in Holmlea Road.

Physically, the past ten years hadn't been at all kind to Harriet. Her face had sharpened while her body had become sticklike. She smoked incessantly and drank cup after cup of black coffee. These two items to a large extent formed her staple diet.

Businesswise Harriet had prospered greatly since her affair with Lou Dansie. She'd sold the Sunbeam and used the money to buy her own small house in Wilton Street in Glasgow's fashionable West End area.

Having completed her typing and shorthand courses, she'd returned from Edinburgh with a wardrobe of smart business clothes to set about finding herself a job suited to her new skills.

The Scottish Amalgamated Insurance Company was situated in Hope Street where in a large gothic building it had both its Head Office and Glasgow Branch.

Harriet's position had been in the communal typing pool serving the Head Office's Accident Department and the Glasgow Branch but after a few years she'd landed the plum post of personal secretary to the manager of Glasgow Branch. This position was the second highest post open to a female within the company, the highest being personal secretary to the general manager himself.

During this time Harriet received several wistful letters from Lou Dansie asking after her and also informing her he and his wife Bess were succeeding in making something of a go of it for Bonnie Sue's sake.

Ruthlessly she'd never replied to any of these letters. A finish had been made that was neat and clean which was how she wanted it to stay.

After a while the letters had stopped coming and now her only reminders of Lou Dansie were Mary Pickford's ring which she wore on a gold chain round her neck and his name when it flashed up on the cinema screen credits as it did from time to time.

There had been no more men after Lou, partly because for a long time after he'd gone she hadn't wanted another relationship, but also because she hadn't been given another opportunity.

So Harriet had thrown herself into her work, so much so that within the company she'd soon gained enormous respect for her ability and dedication.

Carrie was less than delighted to see Harriet as she'd been trying to avoid as many people as possible until her face was more or less back to normal. However she made her sister welcome, ushering her through to the kitchen where she put the kettle on for tea.

The first thing Harriet did was to light the inevitable cigarette. She had a dreadful smoker's cough and as a result of this was forever clearing her throat. The second thing was to inquire after Angus whom she was told was out playing with one of his pals. That pleased Harriet as with Sheena also out of the house it meant she'd managed to catch Carrie on her own. At first Carrie was reluctant to be drawn, but, with a little bit of coaxing, the words were soon tumbling forth.

Even before Carrie had started telling her about how Marjoribanks carried on Harriet worried about her sister. She found Carrie terribly pale and drawn with skin the colour of fresh putty and ribs that jutted where once they had been encased in firm flesh.

Harriet roughly estimated Carrie had lost a stone in weight since the pair of them had last been together a little over six months previously.

Carrie was philosophical about Archie, considering his tempers and violence something that had to be endured. According to her, the beatings weren't as frequent as they'd once been nor were they as severe. The incident of the black eye was a particularly harsh one.

As Carrie spoke, a tale of sleepless nights, headaches, abdominal pains and a more or less general loss of interest made Harriet even more convinced her sister was seriously ill. Whether or not this illness had anything to do with the beatings she could only speculate on.

Completely caught up now, Carrie began to describe some of the sexually perverted practices Archie was so fond of indulging in and which she found totally repugnant.

Harriet swallowed hard, her insides fluttering as her imagination ran riot. Despite herself she couldn't help but picture Archie doing to her some of the things he did to Carrie.

Ten years was an eternity to go without a man, especially for someone like her who was a passionate woman. Besides there was a dark side to her nature she'd long been aware of which secretly hungered after the sort of treatment Archie was so fond of dishing out.

In the end it was established Carrie would stay on with Archie – unless he attacked Angus in which case she would leave – intent on making the best of it.

Harriet's advice to her sister was to go and see Dr Robertson for a thorough check up as it seemed obvious to her there was something physically wrong with Carrie which needed attention.

Shortly after that Sheena arrived home and Harriet took her leave to pay Tallon Street a quick visit in order to give Donald an edited version of what she'd learned.

That night Harriet had great difficulty in getting to sleep.

11

Weeks passed and Angus didn't see Rosemary again until the Christmas holidays which meant a fortnight's glorious release from school.

On the third day of the holiday he went personally as usual to deliver the milk to Arnprior House where he found a note addressed to him stuck in one of the empties. It was from Rosemary asking him to meet her at one-thirty inside the castle.

Foolishly he mentioned the note to Kitty and for the rest of the morning had to endure taunts and innuendoes which, no matter how much he threatened Kitty, laughingly persisted.

The castle was situated just up the hill from Arnprior House and was now a mere shell of its former glory. It went back at least to Mary, Queen of Scots but beyond that Angus knew nothing of its history.

After his dinner, Angus cycled to the castle. Then, leaving his bike, he climbed the stone wall surrounding the ruin on three sides.

Rosemary was waiting for him, sitting in a downstairs

window opening staring across at the heavily wooded area on the other side of the Cart.

'Hello. I'm glad you could come,' she said and smiled.

Angus was so overcome that what was supposed to be an accomplished lighting of a cigarette turned into a ham-fisted fumble. He succeeded in getting the cigarette alight only after two matches had blown out and he'd very nearly burned himself.

Rosemary had changed considerably since their first meeting the previous year. Her face was well on its way to losing its childish lines while her figure now boasted small firm breasts.

'I thought I might have seen you before this,' Angus said, immediately wishing he hadn't as it tipped her off he'd been thinking about her.

Before replying Rosemary asked for a cigarette, and using a lighter produced from her pocket, proceeded to light up in precisely the sort of expert manner he'd intended impressing her with.

There was a teasing note in Rosemary's voice when she informed him he might not have seen her but she'd seen him when he was delivering the milk.

Part of him was gratified to know she'd also been looking out for him but another part was mortified because of the many times he'd stood unashamedly goggling up at Arnprior House wondering which window was hers.

My God, but he must have looked glaikit standing there with his mouth hanging wide open! Quickly he turned away so she couldn't see the sudden flush which flooded his face.

Rosemary puffed on her cigarette and wondered what it was about this tall, gangly boy which intrigued and attracted her so much? Certainly there was an affinity there which she hadn't encountered in any other man and that puzzled her, as she couldn't think why it should be.

'Come and sit here and tell me about yourself. I'd like to know,' she said, sounding strangely grown up.

Angus sat on the spot indicated and instantly became aware of the warm, soapy smell emanating from her. It had the effect of making him feel all sort of jumpy and peculiar inside.

He couldn't bring himself to stare directly into her eyes so he pretended great interest in his cigarette.

'Well?' she prompted.

Slowly and hesitatingly he began telling her about life in Holmlea Road. How he hated his step-father. And how someday when he'd saved enough money he would buy a small house where he and his mother and step-sister could live in peace away from Archie Marjoribanks.

The more he spoke the more confidence he gained and soon he was telling her all about his real father who'd been killed the day he was born in an accident at Armstrong's. As he talked about John McBain his voice filled with pride and his eyes shone with a combination of admiration and love for his dead parent.

His tone became bitter as he recounted to Rosemary how Sir Alan Armstrong had refused his mother compensation for his father's death and because of this Carrie had been more or less forced into remarrying a brute who bashed her about.

Having finally found enough courage to look directly into Rosemary's eyes, he glanced up to find her shrunk back against the side of the window staring at him as though he'd turned into some sort of horrible monster.

'What's wrong?' he asked.?

'Don't let me hear you speak about Sir Alan that way ever again,' she replied coldly.

In that instant it clicked with Angus the name on the milk book for Arnprior House was Armstrong but he'd never made the connection as there had to be hundreds with that name in Glasgow.

'An uncle?' he queried.

'My *father*,' she stated.

How could Angus speak about her father like that! Why, everyone knew daddy was the most warm hearted, generous man you could ever hope to meet.

'How was Mr McBain killed?' she asked eventually, her voice dripping ice.

'He was crushed to a pulp by a casting that got out of control,' adding as though an afterthought, 'strawberry jam.'

The colour fled Rosemary's cheeks.

Angus went on. 'The union tried to get Sir Alan to give my Ma compensation but your father wouldn't entertain the idea. He maintained my Da was responsible for getting himself killed which meant he wasn't liable.'

'And was it your father's fault?' Rosemary asked quietly.

Angus thought of the snapshots he'd seen of his dad. A man of medium height. Broad-shouldered. With an open smiling face. Hair cut short. Greased and swept back from the forehead.

Apart from the snapshots the only mementoes Carrie retained were the medal John McBain had won in the tug-of-war championships when he'd been a member of the Armstrong team, and an old black leather wallet, ripped on one side, with the initials J.McB. in faded gold lettering on its front.

Angus had always found it difficult to broach the subject of his father's death with Carrie, partly because he found it acutely embarrassing to do so and partly because of the pain and anguish it caused her to be reminded of that day. Consequently it was his uncle Hugh he'd turned to for the details of what had happened in Armstrong's foundry on the morning of 12 August, 1921 when John McBain was killed.

'Well?' Rosemary prompted.

'My father was on a gantry that had been declared out of bounds because it was unsafe. We don't know why he was there, only that he was. The casting was being moved when the craneman lost control, allowing it to smash into the gantry. That was the end of my dad.'

Angus paused before continuing. 'My father was in

the wrong but then so was the craneman. Also what Sir Alan might have taken into consideration were the number of years my dad had worked for him. And my grandfather. But he didn't. Despite union pressure he disclaimed all liability and that was that.'

While Angus spoke Rosemary was fiddling with her charm bracelet, hooking a finger under it and tugging outwards. Her anger had dissipated, the last vestiges of it blown away by the sad and hurt expression on Angus's face as he told her about his father.

She desperately wanted to reach out and touch Angus. To draw him to her. To mother him. At that moment she felt as old as Eve.

'I'm going to marry you when we're grown up,' she stated abruptly and in a matter of fact tone of voice.

Angus blinked, not quite sure he'd heard correctly. 'Eh?' he queried.

'I'm going to marry you when we're grown up,' Rosemary repeated. 'I knew it that day at the reccy ground when you saved me from those roughs.'

Laughing when she saw the stunned expression on his face, she went on, 'Don't ask me how I knew. I just did.'

Angus tried to digest that. There was an inevitability about the pair of them he had felt that first day same as she had. But marriage! He hadn't quite got round to projecting their relationship that far ahead.

'Aren't you going to kiss me?' she asked, dropping her head fractionally to one side and looking at him quizzically.

'If you like.'

'Well, if you'd rather not!' she said mercurially and made to move. Her huffiness was replaced by a smile the moment he reached out to restrain her.

Angus knew he was being awkward and clumsy but somehow it didn't matter. All thoughts of denied compensation and Sir Alan Armstrong fled his mind as he took her in his arms.

He started when her tongue licked out to probe the

inside of his mouth. He'd heard about french kissing but this was his first experience of it.

Her hands worked up and down his back and as they did so her bracelet caught in his coat. Snapping open, it flew from her wrist.

'Oh no!' she cried as she saw the bracelet bounce and slide down the rockface to land in a crevice about twenty feet below the window.

The pair of them leaned out of the window to stare at the bracelet so plainly and tantalizingly in view below them.

Rosemary was distraught. Not only was the bracelet an expensive one it was also her favourite piece of jewellery.

Angus knew he was going to have to make an effort to retrieve the bracelet. He studied the sheer rockface falling away beneath them to the Cart below.

Section by section, hold by hold, he worked out a route that would take him down to the crevice where the bracelet was lodged. It wasn't too difficult a descent, he told himself. The trick would be to go slowly and whatever happened not to panic.

Taking off his coat he folded it and placed it on the castle floor. He was nervous. His stomach turned over and his heart thudded in his chest.

He wiped sweaty hands on his trousers before taking off his jacket and placing it neatly on top of his coat.

'Don't be daft!' Rosemary said, placing a hand on his arm.

'Did you really mean what you said?' he asked.

'About what?'

'Us getting married when we're old enough?'

Her mouth creased into a grin. 'Of course.'

Angus took a deep breath. 'It'll be all right,' he said moving to the window and swinging himself up on the sill. 'You'll see.'

He dropped his legs over the side and carefully groped with his right foot for the toe hold he'd picked out. There was a stiff breeze blowing which caused his hair to flap and the back of his shirt to fill out like a sail.

Adrenalin pumped through him as he crabbed his body down. Sliding his left hand across the rockface in search of the grip he knew to be there. From the safety of the window twenty feet hadn't looked very far but once out on the rockface that twenty feet was more like twenty miles.

Rosemary was leaning out of the window staring down. She thought Angus a crazy, impetuous fool and she loved him for it. Without taking her eyes from him she offered up a silent prayer on his behalf.

Angus paused to catch his breath. Already his arms and legs were aching with strain. What really worried him, however, was the possibility of a paralysing cramp setting in, the outcome of which didn't bear thinking about.

A sudden picture flashed through his mind of himself and Rosemary dressed in wedding clothes coming out of a church together. Hand in hand they climbed into a car and then he was throwing handful after handful of coppers out the window, while on the pavement a horde of children dived and swooped, grabbing what they could from the scramble.

With a shake of his head he chided himself to concentrate or it wouldn't be an imaginary wedding he'd be playing a chief role in but rather a very realistic funeral. Glancing up he saw Rosemary staring anxiously down at him.

'Are you all right?' she called.

He nodded and then brought his attention back to the rockface. He was more than halfway to the bracelet and coming up to a traverse which would be the most difficult part of the descent.

Inch by inch he edged his way down and then across. Crying out once in pain when his hand slipped, tearing a patch of skin from his palm.

The wind was worrying him a lot now. It had changed direction in the last few minutes and seemed to be both trying to pry him off and suck him from the rockface at the same time. Gritting his teeth he pressed his body hard against the rock and continued on into the traverse.

He was well aware he was being foolhardy if not downright stupid in trying to retrieve the bracelet. But after what Rosemary had said to him it was important to him to do this thing in order to prove what he felt for her – tangible proof of what he truly felt and believed.

Coming out of the traverse he descended a few more feet which brought him to the crevice where the bracelet was. Carefully bending down, he picked it up and dropped it into his pocket.

He took a few moments to catch his breath and then he started retracing his steps.

Rosemary wanted to shout words of encouragement but wisely decided not to in case she distracted him.

Angus was tiring fast now. His shoulders ached abominably and his legs threatened to buckle under him at any moment.

He wondered what the sensation would be like if he was to fall? Would he be conscious all the way down or would he know very little about it, having been knocked senseless on the first bounce? Was there life after death, or nothing at all?

Rosemary knew something was wrong. Three times he'd reached up to grasp the next hold and three times his hand had fallen away again.

Angus laid his cheek against the cool rock and sucked lungful after lungful of air down the raw barbed tunnel of his throat. He could go no further. He was buggered.

Far below he could hear the fast flowing Cart while in the distance there were voices calling to one another. Off to the left a number of herring gulls were crying as they wheeled towards some unknown destination.

A muffled sob escaped him. He didn't want to die. He didn't want to die at all!

'Angus?'

The word was a whisper in his ear. A vocal caress that might have been an angel beckoning him.

'Are you ok?'

Of course he wasn't bloody ok! Any second now he

was going to fall backwards off this bloody rockface to be smashed to smithereens.

Suddenly he started to chuckle and that eased the tension which had seized his body. He was desperate for a pee! Of all the times and places for that to happen! His chuckle became a giggle with a hysterical ring to it.

He nearly jumped out of his skin when a hand touched his. 'Jesus!' he exclaimed and twisted his head round to find Rosemary right there beside him.

'I'll help you the rest of the way,' she said.

Her hand on his was the contact through which strength poured from her to him. He could feel his body recharging, coming alive again.

And he knew then he was going to make it. With Rosemary beside him there was nothing he couldn't do.

'Careful now!' he warned as she broke the grip and started to make her way back up to the window.

When she reached the window she swung herself onto the sill. Dropping her legs into the room and then screwing round to grasp hold of Angus's extended arm.

She pulled him up till his head and shoulders were framed in the window and then, grabbing his braces, hauled on them so he came tumbling headlong into the room where they both landed in a heap on the floor.

For what must have been been a full five minutes Angus didn't attempt to speak, happy just to lie there revelling in the fact he was still alive.

Finally he produced the charm bracelet from his pocket and laid it in her hand.

Rosemary's eyes were shining as she snapped the bracelet round her wrist. 'Thank you,' she said.

'It was nothing,' he replied and they both burst out laughing at how silly and masculinely vain that sounded.

'I'll never forget today as long as I live,' Rosemary said.

This time he put his tongue into her mouth causing her to squirm and rub up against him.

When they eventually broke apart he had to excuse

himself as the desperate need to relieve himself had returned.

Going to another part of the castle he did it against a lichen spattered wall.

He was fastening his buttons when he became aware of being watched from the doorway.

'I've never seen a man doing it before,' Rosemary said, no hint of awkwardness in her voice.

Angus was acutely embarrassed and quickly did up the remainder of his buttons. 'You gave me a fright sneaking up like that,' he said, forcing out a laugh.

Rosemary stared at the long ribbon flowing along the floor and said men must have far bigger bladders than women to be able to pass as much water as Angus had just done.

The streaming pee reminded Angus of an old Scots custom which he now told her about. He felt he had to say something this was the first thing that came to mind.

According to tradition if a couple were to join hands, jump over a stream and on landing proclaim themselves man and wife then this was as binding in the eyes of God and the community as if they'd been legally married in church.

Hearing this, Rosemary came straight to his side and took one of his hands in hers. Nodding towards the still flowing pee she said if that didn't constitute a stream then she didn't know what did and would he marry her here and now, please?

They had to run to catch up with the pee. Jumping over it they declared they took one another for spouse.

Rosemary was suddenly shy then, giggling a little till Angus sealed their oath with another kiss.

Once over the outside wall and back on the road they crossed over and squeezed through a hedge which brought them out onto a cleared part of the hill. Climbing to the memorial to the ill-fated Mary, Queen of Scots, they stood looking out over Glasgow lying before them.

Anxious to cement over their previous rift as well as being genuinely curious, Angus asked Rosemary what sort of man Sir Alan was?

As Rosemary spoke a lifestyle completely outwith Angus's experience gradually unfolded. He heard of Balls. Dinner parties. Holidays abroad in France and Italy. Of huntin' shootin' and fishin'. Of fast cars and expensive ones. Of clever conversation where wit was the commodity prized above all else. In fact all the glamorous things money and position can provide.

The thought of being a rich businessman fascinated Angus. Not for him the total renunciation of the capitalist class as propagated by Big Donald. And the more he thought about it the more he was attracted to himself in that image.

Intense excitement gripped Angus with the realization that he'd arrived at a major juncture in his life. Suddenly the way ahead was crystal clear and he knew precisely the direction he wanted the rest of his life to take.

There would be no apprenticeship and going to sea after it was completed. Instead he would stay on at school to take his Highers, after which he'd enter the business world. That was where his destiny lay. He was convinced of it.

In a halting voice he told Rosemary of his revelation and as he spoke she too was caught up in the mesmeric dream now holding him fast in its spell.

Of course, all this was a long way ahead, an eternity it seemed at the moment. But all would come to fruition with the passage of time.

Just how he was going to make his fortune wasn't clear to him yet but he had no doubt the details would come with more thought on the subject. The important thing for the moment was the overall concept which lay dazzling and glittering with promise in his brain.

Not for him the anonymity of the proletariat. He was going to be a *somebody*.

In mock anger he shook his fist at the dirty industrial metropolis that was his birthplace and where his roots ran deep. 'I'm going to beat you! I'll have you dancing to my tune before I'm finished! Just you wait and see!' he roared defiantly.

Radiantly happy Rosemary put her arms round his waist. The world was truly a marvellous place. Angus had found his dream and they'd both found one another.

Her cup was running over as hand in hand they ran back down the hill towards the hedge.

When Rosemary eventually returned to Arnprior House she found her father back from the latest of his many recent London trips. There were also several guests being entertained, Sir Hamilton McLaren, a wealthy landowner and friend of her father, and his two sons, Iain and Peter.

Although she'd met Sir Hamilton before she'd never met his boys so when introductions were made they all trooped through for tea.

Iain was the elder son, being several years older than she was. While Peter was a year younger than she.

Iain, several years older than Rosemary, was dark and brooding with thick, heavy eyebrows and a face that had a saturnine quality about it. His skin was sallow and shone as though polished. His eyes black introspective and inclined to flash from time to time. He was an extraordinarily handsome young man in the blazer and tie of the Glasgow Academy.

Peter, a year younger than she, was the complete antithesis of his brother. Chunky in build, with yellow hair, he had a marvellously outgoing personality.

Cordelia Armstrong was the perfect hostess as she presided over tea, happy because for the first time in a long while her husband was too.

Before Hamilton's surprise arrival he'd had time to tell her the good news. The money he'd been so desperately in need of to keep the works afloat had been found. Armstrong's had been saved, or its fate postponed for some time anyway – literally at the eleventh hour, for if the money hadn't been forthcoming within the next few days then final notice would have had to have been served on all employees.

Sir Alan was jubilant as he sipped his tea. Later when the girls were in bed he would crack a bottle of their favourite champagne and together he and Cordelia would toast this last minute reprieve.

My God, but it had been hard graft convincing the board of the merchant bank he'd been conferring with to part with the capital he needed. But by dint of perseverance and hard fought argument he'd eventually won them round.

Mind you, he was paying a terrifically high rate of interest on the loan but what else could he expect? If he could only survive the next couple of years he was sure the works could establish itself in the black once more. His reason for thinking this was based on the disturbing rumours that were beginning to reach Britain from the continent. Mutterings of discontent with the threat of more than words to come.

Over in Spain the new republic wasn't proving at all popular while the Fascists under a certain General Franco were growing in strength daily. Those in the know were convinced an armed conflict between the two parties was inevitable.

Then, of course, there was this fellow Herr Hitler and his National Socialists over in Germany. Now if that man attained power then Germany would be bound to initiate an expansionist programme to try and win back some of the territories she'd lost as a result of the Great War.

It didn't matter if Britain was directly involved or not. Any hostilities in Europe were bound to stimulate the British shipbuilding industry. In fact this stimulation had already begun if he was reading the signs correctly. Weren't many of the ships that had been lying in mothballs for years being dusted off and sold to a suddenly demanding market in secondhand tonnage.? Something was afoot all right. Every instinct he possessed told him so.

Perhaps he hadn't been so persuasive in his arguments to the merchant bank after all. It might just be they knew even more than he did about the current European situation.

He was musing on that when his eye lit on Rosemary. How grown up she'd become recently. When she left Park it would be a finishing school for her. In Edinburgh perhaps or else one down in England. The continent was, of course, now ruled out.

His ruminations were interrupted by Sir Hamilton McLaren suggesting the entire Armstrong family come over to the McLaren house in Carmunnock for dinner sometime in the near future.

Hearing Cordelia accept, a date was set there and then.

This invitation secretly pleased him as he'd been cultivating McLaren for a number of years now and this family get together heralded a breakthrough in their relationship.

It was some hours after the McLarens had departed before Rosemary was able to get her father alone, finally cornering him in his study where he was attending to a pile of personal correspondence.

What Angus had told her about John McBain had been preying on her mind so she'd decided to ask her father for his side of the story.

Sir Alan was astonished when she put the question to him and asked how she'd come to hear of the case after so many years. She shrugged her shoulders and made some vague reply.

Sir Alan took time to collect his thoughts by pouring himself a stiff brandy and soda. He remembered the details of the John McBain affair quite clearly. At the time it had been a stroke of luck that he'd managed to wriggle out of paying the then Mrs McBain compensation, as money had been tight.

What no one knew apart from him was that McBain had been up on that gantry on his express orders to deal with a small matter that had needed attending to.

After the accident he'd naturally kept stum. To have

done otherwise would have been to admit liability. He'd felt sorry for Mrs McBain. But it was a hard world they lived in. Then and now.

Putting a smile on his face he recounted what had happened to Rosemary. The only detail he omitted was the one that mattered most.

When the interview with her father was finally concluded Rosemary was in no doubt that he'd been in the right.

When Angus arrived home after being with Rosemary he was bursting with good humour. The good humour and the whistling died when he discovered Archie to be the only one in.

With a glass of neat whisky in his hand and a half bottle at his feet Archie sat gazing into the kitchen fire. The ruddy glow from the flickering flames giving him a demonic look that accentuated the closeness of his eyes.

Archie had been at times viciously cruel to Carrie but in his own twisted way he'd come to love her. So it was with a sense of shock he'd taken a telephone call in the station manager's office that afternoon to be informed by Dr Robertson that Carrie had collapsed while out shopping and had been taken to the Emergency Department of the Victoria Hospital where she'd been found to be suffering from advanced TB. Tuberculosis. The very mention of the word was enough to still conversation and cause the heart to grow chill with fear. How many poor souls had died from that dread killer in Glasgow alone? The answer was incalculable.

Archie gulped back his drink and then poured himself another. He knew Angus hated him but it wasn't an emotion he returned. If anything, he rather respected the boy for the obvious guts the lad had. He would have liked to get close to Angus but somehow had never been able to.

Archie sighed. He was still in his dungarees with hands and face black and ingrained with oil. He knew he should get up and wash himself but he couldn't find the energy.

Sheena would be back from work soon and he'd get washed then while she made the tea. If there was anything in the house to make that was. Carrie had been out shopping when she'd collapsed.

He'd wanted to go round to the Victoria right away but had been dissuaded from doing so. He was told that Carrie would have already been dispatched by ambulance for Bellfield Sanatorium near Lanark where a bed was waiting for her.

It had been agreed he'd go to the sanatorium first thing in the morning, taking along a number of articles Dr Robertson had suggested Carrie would need.

He could hear Angus through in the boy's bedroom and knew the lad would stay there until teatime, it being Angus's habit to stay well clear of him whenever possible.

He hawked into the fire and watched while the thick phlegm sputtered and hissed on a burning coal, offering up a silent prayer of gratitude that it wasn't he who'd come down with TB. He certainly wasn't a coward but there were things he was deathly afraid of and illness was one of them.

He would go to the sanatorium but hate every second he was there. The smell common to all hospitals always succeeded in putting the fear of God into him.

The outside door opened and banged closed again which meant Sheena was home. He'd been waiting her arrival before breaking the news to Angus.

'Angus! Sheena!' he called out. 'Come away ben. I want to talk to the pair of you!'

Sheena came first, taking the long pearl-tipped pin out of her hat and allowing her hair to fall free to her shoulders. Somehow she contrived to remain voluptuous and seductive looking in spite of the severe green uniform encasing her from neck to mid-calf.

Angus entered the room, annoyance at being disturbed written all over his face. He'd been cutting up a length of red inner tubing which was going to form part of his new catapult.

Archie stared Angus straight in the eye. 'I've got some bad news for you lad,' he said. 'Your Ma collapsed in the street this afternoon and has been taken into hospital. The doctors say she's got TB.'

Angus's mouth fell open and he stared blankly at his step-father. It was some sort of cruel joke. It had to be! Archie was having him on. Taking the mickey.

'Jesus Christ!' Sheena said and sat down.

'You're kidding me?' Angus husked, wilting when Archie shook his head.

'She's been taken to a place out by Lanark. I'm going to see her in the morning. You can come with me if you like,' Archie said.

Angus looked down, seeing nothing. He wanted to run away. To hide. In fact to be anywhere except where he was. Turning abruptly, he fled the room.

Sheena was about to go after him when she was brought up short by Archie telling her to look in the press and see if there was anything there they could have for tea. When she replied there was only a loaf in he said he would go over to Tallon Street and break the news to the Chisholms. He'd pick up some fish suppers on his way back.

He had another dram before going through to the bathroom for a wash. Ten minutes later when he quietly let himself out the front door Sheena's voice could be heard coming from Angus's bedroom where she was doing her best to comfort her distraught step-brother.

The next morning Angus didn't run with the milk nor did Archie go to work.

Angus went down to the front close at his usual time to find Kitty waiting for him. He explained to his pal why he couldn't manage that day and Kitty promised to relay what had happened to Hugh.

Sheena made them a cup of tea and a slice of toast each for breakfast and then he and Archie, both dressed in their Sunday best, left the house to catch a tram.

During the entire journey Angus sat rigidly beside Archie staring out at the passing scenery. His eyes were red and puffy from being awake most of the night.

Arriving in Lanark, they inquired the way to Bellfield Sanatorium from a passer-by who informed them they had a mile and a half hike in front of them. It was either that or wait nearly two hours for the next local bus. They elected to walk.

The sanatorium was a large, imposing early Victorian building surrounded by well-tended lawns and a sprinkling of trees. It sparkled in the weak sunlight, giving the impression it was regularly scrubbed outside as well as in.

Loathing all institutions, Archie hated the place on sight. He shuddered as he and Angus walked through the heavy wooden doors opening into the marbled reception hall.

For half an hour they waited and then a young nurse arrived to escort them to the ward where Carrie was. The nurse's eyes opened fractionally when she saw Angus but she didn't pass any comment.

With the nurse leading the way they tramped along a seemingly endless maze of wood and marble corridors.

The thing that struck Angus most about the sanatorium was how cold it was. Despite the time of year every window was open wide so that the temperature inside the building was the same as it was out.

At the entrance to Carrie's ward they were again instructed to wait and this time they had to stand as there were no chairs or benches available where they might sit.

Within minutes a hatchet-faced woman approached them and announced herself to be Sister McMillan in charge of the ward.

The sister's next words caused Angus great consternation when she declared it was against the hospital's rules for children under the age of fifteen to be allowed into the wards.

Angus shot Archie a beseeching look which he transferred to the sister who stared back at him pityingly but resolutely.

Archie Marjoribanks may have done some terrible

things in his life but he did something then which went a long way to absolving many of them. Putting a winning smile on his face, he asked Sister if he might speak with her in private and together they moved off to a nearby alcove where Archie began exercising his not inconsiderable charm.

Angus never did find out what Archie said to Sister McMillan but, whatever it was, it secured for him the rare privilege of breaking the hospital rule.

Visitors were only allowed in one at a time and it was Archie's suggestion that Angus go first. Before going behind the screens masking the entrance to the ward Angus was handed a bagful of grapes and a box of chocolates by Archie and told to give them to Carrie, saying they came from him.

'Ach away and don't be daft!' said Archie when Angus tried to thank him.

Angus found Carrie near the end of a long row of beds. She was lying flat out with her eyes closed and the blankets pulled up to her chin.

She looked terrible. Her face was the colour of curds and her cheeks so sunken it gave her a skeletal appearance.

For a few moments he stared at his mother while she dozed. His chest heaved and he had to swallow repeatedly to hold back the tears.

'Ma?' he whispered, a catch in his voice.

Carrie's eyelids flickered and then slowly opened. Pain and suffering stared out. 'Hello, son,' she smiled.

He couldn't help what happened next. With a sob he threw himself beside her and, as his warm cheek touched her cold one, a dam seemed to burst inside him. The tears he'd been desperately holding back since Archie broke the news to him came flooding out.

Carrie stroked his hair while he cried and cried, his face buried in her pillow to try and stifle the racking sobs bursting from him.

'Just let yourself go, son,' she said quietly, thinking how much like his father he was becoming now his face had started to mature. Her guess was he'd end up a far taller, slimmer version of his father. She was still worried by the fact he was painfully thin but she'd reconciled herself to the idea that only time would alter that. It would be another year or two before he started to fill out and lose the gazelle quality he now had.

When his crying had finally run its course he used the corner of her top sheet to dry his eyes. He glanced round to see if any of the other patients were staring at him but they were all busy pretending they'd neither seen nor heard anything. The two ladies on either side of Carrie kept their noses buried deep in newspapers.

He wanted to know how long Carrie would be in the sanatorium but all she could tell him was she'd be there until better which could be anything from nine months to a year. Then she'd be back on her feet and singing like a lintie, she said, which brought a smile to Angus's face and even wrung the faint beginnings of a laugh from him.

A tremendous will to live was born in Carrie at that moment. She had to hang on. Her son needed her.

Angus had reached that terribly difficult stage of puberty and adolescence and if, during this time, the additional burden of being orphaned was thrust on him the consequences could well be disastrous. As the doctors would come to tell her again and again. They could do only so much to affect her cure. The real key to her getting better lay in her wanting to do so. For her, Angus became the key. The prime motivation.

They talked a little while longer and then it was time for Angus to go if Archie was to see Carrie as well.

At the screens he turned back and waved, knowing this would be the last look he'd have of her till she came back home again.

'Oh Ma!' he muttered. His heart felt it must surely snap in two. Swinging round he vanished from the ward.

As things turned out, Carrie's prediction of nine months to a year was somewhat optimistic. It was to be over two years before Angus saw his mother again.

When Archie arrived to sit by her bedside he was told

she'd come to a decision: Angus was to go and stay at Tallon Street until she was better.

Thinking it was him and his temper Carrie was worried about Archie wisely agreed. What he didn't realize was he was only part of the problem.

Carrie had often said she wasn't as green as she was cabbage looking. She knew there was a bond between Sheena and Angus that transcended normal step-sister/brother relationships. She would have trusted the young woman that Sheena had become with her life but she did not want her to be constantly alone with her son.

Archie promised faithfully that Angus would be packed over to Tallon Street that very day. Then and only then did Carrie begin to truly relax.

After a few minutes stilted conversation, Archie cleared his throat and in a whisper said he was going to try and control himself a lot more in future. Picking at his fingers he said he was going to miss her terribly and hadn't realized until this happened just how lucky he was to have a wife like her.

Carrie was astounded by this. These were the first intimate words she'd heard from Archie since their courting days. Furthermore, she could tell by his tone of voice and the expression on his face he meant what he said.

'Is it too late for us to start again?' he asked.

There was something boyish and appealing about Archie when he was like this that made you almost forget the cruel, roaring bully he could be.

Carrie lay back and watched a nurse making a bed on the other side of the ward. The nurse was young and fairly pretty with a face full of hope and expectation. Just like she'd once been so long long ago.

She wondered what she'd ever done to lose John McBain. Get saddled with Archie Marjoribanks. And now contract tuberculosis.

Archie was incorrigible. She knew no matter how hard he tried to reform he'd always revert back to type. The man was sick, not in the body like she was but in the mind where it lay darkly hidden. A malignancy that could be truly awesome when it manifested itself.

She was so tired she felt she could close her eyes and sleep for a hundred years. It was as though her very substance had nearly all melted away, leaving her a pale imitation of the woman she'd once been.

Looking a picture of melancholy, Archie sat staring at Carrie. He might have been a cur who'd been temporarily whipped into submission.

'We'll try again,' Carrie replied, knowing it was a futile gesture but feeling this reaffirmation of commitment was the best thing in the circumstances.

Archie nodded his gratitude, genuinely intending to keep his side of the bargain.

A few minutes later when he started to speak again he discovered she'd drifted off into what looked like a very heavy sleep.

With a rough tenderness he tucked her arms under the bedclothes and kissed her on the forehead. Then with a flashing smile to a hovering nurse he walked swiftly from the ward.

Hugh hadn't been back to Tallon Street since the day he'd left with the wireless on his shoulder. He came now knowing as it was the afternoon Donald would be at work. He didn't want to see his father. It was Winnie he wanted to speak to.

His mother answered the door wearing her pinny, her hands and arms covered in flour.

Exclaiming in delight, Winnie threw her arms round Hugh and hugged him tight. He didn't care that flour was deposited in streaks all over the good tweed jacket he'd bought only a few weeks ago.

When they finally disentangled themselves he was taken through to the kitchen where Winnie put the kettle on.

Hugh hardly recognized the kitchen. To begin with, electricity had been installed in the house which meant the old gas lighting outlets were gone. On one side a brand new cooker stood proudly. The small copper had been replaced by a washing machine. The kitchen had also been repainted as indeed had the hall and living room.

Winnie washed her hands at the sink and then, having masked the tea, buttered some piping hot scones fresh from the oven.

As they were going through to the living room Hugh broached the subject of his quarrel with Donald and was sad to hear his father was still angry with him. If there was to be a reconciliation it obviously wasn't going to be for some time yet.

They talked about Carrie and the shock it had been to hear of her being taken to Bellfield Sanatorium. It was unspoken between them but each blamed Archie for Carrie's present state. By now the entire family had come to know Archie Marjoribanks for what he was and if Carrie found understanding and perhaps pity for her husband she was the only one to do so.

Winnie went on to say Angus was sleeping in the room his mother had once shared with Harriet and seemed to be settling down well although at fifty-eight she was finding him quite a handful to have around the house.

This was just as Hugh had suspected and was the principle reason for his visit. He had come to ask Winnie if Angus might not be better off at the Paterson house with him? His idea was that when he eventually married – as he presumed he would someday – he would adopt Angus as his son.

Winnie could see that although Hugh's intentions were admirable he hadn't quite thought this proposal through. Tactfully she explained it was doubtful if Carrie would be willing to part with Angus or Angus with her.

If Angus had been a babe in arms and Hugh married to someone Carrie knew and approved of then that might have been a different kettle of fish. But it was her opinion, as she was certain it would be Carrie's, it was best for things to remain as they were.

Winnie added she was sure Carrie would be pleased to

know Angus had another place to go where he would be welcome. After all, she and Donald weren't getting any younger and who knew what the next day would bring?

Winnie was pleased Hugh had brought up the subject of marriage. At twenty-eight she thought it high time he settled down and raised a family of his own.

Hugh was in full agreement with this and in fact would have liked nothing better but as he hesitatingly explained he just couldn't seem to meet the right woman.

Somewhat embarrassed he said he'd chaffed enough personable lassies at the dancing but none of them had ever struck the right chord in him. He didn't want to get married just for getting married's sake. He wanted to marry someone he genuinely felt something for, someone he could see himself spending the rest of his life with.

There was very little Winnie could say to that except she was sure it would come out all right in the end.

The last thing she wanted was for Hugh to turn into some sort of eternal bachelor, knowing that would be totally wrong for him.

'I'll know her when I meet her,' Hugh said, eyes clouding with introspection.

Winnie sighed. 'I hope you do, son,' she replied in a voice full of sympathy.

While Winnie washed the tea things and saw to a pineapple upside down cake she had in the oven Hugh went through to the big room where he stood by the window looking up the road to the bend round which Armstrong's lay.

It was a bitter cold day and there was ice on the Cart. The air was heavy with grey chimney smoke while from beyond the bend came the thick black fug which proclaimed the Armstrong furnaces to be going full blast.

He lit a Willy Woodbine and wondered if there was something wrong with him that he couldn't meet a lassie he liked well enough to settle down with? He found it difficult to put into words just what he was looking for. Decent looks certainly. He couldn't see himself being drawn to somebody who was ugly. But the looks were only part of it. There was a lot more to what he was after than that.

He stood at the window pondering till the light faded into late afternoon darkness. Finally he shrugged and dismissed all thoughts of women from his mind.

One thing was certain though whomever he married he'd expect her to deliver him a son in time. Lassies round the house were fine and dandy but a boy was the thing. That was what he wanted.

He said goodbye to Winnie through in the kitchen, slipping a pound note into her pinny pocket and telling her to buy a wee extravagance for herself.

All the way up the road to the tramstop he dreamed of being a father with a son by his side.

Aye, boys were the ticket right enough. They made a man immortal.

12

During the next few years Angus and Rosemary saw as much of each other as was possible and all the while their relationship strengthened and developed.

Angus had moved back to Holmlea Road the same day Carrie returned from Bellfield Sanatorium. The reunion had been a joyous one but it had nearly broken his heart to see how gaunt and pitifully thin his mother had become. She was so changed it had taken him a moment or two to recognize her when she and Archie walked through the front door.

True to his word Archie tried to mend his ways, never

drinking and not once losing his temper, forever fussing round Carrie and even bringing her treats such as flowers and sweets.

At first it was thought amongst the family that Carrie would soon recover her former strength but as the months passed it became evident she would never be the same again.

As Donald remarked, all the sap had been drained out of her leaving only a shell of the woman who'd married John McBain and given birth to Angus.

Sheena had gone from the house and no one knew where. Not long after Carrie had been taken into Bellfield Archie had come home from work one night to discover a note which baldly stated she was leaving for good. Inquiring at the tram depot at the top of Holmlea Road he'd been told she'd handed in her notice with the intention of going south. Several clippies said she'd mentioned London while one was adamant it was Birmingham she was headed for.

From that day on not another word was heard from Sheena. Angus sorely missed her.

Angus was now at Queen's Park Secondary School where he was doing extremely well. An incident occurred in his first year which became legendary and marked him out as something of a wit and character. When asked in music class what a violin concerto was he'd blithely replied it was a small violin.

Perhaps it was the way he said it or the extremely serious expression he wore that convinced the rest of the class he was taking the mickey for, with a sort of combined hoot, they all dissolved into helpless laughter.

That reply earned him four of the belt and for a long time the nickname of Concerto McBain.

Physically Angus had grown even taller so that now he topped six feet, still skinny but wiry with it. He walked with a permanent stoop which made him look rather like a coat hanger on legs.

He'd been staying at Tallon Street only a short while when he'd secretly taken on an evening paper round

which had been something Carrie had been completely
against in case he overtaxed himself.

When Donald eventually found out he'd summoned
Angus through to the front room where the pair of them
thrashed the matter out. The upshot was that Angus
would be allowed to continue running with the milk in
the mornings and papers in the evenings just as long as it
didn't interfere with either his health or school work,
which it never did.

Week after week Angus put money by and soon his
savings began to mount up. He bought a metal box with
a padlock on the front and it was in this he kept the
pound and ten shilling notes which began to accumulate.

His business ambitions remained as strong as ever and
often he and Rosemary would discuss what it would be
like when they grew up and were able to marry.

In this particular vision of the future Rosemary had
replaced Sheena and the house the new triumvirate lived
in was considerably more grand than the simple room
and kitchen that had been his first conception.

The one fly in the ointment so far was he hadn't been
able to decide what line of business he should go into.
But he had no doubts whatsoever this would be revealed
to him in time.

So far he'd been most secretive about his ambitions,
not even disclosing them to Carrie when she came out of
the sanatorium. Only Rosemary knew of his plans and
the motivation behind them.

As the spring of 1936 gave way to summer Rosemary
became much preoccupied with trying to think up something unusual to give Angus for his birthday. Birthdays
were a big thing between them due to the fact they'd
both been born on the same day, he the twelfth of
August, 1921, she exactly one year later.

One of their favourite haunts was Paterson's Dairy,
where Hugh always made them welcome no matter
what the time of day or how busy he was. Although
Hugh knew Rosemary lived in the big house in Old
Castle Road he still wasn't aware she was Sir Alan

Armstrong's daughter.

It was there one Saturday afternoon when she and Angus were helping to muck out the stables that the idea came to her.

Hugh had recently bought a stallion called Royal Standard with the intention of breeding, which would add another string to the dairy's bow.

Angus had been called out of the stables for a few minutes, leaving Rosemary at work on her own. What happened next caused her to catch her breath: Royal Standard having got out of his own stall, reared onto his hind legs and mounted a mare called Gypsy.

The enormous penis sunk to its hilt to be drawn out and sunk again and again. With a most unhorsy low grunt Royal Standard pulled himself free and, as he did so, a gush of sperm exploded from Gypsy's rear.

The most marvellous sensations invaded Rosemary's stomach, making her flesh go all prickly. All she could think about was having that done to her.

She and Angus had petted of course but she'd limited this to her breasts and not beyond. Now she felt she wanted to go further and in that instant it dawned on her what the perfect birthday present for Angus would be.

When Angus returned to the stables he found her flushed and with a peculiar glint in her eye as she wielded her pitchfork with gusto. Asking her what was up he was told to mind his own business and all would be revealed, she giggled, in good time.

Mystified, Angus set to work beside Rosemary and falling into the rhythm of the job the incident passed from his mind.

Sir Alan Armstrong was a happy man as he sat in his office sipping his morning sherry.

Like some great beast, the works rumbled below and around him proclaiming Armstrong's to be in full production once again.

The books lying open in front of him were healthier than they'd been in years with more orders flooding in every day.

As he sat staring out of his window, Sir Alan mused on the fear and trepidation that was abroad in the land and had been ever since 7th March when the German Chancellor Herr Hitler's armed columns had streamed into the Rhineland where they'd reoccupied the main German towns.

All Europe was in a furore over this, especially the French government under M. Sarraut.

France was now looking to Great Britain as the British had guaranteed the French frontier against German aggression. Earlier, they'd put a great deal of pressure on France for the evacuation of the Rhineland.

At one fell swoop Hitler had not only violated the Peace Treaty but also the Treaty of Locarno, throwing into great consternation those powers ranged against him.

Lloyd George's response to this flagrant breach of faith had been placatory: 'In my judgement Herr Hitler's greatest crime was not the breach of a treaty because there was provocation.'

Lloyd George's statement was interpreted to mean Hitler's provocation was the failure of the Allies to disarm themselves more than they had done.

Now massive fortifications were being built in the Rhineland which, according to Winston Churchill, meant a great barrier of concrete was being raised which would effectively alter the whole aspect of Middle Europe.

Sir Alan smiled as he sat back in his chair to light up one of his favourite Cuban cigars. War was now inevitable. There could be no doubt about it. Those appeasers in Whitehall would eventually have to stop playing the ostrich and face reality. Herr Hitler was intent on expanding Germany's diminished colonial power and like Napoleon before him his ultimate aim was the conquest of Europe.

A frown flitted across Sir Alan's face. War meant work, which in turn meant Armstrong's was bound to make money hand over fist. If properly handled, the works would never again be in danger of closure. The other side of the coin was that many good men were bound to die, which genuinely saddened him.

Guilt niggled his insides as he thought of how much he'd hoped and prayed for this coming conflict. He'd been thinking of himself, his family and the works, not the poor sods who were going to get chopped or maimed and the loved ones they'd leave behind.

'Damnit to hell!' he exclaimed and poured himself another sherry. It was a rare occasion when he indulged in more than one at this time of the morning.

He pondered for a little while, desperately trying to salve his conscience and dispel the terrible guilt feelings growing in him with every passing second.

His face lit up in a smile as the idea came to him. When war finally did erupt those working in Armstrong's would find themselves in reserve occupations. Well, the least he could do was take on as much staff as possible thereby assuring a few more local men the chance of escaping the front line.

His conscience now assuaged, he picked up the small brass bell standing on one side of his desk and gave it two sharp rings.

He would dictate a memo immediately and see it was posted on the works noticeboard without delay. Slitting his eyes, he worked out just how many additional time served men he could take on and for good measure tacked on a number of apprentices.

Sir Alan's memo duly appeared on the noticeboard that afternoon: Donald read it en route to the pattern makers' offices. He forgot about it until the evening when the hooter had blown and he was on his way home. He recalled then how Angus had once confided in him he wanted to work for Armstrong's just like his Da before him.

Donald made a mental note to go over to Holmlea Road and speak to Carrie and the lad after tea.

Carrie was sitting knitting while Archie sprawled in the

chair facing her reading the evening paper.

Angus was through in his room counting his money. It was a Friday and he'd been paid for both his jobs.

When Carrie called him to come away ben the kitchen he carefully padlocked his metal box which he then placed in its hiding place behind some odds and ends on a shelf in the cupboard.

Satisfied everything was in order, he went through to see his grandfather whom he'd heard arrive while he was in the middle of his weekly count.

Donald disliked intensely being in Archie Marjoribanks's company nowadays. He always had the overpowering urge to backhand the man for the way he'd treated Carrie and still did as far as he knew, although according to Winnie things were a lot better between them of late.

Fancying he could still take Archie in a fight, Donald didn't appreciate just how much he'd deteriorated during the past few years. He'd shrunk several inches while his chest was now a parody of its former burly and muscular self. The fact was Donald had become an old man without realizing it. In a stand up fight he wouldn't have stood an earthly against Archie.

Carrie told Angus to sit and when he'd done so went on to tell him of the marvellous opportunity that had come his way.

With Donald being a senior gaffer it was certain anyone he put up for a job – and certainly John McBain's son – would be accepted.

Angus was thunderstruck. It had just never crossed his mind this sort of thing might happen. In a great rush of words he told them he didn't want to go to work for Armstrong's any more but wanted to go into business instead.

His confession was greeted by surprise – none of them had even the faintest inkling of Angus's change of heart. When Archie asked Angus what sort of business he would like to go into all Angus could do was blush and reply he didn't know yet. Archie snorted and muttered something about delusions of grandeur.

Donald was filled with consternation as he lit up his pipe. What had happened to the common sense he'd always credited the lad with having? Business wasn't something people of their class got mixed up in. That was strictly for those who went to fancy schools and spoke with a plum in their mouths.

Besides being in business meant you became one of *them*. A capitalist! It was the very nature of the beast.

Carefully Donald unscrewed the bowl of his pipe and knocked dottle into his hanky. As he cleaned the mucky inside of the bowl he thought that it was common for lads of Angus's age to have flights of fancy. Well there was nothing wrong with that as long as they were eventually made to realize the difference between those and the reality of their situation.

He sucked his pipe back into life and then began to speak in the calm, reassuring voice he employed when faced with a difficult situation on the foundry floor. He said Angus wanting to go into business was all very well and good but did Angus appreciate just what he'd be up against?

Angus replied rather stiffly he wasn't quite sure what his grandfather was getting at, wincing as Donald then went on to make pertinent point after point.

Angus hung his head under the gentle but penetrating and most disconcerting onslaught. He didn't have the answers to any of this. All he did have was a dream and enormous faith in his own ability to accomplish what he set out to do.

The more questions thrown at him the more frantic Angus became. He desperately wanted to try and explain his dream but found no matter how hard he groped for the words they just wouldn't come. It all seemed so clear when he was discussing it with Rosemary but here talking to adults it was a different matter altogether.

What he did manage to get out was he considered it imperative to get his Highers for without those behind him he would be at a definite disadvantage for getting on.

As the words jerked from his quivering mouth it suddenly dawned on him with resounding clarity that to men like Donald and Archie formal education beyond being able to read, write and count meant very little. To them a trade was the thing, the be-all and end-all.

Archie was in an irritable mood. The rheumatism which had suddenly started bothering him lately was giving him gyp. He thought if only he could have a wee half gill it might ease the terrible nagging pain.

Archie considered what Angus was saying to be a right load of nonsense. The lad didn't realize just how lucky he was, being handed an opportunity like this on a plate. Times might have eased but there still weren't that many jobs going you could afford to pick and choose. Silly bugger with his high-faluting notions. Secretive, too, the way he hoarded the money Carrie allowed him to keep in that metal box through in his room.

The boy was becoming miserly and that was something he detested. Money was for spending, not for hiding away in the back of a cupboard. It was high time Angus was taught a lesson regarding money (in the hope it would bring him to his senses).

Archie grimaced and rubbed his arm. Bloody rheumatism! He would get Carrie to make him a hot bread poultice after Donald was gone.

Carrie appreciated Angus was highly thought of scholastically at school and that his teachers were keen for him to stay on and take his Highers. The trouble was she'd never thought all that much about it, her assumption being he'd still want to leave Queen's Park when old enough to go up by.

At the end of a further half hour's argument Donald was still maintaining Angus should forget this daft business notion and sign apprenticeship papers with Armstrong's where he would learn a useful trade.

Folding her arms across her chest Carrie declared her mind was made up. Angus would not be going back to school at the end of the summer holidays but would be starting with Armstrong's.

'It's for the best son. I know you'll agree with us in a few years time when you come to see things in perspective,' Donald said slightly pompously.

Angus jumped to his feet. He couldn't bear to stay in this room a second longer. He had to get out. It didn't matter where as long as it was a quiet spot where he could sit and nurse his anguish.

'Angus!' Carrie yelled. But it was no use. He was gone. The front door banged behind him.

'Delusions of grandeur,' repeated Archie, shaking his head and kneading his arm.

Carrie stared at the doorway through which Angus had vanished. She knew she was right in insisting he get settled into a good job, especially now her health was giving her cause for concern again.

Angus leaned into the wind and forced his legs to pump harder and harder. His chest was heaving while his short hair spiked out behind him as he sped along the road on his bike.

It wasn't fair. It just wasn't fair! he raged. His knuckles turned white as he strained at the handlebars as though they were a length of steel he was trying to bend in half.

He would never marry Rosemary now. How could he! She was the boss's daughter while he would never be anything more than an employee. A journeyman. A nothing!

His long legs whirled faster and faster till he and his bike were a blur flashing through the night.

Suddenly as though a stopcock had been opened, his anger was gone leaving him feeling washed out and taut as a thinly stretched wire. His hands were trembling as he stopped pedalling to stare round and see where he was.

Instinctively he'd taken the road he travelled every morning to Paterson's Dairy and even now was coasting into Muirend. That pleased him for if there was anyone he could speak to at a time like this it was his uncle Hugh.

Hugh was humming merrily to himself as he put a Windsor knot in his tie. He was off to the jigging and looking forward to it. Outside the house stood a brand new Wolseley Hornet he'd bought for £175 and which had been delivered from the saleroom that very afternoon.

Moving to the window he twitched back the curtain and gazed down at the bright red car. It was a beauty all right and in his estimation well worth every penny.

For months now he'd been coveting the saleroom models and wondering where he could get £175 from. Then he remembered the wireless set he'd bought for Winnie and which now stood on top of his dressing table.

The Wolseley people had been only too happy to enter into a hire purchase agreement and as a result the shining wee beauty now standing outside was his.

He was still at the window, reluctant to take his eyes off the Hornet, when Angus appeared cycling towards the house.

He frowned when he saw the look on Angus's face. Moments later he was hurrying down to the front door where the bell was already clanging.

'You'd better come away up and tell me all about it,' he said. He gestured towards the stairs leading to his bedroom.

There was a packet of Pasha lying beside the wireless and without asking permission Angus helped himself to one.

Hugh closed the bedroom door and stood with his back to it. 'Your mother?' he queried, for his first thought had been something had happened to Carrie.

'No,' Angus said huskily, smoke rising from him as though he was a newly stoked chimney. He declined when Hugh suggested he sit. Instead, striding up and down the room, the words poured from him.

While Angus ranted Hugh crossed to the press from which he produced a screwtop whose contents he poured equally into a brace of tumblers. Angus accepted his on the move and greedily drank it down.

All the words that had steadfastly refused to come earlier now poured from him as he told Hugh about Rosemary and the plans they'd had for their future.

One of the main reasons for the words not coming in Holmlea Road was because he hadn't wanted to bring Rosemary into it, knowing only too well the derisory reaction he would have had from Donald had he announced that he planned to marry Sir Alan Armstrong's elder daughter. But here with Hugh he had no such inhibitions.

Hugh sipped his beer and listened in silence, thinking about something his mother had once said about still waters running deep. He'd thought he knew Angus and yet here was a completely new side to the boy he hadn't even suspected existed.

It amused him greatly to learn Rosemary was Sir Alan's daughter. Jesus, but Angus aimed high!

When Angus spoke about his ambitions in the business field his eyes glowed, only becoming dull again when hc remembered these ambitions would probably never be fulfilled.

Finally he stopped talking and turned to Hugh with an expectant look on his face, waiting for his uncle's comments and advice.

Hugh was well aware of the responsibility now resting on his shoulders. What he said next could well affect Angus for the rest of the lad's life.

The damnable thing was he could see Donald's point of view only too clearly. Angus came from a working-class background and people from there just didn't aspire to the heady levels inhabited by Armstrong and his family.

It was obvious there was a great deal of love between Angus and Rosemary but how was she going to feel in the future when able to look beyond the bounds of passion? And if she and Angus did get married how would he be affected in the years to come?

A man like Sir Alan would denigrate the lad and treat

him as both an inferior and a lackey, to say nothing about how Angus could expect to be treated by the Armstrongs' friends.

Angus would be a misfit, the proverbial round peg in a square hole. And no matter how strong his relationship with Rosemary this could only lead to friction and eventual unhappiness between the pair of them.

Hugh knew that when Donald spoke of *us* and *them* his father had the rights of it. Maybe someday things would be different. He wasn't a prophet and couldn't say. But certainly in the year 1936 that was how it was.

'Well?' Angus prompted.

Hugh took a deep breath and then proceeded to speak for a good ten minutes. When he finally finished Angus looked the most miserable young man there had ever been.

Hugh's words were a death knell to Angus, each one another brick in the wall that had suddenly sprung up between himself and Rosemary. He'd come to Hugh looking for hope and all he was getting were reasons why he should give up all idea of marrying Rosemary Armstrong.

Hugh could see Angus thought he'd let him down so he apologized saying that was how he saw the position and surely Angus wouldn't want him to lie or pretend otherwise?

For Angus two things were crystal clear. The first was that he loved Rosemary and no matter what happened to him in life she would remain his rightful partner.

The other thing was that he wasn't cut out any longer to work at Armstrong's. There had been a time when he would have slotted neatly into that niche but that was before he'd met Rosemary and the candle of ambition had been lit within him.

They sat and talked for a while longer and then Hugh took Angus down to the front of the house to admire the Wolseley.

Hugh had the idea then of forgetting all about going to the jigging and taking Angus out for a run in the car. But

Angus declined, saying he just wasn't in the mood and perhaps they could go another time.

Angus clambered onto his bike. Hugh reached out and shook him by the hand. Angus appreciated the gesture as it signified that Hugh now accepted him as a man.

After Angus had gone Hugh went through and sat with Greta Paterson for a while. She listened sympathetically as he told her about Angus's problems. When he asked her opinion she said he'd done all he could and to have advised the lad otherwise would have been the sheerest folly.

The Plaza Dance Hall had the name of being a right toffee-nosed place where anyone bearing even the faintest resemblance to scruff was definitely not welcome. Dressed in his good suit with a brand new shirt and tie on Hugh didn't anticipate any difficulty in being admitted.

Having parked his car he made his way to the Star Bar directly facing the dance hall.

The interior of the pub was blue with smoke and there were the usual raucous Friday night voices everywhere. He ordered a pint of heavy and a half of whisky. Knocking the whisky back, in a single gulp, he washed it down with a gulp of beer.

He was deep in thought about Angus when he heard himself being hailed from the other side of the bar. Looking up, he saw a chap called Kenny White whom he'd been friendly with at school edging through the crowd towards him.

The two men shook hands, genuinely pleased to see one another. Kenny offered to buy Hugh a refill which Hugh readily accepted. They toasted each other and drank. Kenny informed Hugh he was waiting for a china who was going to make up a foursome with his girlfriend's pal.

They were deep in speculation about the forthcoming football season and how the 'Gers would do when Hugh saw the two girls enter the pub to stand rather self-consciously while they stared round.

One girl's face lit up when she spied Kenny and after a hurried whisper to her companion the pair of them began making their way over.

'Your bird and her pal I think,' Hugh said out the side of his mouth, thinking Kenny had acquired a bit of taste in his old age as both women were classy looking.

Introductions were made, Kenny's girl being Mary Maude and her pal Janey McIver. Hugh shook hands with both of them and then asked what they were having to drink as it was his round.

Once the drinks were in Hugh found himself standing beside Janey and as Kenny and Mary were deep in conversation on their own he felt duty bound to chat with the lassie, not that talking to her was all that much of a hardship. Besides being pretty like many Glasgow women, she had an incisive wit which could make you laugh one minute and cut you to the bone the next.

Janey informed Hugh they were also off to the Plaza that night. Usually she and Mary went to Barrowland but had decided on a change because she had recently broken off with a boyfriend of long standing and didn't want to run into him in case he caused trouble.

While Janey talked Hugh wondered how Kenny had come to get mixed up with a couple of left-footers like these. For it was obvious to him that was what they were, each having the map of Ireland written clearly across her face.

Half an hour later Kenny glanced at his watch and looked anxiously at the door. Fifteen minutes after that he was downright embarrassed as it was now obvious his china wasn't going to show which meant Janey had been given a dissy.

He went up to the bar and got yet another round. Then, surreptitiously, he gestured to Hugh to follow him to the cludgie.

Kenny was frantic and straightaway pleaded with Hugh to fill in for his missing friend.

With the thought that Janey was a fenian uppermost in his mind, Hugh tried to decline but Kenny wouldn't take no for an answer. Kenny confessed he was loopy about Mary and had been trying to get her to go out with him for weeks. Mary wasn't his girlfriend at all, although he desperately wanted her to be. This was their first date together.

Having made his impassioned plea, he produced a small silver flask from his pocket which he thrust into Hugh's hands, urging him to have a dram.

Under the circumstances Hugh felt he had no option other than to agree to be Janey's partner, leaving Kenny free all evening to dance with Mary rather than having to share himself between the two women.

Kenny was delighted and much relieved by Hugh's capitulation and they each had a large swallow from the flask before heading back to the bar where they found both girls looking miserable as sin.

They chatted for a few minutes and then Hugh suggested that as he was also going to the Plaza why didn't he join them to round off the numbers?

Janey flashed him a grateful smile. Finishing their drinks, they left the pub and crossed over the road.

The decor of the dancehall was very genteel with acres of plush and a great many potted plants. The ages of the clientele varied from teenagers to couples in their late forties and early fifties. A number of the older men were wearing tails.

Janey fitted snugly against Hugh when they took to the floor and soon they were enjoying themselves, having a 'rer ter', as the expression goes.

Much later they were cooling themselves with soft drinks when Kenny materialized to announce with a sideways wink to Hugh that he and Mary were off. Without actually saying so, he made it quite clear he and Mary wanted to leave alone.

Having gone this far Hugh decided he might as well go the whole hog and lumber Janey. During the last waltz he put it to her and she rather shyly agreed.

Reaching the Wolseley, he proudly showed it to her, having first made a quick tour of inspection to ensure it hadn't been vandalized in his absence. Janey was most impressed by the fact he had a car and said it was the first time she'd ever been driven home in one. Hugh replied she was the first Catholic he'd ever taken home. He'd meant it as a joke but somehow it didn't quite come out as one. Janey's eyes flashed as she bit back the retort that had sprung so readily to her mouth.

There it was, out in the open at last, the unspoken barrier that had existed between them all night. Religion.

'Aye, well,' said Hugh sadly, helping Janey into the car.

Janey knew exactly what he meant. There was an enormous gulf of bitterness and hatred between their two sides, a gulf that was rarely successfully crossed. Conditions, environment and prejudice bred at the breast saw to that.

As they drove into the festering area that was the Gorbals, Janey mumbled she wanted to thank him for coming to her rescue earlier on and he mumbled back it had been his pleasure.

Thistle Street was a grey canyon whose floor was strewn with garbage and with walls looking as though they were suffering from an advanced case of leprosy. It was a miracle of human will that such an immaculately turned out lassie as Janey could have come from a slum like this.

Hugh killed the engine and for a moment or two they sat in silence. Hugh finally cleared his throat to say he'd better get on back home as he had to be up at the crack of dawn.

In a flash Janey was out of the car, a wry smile on her face as she reached back in again to shake him by the hand. 'Perhaps we'll bump into one another some other night,' she said.

Then turning on her heel she was gone, clattering up her close.

'Aw to hell with it!' Hugh said savagely, angry and

upset and not wanting to admit to himself the reason why.

The Wolseley roared into life, peeling so fast down the street it left a long strip of rubber behind as a souvenir.

As he glared through the windscreen he told himself Kenny White was a mug. There was no future in getting involved with a left footer. That road could only lead to the worst sort of trouble.

The car had already turned out of sight when a wan face appeared high up in one of the tenement windows to stare out onto a street now empty apart from a drunk clinging for dear life onto a lamp standard while he spewed his guts into the gutter.

Sadly, Janey left the window and started to undress. When she crawled into bed it was to lie beside three of her sisters, two of whom slept up the way while she and the fourth slept down.

There were ten McIver children and all of them slept in that one tenement room.

It was a long time before she fell asleep but when she did it was to dream she was back amongst the plush and potted plants of the Plaza dancing with Hugh Chisholm.

'Property,' Sir Hamilton McLaren boomed, 'That's the thing. You can't go far wrong with property. Mark my words.'

There were four of them round the wrought iron lawn table, Sir Hamilton and his wife Elizabeth – Lize as she was known to her friends – plus Sir Alan and Cordelia.

This was the third time the Armstrongs had visited the McLarens and, as Sir Alan had wanted, a strong bond of friendship was growing up between the two families.

Sir Alan mused on Sir Hamilton's word as he sipped a cold glass of Sauterne and watched his daughters, Rosemary and Diane, riding with Iain and Peter McLaren in the far distance. He thought speculatively and not for the first time how well his girls got on with the McLaren boys, a fact he might well be able to exploit at a later date.

'Take industry like you're in,' Sir Hamilton went on, warming to his favourite subject. 'That comes and goes according to the state of the country's and the world's economy, but with property you don't have to worry because it's a permanent fixture. Well, almost permanent anyway. And as long as there are people needing a roof over their heads you're in business. Recession or boom, it's all one to the property owner.'

Sir Alan wondered if this was the diversification he'd long been looking for. Another two or three years the way things were going and he'd be in a position where he could afford to hive off a substantial amount of venture capital. Property might well be the sort of secondary investment which would suit him down to the ground and ensure he'd never again have to think of using that small automatic pistol lying in the dark recesses of his desk.

A little later Cordelia caught her husband intently eyeing Iain McLaren, sizing the lad up. Then she saw his gaze move from Iain to Rosemary and back again. The hint of a smile blossomed at the corners of her mouth as she correctly guessed what was running through his mind.

Well, why not? she thought. The boy was handsome, intelligent, and one day would be worth a fortune. She doubted there was a better prospect in all Scotland.

With a gracious nod to the attendant butler she accepted more wine. It was turning out to be a most interesting and enjoyable afternoon. Giving a brittle laugh, she turned her attention back to Hamilton who'd just delivered the tag line to some absurd joke he'd been telling.

While her parents and the McLarens laughed Rosemary attacked the plate of salmon set before her. She munched hungrily and as she ate she wondered for the umpteenth time why it was so long since she'd heard from Angus.

Twice she'd been up early enough to look out on the milk cart doing its rounds and neither time had he been with it. Could it be he was ill or had been involved in an accident?

She came to the decision she would rise early again next morning and if he still wasn't on the cart she'd go down and have a word with Kitty to find out just what was what.

With her mind now partially at rest she glanced across to where Diane was deep in conversation with Peter. Those two certainly got on like a house on fire, but then everyone got on with Peter. He was such a laugh and always tremendous fun to be with. Not at all like Iain who was quiet and intense with the loner's habit of often retreating within himself.

She watched Iain carefully wipe his mouth, every gesture neat and precious.

Her thoughts were interrupted by Diane shrieking with laughter as she tumbled down a grassy bank while Peter, who was obviously the culprit, stood grinning from ear to ear.

'Come on!' Diane yelled to Rosemary, as she got to her feet, her face red from heat and exertion. 'Let's give him some of his own medicine!'

Rosemary smiled and jumped up. As she did so, she stretched out her hands and waggled her fingers, knowing Peter was hypersensitively ticklish. Even the threat of it was enough to send him into paroxysms of laughter.

Peter yelped as both girls advanced on him. He'd gone too far and would now have to pay the penalty. 'That's not fair!' he protested and turned to run.

Iain smiled thinly at the goings on, rather enjoying them although horseplay wasn't something he personally liked getting involved in. He invariably found it undignified and degrading but only in himself and not in others.

As Peter ran off with Diane and Rosemary in pursuit a white vapour trail suddenly appeared in the sky above them.

Iain shielded his eyes as he followed the aeroplane from whose fuselage the vapour was streaming. The plane roared closer and then banked to come winging directly overhead.

He held his breath. For a split second every detail of the plane's underbelly was visible to him. Then it was gone, disappearing fast towards the horizon while behind it the vapour trail very slowly began to break up and disintegrate.

His mind filled with the excitement the plane had generated in him. He began to think what it must be like to be high in the air flying like a bird. What a glorious sense of freedom that must be!

Staring up at the sky he pictured the plane zooming overhead with himself at the controls. He found the image almost unbearably exciting.

It was mid-afternoon when Carrie and Winnie alighted from the tram into Scotland Street. It was quite some time since Carrie's last visit to the Smiths so another was well overdue.

Mounting the close stairs they rapped on the Smiths' door. They were about to turn away thinking no one was home when the door opened a few inches and an eye peered out.

'Robert?' Carrie queried. The sudden and bizarre appearance of the eye had given her a fright.

There was a pause during which the eye studied her curiously and then the door swung open to reveal old man Smith.

Both Carrie and Winnie were shocked at the sight of him. His face was ingrained with what looked like coal dirt while his hair was long, matted and tangled.

His shirt was open and collarless and, judging from its state, hadn't been changed in weeks. His trousers were tied round the middle with a piece of manky string below which his flies were completely undone. When he moved his flies opened wide revealing the fact he wasn't wearing any underpants.

His face broke into a sudden grin and extending a gnarled bony hand he invited them inside.

The poor man's completely off his chump, Winnie thought, wondering what Meg was thinking of to allow him to get into such a state. She gestured Carrie to go in first and then followed closely at her daughter's heels.

Both women gagged as the overpowering stench filling the house hit them. Winnie gulped and held a hanky to her nose as she followed Carrie and Robert through to the kitchen.

Despite the fact it was high summer and exremely warm out, there was a fire blazing in the grate but the fire wasn't a coal one. Broken pieces of furniture which had evidently been chopped by the hatchet lying just inside the fender, burnt away.

'Where's Meg?' Carrie asked, trying to act as though everything was normal and just as it should be.

Robert's eyes took on a faraway look and his mouth twisted into a secret smile.

Snapping out of his dwam, Robert started humming to himself, a strange discordant tune of his own composition. And crossing to where the hatchet was lying he picked it up and hefted it in his skeletal hand. Without warning the hatchet hissed through the air causing Winnie to give an involuntary little scream and hastily step backwards.

The hatchet crashed into the remains of a wooden chair, breaking the seat part jaggedly in two. Again and again Robert swung the hatchet till the chair was reduced to an untidy pile of kindling.

With dribble running over and through the growth on his chin he piled every last sliver of this kindling onto an already stacked and roaring fire.

Sweat dripped from Carrie as she squatted beside Robert Smith and forced herself to look into those demented eyes. 'Where's Meg?' she asked again, her voice soothing and coaxing.

The scars from the stitches lining Robert's face appeared angry in the reflected firelight. His mouth opened and he tried to speak but all that came out was more spit and animal grunts.

Then for a brief second his eyes cleared and once more he tried to speak. But it was no use. What emerged had no meaning, at least none Carrie could decipher.

Reaching out, he laid a begrimed hand on Carrie's arm and as he did so several large tears burst from the corners of his eyes. The sanity vanished as swiftly as it had appeared. He snatched his hand away and, hunkering on his feet like a dog, began to snigger.

'I think we'd better look around,' Winnie said.

Carrie nodded agreement and came to her feet while Robert ceased sniggering to gaze in fascination into the roaring blaze.

Side by side Carrie and Winnie ventured out of the kitchen and back into the hallway where the terrible stench seemed stronger. When they entered the bedroom they found it pitch dark and the stench stronger still.

'Oh my God!' exclaimed Carrie when she'd swept the curtains back.

Encased in a thick flannelette nightgown, Meg's decomposing body lay stretched out under the bedclothes. Her white hair was fluffed out halo-like round her head while what remained of her eyes stared sightlessly at the ceiling.

For a minute, Winnie thought Robert might have done for his wife with the hatchet or some other such weapon but a cursory glance was enough to verify Meg had died in her sleep or from natural causes while in bed.

Catching hold of the window, Carrie jerked it open to allow some of the stink out and fresh air in. She then asked her mother what they should do and Winnie replied the best thing would be to inform the police.

The problem was solved for them when from the kitchen came a great whoofing sound, unmistakable to those who have ever had a chimney catch fire.

Carrie dashed back through to make sure Robert was all right to discover him capering in front of the flames, cackling like a banshee.

When the firemen arrived they came charging up the

close to be met at the door by Winnie who explained to them what the situation was.

Carrie and Winnie waited on till the fire had been extinguished and the police had taken Meg away for an autopsy and Robert to Gartnavel Hospital for the mentally disturbed.

Badly shaken by their ordeal, they returned home bearing the sad news of what had happened to the Smiths.

Robert died in Gartnavel before the year was out and was buried alongside his beloved Meg. Officially, the cause of death was heart failure but those who'd heard him keening and calling for his dead wife were convinced it was really a broken heart he'd died of.

But then one is merely a romantic version of the other.

Head bowed and hands sunk deep into his overall pockets Angus trudged homeward having just finished his daily stint at Armstrong's.

He'd been working there for several weeks and, as he'd known he would, he hated every minute of it.

Once he'd seen the big white chief himself stalking across the yard and had been filled with a combination of anger, resentment and shame to think he'd been literally forced to work for the man whose daughter he'd planned to marry.

He now thought of Rosemary in the past tense, convinced their relationship was at an end.

He'd also seen Donald a number of times and had avoided his grandfather, blaming Donald for the fact he'd been apprenticed when where he really wanted to be was back at school studying for his Highers and planning his entry into the business world.

He started out of his melancholic reverie on hearing himself hailed and, turning round, saw it was Kitty who'd shouted and was hurrying to catch him up.

Kitty had also applied for an apprenticeship at Armstrong's but had been turned down. There had been a host of applications but only the lucky and the well connected had received a letter of acceptance, enclosing indenture papers to be signed.

After talking it over with his parents, Kitty had decided he, too, would leave school: with the way things had generally picked up, surely it wouldn't be long before he could land himself a decent job?

In the meantime, he was still running with the milk and had taken over Angus's paper round. He'd just made his final delivery for the evening.

'I want a word with you,' Kitty said, falling in beside Angus.

'Oh, aye?'

'Rosemary came out to see me this morning, asking why she hadn't heard from you. And I may tell you the poor lassie was worried stiff. She thought you must have been ill or had an accident or something.'

The blush swept up Angus's neck to invade his face. Stopping he fumbled for his cigarettes. Somehow managing to keep his face averted, he offered one to Kitty and then struck a match which they both used.

The plain fact of the matter was that he'd been putting off and putting off contacting Rosemary to tell her what had happened. He just couldn't seem to summon up the courage to tell her all his plans for the future lay in ruins and there was now no way he could ever see the pair of them getting married.

His wretchedness showed clearly as he strode along the street, his long legs going at such a pace that Kitty several times had to break into a trot to keep up.

Kitty had been all set to jibe Angus but now wisely decided not to. As they hurried along, Kitty told Angus that Rosemary had sent the message she would meet him in 'their place' at three on the Saturday afternoon after their birthday which was the following week.

What Rosemary was referring to as 'their place' was a spot upstream on the Cart which she and Angus had stumbled onto by accident some years ago on an exploring trip.

It was a small cave halfway up a steep bank, screened by trees and a mass of foliage. They called it the bear cave – the pretence being that it had once been a bear's lair – whose existence they kept secret.

Kitty went on to say he'd told Rosemary the story of the apprenticeships coming vacant at her father's works and how Angus, at his mother's insistence, had been made to apply and that the application had been duly accepted. He'd added ruefully that his had been turned down.

'How was she looking?' Angus asked, his voice shaking a little.

Kitty grinned and replied she hadn't sprouted a moustache if that was what Angus was worried about. Angus laughed and snapped out of his mood.

'Three o'clock on the Saturday afternoon?' he queried.

Kitty nodded and then playfully punched his pal on the arm. 'Go on, you great big long streak of misery,' he said. 'Do yourself a favour. Go and see the lassie.'

Arriving home, Angus quickly washed and then went through to his room where he would wait until called for his tea. As he changed out of his working clothes all he could think of was his forthcoming rendezvous with Rosemary.

Now a move had been made, he couldn't wait to see her again.

The day had dawned a beautiful one – just what Rosemary had been praying for. She was carrying a picnic basket in one hand and an old mac slung over her shoulder as she made her way through the undergrowth towards the bear cave.

There was something primeval about this section of the riverbank, she'd always thought. It wouldn't have surprised her in the least had she suddenly come face to face with an ancient Celtic tribesman daubed with woad, or if a sabre-toothed tiger had suddenly appeared on a branch of one of the many trees surrounding her.

She was feeling nervous and rather tired, having had trouble sleeping the night before. Her mind had been racing with thoughts of today and what she planned to make happen.

In a pocket of her mac was a packet of contraceptives which she'd finally obtained from a school chum called Margie McIntyre who had a reputation for being wild and a great one for the boys.

In the picnic basket were all sorts of goodies she'd scrounged from cook plus a bottle of wine she'd managed to lift when everyone's back was turned.

She stopped when she heard voices and, from a vantage point behind a tree, watched four wee boys dressed as Red Indians making their way in the direction she'd just come from. Judging by the way they were creeping along they were in the middle of a game, so no doubt there would be another band of them somewhere around.

A little further on she had to climb the steep bank, working her way behind masses of foliage, to the spot where the bear cave lay hidden.

The first thing she did was to lay the mac on the ground and then she began setting out the picnic things.

She heard him coming before he actually appeared. Suddenly he was there, standing in the mouth of the cave grinning down at her.

It might have been years since they'd last spoken, both were that awkward and shy.

'Happy birthday!' Angus said and thrust a brown paper parcel into her hands. He sat on the mac beside her and watched while she undid the string.

Rosemary exclaimed with delight when she opened the box. Inside were a pair of matching tortoise shell combs which she knew would look marvellous in her hair.

Although Angus had developed a fetish about making and saving money he wasn't scared to spend it when the occasion arose and could be extremely generous at times. To him money was always the means to an end and never the be-all and end-all in itself.

'They're gorgeous,' Rosemary breathed, her face beaming. Leaning across she kissed him on the lips.

'I'll give you yours later,' she added, a mischievous twinkle in her eye.

Like a lot of people who consider themselves to be at fault, Angus couldn't wait to explain himself. In a great rush of words it all came tumbling out.

According to Angus, his life lay in ruins and their relationship in tatters but Rosemary knew this just wasn't so. His having to go to work for her father might appear a setback but who knew how time might transform this into a positive advantage?

A little perspective was needed, she told him sternly. After all, school certificates were never a guarantee for success. What really mattered was determination and a willingness to work longer and harder than anyone else. An astute mind – if you didn't have that no amount of school certificates were going to give it to you – a shrewd business sense and, above all, motivation.

There was a fierceness in Rosemary as she spoke these words – the mother hen cajoling her favourite chick.

She wanted to take Angus by the shoulders and shake all this ridiculous defeatist talk out of him. So what if he had to spend the next few years learning to be a fitter? With the right motivation spurring him on being a fitter need only be the first rung on the ladder.

Angus stared at Rosemary in amazement, a new shame growing in him at how ready he'd been to throw in his hand. As she was now making abundantly clear there were more ways than one to skin the proverbial cat.

In a moment of insight it came to him that their love was only on the threshold of its potential. There were depths he could plumb with Rosemary that would take them a lifetime to fulfil.

'Well?' she demanded.

He smiled wryly. 'With you beside me I doubt if there's anything I couldn't do. You're all the motivation I'll ever need.'

Her nostrils flared and her breathing became laboured. She'd suddenly started thinking about Royal Standard again and what she'd seen him do to the mare, Gypsy.

She poured wine into cups and having passed one to Angus offered up a toast. 'To us!' she murmured. Her eyelids drooped to give her a catlike appearance.

Lying back on the mac, she beckoned him to her. Mouth met mouth and as they did so she guided his hands to the swell of her breasts.

His hands slid under her blouse to stroke and knead her flesh. He fumbled with her bra, cursing himself for having a handful of thumbs, till she came to his assistance by deftly flicking open the hooks and eyes.

She could feel how ready he was, strong and hard pressing down through her skirt.

She ran her hands over his back and then down to clasp his bottom. When she looked into his eyes he was staring quizzically back.

Groping in the mac pocket she pulled out the packet of contraceptives. 'Happy birthday!' she smiled.

He was dumbfounded. 'You mean . . . ?'

She nodded and then shrugged herself free of her blouse and bra, throwing them to one side where they lay in an untidy heap.

Angus gulped and his face drained of colour. This was a moment he'd often thought and dreamt about and now, incredibly, it had arrived.

'Come on!' she urged, undoing her skirt.

Angus was trembling as he took off his jacket and shirt. He unbuttoned his flies, feeling embarrassed and strangely vulnerable.

'Don't forget your socks,' Rosemary said with a giggle.

The giggle relaxed him with the reminder that it was his Rosemary he was doing this with and not some strange girl who meant nothing to him. There was no need for fear or embarrassment. Not with Rosie.

'Angus?'

She was laying stark naked with her hands by her sides and a soft smile on her face.

His stomach muscles rippled and although it was warm in the cave goose bumps broke out on his back and along the length of his arms.

'Scared?'

'Of course not!' he replied indignantly and just that little bit too emphatically.

'I am.'

'There's nothing to worry about. I won't hurt you. I promise,' he said.

They kissed again and as they did so his hands slid down her body.

'Don't forget the johnnies,' she whispered throatily in his ear.

Somehow he managed to rip the packet open but his hands were shaking so much he would never have got it on if she hadn't helped him.

Theoretically he knew what to do next but faced with the reality it was a different matter altogether. It just wasn't as straightforward as he'd been led to believe. If only he could see what he should have been getting at but he couldn't bring himself to visually examine her there as that would have seemed so clinical.

He poked but didn't seem to be getting anywhere until she reached between them to grasp him. Then there was yielding flesh and he was sinking deep inside her.

Her face screwed up in pain and with a hiss she told him to stop, which he did with alacrity, thinking he'd done something wrong. But after a few seconds the pain passed away and she told him to continue.

'Oh Rosie!' he whispered, feeling he should be saying something and not quite knowing what.

The laughter suddenly filling the cave was like an ice cold douche to the pair of them. Each froze in mid-action, not willing to believe their ears.

Rosemary nearly died of shame when she turned her head to see a group of wee boys gawping at her and Angus from the cave entrance. There were five of them all dressed as cowboys. The other half of the group she'd seen stalking through the undergrowth earlier.

Angus knew he had to do something and fast. Pulling himself free he made a roaring noise and simultaneously contorted his face in simulated anger.

Screeching and laughing the boys turned and fled back down the bank as fast as they could go.

'And don't dare come back again!' Angus yelled, shaking his fist after them, not realizing how utterly ridiculous he looked standing there with a condom hanging from his dangling penis.

In a flurry of cowboy hats and brightly coloured chaps the wee boys were gone.

'It seems our secret place isn't so secret after all,' Rosemary said, and started to laugh hysterically.

Seeing the funny side of the situation Angus joined in and when he sat beside her tears were streaming down both their faces. When the laughter finally subsided he poured them both more wine.

'Are you *sure* they've gone?' Rosemary asked after she'd drained her cup.

He crossed to the cave entrance and peered but of the wee boys there was no sign.

Rosemary had that craving feeling back in her stomach. She stared hungrily at Angus who stared hungrily back.

This time there was no fumbling or uncertainty.

'Oh!' she gasped.

A little later he cried out and as he did so she wrapped her legs tightly round him and exhaled a long, satisfied sigh.

Angus lay limp in her arms. 'That was definitely the best birthday present I've ever had,' he said.

In the years to come, if he'd been asked to pick out the happiest moment in his life, he would have had no hesitation in picking that one.

13

By the winter of the following year Angus had grudgingly become reconciled to working at Armstrong's. He'd also set himself up a rather lucrative sideline by keeping book on the Scottish horse and dog races and was to be found every race day taking bets during the breaks in the toilet.

The idea of making book had come to him when he noticed many men in the works were keen on having a flutter. The nearest bookie operated nearly a mile away, so here was a heaven sent opportunity to cash in on a situation crying out to be exploited by some bright spark like himself.

First of all he'd had to learn the intricacies of betting and this he'd done by paying a fitter and dedicated punter called George Edgar to teach him.

For finance he'd used his savings which at the inception of the book stood at an astonshing £235, most of which he'd saved from his milk and paper rounds.

It appealed to Angus's sense of irony that, as time passed, he was making far more from his book than the pittance he was being paid in his position as apprentice.

He rarely took home less than a fiver a week from his book and on several occasions it had been as much as a tenner – more than double what the highest paid worker at Armstrong's was getting.

He was seeing Rosemary as often as he could and sleeping with her whenever possible.

By now Diane and Kitty had become friendly as it was always easier for Rosemary to get out at night with her sister. Kitty had been introduced to make up the foursome and luckily he and Diane had hit it off right away.

Rosemary and Diane always told their parents they were going somewhere locally – to the pictures or dancing – but invariably went further afield to lessen the risk of being seen with Angus and Kitty.

Their luck held out for a long time until one Saturday evening at a dance in the Croftfoot Boy Scout Hall Angus and Rosemary were spotted by a lad called Tod Gemmill. Tod was the son of Ronnie Gemmill, Armstrong's chief pattern maker and as big an arse-licker as his father.

Tod was an apprentice same as Angus although older and in the third year of his apprenticeship. And he recognized Rosemary, having seen her several times at the works with her father.

It was obvious to Tod that Angus and Rosemary were close and he judged from the easy way they had with one another they'd been winching for some time. That gave him food for thought. He made a mental note to mention it to his father.

Hugh was also at the dancing that night, only in his case he'd gone to the St Andrew's Halls in the centre of the city. It was the back of ten when he decided he'd had enough and would drive home to Muirend.

He was passing another dancehall called the Locarno when he noticed a girl struggling with a burly chap. The girl's face swung round into full profile and it was with a shock he recognized Janey McIver whom he hadn't seen since the night he'd dropped her off outside her house in Thistle Street.

He pulled the car into the kerb, rolled down the window and caled out, 'Everything all right, Janey?'

With a sob Janey succeeded in wrenching herself away from the man and, running across to the car, quickly climbed inside. 'Get the hell out of here quick,' she gasped, looking thoroughly frightened as the man she'd been struggling with started fumbling with the door handle.

Hugh let the clutch out and the Hornet leapt away. The man uttered a curse as he was sent spinning into a passer-by, causing the two of them to go crashing to the pavement.

It took a few minutes and a cigarette to calm Janey down. Once she was capable of speaking coherently she explained the chap had been her old boyfriend who was refusing to get the message and take no for an answer.

She'd been at the Locarno that night when suddenly Francey had appeared at her side, demanding she dance with him.

She'd agreed to have one dance to humour him but at the end of it when she'd tried to excuse herself he'd physically forced her to stay on the floor, at the same time declaring in a loud voice to all and sundry she was his girl and the sooner she learned to accept the fact the better.

She'd been scared stiff by then as she'd known from the smell of his breath and the glassy look in his eye he'd been drinking heavily and in that mood was capable of almost anything.

She'd danced the next half hour with him and then pleaded to be allowed to go to the toilet as she was bursting. It was a request Francey couldn't very well refuse so he'd reluctantly consented saying he'd be waiting for her when she came out again.

Knowing he'd be watching, she'd made a show of entering the Ladies. Chancing her luck, she sneaked out less than a minute later, hoping he'd be looking elsewhere and not expecting her to reappear so soon.

Her luck had held as far as the cloakroom. But as she was hurrying from there with her coat over her arm, Francey had spotted her. The ensuing argument had continued out into the street at which point Hugh had come driving by.

As Hugh listened to all this he couldn't help but think

what an attractive woman Janey was. Furthermore she had a certain something which made him feel relaxed and easy in her company.

When they reached St Enoch Square she thanked him again for coming to her rescue and suggested he drop her off on the corner where she could catch a tram.

Hugh wouldn't hear of it, insisting that as Thistle Street was en route to Muirend anyway, the least he could do was take her home.

Both of them were delighted at seeing one another although neither would have dreamt of saying so. Occasionally Janey glanced at him out the corner of her eye while he used the windscreen mirror to catch a glimpse of her.

When they arrived at Thistle Street there was an awkward pause between them which Janey finally broke by asking if he'd like to come up for a cup of tea and a biscuit?

Hugh agreed. Enjoying Janey's company so much he was reluctant to be parted from her.

They climbed the close stairs to arrive at a badly chipped green door.

The kitchen he was ushered into was warm and friendly. It was also crammed with children of all sizes, shapes and ages.

What caught and held his attention were the holy pictures on the walls. There was one of the Virgin Mary with the infant Jesus, another of Jesus wearing a crown of thorns. One of a kind-faced man surrounded by animals whom he guessed was St Francis. Plus a very large one in a gilt frame of Pope Pius XI. There were also two statues on either side of the mantelpiece – Mary and Joseph.

He gulped at this overpowering display of Popery. Here were all the things he and every other Protestant boy in the city like him had been brought up to hate and despise. Involuntarily he shrank within himself, rueing his folly in allowing himself to come into such close contact with the Roman Church.

Mrs McIver was a stout woman of his mother's age who came forward to shake him by the hand after Janey had recounted what had happened both inside and outside the Locarno and how his timely intervention had saved her from something which might well have ended up nastily.

McIver was furious, saying Francey was a bad lot and should he run into Francey he would give him what for. In the meantime would Hugh care for a wee drop of the cratur rather than the tea his good wife was offering? Before Hugh could reply glasses were out and a bottle was being opened.

Hugh's apprehension about his surroundings melted a little as the whisky warmed and soothed him. And soon he began to relax. It transpired that McIver was even more of a radical left winger than Big Donald and soon he and Hugh were arguing the toss about the pros and cons of the new Coalition Government led by Neville Chamberlain, and the attitude of that government in relation to Spain which was being torn apart by the most dreadful civil war.

After a while a small child of about three came and clambered onto Hugh's lap. Hugh stroked the wee lad's hair and then tickled him under the chin, causing him to snort with laughter.

'You like weans, then?' Mrs McIver asked.

Hugh smiled and admitted freely he did, adding that one day when he was married he was hoping to have lots of his own, especially boys whom he was particularly fond of.

Janey sat silent through all this watching Hugh as he talked with her mother and father, admiring his well-spoken manner and the way he held his own against her Da who was a notorious bully when it came to exchanging views, particularly political ones.

When Hugh finally rose to go he was told by Mrs McIver he'd be welcome any time he cared to call. They shook hands all round, then Janey showed him to the front door. The kitchen door was diplomatically shut behind them after they'd made their exit.

Hugh was in a terrible quandary. He liked Janey tremendously – there was no doubt in his mind about that, just as there was none about her liking him in return. But what use was it trying to start a relationship that was bound to founder on the rocks of religion? Words from the old song came leaping to mind.

T'was in County Tyrone in the town of Dungannon,
Where's many a rumption myself had a han' in.
Bob Williamson lived there a weaver to trade,
And all of us thought him a stout Orange blade.

On the twelfth of July as it yearly did come.
Bob played on his flute to the sound of the drum.
Well you can talk of your piano, your violin or lute,
But there's nothing to beat the old Orange flute.

But Bob the old bastard he took us all in,
He married a fenian named Brigid McGinn.
Turned Papish himself and forsook the old cause,
That gave us our freedom, religion and laws. . . .

'I enjoyed meeting your family,' Hugh said, hating what was coming next.

Janey smiled and nodded, waiting.

Outside a cat began to yowl while from a house somewhere close by came the unmistakable sound of a couple having a barney.

'It wouldn't work Janey. You know that as well as I do,' he mumbled.

Her smile stretched and stretched till it seemed her face must surely be sliced in two. Her eyes had a dead, marbled look about them. She'd known he was going to say this but would have given anything to have had herself proved wrong. He was right of course. Trying to mix the green and orange was just asking for trouble, especially if children were to become involved.

'Goodbye,' she whispered, hesitating for a brief second before going to him and kissing him full on the mouth. Then she was gone. The badly chipped green door closed behind her with a click that had the ring of finality about it.

Hugh stuck his hands in his pockets and trudged downstairs. He felt as though he'd just lost both arms.

He was fumbling for his car keys as he came out of the close but when his gaze lit on the Hornet he stopped dead in his tracks. 'Oh no!' he exclaimed, fury bursting within him.

The Hornet's beautiful red paintwork had been viciously scratched and scraped from nose to boot while the upholstery had been ripped and slashed to shreds.

He felt sick, cursing himself for being so stupid as to leave the car parked in a Gorbals street.

The laugh was low and evil and came from directly behind him. Swinging round he found himself facing a grinning Francey.

'Like your fancy car now, Jim? Maybe that'll teach you to take off with my bird and make me look stupid,' Francey spat.

'You fucker!' Hugh hissed and stepped forward intent on smashing Francey in the face.

Laughing again, Francey brought his right hand from behind his back to reveal a rusty iron bar. The bar whistled through the air in an overhand arc that brought it smashing against the side of Hugh's head.

Hugh's legs were suddenly jelly, buckling under him to send him crashing to the filthy pavement.

Again and again Francey's foot thudded into his ribs and back.

He tried to wriggle out of the way but instead got it full on the chin. There was a splintering sound and blood everywhere as he flipped over onto his back.

He must have passed out, for the next thing he knew Francey was gone and he was staring up at a night sky filled with clouds and smoke from tenement chimneys.

He grunted with pain as he rolled onto his side and shuffled himself to the tenement wall which he used as a steadying post to bring himself to his feet.

He spat out gobs of congealed blood and gritty

fragments of teeth. Many of the teeth left were broken, jagged and excruciatingly sore, as indeed were his chest and back.

Coughing up more blood he staggered into the close and, like a drunken man, made his way upstairs to the McIvers' door which he hammered on with his fist.

Suddenly Mr and Mrs McIver were there and arms were being thrown round him.

'Francey,' he croaked.

There was so much pain wracking his mouth and body it was with relief he greeted the darkness.

Donald fidgeted as he and Winnie sat outside Ward 5 of the Victoria Infirmary. The staff nurse had been in to inform Hugh they were waiting and he'd sent back word his present visitor wouldn't be long.

A few minutes later the swing doors opened and an extremely pretty girl emerged from the ward, smiling to the staff nurse as she passed. The nurse then turned to the Chisholms and said they could go away in now.

Winnie and Donald turned to stare at one another, both of them having noted the Saint Christopher dangling from Janey's neck and wondering what business a Catholic girl could have with their Hugh?

Now the moment had arrived for Donald to go in and see Hugh he was reluctant to do so without first knowing he'd be welcome. Voicing his fears to Winnie she agreed to sound out the ground.

Hugh was a sight, his face puffed up like a balloon, from the combination of the kicking and having the remainder of his teeth extracted.

When Winnie confirmed the staff nurse's message that his father was also here, he fell silent for a few seconds before mumbling she'd best call him in.

'It was his own idea, I assure you. You two might have had your differences but that doesn't alter the fact he still loves and worries about you, son,' Winnie said before walking back to the swing doors and beckoning Donald to come away through.

The two men solemnly shook hands. Then Donald asked what the damage was and how it had come about?

According to Hugh, he'd been lucky. Apart from the loss of his teeth he was merely bruised, which looked a lot worse than it actually was.

He went on to tell them about rescuing Janey McIver and how her ex-boyfriend had been waiting for him after he'd said goodnight to her and her family.

Winnie sat quietly on the one chair provided, listening to the men talk about the violence that was an interwoven part of the city's fabric. She would wait till Hugh was better and out of hospital before chiselling him about this McIver lassie.

She prayed to God there was nothing serious between him and the girl, because there would be the most almighty ructions if there were! Her gaze fastened on Donald emphatically making a point.

Sir Alan Armstrong's brow was deeply furrowed as he read the report presented to him that morning by the private detective he'd hired to find out exactly what was going on between Rosemary and young McBain.

It surprised him just how many times the pair contrived to meet. Going alone with Diane to the local pictures and dancing indeed!

But what really upset him was the detective's statement they were having an affair.

According to the detective, friends of the family had been away on holiday during the past few weeks and Rosemary had somehow contrived to get hold of the key to a small guest flat at the back of the empty house where she and Angus had gone on a number of occasions to make love. Peering through a window, the detective had actually seen them in the act.

Laying down the report Sir Alan made a mental note to thank Gemmill for putting him onto this. A reward would come later.

He could forbid Rosemary ever to see McBain again but, knowing his daughter as he did, a face to face confrontation wasn't the way. What was needed here was something subtle, something devious to cause a break between the pair. And break there would have to be and soon if his plans for her future were to have any real hopes of success.

It came back to him she'd once asked him the ins and outs of John McBain's accident. She must have been seeing the lad even then.

A glance at the calendar confirmed there were only a few days left till Christmas. He would use the holiday to think up a plan to get young McBain out of Glasgow and away forever. For if they were as deeply committed to one another as the detective said it would have to be as drastic as that to ensure the affair was over and done with.

Dismissing the matter from his mind, he turned his attention to a sheaf of papers which had arrived in from his solicitor. Some property was about to come onto the market of the sort he'd been looking for as an investment. Within seconds he was totally absorbed by the details of the buildings under proposal.

On Christmas Day Iain and Peter McLaren arrived at Arnprior House with gifts for the girls.

Rosemary and Diane were delighted with what they'd received – perfume in both cases – and somewhat embarrassed by the fact they hadn't thought to buy the McLarens anything.

Iain shrugged that one off with a suitable comment and then changed the conversation by announcing he'd just passed his private pilot's licence a few days previously.

He'd been taking lessons for some time now and had acquired himself the reputation round the aerodrome as an excellent pupil and a potentially outstanding flyer.

Rosemary thought this news marvellous and immediately pressed him to take her up as soon as it could be arranged.

Iain replied he'd be only too happy to oblige providing

Sir Alan agreed, which Sir Alan did.

Watching Rosemary and Iain together started Sir Alan thinking about Angus McBain again and as he thought he played with one of his cuff links which had been a Christmas present from Cordelia. They were twenty-two carat gold inset with diamond chips.

Suddenly it was there, fully hatched in his mind, a plan to take care of young McBain – neat, simple and very thorough. McBain wouldn't have a leg to stand on.

Reaching for the decanter he poured a round of sherries and the toast he proposed was Iain and Rosemary's flight together.

He smiled as he drank because only he was aware of what he'd really meant by that.

Mid-morning of the first day back to work after the New Year Angus was summoned to Sir Alan's private office. He went convinced Sir Alan had at last found out about him and Rosemary and all hell was about to break loose because of it.

For fifteen minutes he was kept waiting in the secretary's outer office before being ushered through to the inner sanctum.

He tried not to wilt under the accusing gaze knifing into him, forcing himself to stand perfectly still.

'I hear you've been taking bets, making book as I believe it's called,' Sir Alan said abruptly.

Relief surged through Angus. It wasn't what he'd been expecting although this was certainly serious enough. 'Yes sir,' he replied.

Sir Alan made a pyramid with his hands and launched into a reprimand scathing in its severity.

There was no way Angus could defend what he'd been doing and knew it. He did point out to Sir Alan, however, that he'd never made book in the company's time.

Sir Alan took the point but countered by saying the important thing was that an illegal act had been taking place on his property which was something he couldn't countenance.

Angus sighed inwardly. Here was the best money-making scheme he'd had to date about to go down the plughole. But if Sir Alan would only overlook it this time Angus gave his word it would never happen again.

Sir Alan grunted and appeared to consider that. He reached for the humidor and took its top off, exclaiming with annoyance when he saw it was empty.

'Wait here,' he snapped and left the room, closing the door behind him.

For a full five minutes Angus was left in the office alone and then the door opened to re-admit Sir Alan puffing on a fat cigar.

In a few short sentences Sir Alan stated he was willing to overlook the matter this once, qualifying himself by adding he hadn't forgotten John McBain had died in his foundry nor that Donald Chisholm was a treasured employee.

With a wave of his cigar, he told Angus to get back to work and he would expect Angus to keep his side of the bargain.

Angus thanked the still glowering Sir Alan profusely and then hurriedly took his leave, thankful he'd been let off so lightly, as he could well have lost his job or even been reported to the police.

He was hurrying back across the yard when suddenly a figure seemed to fly out of nowhere and crash into him so violently both he and the figure went tumbling to the ground.

'I'm helluva sorry, Angus, my fault entirely. I just wasn't looking where I was going,' Tod Gemmill said, springing to his feet and helping Angus to his. 'No bones broken I hope,' Tod added, patting Angus down.

'I'm fine,' Angus replied and shrugged himself away from the questing hands.

Tod grinned wryly. 'No offence?'

'None taken,' Angus confirmed and hastily resumed his way back to the job.

It was just before the lunchtime hooter when another messenger arrived from Sir Alan to say Angus was wanted back again in his office. Thoroughly mystified, Angus trotted back across the yard and up the stairs to be told to go straight through as Sir Alan was waiting for him.

The moment Angus opened the door to the inner office he knew something was dreadfully amiss. Looking like the wrath of God, Big Donald, with cap in hand, stood at one end of the desk while at the opposite end was a constable and what was unmistakably a plain clothes man.

Sir Alan glanced up. 'Come in McBain and shut the door behind you,' he said.

Completely bewildered, Angus stepped forward to stand beside his grandfather.

In a tight, angry voice Sir Alan introduced Detective Inspector Hammill and Constable Forbes, neither of whom gave Angus any sign of acknowledgement. Then with a wave of his hand in the Detective Inspector's direction, Sir Alan sank back into his leather padded chair and proceeded to light a fresh cigar from the now full humidor.

The detective inspector came straight to the point. Earlier on Angus had been called into this office to speak with Sir Alan on a company matter and was it not true that while he was here Sir Alan had left him alone for a few minutes?

'Yes, that's correct,' Angus admitted. He looked at his grandfather hoping for some clue as to what all this was about but Donald refused to meet his glance.

'Would you mind turning out your pockets?'

The question came from the detective inspector and was delivered in such a way as to leave Angus in no doubt that to refuse would be admitting guilt to whatever it was he stood suspected of.

Angus declared he had nothing to hide but before he complied would they mind telling him what this was all about?

Hammill cleared his throat and then went on to say an extremely valuable pair of cuff links – twenty-two carat gold inset with diamond chips – had gone missing that morning from Sir Alan's desk and all those who'd been in the office were being asked to cooperate in trying to solve the matter.

Angus couldn't remember having seen any cuff links and said so, adding that he was only to happy too co-operate as he didn't want anyone thinking him a thief.

There were five pockets in his overalls and the cuff links were in the right leg one.

The moment he felt the unusual bulges he knew with a sickening certainty what they were. He paled and loked from Hammill to Sir Alan, whose eyes were hooded behind a cloud of smoke.

It was the constable who worked the cuff links up the length of the long pocket till they popped out into his hand. He set them carefully on the desk's well polished top for all to see.

They were gold inset with diamond chips.

Donald took a deep breath which he slowly exhaled.

'There's been some sort of mistake,' Angus said al-most hysterically, realizing only too well how pitifully inadequate and clichéd that sounded.

'That'll be for the court to decide,' said Hammill, scooping up the cuff links which he informed Sir Alan would have to be taken along and used in evidence.

Sir Alan cupped his chin in his hand and looked thoughtful, a pose he held for over a minute while he stared hard at the squirming Angus.

Finally, with a sad shake of his head, he thanked the policemen for coming along and informed them he'd decided not to make any formal charges.

Hammill tried to argue but Sir Alan was resolute in that he intended dealing with the matter himself. With a disappointed shrug Hammill capitulated and returned the cuff links.

Hammill and the constable then took their leave, both shooting Angus filthy looks as they did so.

'Have you anything further to say?' Sir Alan asked.

'It wasn't me. I swear it!'

'Then how did the cuff links come to be in your over-alls?'

Angus slumped. He had no answer to that one.

Sir Alan puffed on his cigar knowing he now had Angus exactly where he wanted him. In his victory, he allowed the triumph he felt to show in his eyes. Angus, who happened to glance directly into his face at that precise moment, noticed it.

Suddenly everything clicked into place and Angus knew without a shadow of a doubt it was Sir Alan himself who'd had him framed.

He remembered then Tod Gemmill careering into him in the yard and that part of the mystery was solved. So he'd been right to start with. Armstrong *had* found out about him and Rosemary and this was the bastard's way of putting the boot in.

Sir Alan busied himself trimming his cigar and said it was, of course, impossible for Angus to continue working for him. Furthermore he felt it his duty not to give Angus a reference as should there ever be a repeat of this type of incident it would only reflect on his good name.

For the second time within minutes Angus was stunned. Without a reference he was virtually unemployable, not only on Clydeside but everywhere.

Still busy with the end of his cigar, Sir Alan went on to say in view of what had happened to Angus's father and bearing in mind Donald was an employee of long standing he was prepared to give Angus a letter of introduction to an old friend of his who owned a firm similar to Armstrong's down in Newcastle.

The letter would set out the reasons for Angus's dismissal but would also plead he be given a second chance.

'You can go now,' Sir Alan said. 'I'll have the letter typed out this afternoon and taken to your home by hand.'

In a completely flat voice Donald said in all the years he'd worked at Armstrong's he'd never asked for time off but he would like some now if it was possible?

Sir Alan told Donald to go home and not come back

till the morning, saying the request was perfectly understandable in the circumstances.

Angus and Donald left the office and went down the stairs and into the yard where Donald told Angus to wait while he collected his coat from the foundry.

Angus was lighting a cigarette when he saw a group of lads hurry out of a door. Amongst them was the unmistakable figure of Tod Gemmill. The cigarette went spinning as Angus ran across the yard.

Gemmill saw Angus coming and froze. His eyes bulged and he went white with fright as Angus ground to a halt in front of him. Guilt was written clearly all over his face.

The other lads looked on curiously, wondering what was up.

Angus told himself this was neither the time nor place to settle with Gemmill. That would be when he could get Gemmill alone and there were no witnesses to see what happened.

Reaching out, Angus tapped Gemmill lightly on the shoulder. 'From now on your jacket's marked,' he said quietly. Rounding on his heel, he strode back to where Donald was now waiting for him.

Once out of the works Donald said they would go into the swing park just a little way down the street. Angus knew then there was going to be a confrontation between them.

In the middle of a grassy expanse Donald stopped and turned to face Angus. 'Now tell me the truth. Did you take those cuff links?' he demanded harshly.

There was no lying to Donald in this sort of mood and thankfully Angus didn't have to try. Starting at the beginning he told Donald about meeting Rosemary Armstrong all those years ago and how things had developed between them. The only fact he omitted was he and Rosie were actually sleeping together.

He went on to say Sir Alan must have found out about their relationship and this was his way of trying to break them up.

He then described the incident with Tod Gemmill: Tod had planted the cuff links either when they were on the ground together or when Tod had been supposedly checking to see he was all right. He added that was what he'd been chiselling Gemmill about while Donald was away getting his coat.

Donald's eyes never wavered from Angus's as he listened to this explanation. He knew it had to be the truth he was hearing for apart from having an honest ring about it the story was just too fantastic and elaborate to be otherwise.

When Angus finally finished he grunted and, gesturing towards a bench, said they should sit and have a smoke.

As he packed his pipe he asked what sort of girl Rosemary Armstrong was. Angus spoke of her in glowing and loving terms.

They sat in silence for a wee while after that. Donald's heart was heavy, knowing Angus was going to come out of all this an all-round loser. There was no way Angus could thwart a man as powerful and influential as Sir Alan Armstrong.

What Angus wanted more than anything else was to talk things over with Rosemary. She had a way of putting everything into perspective that he badly needed now.

He would go and see her as soon as he'd parted from his grandfather.

Rosemary's cheeks were still glowing with exhilaration as Iain turned his father's car into Old Castle Road.

As promised, Iain had collected her that morning and driven her out to the aerodrome where the Avro trainer was fuelled ready and waiting for them.

With a beautifully smooth take off they were airborne and she was revelling in the sheer gut-wrenching excitement of her first ever flight.

She'd hung on for grim death when Iain looped the loop and then threw the aircraft into a steep left hand bank that sent them corkscrewing towards the ground at an incredible rate.

With plenty of altitude to spare Iain had brought the Avro out of its spin to send it winging away from the city and out over the Campsie Hills where snow lay hard upon the ground. The air buffeting them in the face seemed to be composed of countless millions of tiny, stinging icicles.

All too soon the joy ride was over and they were motoring back to Arnprior House with Rosemary plaguing the life out of Iain every inch of the way. At last, as he was opening the door of the car, he relented and agreed to take her up again soon.

Impulsively Rosemary threw her arms round his neck and gave him a big smacker full on the lips.

Coming to try and contact her, Angus had seen the car draw up and had immediately recognized Rosemary in the front passenger seat. Handsome-looking bugger she was with, he'd thought, as he'd watched Iain walk round the car to open her door. He couldn't believe his eyes when he saw Rosemary throw her arms round Iain McLaren's neck and kiss him.

In his already tremulous state this was another body blow which stunned him even more than what had happened in Sir Alan's office.

He stood rooted, watching amazed as the pair of them ran hand in hand towards the front door.

At the door Rosemary paused to peck Iain on the cheek and then they had vanished inside with the door banging shut behind them.

Completely numb, Angus turned and started the walk back to Holmlea Road.

Rosemary. *His* Rosie, had somebody else!

The horrible suspicion dawned she was the one who'd told her father about their affair. After all, why should Sir Alan suddenly *now* discover their secret. Was this her way of getting rid of him so he could be replaced by the new chap?

There could be no denying what he'd witnessed back there in the street, nor that Sir Alan had sacked him in a way that ensured he had to leave the city if not for good then certainly for a long time to come.

Sweat broke on his brow at the thought of the saturnine-looking chap being Rosemary's lover. Nausea rumbled inside him and he had to stop and lean against a standard lamp where he threw up into the gutter.

'Oh, you bitch!' he whispered.

Outrage gave way to a bottomless chasm of despair. Closing his eyes he saw her face and heard her voice whispering the sort of love talk she'd been fond of using.

Was she saying the same things even now to her new bloke? Had she managed to sneak him up to her bedroom where they were . . . ?

Staggering like a drunken man, he made his way down the street. Seeing nothing. Hearing nothing. Thinking far too much.

He was still beside himself when he came to his close. There was a clattering on the stairs and suddenly Kitty was standing beside him saying he'd just been up chapping at his door wanting to tell him the most marvellous news.

Angus forced some sort of composure into his face as Kitty burbled on that at long last he'd landed himself a real job as a stoker aboard a ship called the *Almuria* which was at the moment tied up in the Govan Docks.

Eyes shining, Kitty said he was hoping Angus would go out with him that night for a celebration drink as it wasn't every day he landed a job or left home.

A good bucket was just what he needed Angus decided. He congratulated Kitty and then arranged for the pair of them to meet up directly after tea.

With a whoop of delight Kitty was gone, rushing down the street like some kid who'd just discovered Christmas.

Angus knew Archie wouldn't be home yet so he decided this was as good a time as any to tell Carrie what had happened. He found her in the kitchen standing over a simmering pot of leek and potato soup which he asked her to leave and come and sit down for a little while.

It wasn't easy but he hadn't expected it to be. Starting at the beginning he told her the entire story exactly as he'd related it to Donald.

'That man!' Carrie said when he was finally finished. Putting her head in her hands, she burst out crying. Angus took his mother in his arms and sat there rocking her back and forth the way she'd often rocked him when he was little.

Harriet had been into town to the pictures and was now on a tram swaying along Argyle Street taking her home. To pass the time, she started to read a magazine containing the latest film news she'd bought in the foyer of the picture hall.

The article on page three drew her eye the way a magnet does iron. In heavy type it stated veteran screenwriter Lou Dansie had recently died of a heart attack in his Hollywood home.

Her hands came up to touch the gold chain round her neck, tracing its length till her long fingers came into contact with the heavy ring dangling from its inverted apex.

Turning out of Argyle Street, the tram rattled northward to come eventually to Byres Road where Harriet got off.

She walked up the street, a tall, ugly-looking woman whose skin was a muddy grey colour and whose eyes burned with a strange intensity.

A wee boy in her way took one look at her face and hastily scuttled round her. The wee boy shivered as he hurried along.

He didn't like woman with faces like that. They gave him the willies.

Angus and Kitty were in a West Nile Street pub when Kitty came up with the suggestion they take a taxi down to the Govan Docks and have a look at the *Almuria*.

Half an hour later they were standing on the quayside staring up at a rusty old heap that should have been consigned to the breaker's yard years before. Both had screwtops in their hands.

Already a little maudlin from drink Angus kept maintaining the *Almuria* was as fine a ship as he'd seen and Kitty should be proud of sailing on her, adding he only wished he was, by God.

Kitty fell silent for a few seconds while his alcohol-soaked brain laboriously worked out the possibilities that had just come to him.

Finishing his screwtop, he threw it into the water. 'Want me to try and get you a job tomorrow when I report on board?' he asked in a slurred voice.

Angus blinked. Here was something that bore consideration.

'I don't know if there's anything going, but it wouldn't hurt to ask,' Kitty said, a huge, sloppy grin plastered all over his face.

'Why the hell not!' Angus exclaimed, thinking he'd rather do anything than be forced into going to Newcastle. It was just he hated the thought of having to comply totally with Sir Alan's manipulations.

'You serious?'

'Never more so.'

'Then I'll ask the morn.'

Angus put his arm round Kitty's shoulders. The idea of going to sea with his old china really appealed and he said so.

Laughing, the pair of them headed in the direction of the nearest boozer.

'Do either of you fellows have the time?'

Angus giggled and was about to make a negative reply when suddenly the tart's face was caught in a shaft of light from a nearby ship. He frowned, thinking she looked familiar, and then with a shock it dawned on him just who it was.

'Sheena?'

They stared at one another, then uttering a cry she flew into his arms.

'I'm sorry,' she whispered. 'I didn't know it was you.'

With a sad shake of his head he told her it didn't matter. Then he suggested they go for a drink over which she could tell him everything that had happened to her. They were lucky enough to find an empty table at the back of the pub. Sheena told them she'd gone to London when she'd left Holmlea Road. Work had been almost as difficult to find there as it had been in Glasgow and for a while she'd lived pretty rough. Sally Ann hostels. Rowton Houses. And even Battersea Park.

From London she'd gone to Cardiff where one night in Tiger Bay she'd been forced – as a means of survival, she said emphatically – to cash in on her one asset.

Angus stared into his drink, shocked by this revelation and feeling somehow guilty as though he was partly to blame.

He then asked her the question that had been bothering him all this time. Why had she upped so suddenly and left Holmlea Road?

Her eyes clouded as she told him she'd known it was only a matter of time before Archie forgot himself and under the influence did something they'd both regret for the rest of their lives.

'Jesus!' said Kitty.

With a shrug Sheena added, 'He was always a randy sod as you well know Angus. And with Carrie in hospital and you over in Tallon Street that left just him and me. It would have been inevitable.'

Far too soon time was being called. Having found Sheena Angus didn't want to let her go again. At least not yet. So he suggested Kitty make his own way back to Holmlea Road while he went on to Sheena's place as he had a lot more to talk over with her.

The tenement Sheena took him to was tall, dirty and cankerous. There were three other females sharing the house with her and all of them were on the game plying the dockside trade.

The room itself was neat and tidy and smelled strongly of Sheena, a smell that brought a host of half forgotten memories flooding back into his mind.

Sheena had an almost full bottle which she produced from behind a fancy cushion bearing the legend 'A Present From Shangai' embroidered on its front.

For a while she spoke about herself and then in a quiet, sympathetic voice asked him what his problem was. She'd always been able to read his face like the proverbial book and had known since early on in the pub something was bothering him.

They talked and drank into the small hours and then when there was nothing left to be said or excuses to be made they went to the well-used bed jammed hard up against one wall. They stripped and made love.

He cried out once but it was Rosemary's name which burst from his lips and not Sheena's.

He came apart then, and mercifully screened by the all enveloping darkness, cried his heart out while she stroked and soothed him.

If he'd searched far and wide he wouldn't have found a better comforter than his step-sister who'd loved him since he was a baby.

Two days later Angus, with case in hand, opened his front door bound for the Govan Docks. Kitty had come up trumps in securing him a stoker's job.

He'd left his money box with Carrie, his instructions being she was to open a bank account in her name which she could draw on if she needed to, or if she decided to buy the house they'd so often talked about and which had long been his obsession.

Her parting present was his father's black leather wallet with the initials J.McB. in faded gold lettering on its front.

What Angus didn't know was the previous day Carrie had been to see Dr Robertson for the results of her latest tests. Her TB was active once more.

With a final kiss on the landing, he was running downstairs with Carrie calling after him, 'Look after yourself, son and mind the company you keep!'

'I will, Ma!' he yelled back. 'And you look after

yourself too!'

Carrie smiled grimly at that. Turning, she shuffled back into the house to make out a list of all the things she would need to take with her to the sanatorium.

Part III

The Digger's Dream
1942–1944

14

Physically Angus had changed considerably during the four years he'd been at sea. Long hours working with the shovel had filled him out and now iron hard muscles rippled where once there had been only boyish skin and bone.

There were three of them in the boiler room and they worked stripped to the waist. Lowest on the totem pole was a young lad called Sanderson whose job it was to trim the coal. Angus was stoker, Kitty steam boss.

The ancient *Almuria* was having to steam continually at full speed to keep up with the rest of convoy PQ 17, and consequently was threatening to shake herself apart in the process.

They'd set sail from Reykavik in Iceland heading north for Jan Mayen Island and Bear Island, beyond which they were scheduled to turn onto a southeast course that would bring them down through the Berens Sea into the White Sea and their destination, Archangel.

PQ 17 was carrying vital supplies to help save Stalingrad.

Angus and Kitty sat on a pile of coal and lit up. Both were too tired to indulge in unnecessary conversation so they savoured their cigarettes and thought fondly of their bunks.

The hatch to the boiler room burst open and a greaser called Hay came rushing in to relate breathlessly that a signal had been received on board – the convoy was to scatter. Furthermore, their Royal Navy escort was to withdraw westward at high speed.

Both Angus and Kitty exclaimed aloud on hearing this news. It could only mean the pocket battleship, *Tirpitz*, had set sail from her lair in Norway's Trondheim Fiord. For the convoy to be told to scatter as opposed to disperse must mean the *Tirpitz* was almost upon them.

But why had their escort been instructed to proceed westward when the *Tirpitz* would be approaching from the southeast?

The penny dropped simultaneously. The Admiralty didn't intend losing any more of its warships by sending them up against far superior firepower which could only result in their annihilation.

PQ 17 had been abandoned to face the full fury of the pride of the German Navy.

'My God!' whispered Angus.

Hay fled the boiler room, shouting over his shoulder he would keep them informed of any fresh developments.

Soon the coal was flying as the *Almuria* made its bid for survival by veering onto a fresh course that would take it to the Russian Islands of Novaya Zemla. The *Almuria's* captain had chosen this heading because he judged it to be in the completely opposite direction to the course the *Tirpitz* must be coming up on.

Shortly afterwards in the wireless room, the operator bent to his task as the stories started flooding in. The scattering convoy was already in deep trouble although the *Tirpitz* hadn't yet been sighted.

Aboard the *Bolton Castle* the ship's gunners were busy firing at circling Focke-Wulfs and Shads when suddenly a Stuka came seemingly from nowhere to straddle the ship from port to starboard, obtaining a direct hit.

To those watching from nearby ships it seemed the *Bolton Castle* virtually disintegrated, although, incredibly, the ammunition she was carrying didn't explode.

Aboard the *Paulus Potter* her British gunners kept

attacking planes at bay until for a third time a stick of bombs dropped close to the ship. Earlier misses had sprung her plates and shifted her engines but these latest bombs blew the ship's rudder off and damaged her propeller. The order was quickly given to abandon ship.

As the afternoon wore on a mist appeared and with it fresh waves of German planes.

The deadly U-boats had also put in an appearance, their torpedoes soon notching up an ever increasing toll.

But where was the *Tirpitz*? That was the question on everyone's lips as they anxiously watched the southeast.

Alarm bells suddenly clamoured throughout the *Almuria* and a lookout was frantically pointing at five torpedo planes flying in on the starboard bow. Oerlikons and Bofors started up as one of the planes peeled off to begin its run into attack.

The plane seemed to stagger in mid-air as direct hits were scored on it. But seconds before it broke in two it dropped a single torpedo which ran straight and true for the *Almuria*.

'Hard a starboard!' hissed the captain on the bridge. Moments later the old lady began to swing agonizingly slowly in that direction.

The same lookout who'd first spotted the plane stood watching goggle-eyed as only a few feet away the torpedo ran on a parallel course with the *Almuria*. But the ship had completed its successful evasive manoeuvre and the torpedo was gone.

Down in the boiler room Angus, Kitty and Sanderson were force feeding their complaining charge in an effort to try and wheedle a few more knots out of the old lady who was sorely resenting their exertions.

Hay reappeared with a bottle of whisky in his hand saying he'd been saving it for a special occasion. But he thought he'd better drink it now as he might never get another chance to do so.

Angus gulped down a belter and rifted. He passed on the bottle before crossing to his jacket. From his inside pocket he took his father's old black leather wallet.

The clipping was yellow and faded, the face staring back at him one he'd always see clearly in his mind till his dying day.

Below the blurred photograph of the happy bride and groom was an account of the wedding reception held in the groom's house in Carmunnock.

Less than a year after he'd gone to sea she'd married the chap he'd watched her kissing that day her father had contrived to fire him. Her married name was Mrs Iain McLaren.

It was Carrie who'd cut the photo and attendant story from the *Glasgow Herald* and sent it to him with a note saying she thought he should see this.

Carrie had been in Bellfield Sanatorium at the time, her second incarceration lasting eighteen months.

But Angus didn't know that. At Carrie's insistence the pretence had been kept up she was fit and well, and life in Holmlea Road was carrying on as normal.

Angus was still staring morosely at the newspaper clipping when there was an explosion aft which knocked everyone in the boiler room off their feet.

The whisky bottle went spinning from Hay's hand to crash against the bulkhead where it shattered.

'We're hit!' Kitty yelled, and came to his feet to discover the ship was listing badly.

Tottering, he staggered for the hatch with the rest of them close behind.

'Torpedo's blown the arse right off her!' a frantic seaman shouted.

There was a second explosion aft and the lights started to flicker and go out one by one. The air was filled with screams and curses as terrified men battled their way up from the lower decks. Kitty stumbled and would have fallen if Angus hadn't caught him by the shoulders. 'Thanks mate,' Kitty gasped.

Then the pair of them ran for another hatch beyond which was the sea deck.

The *Almuria* was heeled over at about a thirty degree angle. The great heartbeat of the engines suddenly stilled and in that moment the grand old lady died. All that remained now was the internment which would follow hard upon the death.

Angus blinked as he burst into bright daylight. Running to the guard rail, he peered over to see a lifeboat and raft filled to overflowing already about twenty yards away. Further down the ship men were leaping overboard.

Turning to tell Kitty there was nothing left for them to do but jump, he found himself alone.

Swearing volubly, he scrambled over the guard rail, and ran along the black painted hull. Reaching the point where it curved away to the sea below, he jumped as far out as he could.

His feet knifed into the water and he went down and down into an inky blackness. His last surprised thought was the water wasn't nearly as cold as he'd expected. He was wondering why that should be when unconsciousness claimed him.

When he came to he was coughing and spluttering into Kitty's lap. There was the most awful taste in his mouth and breathing was excruciating. Every inhalation seeming to fan the inferno blistering the inside of his ribcage.

He took in the fact he was in a lifeboat with Kitty and four others. All of them he recognized as lower deck members.

Kitty used his sleeve to wipe Angus's mouth and while doing so informed him he'd swallowed some fuel oil from another ship sunk in the area.

When he heard that, Angus stared up at the gun metal sky convinced he was going to die. He'd heard fuel oil burned the lungs out and the poor bastards who'd swallowed the stuff died screaming in agony unless lucky enough to be shot through with pain killer.

He asked Kitty if there was a medical kit aboard, knowing from the expression on Kitty's face before his friend could reply what the answer was.

'We'll be picked up soon. You just wait and see,' Kitty

said with a smile. But there was no conviction in his voice.

While Angus tried to rest Kitty explained what had happened during those last few minutes aboard ship.

He'd seen the lifeboat they were now in bobbing for'ard and, running to investigate, had got himself out of Angus's line of sight. At that point Angus had jumped overboard.

Guessing what had happened, he'd rowed the boat round to where Angus would have entered the water to find him floating face up.

After another racking coughing fit, Angus said as he was going down he'd imagined the water to be warm which couldn't be so. And yet if it wasn't, why hadn't he frozen to death before Kitty reached him?

Kitty's reply was the water hereabouts was indeed warm which he could only think must be due to some vagary of the Gulf Stream.

Angus closed his eyes and wondered how long it would be before his pain became intolerable? He was still speculating when a black conning-tower broke surface on the lifeboat's starboard side.

The U-boat surfaced fully and several of its crew emerged to bring machine guns to bear on the lifeboat.

'Oh Christ!' said Kitty quietly, convinced they were about to be riddled with bullets.

The U-boat closed in on the now pitching lifeboat and as it did so an officer cupped a hand to his mouth and, in perfect English, yelled, 'What ship were you? And where were you bound?'

Those aboard the lifeboat glanced from one to the other but no one replied.

The German officer tried again, 'Why do you want to go to Russia? Are you Bolsheviks?'

One of the British seamen shook his head in reply which was the only answer to that line of questioning any of them were prepared to give.

The officer leaning from the conning-tower realized this and, with a wry smile, inquired if they had a compass on board?

It was Kitty who replied they hadn't and it was to him the compass was thrown which, despite the lifeboat's pitching, he deftly caught.

The same officer informed them in which direction land lay. Then he apologized for not being able to take any prisoners on board as he was already full.

In an incredibly short time the U-boat was once more submerged leaving the lifeboat yawing on waves created by its disappearance.

Time passed and they lost sight of the other lifeboat and raft which according to their compass had gone off southwards.

They took it in turns – with the exception of Angus – to row in the direction the German officer had told them was landfall. But as there was only one set of oars and they were all verging on the point of exhaustion progress was pitifully slow.

Hope of survival was fading amongst them when, in the early hours of the following morning, a grey warship was spied heading in their direction.

At first they thought she was German. But when she drew nearer and they saw her markings and the flags she was flying a ragged cheer broke out.

The ship was a destroyer called the *Wahroonga* belonging to the Royal Australian Navy.

When the watching sailors saw the state they were in more than a dozen Aussies clambered down the scrambling nets to help.

'You just give him here, sport,' a rangy Aussie said, taking Angus from Kitty.

Angus groaned as he was draped over the Aussie's shoulder.

Halfway up the nets a sudden spasm seized him causing him to spew the most evil looking mess down the Australian's back from where it spattered onto the destroyer's side.

Dimly Angus heard the *Wahroonga's* engines surge with power and then something cold and sharp was pressing into his arm.

He knew no more.

Lazily and reluctantly Angus allowed himself to drift awake. Still with his eyes closed he listened to the rhythmic beat of the engines, thinking the *Almuria* was sounding very different to what she normally did.

Then in a rush it all came back to him, including the fact the *Almuria* was at the bottom of the sea.

There was an antiseptic smell in the air and on opening his eyes he found himself staring up at a white bulkhead. Putting two and two together wasn't hard. He was in the *Wahroonga's* sick bay.

'Orderly, he's awake!' a thickly Australian accented voice called out from close by.

Turning his head, Angus found himself staring at a man about his own age grinning at him from the next bed. He and the man were the only patients in the sick bay.

'G'day how do you feel?' the man asked.

Before Angus could reply the door opened and the orderly entered. The orderly promptly repeated the question. Angus replied he'd felt better but certainly wasn't complaining. He was pleased just to find himself alive.

After the orderly had gone Angus turned back to the patient in the next bed who informed him his name was Sean O'Rourke from Sydney.

Angus introduced himself and asked if his shipmate Robin Kirkpatrick was all right.

With a laugh O'Rourke said Kitty had spent hours by Angus's bedside until ordered to his quarters for much needed sleep.

Angus then learned he'd been unconscious for nearly seventy-two hours.

The doctor, a middle-aged man, was greeted by O'Rourke with the words, 'Hello there, Tom. You're looking a bit crook yourself today.'

Angus was amazed at the informality between officer

and hand and was later to discover this was very much an Australian characteristic.

While examining him, Dr Speke told Angus he'd been extraordinarily lucky as the fuel oil he'd swallowed appeared to have been greatly diluted by its passage through the sea. And spewing as Angus had done while being carried up the *Wahroonga's* side had emptied his stomach of what fuel oil hadn't yet been absorbed into his system.

The summation of all this was Angus was going to live, although it would be some time before he was back on his feet again.

Before taking his leave Speke warned Angus against smoking stating it would probably take his lungs years to recover and to smoke in the meantime would merely be to court disaster

The look on Speke's face left Angus in no doubt as to what the outcome would be should he refuse to give up cigarettes. With a mental shrug he acquiesced. It was a small price to pay for his life.

After Speke had taken his leave Kitty came roaring in to throw his arms round Angus.

News of PQ 17 was bad. In fact, it was downright disastrous.

It wasn't yet known exactly how many of the convoy had been sunk. But piecing together the reports the *Wahroonga* had picked up if more than a handful of the thirty-one merchantmen had escaped it would be a miracle.

As for the *Tirpitz* it seemed she and the pocket battle-ship, *Scheer* had been sighted by a reconnaissance plane. But the time and place of the sighting made it impossible for either battleship to have been near PQ 17 when the Admiralty sent out the order for the escort to head west and the convoy to scatter.

Angus was appalled. For it surely meant the convoy had been abandoned prematurely if not unnecessarily.

'There must be facts we don't know about,' Angus said, to which Kitty raised his eyebrows and shrugged.

Angus's next question was where was the *Wahroonga* bound? And what was she doing in these waters operating on her own so far from the British battle fleet?

Kitty's reply was quite simply he hadn't been able to find out. He'd been summoned to see the *Wahroonga's* captain to whom he'd given full details of the *Almuria's* sinking. But on inquiring where and when the survivors could be expected to be put ashore Captain Tolman had become evasive, saying somewhat obliquely the *Wahroonga's* course and destination couldn't be disclosed at the present time.

All Kitty could add was there were some Russian civilians aboard and he guessed the *Wahroonga's* mission was somehow tied up with them.

Angus and Kitty looked questioningly at O'Rourke who promptly said he didn't know where they were headed for, nor did he even know where they'd been except it had been bloody cold there.

Kitty went on to say he'd been quartered in with the cooks with whom he was getting on handsomely. So far he hadn't been allotted any duties so he was taking life easy.

Angus asked O'Rourke why he was in the sick bay, to be told the Australian's legs had been machine gunned during a recent action. But more O'Rourke wouldn't say.

The next day they put into Reykavik where the *Wahroonga* was swiftly refuelled. But there was no shore leave allowed nor were any civilians, including the Port Authorities, allowed aboard.

Angus assumed he and the other survivors would be off-loaded here but he was wrong. When the *Wahroonga* sailed again they were still on board.

Angus concluded the *Wahroonga* must be headed for a British port but when an entire week passed bringing them into latitudes unmistakably southerly to Britain he had to accept that wherever else the Australian warship was headed it certainly wasn't Blighty.

When they passed the equator Dr Speke informed

Angus he could try walking now, but to take it easy for a while and not overdo things.

Angus discovered the great majority of Aussies were compulsive gamblers so a new way was found of passing the time by playing brag and pontoon.

It didn't take him long to realize he was a far cleverer gambler than the rest of the school. And this he set out to capitalize on, which he did with enormous success.

A number of times Angus and Kitty saw the Russian civilians, heavy set, broody men who stuck together and rarely spoke to anyone other than themselves. But the *Almuria*'s survivors were never introduced and it became an unspoken agreement between the British and Australians that the Russians were never approached or even referred to in conversation.

It was while steaming in the direction of St Helena that Kitty started having trouble sleeping at nights. So much sweat dripped off him, he commented, it was just like lying in a shallow bath. It forced him to get up and prowl the ship, sometimes talking to the night watch, other times sitting for'ard staring out to sea and enjoying whatever breeze there was.

During one such occasion he decided to go below and have a natter to his friends, the cooks, who were preparing the morning meal.

He didn't stay long as the galleys were indescribably hot but while there was offered an ice cold can of beer which he gratefully accepted.

Halfway through the beer he noticed an opened can of dill pickles which he fell upon, having an enormous passion for this delicacy.

When he left the galleys a little later the pickle can was empty.

Angus and O'Rourke were in the middle of their breakfast when Kitty entered the sick bay to sit between them. O'Rourke noticed Kitty was looking pale under his tan and mentioned the fact. Kitty replied he'd been feeling a little nauseous and lightheaded for the last half hour although he couldn't imagine why.

Thinking he was suffering from heat exhaustion, Angus suggested Kitty go back to his bunk and lie down. Even a number of the heat-hardened Aussies had succumbed, so brutal was the weather.

After some coaxing, Kitty agreed and with a wry, apologetic smile got to his feet and lurched from the room.

Angus called after the departing Kitty he would drop by the cooks' quarters later on to see how Kitty was feeling.

Then he and O'Rourke, having finished their breakfast, got the cards out as the off duty members of the gambling school would shortly be dropping by. Soon the incident faded from both their minds.

Lunch came and went till finally the game was abruptly halted – Angus having made his usual killing – by the arrival of Dr Speke to change O'Rourke's dressings.

While Speke was attending to O'Rourke Angus slowly walked the length of the ship, then descended several decks to where the cooks' quarters were situated.

He found Kitty fast asleep, curled into an embryonic position facing the bulkhead.

Kitty's breathing seemed regular enough so Angus decided the best thing to do was leave him sleeping until he awoke of his own accord.

That evening he checked on Kitty again but this time it was difficult for him to see properly as most of the cooks were already in bed which stopped him from putting on the light.

However, from what he could hear, Kitty's breathing was strong and regular so he decided to leave well enough alone.

The heat broke that night with an electric storm. To the accompaniment of far-off thunder, great, jagged streaks ripped the heavens apart. Then the rain came pounding down to lash the *Wahroonga* from stern to prow.

The next morning dawned blissful and quiet with only

an unaccustomed freshness in the air to remind those aboard the *Wahroonga* of the previous night's storm.

After breakfast Angus waited for Kitty. When he didn't appear Angus decided to go below to see if he was still feeling ill.

The moment he placed his hand on Kitty's arm he knew something was dreadfully wrong. Grabbing Kitty by the shoulders, Angus heaved, causing him to flop over onto his back.

Angus stared down at the mottled face and glazed eyes. He knew his friend was dead. It was unbelievable. Yet there was the gruesome evidence before his eyes.

'Oh Kitty what happened, son?' he said, laying a hand on his friend's icy cheek.

For a while he sat thinking back over the many good times he and Kitty had shared together since meeting on his first day at Holmlea Road Primary. The fights where they'd fought side by side. The adventures they'd had. Running with the milk. Going out as a foursome with Rosemary and Diane. Secrets shared. Money loaned and borrowed. Laughter.

Kitty had been as close to him as a brother. Closer in some ways. And now he was gone. Blown away like so much chaff in the wind.

With tears in his eyes, Angus rose and went looking for Dr Speke.

Kitty was buried at sea that afternoon. His body was weighted and wrapped in canvas, draped with the Union Jack, and after Captain Tolman had spoken a few words from the Bible, dropped overboard.

When Angus got back to the sick bay after the funeral he found a double tot of grog and a sympathetic O'Rourke waiting for him. He drank off the rum and then sat silently on his bed waiting for Dr Speke to come and tell him the results of the autopsy carried out on Kitty's body before it had been committed.

Speke arrived to say his findings were that Kitty had

died from a severe dose of food poisoning in which there had been complications.

Just what these complications were exactly Speke didn't know. As he explained to Angus, he didn't have the equipment on board to carry out the tests for their analysis.

What had been established was the pickles Kitty had eaten were at fault. Samples taken from his stomach had shown them to be toxic in the extreme, probably due to a combination of the severe heat and their being left in the can.

Incredulity was stamped all over Angus's face as he slowly shook his head in disbelief. To think what Kitty had been through since the start of the war, including the PQ 17 debacle and the sinking of the *Almuria*. To end up dying because of some stupid pickles!

It was farcical. A grisly joke no one, least of all Kitty, was laughing at.

15

It was nine pm on a Friday night and Carrie knew she was going to be in for another bad time. Archie should have been home hours ago but as he hadn't yet appeared she could only assume he'd gone to the boozer.

Pay night was just another excuse for Archie who since having returned to the drink was now worse than he'd ever been.

He continually complained of pains in his arms and legs but refused to go and see Dr Robertson to find out what was wrong with him. Instead he consumed more and more alcohol, claiming only drink deadened the pain.

And of course the more bevy he put away the more impossible he was to live with, the beatings he constantly dished out more violent and brutal than they'd ever been in the past.

Sighing, Carrie rose and crossed to the oven to have yet another look at his tea which she was trying to keep warm.

Thinking she would make some fresh gravy to try and keep the meal moist she put on the kettle and then returned to her chair in front of the fire.

Carrie was a changed woman since Angus had left Glasgow to go to sea. Her hair was prematurely white while her face had become permanently gaunt and haggard. But the biggest change was in her body, which was skeletal.

The last incarceration in Bellfield Sanatorium had done the trick of completely curing her TB. But what a price had been exacted! It was as though all her bodily juices had been bled from her, leaving her a walking talking shadow of her former self.

She must have dozed off for suddenly she started awake to hear the kettle whistling and Archie's key scraping in the lock.

Her heart sank the moment he lurched into the room. He was so drunk he could hardly stand up.

Just inside the door he stood swaying for a few seconds before staggering to the table and collapsing onto a chair. In a slurred voice he demanded to know where in the hell his fucking tea was?

It was too late now to make gravy. So she switched off the kettle and placed the meal, dry as it was, before him.

Archie prodded it with his fork while muttering under his breath. With a snort he threw the fork onto the plate, then thrust it all to one side.

Taking the initiative – a ploy that sometimes worked – Carrie asked him what he expected when he came rolling in hours after he was supposed to get home? It was hardly her fault his meal was in such a state and why didn't he away through . . .

Her voice was drowned as, with a roar, Archie snatched up the plate and threw it at the wall where it smashed into smithereens leaving a gooey mess sliding floorward.

Carrie blinked and then hastily retreated. Turning, she ran, intending to pick up her coat in the hall and make for Tallon Street. But she never even reached the kitchen door as Archie was too quick for her.

She gasped as his hand grabbed her shoulder. Then she screamed as he threw her roughly against the wall.

'No Archie! Please!' she pleaded to no avail. His balled fist homed in on her shrunken right breast.

'Fuckin' no use bitch!' he spat. He hit her again, this time on the left breast.

What followed was a nightmare for Carrie as his fist thudded time and time again into her defenceless body.

With a cry she fell to the floor while he crouched above her.

Looking up she had difficulty in focusing and his leering face swam as though she was viewing hit through several feet of water. Both her eyes had been hit with solidly connecting punches.

Archie was suddenly limp inside, the anger momentarily burned out of him. He hurried to the bathroom where he was hideously sick.

Carrie whimpered as she rolled onto her knees and then struggled to her feet. In the hall she tugged her coat from its peg and, heaving it round her shoulders, somehow got herself through the doorway and down the stairs.

It was Mrs Kirkpatrick who found her slumped at the close mouth.

'Oh, hen!' Mrs Kirkpatrick whispered sympathetically when she saw the state Carrie was in.

Carrie rubbed her eyes but it didn't help. Her vision was still blurred and out of kilter. In a croaky voice she asked Mrs Kirkpatrick to help her to Tallon Street.

Taking one of Carrie's arms Mrs Kirkpatrick hooked it round her shoulders and that way the two of them staggered down the road.

Harriet was making her weekly visit to her parents' house and it was she who opened the front door to Mrs Kirkpatrick's frantic knocking. Exclaiming in horror, Harriet helped Mrs Kirkpatrick take Carrie through to the living room where Winnie and Big Donald were sitting by the fire.

Winnie's hand went to her mouth when she saw Carrie. Then she was on her feet helping Harriet and Mrs Kirkpatrick seat Carrie in the chair she'd just vacated.

Big Donald was frozen with shock, sickened by the dreadful state Carrie was in. Her two enormous black eyes puffed out even further as he watched.

'Archie?' he asked, his voice cracking with anger.

'Oh Papa!' Carrie mumbled. Turning to Winnie she buried her head in her mother's skirt.

Donald decided this had gone far enough. When his daughter came home in this condition it was high time for something drastic to be done.

He strode from the room to the kitchen where he groped in the coal bin for the heavy hammer kept there.

He was slipping it into his trouser pocket when Carrie supported by Harriet appeared beside him.

'No, Papa. He's not worth it,' Carrie said through a slash of bloodless lips. 'I'm leaving him anyway. Tonight was the finish.'

For a few moments Donald was undecided. Then he nodded. 'Away ben and I'll be through,' he said. But before Carrie could turn to leave the kitchen he swept her into his arms and hugged her close. It was a massive demonstration of emotion from a man rarely given to showing his feelings.

After Mrs Kirkpatrick had left Carrie was given a hot bath and helped into some clothes of Winnie's.

It worried her she'd left behind Angus's money box still containing most of what he'd left her – she never had got round to opening a bank account – behind in Holmlea Road.

If she was going to be on her own from here on she was going to need that money to support herself until she was able to sort things out and get a job.

Convinced Archie would be dead to the world by now in a drunken stupor she was all for returning to Holmlea Road, but when she told the others of her intention they ganged up on her saying she was in no fit state to make the journey there and back.

The last thing any of the women wanted was for Donald to go, so it was decided Harriet would get the money box.

Harriet's heart was in her mouth as she climbed the stairs her sister had fled down a little earlier.

She listened at the door before inserting Carrie's key in the lock. Quietly the door swung open.

Every light in the house was blazing while from the bathroom came the most terrible stench of sick. She put the door on the latch and tiptoed through to the bedroom where she found Archie sprawled across the bed snoring like the drunken pig he was.

Excitement tied Harriet's stomach up in knots as she took various items of clothing from the wardrobe and chest of drawers and packed them in a suitcase.

Archie moved once, suddenly rolling from one side to the other. But after a snort and cough his snoring became regular again.

Closing the suitcase Harriet stole from the room.

She laid the suitcase by the front door, then turning back went into the bedroom that had once been Angus's. The money box was hidden inside the cabinet of an old broken gramophone player.

Tiptoeing back to the front door, she reopened the suitcase and stuffed the money box inside.

Relieved at having successfully accomplished her mission she was just about to close the door behind her when she remembered seeing a framed picture of Angus in his bedroom and thought it was surely something her sister would want.

Leaving the suitcase outside on the landing she quietly made her way back to Angus's bedroom.

The moment she picked up the picture she knew she wasn't alone. Whirling around, she discovered Archie standing swaying in the doorway.

His face cracked into a grin as he grabbed hold of the door handle to steady himself. Without taking his eyes from her he shut the door behind him and stood with his back to it.

Harriet knew there was no use pleading to Archie's better side. In his present state he didn't have one.

'Shite but you're ugly!' he said, tilting his head to one side to watch her reaction.

He'd always wanted to hurt and humiliate Harriet for no other reason than she was the type of woman who provoked that sort of reaction in him.

Slowly and with great emphasis he began to unbuckle his belt.

'Don't be stupid!' Harriet snarled as Archie advanced on her. 'I'm your wife's sister, man!'

Archie took no heed as he contrived to steer her into a corner.

Suddenly he pounced and she was in his arms. Silently they struggled, landing on Angus's bed.

Even before they'd stopped bouncing his hand was up her skirt tugging at her knickers.

His breath was hot and smelly, his chin a strip of sandpaper threatening to rip the skin from her face. 'You bastard!' she spat.

Strong hands clamped themselves on her rear. Then before she'd realized what his intention was she'd been flipped over and a forearm was pushing her shoulders down into the mattress.

Penetration was quick, savage and incredibly painful.

Later that night feeling utterly defiled and degraded Harriet lay in bed staring wide-eyed at the ceiling.

When she'd returned to Tallon Street she'd been able

to carry it off saying Archie had been dead to the world just as Carrie had said he'd be.

She'd desperately wanted to confide what had happened to her. But that hadn't been possible.

One breath of it to Donald and he would kill Archie. She had no doubt whatever about that. Nor could she speak to her mother who would be bound to tell her father.

That left Carrie but how could she tell her own sister when Archie was Carrie's husband? Carrie's cross had been hard enough to bear without her adding to it.

Nor was there anyone else she could confide in about so intimate a matter.

'Oh Lou!' she whispered. Feeling more alone than she'd ever done in her life, she wept long and bitterly.

In the summer of 1943 Hugh came home on leave.

It was a beautiful day, fresh and clear with a hint of salt wind blowing in from the coast.

It was his first trip home since enlisting and he'd been looking forward to it for months now, ever since it had first been whispered in the mess that a leave was on the cards.

He was humming as he turned into the drive leading up to the Paterson house.

For a brief moment he stopped to stare fondly at the house which looked just grand and exactly as he remembered it. Then he was striding forward hoping Greta was home.

She was. With a great cry of delight she flew into his arms where he birled her round and round.

She took him away through to the kitchen where she put the kettle on and brought out the special home made shortie.

Pouring the tea, she suddenly stopped to stare proudly at him sitting in Aly's old chair. His various flashes and badges proclaiming him a sergeant in the Highland Light Infantry.

He was smiling and laughing a lot but there was something in his eyes which hadn't been there before. She'd seen a similar look in men's eyes after the Great War. Once acquired, the look was never lost.

Hugh was eager to be brought up to date on what was happening in the dairy and on the farm, which Stewart had won exemption to stay behind and run.

'And how is Stewart, the old sod?' he asked.

Greta opened her mouth to reply but no words came. She covered her face as great racking sobs were wrenched from her.

Instantly Hugh was by her side, cooing words of comfort and holding her close while she sobbed onto his shoulder.

Her body shook as she told him Stewart and his entire family – his wife and the three children – were all dead.

'How?' Hugh asked in a whisper.

Greta's hands twined and intertwined as she told the story. Just over a month earlier a German bomber had either got lost or funked the attack which had done so much damage to Clydebank that night. Or perhaps the plane had been damaged and unable to continue.

Anyway, the pilot had decided to jettison his load and return to base.

The house and everyone in it had gone up in one enormous, blinding flash seen for miles in all directions. No trace of any of the bodies had ever been recovered.

Hugh listened to all this in silence. Suddenly the day outside wasn't so bright any more.

Greta had another bubble and while she did he whispered various things he hoped might bring her a little consolation.

When Greta had got hold of herself again she washed her face. Then the pair of them went outside.

What was worrying Hugh was with Stewart gone Greta was having to manage the entire kit and caboodle on her own. But she put his mind at rest saying she had some excellent lads working for her. And then there was Mr KcKeand and Mr Farquharson, two retired farmhands who were proving to be a big help in looking after the cows.

In fact Greta was pleased she had the work to occupy her – she was going out in the lead cart herself every morning – it kept her from brooding too much on what had happened.

Inside the stables Hugh inhaled the well remembered smell he'd missed so much. It was the rarest perfume to him.

Returning to the house Greta took Hugh round the side to the make-shift garage where he found his Wolseley Hornet, resprayed black after the Francey affair. It was a little dusty but otherwise in excellent condition.

Petrol was rationed but Greta had managed to save quite a bit from the dairy's allocations. This she'd stored at the back of the garage in tins.

Showing Hugh where the cache was she told him to see he enjoyed himself while his leave lasted.

She hurried away in the direction of the back door.

The one o'clock hooter had just finished sounding as Donald slipped out of Armstrong's and headed in the direction of home.

He'd only gone a few yards when a motor drew up beside him and a voice said, 'Would you like a lift, Papa?'

Big Donald's gaze swept over Hugh, taking everything in. 'Aye. That would be grand right enough, son,' he replied.

When he was comfortably seated he and Hugh solemnly shook hands.

They found Winnie in the kitchen. She laid down the spoon she'd been using and carefully wiped her hands before taking Hugh in her arms and holding him to her.

'When are you going away again then, son?' she asked.

Hugh laughed. 'You might let me get my foot in the door before you ask me that,' he joked.

'Ach ye ken fine what I mean,' Winnie replied, wiping

her nose with her pinny. She was desperately trying not to cry.

Carrie would be home in a few minutes, Donald informed Hugh. He went on to tell him about the Archie Marjoribanks business and how Carrie, having returned to Tallon Street determined to make her own way, had landed a job back at Balogie Clothing as a supervisor, the same position Jakey Sanderson had once held. Jakey like all the other men who'd been employed at the factory was off fighting.

According to Donald, Carrie had been made supervisor because it had been recognized she wasn't up to handling a heavy sewing machine any more. This, coupled with the fact she had previous experience of the factory and was a lot older than the majority of girls currently employed there, had made her the ideal choice for the vacant position.

As things turned out, it had been an inspired placing as Carrie was one of the most popular and efficient supervisors the factory ever had.

While they ate Hugh told his parents about what had happened to Stewart Paterson and his family.

'Those poor weans,' Winnie said and sadly shook her head.

Donald said Sandy and Mary were also dead, Sandy having passed away in his sleep and Mary succumbing a few months after him from a heart attack.

The door opened and Carrie entered.

For a moment Hugh failed to recognize his sister; her new thick pebble glasses somehow completely altered her appearance.

Although she was drawn and haggard, there was a light-hearted expression on her face he couldn't recall seeing since those far off days when John McBain had been alive.

Brother and sister embraced, both genuinely pleased to see one another.

For the rest of the dinnertime Carrie kept them in stitches recounting the trials and tribulations of working for Ballogie Clothing.

As the dishes were being cleared Winnie asked Hugh if he'd be wanting the front room while he was home on leave? A flash of pain flitted across her face when he replied he'd be staying out at Muirend.

Seeing her disappointment, he muttered he planned going out with the milk in the mornings, and as there was a great deal to be done round the dairy it was just as well for him to be there close at hand.

With dinnertime over Hugh elected to drive Carrie round to Balogie Clothing where he deposited her at the front door amidst a gaggle of giggling girls.

He then parked the Wolseley and went for a stroll round old familiar streets and places. As he walked he soaked up the Glasgow atmosphere he'd missed so much.

Presuming he came out of the war intact the last thing he wanted was to leave Glasgow. And yet if things turned out as he planned he might well have to.

For hours he walked the streets of Cathcart and Battlefield, biding his time till five o'clock when he returned to the Wolseley and drove to Thistle Street. He parked in front of Janey McIver's close.

He knew from their correspondence she was generally on her way home from work at this time so he lit a cigarette and sat back to wait.

It wasn't long before he saw her familiar shape walking up the street towards him.

She must have been preoccupied for she didn't notice the car and would have turned directly into her close had he not leaned out and said, 'Hello Janey.'

As recognition flooded her face, her mouth dropped open in astonishment. 'Hugh!' she exclaimed excitedly.

Immediately he was out of the car and at her side, and not giving a damn who was watching, he took her in his arms and kissed her.

They moved into the relative privacy of the close mouth where he asked how long it would take her to get ready to go out for a hurl in the car?

In a trembling voice, she said she would need ten

minutes to change. She was back in five.

Once she was seated beside him a feeling of completeness settled on Hugh, dispelling any doubts he might have had. Janey was the woman for him all right. Together they were a couple.

During the drive he told her where they were going and why. On reaching the farm, Hugh parked beside the barn. An old man appeared as though by magic and, remembering what Greta had told him earlier, he presumed this to be either Mr McKeand or Mr Farquharson. It turned out to be Mr McKeand.

Once he introduced himself Mr McKeand immediately relaxed, having heard all about him from Stewart and Greta in the past.

McKeand accompanied them over to where the house had stood. All that was left was a blackened pit filled with scorched bricks, pieces of burnt wood and some lumps of melted metal.

Hugh squatted and silently did what he'd come to do – pay his last respects.

Mr McKeand went off to attend to some matter concerning the cattle so Hugh showed Janey round the farm.

It was a fine evening and as the gloaming came upon them Janey told Hugh that sad as the circumstances were, she was enjoying this breath of fresh air.

With the wind blowing in her hair and bringing a flush to her cheeks Janey looked as though she might have been born to the country. Hugh's heart swelled at the thought of spending the rest of his days with her in an environment similar to this one. He envisioned the pair of them surrounded by an enormous family of boys, happy as two pigs in the proverbial muck.

He lit cigarettes and placed one between her lips. Then straight out he asked if she'd marry him?

Janey caught her breath, momentarily thrown by the abruptness of the proposal.

Collecting herself, she said she had no doubts at all

about what she felt for him. But what about the old brick wall that had always loomed between them in the past?

Hugh's eyes took on a faraway look. He began to talk about some of the things he'd experienced on active service.

He spoke of the men he'd known, all types, shapes, sizes and religions, including a Buddhist who had been a real eye opener for him.

Men with whom he'd shared life and death. Men of many background from all over the world whom he'd seen at their glorious best as well as their worst.

Hugh groped for words. He wasn't a particularly articulate person but he managed to put over to Janey what he'd come to realize.

When you were in a tight spot and a man braved his life to save yours it didn't matter if he was a Protestant or Catholic. What did matter was he'd laid his life on the line for you.

When a man lay dying with both legs blown away it didn't matter what religion he was. You gave him what relief and comfort you could.

When you hadn't tasted water for days it didn't matter what religion the man was who offered you a swallow from his canteen. You accepted and were grateful.

Catholic and Protestant. *The Sash My Father Wore. The Soldier's Song.* Rangers and Celtic. He had no time any more for that sort of bigoted nonsense. He'd finally come to see it in its true light.

Janey replied that might be so, but it didn't alter the fact this was Glasgow and here such things were given enormous importance.

For a Protestant to marry a Catholic was just asking for trouble and in a halting voice she said so.

Hugh sighed. He wanted Janey as his wife and was prepared to do almost anything to get her, even becoming a Catholic.

She came into his arms and they kissed. She said it wasn't necessary for him to turn his coat as long as he agreed she could continue as a practising Catholic and their children be brought up as such.

Hugh had already considered this alternative and rejected it. He thought it best in the long run for their children if the entire family belonged to the same religion.

He went on to say when the war was over, should they run into any unpleasantness, he was quite prepared to go abroad and start a new life where such things were of less significance.

'And how about your family? How are they going to take it?' Janey asked.

Hugh pulled a face and admitted he was expecting the worst, from his father in particular, but that was something he would have to face and live with.

As they walked back to the Wolseley Hugh wondered what God in His heaven thought of what the Protestants and Catholics and many other religions and branches thereof did in His name. If He had a sense of humour He must be laughing at the sheer hypocrisy of it all. When He wasn't weeping in despair, that was.

16

Sir Alan Armstrong lay back in the plush interior of his Rolls and drew with great satisfaction on a very large Cuban cigar.

He'd just concluded a deal which now made him the biggest single property owner in the Gorbals.

He smiled as the smoke blackened tenements flicked by. When the war was over there was bound to be a building boom. There certainly would be if he had anything to do with it.

He'd kick out the slummies, raze the tenements, and then build for the type of tenant who'd once lived there when the Gorbals had been a superior class of district.

The idea was his brainchild entirely, and one which was going to make him an enormous pile of money.

His enjoyment faded at the thought of the small family supper he was now on his way to attend – once he'd picked up Cordelia from Arnprior House – out at Bearsden where Iain and Rosemary lived.

They'd only been living at Bearsden a few weeks when Iain had announced he'd joined the RAF, a move everyone who knew him at all well had been expecting him to make.

Thinking of Rosemary's marriage brought Angus McBain back to Sir Alan's mind. Rosemary's initial pique at finding herself discarded had quickly given way to anger which in turn had been transplanted by the most awesome fury. In such a state she had been putty in his hands and it hadn't been long before she and Iain were engaged.

It hadn't been a long engagement. He'd seen to that. He'd wanted her wedded, bedded and with an offspring on the way before she regained her equilibrium.

Well he'd succeeded with two of his aims at least. The war and Iain's long partings from Rosemary had so far left the third unfulfilled.

The Battle of Britain had been a personal triumph for Iain: he'd emerged covered in glory and had been swiftly promoted to the rank of Squadron Leader.

After Spitfires he'd been transferred to Lancasters and from there he'd gone on to command a squadron of Mosquitoes. It was in one of these he'd very nearly been brought down by anti-aircraft fire over Caen.

From what Sir Alan had heard, the plane had been extensively hit but against all odds Iain had managed to bring it limping back across the Channel to crash land at his home aerodrome.

That had been a little over a year ago and since then

Iain had been hospitalized from the fearsome burns he'd sustained in the crash.

At first his life had been feared for, so bad were his injuries. But thanks to a great deal of dedicated nursing combined with superb work by the specialist involved he'd been able to pull through.

Iain was due home that evening. The small family supper was in his honour.

Rosemary sat staring into her vanity table mirror, scrutinizing her face which she'd stopped making up for the moment because her hands were shaking so badly.

She was wondering about Iain's face which she hadn't seen, except swathed in bandages, since the crash.

For the umpteenth time in the last hour she glanced at the bedside clock. His expected arrival was drawing inexorably closer. She'd wanted to go to the station to meet him but he'd vetoed that in his last letter saying he much preferred her waiting for him at home.

As she sat staring at herself she thought of the three times she'd been down to the nursing home in the Cotswolds – she'd have gone more often only Iain had been dead against it – where he'd been slowly nursed back to health. The last time the plastic surgeon had taken her aside for a little chat, as he'd called it.

According to him a great deal could be accomplished with plastic surgery but miracles were beyond them. They'd done their best and were pleased with the results. He hadn't elaborated further.

There was a crunching of gravel outside as a motor car arrived. Her mother and father's voices came wafting up. They'd hoped Diane would be able to accompany them but she'd phoned to say she couldn't make it as she had to be on duty. She was an ambulance driver with the ATS.

Hours after he should have done Iain still hadn't arrived and a sort of pregnant depression hung over those waiting as the minutes ticked relentlessly by.

Finally, with an exclamation of annoyance, Sir Hamilton rose to announce this was becoming ridiculous and he was going to ring the Central Station to find out the state of the trains.

Sir Alan poured more drinks in the hope of relaxing the tension holding them all as though they'd been collectively caught in a vice.

Sir Hamilton was frowning when he re-entered the room to say the person he'd spoken to had informed him that, although dreadfully late, Iain's train had arrived in an hour and a half ago. Rosemary began twisting her wedding ring.

'Listen!' said Sir Alan urgently when they caught the sound of a car pulling into the driveway.

All eyes swung to the door as footsteps echoed in the hall.

The door opened and Iain stood revealed. Rosemary's gaze was fixed on the buckle at his middle when she heard the involuntary gasp wrenched from Cordelia.

Slowly, reluctantly her eyes inched up his tunic to be arrested by his neck.

The flesh there was an angry red shot through with streaks of white giving it a sort of marbled effect. It took an almost superhuman effort to lift her gaze that little bit higher.

What caught and held her attention were his eyes. Cold and hard, they glittered like those of a snake. There was a chilling quality about them, so completely different from their previous liquidity.

There were no eyebrows above the eyes. Those had gone, leaving in their place twin lines of puckered scar tissue.

Large patches of skin were shiny yellow. Other areas glistened with the same red and white marbling effect as on his neck.

His cheeks had sunk right in leaving the bones above them jutting out.

He was mainly bald with only a few tufts of coarse hair sticking out here and there.

The overall impression was of a decomposing death's head.

Rosemary was only too aware that Iain was watching her, studying her reaction, waiting for her to say something.

She bludgeoned her numb brain to think of a few kind words. But nothing came. She was completely mesmerized by that death's head with its glittering snake's eyes.

As the silence began to lengthen Sir Alan realized something had to be done and quickly. Snatching up a glass, he poured a very large drink into it and walking swiftly across the room grasped Iain's hand which he vigorously pumped up and down, at the same time saying, 'It could have been worse, lad. At least you're alive. That's the main thing.' He then thrust the glass of whisky into the hand he'd been shaking.

The spell was broken. Lize was suddenly on her feet and rushing to Iain. Large, fat tears oozed from her eyes to run rolling down her face.

Striding across to his son, Sir Hamilton shook him by the hand but couldn't yet trust himself to speak.

Inwardly Rosemary was cursing the plastic surgeon for not giving her more of a warning. Burned and scarred, yes, that she'd been led to expect. But nothing like the horror now confronting her which was straight out of her most terrible nightmares.

She knew what she had to do next and the thought revolted her.

'Welcome home, Iain,' she said, and going up on her tiptoes, kissed the twin lines of scar tissue – identical to those where his eyebrows had been – that were all that remained of his lips.

Wryly Iain said, 'They tell me in time I'll get used to how I look but personally I doubt it.'

Sir Alan went round with the whisky bottle and no one even thought of refusing.

Now feeling in full possession of himself, Sir Hamilton asked Iain what had kept him as his train had arrived a considerable time before he'd shown up at the house.

Iain sipped his drink. Then in a peculiar unemotional voice he requested his mother and father sit as he had some rather bad news for them.

Staring into his glass, Iain went on to say he'd been informed by Sir Hamilton's chauffeur who'd met him off the train that shortly after Sir Hamilton and Lize had left for Bearsden a telegram had arrived in from the War Department. The chauffeur had learned of the telegram having rung Carmunnock on servants' business.

The reason for his further delay was that he'd taken it upon himself to go out to Carmunnock and open that telegram.

His voice remained completely unemotional when he said it was just as he'd feared. Peter who was also in the RAF had been shot down and killed.

Lize sobbed and bit her lower lip. Sir Hamilton's expression was one of complete devastation.

Rosemary thought of Diane who was in love with Peter and had been expecting to marry him when the war was over.

'There may be some mistake? Perhaps he was only shot down?' Lize said hopefully.

Iain shook his head. 'Peter's dead,' he said emphatically.

Collapsing, Lize sank sideways onto her husband's lap where her entire body convulsed with grief.

Sir Hamilton was so stricken by this new blow the best he could manage by way of attempted consolation were some half hearted pats on the back of Lize's head and a few mumbled words it was doubtful she even heard.

A little later their chauffeur took Sir Hamilton and Lize home. And shortly after their departure, the Armstrongs left also.

While Iain went upstairs with the remainder of the whisky bottle Rosemary stayed behind to tidy away a few odds and ends. Finally when she'd run out of excuses for remaining downstairs she took a deep breath and went up to her husband.

The bedroom was in darkness. Iain was sitting on a chair by the window which had its blackout curtains pulled fully back.

As she undressed he said it was perfect flying weather and round about now from all over Britain RAF bombers would be taking to the air and winging towards Germany.

Without changing tone and as though it was the same topic of conversation, he said he would understand perfectly should she want a divorce.

Rosemary's thoughts were whirling at this new turn of events. Here being handed to her on a platter was the perfect way out of what she considered to be their disastrous marriage.

She could remember only too well what had been going through her mind when Iain had proposed. By accepting, she'd imagined she was somehow getting back at Angus, hurting him the way he'd hurt her.

But the only person she'd hurt was herself – and Iain, should he ever find out the truth of why she'd married him.

Here was Iain proposing the divorce she so desperately wanted but with circumstances as they now stood she knew she wasn't going to be able to leave him.

Her original mistake was about to be compounded and there was nothing she could do about it, unless she was prepared to live the rest of her life with his blood on her hands.

That Iain was brave and courageous there could be no doubt. His exploits in the RAF spoke for themselves. But there are more more than one kind of bravery and courage.

If she was to falter now in what he believed to be her love for him she would be killing him as surely as if she'd presented him with a loaded pistol and told him to go ahead and use it.

Within days, perhaps even hours, of her leaving him he'd be dead. A suicide.

She was so certain of that she would have bet her own

life on it.

Here he was prattling on about divorce but in his heart of hearts he was praying she was going to say she would stay on with him.

She knew he didn't think she would. But optimist that he was he recognized there was a possibility she might and because of this had come home instead of killing himself in the nursing home.

She knew he wanted to be certain she was leaving him before he did the deed.

Goddamn you, Angus McBain! She raged inwardly. It's all your fault I'm in this impossible position. Why did you have to run off like you did? And where in hell's name are you now?

Her anger died as suddenly as it bloomed at the thought he, too, like Peter might be dead, a victim of the war.

Realizing Iain had stopped speaking she dragged her attention back to him.

Poor sod whose misfortune it was – apart from this latest tragedy of his face – to love a woman who didn't love him in return.

'Well?' he queried.

With that one word he was asking her whether he was to live or die.

'Come to bed,' she said, fixing a half smile on her face. Perhaps in time they both might get used to the way he now looked. But like him, she doubted it.

'Marry a Catholic!' Donald exploded.

Slowly he climbed to his feet from the chair he'd been slumped in. And as he did the years appeared to melt away from him till he was once more the awe inspiring figure Hugh remembered so vividly from his youth.

Winnie hovered nervously in the background, her eyes fastened on her husband as she waited to see what he was going to do. She was sick with worry for Hugh and terrified of what this might do to Donald who, despite his bravado and self-imposed heavy work schedule – and unknown to Hugh – hadn't been a well man of late.

Donald's nostrils flared, their thick projecting hairs thrilling like a flight of arrows.

'Marry a Catholic!' he said contemptuously. It was a preposterous idea and Hugh must be loony to even consider it. Mixed marriages never worked: they were doomed to failure from the very start.

Hugh's reply was the marriage wouldn't be a mixed one as he intended turning.

Donald caught his breath and for a split second it seemed he was going to stride forward and strike his son. But somehow – and the effort it took was both enormous and evident – he managed to restrain himself.

Picking up his pipe, he began packing it, a device he often employed when wanting time to think.

Hugh seized on this opportunity to try and explain to his father just how much the war had changed him.

Quietly he related to Donald the same experiences he'd told Janey about and how all these had combined to open his eyes about many things, not least of all the sheer ridiculousness and hypocrisy of the Glasgow religious situation.

When Hugh had finally finished there was a brooding silence in the room. It was broken by Winnie asking where he and Janey intended living?

Hugh replied Greta Paterson had insisted they stay with her as there was more than enough room in the big house for the three of them.

Being entirely practical, Winnie approved whole-heartedly of this arrangement.

Donald couldn't help but be impressed by the Hugh the war had moulded, seeing in his son many characteristics he'd always considered missing before. A lot of what Hugh said had struck home, making Donald think again about a lifetime's prejudice.

Donald also reminded himself that in these his twilight years, with Angus grown up, he wanted other grand-children to spoil and get close to.

But *Catholic* grandchildren! It was so completely against everything he'd always believed in and stood for. Winnie caught her man's eyes and silently pleaded with him to make his peace with Hugh – for her sake if nothing else.

It was probably the hardest decision Donald had ever made in his life.

It had hurt him deeply when he and Hugh had been estranged previously. And with a war on who knew what might happen?

He would never forgive himself, nor would Winnie forgive him, should Hugh be killed while sundered from his family. The very thought was unbearable.

They would talk about him at work, of course. That went without saying. See Big Donald Chisholm there. Did you know his son upped and married a fenian and went left footed himself? The bastard actually turned his coat! And they would spit in disgust to emphasize the point.

It would be bloody hard but somehow he'd find a way of living with it. He'd have to. For when it came right down to it he couldn't deny Winnie the only son she had left.

'So when do we get to meet this lassie of yours, then?' he asked.

Winnie's eyes shone when she heard that. Rising, she said she'd away through to the kitchen and put the kettle on. She managed to hold back the tears till she'd hurried from the room and shut the door behind her.

She couldn't remember when she'd been so happy.

When the time came for Hugh to return to his regiment his wife of ten days accompanied him to the station.

They held each other close to the very last minute. Hugh finally boarded the train. A whistle shrilled and the train jerked forward.

He hung out of the window, smiling, blowing kisses and feeling terrible.

Janey waved and waved till the train turned a bend

and disappeared from view.

Turning, she made her way back to the barrier, not yet aware her and Hugh's dearest wish had already been granted them.

She was carrying his child.

17

'Hot by name and hot by nature,' Angus said to the sweat slicked body of the woman he'd just been making love to.

Molly Hotblack laughed, a rumbling, sexual sound that came from deep within her magnificent chest.

Angus stared at her in open admiration. There was a wildness about her which fascinated and attracted him. She was fierce and dazzling like the landscape round the small Queensland township of Bundegai in which they now were. A sun woman who at the height of her passion literally blinded him.

He watched while she lit a cigarette and drew the smoke deep into her lungs. She didn't offer him: he'd given up that day aboard the *Wahroonga* when Dr Speke had told him either to finish with smoking or else it would finish with him.

The *Wahroonga* and Kitty, only a year ago and yet seemingly an eternity away. He never thought of Kitty but it brought a lump to his throat, as it did now.

Molly swung herself from the bed and ran her hands down her golden tanned thighs. Her long, auburn hair danced round her shoulders.

'A shower, I think, and then it's back to the slave mill,' she said.

'You don't have to go back to work again, do you?'

She shrugged. ''Fraid so, I promised to cover for Gilly who's down with a crook tum.'

Angus pulled a face. He'd been hoping they'd have a bite together before he headed back for the digging. Usually when he came into Bundegai it was an overnight stop but this time it was merely a flying visit to pick up some provisions.

He put his hands behind his head and watched as she moved towards the bathroom.

'Leave the door open so I can watch you,' he called out.

'Voyeur!' she shouted back.

'Too right!' he replied, and they laughed, both knowing as far as she was concerned it was true. He could've sat for hours just staring at her naked body.

While Molly enjoyed her shower Angus's mind drifted back to the *Wahroonga* and all that had happened to him since the Australian warship had put him ashore at Sydney. For this had been their destination. Once there, the mysterious Russians had been hurried ashore and whisked off in an official looking car.

Angus had been kept aboard until visited by an Australian army major who'd sworn him in under the Official Secrets Act. It had been made crystal clear to him that if he ever so much as mentioned the Russians and the fact they'd been brought to Australia he'd spend the rest of the war behind bars. And from the look on the major's face he knew that to be no idle threat.

After the swearing in bit had taken place he and O'Rourke had been carted off to an ambulance which had taken them to a military hospital in the suburb of Homebush.

A great many tests had been carried out on him. At the end of the first fortnight he'd been taken aside and the news broken to him. His war was over, nor would he ever be fit enough to go back to sea.

What it all boiled down to was that his lungs had taken one hell of a beating from the fuel oil he'd swallowed and would never be the same again. From now on he had to take it fairly easy. Hard graft such as he'd become used to as a stoker was out. Any job he took would have to consist of light duties only.

It had been an awful blow to him but in his heart of hearts he'd been expecting something like that. After all, he knew you couldn't expect to swallow fuel oil and get away scot free. If anything, he'd been damned lucky and could only thank his lucky stars he'd spewed his guts up while being carried aboard the *Wahroonga*. If that hadn't happened Kitty wouldn't have been the only one to have died aboard the warship.

For three months he'd been in the hospital before being declared fit enough to be discharged.

By that time he and O'Rourke had become even thicker than before. And he'd been only too happy to accept O'Rourke's mother's invitation, Mrs Boo as she was called, to come and stay at the O'Rourke home overlooking Manly Beach.

Mrs Boo was an ancient, gnarled old biddy, tough as an old roo skin, according to O'Rourke. Angus came to think very highly of her.

There was no Mr Boo. He'd died some years previously. So with O'Rourke's return there were three of them in the dilapidated wooden house.

By the time O'Rourke was back home Angus had got fed up lying on the beach and generally passing his time doing nothing. So he'd got himself a job as a clerk with a local building firm.

He liked the job and having a quick, not to say inquisitive mind, was soon picking up a great deal about the building trade. So much so that the boss, a man called Bill Pettigrew who was another ex-patriate Glaswegian, took him under his wing. The two of them became good pals outside working hours, drinking together and Angus often visiting Bill's home.

Bill was desperately homesick, although with his new-found prosperity was sensible enough to know he'd never go back to Glasgow except perhaps on holiday after the war. For hours on end he and Angus would sit talking about their beloved city. After a while Bill came to look on Angus almost as a son.

When O'Rourke got home from the hospital Mrs Boo had held a cookout for him in the middle of which O'Rourke had announced his big news. Because of his wounds, he would walk with a limp for the rest of his life and he'd been honourably discharged from the Navy.

It was at that cookout O'Rourke had introduced Angus to Eric Petersson, an Australian of Scandinavian descent, who was pursuing what O'Rourke called 'the digger's dream'.

By rights, Petersson should've been in the armed forces but due to a stomach condition and poor eyesight he'd been rejected.

'Gold!' Petersson had said. 'I know it's up there on the western slopes of the Great Divide. When I was there last I could smell it.'

'Gold!' O'Rourke whispered, his eyes taking on a far away look.

Angus sat entranced as Petersson went on to talk about his two previous prospecting expeditions, the last of which he'd only returned from the week before.

'You're sure it's there?' Angus asked.

'It's there all right. You take my word for it.'

'Eric knows what he's talking about,' O'Rourke said. 'And so he should after the years he spent studying the subject at the university.'

'You're a geologist, then?'

Petersson nodded.

That fact impressed Angus considerably, elevating Petersson to something more than a mere story teller or enthusiastic amateur.

By the time the cookout was over the three of them were well drunk. Petersson said his goodbyes and slouched off.

Alone by the remains of the fire, Angus sat staring up

at the velvet sky thinking about what Petersson had told him.

'Gold!' he said in a voice that was a loving caress. The very word had a magic about it that made the hair at the nape of his neck stand on end.

And with the stars shining down on him he began to fantasize about what it would be like to become a prospector himself.

The next day after work he and O'Rourke went down to the pub for a couple of beers where he discovered it had been a yen of O'Rourke's for many years to go prospecting. In fact if it hadn't been for the war, O'Rourke would've already tried his hand at it.

By profession, O'Rourke was a sub-editor. His last position had been with the weekly *Bulletin* which was basically an outback paper. There was a job waiting for him there now but with his eyes gleaming he confided to Angus he had no intention of going back to spend the rest of his life poring over boring copy.

Angus finished his middy and ordered up another round. 'You're going to Queensland with Petersson, aren't you?' he said.

O'Rourke nodded.

Angus sipped his ice cold beer and studied his friend. 'If Petersson's so sure he knows where there's gold how come he's taking you along? Surely that must mean divvying up the profits?'

'Money, me old sport,' O'Rourke replied with a grin. 'Eric's right out of the stuff. His choice is simple: either he stays over in Sydney for some months putting a new grubstake together or else he takes himself a partner, one who can supply the wherewithal for them both to get going more or less straight away.'

Angus thought about the savings he had stashed. He'd managed to put some money by from his job as clerk and then there was still the bulk of his winnings from the card games aboard the *Wahroonga* – all in all a fair amount.

'Would you and Petersson consider taking me with

you?' he asked suddenly.

O'Rourke looked amused. He'd known this was coming. 'You'd need to put up your ante.'

'How much?'

O'Rourke mentioned a sum well within Angus's means and Angus replied that was fine by him.

'What about your health? I thought you couldn't do any hard work which is precisely what prospecting and mining are?'

Angus replied that was the one big fly in the ointment. Obviously he couldn't do any digging or anything like that. But surely there must be other lighter duties which would need attending to? It would be up to O'Rourke and Petersson to agree to it, of course, but if they would he would do everything that didn't include heavy manual labour.

O'Rourke laughed suddenly. 'Christ almighty, talk about three bloody cripples!' he said. 'You with your bad lungs, me with my gammy leg and Petersson with his rotten eyesight and stomach condition. What a threesome!'

Angus joined in the laughter. It was funny when you thought about it.

They saw Petersson later that day. He said if he was going to take one partner, then why not two? And anyway, the extra money would come in very handy indeed.

All three of them shook hands on it and Petersson produced a bottle of Corio whisky to cement their new partnership.

It took them several weeks to get everything sorted out and during that time Angus took an intensive course in driving. He passed his test first go.

Bill Pettigrew was most upset when Angus told him he'd be leaving, speaking scathingly of the prospectors he'd seen in downtown Sydney, tramps for the most part bumming the price of a beer and only too willing to pay for it with the story of how close they'd come to striking the big one.

Prospecting was a disease, Bill said. It ate into you like a cancer till you could neither live with nor without it. Like the alcoholic who knows only too well that one day the booze will kill him but in the meantime he'll just have one more drink to see him through.

Sure there was gold in the outback. But for every prospector who struck it lucky there were a hundred who didn't.

Petersson was a trained geologist, Angus replied. And what's more O'Rourke believed in him and O'Rourke was well known to be nobody's fool.

Shaking his head, Bill said if Petersson was so damned clever then why hadn't he come up with a strike before now? And from what Angus had told him, Petersson had certainly had enough chances. Once the outback gets hold of you you're lost, Bill went on to say. The outback was the most seductive of mistresses who rarely lets go. And that was where O'Rourke and Petersson were wrong in thinking they'd be the exceptions, that they could get in and out again with the big one under their belts and lie from then on in a bed of roses. ·

It was the same self deception nearly every prospector starts out with. Eventually they learn the truth that they aren't the exception at all. And that there's nothing left for them but to keep on prospecting and trekking till one day the land claims them and they vanish forever.

And wasn't Petersson already lost to that way of life? Everything Angus had told him about the man indicated that was so.

Angus had to admit he was shaken a little by the strength and vehemence of Bill's argument. The last thing he wanted was to end up the sort of bum Bill had described. He thought again of the now countless conversations he'd had with O'Rourke and Petersson and Petersson's absolute certainty that there was gold up there on the western slopes of the Great Divide.

His mind was made up, he said, the opportunity too good to miss. Nothing Bill or anyone else could say would dissuade him from going to Queensland.

But forewarned was to be forearmed. Angus swore to himself he wouldn't let the outback get into his blood the way it obviously had Petersson's

He'd give it a year. If they hadn't struck paydirt by then he'd return to Sydney.

Angus brought his thoughts back to the present as he watched Molly emerge from the shower and start to towel herself dry.

She was a barmaid in the hotel they were now in, the Southern Cross. He'd met her the first day he, O'Rourke and Petersson had arrived in Bundegai.

During the first proper conversation they'd had together she'd told him she was from Perth in Western Australia and was gradually making her way round the entire continent. She barmaided mainly but if that wasn't available then she'd do whatever presented itself.

He'd made a rude comment about that and come close to having his face slapped as a consequence. After that he'd been a lot more careful about what he said to Molly Hotblack.

'How's the prospecting going?' she called out as she started dressing.

'Nothing exciting yet. But hell, we haven't been at it all that long.'

She smiled. 'That's what they all say.'

Angus shifted uneasily at that. Her words were too reminiscent of Bill Pettigrew.

'We'll get there in the end,' he said.

'That's what I'm counting on. And you won't forget me when you strike it rich, will you?' she retorted.

'You sound like you're just after my money?'

Her eyes twinkled. 'Too right, sport. Except at the moment you don't have very much.

'Someday I'll be another Carnegie.'

'So you keep saying.'

'I will. I've sworn it.'

She laughed. 'Crazy bloody Scotchman. But I like you.'

'And I like you too. A lot.'

She paused briefly to stare at him. 'Yeh. I reckon you do.'

Angus knew he was falling in love with her – the first time he'd felt anything for another woman since Rosemary.

He couldn't think of two more contrasting women: Rosemary with her elegance and sophistication as opposed to Molly's aggressiveness and sheer volcanic charisma. Both were full-blooded women but in completely different ways.

He put Rosemary from his thoughts. Even after all this time there was still too much pain in thinking about her.

'Come on, let's be having you,' Molly said. 'Time I was downstairs pulling a few schooners.'

Angus rolled from the bed and quickly dressed. His body was lean and tanned, his hair several shades lighter than when he'd first arrived in Australia.

With every passing month he felt better and better, and even more so since coming north to Queensland. The round the clock fresh air and continual sun did him the world of good. Even if they didn't strike gold the experience would've been worth it for his health alone.

He finished dressing the same time she did and together they went downstairs to the huge tiled bar. It was more like a public convenience than a saloon, Angus always thought. He had a quick beer before saying goodbye to Molly and arranging to meet her on her night off two nights hence.

Out in the hot, pounding sun he made his way across to the post office thinking there might be some mail for Petersson who got a considerable amount of correspondence. To his surprise and delight there was a letter for him from home, the first to reach him since the *Almuria* went down.

He made his way back to the Holden station wagon that was owned jointly by him and his two partners. Seating himself comfortably in the driver's seat, he ripped the envelope open. Eagerly he read.

According to Carrie everyone, including herself, was fine. Hugh had joined the army and was currently abroad although exactly where she didn't know. Albeit well past retiring age, Donald was still foreman moulder at Armstrong's, and would no doubt continue in harness until either unable to carry on or the war ended.

Winnie was just the same while Harriet was doing extremely well with the Scottish Amalgamated Insurance Company, having far more responsible duties than previous thanks to the acute shortage of men.

Everyone sent their love and Harriet the message she'd once very nearly emigrated to Australia and would be eager to hear all about his stay there once he returned home.

Carrie was naturally concerned to learn of his illness and most relieved to hear he'd recovered all right with only minor after effects.

He'd mentioned, but played down, his lung damage in his letters to her.

She went on to say what a shock it had been to them all to learn of Kitty's death and that his parents had taken it badly, Mrs Kirkpatrick in particular.

The rest of the letter was chit chat but the most significant thing as far as Angus was concerned was not once did his mother either mention or refer to Archie Marjoribanks. That could only mean things were bad between them.

Relief at finally having re-established contact with home was overwhelming, even if there was the worry of his mother and Archie.

He whistled merrily all the way back to camp.

Months passed and two things happened to Angus; on the one hand he became more and more dejected that so far they hadn't even come across a trace of gold, and on the other, he fell more and more deeply in love with Molly Hotblack.

There was something about Molly that drew and held

him like filings to a magnet. He could never get enough
of her company and it was always his complaint that their
time together passed far too quickly.

Five times now he and the others had resited their
camp as they worked themselves away from Bundegai in
a sort of semi-circle.

Petersson's spirits remained high despite the fact their
money was rapidly dwindling. The gold was out there,
he maintained. He could smell it.

Although O'Rourke hadn't said anything to him,
Angus knew he too was beginning to have doubts about
Petersson. And it would be a long time before O'Rourke
would say anything, not being a man who admitted to a
mistake or misplaced faith lightly.

What Angus didn't realize about Molly was that she
wasn't in love with him. She enjoyed his company and
going to bed with him, but as far as she was concerned
love had never entered into it.

The other thing Angus didn't know about her was that
she was getting itchy feet again. She'd been in Bundegai
far too long, she thought. It was high time she was
moving onto her next port of call which she'd already
decided would be the Alice.

Unaware that the cookout she'd suggested was to be
the scene of her telling him she was leaving, Angus drove
into Bundegai early on her day off to find her lying on
her bed sipping from a cold can.

She'd made up a basket of goodies which he loaded
into the back of the car alongside the cold beers he'd
bought downstairs in the bar.

'You're quiet today,' he said with a smile as the
Holden bounced its way out of Bundegai.

She returned his smile and laid her hand on his thigh.
'Where shall we go, then?' she asked.

'You choose.'

It was a scorching day with the sun really blistering
down. There was a heavy smell of eucalyptus in the air
mingled with the warm, earthy odour that the ground
exuded.

'Somewhere there's a bit of shade,' she replied. 'Otherwise we'll fry.'

They'd had many cookouts and picnics together and it had been their practice to tend to head in the general direction of the camp. This time however it was decided they'd go more west. They stopped finally by an outcrop of rock beside which a small stream tinkled by.

A helluva long way from Sauchiehall Street, Angus thought as he unloaded the car.

'Koala!' said Molly, pointing to a nearby gum tree. And sure enough, there was one of the small bears sitting in the gum's branches regarding them quizzically.

Molly opened a couple of cans while Angus gathered a number of rocks for the fire surround.

While he was doing this Molly kept glancing at him surreptitiously. She knew she was going to hurt him badly and was sorry about that.

It didn't take Angus long to get the fire going and once it had died down a little he put on the steaks and sausages.

After they'd eaten they stretched out in a patch of shade thrown out by the rock. The heat and meal had made Angus langorous but sleep was the furthest thing from his mind.

Catching Molly by the halter he drew her to him. His hand sought and cupped her breast.

'Angus,' she said in a soft voice.

Smiling, he laid his lips on hers and kissed her deeply, enjoying the scent of her hair and flesh crowding his nostrils.

Somewhere a kookaburra laughed, a loud raucous noise that caused Angus's eyes to jerk open. He was about to close them again when a yellow glint from the dying fire caught his attention.

Gently Molly pushed him away. 'I want to speak to you,' she said.

Angus's brow was puckered in a frown. 'About what?' he asked vaguely, his attention elsewhere.

'There's something I have to tell you.'

There it was again, the same yellow glint as before. 'Wait a minute,' he said, and rising, made his way over to the fire.

Molly sighed. He wasn't making it easy for her.

Angus knelt and, using a twig, poked at one of the rocks he'd used for the fire's surround.

'What is it?' Molly asked, coming to stand beside him.

'I'm not sure yet.'

Using the twig, he pulled the rock he was interested in away from the others. It was still extremely hot so he kicked it down to the stream and into the water.

The jagged yellow line was less than half an inch long and appeared to disappear into the depths of the rock. Not having a pick handy Angus smashed the rock against another lying on the stream's bank.

The rock from the fire split wide open and what was revealed caused the breath to catch in Angus's throat.

'Bloody Ada!' he swore.

Lifting the two sections of rock he showed them to Molly. The split open surfaces of each were riddled with thin yellow streaks.

Molly licked her lips and then stared at Angus with eyes huge as saucers. 'Is that what I think it is?' she asked.

There was sweat on Angus's forehead that had nothing to do with the heat. He stared in fascination at the dully gleaming yellow streaks. 'You ever seen gold in this state before?' he asked.

Molly shook her head.

'Me neither. Although Eric's described it to me often enough. And from what he's told me, well. . . this could be just that.'

'What are you going to do?'

Angus grinned suddenly. 'I'm going to jump in the car and drive like hell back to camp.' And throwing back his head he let out the most enormous yell after which he swept Molly into his arms and kissed her.

Within minutes they'd loaded the car and were on their way, the two split sections of rock lying in Molly's lap.

They were halfway to camp when Angus remembered she'd been going to say something to him back there under the overhang of rock.

She shook her head when he asked her what it was. 'Nothing important,' she said. 'Nothing important at all.'

'Well?' Angus demanded.

Petersson lifted his glasses off his nose and using two fingers massaged the corners of his eyes.

'So it isn't then?' Angus said, his voice heavy with disappointment.

'On the contrary,' Petersson replied. 'It is and from the looks of it very best quality.'

'Oh my God!' said O'Rourke. Then looking directly at Angus, 'You beauty! You absolute beaut!'

Petersson's hands were shaking as he spread a map before Angus. 'Now pinpoint exactly where you found it,' he said.

Angus studied the map for a few seconds. Then his forefinger stabbed downwards. 'There's the stream and I'd say . . . just about here would be the place.'

Very carefully Petersson marked the indicated spot on the map with a pencil. 'Right. Let's go and have a look,' he said hoarsely.

Angus drove. And as he was later to remark his driving that day was probably the worst of his life.

The next morning found Angus and O'Rourke sitting round a table in the bar of the Southern Cross Hotel with a jug of beer in front of them. Every few minutes Angus glanced nervously at his watch. They were waiting for Petersson.

When they finished their jug Molly brought them a fresh one. 'He's taking his time,' she whispered.

O'Rourke topped up his glass which he proceeded to glower into.

Molly and Angus exchanged a few words and then she moved away to serve a customer who was loudly demanding her attention.

Another half an hour passed and then suddenly the doors swung open and Petersson strode into the bar. Seeing Angus and O'Rourke, he crossed swiftly to sit at their table.

'It's a bitch,' he stated flatly.

O'Rourke groaned. 'Let's have it,' he whispered.

Petersson glanced round to make sure they couldn't be overheard. Then he said softly, 'The strike is on private property. Belongs to Rawlestone who owns the haberdashery shop here in town.'

'Damn!' Angus swore.

Petersson went on, 'A quarter of a mile further east and we could've staked a claim. It's bastarding bad luck but there we are.'

'You're absolutely certain of this?' O'Rourke asked.

'Positive. It's a small property comprising a little over four thousand acres that the Rawlestones sheep farmed at one time. But apparently Rawlestone's stock got wiped out in the drought of a few years back. The story is that sickened him of sheep which he'd never been madly keen on anyway. And he went into haberdashery instead of restocking.'

'Then he should be willing to sell?' O'Rourke asked.

'I don't see why not as from what I'm told he rarely bothers to even go near the place. But two things, Sean. Number one, where would we get the money to buy a property like that? And two, we're known around here now so the moment we start making inquiries about a purchase he'd be bound to realize we were onto something.'

The three men sat in dejected gloom.

Petersson said, 'I've sent samples off to Sydney for analysis and we should get the results back within the week. I'm pretty certain they'll confirm the ore is of highest quality.' His face suddenly contorted with fury. 'Hell and damnation!' he said vehemently.

'Well, there's no use hanging around here,' O'Rourke said. 'We may as well get back to camp and talk things through there.'

'Wait a minute,' said Angus. 'Now look, I know little enough about prospecting but is it possible at all that as the vein is almost slap bang on that small stream there might well be nuggets in the stream itself?'

Petersson looked thoughtful.

'Well?'

'There's a damn good chance of nuggets *and* dust I'd say.'

'So why don't we have another look at that stream and if we're right, then what's to stop us doing some panning there? If the place if virtually abandoned as Eric here says then who's to know providing we're careful?'

'I'm still not with you?' said Petersson.

But O'Rourke was. 'Jesus, that's smart,' he said admiringly. 'You mean pan enough gold out of the stream to be able to buy the property?' he said.

'If it's possible,' replied Angus.

Petersson whistled.

'And of course once we own the place then we can get down to mining in earnest,' added Angus.

'It could just work,' said Petersson.

'Except for one thing,' interjected O'Rourke. 'Let's say we do get enough dust and nuggets to be able to buy the place, there's still the problem that Eric has already mentioned. An inquiry from us is sure to make Rawlestone suspicious.'

'There's a way round that as well,' said Angus, a smile twisting his mouth upwards. 'I've always rather fancied myself as a farmer and now that I'm about to get married and settle down – and as I've taken a great shine, or should I say, my future wife and I have taken a great shine to Bundegai – wouldn't it be the most natural thing in the world for me to approach Rawlestone to see if he'd be interested in selling?'

'I like it, I like it a lot,' said Petersson.

'But *would* you actually get married?' asked O'Rourke.

'Why not? It's been in my mind for the past few

months anyway.'

'Have you asked her yet?' O'Rourke went on.

'No. But I doubt she'll refuse. We're in love, you see.'

O'Rourke sighed. 'Love. There's only one thing better.'

'What's that?' Angus asked frowning.

'Gold!'

The three of them laughed. Then Petersson said,'I don't know that I quite agree. But I'd sure as hell hate to have to make the choice.'

'Poor Rawlestone,' said Angus shaking his head. 'We'll be paying the poor sod with what is in reality his own money.'

'Beautiful,' said O'Rourke. 'Absolutely beautiful.'

They talked further and it was agreed Petersson and O'Rourke would get back to camp leaving Angus to speak to Molly.

Molly took her lunch break and together she and Angus went up to her room where he recounted to her Petersson's news plus the two solutions he'd come up with.

'Hold on a minute,' she said. 'Let me just get this straight. Providing the three of you can pan enough gold out of that stream, assuming there *is* gold to be panned out, that is, you'll use what that realizes to buy the Rawlestone place, the excuse being you and I are going to set up home there?'

Eyes shining, Angus replied, 'I was going to propose to you anyway. This just gives me the excuse to do it sooner rather than later.'

Molly's mind was whirling. To cover her confusion she took her time about lighting a cigarette. And to think how close she'd come to giving him the elbow! She shuddered inwardly.

At long last, her luck had turned as she'd always believed it would. Her ship was about to come home.

Nor was Angus such a bad catch. He was young and fairly good looking. And there was certainly no hardship about going to bed with him.

'You're not going to turn me down, are you?' Angus asked in sudden alarm, thinking she was taking an awful long time in giving him his answer.

Instantly she was in his arms. Her lips brushed against his cheek and then nibbled at his ear. 'I thought you were never going to ask me,' she whispered.

'Does that mean you accept?'

'Of course.'

His hands swept down the length of her spine to encompass her backside. 'You'll never regret this,' he said.

She smiled over his shoulder. 'I hope not.'

'Let's go down to the bar and announce the news.'

'Later,' she whispered huskily. 'For the moment I've got a better idea.'

And pulling him over to the bed flopped onto it with him on top of her.

'Could you just show me again exactly what I'll be getting,' she whispered provocatively, adding, 'And take your time. There's no hurry.'

While Angus made love to her she dreamed behind closed eyes of fancy clothes. A smart car. A big house. All the things she'd ever wanted and never been able to afford.

It wasn't till it was too late that she remembered her contraceptive device which in the elation of the moment she'd forgotten to use.

After further consideration Petersson, O'Rourke and Angus decided only Petersson would pan the stream where dust and nuggets *were* to be found as Petersson had soon established.

The routine they fell into was that every morning just before dawn Angus would drive Petersson to the stream where he would drop him off, returning to pick him up again after dusk and taking him back again to the camp.

In the meantime Angus and O'Rourke kept up the pretence of prospecting round the site where their camp was pitched. They created the impression everything was going on precisely as it had been before.

On several occasions they altered the routine by taking Petersson into Bundegai so he could show his face as he would normally have done.

By this time Angus had started putting it about that he was rapidly becoming disillusioned with prospecting and was seriously considering looking for another line of work.

Then one night Angus came into town expecting to find Molly serving behind the bar of the Great Southern Hotel only to be informed by another of the bar staff that she was upstairs in bed having been taken ill.

He found her pale and wan with a bucket beside her bed into which she'd thrown up several times.

He immediately said he'd get a doctor but she restrained him saying she'd already been to see one. The doctor had confirmed what she'd suspected for the past few weeks.

It hadn't been too difficult for her to put two and two together, she said. Her breasts had swollen considerably and she'd put on weight round the tummy. She'd also taken to feeling nauseous at various times of the day.

'I'm pregnant,' she stated seeing the penny still hadn't dropped.

For a moment Angus was speechless and then his face lit up with joy. 'A baby!' he whooped. 'We're going to have a baby!'

First the gold and now this. Truly his cup was running over.

'That's bloody marvellous!' he cried, kissing Molly on the cheek and then hugging her.

The pregnancy was a mistake, of course. Molly hadn't intended it happening, children not figuring at all in her plans.

If she'd been able to have herself aborted locally she would have done so without telling Angus. But in a small community like Bundegai abortions just weren't to be had.

'We'll have to get married as soon as possible now,' Angus said striding up and down the room. The plan had been to wait until they nearly had enough dust and nuggets to buy the Rawlestone farm and then have the ceremony. But as far as Angus was concerned that was now out. The sooner they were wed the better.

'How about this Saturday?' he asked. When she agreed, he added she was to leave everything to him. He would do the organizing.

'I can't tell you how happy I am,' he said, sitting on the edge of her bed.

'Me too.'

'I love you Molly,' he murmured awkwardly.

A smile lit up her pallid face. 'And I love you,' she lied.

The ceremony itself was a quiet affair with only Petersson and O'Rourke in attendance, O'Rourke as best man.

But the reception held in the largest room The Great Southern could provide was a marvellously noisy do with what seemed at times like hundreds of people drinking and dancing and having themselves a grand time.

Early on, before it all got out of hand, Petersson and O'Rourke took Angus and Molly quietly aside. Acting as spokesman, Petersson said they hadn't known what to give the couple as a wedding present, but they hoped this would do.

He then handed Molly a gold nugget the size of a small prune which was by far and away the largest he'd so far panned out of the stream.

Molly was enthralled by it, staring at it in the palm of her hand as though it were the Holy Grail.

'We thought maybe later we'd get it mounted for you and make it into a pendant or bracelet, whichever you prefer,' O'Rourke said.

But in the meantime don't show it to anyone,' Petersson added cautioningly.

'I understand,' Molly whispered.

'The other thing is,' O'Rourke went on, 'when everything's set up we want to call it the Lucky Molly Digging. What do you say to that?'

Her reply was to give O'Rourke and Petersson each a kiss on the cheek.

'The Lucky Molly Digging,' she said, her eyes shining, 'I think it's terrific.'

Their conversation was interrupted by Sam Keller, the hotel owner, calling out to them that the band was about to strike up the Gay Gordons, a Scotch dance in honour of a Scotch bridegroom, was how he put it.

'Feel up to it?' Angus asked.

Molly slipped the nugget into her bra. 'Try and stop me,' she replied.

Laughing, Angus led his new wife onto the floor where despite her pregnancy she wheeched and danced with the best of them.

Well Mister McBain what can I do for you?' Con Rawlestone asked. He was a small man with a bald head and a face that had the map of Ireland written all over it.

'Angus, please.'

'All right, Angus, and you can call me Con.'

They were sitting in the Rawlestone's front parlour, Angus having called after the shop was shut.

It was over four months since Petersson had started panning the stream. It had taken him that long to get enough dust and nuggets together to cover the cost of what they'd worked out the Rawlestone place was worth.

'As you know I recently got married,' Angus started, 'and now we've got a family on the way . . .

'Congratulations!' Rawlestone interjected.

'Thank you,' Angus smiled, then going on, 'I've decided it's time I settled down and stopped prospecting which, to tell you the truth, I've been getting rather tired of anyway.'

Angus then went on to give Con Rawlestone the spiel that had been agreed on and refined over the past few months by his two partners and Molly.

When Angus had finished Rawlestone rubbed his chin and looked thoughtful. 'If I was willing to sell, and I'm not saying I'm not, would you be able to afford it, Angus? I'd be wanting the full market value you understand.'

'Oh aye, of course,' replied Angus, nursing the small whisky Rawlestone had handed him. 'Well what would be your asking price then?'

Rawlestone named a figure which was slightly less than Angus had been expecting. There was more than enough in a Sydney bank – the money had been deposited in Sydney by O'Rourke a few weeks previously. He'd gone on the pretext of seeing his mother but in reality to cash in the gold Petersson had panned and to credit the money to an account in Angus's name.

Angus nodded slowly, as though turning the price over in his mind. Finally he said, 'Aye, well I think that's fair enough, Con. You stick to that sum and we'll call it a deal.'

Rawlestone looked surprised. 'You've got that much?'

'It certainly hasn't come from prospecting, I can tell you,' Angus replied, laughing.

'No, it's money from home in Scotland, a legacy I've had put by for years for just such an occasion as this,' pretended Angus.

That explanation obviously satisfied Rawlestone who poured more whisky, after which it was agreed they'd start proceedings for the sale the very next day.

Leaving Rawlestone, Angus went straight to the Great Southern Hotel where he found an anxious O'Rourke and Petersson in the bar.

'We're on,' he said with a smile.

The three of them looked gratifyingly at one another.

'For us, the digger's dream is about to come true,' Petersson said in a soft voice.

'Amen,' added O'Rourke.

Angus went up to the bar from behind which Molly had been watching him anxiously.

'We'll soon have a home of our own,' he said.

Big as his smile was, it didn't match hers.

The day after the sale was completed Angus picked Molly up from the Great Southern and drove her out to the farmhouse. Her days as a barmaid were now over.

He'd been out to the farmhouse twice that day already, dropping off bits and pieces of furniture and other household items they'd acquired.

Shooing Angus out the door, Molly set about putting everything just the way she wanted it.

As houses went it was a bit of a dump, she thought. But it would do for a start, considering what went with it.

'The Lucky Molly Digging,' she mused aloud. It was music to her ears.

One day a few weeks later word spread like wildfire round Bundegai that gold had been discovered on the old Rawlestone property now owned by Angus McBain.

Con Rawlestone was beside himself with anger when he heard and the first thing he did was consult a solicitor.

He was even more furious when the solicitor told him there was no legal action he could take. Angus had bought the place fair and square. Con had no comeback whatever.

Con then went about telling everyone he'd been cheated as Angus and his cronies must've known there was gold on the place before Angus bought it.

But rather than gaining sympathy for himself all he accomplished was to make people admire Angus. As one of the townfolk put it, who amongst them wouldn't have done the same thing had they been in Angus's shoes.

When Con heard that he thought about it for a while. Then with bad grace he accepted the situation: in his heart he knew Angus hadn't done anything he wouldn't have had the positions been reversed. Still, it was a bitter pill to swallow.

Molly was dishing out the evening meal to Angus,

O'Rourke and Petersson when the first pain came.

Gasping, Molly staggered and clutched onto the sink for support. Instantly Angus was by her side. 'The baby?' he asked anxiously.

She nodded, grinding her teeth together as a second pain seared through her.

O'Rourke came to his feet. 'You get her to bed and I'll get the doc.' Without further ado he was out the front door and seconds later the Holden roared into life and drove off.

Angus helped Molly through to their bedroom where as gently as he could he stripped her and managed to get her into a clean nightie.

'Jesus, these pains are coming quickly,' Molly said. 'I only hope the doc gets here before the baby does.'

'Me too,' said Angus. The thought of having to deliver the child himself was too awful even to contemplate.

Despite her pain, Molly couldn't help but laugh at the expression on Angus's face. She couldn't remember ever having seen a man look so terrified in such a comical way.

While Angus waited with Molly, Petersson put some water on to boil. Having done that, and with nothing else to occupy him in the meantime, he got down to doing the digging's weekly figures and accounts.

The digging was doing excellently, especially since some heavy equipment they'd sent to Brisbane for had arrived, enabling them to work far more efficiently and at greater speed.

Another six to nine months at their present rate and yield and the money would really be rolling in. By then the work would be far too much for the three of them and they'd have to hire more men.

Through in the bedroom Molly jerked her head back and screamed.

Where's the bloody doctor! Angus thought. Knowing even as he did so that O'Rourke and the doctor would be making as good time as was possible.

'There, there, love,' he soothed, holding Molly's

shoulder as her lips stretched back into a fearful grimace, the prelude to another excruciating pain.

Angus was only too well aware that Carrie had had a most difficult birth in delivering him. Indeed she'd come close to losing her life as a result of his having been in an awkward position. He knew this from having overheard a conversation between his mother and Winnie when he was a young lad. His worry now was – and it had been preying on his mind for the past few months – that being his child Molly was carrying she might somehow experience the same difficulty.

'It'll be all over soon,' he said, the smile on his face belying his sweat drenched forehead.

A little later the pains went off and Molly was able to relax somewhat.

'How do you feel?' he asked.

'What a bloody stupid question! How do you think I feel? Like a screeching bloody sheila whose insides are being ripped apart and whose backside feels like it's getting all set to drop off, that's what!'

Angus grinned. It *had* been a bloody stupid question.

Suddenly Molly grinned back. 'This'll teach me to get so hot and bothered I forget my cap,' she said. And they both laughed, relaxing the tension that had been built up in the room.

Ten minutes later O'Rourke arrived with the doctor who banished Angus from the bedroom while he got on with it.

For the next hour and a half Angus paced up and down, watched silently by O'Rourke and Petersson. Twice the doctor called for things which Angus immediately sprang to get. Neither time was he allowed back into the bedroom but handed the articles over to the doctor at the bedroom door.

Suddenly the screams stopped. Those waiting were in no doubt that something had happened. A strange calm settled on the house, a calm that was shattered a few seconds later by the thin, piercing wail of a newborn child.

A few minutes later the doctor emerged looking hugely pleased with himself. 'Congratulations,' he said. 'You've got a son.'

'A son!' Angus echoed.

'As fine a boy as any man could wish for.'

Shaking as though he was the father himself O'Rourke reached for the whisky bottle that had been put out in preparation and poured four large ones.

'Was there any particular trouble?' Angus asked.

'Nope,' the doctor said, accepting a glass from O'Rourke. 'Everything was completely straightforward.

Relief welled through Angus when he heard that.

'To the boy!' toasted Petersson.

'John McBain,' said Angus. It had been agreed between him and Molly that if they had a son they'd call him after his father.

'To John McBain!' O'Rourke, Petersson and the doctor toasted in unison.

'I think you'd better go away in and see them now,' said the doctor.

Squaring his shoulders Angus went through to tell his wife how well she'd done and to see his newborn son.

The months after young John's birth passed quickly for all those involved at the Lucky Molly.

Molly discovered what a full time job it was looking after a baby. With Angus giving what help he could, O'Rourke and Petersson spent long hour after long hour delving ever deeper into the ore bed.

But after such a marvellous beginning things were going from bad to worse, the yield continually decreasing and falling off in quality.

Petersson became gaunt and hollow-eyed with worry, assuring Angus and O'Rourke over and over this had to be a temporary setback and that both yield and quality must pick up again.

Molly lost her exuberance and flamboyance to become more and more withdrawn. When she and Angus found themselves alone during the day he was always aware of her gaze riveted to him as though he was some sort of specimen on a microscope slide.

Then one day their worst fears were realized when the ore bed suddenly and quite dramatically came to an end.

Stunned, the three men stood in the huge excavation they'd created looking at one another.

Petersson attempted a smile which never even came close to coming off. 'Perhaps it's only a break in the bed or then again it might well be that . . .'

'Bullshit!' O'Rourke interjected. 'The fucker's played out. You know that as well as I do.'

'No,' said Peterson, his voice trembling. 'You're wrong.'

'He's right,' said Angus. Then tapping his heart, 'I can feel it here.'

'What do you know about it?' said Petersson scornfully. 'Are you the geologist or am I?'

'You are. But right now you're talking with your emotions and not your head.'

'There *is* more gold down there,' sad Petersson dogmatically. 'There has to be.'

'It looked so promising too,' said O'Rourke wistfully. 'From the way it started I was sure it would go on forever. Just shows how wrong you can be.'

'A bust,' said Angus, shaking his head. 'Who would have thought it?'

Petersson lumbered across to the mechanical digger and climbed into its cockpit. Without another word he set the neanderthal looking machine in action, a look of fierce determination on his face as the digger's metal claw tore and savaged into the hard packed earth they'd discovered beneath the ore bed.

O'Rourke gestured to Angus and together they climbed out of the excavation.

As they walked towards the house O'Rourke said, 'Petersson told me months ago that was the only ore bed on the property. With the quality and yield we were getting then that didn't bother us unduly as we were convinced the bed was a deep one. It seems we were wrong. You might say the Lucky Molly just ran out of luck.'

Angus hated the thought of breaking it to Molly. They'd made so many plans together, built up so many dreams.

Angus said, 'Well we haven't come out of it with nothing at all. There's the property which we can sell plus whatever we can get from the equipment we bought.'

Although the property had originally been in Angus's name it had shortly after purchase been stipulated in the deeds that it was jointly and equally owned by the three of them.

'I think I'm going to get drunk out of my skull,' said O'Rourke. 'And if ever a man needed an excuse for doing that then I reckon we three have a beaut.'

Angus was bemused by what had happened. Although he'd seen it coming it was still a profound shock that it had actually happened. Like the condemned man, he'd been secretly convinced there'd be a last minute reprieve.

Once in the house O'Rourke took himself off to his bedroom with a bottle of brandy. Angus found Molly in the kitchen feeding John.

He sat heavily beside her, slumping forward and cradling his head in his hands.

'The bed's run out,' he said.

The colour drained from her face. The threatened nightmare of recent weeks had become reality. 'That's it, then?' she croaked.

'That's it.'

'You're absolutely certain?'

'Petersson seems to think he can pick it up again but he's kidding himself. The Lucky Molly was a nine day wonder and today was day ten.'

Anger bubbled in Molly which she swiftly brought under control. 'What happens now?' she asked.

'I don't know. We'll have to discuss that.'

Molly plucked the now empty feeding bottle from John's mouth who immediately began to cry. Irritation creased her face as she jiggled him up and down on her lap.

Angus stared lovingly at his son. The wee fellow was the spitting image of him which naturally enough tickled him pink.

'Want me to take him?' he asked.

Molly passed John over and then went looking for a cigarette. 'What a mess,' she said through a cloud of smoke.

'It isn't the end of the world,' Angus replied. 'Nothing ever is. And let's look on the bright side. We've got one another and the baby. As far as I'm concerned, that's worth more than all the gold that was ever dug out of the ground.'

Molly looked sour, her expression making it quite clear she didn't agree.

O'Rourke appeared from his bedroom holding the brandy bottle by the neck. 'You've told the little lady I take it,' he said.

Angus nodded.

'A sad day Molly, eh?'

'You can say that again. And are you going to hold onto that bottle forever or are you going to pass it round?'

Molly coughed as the liquor burned its way down her throat. Handing the bottle back, she crossed to the window and stared out, her eyes taking on a faraway look as though she was seeing something way beyond the horizon.

'Penny for them?' Angus asked eventually.

'Nothing important,' she replied. Her voice sounded as though it came from a far distance.

'Come on, tell me,' he coaxed.

She turned and stared at him. 'I was just thinking of all the things we were going to do. Places we were going to go. The house we were going to have. The clothes. The cars.'

'I'm sorry Molly,' Angus said softly. 'I'd cut off my right arm for you if it would change things. But it wouldn't. The digging's a bust and we're just going to have to learn to live with the fact.'

'These little things are sent to try us,' said O'Rourke. 'Very character building you know.'

Molly looked as though she was about to retort angrily when suddenly John was sick all down his front.

'I'll deal with that,' she said wearily, taking John from Angus and crossing over to the sink where she began changing the wee lad.

'She's a wonderful mother,' said Angus proudly.

O'Rourke swallowed some more brandy.

For another week Petersson worked at the digging on his own before finally admitting defeat.

That evening the three men and Molly held a conference during which it was decided to advertise the property statewide in the hope they'd quickly come up with a buyer.

The equipment Petersson would sell through various private contacts he had.

The night Angus and Molly lay wide awake in bed. 'I think we should go to Sydney,' Angus said after a while. 'We'll stay with O'Rourke's mother till we can find a small flat of our own.'

Molly winced at the word small. 'And what about work?'

'I've told you about Bill Pettigrew who employed me as a clerk. Bill was very fond of me, looked on me as a son almost. He said when I left that I could have my old job back any time.'

'A clerk,' said Molly softly, a hint of contempt in her voice.

'There are big prospects in the building trade, Bill says,' Angus went on. 'Give it a couple of years and who knows? I might even start my own firm.'

To Molly it all sounded like pie in the sky. And suddenly she was feeling trapped and deathly afraid. She could see the years stretching ahead of her. No more fun. No more laughter. Instead the worry of having a child and husband to care for with little money coming into the house. What did a clerk earn? She didn't know but she was sure it was hellish little.

As for the brat now fast asleep in his cot at the far side of the room, she'd never wanted him in the first place. Oh, the idea of a child had been bearable when it had seemed she wouldn't be tied down to him indefinitely. A nanny or baby nurse had been high on her list of priorities once the money started flooding in.

But with the collapse of the Lucky Molly there would now be no nanny or baby nurse which meant she personally would have to continue looking after the brat who seemed to be never endingly performing at one end or the other.

And as for Angus, her knight in shining armour had turned out to be like so many other men she'd known in the past. Namely a dead loss. Big on promises but very short on delivery.

Angus with bundles of money was one thing. But Angus as a clerk in a small building firm was quite another.

Christ! she raged inwardly. What a Godawful mess she'd got herself into. Well she was damned if she was going to let herself be sucked into playing the suburban housewife with sprog. The very thought was anathema.

What she wanted was freedom. Laughs. Fun! God-almighty she was still young yet with her whole life stretching ahead of her. And who knew what might be waiting for her round the next bend? Or should she say *who?*

'Molly, you still awake?'

'Uh-huh.'

His hand slipped up her thigh and into the nest of her crotch.

Despite what she'd been thinking she found herself wanting him.

'I'll give you all the things we talked about Molly. I'll find a way. I promise you.'

'Of course you will,' she replied, wriggling under his

probing fingers.

She accepted him into her arms, enjoying what he did to her and how he made her feel.

And as they made love she worked out the best time for her to leave next day to catch the mid-morning bus that went through Bundegai.

Directly after breakfast next morning Molly said she wanted to go into Bundegai to get some things from the chemist's. And as Angus wasn't working would he mind looking after John?

The three men had already decided during breakfast that they'd spend the morning drafting letters to the various agents and newspapers with whom they were going to advertise the property. Petersson had the additional job of writing to his personal contacts regarding the equipment. So it was no great trouble for Angus to take care of the wee lad.

Angus did wonder briefly why Molly was taking a small case with her but at the back of his mind put it down to some other business she probably had in town.

''Bye then,' Molly said when she was finally ready.

'Don't I get a kiss?'

Smiling, she came back from the door and kissed him on the cheek. Then as an afterthought she bent and kissed John.

'Don't be too long,' Angus said.

Molly smiled again, but didn't reply.

With John cradled in his arms Angus stood and watched the Holden roar off towards Bundegai.

'Now shall we get down to it,' said O'Rourke who was seated at the table beside an extremely morose looking Petersson.

Angus turned his attention to the drafting of the advertisements.

Lunchtime came and went. She must've got tied up, Angus thought. But when afternoon gave way to evening he began to get worried.

'Maybe she's had an accident?' he said to O'Rourke.

'Car's broken down most likely,' O'Rourke replied.

'Aye, no doubt you're right,' said Angus, relieved at this most obvious of explanations. After all, hadn't the same thing happened to Petersson a few weeks previously?

A little later Angus put John down for the night, after which the three men sat playing cards.

At one Petersson went to bed shortly followed by O'Rourke.

For hours Angus kept vigil in a chair facing the door. He dropped off just as dawn was breaking.

The next thing he knew he was being shaken by O'Rourke saying John was awake and crying.

He changed the baby's nappy and fed him. Then the three men had breakfast.

'That's the trouble with not having a phone,' O'Rourke said over coffee. 'Makes situations like this a lot more dramatic than they are.'

'I was thinking just before I nodded off,' Angus said slowly, 'if Molly did have to leave the car in the garage overnight surely they would have loaned her one till she picked the Holden up again? I mean isn't that what they usually do when someone lives out of town?' And when O'Rourke didn't have a reply to that he added, 'I'll give her till ten then if you'll watch John for me I'll start walking into town.

On the stroke of ten Angus set out for Bundegai. He trudged for an hour and a half before being picked up by a passing vehicle which dropped him outside the Great Southern.

There were three garages in Bundegai and he was en route to the nearest one when he spied the Holden parked outside the post office. The car's doors were locked but there was a piece of paper jammed up against the inside of the windscreen which said: 'Angus, keys in post office.'

Having retrieved the keys he opened the car door and slid inside. The piece of paper in the windscreen turned out to be a letter.

As he read his head grew numb. It seemed as though he was standing in the middle of an ice cold wind although it was broiling out.

He read the letter through twice, then folded it and put it into his trouser pocket. Seeing and hearing nothing, he drove the Holden out of Bundegai and back to the farmhouse.

As he drew up O'Rourke came out onto the porch with John in his arms. 'Has she been taken crook then?' he called out on seeing Angus was alone.

Angus joined O'Rourke on the porch, taking John from him and holding the wee fellow close.

'She's gone,' he said, his voice trembling.

'What do you mean, gone?'

'Just that. Lit out for parts unknown.'

'You mean she's left you and the baby?'

Angus nodded.

'Why, the rotten galah!' O'Rourke exploded.

'I found the car with a letter in it,' Angus said after a few seconds. 'She says she's sorry but she couldn't yet face life as a suburban hausfrau as she put it. Before leaving she withdrew what money we had in our joint account. She apologized for that but pointed out I'd have my share from the sale of this place to keep me going.'

'I don't understand,' said O'Rourke.

'I do . . . now. I thought she loved me but I was wrong. What she was in love with was the money she saw The Lucky Molly bringing in.'

O'Rourke swore vehemently, his face flushing and his eyes sparking with anger.

Angus stared down at John who was gurgling happily in his arms. 'Well I'll never desert you, boy. You can stake your life on that,' he said.

'You mean you're going to look after the kid all by yourself?' O'Rourke asked.

'I may need some help. But I'll never have him adopted or fostered. He's my son and we're staying together.

That's the way it's going to be.'

O'Rourke remained on the porch while Angus took John inside. He couldn't remember when he'd last been so moved.

During the next month several people turned up to look the property over but none of them made an offer.

In the meantime Petersson had sunk into a deep depression and had taken to camping out at night all on his own. Going walkabout at one point, he disappeared for over a week.

O'Rourke tried his hand at panning the stream but his efforts produced little dust and no nuggets. Petersson had taken out nearly all the gold there was to be had there.

One month became two and still they hadn't found a buyer. Then one afternoon while Angus was changing John and O'Rourke was busy trimming the lamps an excited Petersson burst into the house.

'We've done it! We've done it! We've bloody well done it!' he yelled, dancing on the spot like an Irishman trying to keep pace with a demented fiddler.

'Done what?' queried Angus.

'All this time staring me in the face and me not having the wit to see it!' crowed Petersson.

O'Rourke caught Petersson by the arm and forced him to stand still. 'Will you please tell us just what it is you're raving on about?' O'Rourke demanded.

With eyes seeming about to burst from his head Petersson said, 'I first noticed it early last week. Although God knows I should've seen it long before then. The trouble is I suppose when you're looking specifically for one thing you just don't take in what else is there. Or at least I didn't.'

'I'm lost,' said Angus.

'When it finally did dawn I took samples from all over the property and sent them to Sydney for analysis. I've just come from Bundegai now. The results of those analyses were in today's mail.'

'You haven't found more gold?' O'Rourke asked quickly.'

'Not gold. Bauxite!' Having said that, Petersson looked from O'Rourke to Angus. But if he was expecting a reaction then he was disappointed. Angus and O'Rourke both stared at him blankly.

'Bauxite,' Petersson repeated.

'What's that?' Angus asked.

'The stuff they smelt aluminium from.'

Again there was no reaction.

'Alufuckingminium!' Petersson shouted in desperation. 'There's a war on and that's one of the metals the government is crying out for. And this entire farm is sitting square on top of a mountain of the stuff.'

Slowly it dawned on Angus just what Petersson was saying.

'Does that mean we're going to be rich after all?' he asked.

'Rich! The three of us are going to be each as rich as Croesus!' Petersson roared.

O'Rourke made a sort of gobbling sound and sat heavily on the nearest chair. He looked like a man who'd just been hit over the head with a sledgehammer.

Like O'Rourke, Angus was completely stunned by this bolt out of the blue. 'You're sure there's no mistake?' he asked in a whisper.

'Not this time,' Petersson replied, and whooped with joy.

Angus took a deep breath and then glanced down at John cradled in his arms. That was who the money would benefit in the long run. He'd make sure of it.

The very best of everything. That would be John's life thanks to a mountain of Bauxite and Petersson's unswerving digger's dream.

He thought of Molly then and the irony of her having left when she did. He could just imagine her face when she heard the news.

Then suddenly O'Rourke was on his feet screaming and yelling and dancing an impromptu jig with Petersson.

Angus hugged John tight against his chest. Later a great deal of serious thinking would have to be done, plans to be made, but for now he was content to give himself over to the madness Petersson had brought into their midst.

Part IV

Goodbye Yesterday
1946–1947

Carrie was dying and was reconciled to the fact.

She lay in bed thinking of the letter Harriet, on her instruction, had written Angus a few months previously informing him of the situation.

His reply had come by return saying he and John would be sailing on the first available ship.

Carrie gritted her teeth and stifled a groan. The plaster corset round her middle was giving her gyp. It had done ever since it had been put on. The corset was to help the sciatica the doctor said she had.

But there was a lot more to her condition than merely that. Her body was completely worn out. The ravages of years of TB and mistreatment at the hands of Archie Marjoribanks had finally taken their toll.

She was forty-five years old and looked sixty.

There was a photograph standing on her bedside table which she glanced at occasionally. It showed Angus holding up young John outside the farmhouse where they lived. It had pleased her enormously that Angus had called his son after his father. Thinking of it never failed to bring a lump to her throat.

Over at the window Harriet stood staring out. She was dressed in her inevitable black with her hair drawn severely back in a bun. Like Carrie, she was thin and wasted, but in her case it was entirely self-inflicted by her almost constant diet of cigarettes and tea. Her thoughts were with the Scottish Amalgamated Insurance

Company and its Glasgow branch, in particular. She'd been in charge of the branch for a number of years now. But with the war over and the men returning home she would soon have to step down and resume her previous position of secretary.

She was going to miss dreadfully the power and responsibility. But there was no way the company was going to promote her officially into an executive position, albeit her ability was well proven.

It was one thing for her to step into her boss's shoes in wartime. Another entirely for her to stay there or assume another position of that nature once peace had been achieved.

She saw it as one more major frustration in a life filled with them.

Carrie started coughing, dry, racking spasms that shook her entire frame. The hand she held to her mouth was skeletal, each bone distinct. The skin covering those bones was yellowishly opaque and like an old leaf to the touch.

Harriet immediately left her vantage point by the window to help Carrie reach a glass of water. As she held Carrie close she knew the only thing keeping her sister alive was Carrie's dogged determination to see Angus again and hold her grandson for the first time.

When the coughing fit was finally over Carrie lay back on the bed and closed her eyes. As she drifted off she thought how much more comfortable she'd be without the damned corset. But she also knew she wouldn't order Dr Robertson to remove it in case she somehow reduced the precious time left her.

When she fell asleep she dreamt of the happy days when she'd been married to John McBain and life, though hard, had been glorious for the pair of them.

Through in the living room Donald was sitting in his chair reading the day's paper. He was retired now having been told directly after VJ day his time at Armstrong's was finished.

He had taken over an allotment after Winnie had gone

on at him incessantly to do so. But his heart wasn't really in it. Growing vegetables on a wee plot was fine as a hobby but it was hardly a day's work for a man.

He missed unbearably the bedlam of the foundry, the roar of the blast furnaces, the dazzling liquidity of molten metal, the pride of a job – his type of job – well done.

Rising, he made his way through to the hall where he stood wondering whether or not to go through and see Carrie. He decided against it when he heard the sound of soft snoring coming from her room.

With Harriet in the house to look after Carrie should she wake he decided to take a dauner along by the Cart. That should fritter away a good hour which would bring him home just as Winnie returned from getting in the messages.

As he walked down the close stairs he thought about Alex being the first of their brood to go. And now Carrie was about to be the second.

The one blessing was she wasn't in the least scared of dying. If any thing, she was looking forward to it as she was convinced somewhere in some form John McBain would be waiting for her.

He could only hope and pray she was right.

Clad in a badly fitting demob suit Hugh stepped off the train at the Central Station. He still couldn't believe he'd emerged from the war completely unscathed. After what he'd been through it seemed a miracle to him he was actually home again in one piece.

Not only that, but there was a wife waiting to greet him and a wee baby daughter whom he hadn't yet seen.

It had been a great disappointment to him to learn Janey had given birth to a girl. But he'd consoled himself in the knowledge the wee lassie was perfect in every detail. And there was nothing to stop him and Janey having a boy next time round.

He made for the Broomielaw from where he'd be able to catch a tram for Muirend. On a sudden impulse he continued on down to the suspension bridge which took him over the gently flowing Clyde and into the Gorbals.

To another's eyes, the dirty, squalid tenements – the air hard and rasping from the sooty smoke belching out of their innumerable chimneys – might have jarred. But to Hugh they were a joy to behold as they confirmed he was home again in the city where his roots ran deep and which he so loved.

He walked as far as the Star Bar and Plaza dancehall opposite. My God, he remembered that night all right! He ran the last few yards to a stop where he caught a tram. As the tram rattled on its way he thought of Kenny White who'd introduced him to Janey. He'd been killed in North Africa.

Janey was scraping potatoes when she heard the front door open and close again.

At first she didn't recognize the man standing in the kitchen doorway staring at her in such a quizzical fashion. Then with a cry she dropped the knife and potato and rushed across the floor into his arms.

There was so much she wanted to say but for the moment no words came.

Lifting Janey's chin, Hugh kissed her, not a passionate kiss but rather one of sheer pleasure at their reunification.

Breaking away, Janey used the edge of her hand to wipe the tears from her face. Still too overcome to speak, she beckoned him to follow and hastened towards the door.

The child lay fast asleep in her cot, her face pink and angelic, the mouth puckered up as though she was blowing him a kiss on this the event of his seeing her for the first time.

'Mary Agnes,' Janey said, the words trembling from her mouth.

She was a bonnie baby with a definite look of the Chisholms about her. His heart went out to the wean and he quickly put to the back of his mind the regret she wasn't a boy. A lassie would do him just fine – for the moment.

Janey would have woken Mary Agnes but Hugh restrained her. They returned to the kitchen where Janey busied herself brewing a pot of tea.

She was putting this by to mask when he asked her where Greta Paterson was? He was looking forward to seeing his old friend again.

Janey turned a suddenly stricken face towards him and asked if he hadn't got her recent letters?

He replied that the last letter he'd received had been a little over six weeks previously.

Janey poured him a cup and as she handed it to him said Greta had been dead and buried a month now. Death, according to the autopsy, was due to kidney failure.

Janey went on to say how close she and Greta had become during the past few years, particularly after Mary Agnes had been born as Greta had doted on the child. She'd seized on Mary Agnes as a substitute for her own grandchildren so tragically killed by German bombs.

Janey said Hugh had taken the place of the dead Stewart in Greta's mind with herself replacing Stewart's wife. Greta had come to think of and refer to their small family as her own.

Hugh was well pleased his old friend had found some comfort in having Janey and Mary Agnes to stay with her. That at least went a little way to repaying the multitude of kindnesses she and Aly had lavished on him.

Hugh frowned suddenly, the thought striking him their position here at Muirend was now extremely precarious. After all it was unlikely the new owners – presumably Greta's next of kin – would be keen on their presence in the house and no doubt they'd be given notice to quit.

It was also quite feasible a new manager would be appointed in his place – new broom and all that.

A soft, loving smile curled the corners of Janey's

mouth as she stared at the dejected Hugh. It was almost worth her last letters going astray so she could tell him the good news herself.

Her smile widened as she told him that directly after the funeral she'd received a communication asking her to call on Greta's solicitors. On presenting herself she'd been ushered into the presence of the senior partner who'd told her in accordance with his late client's will the entire Muirend estate plus the farm on the East Kilbride road had been left to one Hugh Chisholm, a Paterson employee currently serving with His Majesty's Armed Forces.

So taken aback was Hugh he made Janey repeat what she'd just told him.

'My God!' he whispered when she'd finished for the second time. Crossing to the window, he stared out over the yard to the stables beyond. To think all this was now his was simply unbelievable! And the last thing in the world he'd expected.

He knew Greta had some distant relatives but Janey said that Greta hadn't wanted them to have the place as they would've only sold it. And anyway, they were more than comfortably off and didn't need any addition to their bank balances.

Hugh and Janey both loved the house and dairy and because of this she preferred everything to go to them, just as it would've gone to Stewart and his family had they still been alive.

Hugh was suddenly aware of Janey standing by his side, her face beaming as she stared up at him.

Catching her in his arms he announced his intention of taking her upstairs to bed to celebrate his safe return and their stroke of stupendous good luck.

They were halfway up the stairs when Janey remembered to tell him on top of everything else there was also £2653 in a joint bank account she'd opened in their names. This was the cash savings Greta had left and which had also come their way.

Their combined laughter was so loud it woke Mary

Agnes so they didn't get to bed right away after all. . . .

Three weeks to the day after Hugh arrived back in Glasgow the late train from London brought Angus and John. With them was a girl from Bundegai called Dawn Schroeder who'd been acting as nanny to John since shortly after Molly had flown the coop.

Having disembarked from the train Angus booked them into the Central Station Hotel where Angus had no trouble getting them a suite with two bedrooms, one for him and the other for Dawn and John.

After being shown to their suite Dawn busied herself with John who'd been fractious during the latter part of their long journey up from Southampton.

While Dawn got John ready for bed Angus stood by a window looking out on the city, which gave the impression of having had its life juices bled from it. The people he'd seen so far had thin, pinched faces as grey as the buildings surrounding them.

Tanned and fleshed out, he might have belonged to another species altogether so stark was the contrast.

Sighing, he poured himself a glass of whisky. As he sipped, his mind flew back to Australia and his affairs there. The bauxite strike had been everything, and more, Petersson had said it would.

The original digging had been abandoned and a new site opened. This had grown rapidly into what was now known as the Lucky Molly Bauxite Mine – LMBM for short – employing close on a hundred people.

O'Rourke had taken over as overall administrator and was proving superb at the job. As for Petersson, once the mine had been opened, he'd moved on to pastures new. He'd been last heard of up on the Northern Territory prospecting for silver he was convinced was to be found there.

Of course Petersson didn't need to do any further prospecting as he, like Angus and O'Rourke, was now a very rich man with the prospect of those riches reaching mind boggling proportions. But with the outback and

prospecting deep in his blood he needed – as Bill
Pettigrew had once warned Angus nearly always
happened to prospectors – to keep up his erstwhile mode
of life the way a junkie needs another fix.

O'Rourke also had caught the bug although to a lesser
degree than Petersson. With him it was merely the
outback. As he often said, he could no more imagine
himself going back to live in an urban situation than he
could flying in the air.

If asked, Angus would have had to admit he too had
almost fallen for the seductions of the outback. But what
had saved him was an older love and craving – that for his
native Glasgow which surmounted all else.

As for Molly, and he smiled grimly thinking about it,
she'd been back like the proverbial shot once she'd
learned of the bauxite strike. In vain she'd pleaded with
him for them to take up where they'd left off but he'd
have none of it.

He'd loved her once. But that love had been blown
away like so much chaff in the wind the day she deserted
him and John. Stripped of the emotional tie he'd even
come to feel quite repulsed by her.

In agreement for a divorce he'd made a reasonable
settlement on her, far more than she deserved, he
reckoned. But she had given him John and for that he
owed her something.

Angus's musings were interrupted by Dawn calling
out to say John wanted to be kissed goodnight. This he
did with all the warmth and love he bore his son.

It didn't take John long to drop off, worn out as he was
by the journey and excitement.

Dawn joined Angus for a drink. The relationship
between Angus and Dawn was strictly a business one.
They liked one another, enjoyed one another's company, but that was as far as it went. The truth was that
physically neither was particularly attracted to the other.

Angus nervously paced up and down the room,
desperate to go out to Tallon Street and see Carrie.

When he told Dawn he was considering going on his

own she pooh-poohed the idea saying it was far too late and all he would succeed in doing was waking his mother when no doubt what the poor woman needed was all the sleep she could get.

Dawn was right, he decided reluctantly. It was best be bided his patience till the morning when he could take John with him.

It was a decision he'd regret for the rest of his life.

Tallon Street was smaller and meaner than he remembered it.

His heart was thudding as he rapped on the so familiar door at the top of the close. Behind him Dawn wiped John's nose and checked the wee fellow was neat, tidy and a credit to his father.

The door opened and Winnie was there staring at Angus as though he were a stranger. Then the penny dropped.

'Oh, son!' she said in a tremulous voice.

He knew then he'd come too late. 'When?' he asked.

'Last night,' Winnie replied. Had he come to Tallon Street when he'd wanted to he would have caught Carrie just before she'd died.

Realizing she was keeping them standing on the doorstep Winnie brought them in, gesturing towards the living room where she said Donald and Harriet were.

Hugh had already been but had returned to Muirend to see to the milk. He'd be back as soon as he could.

The family knew all about Dawn, Angus having carefully explained about her in the last letter he'd written.

As John came abreast of Winnie she bent and swept the wee fellow into her arms. Kissing him on both cheeks. Then holding him at arms' length she said, 'A fine lad, the living image of his dad. Carrie would have been so proud.'

Donald was waiting just inside the living room door and the first thing he did when Angus entered the room was to throw his arms round Angus's shoulders and squeeze his grandson tightly. All he said, was 'Aye, well there we are, then.'

Harriet had been crying as was obvious from her red rimmed eyes. She embraced Angus after her father had let him go.

When everyone had been introduced and a bit of a fuss made of John, Donald said to the very last Carrie had been smiling and joking, assuring everyone they weren't going to get rid of her until she'd seen Angus again and held the wee chap named after her John in her arms. But she'd been wrong.

When she died Angus's name was on her lips.

Dawn was distraught remembering it was she who'd dissuaded Angus from coming the previous night. But he dismissed her self condemnation saying the argument she'd put forward had been a valid one.

If he blamed anyone it was himself. He should've followed his instincts.

He asked to see his mother's body and Harriet volunteered to take him through to the bedroom where Carrie was laid out.

He'd brought a number of presents along and one of these he now sorted out from the rest.

It was a leather handbag he'd scoured Sydney for, knowing precisely the type and design Carrie would like.

Entering the bedroom, he came to an abrupt halt, his face plainly registering shock. If he'd met his mother alive in the street he'd have walked straight past her.

She was so *old* looking! A crone nearer Winnie's age than the actual forty-five she was.

Stiff-legged, he walked forward to sit on the edge of the bed. Slowly he unwrapped the handbag and laid it on the pillow beside her head. 'A wee minding, Ma,' he said.

Coldness gave way to heat which exploded into a blast furnace of bubbling anger. 'What happened to her?' he demanded, his voice a thrumming stretch of wire.

Harriet wilted under his terrible gaze.

'It was Archie, wasn't it?' he hissed taking hold of the front of Harriet's dress.

All this while Harriet had kept her dark secret, never

once breathing a hint of it to anyone. Time had pushed it to the back of her mind where, like a bad dream, it had gradually faded to nothingness.

But seeing Carrie dead had brought it all rushing back. Her skin crawled with the memory of what the animal had done to her. And how many awful times had Carrie endured the same?

Her nerve shredded. It came out in a rush, the words tumbling from her mouth.

When she finally finished speaking she gave a great shudder as though an enormous weight had been lifted from her.

Angus whimpered. His mind filled with dreadful pictures. It was unbelievable. Inconceivable. And yet Harriet said it was true.

He dashed from the room and before anyone realized what was happening was through the front door and running down the close stairs.

Behind him Harriet wept volubly.

Once out in the street, he hesitated, not quite knowing what to do next. Then remembering it was a Sunday and there was a good chance Archie would be at home, he ran, all the while thinking of the life Archie had given his mother. It had transformed Carrie into the raddled corpse now laid out in Tallon Street.

The time had finally arrived for the reckoning. He was no longer the wee boy Archie could contemptuously knock to one side. It would be man to man and he doubted there were many could have stood up against him the way he felt right then.

Reaching the front door he formed a fist and hammered. And hammered. And hammered.

'Christalbloodymighty, I'm coming!' the well remembered voice called out followed by a dragging sound as though Archie was pulling something heavy across the floor.

The moment the door started to open Angus leapt at it, hitting it hard with his shoulder so it was thrust suddenly and violently back in on itself.

For an instant he glimpsed Archie's startled face. Then, with a cry, Archie toppled backward to fall heavily onto the manky floor.

Angus advanced on his quarry. He was going to enjoy this.

'You!' Archie exclaimed, his face contorted with what Angus mistakenly thought was hate.

'Get up!' Angus spat.

Archie's hands scrabbled for two rubber tipped sticks lying next to him. Using these he tried valiantly to regain his feet.

Angus frowned, wondering what his step-father was playing at. Why the sticks?

For the first time he noticed how twisted and grotesque – the legs especially – Archie's limbs had become.

Raising his eyes he saw a wheelchair standing further along the small hallway.

Finally, having tried repeatedly and failed, Archie sank back onto his bottom. Glaring, he said he couldn't get up under his own steam and that Angus would have to help him.

Sitting there almost helpless as a babe Archie was a pitiful sight, and one which drained the tumultuous anger out of Angus. It just wasn't in him to ladle into a man in this condition.

Angus took Archie by the hand and after something of a struggle got him back on his feet.

Angus asked what had happened and Archie replied his old pains which had bothered him for years had been the early stages of arthritis. He turned and shuffled – making the dragging sound Angus had heard while waiting for the door to be answered – to the wheelchair which he sank into with a sigh of relief.

There was a certain classic irony about all this which wasn't lost on Angus. That Archie's arthritis caused him continual, excruciating pain was plainly evident. The man who'd caused so much misery and suffering to others was now doomed to suffer miserably himself.

Staring at his step-father Angus could find no forgiveness in himself. The picture of Carrie was too fresh in his mind. And anyway he wasn't the forgiving kind.

He hoped Archie lived to a ripe old age, and during every day of the time left him suffered all the pains and agonies of hell.

'She died last night,' Angus said abruptly.

Archie blinked and frowned. 'Who?'

'My mother.'

Archie's lips shrivelled into a thin line and he dropped his head to stare at the floor. Nor did he lift his head again until Angus turned to go.

Revenge had already been exacted on Archie and in a far more terrible manner than anything Angus had had in mind. His hand was on the doorknob when Archie suddenly spoke softly behind him.

'You may be grown up but don't think you know it all yet. In my own way I loved your mother even though I did treat her badly from time to time. For what it's worth I'm truly sorry. She'll be sorely missed for she was a good woman.'

When Archie had finished speaking Angus walked from the house out into the street where he stood feeling sick. He wondered why Harriet hadn't told him about Archie's condition.

The simple answer was she hadn't known. Archie Marjoribanks had become virtually a taboo subject in Tallon Street as Carrie couldn't bear to hear his name mentioned. Consequently Harriet had been in the dark about his illness.

Just then a face from the past arrested Angus's gaze and instantly rekindled his anger.

He watched as Tod Gemmill strolled by on the opposite side of the street. Tod was another he owed and now was as good a time as any to repay that debt.

Crossing the street he hurried after his man. When they came to Angus's old primary school, Angus maintaining a respectable distance behind Tod while he waited his chance, Tod suddenly headed off at a tangent.

Being Sunday and at a time of the morning when most

folk were either still abed or else getting ready for church the streets were more or less deserted, which suited Angus down to the ground.

Breaking into a trot he caught up with Tod in front of the Rialto picture house and tapped him on the shoulder. 'I'm claiming you,' he said.

Recognizing Angus, Tod's jaw literally fell open.

Angus jerked his thumb towards the ash and cinder track leading round the back of the picture house and Tod got the point. With a shrug Tod walked in the direction indicated.

Angus had always had extremely fast reflexes and it was these that saved him now.

In a well practised movement Tod whipped the cap from his head and flicked the brim straight at Angus's face.

Angus registered the blur and hastily jerked his head back. The cap brim missed his eyes by a few inches. Realizing what it was Tod had tried to hit him with he closed on Tod.

Tod flicked the cap again and this time its brim brushed against Angus's outstretched hand. A large gash suddenly opened up from wrist to little finger.

Grunting in surprise, Angus backpedalled.

The next time the cap sliced the air in front of him he glimpsed a flash of metal which told him the brim had been doctored in some way.

The two men circled one another, Tod swaying from side to side holding the cap bunched in his hand with its brim projecting outward.

The rim contained a row of razor blades stitched between the two layers of fabric so only their cutting edges protruded.

Suddenly Angus's opening was there as Tod overreached himself and stumbled. His hands automatically dropped to steady himself and as they did Angus leapt.

He got round behind Tod to put a crushing stranglehold on Tod's windpipe at the same time securing the hand holding the cap.

For a few seconds they struggled. Then Angus brought his heel smashing down on Tod's right instep.

Tod screamed and bucked. Dropping the cap, he reached back with both hands to tear and claw at Angus's face.

Angus exclaimed as a thumb jabbed him in the eye. Shifting his grip, he grasped Tod by a shoulder and using a combination push/pull movement, knocked him off balance. Then he threw him over his leg onto the ground.

He dropped his full weight onto Tod's chest, landing on his knees, which brought another scream from Tod.

'I give up! I give up!' Tod pleaded.

'Like fuck you do,' Angus said, drawing his fist back with the intention of bursting Tod's nose.

'I can tell you about your Da!' Tod wailed.

Angus's fist stopped in mid punch. He thought he couldn't have heard correctly. 'What did you say?' he demanded.

'Your Da,' Tod sobbed.

'What about him?'

'Promise you'll let me go?'

'If it's worth it,' Angus said slowly.

Tod sucked in a breath and groaned. He licked his lips. 'Well?'

'Your Da on the gantry, no one ever knew why he was up there.'

There was a vice in Angus's chest. 'Go on,' he whispered.

'Armstrong himself gave the order. It was to inspect something or other. I know for a fact because *my* Da overheard.' Tod gulped. 'He could never tell your Grandpa or speak up. It would've meant his job.'

So there it was. Sir Alan *had* owed Carrie compensation and the bloody man had never said a dickey bird. He'd kept stum to save himself a pittance, for that's all it would have been to him.

'Please?' Tod pleaded. 'You'll keep this to yourself? If Armstrong was to find out. . . .'

But Angus had stopped hearing. Rising, he started

back for the street, his anger completely gone leaving a great calm behind.

'He'll pay, Ma. I promise you,' he whispered.

He'd never meant anything more in his life.

19

In Scotland the best summer months are often May and September. It was the middle of May now and the sun was cracking the skies.

Diane Armstrong stood in the downstairs bay window of her sister's house in Bearsden watching several blackbirds squabbling over a worm one had dug up.

Rosemary was sitting by the fireplace mending a slight tear in one of Iain's best shirts. Diane said, 'By the way, an old friend of yours has been making inquiries about buying a house that's up for sale in Newton Mearns.'

Rosemary was engrossed in her task, nimbly sewing the tiny stitches required. 'Who's that, then?' she asked.

Diane sprung her bombshell. 'Angus McBain.'

The shock that swept through Rosemary was like having a bucket of ice cold water emptied over her head. 'Is that a fact?' she replied and somehow continued sewing.

In a quiet voice Diane went on to say Angus was apparently interested in buying a mansion that had only recently come onto the market. It was an old property with something like twenty rooms, a conservatory and outhouses.

Rosemary said it couldn't be the Angus McBain they knew as he couldn't possible afford anything like that.

But Diane was adamant. It was the same Angus McBain who'd lived in Holmlea Road and run off leaving Rosemary in the lurch.

A lump filled Rosemary's throat as she pretended to be still interested in her sewing. But she wasn't fooling Diane one little bit and she knew it.

She asked Diane if she knew where Angus had been and what he'd been doing? But these were questions her sister had no answers for.

All Diane could tell her was that Angus was back. And if he was able to consider buying a house like the one in Newton Mearns it was to be presumed he wasn't still the poor lad he'd been when they'd known him.

Rosemary smiled grimly to herself. Angus had always sworn he'd one day be a somebody with lots of money. It would seem he'd at least got the money.

Further discussion was halted by Iain's entrance.

Now he was back in civvy street Iain was being reluctantly drawn more and more into running his father's property business. Both his parents had virtually lost all interest in everything since the night he'd returned home from hospital to give them the combined shock of seeing the ruin his face had become and telling them the news of Peter's death.

Hyper-sensitive about his looks, he'd become something of a recluse, only leaving the house when absolutely necessary. The telephone was his lifeline through which he conducted the vast majority of his dealings with the outside world.

His personality had changed considerably since leaving hospital. He'd always had a tendency to be brooding and introspective: Now it wasn't unusual for him to spend days locked away in his study.

After Iain had left them the two women chatted for some time about the reappearance of Angus McBain.

Then, having seen her sister off, Rosemary went into the garden where she strolled deep in thought. Questions crowded her mind. Had Angus altered much? And if so, what did he look like now? How had he made enough money to be able to contemplate buying a mansion?

And, of course, the big question that had plagued her this long time – why had Angus run off the way he had?

As Rosemary wandered through her garden thinking about Angus, he was mounting the stairs to the solicitors who were dealing with the sale of the Newton Mearns property.

The house was an old one with an enormous amount needing done to it. But rather than being a black mark against it this appealed to Angus as it gave him the excuse to have the place modernized to his own specifications

The house was to be the first stage of the promise he'd made the day Petersson announced the bauxite strike. His son was going to have the very best of everything which naturally included a place to live.

Having stated to the solicitor that he wanted to purchase, he was entertained with sherry and digestives over which he was informed the legal documents would be drawn up in due course.

Before leaving he inquired about rented accommodation and was told the matter would be looked into right away.

Feeling well pleased with himself and the way things were going, he drove out to Cathcart and Tallon Street. Winnie was in but Donald whom he'd really come to see was at the allotment.

Over a cup of tea Winnie told him Hugh and Janey's big news. He said he'd drop by Muirend and see them after he'd had a word with Donald.

Angus found his grandfather at the plot. The two sat on an old wooden bench and for a wee while they blethered about inconsequentials, Donald using the respite to enjoy a pipeful of tobacco.

Retirement was proving a heavy burden for Donald to bear. Despite constant nagging from Winnie he was beginning to neglect himself. It was this personal neglect which was worrying Angus and had given him the idea of

how he could help his grandfather and at the same time
do himself a good turn.

In a mild voice Angus asked Donald if he'd be interested in holding down a job again?

Donald slowly took the battered briar from his mouth
and turned to stare at his grandson. Trying desperately
hard not to betray his eagerness he asked just what it was
Angus had in mind?

Angus explained about buying the house in Newton
Mearns and the state the place was in. Once an architect
had drawn up plans for modernization a gang of workmen would have to be employed to carry them out. What
he wanted was Donald to be gaffer over this lot.

Rubbing his jaw Donald said it was certainly an interesting proposition but had Angus forgotten all his
experience was in the foundry?

It was fair comment and one Angus was pleased his
grandfather had made. What he wanted Donald on the
payroll for was Donald's expertise in handling men and
getting the best out of them. Any problems over the job
in hand and all Donald had to do was refer back to him.
He'd soon get on site and work it out. After all, Donald
was a practical man who'd worked with his hands all his
life. He didn't have to be a journeyman in a particular
field to know if a job was well or badly done. Common
sense and a craftsman's eye would tell him that.

Donald nodded. Taking out his smoker's knife he
busied himself cleaning the briar's bowl and while doing
so quietly asked about money.

Angus replied he'd pay his grandfather a pound more
per week than whatever Donald had been earning at
Armstrong's

Donald was completely taken aback by this generous
offer and for a second actually gawped. Pulling himself
together, he resumed cleaning his pipe. After a suitably
dignified time had elapsed he cleared his throat and said
he'd be happy to accept.

Angus said Donald could consider himself on pay as
from the following Monday although it would be a wee

while yet before actual work started.

Together the pair of them left the allotment. Donald walked very straight and with his head held high. Back at Tallon Street an excited Donald broke the good news he was a gaffer again.

Angus made it quite clear to his grandfather the job had a limited life span after which he couldn't promise anything.

Donald said he fully understood. Then he hurried away through to the hall cupboard to root out his boiler suit for Winnie to wash and get ready for when it was needed.

Out on the landing Winnie drew the door behind her and Angus. There was more than a hint of tears in her eyes. 'Thank you, son. God bless you!' she whispered. Then wiping her face with the hem of her pinny she retreated swiftly to the hall where a voluble Donald was demanding to know where in the name of the wee man his boiler suit was!

As he dove out to Muirend Angus reflected Donald was a gaffer *par excellence* and would see to it every man jack gave a full day's work for the full day's pay they'd be collecting. Furthermore, with Donald in charge, he could rest assured no materials would go for a walk nor would there be any other petty finaglings of that ilk. The money and time saved would more than cover his grandfather's wages.

Humming to himself he arrived at the dairy to find Hugh in the stables attending to the horses. He loved coming to the dairy for the marvellous memories it held for him.

Looking round it wasn't difficult to hear and see himself and Kitty as young lads. There was a choke in his throat when he congratulated Hugh on Janey expecting again.

They found Janey in the kitchen baking and the first thing Angus did was to sweep her into his arms and give her a big hug and kiss.

Hugh was jubilant he was to be a father again. He kept

saying this time it was sure to be a wee boy.

After ten minutes non-stop talking about the forth-coming baby Hugh was told to shush by Janey who said he was beginning to sound like a big jessie the way he was going on.

Hugh mumbled something about not being able to help how pleased he was. To change the subject he said a little defiantly he was regularly attending classes down at the chapel where he was doing just fine. The priest had told him only the other day if he continued at his present rate of assimilation it wouldn't be too long before he was eligible for confirmation into the Catholic church.

Screwtops were opened and while Hugh did the honours Janey said she'd had some worrying news about Thistle Street. One of her sisters had been over to say her mother and father were near beside themselves because of the rumours flying round that the entire area had been bought up and the new owners intended giving them all notice to quit.

There were a dozen conflicting stories about what was to happen once the rows of tenements were finally empty.

One said they were to be demolished and new private middle-class accommodation built in their stead, another that a huge works was to be constructed on the site. Yet another rumour was that a Corporation scheme was to be erected in which many of the former inhabi-tants were to be rehoused.

As to who'd been buying up the area there were as many candidates as there were rumours to support them.

Those who favoured the housing scheme idea natur-ally enough said it was the Glasgow Corporation while others were adamant it was a titled Englishman out to exploit Scotland the way his hated race had always done.

Those believing the works story insisted it was a con-sortium of Scottish businessmen, the most well known of whom was Sir Alan Armstrong. Angus's ears pricked up the moment Sir Alan's name was mentioned.

Janey went on to say her father was terrified of losing

his job. At his age and with the surplus of young man-power suddenly swamping the market as a result of thousands of demobbed soldiers looking for work, the chances were he would never get another job again.

Hugh's bonhomie and wellbeing gradually faded as he listened to all this. Much as he liked his in-laws he didn't particularly want them descending on him for what might turn out to be an indefinite period. He chided himself for the unworthy thought. Nonetheless it was how he felt.

Angus decided he was going to have to have Armstrong's rumoured involvement in the Gorbal's investigated. Anything Armstrong had his snout into interested him.

As it happened he already had a private investigator called Otis Bitu under hire. When he next saw Bitu he would ask him to take on this new assignment.

They spoke about the McIvers possible predicament a little while longer, then Angus excused himself, saying it was high time he went.

Motoring up the drive he decided on impulse to visit Carrie's grave which was close by.

Having parked the car, he walked down an incline past row upon row of graves until he came to the one where Carrie and his father were buried.

The gold lettering recently scored into the marble headstone shone and glinted in the sun. The grave itself still had a freshly dug look about it.

To have come all the way from Australia only to miss her by a few hours! It was heartbreaking.

There had been little of Carrie's he'd wanted to hang onto: her wedding ring, the one his father had given her and not Archie's, several hand stitched pictures she'd done herself, and the tug-of-war medal his father had won against the City of Glasgow police.

What had been his other treasured possession, his father's wallet with the faded initials J.McB. on its front, was at the bottom of the sea, having gone down with the *Almuria*.

All in all not a lot to be the only keepsakes he had of his parents, but for Angus they were enough.

Sir Alan Armstrong was being entertained by his mistress in the house he'd bought her in Partickhill.

Margaret Cunninghame was twenty-four years old, the same age as Rosemary, whom she'd been to school with. Margaret had been the other girl with Rosemary all those years ago when Angus and Kitty had saved the two Parkie lassies from the toughs in the Queen's Park reccy ground.

She was a tall woman with mouse brown hair, frightfully well spoken, and languid in all her movements.

She was a war widow. Her husband, an officer in the Scots Guards, had been blown to smithereens by a German landmine.

Her family were landed gentry, at least they had been until just before the war when everything they owned had disappeared into the open maw of the Glasgow stock market which her father had played addictively and badly.

As a result of her family's penury Margaret had married for money. But her husband had been killed before he'd come into his inheritance and, as she hadn't got on at all well with her in-laws who'd guessed her reason for marrying their son, she'd found herself more or less back to square one.

Being Sir Alan's mistress was a solution to her problem. It was an indolent life she led but then she was an indolent person. Her only worry was keeping Sir Alan happy when he visited her every Tuesday and Friday nights.

His permanent alibi was that he travelled through to Edinburgh on those nights to stay with friends with whom he conducted east coast business. And in case Cordelia ever decided to ring him there a plan had been worked out whereby his friends would say he was tied up and would ring her back. They would then contact him and he would ring her from the Partickhill house pretending he was speaking from Edinburgh.

The reason Sir Alan had taken a mistress was a quaint one: having made a great deal out of the war he had to think of new ways in which to spend and enjoy his money. The idea of a mistress had originated from one of his friends who'd let drop in conversation that a third party they both knew had installed a fancy lady in the West End.

Now Sir Alan's marriage was a happy one with which he was well pleased. Nonetheless the thought of another woman was an exciting one. So there and then he'd decided he too would have a mistress.

Propositioning Margaret had taken him ages and caused him much anxiety in case he was making a mistake as to the sort of person she was.

In the end it was Margaret, no fool at seeing what was in a man's mind and what his intentions were, who'd steered a conversation between them in such a way it had seemed the most natural thing in the world for him to suggest she became his mistress.

Later he'd wondered just who had propositioned whom?

Sir Alan sat back and gazed into his glass of whisky while through in the bedroom Margaret went about making down the bed. He reflected life had been extraordinarily good to him of late, thanks to the war.

Business in the works was falling away, of course, now the conflict had come to an end. But he'd diversified his capital into property. He positively swelled with pride and pleasure thinking of the amount of property he now owned. Nearly half a square mile belonged to him and soon it would be time for the tenements to be razed and the new constructions started.

The one fly in the ointment was there were still several streets eluding a Phoenix takeover.

With a smile of gratification he pictured the plans his architects had drawn up for the area. Once those bright, shiny houses were built they would radically alter the face of south Glasgow, at the same time earning Phoenix

Development Ltd a massive fortune.

The Gorbals would return to what it had been originally – an area where decent middle-class folk lived rather than the appalling, festering blot on the landscape it had degenerated into.

A frown creased his face at the thought of that pocket of resistance holding out on him. It was owned by a cantankerous old besom called Miss McCallum with whom he'd crossed swords in the past, and who, despite a number of most generous offers, steadfastly refused to sell.

Unfortunately the streets owned by her were situated slap bang in central Gorbals, occupying the prime site of the redevelopment area.

The one good thing was she was eighty-six years old with one foot in the grave from stomach cancer. It was thought she wouldn't last out the year.

Once she died he intended stepping in and buying her properties from her next of kin, a nephew in Inverness whom he'd ensure would be only too happy to sell.

The Gorbals! A name as hard as the people currently living there. Well, he was going to arrange it so the name was eradicated forever. It would become a mere historical reference.

Hutchesontown was the correct name for the district and the one he intended it to be known as in the future.

Leaving John and Dawn in the excellent rented accommodation, a house in Barrhead the solicitors had acquired for them, Angus drove into town to Otis Bitu's office. He rather liked Bitu, tiny, dark-haired, swarthy American of Middle European ancestry.

Otis Bitu had come to Scotland as a flyer with the United States Air Force and had married a Scots lassie by the name of Morag. Tall as he was short he worshipped her as though she was a goddess come to earth.

When Morag had announced at the end of the war she had absolutely no intention of leaving Glasgow – she wanted to stay near her Mammy – he'd seen no alternative to remaining behind while the rest of his comrades went home.

Born and bred in Lansing, Michigan, he'd done well for several years until being drafted.

Finding himself a civilian again and unable to practise his profession in Scotland, he'd elected to work as a private investigator for the simple reason it was a crazy sort of job which suited him down to the ground.

He enjoyed getting out and about and meeting people from all walks of life, finding it a sort of balm after the rigours of war.

It was through having performed some minor services for the Central Station Hotel that he'd come to be recommended to Angus. For here Angus had stayed on his return from Australia.

Angus knocked on Bitu's office door, letting himself in when Bitu called out the door was open. Bitu was on the phone and gestured he sit in the visitor's chair. Cradling the phone, Bitu launched into a verbal report outlining the results of his investigations on Angus's behalf.

To begin with he'd gone to the address Angus had given him down by the Govan Docks where he'd found the house still inhabited by prostitutes. But none of them had ever heard of Sheena Marjoribanks.

In a local shebeen where only red biddy –a lethal concoction of rough red wine and meths – was served he'd come across a played out brass called Wild Irish Maeve who for the price of a Parazone bottle filled with the nightmare mixture told him Sheena had left the Govan address to move to the Gallowgate.

Again it had been doing the rounds, asking in shops, speaking with the local police.

He'd come up with another address which had taken him out to Pollokshaws where he'd learned Sheena had moved on to Egypt, an area between Shettleston and Tollcross.

In Egypt he'd discovered Sheena had flitted yet again, this time to the centre of town because she'd landed a job as a barmaid in a boozer called the Capitol Bar.

Angus had never actually been in the Capitol Bar but knew it had a reputation as being a place where a lot of hard men drank. At least that's what it had been like before the war.

Angus was pleased with Bitu and said so. Producing his cheque book, he wrote out the balance of the American's fee, adding a tenner because he appreciated a task well done.

Handing over the cheque, he asked if Bitu would be interested in doing another job for him?

Bitu was only too happy to oblige and hurriedly got out some scrap paper and a pen to take down the details.

Leaving Bitu's office, Angus drove up Sauchiehall Street to just before Charing Cross where he turned off left.

The Capitol Bar was grimy outside but then so was nearly all of central Glasgow. He parked the car and went inside to discover there was an upstairs and downstairs bar. Sheena was in neither.

Thinking she might appear at any time he stayed in the downstairs bar and ordered a pint of heavy. He could have asked for Sheena but didn't want to, preferring to give her a surprise. When at the end of an hour she still hadn't put in an appearance he decided to leave it and return later.

After the evening meal he drove back to the Capitol Bar which was packed.

Downstairs he found an arty crafty crew far different to the hard men he'd been expecting. The clientele had been so sparse in the morning it had been difficult to judge what sort now frequented the place.

He squeezed past two young lads talking about Cubism and sidled up to the bar.

She was dressed entirely in black and standing directly facing him pulling a pint. As she lifted the pint onto the bar she looked straight into his eyes. As she did so her own eyes filled with amazement, then pleasure.

'Another pint of that when you're ready,' he smiled.

When she took his money their hands briefly touched.

She nodded as if to say it was as though he'd never been away.

Handing him his change, she whispered, 'Can you hang on until we're closed?'

He replied that he could. So she added if he'd wait for her outside the front door she'd meet him there.

At a quarter past nine the doors to the pub opened and she slipped out. Without any hesitancy she came into his arms and he held her close.

'A long time, Angus,' she said.

'It is that,' he replied. 'Did you know Carrie's dead?'

She stiffened and then pulled herself away from him. Slowly she shook her head.

There was far too much to talk about standing out in the road like this so he asked her if there was somewhere close by where they could go? She replied she had a wee place only a few streets away.

The room was a large kitchen with a box bed tucked away at the far end. It was neat and tidy and shone like a new pin.

While she hung up her hat and coat Angus sat and studied his step-sister. She was certainly older looking with a few splashes of grey in her hair. She was carrying a little more matronly weight than he remembered. And the stamp of a terrible loneliness was on her.

She produced a bottle of gin from which she poured two generous measures into tumblers. They drank it neat because she had no mix.

Missing nothing out he told her all that had befallen him since they'd last been together.

After he'd finished they sat for a few minutes in silence. Then he prompted her to tell him what had happened to her during the long years of separation.

At first she was reluctant. But he got round her with a bit of coaxing and slowly she began telling him her tale.

She'd remained on the game for quite a while after he'd gone to sea until getting an awful scare by coming down with a bad dose of VD.

The cure had been excruciatingly painful but had

brought her to her senses. When she was discharged
from hospital she'd gone looking for a straight job,
ending up as a conductress on the trams again.

For a time there had been a man. Then one day he just
wasn't around any more and she'd had to accept he'd
gone for good.

The funny thing was she hadn't been sleeping with
him, having insisted they wait until after they were
married. What she'd wanted more than anything was his
respect.

She could only think he'd disappeared out of her life
because he'd got fed up being denied sex or else had
somehow found out about her past. She was inclined to
think it was the latter.

'If you're interested I'd like you to be John's nanny,'
Angus said. 'That's been in my mind since I knew I was
coming home and Dawn who looks after him now, wants
to go travelling.'

'Look after your wee boy?' Sheena said, her voice
cracking with emotion.

'Would you like that?'

'Oh yes,' she whispered. 'You know damn well I
would.'

'Then it's settled. When can you start?'

'I've got to give forty-eight hours notice at the pub. I
wouldn't run out and leave them, you understand.
They've been decent to me.'

Angus nodded. He would've expected nothing less.

There were tears in Sheena's eyes as they made the
arrangements. She would overlap with Dawn for a week
and then Dawn would be free to start her tour of Europe.

Later, when Angus had gone, Sheena went to bed
taking the remains of the gin with her. And there she
cried her eyes out. Thanking God time and time again
for this new chance.

In the morning she felt a woman reborn.

Donald stood with his arms akimbo staring up at
Craiglea – the name of the Newton Mearns house –

which now belonged to Angus. It was a handsome place albeit in his estimation a wee bit dark and forbidding.

He couldn't help but be filled with pride to think *his* grandson was the owner of such a fine mansion. My God, it was a far cry from the hovel he'd been born into in Invershuie or the one Winnie had first seen the light of day in in Fanagmore!

The family had come a long way in three generations. There was Angus with his grand Newton Mearns mansion and his Australian bauxite mine. And Hugh the owner of a prosperous dairy as well as an equally thriving farm out on the East Kilbride road.

Mind you, Hugh had been enormously lucky in having Greta Paterson leave him the dairy and farm but that didn't detract one whit from the achievement. After all, Hugh had grafted damn hard to get in her good books in the first place and Greta had left him what she had knowing full well he'd make a go of it.

He'd come to think an awful lot of his son these past few years although it still pained him greatly that Hugh had married a Catholic and even worse, was in the process of turning one himself.

Not that he could fault Janey on anything bar her religion. Apart from that flaw he couldn't have asked for a better daughter-in-law.

With regards to Angus, it saddened him enormously that Angus's marriage had folded, and so quickly too. The poor boy's mother had gone through so much in that department you would've thought he'd be spared similar problems.

Donald was inordinately proud of what Angus and Hugh had achieved but there was another side of him that was highly suspicious of the way in which they seemed to be joining the capitalist classes.

He still considered it wrong and grossly immoral for individuals to be so well off when countless others in the world were either starving or else barely getting by on subsistence level. In Britain, at least, with a Labour government under Clem Attlee in power, the future looked good and getting better all the time for the working classes. He firmly believed the corner had been turned and what the country was now witnessing was the dawn of a glorious socialist age.

In the meantime he had a job to get on with – and the irony wasn't lost on him – thanks to his capitalist grandson.

He made his way across to where the first of the workmen he'd hired were waiting to be told what to do.

20

Angus was whistling as he parked his car and ran up the stairs leading to Bitu's office, where he found the American primed and ready for him.

Bitu said his inquiries about the Gorbals had thrown up the name Phoenix. He'd gone to London where he'd spent an entire day in Companies House in the City Road where a record is kept of every company formed in Britain. Eventually he'd turned up a company called Phoenix Development Ltd which had two directors, Sir Alan Armstrong and Sir Hamilton McLaren. Between them these two gentlemen now owned nearly all of the Gorbals.

Angus nodded his satisfaction. Bitu had again done well. The question now was what did Sir Alan and Sir Hamilton – whom he knew to be Rosemary's father-in-law which made it even more interesting – propose doing with the properties they'd acquired?

Bitu's new brief was to find out precisely what these

proposed plans were. It seemed a safe bet to assume something had to be in the wind to account for the many rumours currently flying round the area.

They shook hands at the door as Bitu promised to be in touch as soon as he'd come up with something.

Back on the street Angus walked round the corner to a little coffee shop he'd fallen into the habit of frequenting at this time of day when he'd been living at the hotel.

The coffee shop was in the rear of a barber's and was extremely masculine. It was mainly patronized by businessmen who in their pin-striped suits and starched collars blended in perfectly with the wood-panelled decor and faded genteel atmosphere.

He was surprised to see a woman sitting alone at a table. Even a woman in the company of a man would've been unusual as it was just not that sort of establishment. He was even further surprised when she smiled at him.

For a moment he thought she was a high class tart. Then with a start he realized he recognized the face.

'Hello Angus,' she said, extending her hand to be shaken.

She'd changed a lot since they'd last met but then so had he. 'Hello Diane,' he replied. And having sat, he waved to the hovering waiter to bring coffee for him and a refill for her.

They smiled and stared at one another. Finally Diane said, 'I heard on the grapevine you'd bought Craiglea so I went out there this morning hoping to see you but met your grandfather instead. He told me if I was to come here at around this time I might well run into you.'

Angus raised an eyebrow. 'Does Grandpa know who you are?'

'Oh yes. He's seen me many times in the past.'

Angus wondered about Donald knowing he frequented this particular coffee shop. He couldn't remember ever having mentioned the fact to his grandfather. But then that was Donald all over, always full of surprises.

Her voice suddenly betraying her eagerness, Diane

asked if Kitty had returned to Glasgow with Angus and, if so, how was he?

'Kitty's dead,' Angus replied and watched her face crumple in on itself. She and Kitty had been extremely fond of one another.

Angus had always presumed the Armstrong girls would have found out he and Kitty had gone off to sea, but apparently not.

Starting with the *Almuria* he spoke briefly of what had befallen them up to the point where Kitty had died from eating poisoned pickles aboard the *Wahroonga*.

'My God!' said Diane, shocked at the absurdity of Kitty's death.

Angus could hold his own question back no longer. Affecting a nonchalent attitude he asked, 'How's Rosie?' adding what he hoped appeared as an after-thought, 'Didn't I hear or read somewhere she'd got married?'

'She's fine, And yes she is.'

Angus lowered his head and sipped his coffee. He didn't want Diane to see his face.

Diane knew only too well she'd been manipulated by her sister into this meeting. Rosemary's intention was that while Diane was inquiring about Kitty she'd also find out the answer to the question tormenting Rose-mary all these years: namely, why had Angus run off and left her the way he had? Without frills or preliminaries Diane now put it to him point blank.

Angus blinked and sat back in his chair. That Diane had needed to ask the question gave him a great jolt.

He remembered the intense anger and wounded pride he'd felt that day in the Old Castle Road when he'd witnessed Rosemary kissing the man later to become her husband, and whom he'd presumed ever since she'd been two timing him with.

And yet staring into Diane's frank, open face the first suspicions of doubt began to niggle him. If what he'd believed was true all these years then why was Diane demanding an explanation from him as though *he* were the guilty one?

He knew then he was going to have to tell Diane his side of the story. He started with the episode of the cuff links.

As his tale unfolded Diane's reactions couldn't have been more genuine. Disbelief was followed by incredulity which in turn gave way to anger.

In a voice cold as winter she said her father would never have done such an underhand trick and he must be mistaken!

But Angus continued describing how feeling wretched and completely distraught he'd gone to Arnprior House only to witness Rosemary and Iain McLaren kissing in a way that could hardly be described as platonic. It hadn't been difficult to put two and two together.

Diane's face creased in a frown as she searched her memory. As for the reason behind the kissing she couldn't say. But she was certain Rosemary and Iain hadn't been involved at that point.

They sat in silence for a while, accusation and denial having given them both a great deal to think about.

Finally Diane said she would do her best to get to the root of all this and when she'd done so she'd contact Angus again and tell him of her findings.

Then by mutual consent they changed the subject.

For a while Diane talked of herself and what she'd done during the war. Then she tried to pump Angus as to how he'd come by enough money to be able to afford a house the size of Craiglea.

He skilfully parried all her questions with vague answers. For the time being he didn't want any of the Armstrongs, even friendly ones, knowing how wealthy he'd become.

They said goodbye on the street corner.

Diane was nearly a block away when, like a bolt from the blue, it came to her her father did indeed own a pair of cuff links horribly similar to the ones Angus had described.

Furthermore, unless her memory was playing her

false, they'd been a present to him from her mother the very Christmas before the January during which Angus and Kitty disappeared.

She would go straight to Rosemary's to relate everything Angus had told her.

Sir Alan knew the moment he walked into the room and saw Rosemary's face something was dreadfully wrong.

When he asked her if she'd care to join him in a drink she didn't reply, instead holding out her right hand on the palm of which lay two small objects.

Intrigued, he came closer until he could make out what they were. When he recognized them he knew immediately what this was all about.

'Well?' she snapped, her eyes flashing cold fire.

'How did you find out?'

'So it's true,' she said.

He shrugged and busied himself at the decanter. Almost casually he said, 'It was for your own good, lass. McBain was a nothing, a nobody. And you after all are *my* daughter.'

She'd realized long ago he'd manipulated her into marriage with Iain but she'd always believed he'd merely capitalized on Angus's disappearance. It had never crossed her mind he'd engineered that disappearance.

Bile churned in her stomach and it took every ounce of self control she possessed not to fly at her father and rake him with her nails.

Through the open window she could see the very spot where Iain had parked Sir Hamilton's car that fatal day she'd kissed him as Angus had looked on.

If only Angus had come to her she could've explained. Instead he'd run away to sea and out of her life.

Her hand whipped in a savage sideways motion to send the cufflinks sailing out the window to fall somewhere in the garden.

Without another word she walked stiffly from the room.

She was halfway home when the dam broke and her

pent up emotions overflowed in a flood of hot, salty tears.

Iain banked the Tiger Moth and brought her onto a course that would take him directly over Stirling Castle. The plane was a recent acquisition he'd been lucky enough to snap up at a bargain price.

The sky was duck egg blue with clumps of cumulus moving at between 4000 and 5000 feet. He was flying at 3000 so the cloud wouldn't interfere with the splended panoramic view spread below him.

He tried to get up as often as he could for only in the air did he feel whole again and at peace. In the confines of the cockpit he could forget about his face for a little while.

If it had been possible for him to remain airborne for the rest of his life he would've elected to do so. His only regret would have been losing Rosemary who was his strength and whose very strength he found so comforting.

Once over Stirling he executed a wide turn, bringing him onto a south-westerly course that would take him back to the small aerodrome in Renfrew where he kept the plane.

It was worrying him that Armstrong was insisting they start demolition work in the Gorbals as soon as possible, albeit they hadn't yet been able to acquire Miss McCallum's properties.

He wasn't at all convinced starting work at this juncture was wise. He much preferred the prudence of actually waiting till the old woman was dead and Phoenix actually owned her properties.

It also bothered him how obsessive Armstrong was becoming over this particular project.

As a means of self-preservation he'd learned to be extremely chary about this type of subjectivity while in the RAF. Fanatics might make excellent Kamikaze pilots but were hardly the best co-pilots when you yourself weren't interested in becoming part of the Divine Wind.

If only he'd been able to turn to his father for advice. But Sir Hamilton absolutely refused to discuss business, declaring that side of things to be his responsibility now.

He considered his father's attitude a great pity as there was so much he could have learned, and indeed desperately needed to learn, from Sir Hamilton, whom Iain was convinced wasn't long for this world.

During the war he'd become sickeningly familiar with the peculiar aura exuded by many people who have an approaching rendezvous with death. His father had been exuding that aura for months now.

When Otis Bitu met up with Angus some weeks after being instructed to find out what Phoenix Development Ltd had planned it was to report failure.

Try as he might, he just hadn't been able to uncover what Sir Alan Armstrong and Iain McLaren – whom he'd established was acting on behalf of Sir Hamilton McLaren – intended for the Gorbals

Demolition had already started near Ballater Street where a great many families had been evicted and a sizable area razed in the short time the bulldozers and wrecking crews had been at work.

Bitu went on to say he'd even gone as far as making inquiries of the Clerk of the Dean of Guild Court. But according to that worthy, Phoenix hadn't yet submitted plans for re-development.

While Angus digested this Bitu coughed and, looking vaguely embarrassed, shifted several times in his seat.

When asked by Angus what was on his mind he replied he'd accidentally stumbled across a piece of information which if Angus cared to exploit it might just be the key to solving the problem.

Prompted by Angus to continue he went on to say he'd discovered Sir Alan's chief accountant, a man called George Hetherington, was deeply in debt to a bookie by the name of Joe Field.

Angus grinned to hear Hetherington, whom he remembered well, had taken to playing the gee gees. A dry stick of a man, Hetherington always gave the appearance of being the very epitomy of self-righteous presbyterianism. It seemed Hetherington wasn't such a dry stick after all.

It was a few minutes past eight pm when Angus knocked on the door of Hetherington's house in the smart district of Clarkston, not all that far from Muirend where Hugh and Janey lived.

Hetherington himself answered the door and asked in a not particularly friendly manner what Angus wanted.

It was plain Hetherington didn't recognize him so he introduced himself and asked if he could come in as he had a business matter to discuss.

Hetherington was startled to find out who Angus was and after a moment's hesitation started closing the door in Angus's face.

He exclaimed in surprise and annoyance when Angus first jammed his foot in the door, then leant heavily against it. Smiling softly, Angus told Hetherington he wasn't being very polite towards someone who'd come to do him a good turn.

Extremely agitated, Hetherington wasn't at all sure what to do next. Finally he decided prudence was the better part of valour and with bad grace invited Angus through to the parlour where they could discuss whatever it was Angus had in mind.

Angus had already been to see Joe Field – spinning him a yarn that had opened the bookie's mouth – to get the facts and figures right. So he came straight to the point.

'How would you like to earn £419?' he asked.

Hetherington gulped and had to hold onto a chair for support. The figure was too precise for there to be any mistake.

In a trembling voice he asked how Angus had found out about his gambling debts and what Angus intended doing about it? Both he and Angus knew if this came to

Sir Alan's attention he'd be sacked immediately.

Before Angus could reply the door opened and Mrs Hetherington entered. She was a kindly looking soul although shockingly thin with a positively haggard face. She was the sort who is always cheery with never a bad word to say about anyone. Angus warmed to her right away and wondered how she'd got tied to such a dreich colourless man as her husband was.

Seeing Hetherington wasn't going to do the honours, Angus introduced himself and shook Mrs Hetherington by the hand.

She was taking her leave to put the kettle on when she started to cough and wheeze simultaneously, causing her to stop and bend over in an effort to catch her breath.

Straightening up again she said to Angus it was just a wee dry tickle she had in her throat. Throwing him a beaming smile, she hurried away through to the kitchen.

Angus sat unbidden facing the accountant and while Hetherington stared concernedly after Mrs Hetherington he went over what he'd learned from Donald that afternoon regarding the man.

During the many years he'd been with Armstrong's Hetherington had made a name for himself as being highly conscientious and exceptional at his job. He thrived on anything to do with figures, having a natural understanding of money matters and all their various facets.

He also had a shrewd head on his shoulders and was often consulted personally by Sir Alan. And more often than not his advice was acted upon.

As chief accountant he was naturally in charge of the Armstrong books. What Angus was hoping was that he was also in charge of the Phoenix ones, or at least privy to their contents.

Hetherington slowly brought his attention back to bear on Angus. As he did so guilt and apprehension crept over his face.

Licking his lips, he asked what Angus intended doing,

adding dourly that if it was money Angus was after then Angus was out of luck as he didn't have any.

Angus shook his head. On the contrary he was hoping to give Hetherington some in exchange for a little information.

Hetherington was clearly puzzled and asked how an ex-apprentice fitter could afford to hand over the sort of money he was in debt to the tune of? Unless, of course, Angus was working for someone else, in which case who?

Angus replied he was working for no one but himself. When he saw Hetherington didn't believe him he crossed to the telephone and gave the operator the number which would connect him with the solicitor who'd handled the purchase of Craiglea for him.

When the man came on the line Angus told him what was required. Then gesturing Hetherington over, he left it to the solicitor to confirm his financial *bona fides*.

Hetherington returned to his chair to admit grudgingly it would seem Angus was now a man of considerable means.

Angus wrote out a cheque for £419.00 which he passed over to Hetherington. He wanted the accountant to hold his salvation in his hands for the psychological effect it would have on him.

The door opened and Mrs Hetherington wheeled in a trolley overflowing with goodies. She helped Angus and her husband to what they wanted and was about to help herself when Hetherington said gruffly he wanted to be alone with Angus.

Without a word of argument or dissent Mrs Hetherington left the room. Hetherington stared after his wife. There was something very poignant and touching in his expression which impressed Angus.

Hetherington's gaze dropped to the cheque still clutched in his hands.

Angus smiled and said for reasons of his own he wanted a friend – Hetherington winced at the euphemism – in Sir Alan Armstrong's camp and was willing to pay handsomely for the service.

If Hetherington agreed the £419 would only be a down payment with regular monthly sums to follow.

When Angus mentioned the sum of fifty pounds Hetherington looked startled for a second, then quickly nodded.

There was something wrong here. Angus could feel it. Although having little choice in the matter of capitulation Hetherington, for the man of honour and integrity Donald assured him he was, had done so too easily. That bothered Angus so before putting his question about the Gorbals he demanded to know why it was so?

Hetherington took so long in replying that Angus was beginning to think he wasn't going to. But suddenly he started to speak in such a low voice that Angus had to strain to hear.

Hetherington said his wife had always been asthmatic but her condition had worsened drastically during the war years as a direct result of the prevailing conditions. Her asthma was now so bad that unless they could move to a warm climate within the next year her chances of surviving much beyond that were extremely slim.

As Hetherington spoke Angus felt awful about how he'd misjudged the man. He'd presumed Hetherington to be just another punter with gambling fever whereas the truth of the matter was it had been a frantic effort on Hetherington's part to try and raise the money to take Mrs Hetherington to the sort of climate the doctor said was necessary for her survival.

Angus asked if they owned the house, thinking they could have sold and raised capital that way. But the answer was no. Like the vast majority of Glaswegians the Hetheringtons rented.

What little savings they'd had had gone on financing his gambling venture which Hetherington had hoped and prayed would bring them in the sort of return to solve their problem.

It had been clutching at straws, of course. And Hetherington had come horribly unstuck when, after a short winning streak, he'd hit a seemingly non-stop losing one.

That left the obvious question. Why hadn't Hetherington gone to Sir Alan for the sort of money that would enable him to send Mrs Hetherington abroad while he remained behind until the loan was repaid?

Hetherington replied he had indeed approached Sir Alan only to be callously turned down. He thought Sir Alan considered him far too valuable an employee to lose which would've eventually happened had the loan been forthcoming.

As an afterthought, Hetherington added he'd actually considered embezzlement and would have committed it had he thought there was any possible chance of getting away with it. But there wasn't thanks to a checking system he himself had introduced.

Angus asked why Hetherington had elected to try Joe Field's when surely the Stock Exchange would have been a far more suitable hunting ground for a man of his abilities?

Hetherington's reply was that the Exchange was still very firm after the conditions imposed on it during the war. As such it would've been virtually impossible, in the relatively short time available to him, to turn his small amount of savings into the capital sum needed.

Angus now appreciated why the poor bugger had caved in so easily.

Much as Sir Alan prized Hetherington as an employee he would be forced to sack him, especially if Joe Field made the matter public as Field was threatening to do.

Besides, from Sir Alan's point of view Hetherington would now be untrustworthy. Not only would Hetherington be sacked but undoubtedly there would be no letter of recommendation – and how that brought back memories for Angus! – which would mean the middle-aged accountant would never work again.

Angus's proposal was this. He would advance Hetherington over and above the £419, one year's money which amounted to £600, enabling Mrs Hetherington to go abroad right away.

Hetherington was dumbfounded. He stared incredulously at Angus, hope dawning joyously in his eyes. 'Why?' he croaked.

Angus explained it was merely a case of each of them having something the other wanted; Hetherington money, himself access to Sir Alan's innermost financial secrets. It seemed stupid for them not to help one another to their mutual advantage.

There had been a time when Hetherington would've refused outright in the name of loyalty to have anything to do with such a deal. But Sir Alan had forfeited that loyalty in turning down his plea for a loan, and condemning his wife to an early grave.

Angus and Hetherington shook hands on the agreement. Then Hetherington told Angus everything he wanted to know about the Gorbals project.

En route home it came to Angus there were parts of Australia – although unfortunately not Queensland – ideal for Mrs Hetherington's condition. He would put it to Hetherington the next time they spoke that she go there.

It had been a fruitful night which had brought him one step closer to Sir Alan's jugular. He wasn't quite sure yet just how he was going to effect his revenge. But he was certain that he was on the right track.

The next morning Angus was up early and, having breakfasted alone, collected the mail from the postman as he made his way out to the car.

It was a beautiful day so he thoroughly enjoyed the run down to Largs on the Firth of Clyde's coastline.

Arriving in Largs he embarked on the P.S. *Jeanie Deans* for Rothesay on the Island of Bute.

Halfway across a sudden squall came up. Leaving the outdoor passenger deck, he made his way to the aft saloon where he settled himself amongst the rose pink furnishings and light oak woodwork.

Remembering the letters he'd stuffed in his pocket earlier, he pulled them out. It was the last letter which interested him most coming as it did from Diane Armstrong and suggesting they meet again in the same coffee shop where she'd previously waylaid him. She said she'd be there on the following day at the same time unless she heard from him – her telephone number was enclosed – to the contrary.

As she'd said she would contact him again when she'd investigated the allegations he'd made about her father, Angus was curious to hear what she had to say.

When the boat docked Angus drove ashore. He had to ask directions twice before he found the house he was looking for.

He knocked, knocked again, and then again.

He was on the point of turning away thinking there was no one at home when the door opened to reveal an ancient, gnarled crone with a crabbit face.

'Miss McCallum?'

'Aye, sonny. What do you want?'

Angus hated people who called him sonny in that patronizing way. Nonetheless he fixed a smile on his face and introduced himself, asking if he could come inside as he had some business to discuss.

Miss McCallum looked suspicious and it was only when she realized he had a car – he could only wonder what association that had in her mind! – she agreed to let him in.

The place stank appallingly which was hardly surprising considering the clart and general debris littered everywhere.

There were the remains of a multitude of meals now covered in a virulent looking fungus atop a table. The sink was stacked high with unwashed dishes. There was another load piled in a cracked and mottled basin under the open-faced sink stand.

From the state of the house's interior it wasn't difficult to believe it had been many years since a cleaning hand had been raised in anger against it.

The *piece de resistance* was a rabbit hutch complete with long-eared rabbits tucked away in the far corner of the living room.

Miss McCallum asked if he'd like a cup of tea which he hastily refused. She sat down in a threadbare armchair whose bottom was threatening to fall out. A grizzled scotty dog nuzzled at her feet until she picked it up and deposited it in her lap. Gently she stroked the animal.

Angus wasn't quite sure what he'd been expecting – probably some genteel old lady amid a quaint Victorian setting. Instead he was faced with someone who might have stepped straight out of the first scene of *Macbeth*.

Opening the conversation, he said he understood she'd been ill and in the circumstances had been surprised to learn she was still at home. Surely she would have been far more comfortable in a hospital?

Miss McCallum replied waspishly that might well be so but hospitals didn't take in dogs and she had no intention of leaving dear Bella here to fret and pine which the beast would do if the two of them were parted.

In a whisper she added – perhaps she thought Bella would overhear and understand – her wee friend was also getting near the end of her days. They chatted for a while about Bella.

Then Angus brought up the object of his visit. He was interested in purchasing the properties owned by Miss McCallum in the Gorbals and was prepared to make a generous offer for them.

Miss McCallum snorted, replying he was the second person who'd wanted to buy those houses in recent years, the other being a certain Sir Alan Armstrong whom she couldn't abide at any price, being a rude and horrid man.

Angus said he knew Sir Alan and stressed he and Armstrong were far from friends.

Suddenly and without warning Bella was sick all down Miss McCallum who exclaimed in sympathy. She explained Bella had been suffering from a gyppy tummy of late which she thought had been cleared.

Leaving Bella whining in the chair, Miss McCallum hurried to a cupboard to fetch a far from clean cloth.

Hating to see the animal in distress Angus crossed to it and stroked its head. Then Miss McCallum was back wiping away the sick and fussing over the stricken beast.

Angus recalled a conversation he'd once heard between some Australian associates, both of whom were mad keen on dogs. It included a tip for canine upset tummies which he told Miss McCallum about. The mixture was warm milk with a tablespoonful of bicarb of soda stirred into it.

Miss McCallum had never heard of this particular cure and decided to give it a try. Luckily she had both ingredients to hand.

When the mixture was ready it was placed in a saucer before Bella who after a tentative sniff and taste eagerly lapped it all up. The dog appeared a little eased after that, soon curling up and falling asleep.

Miss McCallum was full of Angus's cure and insisted he take a glass of sherry with her. The sherry was sickly sweet and cloying, the glass it was served in manky. Somehow he got it down.

Again he broached the subject of the Gorbals properties to be told although he was a nice young man who'd just done her a service she had absolutely no intention of selling.

She'd originally purchased these properties on the advice of her man of business, a Mr Tait, now deceased, who'd told her never to part with them under any circumstances as they were the best possible investment a body could have.

The more she talked about this Mr Tait, who came over as having the wisdom of Solomon and the business acumen of a Rothschild, the more it became obvious she'd been a wee bit in love with him.

She said she sympathized with Angus and would like to have helped him as opposed to Sir Alan who in his efforts to get her to sell had caused her severe harassment in the past. But what it all boiled down to was her

Mr Tait had sworn her to holding onto these properties for the fine investment they represented and the regular income they provided.

She was adamant. She would hold onto these properties until her death after which they would go to her only surviving relative, a nephew living up in Inverness.

Angus asked if she was sure the nephew wouldn't sell to Sir Alan? But she pooh-poohed the idea, saying she'd written to him a number of times making it quite clear he was to abide by her wishes in this matter.

Angus could see there was no use discussing the subject further. So having left Miss McCallum his rented Barrhead address with the instructions to contact him should she ever change her mind, he climbed into his car and returned to Rothesay Pier where he awaited the next boat to Largs.

He was bitterly disappointed for he'd seen this as the perfect opportunity to initiate an attack on Sir Alan. Still it would seem Armstrong was going to have enough problems to contend with if Miss McCallum's nephew kept faith with her wishes.

According to Hetherington Sir Alan was confidently expecting to pick up the properties at bargain prices once Miss McCallum was dead and the houses transferred into the nephew's name.

With massive initial investment already sunk into the project and demolition work under way it was going to be a terrible headache to Phoenix to discover things weren't going to quite fall out as they'd planned after all.

During his return trip to Glasgow Angus tried to be philosophical about his failure. Other ways of getting at Armstrong would present themselves. All he needed to do was recognize and grab hold of them when they did.

He suddenly burst out laughing at a thought which flashed through his mind. Wouldn't it have been marvellous to have knocked down Miss McCallum's properties and built a glue factory in their stead!

He would love to have seen Phoenix try and sell their middle-class houses with that little lot belching out the most noxious fumes right in their midst.

Mid-morning the next day at precisely the time Diane had stated in her letter Angus presented himself in the coffee shop.

He was halfway to the table where the solitary woman was sitting before he was able to glimpse her face. The moment he did so it was as though he'd been hit a sledge hammer blow in the solar plexus.

He stood by the table and they stared at one another. Angus drank in every well remembered feature of her face.

'Hello Rosie,' he said and sat.

A waiter approached and, seemingly from a long distance away, he heard himself ordering coffee and biscuits.

'I was very upset to hear about Kitty's death,' Rosemary said.

Nothing had changed between them. It was the same as it had always been, the same empathy, the same ease. They fitted.

Taking a deep breath he launched into the tale which ended with Kitty's death aboard the *Wahroonga*.

The impulse to touch her, to hold her, was almost overpowering.

When he finally concluded she was sad and withdrawn. She said she hoped he didn't mind her coming in Diane's place but she'd felt it only right she did.

Jesus, the smell of her was so good! Time had dulled his memory of it. He inhaled to let it wash through him.

Continuing, Rosemary said she'd challenged her father about the cuff link incident which he'd admitted to.

Angus grunted.

The entire affair had been a complete set-up to get rid of Angus and have her married to Iain McLaren.

'And the kiss?'

She smiled bitterly and said she had, indeed, kissed Iain McLaren that day. But not for the reasons Angus had thought.

The kiss had been a purely spontaneous action because she'd just talked Iain into taking her flying again. That was all it had been. She gave him her oath on it.

'Aye, well there we are then. We were both played for a right couple of mugs,' Angus said, his intense hatred for Sir Alan Armstrong deepening even further.

That Rosemary hadn't been two timing him was a relief on the one hand and galling on the other. If only he'd kept his head how differently things might have turned out! As it was, he'd played right into Armstrong's hands.

Rosemary said Diane had told her Angus had married an Australian girl from whom he was now divorced. And that he'd brought his boy back to Scotland with him who, from all accounts, was a right smasher.

Angus dug in his wallet for a snapshot he carried of himself and John. John was positively beaming into the camera: it would have been impossible to find a bonnier or more appealing wee laddie anywhere.

Rosemary smiled as she stared at the snap. But it was a smile belying the pain lancing through her. She couldn't help but think if only circumstances had been different this wee chap might well have been hers.

'I'm sorry about the divorce,' Rosemary said.

Angus shrugged. 'Just one of those things.'

'Are you over it?'

'Oh yes.' Then to change the subject Angus said, 'He's a good looking chap, your Iain. I hope you've had and continue to have a lot of happiness together.'

For a split second she thought he was sticking the knife in. Then she realized from his expression he genuinely didn't know about the tragedy that had befallen Iain.

She considered telling him and decided not to. The last thing she either needed or wanted was his sympathy.

They talked for a little while longer, each dragging the minutes out and hoping the other wasn't noticing.

Finally after four cups of coffee and being nearly awash they ran out of excuses for prolonging the meeting any further.

Angus paid and then ushered Rosemary outside where they stood blinking in the harsh sunlight. There were creases round her eyes and mouth he hadn't noticed inside. She too had aged.

She pecked him chastely on the cheek and, without further ado, turned and went.

His heart in his mouth, he watched her till she'd rounded a corner and disappeared from sight. He'd thought she might look back. But she hadn't.

He remembered then Otis Bitu kept a bottle in his office for emergencies. If feeling the way he was didn't constitute an emergency he was damned if he knew what did.

A few weeks later Angus received a letter date stamped Rothesay. It came from Miss McCallum.

Miss McCallum had given a great deal of thought to their conversation and as a consequence had written her nephew in Inverness ordering him to travel down and see her. The nephew had come hot foot only to find himself subjected to an immediate interrogation. Riddled with guilt, he'd soon confessed to having been approached recently by Sir Alan Armstrong's partner with whom he'd made a gentlemen's agreement regarding the Gorbals properties once they became his.

Miss McCallum had been furious and lambasted the poor unfortunate who in an effort to make her see his side of things had explained he wanted to expand the wee grocery shop he owned and if possible open up another. The income from the Gorbals properties, while steady, was low whereas what he wanted was a lump sum in his hand.

After thoroughly vilifying her nephew for planning to go against her wishes Miss McCallum dispatched him back to Inverness with a gigantic flea in his ear, threatening to leave everything to a charity for dogs should he have anything further to do with Phoenix Development Ltd.

The upshot of all this was Miss McCallum was more determined than ever Sir Alan wouldn't get his hands on her properties. The cheek of the man and his partner going behind her back like that!

So to spite Sir Alan and this Iain McLaren she'd decided to sell to Angus, the proceeds of which would go to her nephew whom she still had a soft spot for. And his wish for a lump sum would then be fulfilled.

Angus was delighted by this. It meant it was now possible for him to move against Armstrong and hit the man where it would hurt most – in the pocket.

This operation he would tie in with another, something he and O'Rourke had discussed at length and come to agreement on before he left Australia. A great deal of what LMBM was producing was being exported. The bulk of what was going abroad came to Britain.

What Angus and O'Rourke intended was for Angus to set up a UK office of LMBM to handle the importing of the bauxite ore and its distribution. With the various middle men cut out they reckoned the company's British profits would leap by as much as one hundred per cent.

Angus intended setting up the company office in Glasgow for two reasons. The first was that he would be the chief executive of that office and Glasgow was where he wanted to live. For the time being, though, he would remain anonymously in the background, not wanting Sir Alan to know he was the puppeteer pulling the strings. His second reason was that LMBM ore coming into Clydeside would be work for the Docks, his small contribution to the prolonged life of his beloved city's main artery.

What he needed now was a front man, a lieutenant who'd apparently be in charge but in reality be under his command. And he was convinced he'd found just such a man in Otis Bitu whom he was sure would grab at the opportunity as Bitu's private investigation line of work – outside what Angus was putting his way – wasn't proving too lucrative.

The idea of the glue factory came back to Angus

making him laugh out loud. Glue factory it would be!

21

Sir Alan Armstrong stared lovingly at the plans for the new Hutchesontown spread before him.

These plans had actually been ready for some time but he'd always managed to find some small additional improvement to suggest which necessitated sending them back to the architects for incorporation.

When he finally came to submit the plans to the Dean of Guild Court he wanted them perfect in every detail. He wanted to submit a work of art which would reflect on him personally.

He started slightly, then smiled benevolently as Margaret Cunninghame slid her arm round his waist.

She said she enjoyed seeing him this way when he was so obviously happy, but thought sometimes he derived more pleasure from these plans of his than he did from her company.

Breaking away, he crossed to a trolley laden with drinks and poured them each a stiff one.

Handing Margaret hers he told her to sit and he would try and explain what the Gorbals project meant to him.

The engineering works was his father's creation. Sir William had conceived and brought into being the works of which he was now owner.

Armstrong's might be his responsibility but it wasn't his brainchild. The Gorbals project was. The fact he was deriving enormous self satisfaction out of it was enough.

But there was a lot more to it than that.

By building this whole new housing redevelopment scheme he was leaving his personal mark on Glasgow. For the next hundred years or so there would be a great slice of the city owing its existence to him – his memorial so to speak.

Not that he wouldn't be making a huge profit out of the redevelopment. He would. But the money wasn't primarily what this was all about.

The project was going to be the pinnacle of his life – what he would be *remembered* for.

Angus discussed the matter thoroughly with Hetherington who'd advised him to exploit without further delay the fact Sir Alan hadn't yet lodged the plans for the redevelopment of the Gorbals with the Dean of Guild Court.

Angus had therefore instructed the same architect working on Craiglea to cannibalize a past design into one for an animal by-products factory.

The reason it was necessary for him to lodge his factory plan first was by doing so he would have precedence over anything coming after, even something on such a grand scale as Sir Alan's plans. The smaller wouldn't have been allowed to intrude on the larger had the larger already been established.

Speaking further with Hetherington, Angus had been able to establish that one member of the Dean of Guild Court if approached the right way – by which Hetherington meant the man took backhanders – could be persuaded to argue their case, more or less ensuring LMBM's factory plan won aproval.

Otis Bitu – who'd accepted the job and who to all intents and purposes was now the UK representative of LMBM (Pty) Ltd – had consequently approached a civil engineer called Graeme McAskill who'd agreed to give LMBM's case due consideratioon.

This was McAskill's way of saying he was waiting to see what was offered before committing himself. Bitu

had then suggested he and McAskill get together for a
few drinks to solidify the situation. McAskill readily
agreed.

McAskill's sweeteners usually came in the form of
hard cash. But Angus intended introducing another
element into the proceedings which he was convinced
would really win McAskill over to LMBM's cause.

Angus explained to Sheena what he needed and asked
if she could help? Sheena laughed and replied with her
contacts from the old days it was the easiest thing in the
world for her to arrange.

That Saturday night Bitu met McAskill in a pub. The
pair of them made their way to a hotel where Sheena and
a beautiful prostitute were waiting for them in the best
suite the hotel had to offer.

Janice was what is known in Glasgow as *a right
brammer*. She was petite with finely chiselled features
and a figure any movie actress would've been proud of.

Perhaps her most winning asset – bearing in mind
many middle-class Scots such as McAskill are most
impressed by this sort of thing though they deny it – was
her accent which was so refined as to be almost good
enough to pass for a southern English one.

One look at the gorgeous Janice and McAskill was
completely smitten. Glancing across at Bitu he was
tipped the wink he wasn't misreading the situation.

For appearances sake and to help matters along Bitu
had been paired with Sheena. But this was only a façade
for McAskill's benefit. Neither Bitu nor Sheena intending anything other than a few drinks and conversation.

McAskill wasn't a widely experienced man when it
came to women and Janice was something out of his
wildest dreams. She had tricks to her repertoire that left
him pop-eyed and gasping for more.

And more he got in abundance. When morning finally
came McAskill was a man who'd already tasted paradise.

After the women had left, Bitu handed McAskill a
wad of used fivers with the promise there would be more
plus another party with Janice as soon as LMBM's plan

for an animal by-products factory was given the go ahead.

As Bitu later reported to Angus, they could be certain McAskill would wax most eloquent on their behalf. Janice had seen to that.

The same night McAskill was being entertained, Hugh and Janey were wakened a little before midnight.

They lay in silence for a few minutes listening. Then they heard quite distinctly the chink of a foot knocking against a stone followed by the furtive whisper of voices.

Thinking burglars were paying them a call, Hugh swung out of bed and reached for his dressing gown.

In a whisper Janey asked if she should ring for the police?

Hugh replied he didn't think that necessary. He crept downstairs to the hall stand where a stout walking stick was kept. Grasping this, he stepped out into the night chill.

Again he heard voices, this time off in the direction of the dairy. Being as quiet and stealthy as he could he tip-toed towards them.

Suddenly a dozen or so figures erupted out of the darkness to go hurtling past. Although he managed several good swipes with his stick he failed to make contact with any of the ducking and weaving bodies.

Several of the figures turned in the driveway. It was evident they were teenage lads. They called out:

'Fenian bastards!'

'Left footed whoor!'

'Ya fuckin' turncoat!'

Hearing these vitriolic mouthings, Hugh knew with a sinking heart what this was all about. Taking a deep breath, he returned to the house, confident whoever those boys were they wouldn't return that night.

Janey was waiting for him at the top of the stairs to say Mary Agnes hadn't been disturbed.

They went back to bed where he told her what had been shouted at him downstairs.

Suddenly he was deathly afraid, not for himself but for

Janey, Mary Agnes and the unborn child.

Next morning they were up at their usual early hour.

When Hugh stepped outside what he saw stopped him dead in his tracks.

The sides of the house plus stables and dairy had all been daubed with various slogans in bright orange paint.

Catholics ya bass!

King Billy won at Benwater!

Remember the Boyne!

Clutching Mary Agnes to her bosom Janey came out to stand at Hugh's side. 'Holy Mary Mother of God!' she whispered.

Hugh felt sick. He'd secretly dreaded this happening.

The news of his defection to the Catholic church had finally come to the ears of those who weren't prepared to sit back and allow such a thing to happen without exacting some sort of revenge. The bully boys and wild element had become involved.

'Hugh?' Janey whispered. Leaning close and staring up into his face, she was remembering the terrible sights she'd witnessed in the Gorbals and elsewhere when the Green and Orange had clashed.

Men with faces shredded by razors. Others being carted away with hatchets embedded in various parts of their anatomies.

Quite clearly she recalled the awful picture of a man lying dead with a knife sticking out of his chest. Mindlessly drunk, the silly bugger had worn a bright blue suit and shouted 'Up the Gers!' at a dance where those present had been predominantly Catholic.

'Never mind, lass. It'll soon scrub off,' Hugh said. And giving her a squeeze he went in search of a bucket to fill with hot water. He wanted to erase as much of the daubings as possible before the milk boys came.

As he worked up a sweat scrubbing it came to him it would be a good idea to get a guard dog to let loose on the premises at night when they were all indoors.

He laughed suddenly thinking he would get a brute of an alsatian whom he would call King Billy.

Let those lads come back and he'd give them King Billy all right, a mouthful of slavering fangs where it would hurt like hell, in the arses of their trousers.

Whistling, he bent to his task, the situation not appearing nearly as black as it had done a few minutes previously.

King Billy! He couldn't wait to tell Janey.

Iain McLaren sat across from Rosemary in the drawing room of his parents' house. Upstairs with his mother and a specialist in attendance his father lay dying. According to the specialist it was doubtful if Sir Hamilton would last till morning.

He and Rosemary had been with Sir Hamilton for some hours but had broken their vigilance to come downstairs for a much needed cup of tea and smoke.

There was a knocking on the outside door which the butler answered. Sir Alan's voice filled the vestibule.

Sir Alan burst into the room with a face like fizz. He was about to launch into a tirade when, remembering the solemnity of the occasion, managed to keep himself under control long enough to ask what the up-to-date position on Sir Hamilton was?

Unable to contain himself any longer and not even making a pretence of listening to Iain's reply, he exploded with his news.

The old bitch Miss McCallum had gone and sold to some Australian firm who that very afternoon had been granted permission to build an animal by-products factory on the site where her properties now stood.

'A bloody glue factory!' he fumed.

Purple with rage, he stalked over to the whisky decanter and poured himself a large one.

Staring at the irate Sir Alan, Iain was filled with contempt for the man's insensitivity.

Sir Alan strode up and down the room furiously trying to think.

He would have to put in a bid to this LMBM (Pty) Ltd for the properties involved. Perhaps they would be understanding once he explained the situation to them. After all, there had to be a hundred places in Glasgow where such a factory could be sited without causing undue inconvenience.

What he could suggest was he give them the benefit of his local knowledge in their purchase of an alternative strip of land. Naturally he would ensure it was worth their while financially obliging him this way.

Coming up with a possible solution mollified him somewhat and whirling on the whisky decanter he poured himself another.

Turning back to Iain he began to explain what he had in mind only to be brought up short by Iain saying firmly no business would be discussed in this house that night.

Sir Alan had been somewhat dismissive of Iain in the past but hearing the steel now in Iain's voice caused him to pause and look at Iain afresh.

Part of the trouble was Iain's badly damaged face was so damned difficult to read because it so rarely betrayed the emotions behind it.

In a flash of insight Sir Alan realized there was far more to Iain McLaren than he had previously given him credit for.

Iain rose and stared at Sir Alan who was suddenly acutely aware their business relationship had just undergone a shift of emphasis.

Never again would he be able to ride roughshod over Iain who was on the brink of succeeding to the family title and, more importantly from his point of view, fortune. A large part of that fortune was pledged to the building of the Gorbals project.

Rosemary sat quietly amused by this silent interplay. It was a rare sight to see her father stopped dead in his tracks.

Sir Alan coughed, using that as an excuse to turn his eyes away from Iain.

He laid his glass beside the decanter. Then acting as though nothing had happened, declared he must be getting on his way as it was getting late and Cordelia would be worried.

At the door Sir Alan said if there was anything he could do Iain wasn't to hesitate getting in touch. But it was an offer he should've made on entering the house rather than on leaving.

Iain had just seen Sir Alan out when the specialist appeared at the top of the stairs. 'You'd better come quickly,' the specialist said.

Iain took the stairs two at a time with Rosemary coming up behind him as fast as she could. He was only a few feet away from his parents' bedroom when an agonized wail erupted from within.

They found Lize lying prostrate over her husband's body. She was weeping profusely, quite beside herself with grief.

Next morning tragedy struck the McLaren family afresh when Lize, the shock of losing her husband having proved too much for her, was discovered dead in bed.

Her face was in repose, a soft smile on her lips, as though she'd just seen someone she hadn't expected to see again so soon.

Angus wheeled his car in Craiglea's front drive. Switching the engine off, he sat back to listen to the cacophony of sound made by hammers and saws all going nineteen to the dozen.

It pleased him that within forty-eight hours of LMBM having been granted permission to build an animal by-products factory an approach had been made to Bitu by Phoenix Development Ltd.

Bitu's reply to the letter had been LMBM hadn't been aware of Phoenix's plans. But now these had been made known to them he was certain Mr O'Rourke, LMBM's head man in Australia, would view Phoenix's offer with sympathy.

This was a purely delaying tactic to allow Angus to come up with the next move.

Angus made a fist and gently bashed his thigh. Now he

knew what was niggling him.

All this was very well but where was it ultimately leading? Was he merely going to use the former McCallum properties to eventually extort a monstrous profit out of Armstrong or was there a way in which he could use this lever to hurt the man even more?

What he wanted was a gutting stroke – the infliction of maximum pain combined with maximum damage.

Suddenly what his goal should be came to him and the very rightness and irony of it caused him to exclaim. It should have been obvious to him all along!

It would be an incredibly difficult coup to pull off, and one that in the end might even prove impossible. Only Hetherington would know its feasibility so the sooner he saw the chief accountant the better.

Hetherington was full of the letter he'd received in the morning's post from his wife who'd arrived safely in Perth, Western Australia.

According to Mrs Hetherington her health had picked up almost immediately she crossed the equator. And now she had experienced the warm, dry Westralian climate she had no doubt it would improve her condition immensely.

Angus allowed Hetherington's excited chatter about Mrs Hetherington to run its course before sitting the man down and disclosing his idea.

Hetherington was dumbfounded. Then ever so slowly his face cracked into a grin and he began to laugh.

'You really do hate Sir Alan, don't you,' he said: it was a statement, not a question.

Angus thought of his father, dead without compensation; his mother married to that sadistic bastard, Archie Marjoribanks, and the life he and she had undergone as a consequence; and at last but hardly least, the incident with the cuff links which had cost him Rosemary.

'Yes, I hate him,' Angus replied grimly.

Hetherington wouldn't be rushed into giving an answer and insisted on making a pot of tea in order to give himself time to think.

Finally he said what Angus had in mind was possible if handled the right way and luck was on their side.

Armstrong's weakness lay in being short of ready capital, having only a fraction of the works' war profits left. The rest had been ploughed into buying up the Gorbals.

Some time ago Sir Alan had gone to the London Merchant Banks and various private financiers in the hope of raising building capital. Much to his consternation he'd been turned down flat by each and every one of them.

The general consensus of opinion had been the Gorbals project was not a viable one and could only be doomed to failure. None of them could believe with the terrible name the district had that middle-class people would ever be persuaded to live, far less buy private homes there.

Despite a great deal of correspondence and to-ing and fro-ing on Sir Alan's part, he'd been unable to make the money men change their minds. Rebuffed by London, Sir Alan's solution to his problem had been to approach Sir Hamilton McLaren – already involved in a minor way – and propose Sir Hamilton put up the money.

The Phoenix partnership had then been drawn up with each director having equal standing. Sir Alan's capital had bought the Gorbals. Sir Hamilton's would re-develop it.

Excited now, Hetherington leaned forward to say Sir Alan's dependency on the McLaren fortune was the key to his possible undoing. If one could somehow be separated from the other, Sir Alan would have to fall back on his own resources which would leave him with only three options.

The first was to abandon the project altogether and in time recoup his investment by selling off the Gorbals piecemeal. This Hetherington was convinced he wouldn't do as he was so committed to the project that as long as there was a way open for him to continue he would use it.

Apart from the Gorbals, Sir Alan's other major asset was the works on the River Cart and this he could raise money on by either mortgaging buildings and plant or else going public. These were his second and third.

In his privileged position as chief accountant Hetherington would be expected to give advice on the matter. He would strongly advise the latter which Sir Alan would undoubtedly plump for once it had been explained to him a greater amount of capital could be raised that way.

Angus asked why Sir Alan hadn't approached Sir Hamilton in the first place? Hetherington's reply was that Sir Alan had never wanted to share the glory of redeveloping the Gorbals: this he would be forced to do with another prominent Glaswegian in partnership with him.

Hetherington went on to say a detailed plan of action would be needed and this he'd get cracking on from the financial point of view. It was agreed they'd meet several days hence to discuss the matter further.

On an impulse Angus drove down to the Cart where he stopped, facing Armstrong's. Emerging from his car he crossed the road to stand by the iron railings over which he'd climbed to get to the river countless times as a boy.

Lines from an old street song he'd sung in his youth came suddenly to mind: 'I'm the king of the castle, and you're the dirty wee rascal!'

He glanced across to the brooding pile on the opposite bank – the king of that particular castle was about to discover just how dirty this ex-wee rascal could be.

And it wasn't hygiene he was referring to.

When Angus and Hetherington next met, the accountant had already drawn up rudimentary financial plans for Angus's eventual takeover of Armstrong's. These he would continue to work on.

In the meantime, phase one of their ultimate realization was to cause a breach between Iain McLaren and Sir Alan.

Angus had been thinking about the correspondence Sir Alan had conducted with the London Merchant Banks and private financiers. He was now able to verify from Hetherington that the contents of this correspondence had never been disclosed to Sir Hamilton either before or after Sir Hamilton had pledged McLaren money for the Gorbals project.

What Angus wondered was if Sir Iain (Iain having succeeded to the title) were to see that correspondence now would it persuade him to pull out of the Gorbals venture?

For a start, withholding vital information was hardly conducive to inspiring future trust within a partnership.

Secondly, London were certainly no fools when it came to matters of investment. So if it was their opinion the Gorbals project was a non-viable one that opinion just had to be given deep and careful consideration.

According to Hetherington this correspondence was kept in a locked filing cabinet in Sir Alan's office to which Sir Alan had the sole key.

Hetherington was in a position to remove this correspondence but for him to do so, and it subsequently turning up in Sir Iain's possession, would necessitate giving himself away. His future use to Angus within Armstrong's would be non-existent which was the last thing Angus wanted.

So Angus decided to call in an expert to acquire the correspondence for him. But before going into action he had a little ploy up his sleeve which would be the opening shot in his bid to sunder relations between Sir Iain and Sir Alan.

It was the morning of Sir Hamilton and Lize McLaren's funeral: Sir Alan was dressing to attend when he was informed there was an urgent telephone call for him.

Otis Bitu was on the line to say he'd received a telex only minutes previously informing him Mr O'Rourke was ringing through at eleven am and wanted to speak personally with Sir Alan about the former McCallum properties.

This put Sir Alan into a terrible quandary as he naturally wanted to settle the McCallum business – and from Bitu's tone he guessed it was going to be in his favour. On the other hand, it would be a dreadful insult to the McLarens if he was to turn up late for the funeral.

Bitu expressed sympathy with Sir Alan's position, then pointed out as the funeral service didn't start until twelve-thirty surely Sir Alan would have time to speak with Mr O'Rourke *and* attend the service?

Sir Alan was uncertain. Bitu said he could understand if Sir Alan didn't come into the office but O'Rourke might not.

The insinuation was crystal clear. Sir Alan assured Bitu he would be on his way shortly.

Angus was in the new LMBM office which Bitu had moved into listening to Bitu on the phone to Sir Alan. When Bitu hung up and turned to him with a smile he knew the bait had been swallowed.

As it would be a little while before Sir Alan arrived they lingered over a cup of coffee. Then Angus left the office to go across the road to where his car was parked. He settled back to wait the arrival of his adversary.

The Rolls Royce was different to the one he remembered. As Sir Alan climbed out of the Rolls he was afforded a clear view of the face he hated so much – the face he'd last seen the day he'd been framed for the supposed theft of the man's cuff links.

As Sir Alan disappeared into the building where the LMBM office was Angus got out of his car and crossed to the Rolls. It was a trick he'd learned as a lad, effective now as it had always been. He waited till the coast was clear. Then bending down to the nearside front tyre, he whipped the valve cap off and rammed a matchstick into the valve itself so it was jammed in the *on* position.

He did this with all four tyres, waiting a little way off

until the last one was flat. Hastily he removed the match-stick evidence before returning to his car.

When he was again settled in the driving seat a glance at his watch told him it was one minute to eleven.

At eleven am precisely Morag Bitu dialled her husband and, pretending to be the operator, said a call was coming through for LMBM on the radio link with Australia. It would be delayed for a few minutes due to trouble on the Australian side.

Bitu relayed this to Sir Alan and then urged him to tell him more about the alternative site for the animal by-products factory Sir Alan had discovered out in Polmadie.

Sir Alan went on at length praising the virtues of the site which in his estimation was ideal for LMBM's purposes.

Morag called again at eleven fifteen to say the call from Australia was still delayed but should be coming through any minute now. This an apologetic Bitu relayed to Sir Alan.

At eleven thirty Morag rang to say the call was on the line but due to appalling interference they were holding it for a few minutes more in the hope the interference would clear itself.

By now Sir Alan was becoming extremely agitated and kept glancing repeatedly at his gold hunter.

Bitu talked non-stop, pointing out again and again it would be ridiculous for Sir Alan to leave now and jeopardize the Phoenix position when Mr O'Rourke would no doubt be getting through at any moment.

Outside the next phase of the charade had appeared in the shape of a black cab whose driver Angus had sought out and bribed earlier. The driver would now wait a little way up the street until Angus tipped him the wink.

The minutes ticked by and as they did so Sir Alan became more and more frantic. When yet another look at his hunter told him it was noon he knew he was going to be late for the service.

And still Morag kept ringing to say the call was being

variously held or detained and should be coming through loud and clear directly. Finally at twelve fifteen she rang to say the Australian party had cancelled.

Sir Alan was apoplectic, Bitu full of apologies but argued that no fault could be attached to him for what had happened. The blame rested fairly and squarely with the telephone people.

At the door Sir Alan muttered hasty goodbyes, then went galloping downstairs intent on getting out to Carmunnock to join the other mourners who'd been invited back to the McLaren house.

The moment the Rolls started forward he knew something was wrong.

Bringing the car to a halt, he got out to examine the tyres thinking one of them had gone soft. When he saw all four were completely deflated he jibbered with anger.

Cued by Angus, the taxi moved forward to be hastily flagged down by a relieved Sir Alan. The taxi disappeared in the direction of Carmunnock – not that it was ever going to arrive there.

Once out of the city and at a rural spot previously agreed on, the driver would suddenly take ill and insist on dropping Sir Alan so he could return to Glasgow and his bed. From there, Sir Alan would have to walk a good two miles to the nearest public transport which was infrequent at the best of times and downright non-existent at others. It would be a miracle if he succeeded in reaching the McLaren house before the mourners dispersed.

Angus was well aware there were elements of farce about all this and it seemed more like a schoolboy prank than the action of one grown man against another. But there was a serious side to this apparent frivolity concerned directly with loss of face.

Even though Lady Armstrong had been present at the service and gathering after, the fact Sir Alan had elected to go off and attend a business meeting would be seen as a lack of respect for the deceased. Sir Iain couldn't fail but take offence.

Returning to the LMBM office, Angus found Bitu on the phone congratulating Morag on her successful excursion into amateur dramatics. Angus congratulated her also.

Hanging up, he announced what he needed now was a first class burglar and could Bitu please find him one?

The smile on the American's face changed fractionally to become a trifle strained. So far Bitu had done everything Angus requested with no questions asked. But now he thought it time to be told what all this was about.

Angus had been intending to confide in Bitu as more and more he was coming to think of him as a friend rather than employee. So he started at the beginning with his father's death.

In Angus's estimation Hetherington had done a brilliant job on the financial plans. If they worked as well in practice they would make him, as majority shareholder, head of Armstrong's.

This was going to take an enormous amount of capital so to ensure enough was available he'd approached the Bank of Scotland to arrange an advance set against his future earnings from LMBM which were guaranteed into the next century.

He'd also asked the Bank of Scotland to act on his behalf regarding a large number of shares he intended purchasing in the new year.

Besides the Bank of Scotland he'd also approached a number of other Scottish banks, none knowing about the other's consent to act on his behalf with regards to shares yet unbought, and all of them had agreed.

Another part of Hetherington's plan called for Angus to set up a construction company which Angus duly did, registering it under the name of Jocar Ltd whose directors were listed as D. Chisholm and W. Chisholm. Donald and Winnie had only reluctantly agreed – after Angus had pleaded with them, saying it was of vital importance to him to have people fronting the firm whom he could trust implicitly.

The name Jocar was a play on words as well as being a combination of parts of Angus's parents' Christian names, Jo/hn and Car/rie coming together to make Jocar. Angus's joke was to be at Sir Alan's expense.

As Angus intended they would never meet, he thought it highly unlikely Sir Alan would tumble to the fact D. Chisholm and W. Chisholm were his retired foreman moulder and wife.

Hetherington had explained to Angus in the first instance Sir Alan would no doubt retain fifty-one per cent of the shares issued, thereby giving him the majority holding. Jocar had been brought into existence to trick him deviously later into relinquishing this majority.

In the meantime there was still the business of engineering a split between Sir Iain and Sir Alan which the success of everything else depended on.

The man Bitu eventually found was called Shughie Reid who'd been a cat burglar all his life.

A layout of Armstrong's office and the exact location of the filing cabinet containing the correspondence was drawn by Hetherington.

To disguise the real motive behind the burglary Shughie was instructed to take other bits and pieces including the petty cash kept in Sir Alan's secretary's office.

One week after Bitu had first contacted Shughie Reid the burglary was successfully carried out and Bitu able to hand over the correspondence to Angus.

The correspondence verified everything Hetherington had said. London was unanimous in its opinion that the Gorbal's project was non-viable in its present form and could only turn out to be a white elephant.

Certainly if Angus himself had been considering investing money in the project this would have turned him completely against it. He could only hope it would have the same effect on Sir Iain McLaren.

* * *

The ball was being held in the home of the Duke of Renfrew, a stately mansion just outside the small village of Carmunnock.

Angus had received his invitation at Craiglea the previous week and after dithering over it had finally decided to attend. Now that he belonged to this strata of Glasgow society he might as well find out whether he liked it and vice versa.

The ball was on behalf of the area Conservative and Unionist Society. The night it fell on was Hallowe'en.

Angus parked his car amongst the Rollses, Bentleys and Armstrong-Siddeleys, then made his way to the front door and the liveried flunkey in attendance there.

Standing beside Iain with whom she'd had a terrible battle earlier on in order to get him to attend, Rosemary saw Angus the moment he entered the great hall. Although she continued making the correct responses to a couple talking to her and Iain, her eyes were riveted on Angus.

Sensitive to all his wife's moods, Iain noticed immediately the change in her focus of attention. When he was able to, he glanced swiftly across at the man she was staring at but failed to recognize him.

Diane Armstrong was talking to her mother and father when out of the corner of her eye she spied Angus. Initial surprise gave way to pleasure and, excusing herself, she crossed to where he was hovering on the periphery of a group who were talking about what a disaster it had been for Winnie to be defeated at the polls the previous year.

Angus was delighted to see someone he knew, greeting Diane warmly and affectionately. He was brought up short when she asked him if he'd spoken to Rosemary yet?

Just as he was shaking his head he caught sight of Rosemary and a man with a hideous face moving slowly in their direction.

He knew from Bitu's report – compiled since his meeting with Rosemary in the coffee shop – that Sir Iain had been disfigured in the war. But it was a shock to see just how hideous the actual disfigurement was. He couldn't help but feel sorry for the poor sod.

A few minutes later he sensed Rosemary intended to joining them and wondered if Sir Iain knew about him.

'Angus, what a pleasant surprise!'

The moment Iain heard Angus's name he knew why Rosemary had been showing such great interest in the man.

She believed he didn't know about her and Angus McBain but he did, having learned it from his brother Peter who'd wormed it out of Diane when she'd inadvertently let something drop one night during the early war years.

He'd made discreet inquiries and found out Angus McBain had vanished suddenly from Glasgow although for what reason he'd been unable to determine.

Since then he'd come to suspect Rosemary retained a great deal of feeling for McBain which hadn't bothered him unduly as McBain was safely out of the way and out of her life.

Only now McBain was back.

During the ensuing chat Angus turned to Sir Iain and said he understood Sir Iain was interested in flying?

Replying, Iain told Angus about the Tiger Moth he'd recently bought and what a joy she was to fly.

Throwing leading question after leading question, Angus encouraged Iain to talk about flying which he did with enormous keenness and passion.

Sir Iain was waxing lyrical about Mosquitoes which he'd flown during the war when he was interrupted by a new voice asking to join their circle.

Angus went ice cold inside. Glancing across at Rosemary he saw she was frowning sympathetically at him.

The muscles in his face were rigid as he turned towards Sir Alan and Lady Armstrong.

Sir Alan stared directly into Angus's face, his brow creasing in thought as he tried to place where he knew this young man from.

Unable to help herself, Rosemary smiled sweetly and said, 'Surely you remember Angus McBain father? You loaned him a pair of cuff links once.'

Inwardly Sir Alan cursed her for her impertinence. McBain! Where in God's name had *he* come from!

The atmosphere between Angus and Sir Alan was almost a static crackle. They were like two fighting dogs suddenly come face to face in an alley.

It was Sir Iain who saved the explosive situation from erupting altogether. His scarred and mangled face lit up in a gruesome smile as he asked Diane for the pleasure of the next dance. Casually he suggested Angus might like to take the floor with Rosemary.

The ferocity of the looks Angus and her father were exchanging sent shivers racing up and down Rosemary's spine. Hurriedly she took Angus by the arm and steered him in the direction of the dance floor

The arm in hers was like a steel pole.

Later that night as Rosemary sat brushing her hair in front of her dressing table Iain approached her from behind to put his hands on her shoulders.

'Tell me about the cuff links?' he asked.

She started but swiftly recovered her composure. Shrugging, she said it was something that had happened a long time ago and wasn't worth talking about now.

'I'd still like to know,' Iain said softly. Adding when he saw she intended to prevaricate, 'I know all about what went on between you and McBain if that's what's holding you back.'

This time she wasn't able to recover her composure. She was rattled and clearly looked it. 'How did you find out?' she whispered.

He told her. Then he asked again.

Rosemary nervously lit a cigarette. She had enormous affection for Iain and didn't want to hurt him in any way. But if he knew part of the story it was probably best he knew all.

Hoping she was doing the right thing she started at the beginning – the time Angus and Kitty had saved her and Margaret Cunninghame from the louts in Queen's Park Recreational Ground – and told him everything with the exception of having met up with Angus in the coffee shop. That and the fact she was still in love with Angus.

For Angus the night at the ball had proved constructive in one respect: he'd discovered just how passionate Sir Iain was about flying.

He therefore continued to hold on to the burgled correspondence while Bitu went on yet another quest for him.

Some LMBM business had come up which took Bitu to London anyway and while he was there he contacted a number of planemaking firms and flying organizations whom he enlisted to his aid.

It was finally through the Handley-Page people that he came to hear of a young man call John Muir who lived in Kilwinning, a small village in Ayrshire.

Like Sir Iain, Muir had been in the RAF during the war only instead of flying as Sir Iain had done he'd been one of the backroom boffins.

Since the war and working entirely on his own Muir had come up with a design for a revolutionary new passenger plane intended for the Middle and Far East runs. He'd tried every planemaker in Britain but his design had been turned down flat by all of them.

The simple reason for this was that money was desperately short in the planemaking world and what capital the planemakers had was already committed to schemes of their own.

According to Handley-Page who'd kept tabs on Muir he was now back in Kilwinning where he was contemplating going to America to see if they would buy his design.

What Angus had been looking for, and was sure he'd now found, was an alternative investment to the Gorbals project for Sir Iain. And where better to look for that potential investment than in the world of aeroplanes in which Sir Iain was so interested?

Janey was kneading dough when the pains started. She gasped and bent over the table till the first one had passed. Then very carefully she crossed to a chair and sat.

She gritted her teeth as the second searing pain tore at her insides. When that pain had passed away she came to her feet and stumbled to the door and out into the front yard. There was no need to worry about Mary Agnes for the moment. The wean wasn't long down for her sleep.

Hugh was in the stables mucking out.

Yet another pain exploded in her. As she lurched into his arms her fingers dug deeply into his flesh.

'It's coming!' she whimpered.

She was a hefty lump but Hugh would've managed had she been twice the weight. Staggering, he carried her back to the house and up to their bedroom where he laid her on top of the bed.

He flew down the stairs to the telephone and rang Dr Robertson's surgery to be informed by the receptionist the doctor was out doing house calls but should be ringing in soon.

His second call was to a neighbour in Tallon Street who'd go and tell Winnie that Janey's labour had started and she was needed right away.

He was filled with a curious combination of fear and elation as he raced back up the stairs to Janey. The baby was several weeks early.

Winnie and Dr Robertson arrived almost simultaneously to find Hugh with the situation well in hand. Mary Agnes was playing quite happily down in the kitchen on her own while Janey was sitting up in bed wearing a clean nightie and sipping a cup of tea between spasms.

Banished to the kitchen, Hugh strode up and down like the proverbial cat on a hot tin roof. Winnie told him to go back to work and she would give him a shout when there was news. But he would have none of her suggestion.

Suddenly he burst out he and Janey had agreed to call the baby Alexander after his dead brother providing it was a boy which of course it would be.

Winnie was most touched by this gesture and said it was a grand idea. She knew Donald would be pleased and said so.

Exactly six hours after the pains had started the baby was born without any complications.

When Dr Robertson handed it to Janey there were tears streaming down his face as a result of what he'd had to tell her after his examination of the wee one.

'I'll send Hugh to you,' Robertson said, turning in the doorway to add, 'I'm awful sorry, lass.'

The moment Hugh saw the doctor's face he knew something was wrong. 'Well?' he demanded, his voice suddenly harsh and ugly.

There were times Robertson hated being a doctor and this was one of them. 'Janey and your baby daughter are both well,' he said.

'A girl?' Hugh replied quickly and Robertson nodded affirmation.

Hugh was bitterly disappointed but consoled himself with the fact they could always try again and next time it was *bound* to be a boy.

As though reading Hugh's mind Robertson said unfortunately Janey wasn't going to be able to have any more children.

The he dropped the real bombshell. The wee girl was a mongol.

For a few seconds the whole world spun and the only thing Hugh was aware of were the doctor's pitying eyes.

'Oh, son!' said Winnie.

'I think you'd better away up and see Janey,' Robertson said. 'She needs you now.'

'Aye,' said Hugh.

He trudged up the stairs with shoulders hunched and head low. His face was grey and lined. He seemed to have aged a dozen years in the past few minutes.

He knew it was selfish but the thought running

through his mind was there would be no immortality for him after all.

'Why are you crying, Granny? Aren't you happy I've got a new babby sister?' Mary Agnes asked.

Winnie couldn't answer, the words sticking in her throat when she tried.

Dr Robertson let himself out.

John Muir wrote to Sir Iain McLaren who replied asking him to present himself at Carmunnock which Muir duly did.

They started talking mid-morning and became so involved in the conversation they missed lunch. Undoubtedly they'd have missed dinner as well had Rosemary not interrupted to demand their presence at table.

After dinner they disappeared back into Iain's study where they continued talking till well after midnight when Rosemary interrupted again to say Muir had better stay the night and that a bed had been made up for him.

Iain's conversation with Muir resumed over breakfast and continued through till late afternoon, at which time Iain suggested they go for a walk to clear their heads with a breath of fresh air.

On the return leg of this walk Iain thought to ask about the American Muir had mentioned in his letter who'd recommended Muir to contact him.

Muir explained the man had arrived at his door one day out of the blue with some knowledge of his design. To begin with he'd thought the man represented one of the American aero firms but it had transpired this wasn't the case.

The man had been extremely vague about just who and what he was. His one definite action was to recommend in the strongest terms that Muir contact Sir Iain McLaren whom the American was convinced would be interested in the design, perhaps even to the extent of financing its production.

Sir Iain was intrigued by this report and couldn't help but wonder who this mysterious American was who seemed to know so much about him.

Then he thought of the correspondence that had arrived anonymously through the post a few days previously regarding dealings Armstrong had conducted with London banks and financiers.

Suddenly he began to smell a rat. All this was too pat and far too coincidental.

Over a month had passed since the correspondence burgled from Sir Alan's safe had been mailed to Sir Iain. According to Hetherington there was as yet no sign of discord between these two worthies.

Angus was beginning to despair that his plan had failed and that he would have to find some other way of splitting the two Phoenix directors when suddenly his telephone rang one morning with Sir Iain on the line suggesting they meet.

Angus was taken aback by this invitation, but nonetheless agreed to do so the following afternoon.

Angus arrived dead on time to find Sir Iain waiting for him. They strolled for a little while in silence. Then Sir Iain's glittering, snake-like eyes swung slowly round to fix themselves on Angus's face.

They were cold as ice those eyes and made Angus wilt a little inside. In a voice as chilly as his gaze Sir Iain said he would be obliged if Angus would tell him just what in the hell Angus was up to?

The fact Sir Iain was accusing him meant the man knew something. But how much?

Angus phrased his reply in such a manner he neither pretended innocence nor committed himself in any way.

With a sigh, Sir Iain said he'd been able to prove conclusively that Otis Bitu of LMBM and the mysterious American who'd visited John Muir at Kilwinning were one and the same. And weren't Angus and Bitu often to be found in one another's company?

Furthermore, a cablegram to an Australian contact

had eventually resulted in this contact discovering that one of LMBM (Pty) Ltd's directors, who employed Bitu in Glasgow was one Angus McBain. And hadn't Angus recently returned from Australia?

Taking all this into consideration plus the fact LMBM owned the former McCallum properties which Phoenix Development Ltd were desperately after – not to mention some incriminating correspondence he'd received regarding his Phoenix partner whom Angus quite understandably hated – had led to the logical conclusion. Angus was the common denominator in all these events with the exception of the correspondence which Iain suspected Angus was also involved in but couldn't prove. Angus was up to something and would Angus please tell him precisely what that was?

Angus digested this, thinking his convoluted machinations had come to naught. Or had they?

He asked Sir Iain quickly if Sir Alan was aware of his connection with LMBM?

'Not as far as I know. I've certainly said nothing to him,' Sir Iain replied.

That was an enormous relief to Angus as it meant all wasn't yet lost. If only he could win Sir Iain to his cause he might still carry off the plan Hetherington had devised.

They walked a little further, Angus with head bowed in thought as he tried to work out how best to put what he wanted to say to Sir Iain.

Finally Sir Iain said, 'I found out about you and Rosemary a long time ago although it wasn't till recently I discovered how Armstrong separated the pair of you. Will that make it any easier?'

Angus nodded, grateful to Sir Iain for clarifying the position.

'Let me say I bear you personally no malice whatsoever. It was hardly your fault the way things happened and how they turned out. It's Armstrong I'm after. Him and him alone.'

And having said that, Angus launched into an explanation of his recent actions.

* * *

Iain was jealous of Angus and had been ever since Peter had told him of the milk boy who'd been having it off with the girl who was later to become his wife. Of one thing he was now certain – Rosemary and Angus still hankered after one another. The signs were all there and not too difficult to read.

So what should he do? Should he put a spoke in Angus's wheel by ensuring the Gorbals project went ahead as planned? Or should he follow the dictates of common sense and jettison Armstrong as Angus had been trying to manoeuvre him into doing?

There were no words to describe what he felt at the thought of losing Rosemary. On the other hand he didn't want her staying with him out of pity and doubly so when there was another man she wanted to be with.

He decided the best thing he could do was not to put the boot in as far as Angus was concerned. He wouldn't do anything against Angus that could later be held or used against him in any way.

He was only too well aware this course might prove disastrous in the long run. But it was the one he was determined to pursue.

Iain heard Angus through to the end, then said he would see Armstrong the following week and dissolve their partnership.

He'd never been happy in property anyway, and especially since Armstrong had become so fanatical about the Gorbals project.

John Muir's aeroplane was far more to his taste as an investment and it was into that he would now channel his energies and capital resources.

Nor was he doing this for Angus's sake but rather because of the correspondence Angus had sent him.

He wouldn't allow himself to remain in partnership with a man he didn't trust to be as honest with him as he was in return.

Angus asked Sir Iain to keep his own involvement in all this quiet, which Sir Iain promised to do.

They shook hands on what had passed between them and without a further word Sir Iain strode off.

Angus's breath misted the air as he rubbed his hands together in self congratulation. He would telephone Bitu with the good news immediately and later Hetherington.

His head whirling with plans, he followed Sir Iain out of the park.

22

Angus and Bitu waited till the end of the week after Angus's meeting with Sir Iain before Bitu telephoned Sir Alan to say he'd now had the go-ahead from Australia to sell the former McCallum properties to Sir Alan provided terms could be agreed.

Sir Alan was still in a state of shock when Bitu rang. He had been since Sir Iain McLaren had confronted him with the various letters stolen from his office which Sir Iain had said had come to him anonymously through the post.

It had been a terrible blow to have the McLaren money withdrawn from the project which, in a momentary panic, he'd suddenly seen as having to be abandoned.

Then he'd somehow pulled himself together again and forced his benumbed brain to consider the financial alternatives.

In grey despair he turned over all the possibilities in his mind – which individuals he could approach with a view to making them a partner, including the proposal put forward by Hetherington that he turn Armstrong's into a public company.

His initial reaction to this had been one of rejection. But the more he thought about it the more it appealed.

He'd never wanted the McLarens or any other local individuals involved in the first place. And it was only dire necessity that had made him approach Sir Hamilton.

But here was a viable alternative which would ensure all the eventual credit and glory would fall squarely to him. It would be just as he'd always seen it. His project and his alone. The new Hutchesontown. *His* creation!

He summoned his secretary and told her to fetch George Hetherington. He had a host of eager questions to ask his chief accountant about the technicalities and ramifications of going public.

The Monday following his telephone call Bitu was ushered into Sir Alan's office. Bitu repeated what he'd already told Sir Alan on the phone – O'Rourke had finally agreed to resiting the proposed animal by-products factory and selling the former McCallum properties to Sir Alan.

However, there would be several stipulations, one of which was that the actual sale didn't take place until after the old woman's death, as knowing how she felt about Sir Alan, they didn't want to cause her any further upset and pain.

Bitu then mentioned the price LMBM wanted for the properties. Sir Alan replied hoarsely that such an astronomical sum was way above their real value.

Bitu smiled thinly and said of course it was way above their real value. But what Sir Alan had to consider was their value to *him*.

Sir Alan made some rapid mental calculations. He could just afford to buy the properties out of the remainder of his capital. But it would mean his financial resources were more or less wiped out.

Still smiling, Bitu stuck the knife in even further by saying if Sir Alan wasn't agreeable to an immediate purchase his instructions were to raze the site and start building the factory within the month. Once that happened, the opportunity to buy would be lost forever.

Fearing the worst, Sir Alan asked what the remaining stipulations were?

There was only one, Bitu declared, which was that a construction firm called Jocar Ltd whom LMBM had connections with be given the overall contract for the Gorbals project.

Sir Alan naturally seized on this second stipulation as a bargaining point – as Angus had foreseen, hence the outrageously high asking price – to beat down the figure for the former McCallum properties to a little over half what had been initially demanded.

Angus didn't really care what price he got for the properties as they were now merely a device to secure Jocar the contract.

As it transpired he still made a substantial killing.

It was a Saturday afternoon when Angus drove John and Sheena into the driveway at Craiglea to find Donald waiting for them. Only hours previously the finishing touches had been completed and Craiglea was now ready to be moved into.

After the tour of inspection was over and the appropriate comments made, Angus sent Sheena and John into the kitchen to make tea while he took Donald to one side.

'You've kept on the Craiglea workforce like I told you?' he said.

'Aye, that's right.'

'Good. Now what I want you to do is expand that gang to at least ten times its present size.' Angus laughed a little when he saw the mystified expression on his grandfather's face. 'Jocar's been contracted to rebuild the Gorbals.'

'Help ma bob!' exclaimed Donald.

'But somehow I don't feel it's going to be a very long job,' said Angus mysteriously. He hadn't yet confided in Donald as to what his ultimate goal was nor what part Jocar was to play in achieving that goal.

'Are you going to tell me what this is all about?' Donald demanded.

'Not yet. I want it to be a surprise.'

'Always did have a mind like a bloody corkscrew,' Donald muttered later after the tea had come.

Angus smiled broadly. 'Flattery will get you everywhere.'

'Away to hell!' Donald retorted but secretly he was highly chuffed as it meant he was still in a job.

Later that night after John had gone to bed Sheena came to sit opposite Angus by the fire.

Although Angus had the evening paper up in front of him he was actually thinking about Hannah – Hugh and Janey's new wee girl – whom he was in the habit of dropping by to see whenever he could.

He felt so sorry for Hugh who, although trying to put a bold front on things, was a changed man since Hannah's birth.

He thought again of that little face and shuddered.

According to Dr Robertson a mongol could live a good twenty years or more. Poor soul, he thought, then poor Hugh and Janey.

'Angus?'

Dropping his newspaper, he discovered Sheena smiling at him.

'I've never really thanked you for asking me to look after John. Doing so has made me very happy, in fact happier than I've ever been before,' she said.

He returned her smile, a wealth of understanding between them.

Crossing to his chair she kissed him tenderly on the forehead, then left the room for her bed.

Angus stared after his step-sister. Next to Rosemary he loved her more than any other living female.

                    *   *   *

Sir Alan was in his dressing gown having just enjoyed a piping hot bath. He sat now on the toilet seat with a glass of whisky in his hand watching in admiration as Margaret climbed into a freshly drawn tub.

From time to time he enjoyed talking to her about business which was what he was now doing.

That very day the manifesto for the new public Armstrong's had been issued. It had finally been decided between himself and Hetherington there would be 1,500,000 one pound shares selling in the first instance for fifteen shillings per share of which he would retain a majority holding of fifty-one per cent.

The remaining forty-nine per cent would be made available on the Glasgow and London Stock Exchanges on a day still to be decided the following month.

There would be a board of directors of which he would be chairman. And to accommodate the monthly and annual general meetings he was having a boardroom built as an extension onto the side of his office.

There was also good news concerning Miss McCallum who'd finally reached the stage of being unable to continue on her own. She'd been admitted to a hospital in Greenock: her end was evidently imminent.

All of a sudden he grunted in agony and bent over double, his face suffused with blood.

'Alan!' Margaret exclaimed in alarm. Clambering from the bath, she quickly crossed to enfold him in her wet, soapy arms.

'It's nothing, lass,' he wheezed. Disentangling himself from her embrace, he sucked in a large lungful of air,

She wore a worried frown as she studied him. 'Can I get you anything?' she asked.

'Have you any antacid powder or milk of magnesia?'
She shook her head.

'Then a glass of water,' he smiled.

While she got the water he massaged his chest.

Within a minute his face was back to its normal colour. And within five they were laughing at the terrible fright he'd given her.

It was only a bad attack of indigestion he assured Margaret. And not the first he'd had like it either.

Usually the antacid powder or milk of magnesia cleared it up. But as she had neither he was just going to have to settle for another glass of whisky.

He started talking about the Gorbals project again and soon the incident had passed from both their minds.

Angus entrusted the drawing up of the Jocar contract to Otis Bitu.

There were two important clauses incorporated into the contract. One featured reasonably prominently while the other was buried deep in the mass of small print comprising the latter part of the document. The first clause stated all aluminium used in the constructions to be built had to come from bauxite ore originating from LMBM (Pty) Ltd.

The reason Bitu would give Sir Alan for the clause's inclusion was that LMBM wanted to encourage the importation of their ore into Britain and this was a device to set the ball rolling.

Angus, Bitu and Hetherington all agreed that Sir Alan would accept this clause as he would think it the reason why LMBM had stipulated Jocar get the Gorbals contract. He would imagine it was a case all round of 'If you scratch my back then I'll scratch yours'.

The trick was going to be to get Sir Alan to sign the contract without tumbling to the timebomb ticking away in the small print.

Directly Angus learned Miss McCallum had been taken into hospital he drove to Greenock to check she was being properly looked after and to see if there was anything she needed.

'Oh it's yourself, sonny,' she whispered out of the crabbit face he remembered so well.

He'd brought her a bunch of flowers plus a bottle of

lavender water which he'd suspected correctly she would like.

She thanked him for these gifts then launched into a tirade against the tyranny that insisted on carting her off to hospital away from the rabbits and poor Bella whom she missed so much and was so worried about it fair made her heart hurt.

Angus inquired who was looking after the animals? A distraught Miss McCallum told him that having collapsed in the street she'd been wheeched off to hospital without being allowed home to make arrangements for the poor beasties.

Angus earned her eternal gratitude by saying he would go to Rothesay straight from the hospital and, having collected Bella and the rabbits, would take them back to his house where he would see they were well provided for.

When he added he had a wee boy who'd be delighted at the prospect of having pets to play with Miss McCallum replied she couldn't have asked for anything more for them. 'And God bless and look after you, sonny.'

He stayed and chatted with her for about half an hour, then as he'd promised, he left the hospital to drive down to the quayside from where he caught a boat for Rothesay.

He found Bella in a pitiful state lying whining in the old woman's bed. It was patently obvious neither dog nor rabbits had been fed or watered since Miss McCallum had last done so.

Once Bella and the rabbits had been attended to Angus put the hutch into the back of his car. Then with a satiated Bella lying beside him he made the journey back to Craiglea where he and the animals were welcomed by an ecstatic John.

That night Angus wrote to Miss McCallum assuring her all was well with her animals and she could now set her mind at rest.

He also wrote to Sean O'Rourke telling O'Rourke what he wanted done, when it was to happen and why.

O'Rourke's brief was to arrange matters so that on a signal from Angus all LMBM ore to Great Britain would be blacked indefinitely by the Mine Workers' Union.

The actual securing of the Armstrong shares when they appeared on the exchanges was conducted by Angus with all the thoroughness of a military operation.

A number of brokers in Glasgow and London were instructed to snap up the shares the moment they became available, which the brokers did with such success that within one minute of their appearing Angus owned forty-six per cent of the forty-nine sold.

The remaining three per cent somehow eluded Angus's brokers to be bought on behalf of a Major Cattermole residing in Richmond, Surrey who, despite the offer of a most handsome profit, stubbornly and steadfastly refused to sell.

This didn't worry Angus unduly as he considered forty-six per cent a more than satisfactory haul..

The next step was to parcel the shares out to the various banks he'd previously approached and whose managers would now be acting as his nominees.

None of the nominees knew the others were also acting on his behalf or that they all had the same instructions – to rubber stamp *everything* Sir Alan proposed.

When Armstrong's board of directors was finally announced it consisted of Sir Alan as chairman, four men of his choosing of whom one was Hetherington, and the four bank managers acting as nominees on Angus's behalf.

At the beginning of December the Greenock Hospital phoned Angus to say Miss McCallum had sunk into a coma the previous day and had passed away in the night.

He thanked the Sister for ringing him and asked if she'd let him know what funeral arrangements were made as he wished to attend.

Three days later he went to Miss McCallum's funeral

in the local Greenock cemetery where he was the only mourner.

It seemed the nephew hadn't wanted the additional expense of shipping the body back to Rothesay. Nor had he even bothered to put in an appearance, having arranged everything by telephone from Inverness.

'Bastard!' was Angus's sole comment when he found this out.

A week after Miss McCallum's death the contract from LMBM for the sale of the former McCallum properties plus the Jocar contract arrived simultaneously on Sir Alan's desk, both of which he immediately handed over to Hetherington for perusal.

The same morning Bitu rang Sir Alan to give LMBM's reasons for the inclusion of the ore clause in the Jocar contract. This explanation Sir Alan readily accepted.

Hetherington sat on the contracts for several days, then returned them to Sir Alan saying as far as he could see they were both perfectly straightforward.

Hetherington had already warned Angus that Sir Alan would give the contracts to a solicitor whose job it would be to go over the documents with a fine tooth comb. To prevent this happening and the delay clause being discovered Angus had come up with a plan which now swung into operation.

Informed by Hetherington that the contracts were now back with Sir Alan, Bitu made another phone call to Armstrong, consisting in the main of a well rehearsed speech.

With panic in his voice Bitu said he'd just received an urgent cablegram from Mr O'Rourke saying for reasons unspecified there had been a change of heart about the former McCallum properties which were not now to be sold under any circumstances.

Sir Alan reacted exactly the way Angus anticipated in replying it was too late for LMBM to go back on the deal as the contracts had already been signed and witnessed.

Having inveigled Sir Alan into committing himself,

Angus further pressured the man by having Bitu announce he was leaving for Armstrong's right away and would expect to see the signed contracts on arrival.

Hanging up, a smiling Sir Alan immediately signed both contracts. Hetherington witnessed them. They were then laid aside for Bitu who arrived half an hour later seemingly frantic and consumed with worry.

Within days of the contracts being signed Donald and the Jocar workforce started building on part of a Gorbals site previously razed by a demolition firm contracted to Sir Alan.

Word went swiftly round that Jocar were looking for time served men. Within hours of work being started there were long queues of eager applicants.

Acting on Angus's instructions, Donald hired a large number of these hopefuls to further double the Jocar manpower before the week was out.

As was traditional, the Jocar men toiled over Christmas then got three days to themselves at Hogmanay, *the* festival in the Scottish calendar.

Normally Donald wouldn't have dreamt of leaving his own house on that night of nights. But when Hugh and Janey invited him and Winnie up to Muirend they decided to go for wee Hannah's sake.

Harriet was also invited, as was Angus. So too were Sheena and John but she swiftly declined saying she'd had enough of partying to last her the rest of her life. And anyway John should be in his bed, Hogmanay or not, and not up to all hours. So Angus left Craiglea on his own on Hogmanay and drove to Muirend where he was the last to arrive.

Nobody spoke much about Hannah but it was understood they were all there as a sign of family unity and strength for which Hugh was pitifully grateful.

After a while it was suggested by Hugh the men go to the pub for an hour to allow the women to have a good old blether amongst themselves.

The pub was jam-packed with alcohol being consumed as though it were going to be banned come morning.

A group of men started to sing but were told to keep quiet by the landlord as they knew damn well singing was against the law.

Donald insisted on getting the first round in so while he fought his way to the bar Hugh asked Angus how John was getting on?

Angus gave Hugh a quick rundown on the wee fellow's latest exploits and activities then subtly changed the subject, thinking that the wisest thing to do in the circumstances. He knew only too well what a bitter and compounded disappointment Hannah had been to his uncle.

While they chatted Hugh was thinking about the gang of teenage boys who'd daubed his walls earlier in the year. They'd tried again another night only to encounter King Billy, a huge fearsome black beast whose very growl was enough to chill the marrow.

He didn't think he'd be seeing them or their like back again which was a relief. But it was still depressing to be the object of so much scorn and hatred. Nor could he even emigrate now as no country would accept a family which included a mongol. For better or worse he would have to stand his ground and take whatever was dished out.

When the pub closed they drove back to Muirend where they settled down to await the bells which would start to dead on the final stroke of twelve.

At ten to twelve Janey decided she wanted Angus to be their first foot. So armed with shortie, a lump of coal and his bottle he had to go out into the yard where he would have to wait till the bells.

Earlier in the day it had been freezing cold. But during the past few hours the temperature had risen considerably making Angus think they might well be in for a fall of snow.

He took a deep swig from his bottle then listened lovingly to one of the horses snickering in the stables. He had so many fond memories of this place which had been such an oasis to him in the dark days of Archie

Marjoribanks.

He remembered again the many mornings he and Kitty had cycled here to run with the milk.

Thinking of those times inevitably brought Rosemary to mind. As it did now. Raw emotion rose in his throat which he forced down again with several more swigs from his bottle.

'Oh, Rosie love,' he whispered to the wind. Having met up with Rosemary again he'd come to realize that what he'd felt for Molly Hotblack was a mere counterfeit when put up against the real thing.

Suddenly the bells were pealing in the far distance. With the broadest of smiles plastered all over his face he chapped the door.

'Happy New Year!' he said to Janey when she answered.

And having been solemnly invited in he equally solemnly presented her with the shortie, coal and whisky after which he swept her into his arms and hugged her tight.

For the next several hours Angus drank with a savagery awesome to behold. Dram after dram vanished down his throat. And each time it seemed to those watching he must surely have reached his capacity. But he dumbfounded them by again reaching for the bottle.

Hugh was another hitting the cratur as though he intended drowning himself in the stuff. And the more he drank the more morose and sullen he became.

At a little past three Winnie and Donald decided they'd had enough and, overhearing this, Angus insisted on driving them home.

A few friends and neighbours had dropped by so there was something of a party going on. Angus announced to Janey that he wouldn't be long.

His excuse for taking a bottle along with him was he might bump into someone he knew en route in which case he'd have to exchange drinks as was the custom.

There were quite a few people out and about first footing and visiting but luckily not many cars on the road. Angus drove with a drunken concentration and somehow – much to their obvious relief – managed to deliver Donald and Winnie home all in one piece.

Waving goodbye he turned the car around and headed back the way he'd come.

His thinking was completely muddled and confused now. Every so often he spoke aloud addressing Kitty as though Kitty was sitting there in the car with him.

He confided to Kitty he was on his way to the bear cave where he was to meet Rosie just like in the old days.

He swung the car away from Muirend in the direction of the Linn Park. Things became indistinct and hazy after that. But he was aware of parking the car and then climbing a wall down which he dropped on the other side.

The River Cart was black and ominous as it moved silently on its way. A slight wind had sprung up causing the denuded trees to rustle and sway. Somewhere close by rooks were cawing.

He staggered through the long grass almost to the water's edge. Something wet hit and clung to his face again and again. In his befuddled state it took him a little while to realize it had started to snow.

Within minutes the snow had intensified to such an extent it was difficult seeing more than a few yards ahead.

His foot slipped once and he went tumbling over and over to end up sprawling only inches from the lapping water. Luckily he wasn't hurt nor was his bottle broken. To celebrate he treated himself to another drink.

The snow had started to lie immediately and even before he reached the bear cave the world had turned white and he was a stumbling snowman.

It was warm inside the cave where he sat huddled listening to tiny rivulets of melted snow running down its sides.

She would come soon he told himself. And when she did they'd make love just like they used to.

Once he thought he heard her and smiled in anticipation. But it was only a fall of snow or else some creature being less stealthy than it should.

After a while he could fight the tiredness no longer. His head slumped forward as he pitched into a deep and troubled sleep.

Sheena was in the process of giving John a late breakfast when Angus stumbled into the kitchen.

His face was grey and pinched, his eyes red rimmed with red bags under them, his clothes muddy and wet as though he'd been rolling around on the ground.

A long shuddering spasm wracked his body. 'Christ, I'm so cold,' he mumbled. Then suddenly all arms and legs, he slumped to the floor.

The briefest of examinations confirmed he had a raging temperature. Grasping him under the arms, Sheena dragged him across to the fire and there began stripping him.

John stared in horror at his prostrate father. He began to wail in a high, shrill voice.

Angus was soaked through and positively stinking of alcohol. Sheena stripped him stark naked, then getting a large towel from the press, rubbed and buffed him dry.

Somehow she got him into clean pyjamas which, within minutes, were wringing wet from the sweat suddenly oozing from him.

He was a good fourteen stones to her eight and a half but alternatively coaxing and shouting at him she managed to get him to his feet where he stood swaying and clinging to her for support.

Buckled under his weight, she manoeuvred him out of the kitchen and into the hall. Ascending the stairs to the first floor landing, in through the door of the closest bedroom and onto the bed.

His teeth began chattering as she wrapped the bedclothes round him. Every so often his body jerked as though an electric current had been shot through it. Each time that happened he gave a horrible groan.

Running downstairs she hurriedly put the kettle on for hot water bottles. Picking up the telephone she rang Dr

Robertson's surgery, to get no reply.

Cursing, she hung up and redialled, this time the doctor's home number.

She was profuse in her apologies in disturbing him at a time like this but she was sure it was an emergency.

After hearing her description of Angus's condition Dr Robertson said she was quite right to ring him and he would be at Craiglea within the hour.

With that weight off her mind Sheena hung up to find John standing by her side clutching her pinny. His face was streaked with tears and his eyes huge with concern as he asked her what was wrong with his daddy?

She replied she didn't know but the doctor was coming to find out. So John would have to be a big man and let her get on with organizing things for the doctor's arrival.

When she returned to the bedroom she found Angus writhing deliriously repeating the same word over and over again.

'Rosie . . . Rosie . . . Rosie . . . '

On arrival Robertson gave Angus a thorough examination at the conclusion of which he looked most grave.

In his opinion Angus had a pleurotic involvement compounded by an almost certain local pneumonia. Angus should really be in hospital but he was against moving him as to do so now would undoubtedly cause further complications.

He intended giving Angus an intra-muscular penicillin injection for the pneumonia. He would return in several hours with further medication.

John bit his lip and clung to Sheena as the needle slid into Angus's flesh. He whimpered when the needle was withdrawn and a spot of blood spattered the sodden whiteness of the bed's bottom sheet.

'Is there any chance of him . . . ? I mean, is it possible he could . . . ?' Sheena stumbled over the words, not quite knowing how to put the question without it seeming over-melodramatic.

Robertson looked up from where he'd stooped to

ruffle John's hair. 'Yes, it is possible,' he said evenly.

After the doctor had gone she rang Hugh and Janey to say she needed help and could Hugh go and fetch his mother for her? Hugh said he'd leave for Tallon Street right away.

Harriet was still at Muirend and offered to come over. But Sheena declined, thinking the domineering Harriet would try and take over, which she didn't want.

In his delirium Angus talked of many things. But time and time again he came back to Rosemary, calling for her and asking where she was.

Winnie and Hugh arrived and sometime after that Dr Robertson returned with a freshly charged syringe of special anti-toxin.

Robertson injected Angus after which he contrived to make him swallow several pills. He then took Angus's temperature.

Robertson perched himself on the edge of the bed and said he would hang on for a wee while as he wanted to observe the effects of the jab.

Half an hour later Robertson again took Angus's temperature, shaking his head when he saw it was unchanged.

There was a look in his eyes which told Sheena and Winnie he was becoming more and more concerned for Angus's life.

They were sitting drinking tea Winnie had made when Robertson asked who this Rosie was Angus was continually asking for? And was it possible to get this Rosie here as her presence just might help?

Sheena's gaze was riveted to Angus's sweat slicked face as she considered that. 'It's worth a try,' she said eventually. She went in search of Angus's address book.

When Rosemary came on the line Sheena explained who she was and why she was ringing.

Rosemary was taken aback to get this call so out of the blue. When she mentioned Angus by name she was aware of Iain raising his head from the book he was reading to stare at her.

Her heart was thumping when she finally hung up.

Iain sat apparently engrossed in his book but his eyes remained fixed to one spot on the page.

'Iain?'

'Yes, my dear?' he replied, looking up and smiling.

Rosemary sat and related precisely what Sheena had told her. When she was finished she waited for Iain's reply.

That the telephone had announced a crisis point in their marriage Iain had no doubt. He could feel it with a certainty that was absolute. His smile became strained as he considered what his reaction should be.

Finally and with a lightness he certainly didn't feel he said if Angus was as ill as his step-sister purported then Rosemary had better get over there to be of what assistance she could.

Rosemary's heart went out to Iain. She knew how difficult this must be for him. Kissing him quickly on the forehead, she turned and strode from the room.

For a long time after she'd gone Iain stared at the doorway through which she'd vanished. He'd known since the night of the Ball this moment was going to come when Rosemary would have to make a choice.

When he tried to concentrate on his book again what he saw was a blurred page from which Angus's face stared up at him.

On arriving at Craiglea, Rosemary was met at the door by Sheena. For an instant the two women stood eyeing one another. Then Sheena stretched out her hand and said how good it was of Rosemary to come.

As they walked up the stairs Sheena explained that Angus had needed someone to look after him and John and had very kindly asked her to be his housekeeper.

Rosemary had known Angus and his step-sister were close but hadn't been expecting whatever it was she now saw in Sheena's face.

In a moment of insight it came to her that Sheena was in love with Angus in a more than sisterly way and yet less or perhaps differently than she herself felt towards him. Surprisingly she sensed in Sheena she had an ally.

Angus lay bathed in sweat, his eyes open but unseeing, his face flushed to a ripe shade of candy pink.

Rosemary's stomach flipped as she stared down at him. Her whole instinct was to take him in her arms, gather him to her and tell him everything was going to be all right now she was here.

'He's been desperate for you to come,' Sheena said.

'I'll stay as long as I have to,' Rosemary replied simply.

Sheena nodded. They understood one another. 'I'll be downstairs if you need me. Just call,' she said, and flitted from the room.

Angus didn't know where it was he'd been but he'd wanted to stay there forever. But someone had called him back. He wasn't ready for that other place yet. There were still things to be done here.

'Rosie?' he croaked.

A hand tightened round his. 'I'm here,' she replied.

He blinked, feeling so weak it was an effort even to open his mouth.

When he tried to focus, his vision became blurred and watery. 'Is it really you? I mean, I'm not dreaming, am I?'

'You're not dreaming,' she replied.

Closing his eyes to stop his head going round and round he said he'd gone to the bear cave to wait for her but she'd never come.

She replied softly no such arrangement had been made between them.

'Must have been the bevy then,' he said. 'So many dreams and imaginings. Hard to know just what was real and what wasn't.'

She bent over to wipe his forehead and suddenly found their lips scant inches apart.

'What have we done to one another?' he asked in a whisper.

She bent her head further and their lips met in a kiss.

There were tears in her eyes when she finally drew away.

He struggled higher up the bed onto his pillows, a fever in him now that had nothing to do with the illness. 'It's still not too late,' he said urgently. 'Leave Iain and come to live with me. We'll get married just as soon as you can get divorced.'

Before she could reply the door opened and Sheena ushered Dr Robertson into the room. They both exclaimed with surprise and pleasure when they saw Angus was sitting up and talking.

Dr Robertson felt Angus's forehead, then said he'd prescribed the right medicine in asking Rosemary to come. A check with the thermometer confirmed Angus was now on the road to recovery.

Sheena announced Winnie had some leek and potato soup on downstairs and Angus was going to have some whether he wanted it or not.

'Bully!' Angus called after her and grinned.

Rosemary was in a turmoil inside. There was nothing she wanted more than to come and live with Angus. And yet she couldn't help but think of the poor man she'd left at home. She knew Iain would be sitting there, watching the clock, fearing the worst.

Before taking his leave Robertson gave Angus another injection. To observe the proprieties Rosemary stepped outside while Angus bared his bottom.

She was just about to go back into the bedroom when Sheena appeared with the bowlful of soup.

Thrusting the bowl into Rosemary's hands Sheena told her to take it, adding Angus was probably too weak to feed himself so she would have to do it.

Sheena was at the top of the stairs when she suddenly paused to say over her shoulder, 'And thank you for what you did. I think we might have lost him if you hadn't been there for him to come back to.'

As Rosemary rejoined Angus and Robertson it was to hear the doctor say he'd return the next day but from now on he expected it to be all uphill for Angus. What Angus needed was rest and plenty of it.

After the doctor had gone Rosemary sat on the edge of the bed with the intention of feeding Angus. But before he would accept any soup he demanded to know the answer to his question. Would she leave Iain for him?

They were right together and always had been, he said – like bacon and eggs they fitted. They were a natural couple.

'Well?' he demanded, and when there was no reply, 'It's now or never, lass. Let this moment go and we'll both rue it the rest of our lives.'

She was so choked with emotion she could hardly get the words out. But eventually they came in a tight crackling whisper. 'Yes, I'll live with you,' she said.

'When?'

With her thoughts whirling she replied it would be best if they waited a little while, at least until Angus was better.

Telling Iain she was leaving him wasn't going to be easy. She needed time to work out just how she was going to do it.

Angus wanted to kiss her again but she said there would be more than enough time for that once he was better. What was important now was he got this hot, nourishing soup inside him to build his strength back up.

He laid his head against the headboard and accepted the first spoonful into his mouth. With Rosemary feeding him he ate every last morsel.

Over the next fortnight Angus grew steadily better until finally Dr Robertson announced he could be taken off the sick list.

During those two weeks Rosemary came to see him every day and each visit was an inspiration to him. He was happier than he'd been in years which went a long way to aiding his recovery.

Early on he told Sheena that Rosemary would be coming to stay and eventually they planned to marry.

Sheena was genuinely pleased to hear this news. She

knew what Rosemary meant to him.

She said it would be best if she left as she wouldn't be needed now. But Angus wouldn't hear of it and nor would Rosemary.

As the days passed Angus pressed Rosemary to tell Iain. Again and again she put it off saying it was her prerogative to choose the right moment.

Iain grew desperately morose and despondent during this time, sitting in his study and staring vacantly at the wall for hours on end.

Even his enthusiasm for John Muir's aeroplane waned as he became more and more resigned to the fact Rosemary had taken up again with Angus McBain and consequently it was only a matter of time before she left him.

Finally Angus forced Rosemary into naming the date she would come to Craiglea.

On the coming Saturday she would ensure she and Iain were alone for the evening and tell him then. Angus would be outside waiting for her in his car.

On the Friday Rosemary paid her daily visit to Craiglea to discover Sheena had gone into town taking John with her to do some shopping. This meant she and Angus were alone in the house.

When she saw the gleam in his eye she knew right away what he had in mind. Nor was she averse to it providing his health was up to it which he assured her it was.

He took her by the hand and led her up to the bedroom where they both stripped and hurriedly crawled beneath the bedclothes.

He was nervous to begin with as was she. But soon those barriers fell away and it was even better than it had been all those years previously.

Life was truly wonderful after all, Angus decided.

By lunchtime on Saturday Iain knew this was the day Rosemary had chosen to tell him she was leaving. He could feel it. Sense it. Read it in her face.

He'd already decided he'd make it easy for her. There would be no row or vain pleadings – merely the statement he wanted her to be happy and if she thought being with Angus McBain would bring her happiness then so be it. He wouldn't stand in her way but rather wish her well.

Dinner that night was a sombre affair, the main course a great favourite of his, a last minute sop, he thought grimly.

After the meal they sat round the fire, he waiting for the prepared speech she was so obviously working up to.

Eyeing the clock, Rosemary knew Angus would be outside waiting for her. Upstairs she had a small case packed ready for the moment of departure.

All that was left for her to do was speak. And yet, for some reason she couldn't.

She loved Angus and always had done. There was absolutely no doubt about that. If things hadn't turned out the way they had she would've undoubtedly married him all those years ago.

As coldly as she was able, she examined her feelings towards Iain. She didn't love him in the grand manner she loved Angus. But she was inordinately fond of him – loved him in a minor way.

Over the years she'd come to accept her situation and together she and Iain had built a successful life by many people's standards. If Angus had never reappeared their marriage would have gone marching on without even a hiccup to disrupt it.

There had been the time she was going to leave Iain. But that had been before his disfigurement.

If the break had been made in those early years it would've been neat and clean. But she'd been unable to bring herself to leave him after his crash, knowing to do so would be to literally sign his death warrant.

The intervening years had altered Iain, however. He was now far tougher mentally and had come to terms with his disfigurement. This time there would be no question of him killing himself.

Staring into the fire's cheery blaze she thought of the good times she and Iain had enjoyed together. There had been many.

She remembered the innumerable kindnesses he'd done her, the way he'd always been there to give her strength and support whenever she'd needed it, the love he'd unabashedly and unstintingly lavished on her.

It came to her that their marriage was a number of daily bricks they'd built together and which formed a bond between them, a bond consisting of many little things put together to comprise a whole.

And it surprised her, thinking of it like that for the first time, just how strong and worthwhile that whole was.

Then there was the question of need. Angus loved and needed her. That was indisputable.

But Iain loved and desperately needed her too – and if she was honest about it – undoubtedly more than Angus did. For it was always possible Angus could find someone else whereas in Iain's case it was either her or no one.

Another item to be taken into consideration was that Angus was a born survivor. Naturally he could be wounded and deeply. But he was the type who would overcome that wound and flourish despite it.

Iain, on the other hand, like some plant whose roots have been badly damaged, would eventually fade and wither away.

She would be happy with Angus but her happiness would be marred by the knowledge that it had been achieved only at Iain's expense. She would be forever feeling guilty and might that not be the fatal flaw that would ultimately destroy her relationship with Angus?

For she knew herself only too well. Once her guilty conscience was activated it would gnaw and gnaw away at her with never any relief except the eventual one of death. She just wasn't the sort of person who could walk out on a marriage and conveniently forget the devastation she'd left in her wake.

What had seemed so easy only hours before, and

especially the previous day in bed with Angus, was now a skein of complications.

However, of one thing she was certain. Angus had been right when he'd said it was now or never. If she didn't make the break tonight she never would.

She glanced across to where Iain sat apparently immersed in a newspaper. He didn't fool her. They'd been together too long for that. She knew he knew and was even now waiting for her to utter the death knell to their marriage.

It was funny how she'd grown accustomed to his face over the years, she thought. To begin with it had horrified and revolted her. Now she hardly even noticed it.

She knew then she was going to stay with Iain and not go off with Angus.

For better or worse she was married to Iain. That was where her commitments lay.

With a sigh she rose and straightened her dress. For a few brief moments she considered going out to the car and telling Angus her decision face to face. But in the end she chose not to, whether because of cowardice or a reluctance to put her decision to such an immediate test she wasn't quite sure.

'I'm going to bed. Are you coming?' she said.

Iain tried to hide his surprise. Had he been wrong? Had her intended decamping been a product of his imagination?

Looking deep into her eyes he saw he'd been right and for some reason she'd changed her mind and was staying with him.

Pity? He didn't think so. He could see many things in her eyes but pity wasn't one of them.

'I'll be right behind you,' he replied, his voice not betraying one whit of the drama that had just passed unspoken between them.

He checked the gas and electricity as he did every night. And only when he was certain everything was as it should be did he climb the stairs to his wife whom up until minutes previously he'd been convinced he'd never sleep with again.

Outside in his car a chilled Angus frowned as the lights in the house went out one by one. His frown deepened to puzzled perplexity when the last one blinked off to leave the house in total darkness.

Something must have gone wrong. There had been a fight. Iain was forcing her to stay against her will.

These and a dozen other explanations for Rosemary's continued non-appearance flashed through his mind.

The minutes ticked by and, as they did so, came the horrible realization Rosemary wasn't going to come with him after all. Nor was she being held against her will. She'd *elected* to stay on with Iain. That had to be the way of it.

His head sagged forward to rest against the wheel. His breath was laboured and there was a burning sensation in his chest.

He would be daft to stay here further considering he wasn't all that long out of a sick bed, he told himself.

But still he hung on, hoping against hope he was wrong and she would suddenly appear full of apologies and saying she'd been detained for some reason or other.

Midnight came and went. Then one o'clock and finally two.

At the back of two he admitted defeat. He headed for Craiglea and the bed that was going to seem empty even when he was in it.

The drive home remained a blank in his mind for the rest of his life.

By June of 1947 Angus had Sir Alan over the proverbial barrel.

Jocar had built a considerable amount of houses in the Gorbals by this time, none of which were finished thanks to the fact all aluminium bits and pieces – and there were a great many in each unit – couldn't be installed due to LMBM's ore being blacked at source from coming to Britain.

O'Rourke had done his job well.

Sir Alan grew more and more worried as his remaining capital rapidly dwindled. His plan had been to sell off blocks öf units as they were completed thereby financing the next section to be built. With nothing being sold it was all outgoings and no incomings.

In vain did Sir Alan contact D.Chisholm and Bitu – he spoke to the former a number of times on the telephone and never recognized the voice as being that of his one-time foreman moulder – to try and get them to use British aluminium in the meantime until the Australian ore could reach this country and be processed.

But Donald and Bitu – carefully stage managed by Angus – were adamant. According to the contracts only aluminium derived from LMBM ore could be used. And that was the way it was going to be.

Feeling he had no other recourse left to him, Sir Alan notified Jocar that all further construction was to be cancelled until such time as the Australian ore was in this country and processed ready for use.

Angus then played his trump card – the delay clause buried deep in the Jocar contract small print.

From now on until construction started again all costs incurred by Jocar – including the wages of the entire Jocar workforce – were the responsibility of Sir Alan who as contractor was liable.

Beside himself, Sir Alan had looked up the named clause. Apoplectic with rage, he consulted his solicitor to be informed the contract was wholly binding in law and as such he was liable for all Jocar's delay costs whether he liked it or not.

At the end of the first delayed week a massive wages bill was sent to Sir Alan which he had no option but to pay.

By the end of the second delayed month Sir Alan had been so reduced financially he was actually considering approaching the Glasgow Corporation to try and offload his Gorbals holdings for whatever price they would pay.

At this point word arrived from Australia – again

carefully orchestrated by Angus – that the end of the union's blacking was imminent. All being well, the first consignment of ore should be on the high seas within the next few days.

This news put Sir Alan into a terrible quandary. If only he could lay his hands on enough capital to tide himself over until the ore arrived in Britain, was processed and made up, all could yet be saved.

It was Hetherington who again came up with the solution. He pointed out that the members of the Armstrong's board had proven themselves to be a most accommodating lot; without exception they'd approved of everything Sir Alan had either suggested or put before them. With so much control over the board, why didn't Sir Alan put it to those directors representing outside interests that he sell them a further twenty-five per cent of his shares with the proviso that those shares would never go on the open market and could only be sold back to him?

According to Hetherington's calculations, the money so raised would be sufficient to allow Sir Alan to ride out his current financial nightmare.

Of course this would necessitate Sir Alan losing his majority holding in Armstrong's. But with such an amenable and malleable board of directors what did that matter as he would always get his own way anyway?

In desperation Sir Alan came to the conclusion that Hetherington's suggestion was his only salvation.

So he called an extraordinary general meeting of the board in which he put it to them he was willing to sell another twenty-four per cent of his shares – this a further refinement of Hetherington's – and would offer each director acting as nominee for outside interests the option on six per cent of them.

This way he could still retain – so Hetherington had smoothly argued – the most individual shares and therefore the right to the position of chairman.

The nominee directors agreed to inform their various clients of this development. All came back saying their clients were willing to take up the options.

It was a day Angus had long been looking forward to. It was the first of August and on the twelfth of the month he would be twenty-six years old. He felt twice that age.

The day dawned warm and sunny with blue sky stretching from horizon to horizon. He ate a leisurely breakfast before returning to his bedroom where he dressed himself in a brand new suit he'd had made especially for the occasion.

Outside in the drive stood something else he'd bought especially – a 1932 Rolls Royce in immaculate condition.

When it was time to leave he went downstairs where he shook John solemnly by the hand and kissed Sheena on the cheek.

Whistling merrily, he went out to the Rolls and eased himself behind the wheel.

En route, he thought of George Hetherington now on his way to Australia where his wife was eagerly awaiting his arrival.

Hetherington had taken with him a nice little additional nest egg courtesy of Jocar and Angus. Angus reckoned he'd earned a good bonus.

At the gate into Armstrong's Angus was automatically waved through by the guard. The guard was someone he'd known all his life and yet he went by unrecognized. It seemed guards didn't look too closely at the faces of those who drove a Rolls, the car being credential enough.

He drove slowly across the yard, glancing briefly at the spot where Tod Gemmill had bumped into him and planted the cuff links in his overalls. He smiled grimly at the memory.

He parked the Rolls beside Sir Alan's and climbed out into the sunshine. A glance at his watch told him the meeting was scheduled to have started one minute previously. He had timed it to perfection.

He strode up the stairs that brought him to Sir Alan's office where in a small reception area a middle-aged secretary asked him what his business was?

He replied he'd come for the board meeting and he looked so much the part he was shown straight through. When he entered the boardroom he did so as though to the manner born.

As he expected, there were four of them grouped round the table – Sir Alan plus Sir Alan's three tame directors. He stared boldly at Sir Alan.

'You!' Sir Alan exclaimed and looked thunderstruck.

Angus took his time about walking to the seat furthest away from Sir Alan. He smiled softly and waited.

'Just what in God's name do you think you're doing here, McBain?' Sir Alan demanded angrily.

Angus laid his brief case on the table and slowly opened it.

The penultimate twist of the screw had been applied to Sir Alan that morning in the form of a telegram from O'Rourke informing him the Mine Workers' Union had reconsidered their position. As a result they were once more blacking all LMBM ore to Great Britain.

This was in effect the death blow to the Gorbals project for it was impossible for Sir Alan to financially survive the consequences of this action.

Angus leant across the table to hand the man nearest him certificates and statements showing the absent four nominee directors had all been acting on his behalf. With seventy per cent of the Armstrong shares he was now the majority shareholder.

Having noted the contents of these papers Sir Alan closed his eyes. It was as though he'd been reduced to a shell with a cold wind blowing through the empty spaces where flesh and blood had once been.

Angus reached into his pocket and pulled out an old pair of cuff links which he threw down on the table where they came to rest about a foot in front of Sir Alan. 'Also for Rosemary and the compensation you owed but never paid my mother,' Angus said.

The three directors watched spellbound the drama being played out in front of them. From the expressions

on their faces Angus might have been the very devil
incarnate.

Angus went on, 'As the new majority shareholder I
claim the position of managing director and as such will
assume responsibility for the running of the firm. As
you, Armstrong, still own twenty-seven per cent of the
shares I hereby offer you the post of assistant managing
director which your holdings entitle you to.'

Having said that, Angus swung his gaze onto the three
directors sitting gawping at him. 'In the circumstances
there will now be no further need for a board of directors
which makes you redundant, gentlemen,' he added.

Sir Alan squared Angus's certificates and statements
into a neat pile before coming to his feet.

Without uttering further he walked from the boardroom into his office. His secretary's voice was heard a
few moments later asking if he was all right as he looked
awful.

Mumbling something incomprehensible, Sir Alan
took a last fond look round his office, then left it for his
car parked outside.

The three directors took their leave almost directly
afterwards. En route one of them explained to the secretary there was a change of management and Mr McBain
was now in charge.

After the directors had gone Angus strolled through
to what had been Sir Alan's office, plonking himself
down behind the man's desk.

Strangely there was no feeling of elation but rather a
sense of the anti-climactic.

There was a framed photograph on the desk which he
picked up and studied. It featured a grown woman and
two young girls – Rosemary and Diane as youngsters
with their mother.

His heart crowded into his mouth as he stared at the
young Rosemary's face. With a sigh he slid the photograph into a desk drawer and called out for the secretary
to come through.

The woman entered all wide-eyed and timorous. He

introduced himself and told her to take a memo, copies of which were to be distributed throughout the works.

In the memo he informed the workforce of the change of management, then went on to allay any fears they might have had regarding the sort of internal upheaval often occurring in circumstances like these.

He instructed her to tell all heads of departments and gaffers to present themselves in his office in half an hour's time. He wanted to introduce himself to these men without delay.

When Miss Morrisson had left he crossed to the window and stared out. There was an enormous amount he was going to have to learn about running a business like this. But learn it he would and quickly.

He was going to see Armstrong's prosper like it had never prospered before. Before he was finished Armstrong's was going to be a by-word not only in Glasgow but throughout Britain and beyond.

'Mister McBain?'

He turned to find himself staring at a pretty blond lassie of about twenty-two or -three.

'I'm Miss McPhail, Miss Morrisson's assistant. I was wondering if you'd like a cup of tea? We usually have one about this time.'

There was something about the girl, a certain unmistakable Glasgowness, that appealed to him. 'What's your Christian name, Miss McPhail?' he asked.

She blinked in surprise. 'Irene.'

'Well, Irene, I'd love a cup of *coffee*,' he said.

She smiled hesitatingly, then was gone.

Angus rubbed his hands briskly together. The sun was shining outside and he'd achieved what he'd set out to do. True, he'd lost Rosemary but then perhaps there was a law somewhere which stipulated a man couldn't have everything he set his heart on.

Looking on the bright side there was an awful lot he had to be thankful for including a smashing wee son whom he idolized and would have sold his soul for.

Returning to his desk he mused he was going to need a

personal assistant-cum-secretary now, someone clever and efficient to be by his side as he constantly flitted between LMBM and Armstrong business.

He wondered if the pretty Irene McPhail would be interested?

For three days after Angus's coup Sir Alan sat at home and brooded. Surly and taciturn, he refused to discuss the situation with anyone, including his wife, Cordelia.

He drank a great deal, consuming bottle after bottle of his favourite malt.

On the evening of the third day he announced abruptly that he was going out.

He drove to Partickhill, having a desire to see Margaret Cunninghame, and as this was one of his usual nights for going there he'd decided to keep the tryst.

Not feeling the same sense of shame with Margaret as he did with Cordelia he was telling her everything within minutes of his arrival.

Appalled, Margaret fetched him a stiff drink, made sure he was sitting comfortably and generally fussed over him.

They talked and drank, he downing the whisky as though it was water. The more alcohol he consumed the more flushed and agitated he became.

Like many courtesans, Margaret eventually related most things to sex and bed. To her, intercourse was the great panacea which, if not exactly the cure for all ills, couldn't fail but help.

With that in mind she began coaxing Sir Alan to come to bed.

To begin with he wasn't interested but when she began touching him in a way he especially liked he soon became aroused.

As she'd intended, all thoughts fled from his mind other than lust and bodily satisfaction. Hand in hand they hurried to the bedroom where they both quickly undressed.

Their lovemaking was fiercely urgent – far more so

than normal.

Suddenly, he gave a long, shuddering sigh and collapsed on top of her where he lay heavily pressing her into the bed.

'Oh love, that was wonderful,' Margaret crooned, stroking the side of his sweat slicked neck.

She continued stroking him, then frowned when she got no reply.

'Alan?'

For the first time it dawned on her there was something peculiar about the way he was lying so heavy and unmoving.

'Alan?'

Her hand groped for the bedside table and the lamp sitting atop it.

His face was suffused with blood, the way it had been when he'd had the previous attack in her bathroom.

His eyes were wide open and bulging as though being forced outward from internal pressure of some kind. The expression was a grotesque parody of sexual ecstasy.

There could be no mistaking he was quite dead.

A few days after Sir Alan's funeral Angus stood by the man's grave in the Linn Park Cemetery with a huge bunch of magnificent red roses in his hand.

For a long time he stared down at the grave. Then turning he made his way to another part of the cemetery where his mother and father were buried together.

On top of their grave he laid the roses.

It was a puerile thing to say but he said it nonetheless. 'You got your compensation at last, Ma. Armstrong finally paid up. And with interest.'

Tears oozed from his eyes which he hurriedly wiped away. It wouldn't do for anyone to see a grown man greeting like a wean. They'd think him a big jessie.

Taking a deep breath, he thought Armstrong's death was the passing of a personal era. Yesterday was now gone. Tomorrow lay fresh and inviting before him.

It was with a light heart that he made his way up the

path to the cemetery gates beyond which his Rolls was parked. Off on the horizon he could see the grey pall of chimney smoke that hung forever lowering over central Glasgow.

It might be a dirty horrible violent place but he loved it.

It was home.

When Dreams Come True

Contents

Part 1

THREE LITTLE WORDS
1932–36

Chapter One

March had been a rotten month filled with rain, wind, cold and sleet. But with the arrival of April the weather had changed, with the sun appearing and the grey skies turning to blue.

Norma McKenzie hummed happily to herself as she walked along the path which would take her home. She'd just been to the wee town of Kirn about a mile away on the Argyllshire coast to get some messages for her ma, and while there had had a good crack with Marion Cockburn, a school pal of hers in the same class. During the school holidays – and it was now the Easter ones – Marion helped in the family shop, a licensed grocers.

Norma stopped to stare out over the Firth of Clyde, and watched the paddle-steamer *Maid of Lorne* head for Kirn pier, *en route* from Gourock. She knew all the steamers on the Clyde, having been able to recognise and name them before she could read or write.

Then something on the road running parallel to the seashore caught her eye. It was the big swanky car that belonged to the new owner of Kilmichael House, her da's new boss.

As the car turned in at the drive gate she caught a glimpse of Mr Hodgart, and beside him his wife. The Hodgarts had a son called Rodney and a daughter Caroline who was just a little older than herself.

Norma didn't like the Hodgarts very much. There was an aura about them – Mr Hodgart in particular – which made her uneasy. The one time she'd bumped into Mr Hodgart he'd smiled at her, but it had been a smile she hadn't believed. There was a bully at school who smiled in exactly the same way as he was nipping you or giving you Chinese Burn.

Despite their wealth, the Hodgarts weren't real toffs in the

3

way the previous owner, the Earl of Arran and Clydesdale, had been. They might be stinking rich but they didn't have class. Their money was new – and it showed.

The Earl's family had owned Kilmichael House, and the ten acres of grounds belonging to the house, for over three hundred years, but the Earl had fallen on hard times financially and, after a long struggle, had been forced to put the property on the market where it had soon been snapped up by Mr Hodgart.

Mr Hodgart was a general importer and exporter who also owned a big factory in Greenock. A factory, according to her da, that made pipe fittings and ball bearings.

'Norma!'

She turned at the sound of her da's voice, and there he was striding towards her, coming round from behind a stand of rhododendron bushes.

Not for the first time it struck her what a fine upstanding-looking man her da was. There was a dignity and purpose about him which suited his position as head gardener to Kilmichael House. He had three other gardeners working under him.

'I've just been to Kirn to get some messages for Ma,' Norma explained.

Brian McKenzie glanced at the basket she was carrying and nodded. Effie had mentioned earlier she was going to send Norma in for a few things, adding tobacco to the list when he'd told her he was about to run out.

'Did you get my 'baccy?' he asked, accepting the tin when Norma handed it over.

'McLean from the House came searching me out to say that the master himself wants a word when he gets back. As that was his car I spied I'd better away up and see him.' McLean was a footman.

Gardening business, Norma presumed, as had Brian.

'Tell your ma where I've gone and that I may be late for dinner as a result. I'll try and get home as soon as I can.'

'I'll tell her da.'

Brian smiled softly at his eldest daughter, the eldest of three. Norma was fourteen, Lyn a year younger, and Eileen, the baby, eleven. He loved them all but – maybe because she was his first-

4

born – he loved Norma the most, something he'd never confided to a living soul, not even to Effie.

Brian slipped the tobacco tin into his jacket pocket. 'Away with you then and I'll see you by and by,' he said.

Norma waved to her father, then he was gone, hidden from view by another stand of rhododendron bushes.

When she arrived at the cottage Norma found Lyn laying the table while Eileen was cutting bread into slices and buttering them. Her ma was at the range stirring a pot of stew. The smell from the stew and from the potatoes baking in the range oven filled the kitchen, and was delicious.

'I saw Da,' Norma said, then proceeded to give her ma his message.

Effie wiped her hands on her pinny, then pushed back a stray wisp of hair which had tumbled down onto her high forehead. She was wearing her hair in her usual way, swept up and held in place by a great many pins and a brace of tortoiseshell combs. It was only when going to bed, or washing her hair, that she let it down.

'Well I'm glad we don't have to wait. I'm starving,' Lyn said hopefully.

'Who said we don't have to wait?' Effie queried, the corners of her mouth twitching upwards.

Lyn dropped her gaze. 'I just thought that's what Da's message implied,' she mumbled.

'Trust you to think that Podge,' whispered Eileen.

Lyn glared at her younger sister. She hated her nickname, positively loathed it. If Ma hadn't been there she'd have skited Eileen round the ear for using it. And she might still, later, if she could get the wee so-and-so alone.

'I don't see how you can be that hungry after the breakfast you've eaten,' teased Norma. Lyn had eaten a whopping breakfast – but then she always did. She ate as much as Norma, Ma and Eileen put together.

'We'll wait for Da. Not that he'd mind if we went ahead, but I would,' Effie said.

Lyn sniffed, and listened to her belly rumble. It rumbled a lot; she was known for it.

When she thought Effie wasn't looking Lyn swiped a bit of breadcrust from the table and quickly popped it into her mouth.

5

It wasn't her fault she had a healthy appetite, she told herself. Ma and the others were just pickers anyway. Why, a bird ate more than they did!

'I saw Caroline Hodgart while you were out, she was riding that horse of hers,' Eileen said to Norma.

'It's a smasher, that chestnut mare,' Norma replied, her voice tinged with jealousy.

Eileen sighed. 'I'd give anything to own a beastie like yon.'

Me too, Norma thought, as daft on horses as Eileen was. The pair of them did get the chance to ride from time to time, but only on the old broken-down hack over at Boyd's Farm. There was no comparison between Tom-Tom and Caroline Hodgart's chestnut mare.

It must be great to be rolling in it, Norma thought, to be able to afford anything you want. Just a snap of the fingers and there it was – a horse, a dress, whatever.

She fell to day-dreaming about being rich, and in that day-dreaming did an awful lot of finger snapping.

They all looked up when the door opened and Brian came in. It was over an hour since he'd met Norma returning from Kirn.

Brian's face was tight and drawn. His expression was strange, sort of bemused. Going to his favourite chair he plonked himself down.

'I'll get the dinner out now you're back,' Effie said with a smile.

Brian didn't answer, just stared straight ahead.

'Lyn's been fair champing at the bit, you'd think she hadn't eaten for a month,' Eileen said to her da.

Brian produced his pipe and a new tin of tobacco. Still staring ahead he opened the tin and began filling his pipe.

'Da, dinner's going on the table,' Norma admonished.

'I've had the sack,' Brian said.

Effie went stock still, ladle filled with stew poised in mid-air.

Lyn laughed. 'He's at it again!'

Effie's face cracked into a grin that became a large smile. 'Och see you, you're terrible so you are!' she said to Brian, filling the plate she was holding.

Norma stared at her da. He was an awful joker, mickey-taker, forever saying the most outrageous things. Why only the previous week he'd told them that moonmen had landed in

London and were even then in private consultations with the Prime Minister Mr MacDonald.

Brian put his pipe to his mouth and lit up, then blew out a long thin stream of blue smoke.

'I'm afraid it's true,' he said, his voice leaden.

'Da, will you stop it! We know you're only trying to get us going,' said Lyn, pulling out a chair and sitting at the table.

'I'll have two of those jacket potatoes Ma,' she said to Effie.

Eileen scrambled into her place and reached for a slice of bread and butter. 'Is there anything you want me to do this afternoon Ma? If not I thought I'd go and play with Helen Millar,' she said. Helen was the daughter of one of the gardeners under Brian, and lived in another cottage close by.

'Mr Hodgart said he's nothing against me personally but wants to put his own chap in as head gardener, the chap he had at his last place. He's promised to give me a good reference,' Brian went on.

Norma suddenly saw there was a sheen of sweat on her father's brow. Sweat that glinted as it was caught by the light streaming in from the window by the sink.

Fear clutched her insides. 'Da?' she whispered.

Brian looked at her. There was none of the humour in his eyes that there usually was when he was having them on. On the contrary, there was a deadness about them that she'd never seen before.

'Come on you pair, will you get in at the table. And put that pipe out Brian. Honestly!' Effie grumbled, sitting down at her customary place.

'Pass the butter please,' Eileen asked Lyn.

Lyn helped herself first, putting two huge dollops on her plate.

'If you're not careful you'll be the size of a barn door before you're much older,' Eileen said to Lyn.

'Don't be cheeky,' Effie told Eileen. Then turning to Lyn she went on, 'but she's right, you are eating far too much. Put half that butter back, and no arguments either.'

'Ma, I think it's true,' Norma said softly to Effie.

'What dear?'

'About Da being sacked.'

7

Effie opened her mouth to laugh, but what she saw written on Brian's face stopped her.

'Dear God!' she muttered in a strangled voice.

'We've to be out of here by the first day of June, whether I've got another job or not. In the meantime I'm to take as much time off as I need to find one.'

'It *is* true then,' said Effie, a hand going to her heart.

'Wants his own chap as head gardener,' Brian repeated.

Eileen put down the bread she'd been munching on. A film covered her eyes, then she burst into tears.

'But you've worked for the House man and boy. Didn't he take that into consideration?' Effie asked, desperation in her voice.

'There's no question about the standard of my work, or of my loyalty. It's just that he wants his own chap,' Brian replied.

'It would seem the loyalty's all one-sided,' muttered Norma.

'Nor did Mr Hodgart think I should stay on under the new fellow. He didn't think that would be right for either of us,' Brian added.

Effie pushed back her chair and stood up. Going to Eileen she cuddled her youngest daughter to her.

Norma was not only stunned – she was devastated. Leave the cottage where she'd been born and brought up. Why the idea was inconceivable! And yet, that was what she was going to have to do. What they were all going to have to do.

'I just couldn't believe it when he told me. I thought I was hearing things,' Brian whispered.

'Damn him!' Effie exploded in a sudden burst of anger.

Brian ran a hand through his hair. The hand was trembling slightly, he noted. Then realised that the other one was as well.

'This doesn't need to be as bad as it sounds. I heard there was a head gardener's job going in Innellan, I'll bicycle down there after breakfast tomorrow and apply. With a bit of luck I'll be fixed up again before we know where we are,' he said. Innellan was south on the coast road, about ten miles away.

'Does a cottage go with the job?' Effie asked quickly.

'I don't know, but I'd imagine it would. Anyway, I'll find out the details when I go there tomorrow.'

'When did you hear about this job Da?' asked Norma.

'Last Friday down the pub. It had only come available, so news of it can hardly have spread very far yet.'

'Let's keep our fingers crossed then,' said Effie.

'Aye,' Brian agreed.

Eileen stopped crying, and wiped her cheeks with her sleeve. There was a lump in her throat that felt the size of a turnip.

Effie took a deep breath, then another. 'Well, that was a bombshell and no mistake,' she declared.

'I couldn't face any dinner love. I've no appetite at all,' Brian told her, and took a lengthy drag on his pipe.

'Me neither Ma,' said Norma.

In the end only Lyn ate. She looked guilty as she did, but she ate nonetheless.

Norma was the first to hear the squeak of her da's bike approaching the cottage. The chain needed oiling, a task Brian had been meaning to get round to for some time.

She glanced up from her darning and over to where Effie was bent over the ironing board. She saw her ma stiffen – she too must have heard her da's approach.

Effie bit her lip, then, consciously trying to relax, went back to her ironing. She wanted to appear casual and not betray the inner turmoil she was feeling.

She was whacked, having been awake worrying most of the night. Brian hadn't had much sleep either. And what sleep he had managed to get had been filled with restless tossings and turnings.

'It's Da!' exclaimed Eileen excitedly. She and Lyn were sitting together mending a sheet that Lyn had put a big toe through and ripped. The sheet might be gey thin but it still had life left in it yet according to Effie.

Brian dismounted from his bike, leant it against the cottage wall, knocked his boots on the step – even though he'd polished them earlier he did this through force of habit – and, with a heavy heart, went into the kitchen.

Effie forced a smile onto her face. 'So how did you get on?' she asked.

Brian shook his head. 'You wouldn't credit it, but the job went late last evening.'

9

'You mean ...?' Effie trailed off.

'Aye, that's right. If I'd gone directly after yesterday's dinner instead of waiting till this morning I'd have got it.'

That was cruel, Norma thought. And resumed darning.

'My fault entirely. I shouldn't have waited,' Brian added, anger and bitterness in his voice.

Effie crossed over to the range and placed the iron in a place where it would be reheated. 'Was there a cottage going with the job?' she asked.

'Aye. A nice one too I believe.'

Effie and Brian's eyes locked, then she looked away. The slump of her shoulders betrayed her disappointment.

'Ach well, if it wasn't to be it wasn't to be,' she said, trying to make her voice sound light and unconcerned, and failing totally.

'I'll put the kettle on. I'm sure you could use a cup of tea,' Norma said to Brian.

Brian wanted to take Effie in his arms and comfort her, but didn't because the children were there. 'I certainly could,' he replied to Norma.

'What now Da?' Lyn asked.

'I'll have my tea and then take myself round about, see if anyone's heard of anything.'

'Make sure you buy a paper. There might be something advertised,' Effie said.

'I will. And I'll go into the pub and have a word with John Paul. He's a mine of information that man.' John Paul was the publican of Brian's local The Royal Arms.

Effie couldn't help her gaze straying to the calendar tacked to the wall. The first of June was uncomfortably close – six weeks away, that was all. And what were six weeks? Nothing whatever in their present situation. If only Brian had gone to Innellan yesterday afternoon! Brian blamed himself for that, but wasn't she just as much to blame. She should have thought to make him go straight away. But it hadn't even occurred to her. It was just that ... well, their pace of life was such that they weren't used to doing things in a rush.

While Effie was staring at the calendar Norma noted that the deadness she'd seen in her da's eyes the previous night was back. And was it her imagination or did he seem to have aged?

'I'm glad you missed that job, I don't like Innellan anyway,' Eileen said suddenly, trying to cheer her da up.

Brian turned his attention to his youngest daughter. 'You know something Eileen?'

'What Da?'

'To tell the truth I don't either.'

They all laughed at that, with the exception of Effie.

'I'll make you some scones for later,' Lyn said.

All four females could bake, but Lyn's baking – which she didn't do very often as surprisingly she didn't enjoy doing it – was special. There wasn't another female in the district who could bake as well as her; she was in a class of her own. A lot of it was to do with her very cold hands, Effie had always said.

'I'll look forward to that,' Brian replied, giving a wee nod to show he appreciated the treat.

When Brian had drunk his tea he cycled away again, with Effie and Norma standing at the sink window watching him go.

'If only . . .' Effie started to say, trailing off to bite her lip.

Norma squeezed her mother's hand comfortingly. Then she returned to her darning; Effie to the ironing.

Early evening ten days later Norma was returning home with a pail of milk she'd been to Boyd's Farm for, when there was the ting of a bell behind her, and there was her da on his bike. On reaching her he dismounted.

'Any luck?' she demanded eagerly, knowing he'd been into nearby Dunoon to see the manager of the Marine Hotel. The hotel had large grounds attached and employed a number of gardeners and Brian had heard that one of them was shortly to retire.

'A *year* till the fellow retires, the manager told me,' Brian said ruefully and shrugged.

'So it was a wild-goose chase.'

'I'm afraid it was, pet.'

They walked along in silence.

'Da?'

He glanced sideways at her.

'What happens if you don't find something?'

'There's plenty of time left before we have to worry about that,' he replied quickly.

11

'But if you *don't*?' she persisted.

She waited for an answer, but none came. They walked the rest of the way home with the sort of silence between them that you could have cut with a knife.

Norma awoke suddenly, her eyes snapping open. She stared up into the heavy darkness wondering what had roused her.

She didn't need a clock to tell her it was late, very late. Well after midnight she guessed.

Outside a cat screamed, then screamed again. *That* must have been what had wakened her, she thought, smiling to herself. Snuggling down she prepared to go back to sleep.

Then she heard something else, a voice speaking from the direction of the kitchen. Her da's voice.

Norma frowned. What was he doing still up at this time? He was normally early to bed and early to rise. With the exception of Hogmanay she'd never known him be up after twelve.

Getting out of bed she threw her dressing gown round her shoulders and padded to the door. She opened the door quietly and, without making a sound, slipped out into the hallway.

The kitchen door was ajar and Norma could see her mother and father sitting by the range. A solitary paraffin lamp cast a soft yellow glow round their chairs.

Her mother was speaking now, but in such a low voice that Norma couldn't make out what she was saying.

The pair of them looked terrible, Norma thought. Her mother's face was haggard with worry; her da – this time it certainly wasn't her imagination – looked a dozen years older than before that fateful day when he'd been told of his sacking.

Brian put a hand to his forehead and leant forward in his chair. He was the very picture of despair.

For the first time in her life Norma felt really frightened. Her body tingled with gooseflesh; the inside of both thighs began to quiver.

She went back to bed and lay staring into the darkness. Fear filled her from head to toe, ice-cold, mind-numbing, terrifying fear.

Fear that was still with her when she woke again the next morning.

It was Friday night – bath night for Effie and the girls – and as was usual, Brian had gone to The Royal Arms to give them privacy.

The zinc bath was in front of the range and Eileen was in it. They always shared the same water, starting with the youngest and working their way through to Effie.

On the range itself various large pans were bubbling. After Eileen each new person into the bath got a hot top-up.

Norma glanced away from the book she was reading, over to where Effie was sorting through a pile of dirty laundry.

Effie, clutching a blouse Norma recognised as being one of Eileen's, was staring at Eileen in the bath. Suddenly a stricken expression crumpled her face, and tears welled in her eyes. With a sob she fled the room.

Lyn started to rise, but stopped halfway at a sign from Norma. 'I'll go,' Norma said.

She found Effie in the parlour weeping into a hanky.

'It's four weeks now, only four left,' Effie choked out.

'I know Ma,' Norma replied, lighting the lamp on the mantelpiece.

'Oh Norma!' Effie wailed. The pair of them came together and Effie hugged Norma tightly to her.

She mustn't cry as well, although she felt like doing so, Norma told herself. She must be strong. Usually it was Ma who was the strong one; this time it was up to her.

She stroked Effie's neck and waited for the weeping to subside, which it eventually did.

Effie wiped a nose that had gone red. 'I'm sorry for breaking down like that,' she apologised.

'It's understandable Ma.'

Effie held the hanky between her hands and twisted it.

'It was seeing Eileen in the bath and remembering the first bath I gave her as a baby that did it.' She twisted the hanky even more vigorously. 'If the worst comes to the worst – and it seems it's going to – the family is going to have to split up,' she said, the latter in a rush.

Norma was appalled. 'Split up? How do you mean?'

'Your da's already written to our relations and it's been agreed. You're going to Auntie Josie and Uncle Bill, Lyn to my sister Meg and her husband, and Eileen to Granny and Grandpa McKenzie. Brian and I will stay with his brother Gordon in Hunter's Quay.'

'But ... I mean ... surely there's some other way, a way the family can stick together?' Norma protested.

Effie shook her head. 'We have just over eleven pounds in savings – how far do you think that would get us without a wage coming in? No, your da and I have thought this through. Splitting the family for the time being is all we can do.'

Norma thought of Mr Hodgart, she'd never liked the man, now she positively loathed him for what he'd done to them. 'Everything was so happy and secure here till that Mr Hodgart bought the House,' she said.

'Aye, the Earl would never have got rid of your father. He thought the world of Brian and Brian's work. Said so often.'

Effie blew her nose with the now sodden handkerchief, then wiped her eyes which she knew to be puffy from crying. 'We weren't going to let on to you and the other two till next week, but then I had that wee breakdown just now and it all came tumbling out. You will keep it quiet till then, won't you? Your da and I decided that would be for the best.'

'I'll keep it to myself if that's what you want,' Norma agreed.

Effie kissed Norma on the cheek. 'I hadn't noticed till tonight how grown up you've become. It's good to have another woman to share things with.'

Norma's heart swelled to hear that. The two women clasped one another, never more close than they were at that moment.

'I'd better get on then,' Effie said when they'd released each other.

Norma put out the lamp.

Norma let herself out of the cottage, her mind in a turmoil. She'd lost all notion for having a bath, and Effie hadn't insisted.

It was a fine night, though somewhat chilly. She pulled her shawl more closely about her as she made her way down to the shore road which she crossed to get to the shoreline beyond.

The tide was in as she'd known it would be; the Firth placid, its waters gently lapping against the many big boulders and rocks hereabouts.

She had a favourite rock which she sought out now, and climbed onto. Across the Firth the Cloch Lighthouse winked in and out.

The family to split up and she to go to Auntie Josie and Uncle Bill! The thought made her feel sick. For apart from the split itself Auntie Josie and Uncle Bill were Wee Frees, meaning members of the Wee Free Church.

She didn't know too much about the Wee Frees, except they were very strict, with a lot of talk of hellfire and brimstone. It would be church, church and church again. How many times on a Sunday alone, was it twice or three times?

Auntie Josie and Uncle Bill were a dour and serious couple, as well as religious fanatics. Why, in the many times she'd been in their company she'd never seen either of them laugh. She knew without a shadow of a doubt she was going to loathe living with them.

It would be hard for her, but what about poor Eileen? It would break Eileen's heart to be parted from the rest of them, especially Ma, for at eleven Eileen was still very much tied to her mother.

For Lyn at thirteen, it wasn't quite so bad, but it was going to be an awful blow for her all the same.

Norma gave a sudden grin. Auntie Meg and Uncle Sammy who Lyn was going to were renowned for being tight, which was reflected in the way they ate – wholesome food, but not very much of it. Lyn would suffer there right enough.

But probably the one to suffer most would be Ma. Being parted from her children would be an open wound, daily salted by memories of the past.

As for her da, he wouldn't say much about it but she could imagine what he'd go through.

He was such a terrific man, her da, one of the best. She'd never known anyone not to like him. As Ma had said the Earl had thought the world of a —

The idea came to her in a blinding flash.

Thought the world of him, she repeated slowly to herself.

It might be the answer. It just might be!

Sliding down from the rock she ran back towards the cottage.

When Brian returned home from the pub he found Effie, Norma and Lyn eagerly awaiting him. Eileen had already been sent to bed as it was past her bedtime.

'Norma's had an idea you should hear,' announced Effie.

'Oh aye?' He was a bit muzzy from beer, but not too much so. He sat down and began packing his pipe.

'The Earl of Arran and Clydesdale always thought the world of you and said so often.'

Brian nodded. That was true enough.

'And he's influential, right? Knows all sorts of people, many of whom must employ gardeners?'

Brian considered that as he tamped down his fill.

'It's worth a try. What have you got to lose?' Effie urged.

Not a damn thing, he thought to himself.

'Well Da?' Norma queried.

'Come here,' he said, beckoning her over.

He playfully punched her on the side of the jaw. 'I think it's a smashing idea. And you can write the letter because you've got the best copperplate.'

'I'll get pen and paper,' said Lyn, going to the drawer where these things were kept.

Effie was filled with excitement and new hope, as she'd been ever since Norma had told her of her idea. Surely the Earl, as kindly a man as had ever lived, would come to their rescue and find a way out of their predicament for them. Surely!

'Now what do you think you should write?' asked Effie.

'I'll explain what's happened, what my position is, and ask if he knows of anyone looking for a gardener,' Brian replied, furrowing his brow. He lit his pipe.

'We must emphasise the urgency of the situation – that we're being chucked out of here in a fortnight's time,' Norma stated.

In the end all four of them helped compose the letter.

The following Monday the girls returned home from school to find their parents in a lather of activity. Brian was putting on his best suit – the one he wore for going to church, weddings and funerals – while Effie was packing an overnight case for him.

16

'A telegram arrived not half an hour ago from the Earl asking your da to go and see him in Glasgow,' explained Effie.

Brian stopped what he was doing. 'And I'm going *right away* so that I can present myself on his doorstep first thing tomorrow morning. I lost that last opportunity through taking my time – I'm not about to repeat that mistake.'

Norma nodded her approval.

'Make your da up a piece to take with him; he'll probably feel like a bite before he gets to Glasgow,' Effie said to Norma.

'There's some of that fresh salmon left. Put that in the piece,' Brian added. He regularly got a fresh salmon from a game keeper he was friends with.

Lyn picked up the telegram which had been lying on the kitchen table, while Norma set to cutting bread.

'The Earl just says you've to go and see him, nothing else,' Lyn said.

'But it *is* a telegram. That speaks volumes as far as I'm concerned,' replied Effie.

Brian was knotting his tie, a job he always found difficult because of the thickness and hardness of his fingers. Fingers far more used to a trowel and hoe than to a tie. He stopped to stare at Effie.

'Let's not build our hopes up too high eh? The Earl might want to help, but that doesn't mean he's going to be able to.'

Effie's return stare bordered on being a glare. 'There's no need to be pessimistic about this,' she snapped.

'I'm not being pessimistic, realistic rather,' Brian replied softly.

'But he did send a telegram all the same,' Effie persisted.

Brian shut up, letting her have the last word. She'd got the message anyway, he could read that in her eyes.

'I've put a couple of nice tomatoes and a screw of salt in the poke as well, Da,' Norma said, changing the subject. With a deft twist she closed the brown paper bag containing her da's food.

Five minutes later Brian was ready for off.

'Now be careful where you stay the night – make sure it's respectable. You know the stories about Glasgow, it's the devil's own place,' Effie warned him as they made for the door.

'I'll be careful. Don't you worry about me,' he replied gently, his voice warm with emotion.

17

'Come and give your da a kiss and wish him luck,' Effie instructed the girls.

Norma was the last in line. 'Good luck Da,' she repeated as the other two had done.

Effie kissed him on the cheek – she'd never have dreamt of kissing him on the mouth in front of the children – muttered 'Good luck', and then Brian was on his way, out the door and striding down the path that would take him to the shore road.

Norma crossed two fingers.

Brian didn't return the next day, or the next. It was Thursday evening when he reappeared, wearing the most hangdog and woebegone of expressions.

Effie put a thumb in her mouth and chewed it. She felt sick.

'Well it was a good idea at least,' Brian said, and shrugged. He placed his case in a corner.

'So what happened?' Effie asked, her voice heavy with disappointment.

That was it then; the family would be split up after all and she would be going to stay with Auntie Josie and Uncle Bill, Norma thought to herself, feeling as sick as Effie.

'I brought you a wee minding back from Glasgow, lass,' Brian said, ignoring his wife's question. He produced a key which he handed to Effie.

She stared blankly at the plain, unadorned, gun-metal object in her hand. 'What's this?' she queried.

'A key.'

'I can see that!' she exclaimed, quite mystified.

Norma, knowing her da as she did and being very quick on the uptake, caught on first.

'Well, to be specific, it's a door-key,' Brian elaborated.

'What blinking door?'

Brian pulled a half bottle of whisky out of his hip pocket and placed it on the table.

'The front door of our new house,' he said, his hangdog and woebegone expression vanishing, to be replaced by a huge beaming smile.

Effie staggered. 'You mean . . .?'

'Aye, I've got a job, thanks to the Earl. I start the fourth of June!'

18

'Hooray?' Eileen yelled, jumping up and down.

'Oh see you, see you!' Effie said, shaking a fist at him for doing that to her. On impulse she went to him and hit him, but not too hard. There were bright sparkling tears in her eyes.

Lyn threw her arms round Norma and hugged her. Then Eileen joined in, the three of them all hugging one another.

'The house is in Bridgeton – the Earl helped me get that as well,' Brian continued.

Effie frowned. Bridgeton, she'd never heard of it.

'It's only a room and a kitchen, smaller than we've got here. But that was all the Earl's friend had available. It's not a bad tenement either – a lot nicer than many I saw.'

While Brian had been speaking he'd taken out two glasses and poured drams for himself and Effie. He now topped the glasses up with water.

'Where is Bridgeton?' Effie asked.

'Central Glasgow.'

'But . . . You mean . . . Are you saying we're going to live in Glasgow?' Effie demanded.

Brian sipped his drink. He'd known this was going to hit hard. 'My job is as a gardener with the Glasgow Corporation Parks Department, with me based at Glasgow Green. Bridgeton will be handy for my work,' he replied softly.

They were to go and stay in Glasgow! Norma hadn't even thought of the possibility · when she'd made her suggestion to her da. She'd presumed the Earl would find Brian another position in a big house similar to Kilmichael House, a house in a rural or semi-rural setting. The sort of thing they were used to.

'Is this another of your jokes?' Effie queried, hoping it was.

Brian shook his head. 'No, I swear.'

'But Glasgow, Da! It's filthy there, and full of criminals,' protested Lyn.

'Well it certainly isn't as clean as it is round here, there's no disputing that. But not all Glaswegians are criminals; some of them are really quite nice, just ordinary, hard-working folk like ourselves.'

'You're telling us there's no choice, Da,' Norma said quietly.

Brian directed his reply to all of them. 'The Earl made a number of enquiries on my behalf, and this was the only one

19

that came up. So it's either Glasgow and the Parks Department or else . . .' After a quick glance at Effie. 'Or else the family will have to split up.' He explained to Lyn and Eileen the contingency plans he'd made. When he'd finished the pair of them were as white as ghosts.

Brian took another sip of his drink. He was just as worried as the rest of the family about going to live in Glasgow, but had no intention of letting on he was. Not even to Effie later.

Effie appeared to be making a decision. Straightening up, she squared her shoulders and thrust out her chin. 'We must look on this as a challenge. If staying together means going to Glasgow, then go to Glasgow we will – and make the best of it,' she said, her voice iron with determination.

'That's the ticket lass!' Brian smiled and silently toasted his wife, his love for her, and the pride he felt for her creeping into his face.

Eight days till they had to vacate the cottage. They'd cut it fine, Norma thought.

But the family *was* going to remain together. That was all that really mattered.

Though God alone knew what they were going into.

All their friends and neighbours came to see them off at the harbour, a hundred folk or more. The gardeners and their families from the House, and the servants too, shopkeepers, school pals, old cronies – even a bevy of ladies from the WI of which Effie had been a keen member.

The paddle-steamer *Strathmore*'s gangplank was taken on board, the funnel hooter sounded, and that was it, they were away.

Norma, standing on the main deck with the rest of the family, was waving frantically to her friends: to Marion Cockburn and Isabella Doig whom she suddenly remembered owed her thruppence, to Mr Annan the baker – she'd aye been a special favourite of his, he slipping her fly buns and cakes for as long as she could remember.

There was Norman Rae, the first boy she'd ever kissed seriously, Norman waving to her fit to bust and looking sad as could be.

And there was Mrs McLure galloping onto the pier, late, but

not too late to have missed them. Mrs McLure ran the Post Office and had closed up especially to be there.

The *Strathmore* was stopping at Wemyss Bay where they'd get off and board the train to Glasgow.

Their furniture and all other belongings had left early that morning, being taken to Glasgow by the far longer inland route. the lorry carrying their things would arrive in Bridgeton some hours after they themselves had got there.

They waved and waved, only stopping when they came abreast of Kilmichael House and – just visible behind – the chimney-stack and -pot of what had been their cottage, and much loved home.

Finally the pier, Kirn and Kilmichael House disappeared astern.

Brian turned to Effie. 'A new beginning,' he said.

'A new beginning,' she echoed.

Rain had been threatening all day and now, heralded by a flash of lightening and a loud clap of thunder, it started bucketing down.

She hoped this wasn't an omen, Norma thought to herself as they raced for the nearest hatchway.

The rain was stotting off the deck as they went below.

Chapter Two

Outside the Central Station they caught a tram that took them along Argyle Street and into the Trongate. Norma stared in fascination; she'd never seen so many buildings or people. As for the tram they were on, clanking and swaying, she found that just a wee bit frightening – like being aboard some metal prehistoric monster.

They left the Trongate to enter Gallowgate, with the district of Calton to the right of them.

Norma wrinkled her nose at the smell which suddenly pervaded the tram. It was a sooty smell, with other nasty odours mingled with it.

There was the smell of heavy industry – a bitter tang that left a bad taste in the mouth. That and the smell of unwashed bodies, excrement, urine, general dirt, decay and the rubbish bins. Together they formed the distinctive smell of the Glasgow slums.

'Ugh!' said Norma, pulling a face.

Effie sat tight-lipped staring at the tall, grey and – to her eyes forbidding – tenements of the Calton. They terrified her.

Lyn gawped at a wee boy strolling past the tram. His trouser legs were raggedy, stopping halfway between his knee and ankle. He had no shoes or socks on and his exposed feet were disgustingly filthy – not with the filth of the day, but with the accumulated filth of weeks.

They passed a street where two men were fighting in the gutter.

'Look Ma!' Eileen cried out, pointing.

There was the crash of a breaking bottle. One man fell to the ground, blood spurting from his face. The other began putting the boot in.

A teenage lad shot out of a closemouth, legs going sixteen to the dozen. He took off up the street like a runaway greyhound.

There was the piercing blast of a whistle, and a pair of policemen came charging out of the same closemouth to go thundering after the lad.

'I said they were all criminals here,' Lyn mumbled, but not loud enough for her da to hear.

'Bridgeton's not nearly as awful as this,' Brian whispered to Effie, giving her a reassuring smile. Her lips tightened.

Norma gazed in amazement at a man sitting on the pavement propped up against a tenement wall. From the way his head was lolling he was clearly drunk. Then, to her total horror, he threw up all over himself.

Calton gave way to Bridgeton, and as Brian had promised there was an improvement, but hardly a big one.

'Our stop!' said Brian, and they all got off, with Eileen clinging to her da's hand.

Norma thought of all they'd left behind: the fresh air from the Firth, the trees, flowers and plants, and the beautiful, glorious sea. All that for – *this?* A huge black cloud of depression settled over her.

They crossed over Gallowgate to a narrow street leading off. 'Cubie Street, where our house is,' Brian announced, thinking it looked a lot meaner and scruffier than he remembered it.

The tenements were grey; the street itself and pavements were grey; even the sky above was grey. The complexions of the children playing peerie in the street were the same colour, in complete contrast to their own healthy complexions.

They passed a broken window, taped up inside with a bit of cardboard. From the room behind came the sound of a woman's hacking cough.

'Here we are, number thirty-eight,' said Brian, stopping outside a close.

'Janice Morton has a big bum' had been chalked on the front of the building.

'That's not all she's got that's big!' had been chalked in a different hand below.

'We're two flights up,' Brian said, and led the way, Eileen still clinging to him as though for dear life.

On the half landing between the first and second flights of

stairs Effie insisted on stopping to inspect the communal toilet.

There was an ancient wooden seat that was scarred and scratched all over; it was even burnt in one place. The toilet bowl was yellow inside, but did give the appearance of having been regularly cleaned and disinfected.

The stone floor was badly cracked, as were the walls – walls painted a vile shade of green.

'It's not that bad,' said Brian quietly.

The toilet was better than she'd expected, Effie had to admit to herself. She'd feared something truly dreadful. It was the fact the family had to *share* it she found off-putting.

They continued on up the stairs.

There were three main doors on each landing, theirs the one on the left. Brian unlocked it and the door swung open.

'Now watch this!' he said, going into the small hall. He flicked a switch and the hall flooded with light.

'Electricity,' he smiled. There had been none at the cottage where they'd had to make do with paraffin lamps.

There were two doors leading from the hall, Brian led them through the one on the left.

They found themselves in a good-sized kitchen, which would also double as a bedroom for Brian and Effie, who would sleep in the cavity bed sunk into the wall that the kitchen shared with 'the room'.

'Modern fireplace, no more cooking on a range,' Brian said to Effie.

The gas stove was already installed, and stood in a corner. Gas was another convenience they hadn't had in the cottage.

Effie turned a brass tap, and immediately there was the hiss of gas. Cooking on gas was going to take getting used to she thought to herself.

Norma peered into the cavity bed. It was like looking into a wee cave she thought. It would be comfy though. She decided she liked it, and was disappointed she wouldn't be sleeping in it.

There was a good linoleum on the floor, while the walls had been distempered not long since. They were painted in a pretty primrose shade which cheered up what might otherwise have been a darkish room.

Norma crossed over to the window above the sink, facing the cavity bed, and peered out.

24

The communal back court was devoid of grass, except for a few forlorn tufts growing here and there. A great deal of rubbish lay scattered over the brown earth: tin cans, broken glass, old newspapers, these sort of things. The brick middens containing the bins were overflowing with refuse.

She turned on the cold water tap, cupped her hands, and took a mouthful of the water.

Her face lit up in surprise. The tap-water was almost as pure, and pleasant to drink, as the well-water they'd been used to.

She said so to Effie who came over and tried it for herself.

'You're right,' Effie said, agreeing with Norma. It was a relief to know she was still going to be able to brew a nice pot of tea.

At Brian's suggestion they all trooped through to 'the room'.

This was a little larger than the kitchen and its walls were papered. The paper was a floral pattern which Norma and Lyn said they didn't mind, but which Eileen declared to be horrible.

'Hard cheese,' Lyn said to her.

The mahogany-brown linoleum was on its last legs, with a gaping crack running right down its centre.

'That'll have to be replaced,' Effie said.

Brian nodded his agreement.

Norma went to the window and looked out. The window was clarty, just as the other had been. They both needed a right good clean.

Across the street two women were leaning out of adjoining windows, having a natter together. Both were wearing full-length pinnies and one had a scarf tied round her head.

There was the clatter of an empty can being kicked. The boy doing the kicking had on tackety boots, several sizes too large for him.

'I'm starving hungry!' Eileen suddenly announced. They had had sandwiches on the train but that seemed ages ago now.

'Well I can't cook anything till my pots and pans get here and that won't be for a while yet,' said Effie.

'Tell you what, why don't I nip out and buy fish suppers?' Brian suggested.

'That's a smashing idea!' Lyn enthused.

'While your da's getting the fish suppers you can get me some messages Norma. We'll need tea, milk and sugar for later tonight, and things for tomorrow's breakfast,' Effie said.

'I don't want to be out there on my own!' Norma replied in alarm.

'Don't be soft. We're going to be living here so you'll have to get used to going to the shops and round about. But as it is your first time Lyn can go with you,' Brian replied.

Lyn wasn't too keen either, but knew her da to be right. And like swimming, the sooner you took the plunge the better.

Effie reeled off the items she wanted, then extracted a ten shilling note from her purse and handed it to Norma.

'Mind check your change and not get diddled!' she warned, not trusting Glasgow shopkeepers one little bit.

Brian, Norma and Lyn walked back to Gallowgate where Norma immediately spied a wee place that would sell what she and Lyn had been sent out to get. The pair of them went in, leaving Brian to find a chippie.

There was a chap in a white apron behind the counter and another chap lounging in front of the counter talking to him. They broke off their conversation as Norma and Lyn approached.

The chap in the white apron couldn't have been nicer or more helpful, putting their messages in a cardboard box when he learned they didn't have a shopping bag.

While they were being served, the second chap, obviously a pal of the other, kept glancing at Norma. When their gazes met he smiled. She didn't smile back.

Lyn waited till they were outside the shop before bursting into laughter.

'I think he fancied you,' she teased.

'Who's that?' Norma replied, pretending innocence.

'You know who. The chap who kept giving you the glad eye.'

'Can't say I noticed,' Norma answered keeping up her pretence of innocence.

'You noticed all right. You'd have to be blind not to.'

'I must be blind then.'

'Oh come off it Norma McKenzie!'

He had been attractive, Norma thought. And wondered who he was.

On reaching what was now their home she promptly forgot all about him.

* * *

26

'What time is it now?' asked Effie.

Brian took out his pocket watch from his suit waistcoat. 'Ten past eleven,' he replied.

The entire family was sitting on the kitchen floor, their backs against various walls. Eileen had long since fallen asleep.

Effie exhaled sharply in exasperation, 'It's not coming tonight, I just know so,' she said, referring to the lorry bringing their furniture and other belongings. It was hours overdue.

'It must have broken down somewhere. That's the only explanation,' Brian replied.

Lyn yawned; she was dead tired. Completely whacked.

'So what are we going to do?' asked Norma.

'The four of you can crowd into that cavity bed while I doss down here. There's nothing else for it,' Brian answered. Luckily there was a mattress in the cavity bed.

'It may be June but it'll be cold during the night,' Lyn complained.

'It'll be colder for me than it will be for you. At least you can cuddle up,' Brian retorted.

'Lift Eileen in will you Brian, she can go to the back of the bed,' Effie said.

Brian went to Eileen and was just about to pick her up when there was a timid knock on the outside door. He looked at Effie who shrugged. She couldn't imagine who it was either.

Going into the hall Brian put the light on, then opened the outside door. A middle-aged woman in a purple cardy stood revealed. The door behind her was ajar.

'I'm Mrs Fullarton, your neighbour,' the woman said, smiling uncertainly.

'Pleased to meet you. I'm Brian McKenzie. We've just moved in, as you no doubt know,' he smiled back.

'Aye, well, that's why I'm chapping. I hope you don't think I'm sticking my nose in or anything like that, it's just that I saw you arrive but no flit with you. Is everything all right?'

'Come away ben and meet the wife and family,' Brian replied, and ushered Mrs Fullarton through to the kitchen where Effie, Norma and Lyn were now standing waiting to be introduced.

'Brian was just saying the lorry must have broken down,' Effie explained.

'It was coming from Kirn so it could well be stuck in the middle of nowhere,' Brian added.

Mrs Fullarton tut-tutted, then said, 'I went to Kirn on a mystery tour once. I thought it a lovely spot.'

'It is indeed,' Effie agreed.

Mrs Fullarton had a great many questions she was dying to ask, but now was hardly the time.

'And another lassie there fast asleep,' she said, nodding at Eileen.

'That's Eileen, my youngest. It's been a long day for her. For all of us,' Effie replied.

Mrs Fullarton's gaze swept round the kitchen taking in the messages that had been bought now standing on the board by the sink. 'Well, we can't let you spend the night like this. I'll organise sheets and blankets for you.'

'Can you do that?' exclaimed Brian.

'Oh aye. A wee knock here and a wee knock there and I'll soon have what you need. Leave it to me.' And with that Mrs Fullarton bustled from the kitchen and out into the house.

Ten minutes later she was back with a lad she introduced as her son Jacky. They'd brought two quilts with them, three large sheets, half a dozen beige blankets and four pillows. They'd also brought a kettle so the McKenzies could make tea.

Effie was visibly moved by all this kindness. 'It's awful good of you,' she said

'Ach away with you. It's what neighbours are for. We all give each other a helping hand round here. It's the only way to get by,' Mrs Fullarton replied.

'Is there anything else you need?' Jacky Fullarton asked. He was a lad in his late teens.

'Nothing I can think of,' Effie replied.

'We'll leave you to it then. Cheerio for now,' Mrs Fullarton said, shooing Jacky out the door.

'Would you credit that,' Effie said when the Fullartons had gone.

'I told you Glasgow folk weren't nearly as bad as they're painted,' Brian beamed.

Effie picked up one of the sheets and smelt it. 'Freshly laundered,' she said. In fact it and the others had been to the steamie that morning.

Norma and Lyn helped Effie make the cavity bed. Brian still had to doss on the floor where, although he spent an uncomfortable night, he at least was warm.

The lorry arrived in at one o'clock the next afternoon; the driver full of apologies. It was as Brian had thought; he'd broken down with engine trouble in an out-of-the-way spot and hadn't been able to get a tow and the engine fixed till that morning. He and Brian set to unloading the heavier things; the girls the lighter.

An oak wardrobe was proving something of a problem, being not only unwieldy but weighing an absolute ton, when two men came along the street to halt beside Brian.

'Mr McKenzie?'

'That's me.'

'I'm Jim Fullarton and this is Sandy Reid who lives the next flight up. Can we help?'

Brian smiled his gratitude. 'That would be tremendous. I'd be fair obliged.'

Jim and Sandy pitched in, and it wasn't long before the lorry was cleared, the entire flit indoors.

Brian was profuse in his thanks, but Jim and Sandy shrugged off what they'd done, Jim echoing his wife's words of the night before that that's what neighbours were for.

Back in the kitchen, Brian put an arm round Effie. 'Living in Glasgow isn't going to be as bad as we'd feared,' he said softly.

Effie agreed.

The Friday that marked their having been in Cubie Street a fortnight was Norma's fifteenth birthday. Effie made an Albert sponge with vanilla icing on top for her, and when Brian arrived home from work – where he'd settled in no bother at all – he was carrying a rectangular shaped parcel wrapped in brown paper.

'Happy birthday, girl,' he said, kissing Norma on the cheek and giving her the parcel.

His eyes twinkled as he watched her undo the string and unwrap the paper. She found a shoe-box inside.

Norma gasped with delight when she took the lid off the box. Nestling in a bed of tissue were a pair of blood-red high-heeled shoes.

'I hope they fit,' Brian smiled. Effie had told him what size and width to buy. But still, you never knew with these things.

Norma slipped first one on, then the other. 'Absolutely perfect,' she pronounced.

She walked up and down, showing them off. 'They're just fabulous Da! I hate to think what they cost.'

'Aye well, as it was your idea to write to the Earl, which saved the family from being split up, I thought you deserved something a wee bit special this year.'

'My first high heels,' she breathed, more to herself than anyone else.

'Can I try them on?' Eileen asked eagerly.

'No you cannot! And no fly goes behind my back. If you do you'll get a clout round the ear.'

Lyn didn't even bother to ask, knowing she'd get the same answer as Eileen.

After they'd had their main course Effie brought out the sponge she'd made and Norma cut it while everyone else sang 'Happy Birthday'. She put five pieces on to the plates laid out.

'My piece is smaller than the rest,' Lyn complained.

'They're all the same, I was careful about that,' Norma told her, thinking no matter what piece she'd given her Lyn would have seen it as smaller than the others.

Lyn didn't argue further, but wasn't at all convinced she hadn't been 'done'.

The table had been cleared; the dishes washed and put away, and Brian was talking to Effie about how different Glasgow Green was to the grounds of Kilmichael House, when suddenly the strains of music came wafting into the kitchen.

'Somebody must be playing a gramophone,' Effie said.

'Don't be daft, that's live or I'm a monkey's uncle. And it sounds like it's coming from the street,' Brian replied.

Eileen scampered through to the room to look out the window.

'You're right Da, there's a band out there!' she called through.

The rest of them went into the room to stare out, and sure enough, there was a band comprising two fiddlers and an accordionist playing just a little further down the street.

Several couples were dancing to the music, while others were standing by watching.

'I wonder what this is in aid of?' Brian mused aloud.

There was a knock on the outside door. Norma answered it to find Mrs Fullarton there, who asked if she could speak to her ma and da. Norma took her ben the room.

'Jenny Elder, who lives a few closes down on this side, has got engaged to Murray Muir who lives further up the street on the other side, and as both their fathers are idle they're having their engagement party in the street. I was instructed to tell you you're all welcome, and both sets of parents hope you'll come down and join in,' Mrs Fullarton said.

So that was the explanation, Norma thought. She glanced out the window again to see that more couples were now dancing. It looked like fun.

'It'll be a good chance for you to meet everyone, and they you,' Mrs Fullarton added.

It would too, Brian told himself.

'Would we be expected to bring anything?' Effie asked.

'Well those men who can afford it will probably take a few screwtops, but that's all,' Mrs Fullarton replied.

'Please Da?' Eileen pleaded.

Brian looked at Effie who gave him a nod. She also thought it a good idea.

'Right then, we'll be glad to accept. We'll be down shortly,' Brian said, knowing Effie would want to change her clothes and generally do herself up a bit. No doubt so would the girls.

'That's grand. Jim's just about to away up to the off-licence to get a few bottles and then we'll be going down.'

'Can I go with him? I'll get some screwtops as well,' Brian said, correctly thinking that what Mrs Fullarton had meant by those who could afford it being men in work, while those 'idle' wouldn't be expected to.

'Aye, he'll be out in a jiffy. You can meet him on the landing,' Mrs Fullarton replied.

Effie found it a daunting prospect having to go out and face so many new people. But she'd do it, and with a smile.

Norma was already rummaging through the wardrobe she shared with Eileen pulling out the dress she intended to wear. It was a cream colour, which would be set off perfectly by her new red shoes.

From outside came the sound of someone wheeching. The party was hotting up.

Effie dabbed on a wee touch of powder, then put a drop of the Evening in Paris perfume behind each ear. That completed her make-up. She never ever wore lipstick. Not that she had anything against lipstick, it was just that she'd always felt it was too much for her. She preferred things plain and simple.

There was a minor scuffle when Lyn discovered that Eileen was wearing a bracelet of hers, but Effie soon sorted that out, making Eileen return the bracelet to Lyn who put it on even though she hadn't intended wearing it.

'Can I have a dab of your powder Ma?' Norma asked.

Effie considered the request, then nodded. How grown up Norma was becoming. Why, it only seemed like yesterday that — She smiled to herself. Was there ever a parent who'd never had the same thought? She doubted it.

Effie took a final look at herself in the wardrobe mirror, and rearranged one of her tortoiseshell combs. She wasn't bad for someone of thirty-four who'd had three children and a miscarriage, she told herself. Not bad at all.

Brian returned with his screwtops to say that Jim Fullarton had suggested the two families go down together, which was what they did a few minutes later.

There was quite a gathering in the street now, with a good two dozen couples up dancing.

In quick succession the McKenzies met the Vicarys, Mathers, McNaughtons, Carrs, Galbraiths and Laidlaws. The Mathers and Laidlaws lived in their close.

'I was wondering if you'd care to have a birl?' Jacky Fullarton asked Norma, stammering a little.

Eileen giggled, and Norma glared at her, giving her a right sinker.

'I'd love to Jacky, thank you,' she replied and, taking his arm, crossed over with him to where the dancing was taking place.

The three-piece band, if you could call it a band, was playing a polka, and giving it big licks, the fiddlers sawing madly with their bows; the accordionist attacking his instrument with such vigour it might have been a demented bellows about to run amok.

While Norma was up with Jacky Fullarton, Brian and Effie met the Muirs and Elders, whose son and daughter's engagement hoolie it was.

The band took a break, so Norma and Jacky came off 'the floor', Norma rejoining Lyn and Jacky his parents.

'Look who was watching you,' Lyn said quietly, giving a sideways gesture of her head.

Norma glanced in that direction to see a vaguely familiar face staring back at her. He was tallish, with fair hair and – even noticeable at that distance – bright blue eyes.

'Recognise him?' queried Lyn.

The penny dropped. 'The chap in the shop we met that first night here. The one in front of the counter,' Norma replied.

'That's him, and he hasn't taken those gorgeous blue peepers off you the whole time you've been up with Jacky Fullarton.'

Norma had found him attractive before, and still did. In fact, he was quite a dish. She wondered if he'd ask her up? He must be interested if he'd been watching her the way Lyn said he had.

'He's on the move,' Lyn whispered.

'Is he coming over here?' Norma asked, having immediately looked the opposite way.

'The Pride of Erin!' one of the fiddlers announced. The band struck up, and dancing resumed.

'He's gone over to speak to Jacky,' Lyn replied.

Eileen went dashing past, playing tig with some of the street's other children. She was having a whale of a time.

'I think he's coming over now, with Jacky,' Lyn whispered. Norma put on her most nonchalent expression.

'Norma, I'd like you to meet a pal of mine, Midge Henderson – Midge, this is Norma McKenzie, and her sister Lyn,' Jacky said.

Norma focused on Midge, as if noticing him for the first time.

'Hello, pleased to meet you,' he smiled.

He had a typical Glasgow voice, grey with a hint of gravel.

'Midge? What sort of name is that?' she queried.

'It's short for Michael, and not because I used to play round the midgies as a wee boy,' he answered, his smile widening.

Norma's face went blank. 'What's a midgie?'

'They're new to Glasgow, flitted here from Kirn down the Clyde coast,' Jacky explained.

'I knew you'd moved here recently, but didn't realise it was from outside Glasgow: A midgie is a midden,' Midge replied.

'You learn something every day!' Lyn said and laughed.

'Would you like to dance?' Midge asked Norma.

She hesitated for a brief moment, not wanting to appear too eager. 'Yes, that would be nice. Thank you,' she said.

Lyn was hoping that Jacky would ask her up, and was disappointed when he excused himself, and went elsewhere. She watched in envy as Norma and Midge took to 'the floor'.

'What brought you here from Kirn?' asked Midge.

'My da landed a job with the Parks Department, he's a gardener.' She then explained about Mr Hodgart and Kilmichael House, but not about Brian writing to the Earl, thinking that a private matter. If her da wanted to tell people then that was up to him.

'Your da was lucky to get another job so quickly, unemployment being as rife as it is. And Glasgow's no better than the rest of Scotland – worse I'd say. Why, half the men in Cubie Street are idle, maybe even more than that.'

'What about yourself?' Norma asked.

'I'm an apprentice with the North Woodside Flint Mills on the Garriochmill Road. I finish my apprenticeship next year when I'm eighteen.'

Norma was intrigued. 'What happens in a flint mill?' she queried.

He grinned. 'Basically, we reduce the flint to a fine powder by a process of burning and grinding. It's then used in the making of glaze for sanitary earthenware. Right now I'm mainly concerned with the kiln where the flint is calcined, which is to say burned.'

'Sounds interesting,' Norma commented.

'Yes. And they're a good bunch that work there. But what about you, what do you do?'

'I was at school in Kirn, but left on coming here. I'm on the look-out for work, but haven't found anything so far.'

School! He'd taken her for older than that. He'd thought her his own age.

However, she was certainly a looker. Tall for a lassie, as tall as himself, with honey-blonde hair, a deepish voice and eyes that kept changing from grey to green and back again. He thought her a knockout.

'I like your shoes,' he said.

'I only got them today. They're for my birthday.'

'Your birthday!' he exclaimed. 'Congratulations. What does that make you then?'

'Fifteen,' she smiled.

Which meant she'd been only fourteen when he'd seen her in Chic's shop a fortnight previously. 'Ach you're no more than a bairn still!' he teased.

That annoyed her. Bairn indeed! She felt herself going right off him.

'I live in number six,' he said.

'Do you,' she answered coldly, making it sound as if that was of no importance whatever to her.

He burbled on till the end of the dance.

'Thank you,' she said the instant the dance was finished. Before he could ask her to stay up she strode off, leaving him standing.

'What happened there?' Lyn asked when Norma rejoined her.

'He was impertinent. I didn't like that,' Norma snapped in reply.

Lyn pulled a face. '*Impertinent was he! Dear me.*'

Trust Lyn to take the mickey, Norma thought. She was forever doing it, something she'd inherited from their Da.

The band struck up again, this time a schottische. Lyn looked round hopefully, but there was no lad making in her direction.

'I think I'm destined to be a wallflower,' she sniffed.

'What about me, will I do?' Norma said.

'I thought you'd never ask,' Lyn replied, and giggled, thinking what the heck! Your sister was better than nothing. Arm in arm, the pair of them took to 'the floor'.

Effie was thoroughly enjoying herself. It had been no ordeal whatever meeting all these folk; in fact it had been easy as pie. Right then she was having a fine old chinwag with Mrs Vicary who'd invited her in for a cup of tea the following day, an invitation she'd eagerly accepted.

Brian was drinking beer. The screwtops that had been brought had all been placed on a bench that had been set out,

35

and anyone who wanted one just helped themselves, irrespective of whether they'd contributed or not.

Norma was dancing and laughing with Lyn when suddenly she found herself whisked out of Lyn's grasp and into that of a man. It was Midge.

'Lassies aren't allowed to dance with lassies here so we've come to split you up,' he said.

Lyn was with Jacky Fullarton, who'd been dragooned into this by Midge who'd wanted to dance again with Norma.

'You're persistent aren't you,' Norma said.

He gave her a cheeky grin. 'Did you take the hump because I called you a bairn?'

She'd give him the frozen treatment, she decided. She looked off to the side, and didn't reply.

'Ach come on, it was only a wee joke. No need to take it that way.'

She continued looking to the side.

'All right, I'm sorry if it upset you. That was the last thing I intended.'

She was stiff in his arms, like dancing with a stookie he thought. Her feet might be going through the motions, but apart from that she was totally unresponsive.

He felt his confidence draining away. He'd made a mistake in saying what he had, and a further mistake in splitting her from her sister. He stopped dancing.

'I didn't mean to force myself on you, and won't bother you anymore. I really am sorry you took such offence where none was meant. Thanks for the dance,' he said, and made to move away.

She didn't know why she did what she did next, but nevertheless she did. Perhaps it was something in his tone; perhaps it was because she really did like him and knew if he went now that would be the end of it.

She reached out and took hold of an arm, stopping him. 'I'll tell you what, let's start again shall we?'

His bright blue eyes sent a shiver through her insides. Then she was once more in his arms and they resumed dancing.

When that dance was finished she stayed where she was. She didn't have to be asked if she wanted to stay up. Both of them wanted to, and both knew that. It didn't have to be said.

A wee while later the band broke for a breather, and a woman called Belle McHarg got up to sing. She launched into a folksong called 'The Dundee Weaver'.

Oh I'm a Dundee weaver and I come from bonnie Dundee,
I met a Glesca fella and he came courting me.
He took me oot a walking, doon by the Kelvin Ha',
And there the dirty wee rascal stole my thingummyjig awa' ...

Norma tapped a foot in time to the tune, there'd been a lot of folksongs sung in and around Kirn, and she'd always enjoyed them. But this was a new one to her.

He took me oot a picnic, doon by the Rouken Glen,
He showed to me the bonnie wee birds and he showed me a bonnie wee hen.
He showed tae me the bonnie wee birds frae a linnet tae a craw,
Then he showed tae me the bird that stole my thingummyjig awa' ...

Norma frowned, she didn't understand the words.

So I'll go back to Dundee looking bonnie, young and fair,
Oh I'll put on my buckle and shoes and tie up my bonnie broon hair.
Oh I'll put on my corsets tight tae mak' my body look sma',
And wha' will ken with my rosy cheeks that my thingummyjig's awa' ...

Norma turned to Midge. 'What's her thingummyjig?' she asked.

He raised an eyebrow, saw she was serious, and wondered whether he should tell her or not. After all he'd only just met the girl.

He decided he would. Putting his mouth to an ear he whispered.

Norma's face flamed. How could she have been so dense! And how embarrassing. She felt quite mortified.

It was too much for Midge, he burst out laughing which made her face flame even more.

So a' you Dundee weavers take this advice from me,
Oh never let a fella an inch above your knee.
Oh never staun at the back of a close or up against a wa'
For if you do you can safely say your thingummyjig's awa.
For if you do you can safely say your thingummyjig's awa'.

37

'I shouldn't laugh but your expression after I told you was priceless,' Midge said.

Norma didn't know where to put herself. She wished the ground would open up and swallow her.

'I'd better get back to the others,' she mumbled, and started to go.

This time it was he who reached out and stopped her. 'Please don't?' he pleaded.

'I ...'

'Please?'

'I feel such a fool.'

'You're anything but. You're the prettiest lassie here tonight, and you'll break my heart if you don't stay up.'

'Your heart must be easily broken then?'

He was amazed at his own audacity. He'd never said anything even remotely like that to a girl before.

The fiddler doing the announcing said they'd had a request for the 'dinky one-step'.

'Can you do it?' Norma asked. It was a favourite of hers, and a dance she'd learned at school. She'd had a teacher there who'd taught her a number of dances.

'Just try me,' Midge replied.

Right, she thought. She would.

It was a waltz-hold, with the man facing the line of dance, or direction in which the dancers move round the ballroom, which is to say anti-clockwise.

Afterwards Norma couldn't say how it happened, only that it did. She and Midge somehow fused, to become as one. She knew exactly what he was going to do, and how he was going to do it. And it was the same with him. They might have been telepathic.

When the dance ended there was applause, and the applause was for them alone. Glasgow is the most dancingest city in the Empire, and Glaswegians know good dancing when they see it.

'Well,' said Norma, lost for words.

'You're not half bad,' Midge told her.

'You're not half bad yourself.'

'Listen, there's a big dance on tomorrow night at the Magic Stick – Roy Fox and his band will be playing. Would you like to go with me?' Midge asked eagerly.

Norma laughed. 'What's the Magic Stick when it's at home?'

'It's the nickname for the Majestic, a dancehall in town.'

Roy Fox and his band, why they were famous! She'd heard them a number of times on the wireless.

'I'd love to but ...'

'But what?' he queried anxiously.

'I really would have to ask my da first.'

'Then do that. Do you want me to come with you?'

'No, I'll speak to him on my own,' she replied, hoping Brian was going to say yes. Oh please God he would!

She told Midge she'd see him again in a few minutes, then left him to seek out her da whom she found amongst a knot of men chaffing one another.

'That was a fine bit of dancing there. You and the lad were quite a sight,' Brian said.

She drew her father aside. 'His name's Midge Henderson and he's asked me to go out with him tomorrow night. Can I Da?'

Brian's brow creased with doubt. She was just turned fifteen that day after all. If he agreed this would be the first time she'd ever been out properly with a lad.

'Take you where?' he queried.

'A dancehall in town.'

Brian didn't like the sound of that, not one little bit. He listened intently while she told him why Midge particularly wanted to go to the Majestic.

'Jim, can I have a word?' he called out to Jim Fullarton, who immediately came over.

He explained the situation, then asked Jim's opinion of Midge.

'Midge was born into the street, and I've known him all his life. Let me put it this way, if I had a lassie and Midge asked her out I wouldn't put the stoppers on it,' Jim replied.

'Would you let this supposed lassie of yours go into town with him though?'

'Norma will be all right with Midge, I assure you.'

'So can I go Da?'

She was clearly mad keen. It would be an awful blow to her if he did say no, and he didn't really see how he could refuse after Jim's strong recommendation of the boy.

His face cracked into a smile. 'I wouldn't mind seeing and hearing Roy Fox in the flesh myself. He's rare.'

Norma kissed him on a cheek. 'Thanks Da.'

Brian watched his eldest daughter walk away from him with a lump in his throat. This was the start of it, he told himself. She wasn't his wee Norma anymore.

'Well, what's the verdict?' Midge demanded when Norma joined him.

She nodded. 'It's on.'

'I'll pick you up at half six then.'

'I'll be ready.'

The 'dashing white sergeant' was announced. Brian got Effie up, and a chap asked Lyn if she'd care to trip the light fantastic with him.

Norma and Midge went back onto 'the floor'.

'How do I look Da?'

'A real treat,' he assured her.

Norma was wearing a black dress that Effie had found in a WI jumble sale, and which was the very thing for this occasion. She had her new red shoes on, of course, and a brand new pair of Ballito stockings which Effie had gone out that afternoon and bought for her.

'Will you kiss him when you get back?' Eileen asked wickedly, puckering up her lips and making kissing sounds – sounds that quickly degenerated into a fit of giggling.

Lyn laughed. 'And will it be in the back close?'

'There will be no kissing or back close for me!' Norma retorted sharply, thinking of the song from the night before.

'I should think so. And you two stop it!' Brian said, wagging a finger at Eileen and Lyn.

Brian was doing his best to put on a brave front, but was worried sick. It was all right Jim Fullarton saying Norma would be fine, but Glasgow was Glasgow.

'Home by ten thirty mind, no later,' he said to Norma.

'I'll tell Midge that,' Norma replied.

'Make sure you do.'

Brian tried not to think of the big gang fight that had taken place in Sauchiehall Street the weekend before last. The accounts of it in the newspapers had been enough to make your hair stand on end.

Effie glanced over at Brian. His brave front wasn't fooling her any and his eyes gave the game away. They told her how he was really feeling. Nor was she all that happy either, she had to admit it.

There was a knock on the outside door.

'I'll get it!' Eileen said, leaping up from her chair.

Lyn, just to annoy her, beat her to it.

'You're awful quiet the night,' Norma said to Midge. They were on top of a tram taking them into town. He couldn't have said more than a dozen words since picking her up.

'Am I?' he replied, pretending he hadn't realised he'd been.

He's gone right off me, Norma thought. He doesn't fancy me anymore.

But it wasn't that at all. He'd been looking forward all day to seeing her again, and then chapping her door he'd suddenly felt himself clamming up, going all shy. That had surprised him, shocked him even. For he was anything but a shy person. In fact he was normally quite the opposite. No girl had ever had this effect on him before.

He forced himself to make small talk till they came to their stop. From there, it was a short walk to the Majestic. They had to queue to get in.

The hall where the actual dancing took place was a gilt and plush cavern. Norma gaped, she'd never seen the like.

'It's gorgeous,' she breathed, quite overawed.

Roy Fox and his band were already playing. Al Bawley was the vocalist, giving his famed megaphone delivery. Thanks to the megaphone his words rang round the hall like bullets, each bullet crisp and clear.

'Would you like to sit for a bit, or get up right away?' Midge asked.

'Sit I think and ... well just take it all in,' she answered.

They had trouble finding a table, but when they eventually did, secured one that afforded them a good view of the bandstand.

Norma sat entranced, feeling as if she'd strayed into another world, a fairyland.

41

Eventually they got up to a foxtrot, and it was the same as the previous night. They fused together, to dance as one.

'I enjoyed that, I really did,' Norma enthused as they sat down again.

'I did too.'

She sighed with pleasure, having completely forgotten that he seemed to have gone off her.

For his part Midge was beginning to unclam, his shyness starting to disappear.

'Did you hear those American voices when we were on the floor?' he asked.

She shook her head. 'No.'

'Well I did.' His eyes took on a faraway, dreamy look. It was as if he was seeing something in the far, far distance, something she couldn't.

He went on, now speaking very softly. 'That's one place I'd give my eye-teeth to go to. And one day I will. I've promised myself.'

'What, America?'

'New York, Chicago, San Francisco and the Barbary Coast, all magic names to me, just as Sydney, Cape Town, Bombay, Cairo and many others are. It's not only America I want to see, but Australia, South Africa, India, Egypt and a dozen other countries I could name.'

'Sounds like you've got a real wanderlust,' she replied, smiling.

'I can't think of anything more exciting than travelling. Can you?'

'It doesn't really appeal to me all that much, I'm afraid. I should imagine it would get boring after a while.'

'Boring!' he exclaimed, shaking his head in disbelief. How could travelling possibly be boring!

'And how will you manage this travelling to all these foreign parts?' she asked.

'I don't know yet. But I will somehow. I'm determined.'

A young man's flight of fancy, she thought. And why not, it didn't do any harm to have dreams. It showed imagination, which was a good thing. But probably, like so many working-class Glaswegians, the only travelling he'd end up doing was 'doon ra watter fur ra Fair', which was to say

42

down the Clyde for the Glasgow Fair holidays.

After a while they got up to dance again, and Norma couldn't help noticing that a number of pairs of eyes followed them round the floor. A compliment indeed in a Glasgow dancehall.

The following Wednesday evening, just as the McKenzies were about to sit down to tea, there was a knock on the outside door, which Eileen went to answer.

She came back into the kitchen. 'It's for you, Romeo himself,' she said airily to Norma.

Norma glared at her wee sister. 'Do you mean Midge?'

'Who else do you think I mean!'

'Didn't you ask him in?' Effie called out from the sink where she was draining the potatoes.

'He said he wouldn't as he was wearing his work boots. Maybe he didn't want to take them off because his feet smell,' Eileen jibed.

'Ssshh, he'll hear you!' Norma whispered.

She hurried through to the hall, closing the kitchen door behind her, which made Effie smile, and Brian frown. Her own da's work boots, covered in their usual clart, were just inside the front door where he'd left them on arriving home from work. He cleaned them once a week, on Sunday mornings after he'd had his bacon and egg and read the paper.

'Hello,' said Norma with a smile, wishing her hair wasn't so greasy-looking. She was going to wash it later on.

'I just met a lassie I know called May Hastie who works for the SCWS – that's the Scottish Cooperative Wholesale Society – in Morrison Street, which is off the Paisley Road. She's an office junior there – or at least was. She was informed this morning that she's been promoted and her promotion will take effect as from next week. That means her present job will be going vacant,' he said quickly.

Norma saw right away what he was driving at. 'And you think I should apply?'

'May says she's pretty certain they haven't got anyone lined up.'

There was a warmness in his voice when he spoke the girl's name that was a giveaway. A pang of jealousy stabbed through Norma. 'Is this May an old flame of yours then?' she teased.

Midge looked down and shuffled his feet. There she was making him feel, well, positively shy again. He found that profoundly disturbing.

'Aye she was, but it was a long time ago,' he mumbled.

'It's good of you to think of me Midge. Thank you.'

He cleared his throat. 'It's a huge warehouse in Morrison Street, you can't miss it. May says you should ask for a Mr Scully who does the hiring and firing.'

'I'll be there first thing tomorrow.'

'Good luck then.'

He was on the half landing when she called out. 'And thanks again Midge.'

He gave her a brief smile, then clattered away.

She flew back to the kitchen to tell Brian and Effie.

'How do you feel?' asked Effie.

'How do you think?'

Effie had come with Norma to Morrison Street and the pair of them were now sitting outside Mr Scully's office. Norma would go in alone.

'Now remember, only speak when you're spoken to, and don't ask any questions unless he asks you to.

'I understand,' Norma replied, nodding. Her insides were churning, for she was convinced she had a definite chance. She only prayed her face fitted.

Effie's gaze swept again over Norma, checking for the umpteenth time that she was neat and tidy; that everything was just as it should be. She didn't tell Norma, but she had the collywobbles herself.

'I wonder what the pay is?' Norma whispered.

'Whatever it is, tell him that's fine if you're offered the job. And tell him you can start right away, today if needs be. Let him see how keen you are.'

Mr Scully's door opened and his secretary emerged. 'Miss McKenzie, if you'll just step this way please,' the secretary said.

Norma rose. Her insides weren't just churning anymore, they were in her throat trying to jump out of her mouth.

'Good luck lass,' said Effie.

Norma went through the door feeling as though she was walking to her own execution.

She hung out the window, waiting for Midge to turn into the street on his way home from work. Then she saw him, talking to a couple of other lads he'd met in Gallowgate.

'Midge!' she shouted, gesturing that she was coming down.

When she reached the closemouth she found him waiting for her, the lads he'd been with having gone on.

'I got it! I start Monday,' she blurted out, hugging herself with glee.

'Oh that's smashing, it really is,' he beamed.

'Ma went with me. The warehouse was still closed when we arrived and we had to wait until it opened. Then we had to wait another half an hour before I got in to see Mr Scully, but when I did he was nice as pie. I just know I'm going to enjoy working there.'

'I'm pleased I was able to help, jobs being as scarce as they are and all.'

'Aye, like gold dust,' she agreed. For the chronic unemployment situation was something that had really come home to her since she'd started looking for work.

'Right then, good,' he said.

She placed a hand on his right arm, a gesture that said 'thank you' but in a more intimate way than just speaking the words, then turned, intending to run back up the close.

'Norma?'

She stopped, turning to him again.

'There's a dance on this Friday at Bridgeton Public Halls. The band won't be Roy Fox, but they shouldn't be bad all the same.'

Something flipped inside her. Flipped, fluttered and made her feel warm.

'I'd love to go with you,' she told him.

'Seven o'clock?'

'Seven o'clock. I'll be ready.'

Halfway up the stairs she started to sing.

45

Chapter Three

It was February of the following year, 1933, and Midge was having a double celebration party at home. Firstly to celebrate his birthday – he'd turned eighteen the previous week – and secondly to celebrate the fact that his three-year apprenticeship was over and that he was now time-served. This meant that he would now be paid a full man's wage instead of a boy's.

Leslie and Alice Henderson, Midge's parents, had two rooms and a kitchen; the party being held in the larger of the two rooms.

The carpet had been rolled back, and a gramophone borrowed to provide music. Leslie had also laid on a couple of crates of beer and a couple of bottles of whisky.

Norma was there, for she and Midge had been courting all this while. So too was Midge's younger sister Katy, who was the same age as Norma, and there were other close friends from the street and round about, about twenty folk in all, a number Alice had declared to be just right for the amount of space they had available.

'Here, have some of this, you look like you could use it,' Midge said to Norma, handing her a glass of beer.

She drank some down, then handed back the glass. She'd just finished an energetic bout of dancing with Billy McManus, a neighbour who was also great pals with Midge.

'Enjoying yourself?' Midge asked.

She nodded. 'And you?'

'Thoroughly.'

She linked an arm round one of his, thinking how happy she was. She was always happy when she was with Midge, and she believed he felt the same way about her. At least that was what he said.

Bob Gillespie who was operating the gramophone now held up a hand and called for silence. The Gillespies lived in Graham Square adjacent to the Cattle Market; he and Leslie Henderson had fought side by side in the Great War.

'A wee bit of hush please!' he yelled.

The noise died away. 'That's better. Now as some of you might know, Midge and his girlfriend Norma there have been going a lot to the jigging lately, and a wee birdie has told me they're rather good. That being the case, and this being his party, I think he and Norma should give us an exhibition. So come on you two, it's a slow waltz.'

Midge looked at Norma. 'Well?'

'Why not,' she answered, and they took the centre of the floor to loud applause.

Bob Gillespie wound up the gramophone and placed the needle on the record. The music of the Savoy Orpheans filled the room.

It was as it always was when they danced together; they fused to become as one. As they swirled round the floor Bob and Beryl Gillespie nodded their appreciation.

When it was over Norma and Midge, more for a laugh than anything else, bowed solemnly first to one side, then to the other, then returned to where they'd been standing.

'That was smashing so it was,' Katy Henderson said to Norma, when the applause that had greeted the end of their exhibition was beginning to die away.

It was funny, Norma thought. It didn't bother her to perform in front of others, in fact she thoroughly enjoyed it. Whereas with other things, such as her interview with Mr Scully at SCWS, she'd go rigid with fright and embarrassment.

Later in the evening Bob and Beryl Gillespie came over to join Norma and Midge, Bob saying he wanted to speak with them.

'Did you know Beryl and I used to go ballroom dancing?' he asked.

'No I didn't.'

'Oh aye, for a number of years actually. We were nothing startling mind, but we both enjoyed it.'

Beryl Gillespie chipped in. 'We had to stop in the end because of my recurring hip bursitis. When something becomes a torture

47

rather than a pleasure then you realise it's the time to give it up.'

'We still go spectating occasionally, but it's not the same thing,' Bob Gillespie said.

'You two have real talent, there's no doubt about it. Have you considered going in for proper ballroom dancing rather than the dancing you go to now?' Beryl asked.

Midge glanced at Norma. They had discussed it vaguely once, but never pursued the subject. 'Not really,' he said slowly.

'You'd find the standard a lot higher than those you're mixing with now, and of course, the most exciting thing about ballroom dancing are the championships. They give you something to aim for. And what an achievement if you could actually win a championship eh? Beryl and I would have given our eyeteeth to have done that, but we were nowhere near good enough,' Bob Gillespie said.

'Isn't it an expensive business though?' Norma asked.

'You mean buying the gowns?' Beryl queried.

'They must cost an awful lot.'

'They can do, if you buy them. But I used to always design and make my own. A lot of the women do that – it's a great deal cheaper that way. But if you were interested, to get you started, I could give you all mine – they're just taking up space in the wardrobe anyway, and your ma could alter them for you. Could she do that?'

'Oh aye, we have a Singer that she's a dab hand with. But I wouldn't have to ask her, I could do the altering myself. I can do everything except cutting out – for some reason I've never been able to get the hang of that so Ma always does it.'

'It can be very very glamorous. Out there with a spotlight on you is an experience that takes some beating,' Beryl went on.

Norma liked the idea of that, and so too did Midge.

'If you are interested why not jump right in at the deep end? This year's Glasgow Latin American Championship is to be held at the Albert Ballroom next month; why not put yourselves in for it?' Bob Gillespie suggested.

'It could be fun,' Norma said, smiling at Midge.

'Aye, but what about tails, he'd need a set of those and they must cost a small fortune,' commented Leslie Henderson.

'It's a pity but I sold mine after Beryl and I gave up, otherwise he'd have been welcome to them,' Bob Gillespie said.

'You certainly couldn't go ballroom dancing without a set,' Alice Henderson said.

'I'm afraid buying a brand new set of tails would be too much for my pocket. Even with my increase in wages it would be way beyond me,' Midge said.

'Then why not buy second-hand? Surely you could pick up a second-hand set somewhere?' Norma suggested.

'I could try.'

'Shall we put our names down then?'

'Do you want us to?'

'Do *you*?'

Midge laughed. 'Let me get the tails first. If I get them then we will.'

'I'm sure you'll find you'll really enjoy yourselves,' Beryl Gillespie beamed.

'And we'll come along to watch and give you support,' Bob Gillespie added.

'I'm looking forward to it already,' Midge said.

So was Norma. She was looking forward to it tremendously, and was glad the Gillespies had suggested it to them.

'I'll drop those gowns in to Alice and she can bring them over to you. You'll have them within the next few days,' Beryl Gillespie told Norma.

Norma couldn't wait.

Early evening two Saturdays later found Norma waiting for Midge to call – they were going out dancing at the Bridgeton Public Halls. She was anxious to hear how he had got on with his latest expedition to find a suitable set of tails.

Midge arrived on the dot of seven, wearing a glum expression.

'I've tried every second-hand clothes shop I know and not one of them has a single set of tails for sale. You'd think such things just didn't exist,' he announced.

'Aye well, it's Glasgow you see. Apart from your ballroom-dancers how many men would own the likes? Precious few I would imagine. And I suppose the toffs who do have them either wear them out or else pass them on to their sons, that sort tending to be mean,' Brian said from where he was sitting by the fireplace.

He had a point, Norma thought. Toffs – real toffs that is and not new money like the Hodgarts – did tend to hang on to things. They were known for it.

'Have you tried the Barrows?' Eileen piped up. The Barrows was a large street market near Glasgow Cross. She went on. 'They say you can get anything there from a stuffed parrot to French postcards.'

'Eileen!' exclaimed Effie. What did she know about French postcards!

Brian gave his youngest daughter a sinker, a look that plainly said, 'We'll have no more mention of things like that young lady, *or else.*'

Eileen smiled sweetly back, and wondered what they'd have said if she'd told them she'd seen half a dozen French postcards that Tommy Jack in her class had got from his brother in the Merchant Navy. But that was her secret, she wasn't telling anyone.

'I haven't tried the Barrows, that's a thought,' said Midge. It was possible he might just get a set there.

'I'll go tomorrow morning,' he told Norma, the Barrows being a Saturday- and Sunday-only market.

'And I'll come with you. I've never been.'

After Norma and Midge had left for the dancing Brian went back to his paper, to the news article about the German Reichstag having been set on fire.

Chancellor Hitler worried him, there was something disturbing about the man. Something very dangerous.

The Barrows was in full swing, with throngs of people surging to and fro on the hunt for bargains. There were a number of stalls that sold second-hand clothes. Norma and Midge began rifling through them.

It was she who found the set of tails, and a smashing set they were too. Hardly worn at all.

'Over here!' she shouted to Midge, and when he joined her she held them up against him for size. He tried on the jacket which was near as dammit to being a perfect fit. The trousers would need to be taken in a bit round the waist.

'How much?' Norma asked the stallholder.

'A fiver and you can take them away.'

Norma glanced at Midge; she knew three pounds to be his maximum. And that was a full week's wage at his new rate.

'That's daylight robbery. You should be wearing a black mask and carrying a pistol,' she replied to the stallholder.

The stallholder grinned. He enjoyed a bit of banter and suspected he was going to get some here.

'A fiver it is missus, and worth every farthing,' he said.

Norma smiled to herself to be called missus; it was really a term for an older woman. She knew he was getting at her.

'There can't be much call for a set of tails in Glasgow. You'll still have them here this time next year if we don't do you a favour by taking them off your hands,' she replied.

'I'll sell them all right, no bother at all.'

'Sez you!'

The stallholder stared at Norma. She stared straight back at him, holding his gaze.

He shrugged. 'Tell you what, as a gesture of goodwill I'll knock a dollar off the price. Four pounds fifteen, I can't say fairer than that.'

She laughed. 'Where do you think the likes of us are going to get that sort of money for a set of tails? We're only working-class folk you know, not blinking royalty.'

'Then why not a nice serge suit? I've got one here I can let you have for thirty bob.'

'I need tails for the dancing,' Midge explained.

'Oh aye?'

'Ballroom dancing,' Norma elaborated.

'I get you now. The real fancy stuff?' he said, and did a few quick steps behind his stall, much to the amusement of the others round about.

'Have you always had club feet?' Norma asked blithely.

The stallholder scowled; he considered himself to be a fairly good dancer. 'Those tails are worth four pounds fifteen. Why, they're almost new,' he said.

Norma looked down at the set of tails. She had her heart set on that Latin American Championship and these were the only set of second-hand ones they'd been able to find.

'I'll tell you what. I must be off my chump but I'll give them to you for four pounds ten. Now how about that?' the stallholder offered.

Norma had ten bob of her own money she could add to Midge's three quid, but that still left them a pound short. She looked again at the set of tails spread before them; she was determined she and Midge were going to walk away with them. *Determined.*

'Give me your three quid,' she said to Midge, holding out her hand. Taking the money from him she put it on the stall, then placed her ten shillings alongside.

'That's all we've got. I swear to you,' she said to the stall-holder.

The man eyed the four crumpled notes. He was tempted – but not tempted enough. He was convinced he could do better.

'Sorry hen,' he said, shrugging his shoulders.

'Let's go,' Midge muttered, making to pick up the cash. But he was stopped by Norma tugging his arm.

'Four pounds seven and six, and not a penny less. That is my *final* comedown, I promise you.' the stallholder said, folding his arms resolutely in front of him.

Norma suddenly realised that a crowd had gathered round, all of whom were watching expectantly, waiting to see what was going to happen next.

'It's hopeless,' Midge said to her.

And so it seemed, for it was clear that the stallholder meant what he'd said about not coming down any further.

'Hell's teeth!' she swore, seeing the Latin American Championship fast disappearing down the plughole.

Then she spied a gramophone on an adjacent stall, which gave her an idea.

'Does that grammy work?' she called out to the owner of the stall, pointing at the machine.

He nodded.

'Then would you play it for us please? Something we can dance to.'

'What are you intending to do?' Midge asked in a low voice.

'We're seventeen and six short, so let's see if we can earn it,' she replied and, going over to an old gaffer in the crowd, asked if she could borrow his cap.

The owner of the gramophone was only too happy to oblige; what had he to lose after all? Someone might buy the gramophone as a result. Quickly he wound it up, and put a record on the table. It was a tango.

Realising that something unusual was happening, people were joining the ever-swelling crowd from all directions.

'Right, let's give them an explanation,' Norma said to Midge. Then, in a loud voice so all could hear, 'And all contributions will be welcome so that we can raise the seventeen and a kick we need!'

Glaswegians have a great sense of humour, and this ploy of Norma's appealed. It also showed originality and the refusal to be beaten, both qualities much admired by Mungo's children.

Midge entered into the spirit of the thing, what else could he have done? He bowed to Norma, she to him, and sliding into each other's arms they were off.

The glorious daftness of it all made the day for those watching; soon ha'pennies, pennies, wooden and silver thruppennies, and sixpences were flying through the air to land in and around the borrowed cap on the ground.

They danced the same tango again and again to a crowd that, forming in a semicircle round them and standing back to give them room, cheered, clapped, whistled and generally urged them on. They only stopped when it was clear that no more contributions would be coming their way.

Norma gathered up and counted the money. 'We're still one and two short,' she said to Midge.

'Ach tae hell with it. If you want that set of tails so bloody much, and because I enjoyed your dancing, you can have them for what you've got now,' the second-hand clothing stallholder announced, a comment which was greeted by a storm of applause from the crowd.

Norma's cheeks flushed with pleasure. She'd won – they'd got Midge's set of tails after all.

'As we're skint we'll have to walk home,' Midge said to her.

'I don't mind. Do you?'

He shook his head. 'Not one bit.'

The tails were wrapped in brown paper and the parcel tied with string.

The stallholder presented the parcel to Norma. 'You know

what lassie, you'll either end up being somebody in life, or being hung,' he told her.

'Hung probably,' she replied with a laugh.

When the Barrows were behind them Midge took the parcel from her. 'You're something special Norma, very special indeed,' he said quietly, with emotion.

Her reply was to take him by the hand. She was fair bursting with happiness and pride. Fair bursting with it to have had him say that.

'No!' Norma exclaimed and broke away from Midge. Her bosom was heaving, and she'd gone prickly all over.

They were alone in Norma's house, the rest of the McKenzie family having gone to the pictures to see Douglas Fairbanks in *Mr Robinson Crusoe*. Effie was a devoted fan of his.

Norma had stayed in to do some more work on the ballgown she'd decided to wear at the Latin American Championship. Midge had come over by chance to discover her alone.

'I only wanted to ...'

'I know what you wanted to do and you're not going to,' she replied hotly.

'There's no harm in me just ...'

'One thing leads to another, and before we know where we are we'll have gone the whole way. Kissing and cuddling are fine but that's it, that's where I draw the line,' she told him.

Midge threw himself into a fireside chair and put his head in his hands. His expression was thunderous.

'And there's no use doing a big moody on me, I won't change my mind,' she said.

'Other couples ...'

'I don't care what other couples get up to, that's their business, not mine. Or yours either come to that. And anyway, if they are doing such things they shouldn't say, which makes me wonder if they actually are or just pretending in order to impress.'

Midge took a deep breath.

'I know it's supposed to be more difficult for a man than a woman, but that's how it's going to be,' she said, softly this time.

She went to the kitchen window and looked out. It was

54

pelting with rain outside and bitter wind was blowing, rattling the window panes up and down the tenements.

She tensed slightly to hear him approach her from behind. His arms slid round her waist, and he nibbled her neck.

'That's lovely,' she whispered.

He blew in her ear, then kissed it, his tongue probing deep inside.

Norma's stomach turned to jelly; she felt positively weak at the knees. Her nipples started to ache.

'Don't kid me you don't really want to go any further?' he whispered.

'I didn't say I didn't want to. I said I wasn't going to.'

'Oh Norma!' He spun her round, his mouth seeking hers. As they kissed his left hand brushed against her right breast.

She pushed him away to hold him at arm's length. 'You don't take a telling do you?' she smiled.

'I didn't do anything!' he protested.

She didn't reply, letting the silence between them stretch out. She made her bosom heave as it had done earlier, and slitted her eyes.

'There is one thing I'll do for you,' she husked, her voice thick with passion. Her gaze flicked down to the front of his trousers, then back to his face.

Hope dawned in his eyes. 'What?' he breathed.

She pulled herself close to plaster herself all over him. With one hand she slowly drew his head down to her mouth. He shivered in anticipation.

'Make you a cup of tea,' she whispered into an ear.

For a couple of moments it didn't sink in. Then it did. 'Why you ...'

She laughed loudly, and just a trifle mockingly, as she released him.

'I'll make you a cup of tea,' she repeated, this time in her normal voice.

'See you!' he said, shaking a fist at her. He was more bemused than angry.

Still laughing she picked up the kettle and went back to the sink to fill it. She was doing that when he got his revenge.

There was a loud crack as the flat of his hand connected hard with her backside. She jumped, exclaiming with pain.

'That hurt!' she complained. And it did. Her bottom was stinging. She knew if she'd been able to look there'd be a red weal there.

'Want me to kiss it better?' he asked innocently.

This time it was Midge who laughed loudly.

It was by far the most exciting occasion Norma had ever been to. The atmosphere inside the Albert Ballroom was absolutely electric, the tension at fever pitch.

And the spectacle of the gowns was stunning. It was as if a flight of wildly exotic birds, all colours and combinations of the rainbow, had descended on the hall. The first sight of the gathering had literally taken Norma's breath away, so impressive was it.

The championship had started with forty competing couples, which had now been reduced to twenty. Those twenty were now in the process of being reduced to ten. Norma and Midge, each wearing the number eighteen, were up next.

Norma stared in admiration, and jealousy too, at one of the two couples now on the floor. That particular couple, number thirty-four, were simply magnificent. She was almost openmouthed to watch them.

'They're terrific eh?' Midge whispered to her.

She nodded agreement. They were indeed.

Norma glanced over to where the Gillespies were sitting. Bob Gillespie gave her a wink, and a thumbs-up sign.

She was wearing the red shoes she'd had for her last birthday, the day she'd met Midge at the street party. She'd chosen the gown she had on specifically because it went with them.

The music ended, and both couples got a round of applause, as everyone did. The five judges sitting on a rostrum at the side of the ballroom went into a huddle. When all twenty of the remaining couples had danced, the chosen ten would be announced.

Norma and Midge rose as the two couples left the floor. Another couple rose also, the other part of their pair.

'Here we go then,' Midge whispered out the side of his mouth. Taking her by the hand he led her onto the floor.

It was a marvellous feeling to have a spotlight on you, Norma thought. It made her bubble inside. Whatever the outcome of the evening she knew she was hooked, and knew that Midge was too.

'Again a jive, this time to Cy Oliver's Opus 1,' the MC announced. As he was backing away the band struck up.

As was required in the jive Midge stayed in the one spot while taking Norma through a series of underarm turns and spins.

Their allotted time was two minutes and it whizzed by so quickly it seemed to Norma that they'd only been up for a handful of seconds. When it was over they bowed, accepting their applause.

'How do you think we did?' Midge asked her in a whisper when they'd sat down again and the next pair of couples were on the floor.

'Hard to say,' she whispered back. For in truth the general standard was very high. Far higher than she'd expected.

A little later the ten couples to go on were announced. They weren't one of them.

Norma bit back her disappointment. She'd hoped . . . Aye well maybe she'd been silly, not to say naive, to hope too much.

In the end the championship was won by the couple, number thirty-four who Norma and Midge had so admired, their final dance a paso doble to El Gato Montez.

Norma lay in bed staring up at the ceiling – Lyn and Eileen were sleeping in the other bed, a double, and Lyn was snoring – she was a terrible snorer, like her da.

Tonight had been a real eye-opener, Norma thought, her mind filled with the championship. She'd enjoyed it, oh thoroughly, but was ... what? She decided the word she was searching for was *frustrated*, yes that was it, she was frustrated that she and Midge hadn't done better, that they'd been so outclassed by many of the other couples taking part.

The way she and Midge danced was raw, simplistic and in many cases purely instinctive, she now realised. Which was well and good as far as it went. But if they were going to go in for other competitions – and she had every intention they would – they were going to have to build on that. In other words, a great deal of learning was going to have to be done by her and Midge if they were to achieve the sort of class they'd seen in the Albert Ballroom.

'What an achievement to win a championship,' Bob Gillespie had said the night of Midge's party. She now knew exactly what he meant, and swore to herself she was going to make that dream come true for her and Midge.

Eventually she fell asleep to dream of the championship, only this time it was herself and Midge who were couple number thirty-four, and who danced that final paso doble to win.

'If you want proper lessons then there's only one place to go, and that's Silver's over by the Citizens' Theatre,' Bob Gillespie said in reply to Norma's question.

'Have you any idea what the cost of lessons are?' Midge asked, worried about the money. Now that he was earning a full wage he was expected to contribute the same amount as his father did into the house. He wasn't left with hellish much after, though quite a bit more than he'd had as an apprentice.

Bob Gillespie looked at his wife Beryl who shook her head; she didn't know either.

'Sorry, can't help you there. I only know the place by reputation, nothing else,' Bob Gillespie said.

'And it's the Citizens' Theatre, that's in the Gorbals isn't it?' Norma queried.

Midge nodded.

'Not too far from where I work. I'll drop by tomorrow and find out what they charge,' Norma said.

She and Midge stayed with the Gillespies for an hour after that, talking about the Latin American Championship and how much they'd enjoyed it.

Finlay Rankine looked up from where he was sitting as Norma came in through the door of the studios. He was immediately struck by her, forcibly so.

A real cracker, he thought, eyeing her up and down. Deliciously nubile, just the way he liked them best.

She gave him a hesitant smile, and walked over to him. He noticed how sensuous her walk was – it was the walk of a born dancer.

There were three full-time instructors at Silver's, of which Finlay was one. Between them they virtually ran the place, the

58

owners only appearing roughly every fortnight or so, sometimes not even as much as that.

'Can I help you?' he asked, rising to greet her.

Norma introduced herself, and explained why she'd come. Finlay replied that before they talked about money he'd show her round.

The smell of her made Finlay's nose twitch in appreciation. And those eyes, were they grey or were they green? They seemed to go from one to the other. He found them mesmeric.

Norma was impressed by what she saw, very much so. She'd thought that being in the Gorbals, Silver's might be quite tatty but she couldn't have been more wrong.

Finlay showed her all the facilities, ending up in the studio where he was about to teach. As they'd gone along Norma had explained about her and Midge having just taken up ballroom dancing, and how keen they were to improve.

'Let's see what you can do now,' Finlay said, and put a record on the gramophone. It was a foxtrot.

He'd been right, he thought as they glided round the studio, she was a natural mover. She was also very sexy; sexier than Trish whom he'd just broken off with. He'd met her at Silver's also.

When the record was finished Finlay reluctantly released Norma.

'There are three important considerations to remember when dancing the foxtrot: direction, follow-through and dance position. I would teach you to achieve all three to the best advantage. Also, amongst other things, the length of your stride is too long at the moment and because of this you're frantically losing control of your balance. And then there's contrabody – you're not employing that at all. If you're going to compete, it's essential you do,' he said.

'I'm afraid I don't even know what contrabody is.'

He gave her a thin, crocodile-like smile. 'Contrabody is when if I take a step with my right foot, for example, I swing the left side of my body towards that foot and vice versa. This action of turning the opposite hip and shoulder towards the moving leg facilitates the art of rotation. Understand?'

'I think so,' she said slowly.

Finlay glanced at the wall clock. His client would be arriving at any minute. He brought his attention back to Norma. She was so tempting, he could have gorged himself on her there and then.

'*You* have talent – what about your boyfriend?' he asked.

'Let me put it this way, if I've got talent then so has he,' she replied.

He grunted, believing her. A dozen steps or so is all it takes for one good dancer to recognise another.

'So what do you charge then?' Norma asked.

'We don't do individual lessons but courses. The minimum course is twenty lessons which for a combined lesson – that's you and your boyfriend together – would be thirty pounds,' Finlay replied.

Norma's eyes opened wide. 'How much?'

'Thirty pounds, payable in advance.'

Norma was staggered. After seeing the place she'd expected the prices to be steep, but nothing like that.

'And are those lessons an hour each?' she queried in a weak voice.

'No, half an hour.'

Worse still, she thought. Well that was it, Silver's was out for her and Midge, the prices were quite beyond their reach. Thirty quid! She wasn't just staggered; she was stunned.

'I'm sorry I've wasted your time,' she said to Finlay.

He'd already guessed she wouldn't be able to afford Silver's; it was unusual for them to have a client who was other than middle-class. Most of their clients were bored wives – often childless – who took the lessons as a hobby. Trish, a member of the childless contingent, had been one such, her husband a bank manager.

'A pity, you being so keen,' Finlay said slowly.

'Yes, I'll just have to find some other way to learn,' she replied.

'There are no alternative dance studios in Glasgow; we're the only one.'

She looked around to check where the door was, preparing to leave.

'However there *is* a way you can have a course here, for nothing,' he said silkily, treating her to another of his crocodile smiles.

60

Norma frowned. For nothing? What did he mean?

'I would teach you in the evenings, my final client of the day,' he continued, still smiling.

'And my boyfriend?'

'No boyfriend. Just you.'

'But we . . .' She stopped as the penny dropped. 'I wouldn't be paying?'

He nodded.

'And no boyfriend?'

He nodded again.

Outrage filled her. That and anger, and fear too. 'Are you propositioning me?' she demanded, voice tight.

'I find you exceptionally attractive. So I'll be nice to you if . . . you'll be the same to me.'

She couldn't believe she was hearing this. Why the dirty sod, what did he take her for!

'Enough lessons and I could make you, if not *the* best then certainly one of the best ballroom-dancers in Glasgow,' he purred. He had a flat in the West End with a big double bed in it, and could just picture her, naked, lying on it. He could feel himself getting excited at the thought. Excited, and he hadn't laid a finger on her yet.

'I wouldn't go with a slimy creep like you if you were the last man on earth,' she exploded in a vehement hiss.

He came forward very quickly to grab her by the waist. 'Don't turn my offer down out of hand – at least mull it over when you get home. I can always be contacted here should you change your mind.'

'I won't be changing my mind. Now let me go!'

He released her, still smiling his crocodile smile.

Heart thumping, she marched to the door and wrenched it open. She knew tears weren't far away.

'Your boyfriend's a lucky fella. I envy him,' Finlay said.

She turned in the doorway; she'd wipe that bloody smile off his face. It had just come to her how to do so.

'I didn't mention my boyfriend's name, did I?' She paused for effect, then said, 'Sammy McGuigan. His name's Sammy McGuigan. Maybe you've heard of him?'

The smile vanished as though by magic, and Finlay's face went a sick, milky-white. Sammy McGuigan was a notorious gang leader and razor king. Everyone in Glasgow had heard of Sammy McGuigan, he was regarded as a local Genghis Khan or Attila the Hun.

'Are you ... will you ...?' Finlay croaked from what were now bloodless lips.

'Tell him about your proposition? You'll just have to wait and find out, won't you?' she replied, and made off up the corridor that would take her to the reception area and out of the building.

She left a stricken Finlay behind her, so rigid from shock and terror he might have been carved out of stone.

She managed to reach the street before the tears came. What a horrible, dirty thing to have happened. And then with the tears came laughter, so that she was laughing and crying at the same time.

Oh by God she'd wiped that smile off his face all right! Sammy McGuigan, she'd been inspired to come up with that.

She'd left Finlay Rankine with a lot to think about. She must have scared him out of a year's growth.

It was several minutes before she was able to compose herself sufficiently to continue her way home.

'Aye of course we'll be happy to pass on all we know,' Bob Gillespie said.

After Silver's had fallen through – she hadn't told Midge about Finlay Rankine in case there had been a fight and he'd got into trouble with the police – they'd discussed what to do next, and it had seemed logical to them to approach the Gillespies to ask if they would help.

She and Midge had arrived at the Gillespies' about half an hour previously, but had to wait for Bob Gillespie to arrive home from work. He worked at the Cattle Market, a stone's throw away, where his job was to look after the cattle while they were on the premises, and herd them round during auctions, keeping them on the move so that bidders could satisfy themselves that none of the beasts were lame.

'That's very good of you, thank you,' Midge replied.

'We've already got a gramophone so there's no worry there,' said Beryl.

'Yes I think it best if we do it all here, at our home. Is that all right with you?' Bob Gillespie asked.

'Fine,' Norma nodded.

'How about two sessions a week, Tuesdays and Thursdays say?' Bob Gillespie suggested.

Norma glanced at Midge. 'Sounds excellent to me,' he said.

And so it was agreed, seven o'clock on Tuesdays and Thursdays – from then on Norma and Midge would present themselves at the Gillespie house to be taught what the Gillespies could teach them.

Friday night six weeks later Norma was in the room getting herself ready to go out with Midge. They were going to the Locarno Ballroom in Sauchiehall Street which had become something of a favourite of theirs of late. The night was going to be a big one; Victor Silvester and his band were playing.

Brian was away for a drink with Jim Fullarton and Sandy Reid; Lyn out somewhere, Norma didn't know where; and Eileen round at a pal's. Effie was through the kitchen knitting a new sleeveless pullover for Da.

Norma decided she needed the toilet and went. On returning to the house she went into the kitchen for a lipstick she'd left there, to discover Effie sitting in a fireside chair, knitting in front of her, tears rolling down her face.

'Ma! What's wrong?' Norma exclaimed, and hurried to Effie's side.

'Get me a clean hanky will you lass,' Effie said.

Norma went and got a hanky from the drawer where they were kept, came back to her mother and handed it to her. Effie wiped the tears away, dabbing her brimming eyes.

Norma knelt beside her ma. 'What is it? Is something wrong?'

'Not wrong, I was just...' Effie blew her nose, and wiped away more tears that had found their way onto her cheeks. 'Just thinking about our wee cottage at Kilmichael House, and what it used to be like living there. The flowers, the trees, the sea, the freshness of the air, and the cleanliness of it all.'

'I miss it too, I'm sure we all do,' Norma said quietly.

'You may miss it, but you and the other two have completely

settled in here. You're young you see, and the young can adapt a lot easier than us old ones.'

'If only there was a Womens' Institute branch hereabouts,' Norma said, Effie having been previously much involved with the WI. But there wasn't a WI in Bridgeton, it just wasn't the sort of area to support one.

Effie wiped away more tears. 'It's the countryside I miss more than the WI. A thousand and one things, the droning of the bees, the flitter of butterflies in flight, cows on their way home to be milked, daisies and clover – all the things I took for granted for so long, all of which have been totally removed from my life. And in their place? The sour stink of Bridgeton, filthy streets, soot-laden air, dirt and grime everywhere.'

Norma took one of her mother's hands and squeezed it. 'Have you spoken to Da about this?' she asked.

Effie shook her head. 'No, I don't have to tell him how I feel, he knows. Just as I know he doesn't enjoy working at Glasgow Green one iota as much as he did at Kilmichael House. He's never said, nor will I.'

'You're right about us younger ones getting used to Glasgow. When we first came here I used to think about our cottage at Kilmichael House and Kirn all the time, now I rarely do.'

'And that's how it should be if we're going to live here,' Effie replied.

Effie took a deep breath, then another. 'I'm all right now, I'm over my silliness. Have you got time for a cup of tea before you go?'

Norma glanced at the clock on the mantelpiece. Midge would be there at any moment, for he was always prompt. Well he'd just have to wait.

'A cup of tea would go down a treat,' she smiled back.

From somewhere nearby came the sound of voices raised in anger. There was a shout, followed by the crash of breaking glass. A window had either been put in or out.

Norma and Effie pretended not to hear a thing.

Norma and Midge came out of Green's Playhouse in the town. They'd just been to see Fred Astaire in *Dancing Lady*. They'd both been entranced, never once having taken their eyes off that mesmeric figure up there on the silver screen.

'Wasn't he just ... unbelievable!' Norma breathed.

'You can say that again.'

They walked a little way in silence, heading for their tram-stop, both lost in the memory of what they'd just seen.

'Imagine dancing alongside him, wouldn't that be the ultimate.' Midge said, awed at such a prospect.

A small smile curled Norma's lips upwards. 'No, to be as *good* as him, *that* would be the ultimate,' she replied.

Midge barked out a laugh. She was quite right of course. Trust Norma to see it that way.

They arrived at the tramstop and joined the queue. There would be a tram along soon. It was a regular, and busy, service.

Norma said in a quiet voice. 'You know that we've gone as far as we can with Bob and Beryl. We've learned a fair amount from them during these past four months. But that road's one we've come to the end of.'

'Yes, I agree. They've been floundering these last few weeks trying to think up something new to teach us,' Midge replied.

The Gillespies, bless them, had been helpful, but only to a degree, thought Norma. There was still much more, particularly in the realms of technique, for them to learn if they were ever going to win a championship.

So what to do next? What they really needed was to be taught by a top-ranking couple like the one, number thirty-four, who had won the Glasgow Latin American Championship. But Norma knew, as did Midge, that there was little hope of that. Bob Gillespie had explained to them that the top rankers never willingly passed anything on, such was the intense rivalry at that level.

'I suppose all we can do now is keep watching and pick up what we can that way,' Midge said.

Norma agreed reluctantly. She couldn't see any alternative, not for the moment anyway. But it was a very unsatisfactory, not to mention roundabout, way of doing things.

A tram rattled along, and they went on board, going on top to please Midge who preferred travelling there.

'I enjoyed the wee picture as well, it was a real bobby dazzler right enough,' Midge enthused. The *B* picture had been a travelogue on the Kalahari Desert.

'Wasn't that scenery breathtaking,' he continued. 'And what

65

about those bushmen with the big fat backsides who live there, weren't they absolutely fascinating.'

'I didn't think the scenery breathtaking at all, in fact I thought it looked pretty horrible. Sand and scrubland, what's breathtaking about that? And as for your bushmen with the big fat backsides...' She shuddered.

'But didn't you see that blood-red sunset. I've read about sunsets like that and always thought the description was an exaggeration. Now I know it isn't.'

He paused. Then, eyes miles away, added, 'I'd give anything to experience a sunset like that. To actually be there and watch it happen. It must be... well, it must be out of this world.'

Norma stared at Midge. Him and his wanting to travel, pipe-dreams he should grow out of.

After all how would he, a Glasgow flint mill-worker, ever get to the Kalahari? The idea was ludicrous.

She went back to thinking about Fred Astaire, and *Dancing Lady*. What he'd done with his feet and body had been poetry, sheer poetry. The man was a genius.

'I thought so, ten days overdue. Do you know how much that'll cost you in a fine? And it'll cost *you* young woman for neither your da or I will pay it,' Effie said, waving a library book at Eileen.

'There's no panic, don't worry,' Eileen replied, looked completely unconcerned.

'So you're not worried about money, you've found a tree that grows the stuff have you? For if you have I wish you'd show it to me, I could certainly use a handful of what it grows,' Effie went on waspishly. She hated money being wasted, and paying out fines on library books was a waste as far as she was concerned.

'I won't have to pay any fine,' Eileen said.

Norma glanced up from where she was doing some hand stitching on a new ballroom gown she was making, the first that was truly hers and not an alteration or remake. Not that there was anything wrong with those Beryl Gillespie had so kindly given her, just that in their design they were older than she would have wished. The material she was now working on had come her way from a lad at the SCWS who'd sold it to her dirt cheap, warning her not to mention where she'd got it from as it had 'fallen off the back of a lorry'. Nor had she told anyone, certainly not her ma. If she had told Effie it was nicked Effie would have had a canary.

'And why's that?' Effie demanded, thinking the girl was havering. But Eileen wasn't.

'Because of Charlie Marshall, one of the librarians. I often take books back late and he always slips them through for me,' Eileen replied.

Effie stared at her daughter. 'And why does he do that?'

'Why do you think Ma! Because he *likes* me, that's why. Norma giggled.

'I'm not a baby anymore you know, though I'm treated as one round here often enough,' Eileen protested, worried now about Effie's reaction. Maybe she should have kept her mouth shut.

'And how old is this Charlie Marshall?' Effie asked quietly.

'Seventeen. He started in the library last year.'

Effie threw the library book onto the table, then went over to the sink so she could turn her back on Eileen. She didn't want her youngest to see her face.

'Does he know how old *you* are?' Effie queried.

'Oh aye, thirteen next month. That came out in a conversation I had with him a week past Thursday. We met in the street and stood chaffing for a while.

Effie rinsed through some cloths she had boiled, then wrung them out. Eileen was right, she was growing up fast, and a lot more quickly than the other two had done. She supposed she could thank Glasgow for that.

Effie looked at Eileen's reflection in Brian's shaving mirror that hung on a nail by the side of the window. She kept forgetting that Eileen was technically a woman now, and had been for a while.

'You just make sure that chaffing in the street and his slipping books by for you is all that happens,' she said ominously.

Eileen completely lost her bravado on hearing that, and blushed. 'Aye of course,' she muttered in reply.

It wouldn't be long before her youngest was courting, Effie thought with mixed emotions. How time flew, particularly where children were concerned.

She gazed out at the middens down at the back - their bins

overflowing as usual – only it wasn't the middens she saw, but a secret place in Bluebell Wood where she and Brian had done a lot of their courting. A beautiful spot, particularly when the bluebells were in bloom.

Why she could remember . . . She nodded at the memory, one of dozens that came flooding back.

Normá realised she needed to go to the toilet, and laid her stitching aside. She'd take it up again when she returned.

She was collecting the toilet roll from where it was kept in the hall when the outside door opened and Lyn came in.

'You've got chocolate on your mouche,' Norma said to Lyn who, brushing past, mumbled something about an éclair she hadn't been able to resist.

Her sister was getting bigger all the time, Norma thought as she went into the toilet and snecked the door. She was far more than a podge now; she was becoming a right fattie.

Norma sat and, having forgotten to bring something to read, her mind turned to the conversation that had taken place upstairs between Eileen and Ma.

Slowly a smile spread across her face. That could just be the answer to her problem. It could just be indeed.

Charlie Marshall was skinny, even by Glasgow standards, with a wispy moustache and a couple of plooks on his forehead. But he wasn't bad looking at all; Norma had seen a lot worse.

'How are you today Charlie?' Eileen asked coyly.

'Fine Eileen, and yourself?'

'Feeling guilty about this,' she replied, handing him the library book that was ten days overdue.

Charlie looked at the date page, then up at Norma, wondering who she was.

'This is my eldest sister,' Eileen explained.

The book disappeared under the counter. 'You're a naughty girl you know,' Charlie admonished Eileen.

'I know,' Eileen whispered in reply, and blinked her eyes at Charlie.

Why the little minx, she was flirting with the lad! Norma thought in astonishment. And Charlie, grinning foolishly back at Eileen, appeared to be loving every minute of it.

'My sister wants you to do her a favour, will you Charlie?' purred Eileen, then gave him an appealing smile.

Norma had never seen this side of Eileen before. Talk about a budding *femme fatale*! She had Charlie eating out of the palm of her hand.

'Of course I will,' Charlie replied.

With a hint of triumph in her eyes Eileen made a gesture to Norma indicating she should speak.

Norma explained to an attentive Charlie what she was after, and he replied that though he had nothing worthwhile on the subject in his library, leave it to him and he'd do his best for her.

A week later Norma left the library with half a dozen books on ballroom dancing that Charlie had obtained for her from other libraries. He'd tipped her the wink not to be too concerned about getting them back on their due date; just as long as they came back through him everything would be hunky dory. And when she'd done with those he'd have others waiting for her.

Hurrying home, Norma took the books into the room, stretched out on her bed and picked up the top one. The book was brand new, the first item it dealt with the rumba, a dance that had recently taken the United States by storm.

Basic box step, open cuban walk, side break, forward rock ... Brow furrowed in concentration, she began to read.

Chapter Four

Norma felt sick; she had felt sick all evening since seeing who was on the panel of five judges – the instructor from Silver's, Finlay Rankine. Up until the moment of clapping eyes on him she'd thought that she and Midge had their best ever chance yet of winning a championship. Now she was convinced Rankine would do the dirty on the pair of them in retaliation for her turning him down and giving him such a fright about Sammy McGuigan.

The date was 5th November 1934, the venue the Plaza Ballroom in Glasgow's Southside where the All Lanarkshire Open Championship was being held. Norma was now seventeen and a half years old while Midge was nineteen, twenty that coming February. They'd been dancing competitively for twenty months now, and in that time had taken two second places and three thirds. But still the number one, that winning place, eluded them.

There were six couples left who would dance as individual couples one after the other. Rankine had let them come this far, Norma thought grimly. Now he'd slide the knife in.

For the umpteenth time that evening she glanced across to where Rankine was sitting, and for the umpteenth time he refused to meet her gaze.

She brought her attention back to the floor as the first of the six got up to dance.

The minutes ticked by as couple followed couple onto the floor, all of them turning in excellent performances. Then it was their turn.

As she stood up she suddenly relaxed, the tension, anxiety and disappointment caused by Finlay Rankine's presence suddenly draining out of her. It was all a formality anyway, their fate had already been decided, she told herself. But sod it, that wouldn't detract from her performance. She'd give it all she'd got – and then some more.

The dance was a saunter revé, the tune they would be dancing to 'In My Solitude'. The band struck up, and they were away.

As they took their bow she knew they'd done well, had been in cracking form. The magic between her and Midge had never been stronger. Bob Gillespie, sitting among the spectators with his wife Beryl, gave her a beaming smile and the thumbs-up sign.

Then it was all over, and time for the results to be announced. The MC returned from the judges to take the centre of the floor. He held up his hands for hush, and the excited buzz turned to silence.

He made a short speech, interspersed with a few not very funny jokes, thanking everyone connected with the championship. He made a special point of saying what a high overall standard there had been that night, which was absolutely true, there had been.

'And now the results,' the MC went on. 'In third place, couple number fourteen, Mr and Mrs John Garland!'

The Garlands got an enthusiastic round of applause as they walked over to the judges, where they were presented with a small medal apiece. Still to applause, they returned to their chairs.

'In second place, couple number forty-five, Miss Jane Milne and Mr David Liddell!'

This was another young couple, though older than Norma and Midge. They too got an enthusiastic response as they went up to collect a Waterford bowl.

She and Midge had been better than those two, Norma thought bitterly. She was certain of that. But now it was the winners' turn to be announced and she wondered who they would be?

'And now, in first place, winners of the All Lanarkshire Open Championship.' The MC paused, smiled tantalisingly, stretching the moment out. 'Couple number twenty-one, Miss Norma McKenzie and Mr Michael Henderson!' The last said in a rush of words.

For a second or two Norma didn't take it in, so convinced was she that Rankine would have done the dirty on her and Midge. Then she did.

They'd won their first championship. *They'd won!*

She looked at Midge who was flushed with pride and success.

'We did it,' he choked.

She nodded. They had. They'd done it. And the feeling was a glorious one, like being filled from top to toe with fizzy bubbles.

They rose and crossed over to the judges, where they were presented with a silver cup.

'Congratulations,' the five judges said in unison.

Norma and Midge shook each of the judges by the hand; Rankine smiling at her when she shook his.

Norma glanced over at the Gillespies who were both on their feet clapping furiously.

It was a popular win; that much was clear from the ear-battering applause. Midge waved a few times, and Norma nodded her head. Midge gave her the cup to hold which she did at shoulder height, then above her head. People laughed approvingly at that, and applauded even more fiercely.

The Gillespies came charging over to thump Midge's back and kiss Norma. The pair of them were babbling on nineteen to the dozen.

'I knew you could do it in time, I knew it!' Bob Gillespie raved excitedly to Norma, turning again to his wife, his voice a whole octave higher than it normally was. 'Didn't I always say that Beryl, didn't I?'

It was a little later when things had begun to calm down somewhat that Norma, temporarily separated from Midge, found Finlay Rankine at her side.

'Congratulations again, you and your partner fully deserved to win. It was an outstanding performance, and outstanding is a word I don't use lightly.'

'Thank you Mr Rankine,' she replied, embarrassed not by his praise, but by having to talk to him.

'There was no doubt about the outcome after that saunter revé. At least not in my mind.'

'I thought . . . Well, to be honest when I saw you on that panel I thought Midge and I didn't stand a chance.'

He treated her to one of his crocodile smiles. 'You were referring to that tale of yours about Sammy McGuigan?'

She nodded.

'Most effective it was too. I went around quaking in my shoes for the next fortnight, fully expecting McGuigan to come springing out at me with a razor in either fist, till I read that big article the *Evening Citizen* did on him.'

'I read it too,' Norma said.

Two weeks after she'd been to Silver's the *Evening Citizen* had done a full-page feature on McGuigan in which it had been stated that he had a long standing girlfriend whose name Norma couldn't now recall, but which certainly hadn't been hers. There had also been a picture of the girlfriend with McGuigan.

'And you thought I'd make sure you didn't get placed tonight because of that and because you refused me?'

She nodded again.

'I can understand you thinking that, but no, it's not my style. I may have faults, but cheap revenge isn't one of them. Anyway, I doubt I could have influenced the result against you even if I'd wanted to. You and Mr Henderson were simply streets ahead of the others. And I mean streets.'

'Thank you,' she whispered.

'I mean it, I assure you. By the way, did you tell Mr Henderson, Midge you just called him, about...?'

'No,' she interjected.

'Well that's a relief. He might not be McGuigan, but I'm sure he's quite capable of doing his best to punch my head in. So tell me – I've been dying to know all night – who did teach you, bring you up to the level you're now at?'

'Some friends did help for a while, but we quickly absorbed all they could give us. After that it was me,' she replied.

He stared at her blankly, suspecting his leg was being pulled again. 'You? How so?' he queried.

'Me, and books on dancing. I must have read dozens of books on the subject, and still am. Books by experts, world champions. Books that specialise on the waltz, the foxtrot, the quickstep, the merengue, the mambo. Books on the history of modern dancing, books on various techniques and the application of these techniques.

'For example, let's take the history of the waltz. Did you know it originated in the country folk dances of Bavaria? Or that it didn't become popular among the European middle class until the first decade of this century? Up until then it was the cherished property of the aristocracy. Yet, in the United States, where they don't have a blue blood caste, it was being danced by the ordinary people as early as 1840.

'I can go on if you like?'

Finlay Rankine was dumbfounded, momentarily speechless.

She continued. 'Let's move from history to practice. When you dance the waltz you should do so with your entire body, all side-steps long and wide in order to obtain control and fluidity of movement. Knees should be kept flexed and never allowed to lock, otherwise your leg will move stiffly. However, when step patterns indicate you bring your feet together or cross them, your knees will not be as flexed as otherwise.

'Want me to go on?'

He shook his head, and found his voice. 'You're saying you learned everything from books?'

'Not everything. The books explain in detail how it should be done; we then watch others and see the translation from the page onto the floor so to speak, the realisation of the theory. We absorb both, then try to do better than the people we've been watching, or are competing against.'

'I'll be damned!' Finlay swore. He'd never heard of anyone doing it this way before. It was a novel approach. And very successful too, borne out by what he'd seen, and judged, earlier.

'And it was your idea to get these books and learn that way?' he asked.

'It was.'

'Aren't you the clever one. I'm impressed, very much so.'

'Thank you,' Norma replied, acknowledging his compliment.

'Of course doing what you did is one thing, but it wouldn't have amounted to what it has without the natural talent you and Mr Henderson have in abundance. It's a talent that comes right out and smacks one in the eye. In fact I'll go so far as to say the pair of you have the most potential I've personally ever come across. But . . .' He let the word hang in the air. 'You still have things to learn: nuances, the precisely correct line of a leg for example, that you won't get from a book, or pick up from

74

watching because those you're watching – unless you're at top national and international level – won't be doing it. What I'd like to do is take you under my wing for a spell and teach you those little additions that can ratchet the quality of your performance up another notch or two.'

Norma raised an eyebrow. 'For free I suppose?'

'Yes, because you excite me. In the dancing sense that is.'

'And what about my boyfriend Midge? I don't suppose this generous offer includes him?' She asked sarcastically.

'The offer is to the pair of you as a couple, with no funny business attached. You have my sworn oath on that.'

He took out his wallet and produced a card. 'This is my home telephone number. Talk it over with Mr Henderson, and if you decide you would like my help then have him ring me. Which I may say, I hope he does.'

Norma accepted the card. 'I'll talk to Midge about it later,' she replied.

'Goodbye for now then,' Finlay Rankine said, and walked away.

How about that, wasn't that a turn-up for the book! Norma thought. If Finlay Rankine could do as he'd promised, ratchet their performance up another notch or two as he'd put it, then this was an opportunity to be grabbed with both hands. And grab it they would, she'd see to that.

By golly she would.

Norma had just washed her hair in the sink and Lyn was in the process of doing so while Eileen was waiting to follow Lyn, when there was a rat-a-tat-tat on the outside door.

'I'll get it,' said Eileen, leaving the kitchen.

Brian, puffing on his pipe, was listening to Herbert Tatlock in 'Bitter Brevities' on the wireless and enjoying the rare fire that Effie had made. He was just getting over a cold, and still not feeling his best.

Eileen poked her head back into the kitchen. 'It's Midge; he wants to speak to you da,' she said.

'Wait up!' Lyn exclaimed from the sink, gave her hair a final quick rinse, wrapped it in a towel, and then hurriedly shrugged herself into a dressing gown.

By this time Norma had risen from the front of the fire where she'd been kneeling, drying her hair and combing it through. She too was in a dressing gown, as was Eileen.

Midge come to see her da and not her? She wondered what this was all about.

'I'll make a cup of tea,' said Effie who'd been tidying out the press. A visitor was always an excuse to put the kettle on. She switched the wireless off.

'You can come in now, she's decent,' Eileen said over her shoulder to Midge.

'I've got some news that might interest you, Mr McKenzie,' Midge announced the moment he was in the kitchen.

'Oh aye?'

'Do you know the Smarts who live in a three-room and kitchen on the next landing up from us?'

'He and I say hello and occasionally pass the time of day,' Brian replied.

'Well, I've just been talking to him. He's been unemployed for the past five months, got laid off from a firm over in Springburn, and was beginning to find things very difficult indeed. Anyway, to cut a long story short, he's landed himself a new job in Paisley which, because it's so far away, means he and his family are going to have to move.'

Brian blew out a stream of smoke, not seeing what Midge was driving at. 'That's very interesting son, and I'm certainly pleased for Mr Smart, to be idle being a terrible thing. But what's that got to do with me?'

'It's the house, isn't it?' said Norma, quick to grasp the point.

'If the Smarts flit, the house above us will be available, and it's a *three*-room and kitchen. I remember hearing Mrs McKenzie saying not long ago how cramped you were here,' Midge replied.

'I see now,' Brian said, stroking his chin. They were worse than cramped, bursting at the seams more like. A three-room and kitchen would certainly solve a lot of problems, and now that Lyn was working as well as Norma, and it wouldn't be long till Eileen was also, they could afford the larger house.

Norma had been promoted at the SCWS to filing clerk, and Lyn had been taken on in her old job as office junior. The two of them now went and came back from Morrison Street together.

'Anyone else after it?' Brian asked.

'Not as I've heard. That doesn't mean to say there isn't, mind you. But if you were interested then the quicker you speak out to the factor the better.'

'Oh I'm interested all right.' He looked over at Effie. 'First thing tomorrow morning it's the factor's office for you girl.'

'I'll be there when he opens up,' Effie promised, delighted at the prospect of a bigger place. It had become so that they all felt they were living like sardines in a can.

'Let's hope it comes off then,' Midge smiled.

Brian rose and shook Midge by the hand. 'It's very kind of you to come and tell us. It's not the first time we're indebted to you either,' he said, the latter referring to the fact it had been Midge's tip that had landed Norma her job at SCWS.

'Aye, well that's what friends are for,' Midge replied. He was that sort of person; if he could do a person a good turn he would.

He turned to Norma. 'There's something else. I've also been talking to Bob Gillespie – or I should say he's been talking to me – about the Edinburgh Veleta Championship which is coming up in three weeks time. He thinks we should go in for it and that we have a very strong chance of winning.'

'Let's have a go then,' Norma replied with enthusiasm.

'There's just one snag though. The evening won't finish until after the last train has gone, which means staying the night in a hotel in Edinburgh.'

'No,' said Brian firmly. 'That's definitely out.'

Norma pulled a face. 'I rather fancy the thought of a hotel, I've never stayed in one.'

'No disrespect to you Midge, but Brian's right. It just isn't on,' Effie said.

'I wouldn't ask if it was only Norma and myself, that would hardly be respectable, we've her name to consider after all. But the thing is the Gillespies, whom you've met, would be with us, and would be acting as chaperones.' Midge went on.

Brian took a draw of his pipe. That did alter matters considerably. He glanced across at Effie, and saw she thought so too.

'Please Da? The Edinburgh Veleta Championship is a very prestigious event. It would be a tremendous feather in our caps if we won it,' Norma pleaded.

'The Gillespies know a hotel in Newtown that's very reasonable and which they can recommend,' Midge added.

'What about work the next day?' Brian queried.

'It's a Saturday night event,' Midge explained.

The Gillespies were a fine respectable couple, Brian told himself, everything would be above board – and seen to be – with them in attendance.

'Effie?' he said, looking again at his wife.

'In the circumstances I'll agree if you do,' she replied.

Brian took another pull of his pipe. 'I went to Edinburgh once, didn't like it. The folk walk around with their noses in the air as if there's a permanent bad smell around them. Didn't take to them at all. A cold folk, very cold,' he said, and sat down.

'Does that mean we can go?' asked Norma.

'I'll expect you to bring me back a stick of Edinburgh rock. If there's one good thing ever came out of Edinburgh it's their rock, fair smashing so it is,' Brian said.

'Tomorrow night at my house for practice?' Midge smiled at Norma.

'Tomorrow night for practice,' she agreed.

Norma rewound the gramophone while Midge was away at the toilet, a gramophone he'd found and bought cheap from somewhere. They both bought records for it on a regular basis. They had two large stacks of them; some were new, some second-hand.

She and Midge had been practicing for the Veleta Championship which was now only four days away, and would practice every night until Saturday. Thursday and Friday nights they would be with Finlay Rankine who was proving a tremendous help to them. Norma had come to the conclusion that what Finlay didn't know about dancing just wasn't worth knowing.

She decided she was tired of the Veleta for the moment, and would put another type of music on, the merengue, which the Haitians, who claim to have originated it, call the singing dance.

Midge returned from the toilet. He and Norma had the house to themselves that night, Leslie and Alice having gone to a Burns Supper at the local Masonic Hall while Katy had gone to see and hear Geraldo and his band who were playing in town,

Geraldo's vocalist a young singer called Vera Lynn. Katy was also mad keen on dancing, but had nothing like the talent her brother had.

Norma decided on a wee bit of teasing. Sidling up to Midge she put her arms round him and whispered. 'Three Little Words, what does that mean to you?'

'Eh?' What was she havering about?

'Three little words,' she repeated. 'What does that mean to you?'

He stared at her, then a soft smile curled his lips upwards. 'I love you?'

She broke away from him. 'I thought you might say that. In fact it's a Yankee dance step, a new one we're going to try out. I found it in a book I've been reading.'

'You mean that's what this dance step is called, three little words?'

She nodded. 'So far I've discovered you can use it in the waltz, foxtrot, and merengue. It's a bit different, and a step no one else uses, at least no one I've ever seen. If you like it we can incorporate it into some of our performances.'

'Three little words,' he mused. Very Yankee.

'I love you – that's exactly what I thought when I first came across it,' she said, and went over to the gramophone to put a record on.

'Norma?'

She glanced at him over her shoulder.

His voice was suddenly husky, and far steelier than usual. 'I do, you know.'

She stopped up short. 'Do what?'

'Love you. I've never said before, but I have for a long time now.'

Norma's heart seemed to be turning over in her chest. She'd known for ages how he felt about her, but this was the first time he'd actually come out with it.

She went back over to him. There was a hint of tears in her eyes, and her voice had gone as husky as his when she whispered, 'Kiss me'.

It wasn't a passionate kiss, but one of great feeling on both sides. It seemed to her she could feel the warmth and intensity of the kiss in every part of her being.

The kiss went on and on, both of them reluctant to break the contact. Finally it was she who did so.

'And I love you too, but wasn't going to tell you until you'd said it first.'

'I've been meaning to... It's just, well, I felt embarrassed to say so.'

'Are you embarrassed now?'

He thought about that for a moment, then shook his head. 'Maybe that's because it just sort of happened naturally, without me planning it so to speak.'

'Maybe so,' she agreed.

He took a handful of honey blonde hair, and pulled it tight in his grasp, but not tight enough to hurt.

She stared into those piercing blue eyes of his, thinking how gorgeous they were. She knew why he'd taken so long in declaring his love. Glasgow men were like that, any emotional declaration – particularly love – being complete anathema to them.

'Tell me again,' she asked.

'I love you Norma. I love you.'

'And I love you.'

He took a deep breath, then drew her face close to his. He kissed her again, long and slowly and, as happened when they danced, it was as though they fused together to become as one.

When that kiss was over he took her in his arms. They stood there, holding tightly to one another.

After a while Norma put the record on and taught him how to do three little words.

The MC was a fat man whose face was streaming with perspiration, as it had been for most of the evening. The Usher Hall was jam-packed, so much so Norma couldn't even have begun to put a number to those present, most of them spectators come to watch.

She glanced at Midge. Second and third place had been announced – it was now the turn of the winner.

She caught sight of Finlay Rankine, and beside him the Gillespies. Finlay had insisted on coming through to Edinburgh with them, and had given them a quiet booster talk, as well as

80

going over various technical details with them before the championship had begun.

Midge reached out and took her left hand, holding it clasped in one of his as the next few seconds ticked excruciatingly slowly by.

The MC was talking, but Norma wasn't really hearing what he was saying. They were just so many words that went in one ear and out the other. The only words that would register now was who the winning couple were.

'Couple number twenty-nine, McKenzie and Henderson!' The MC declared, leading the applause.

They'd done it, they'd taken the Edinburgh Veleta Championship! Somebody yelled very loudly. She learned afterwards that it was Bob Gillespie.

Still holding her by the hand Midge led her forward to the judges' rostrum where they would collect their prize. Oh but it was a proud moment right enough.

The prize was a silver salver, and two medals went with it. As the salver was large and heavy Midge held on to it in case Norma dropped it.

It took them ages to get away after that, but when they eventually did, they walked out into the chill night air to discover it had been snowing while they'd been inside, snow that covered the pavements and streets like a blanket.

Finlay managed to flag down a cruising taxi, and said he'd drop them at their hotel before going on to his own.

Norma, knowing Finlay, didn't believe he was staying in a hotel at all, but with some female he knew. A female who'd provide a lot more than he'd get in any hotel.

The taxi ride was a hilarious one, with Bob Gillespie cracking jokes and everyone laughing as though laughter was going to be banned come the morning. There was a certain amount of hysteria about the conversation, natural in the circumstances – winning the Edinburgh Veleta Championship was an enormous coup.

Arriving at the hotel they said goodbye to Finlay, arranging to meet him at the train in the morning. Midge, Bob and Beryl went straight into the lounge to order drinks – Finlay had refused the offer of one, his excuse being he might have trouble getting another taxi – Norma saying she'd join them after she'd been to her room. Midge showed all those present the silver salver he and Norma had won, and the three of them were bought a round by the hotel-owner as a congratulations gesture.

When Norma joined the others in the lounge it was clear that something of a party had developed. Midge was pouring Bob and Beryl whiskies the size of which you could have gone for a swim in. Norma said no to alcohol, settling instead for a glass of Irn Bru which was thirst-quenching, and just what she wanted.

She stayed for a little over half and hour, then left saying she was worn out and desperate for bed. Midge, the Gillespies and several others were in fine form when she took her leave.

Back in her bedroom she removed her make-up, had a good wash – an uppy and downy – then crawled into bed, which two hot water bottles had already made nice and cosy.

She lay in the darkness, going over the evening's events, analysing the better performances to see if there was anything she and Midge could pick up and use to their advantage. She was still doing this when she drifted off to sleep.

She awoke suddenly. What was that? Something had roused her, a noise of some sort, she was certain of it.

Tap tap tap.

There it was again.

She chewed a thumb, wondering who it was, and what she should do.

Tap tap tap.

Getting out of bed she tiptoed to the door. 'Who's there?' she demanded.

'It's Midge; let me in.'

Had something happened? Was something wrong? She quickly undid the snib and opened the door. Midge, wearing his dressing-gown and carrying a bottle, slipped inside.

'Jesus but it's freezing out.' As she shut the door and snibbed it again he flicked on the overhead light to get his bearings. When he had them he flicked it back off.

'Let's get into kip where we can be warm,' he said, and padded over to the bed.

She caught him by the arm just as he reached it. 'What do you think you're doing?' she asked in alarm.

'I've got a bottle of best sekt champagne here, and two tumblers. And as I haven't got any slippers on, my feet are like lumps of ice, so can we get into bed?' he replied.

'No you can't get into my bed! The Gillespies are just across the hallway for God's sake, they might have heard you come in!'

Midge chuckled. 'The state they're in neither of them will have heard anything. The roof could cave in an it wouldn't rouse them. I made sure of that.'

Norma frowned. 'What do you mean?'

'Can we get into bed first, please?'

'Oh all right,' she agreed reluctantly. What was he playing at? And why the sekt champagne? She'd never had champagne, nor did she want any right now. All she wanted was to go to sleep.

Being a single bed it was a tight fit, but they managed it. The pair of them pressed close up against one another.

'Hold these,' he instructed, and gave her the two tumblers, which he'd fished out of the pockets of his dressing gown.

'Just what is all this about?' she queried, totally mystified.

'Our own wee private celebration for what we did tonight,' he answered struggling with the cork. He pulled a face as he pushed as hard as he could with both thumbs.

With a pop the cork flew across the room just as the bedside lamp came on. With a low laugh Midge poured frothing champagne into the tumbler Norma was still holding.

'Terrific eh?' he said, and laughed again.

'What did you mean you made sure the Gillespies couldn't be roused?' she queried.

'I deliberately got them bevied to the gills, while actually taking it easy myself. I wanted them sparked out so that they wouldn't be aware when I came visiting,' he grinned in reply.

'You planned this then?'

'Whether we won or lost I intended coming to see you tonight. If we had lost I'd have got the Gillespies bevied out of disappointment. They're both pretty heavy drinkers anyway – I thought you'd have realised that by now.'

Norma hadn't.

Picking up the tumbler Norma had laid down he poured champagne for himself, stood the bottle by the side of the bed, and then raised his tumbler in a toast. 'To us!' he said, gulping down a mouthful.

Norma took a sip from her tumbler. It was bubbly and quite pleasant, if a trifle sweet for her taste.

'Oh Norma,' he whispered, his mouth seeking and kissing her breast.

She pushed him away. 'None of that now. I don't mind a celebratory drink as you've gone to all this trouble, but that's all.'

He downed what remained in his tumbler. 'Don't be daft,' he said, throwing himself on top of her.

His lips clamped on to hers, and his tongue snaked into her mouth. A hand found the breast he had kissed.

She managed to get her tumbler onto the bedside table without spilling its contents. As she was doing this his other hand shot up inside her nightie to grasp hold of her crotch.

'Stop it!' she exclaimed angrily, tearing her mouth away from his.

He groaned, both his hands working overtime feeling and prodding.

She hit him as hard as she could. A cracking slap that took him across the left cheek. His eyes, closed for the past few moments, snapped open in surprise.

'Let go of me,' she said, her voice hard and angry.

'But Norm...'

'I said let go. This instant, dammit!'

He released her, and she fell back against the pillow where she caught her breath.

He stared at her, perplexed. 'I thought... I thought you'd want me to come. That you'd want us to sleep together.'

'I never allowed anything like this to happen before so why should I suddenly do so now?' she snapped in reply.

'Because I've told you I love you, and you've admitted the same to me.'

So that was it. She was beginning to understand. 'You engineered all this so that you and I could sleep together for the first time, is that what you're saying?'

He nodded.

'You thought because we'd declared our love for one another that I'd sleep with you?'

'Staying in a hotel was a chance not to be missed. That's why I got the Gillespies bevied.'

She pulled the front of her nightie closer together, then reached for her drink. She really felt like one now.

'The answer's no,' she stated firmly.

Disappointment filled his face. 'But why not, I don't understand?'

She marshalled her thoughts, wanting to explain this clearly to him. Finally she said,

'I have no intention of going to my husband as second-hand goods; I want to be a virgin on my wedding night.

'Besides, if I did sleep with you now you might lose respect for me, and I'd hate that.'

'I wouldn't Norma, I swear!'

She gave him a cynical smile. 'I'm told men will swear anything to get you. Only afterwards, when they've had what they wanted, it's a different story.'

'Not with me, honest.'

'I think you'd better go back to your own bedroom now Midge. That would be best.'

'I don't want to go. I want to be here with you.'

'I want you to be here with me – only I'm not going to allow it. You'd just keep on trying, and I'd just have to keep on saying no, which seems a bit pointless when you think about it doesn't it?'

'I do love you,' he pleaded.

'I know, and I love you. But that's not enough. Not for me anyhow.'

He could see she wasn't going to change her mind, that she was determined to keep him at bay.

'I want you so much,' he said, balling his fists.

'And I want you too, but I won't give in to it, or you. I will not go as soiled property to my husband when the time comes because I feel, believe, that is his due.'

'I could force you,' he said.

She stared coldly at him. 'That would be a stupid mistake,' she replied levelly.

He hung his head. 'I'm sorry, I didn't really mean that. I would never force you. Never.'

She touched him very lightly on the arm. 'Goodnight then

Midge, see you in the morning.'

He got out of bed and stared down at her. He was twenty the following month, old enough to get married. And yet . . . What about his dream of visiting foreign places? If he got married those would have to go by the board. On the other hand what had he done to try and fulfil those dreams? Nothing whatever – so far it had been all talk on his part. All pish, wind and sugarally watter as his father would have said.

If he hadn't met Norma, if the two of them hadn't got so involved in this dancing; if he'd run away to sea as a boy as he'd always been going to instead of ending up as an apprentice at the North Woodside Flint Mills . . . Ifs and ands, pots and pans.

He lifted the bottle of champagne from the side of the bed. 'I'll take this with me and have a swig or two before I go to sleep,' he said.

At the door he stopped to look back at her. In that moment he knew what he was going to do, what his future would be.

It would be with Norma.

Success followed success. Already Lanarkshire Open Champions and Edinburgh Veleta Champions, they also became Glasgow Latin American Champions (having deposed the couple they'd so admired two years previously), Lanarkshire Ballroom Champions, Renfrewshire Latin American and Ballroom Champions, Stirlingshire Quickstep and Foxtrot Champions and Aberdeen Ballroom Champions.

That was their current standing when one night in August, they went to a new dancehall that had recently opened in Glasgow called Barrowland which overlooked the Barrows where Midge had bought his first set of tails.

'What do you think?' Midge asked as they waltzed round the floor.

Norma glanced about her. 'It has a good, friendly atmosphere. I like it,' she replied.

Midge nodded, that was his impression as well. They'd come again.

'Quite quiet though,' said Norma.

Midge looked at his watch. It was quiet for that time of a

Friday night, he'd have expected far more people to be there, particularly as the pubs had let out.

At the end of that waltz the band took a break, and they returned to their table. They were sitting there chatting when a middle-aged man in dinner jacket and bow tie approached them.

'I'd like to introduce myself. I'm Joe Dunlop, manager of Barrowland,' he smiled.

Midge rose, and had his hand shaken by Dunlop, who then shook Norma's hand.

'Mind if I join you?' Dunlop asked.

'Please do,' Norma told him. He borrowed a chair from an adjacent empty table.

'I saw you dance in the Lanarkshire Championship, I thought you were marvellous and well deserved to win the ballroom section.'

'Thank you,' Midge replied.

'I was wondering . . . Do you think you might give the patrons an exhibition tonight? Anything you fancy, I'd be most obliged.'

Norma glanced at Midge, and he shrugged back.

'How about a rialto two step to the tune of "Bladon Races"?' she suggested.

'Sounds great.'

'Then that's what we'll do.'

'You're a couple of toffs, thank you,' Dunlop said. 'I'll announce you myself, say in five minutes time?'

'Fine,' Norma replied.

Dunlop hurried off to talk to the band. 'I was hoping to practice our rialto two step tonight anyway, this gives us the chance,' Norma said to Midge, who agreed with her. It was a dance they did need to practice.

The band returned to the stand; then Joe Dunlop picked up a microphone.

'Ladies and gentlemen, tonight it is my great privilege to tell you we are going to be given an exhibition of a rialto two step by a young couple who are the hottest thing to hit the Scottish dancing scene for years.

'Ladies and gentlemen, will you give a big welcome to Miss Norma McKenzie and Mr Michael Henderson!'

Norma and Midge stood, inclining their heads to acknowledge the applause. They then walked out to the centre of the floor.

When the dance was over the response was rapturous, something they were becoming well used to. Audiences loved them, not just because they were top-notch dancers, but also because they positively exuded charisma, and were such a physically striking couple.

On returning to their table they were asked to sign a number of autographs, which they did. That was something else they were becoming well used to.

When the impromptu signing session was over Joe Dunlop came across and thanked them again. He then asked if they'd go with him to his office, for a word in private.

'Whisky?' he offered when the office door was shut behind them.

Norma and Midge both declined. Dunlop poured himself a small one, topping up the glass with lemonade.

'As I'm sure you know, Barrowland hasn't been opened that long and, as you can see from the numbers here tonight, hasn't really got going yet. My brief from the owners is to change that as quickly as possible, and make Barrowland one of the foremost, and popular – if not *the* foremost and *the* most popular – dancehall in Glasgow.

'I've already booked some of the big name bands, bands that have never been to Glasgow before. Billy Cotton for one, Henry Hall for another. I've also booked Stanley Black, Denny Dennis and Nat Gonella and his Georgians.'

'That's quite a line-up,' Midge acknowledged, for Dunlop had just reeled off some of the biggest names of the day.

'I'm also negotiating to have Glenn Miller appear here during his forthcoming British tour. If I can pull that off, and I'm pretty certain I can, it should really pack them in.'

Midge gave a low whistle. 'They don't come any bigger than Glenn Miller,' he said.

Dunlop nodded his agreement. He offered Midge a cigar, which Midge refused. Dunlop lit up, then went on.

'Watching the pair of you tonight I had a thought. What Barrowland also needs to bring people in is a regular exhibition couple, a couple who'd be in residence so to speak, and who'd perform, say, four times a night.'

'You mean professional dancers,' Norma said.

'That's it, a professional couple. What do you think?'

'I think it's an excellent idea. What couple did you have in mind?' Midge replied.

Norma, as usual, saw what was coming. 'I believe Mr Dunlop is thinking of us,' she said.

Midge looked from Dunlop to Norma, and back again to Dunlop. 'Are you?'

'Tuesdays through Saturdays, four exhibitions a night, and I'll pay a tenner,' Dunlop said quietly.

Midge swallowed hard. That was five pounds each, and for dancing! Work was work, but dancing was pleasure.

'I'll have a whisky after all please,' Norma said. She didn't really want one; it was a device to give her time to think.

'It would mean an end to our amateur status of course. It depends how important you feel that is to us,' she said to Midge.

'Certainly I enjoy, revel in, winning championships, I can't deny it. But a tenner a week between us, that's something that has to be considered seriously,' he replied.

He was right. It wouldn't bar them from all championships mind you, Norma thought, only the amateur ones. There were a few pro championships, but only a few. There was one notable exception, the All Scotland Dance Championship – all comers could enter that, pro and amateur alike. It was Scotland's most prestigious championship and the winners were acclaimed as the best dancers in Scotland.

She accepted her whisky from Dunlop. As she did so she searched his face, and what she saw there told her he was dead keen to have them.

Ten pounds was a lot of money, but then Dunlop – if he could afford whatever Glenn Miller would charge – certainly seemed to have access to plenty.

'It would be a huge sacrifice on our part. And once we relinquish our amateur status that's it, there's no going back,' she said softly.

'Do you want time to consider?' Dunlop suggested reluctantly.

'Would there be a contract?' she queried.

'I hadn't thought that far ahead. Would you want one?'

Now was the time to think of the future, Norma told herself. If they took the job and were successful, then who was to say this might not lead on to better, more lucrative things? In which case it would be better if they weren't tied by a contract.

'No,' she replied.

Midge glanced at her in surprise, but held his tongue. If Norma said no then she must have a reason.

Norma took a miniscule sip of her drink, and thought about being a professional dancer. The idea appealed, very much so.

'Fifteen pounds and we start next Tuesday,' she said.

Midge gaped at her. Fifteen nicker! Was she off her chump!

Dunlop stared at her. He hadn't expected to have to bargain. He shook his head; she was only a lassie after all, what did she know about business? And dammit, his offer was a good one.

'That's beyond me,' he replied.

Norma had another miniscule sip of whisky, and waited.

'Oh all right, eleven,' Dunlop said after a while, thinking that would be the end of it. But it wasn't.

Norma still didn't reply. She had looked into his face and seen how badly he wanted them. The seconds ticked by.

Dunlop frowned, he found it most off-putting the way she just sat there saying nothing. He began to believe she'd have sat there in silence for the rest of the night if he'd let her.

'Twelve pounds ten, and that's it,' he said, pouring himself another whisky.

Midge was jumping inside, and there was cold sweat on his forehead. Six pounds five a week each, it was a bloody fortune. Why didn't she agree? He considered putting his spoke in, then thought better of it. He had a lot of faith in Norma. Experience had taught him that when she took a stand she was invariably right.

Slowly and softly, but with a hint of steel, Norma said. 'If I may quote what you said about us in your introduction earlier on: "a young couple who are the hottest, and most exciting, thing to hit the Scottish dancing scene for years".

'Glenn Miller, Billy Cotton, Henry Hall – if you want the best you have to pay for them. You know that Mr Dunlop.'

He gave a grunt that was actually a laugh. Throwing his own words back at him! He liked that. It was what his Ikey friends called chutspah. He also liked the fact that, without actually saying so, she'd ranked herself and Henderson alongside Miller, Cotton and Hall. Now that was real chutspah.

'Fourteen pounds a week, and that *is* it. A matter of pride,' he told her.

This time she knew he meant it. He'd gone up four pounds, she'd have to concede one. As he said, his male pride demanded it.

'You have a deal Mr Dunlop,' she replied.

'Well, thank God for that!' he exclaimed, pulling a face. Which punctured the tension that had built up in the room, and made them all laugh.

When they left Dunlop's office a few minutes later Norma suggested to Midge that they call it a night and head back to Bridgeton, to which he readily agreed. He also wanted out of there, and fast.

He somehow managed to contain himself till they were away from the front of Barrowland, and down the street a bit. Then, giving vent to a loud Red Indian-type whoop, he caught Norma in his arms and, lifting her right off the pavement, birled her round and round.

'Fourteen pounds a week, it's unbelievable!' he croaked, setting her down again.

'You are certain about us giving up our amateur status? For once we do that's it, there's no going back,' she said anxiously.

'I'm certain, seven pounds a week certain. Why, that on top of what I'm earning now makes me rich, and you too.'

It did as well. She'd be the highest earning female in all Bridgeton, no doubt about it. From now on she'd be earning four times what she had been.

Midge let out another Red Indian whoop, and birled her round again. When he stopped Norma was smiling hugely, and her cheeks were flushed with a combination of euphoria, and self-satisfaction.

'Let's hurry home and tell our folks,' she said. She couldn't wait to see the look on her da's face when she broke the news. Or her mother's – the pair of them would be dumbstruck.

Hand in hand, laughing like a couple of dafties, she and Midge ran for the tram that had just pulled up.

* * *

They'd just finished their first exhibition of the evening when Norma spied the old man again, standing beside a pillar and staring at her.

'There he is again,' she whispered to Midge.

'Who?'

'*Him*, the old fella.'

Midge's expression creased into one of worry and concern. The old man had been coming in every night for the past fortnight. He always came alone, and never danced. Just stood, or sat, staring at Norma, his eyes glued to her.

'A joke's a joke, but this has gone far enough. I'm going to speak to Dunlop,' Midge replied.

Norma worried a crimson-painted nail. 'I think you should. He's starting to give me the creeps, that man, just staring at me the way he does.'

Midge was about to go and seek out Dunlop when the manager hove into view, doing his rounds, making sure everything was all right and going as it should.

Midge caught Dunlop's eye and gestured him over.

Norma and Midge had been resident professionals at Barrowland for just over three months now, and were loving every minute of it. Their exhibitions had become firm favourites with the patrons, as had they. Business at the dancehall was booming. And, as Dunlop was the first to admit, a lot of the credit of that was down to them.

When Dunlop joined them, Midge explained in low, hurried tones what was troubling Norma, and giving him cause for concern.

Dunlop glanced over at the old fella, wondering if he was dangerous. You never knew in Glasgow, and, as he had learned to his cost in the past, appearances could be very deceptive. He would take 'Spider' Webb, one of the two bouncers he employed, with him when he spoke to the man, just in case.

Dunlop left them in search of Spider, and shortly after that they watched Dunlop and Spider home in on the old man. A short conversation took place, at the end of which Dunlop led the way to his office with the old man following behind, and Spider behind him.

There were fifteen minutes till their second exhibition of the evening, the Doris waltz, when Dunlop reappeared with the old fella by his side.

'Norma, I'd like you to meet Mr Gallagher. He has an interesting story I think you should hear.'

If Dunlop had brought Gallagher to their table, he must be safe, Norma reasoned, and shook hands with him. Gallagher then shook hands with Midge.

Seeing Gallagher up close Norma realised he was even older than she'd thought. Late seventies? Eighties? He was positively ancient, though still spry on his feet.

'I must apologise for giving you a fright, I really am sorry. It just never dawned on me, with so many folk present, that you'd notice me watching you,' Gallagher said.

He was well spoken, Norma noted. Though hardly what you would have called a toff. His clothes had been expensive when bought, but that had been a fair while ago. The jacket cuff of his right sleeve had started to fray, and there was a distinct sheen to his trouser legs.

Norma invited Gallagher to sit, and Dunlop sat down as well. Norma and Midge always kept several empty chairs at their table, as some of the regulars liked to come over and have a natter, which they didn't discourage, looking on it as part and parcel of the service.

'Show Norma your photograph,' said Dunlop.

Gallagher reached into an inside pocket to produce his wallet. From the wallet he took a small photograph, about three inches square, Norma judged.

'My daughter,' Gallagher said simply, and handed Norma the photograph.

It was a sepia-coloured photograph of a girl in her late teens, or perhaps twenty or twenty-one. She was a very attractive girl, with long hair and smiling mouth. And she was somehow familiar.

Midge, leaning over, looked from the photograph up to Norma. 'It's you,' he said.

Gallagher nodded. 'The resemblance is remarkable. I noticed it the first time I saw your own photograph outside in the foyer, Miss McKenzie. It was that which prompted me to come in, and why I've been coming ever since.'

The photograph of Norma that Gallagher was referring to

93

was a huge blow-up one of her and Midge which was positioned in the foyer so as to be visible from the street. Gallagher had been passing when a glance at the photograph had brought him up short.

Norma stared at the small photograph in her hand. She could see it now. In a strange way it was like looking into a mirror, a mirror distorted by time. For the girl's clothes and hairstyle belonged to an earlier period. Before the Great War, Norma thought. Yes, sometime between the turn of the century and 1914.

'Her name was Morna – even the name is similar,' said Gallagher.

Norma glanced up at him. '*Was?*'

'She died young, of a brain tumour.'

'Oh I am sorry,' Norma said quietly.

Gallagher averted his gaze for a moment. When he looked back at Norma she could see a glint of tears in his face.

'When I saw you in the flesh I just couldn't believe it. It was as though Morna was still alive, though of course you wouldn't have been born until some years after her death.'

He groped for a handkerchief, a large, white, cotton one, which he blew his nose into.

'Excuse an old man his foolishness, but my Morna and I were very close, the way it is sometimes between a father and daughter.'

Gallagher stuffed the handkerchief back into his breast pocket. There were brown liver spots on his hands, hands that trembled slightly.

Norma gave the sepia photograph to Midge so he could study it more closely. It was Norma all right, he thought. Morna and Norma could have been identical twins. Identical, with just those few little differences to enable you to tell them apart. Morna's nose was a shade longer; her cheekbones somewhat more prominent.

'What colour eyes did she have?' asked Midge.

'Grey,' Gallagher replied.

Even that was similar Midge thought. Though Norma's weren't always grey but changed from grey to green and back again.

'And you say she died of a brain tumour,' Norma said.

'Yes, it was a most painful, and protracted death. Towards the end, she was sleeping most of the time, due to the huge doses of medication she was receiving. Then one afternoon she went to sleep and never woke up again.'

'And when was it she died?' Norma asked.

'1908.'

Nearly thirty years ago, Norma thought. Morna would have been fifty or thereabouts now, older than Effie.

'And Mrs Gallagher?' she inquired.

'Died giving birth to Ian, our son. He was killed in the closing months of the war. He was with Allenby when Allenby destroyed the last Turkish army at Megiddo.'

What a sad tale, Norma thought. And what a sad old man. She took the photograph of Morna from Midge, looked at it again, then passed it back to Gallagher.

'Thank you for showing your daughter's photograph to us,' she said.

'It was the least I could do after being so stupid as to frighten you. I never intended any harm, only to look, and remember, and ...' He shrugged. 'Think of things as they might have been.'

Norma glanced at her watch. It was almost time for their second exhibition.

'Listen Mr Gallagher, we don't mind people coming over and chatting to us occasionally. If you'd like to from time to time then please feel free to do so,' Norma said.

His face lit up. 'You really mean that?'

'I do.'

'Is this acceptable to you Mr Henderson?'

Midge nodded. 'Yes of course.'

'From time to time then. And not for too long. I won't make a pest of myself, or outstay my welcome.'

Gallagher took Norma's right hand in one of his, and kissed the back of it the way a Frenchman would.

'Thank you,' he said softly.

There was silence round the table after Gallagher had gone, each of them thinking about the old man and his tragic story. Thoughts that had to be interrupted when the number being played came to an end.

'I'll introduce you,' Dunlop said, rising.

Norma fought back the lump that was in her throat. 'The Doris waltz,' she said to Midge.

From a dark, secluded part of the hall Gallagher watched Norma with tears rolling down his cheeks.

In the flesh he was in Barrowland watching Norma, but in his mind he was in a different place, with a laughing girl.

That Saturday afternoon found Norma and Midge, as they were now to be found most Saturday afternoons, in a hall in their local Bridgeton 'Pineapple' – the nickname used by Protestants when referring to a Catholic Chapel.

Neither Norma or Midge was Catholic, but both were friendly with Father Finn, the parish priest of St Mary Magdalen.

It wasn't common for Catholics and Protestants to be friendly in this way, particularly where one of the parties involved was a priest. But Father Finn was a man who rose above sectarianism, with time for everyone whether they belonged to the Catholic Faith or not. He was, as he'd often been described, a true Christian.

Up till then Norma and Midge had been practising at either her house – now the three room and kitchen – or Midge's. That was until Father Finn had suggested they use one of the halls in the 'Pineapple', which would give them a lot more space to practice in.

They'd been delighted to accept Father Finn's offer, and also the use of the 'Pineapple's' gramophone. They brought their own records along for each session as required.

'Well that's about it,' Midge said, releasing Norma, and going over to the gramophone to take the record they'd been dancing to – 'Kissin' Bug Boogie' with Sid Phillips and his Band – off the turntable.

Norma ran a hand through her hair. It was greasy; she'd need to wash it before she and Midge went to Barrowland that evening. They'd been practising a slight variation of the foxtrot basic one step which made the dance more exciting to watch. She was happy with it now, as was Midge.

She put on her coat, for it was cold in the unheated hall. She'd been dancing wearing a sweater and cardy on top of that. Enough when you were moving, but not when you'd stopped.

'Before I put the grammy away there's something I want to give you,' Midge said casually. He went to his own coat, fished in a pocket, and pulled something out.

Crossing to Norma, the faintest of smiles twisting his lips, he presented the something to her. It was a small black box. The unmistakable sort that rings come in.

Norma looked at the box, at Midge, then back at the box again.

'Open it,' he instructed.

There was white satin inside, and a black velvety panel. Embedded in the panel was an engagement ring consisting of a large diamond surrounded by smaller ones.

'I've been saving up for that. Wanted to give you a decent one,' Midge said, his smile widening.

Norma gazed at the ring. It was a smasher, a real humdinger. She doubted any other girl in Bridgeton had a ring as beautiful as this one. And it must have cost a fortune.

'So, are we engaged then?' he asked.

This was the last thing she'd expected, well, not in these circumstances anyway. It had taken her breath away.

'Engaged to be married?'

He laughed. 'What else do you think I mean!'

She gently pulled out the ring from the slit. As she did the light caught the big stone, sending out rays of flashing fire.

'This is an actual proposal?' she queried.

'An actual proposal,' he confirmed.

Norma was a bit miffed he'd chosen these very unglamorous surroundings in which to pop the question. It was so ... unromantic! And he might have asked her properly. 'So are we engaged then?' sounded like 'Would you like a fish supper for your tea?'

Devilment got into her. 'Aren't you supposed to go down on one knee to propose? Isn't that the tradition?'

Midge looked alarmed. Her tone might be jocular, but he knew her well enough to know she was serious. Down on one knee! He could feel his face colouring.

'No one would see. We're perfectly alone,' she purred.

He knew that was so, but glanced round the hall nonetheless. Just to be sure. 'I don't think I ...'

'Down on one knee,' she repeated, her tone still light,

but with an underlying hint of steel.

He took a deep breath. The things men did for women. Honestly! He went down in front of her.

'There,' he muttered.

'And you say ...'

He groaned.

'And you say, Norma will you marry me?'

'Norma will you marry me?'

'Please.'

He took another deep breath. He felt a proper Charlie doing this, a right heid the ba'.

'Norma will you marry me *please*?' he asked.

She slipped the ring onto the appropriate finger, twisting it round one way, then the other, making it catch the light so that it shot off more flashing fire. During this she kept her face impassive.

Sudden alarm flared in Midge. She wasn't going to refuse him, was she! He'd never even considered the possibility. He'd thought her reaction would be to be all over him like the proverbial rash. Yet here she was, seemingly undecided.

'Norma?' he croaked. If she turned him down it would be a disaster, a catastrophe!

'A girl is supposed to take her time in answering that particular question. She musn't appear too eager.'

'So will you or won't you?' he demanded.

She grasped him by an elbow, and raised him back to his feet. She gazed into those gorgeous blue eyes of his, eyes she'd often thought would mesmerise her if she stared into them long and hard enough. 'Of course I'll marry you,' she whispered.

Relief flooded through him and he drew her close and kissed her. A kiss that made her squirm with pleasure.

When their mouths parted she kissed him back, on the neck, and under the chin.

'Three little words Midge,' she whispered.

He knew full well what she was after, but now it was his turn to tease.

'You want to dance?' he asked innocently.

She shook her head. 'The *other* three little words Midge.'

His expression became deadly earnest. 'I love you Norma,' he said softly.

'And I love you, Oh, how I love you!'

Their faces came together again, and their mouths closed on each other.

They were now officially engaged to be married. She was to be Mrs Midge Henderson, and she was overjoyed at the prospect. One she'd dreamt of for a long long time now.

Mrs Midge Henderson.

A warm, delicious prickle ran up her spine.

She'd been home long enough to wash her hair, dry it in front of the fire, and now get ready for Barrowland and still no one had noticed.

Norma looked over at Lyn. She was amazed old eagle eye hadn't spotted it. She brought her left hand up so that it was resting casual-like, on her left cheek.

'Everything all right Lyn?' she inquired nonchalantly.

Lyn was buried in a magazine of romantic stories she'd borrowed off a lassie at work. The story she was in the middle of was about a nurse, and set during the war. It was a cracker.

'Why shouldn't it be?' Lyn replied, glancing quickly in Norma's direction.

Norma waggled her engagement finger. Come on you stupid cow, the ring's bloody big enough she thought. 'Just asking, that's all,' she replied in the same nonchalant tone.

With a shrug Lyn returned eagerly to her nurse.

'Tea will be ready in a mo,' announced Effie from the stove, where she was making scrambled eggs, fried tomatoes, mushrooms and toast.

Norma looked over at her mother's back, then to her father engrossed in an *Evening Citizen*. She brought her gaze onto Eileen who was sitting staring into the fire.

'How's the job going then Eileen?' she asked. Eileen had left school that summer and was now working in a local bakery tending counter.

'Fine ta,' Eileen replied.

Norma, left hand still on cheek, waggled her engagement finger again. Making it a more pronounced waggle this time.

'The Mavors seem like nice people,' she said. The Mavors owned the bakery.

'Aye, they are.'

Norma glowered at Eileen. Her wee sister hadn't even so much as flicked her eyes at her, but continued staring into the fire.

'Oh dammit to hell, I give up!' she exploded.

Brian's head emerged from behind his paper. 'Something wrong?'

'No everything's right, except nobody's noticed that's all.'

She had everyone's attention now. Even Effie had paused in what she was doing to glance across at her.

'This afternoon Midge ...'

At which point 'old eagle eye' saw the ring. Squealing, Lyn jumped right out of her chair to point dramatically at Norma. 'She's wearing an engagement ring!'

At last! Norma thought with satisfaction. *At last.* She smiled as her two sisters crowded round.

'Let's see. Hold it up properly so we can get a good gander,' Lyn said.

I've been doing nothing but since I came in earlier. I was beginning to think you'd all been struck blind,' Norma retorted.

'Oh it's a brammer!' Eileen breathed.

'And the size of that stone, absolutely ginormous,' Lyn said, her eyes popping.

Brian was staring at his eldest daughter in astonishment, though he couldn't think why. He and Effie had long known this was on the cards. Maybe he'd thought they'd leave it a while longer. But at eighteen, eighteen and a half nearly, she was certainly old enough if that's what she wanted. Which it seemed she did.

Effie wiped her hands on her pinny. There was a catch in her throat as she walked over to a now beaming Norma. 'Let's have a look then,' she said, pushing a stray lock of hair away from her forehead.

'I've been flashing it like mad since I got in. Flash flash, sparkle sparkle!' Norma giggled. 'How you all missed it beats me.'

Effie studied the ring, then shook her head in admiration. 'Well he hasn't made a fool of you, that's for certain,' she said.

Norma suddenly found herself in her mother's arms, the pair of them holding each other tightly. There were tears in Effie's eyes when she finally let Norma go.

Brian shook her solemnly by the hand, his expression one of fierce pride. 'Congratulations lass,' he said, voice thick with emotion.

'Aye, congrats,' Lyn added.

'Can I try the ring on?' Eileen asked eagerly.

'No you cannot, that would be unlucky,' Norma replied instantly. She didn't know whether it was unlucky or not, she just didn't want anyone else, not even a sister, putting it on.

A few minutes later they all sat down to tea, laughing, joking and talking about the engagement.

Late that night Norma and Midge stopped on his landing as they always did coming back together from Barrowland. He'd just started to kiss her when his door opened and Katy poked her head out.

'If I could do a wolf whistle I would,' she grinned.

'Do you mind, this is private,' Midge replied, glaring at her.

'Sorry to interrupt the winching, but Ma and Da are upstairs with the McKenzies and want you to pop up there before you come in by,' she said.

'To the McKenzies, what for?'

'Search me. All I know is that I was to pass on the message.' And with that Katy shut the door again.

Midge looked thoughtful, wondering what this was all about.

'Ach they're probably having a few drams in celebration and want us to join them,' Norma said.

'Aye, that's probably it right enough,' Midge replied. They continued up to the next landing where she used her key to let them into her house.

They walked into the kitchen, and were mobbed. 'Surprise!' shouted Brian, waving a whisky bottle in the air. His flushed cheeks told Norma he'd been hard at it for some while.

Norma's hand was grabbed and pumped up and down by Bob Gillespie; then Beryl was embracing her and saying how marvellous the news was.

After the Gillespies, it was the Fullartons' turn to offer congratulations; Jacky kissing her on the cheek, declaring that right from the word go, from the night he'd introduced Midge to her out in the street, he'd had the feeling the pair of them would end up tying the knot.

'We thought a wee party would be just the dab,' Effie said to Norma.

'This is tremendous Ma,' Norma enthused. Many of the friends from the street and round about were there, and several from further afield, including Finlay Rankine who'd been contacted by telephone.

Katy Henderson came into the kitchen, and gave Norma a fly wink. 'Your da wanted it to be a complete surprise.' she said.

'Well it was certainly that right enough. We didn't even have an inkling, just walked straight into it.'

Most of those present had already had a good drink while waiting for the newly engaged couple to return from Barrowland.

Norma spied Eileen with Charlie Marshall, the pair of them holding hands. Charlie's plooks had long since disappeared, and his once wispy moustache had thickened so that it now looked like a proper moustache instead of some very thin oose stuck to his upper lip.

He and Eileen made a handsome couple, Norma thought. How long till they got engaged? Not too long, she'd bet money on that.

Alice and Leslie Henderson forced their way over to tell her how pleased they were. Their Midge couldn't have found himself a nicer lassie, and that was the truth.

If there was one person not enjoying herself it was Lyn. When was *her* prince going to appear, she wondered despairingly. All the other girls had boyfriends and admirers, but not her. Of course if she wasn't so big it might have helped, but all she had to do was breathe to put on another pound. Well, maybe a wee bit more than breathe. But it was hardly her fault she had a healthy appetite!

Mr Laidlaw poured Norma a dram, having already given one to Midge.

'A toast! A toast!' the cry went up.

The general hubbub subsided. Brian came forward to do the honours.

Brian raised his glass. 'To the happy couple,' he said simply. Speechmaking wasn't exactly his forte.

'To the happy couple!' echoed from all sides.

Norma looked at Midge who grinned rather sheepishly back

at her. She'd never been so happy in her life. She was fair bursting with happiness.

She lifted her glass to him, and he to her. Everybody else present shouted and clapped as they toasted each other, and themselves.

It was late afternoon of Hogmanay and Norma and Midge were at the Central Station to see her family off to Kirn for a holiday. It was the first time ever that Effie and Brian had gone off on one, and it was their first visit back to Kirn.

Brian didn't get time off at Christmas – that was for weans and the English – but he got four days at New Year. That year, thanks to a bit of finagling on his part, he'd managed an extra afternoon, that afternoon, stopping at one o'clock instead of six.

They would be staying with an old friend of Effie's from the WI who owned a small guesthouse which, being out of season, was currently empty apart from herself and husband.

Norma couldn't go because of her commitment to Barrowland. Hogmanay was the biggest night of the year and, much as she'd have adored to go back to the place where she'd been born and brought up, it had never even entered her mind to let Joe Dunlop down.

Effie was full of going back to Kirn, as was Brian, though he refused to admit he was. He was being very casual about the whole affair, but underneath it all was just as excited as Effie.

Lyn was also looking forward to going back, though not nearly so much as her parents. As for Eileen, she hadn't wanted to go at all and was only doing so at her father's insistence. She wanted to be with Charlie over Hogmanay and, at sixteen, felt she was old enough to be left behind. Brian agreed she was old enough, but said it was only right and proper that they were all together for Hogmanay – those who could be, that was. Norma's exemption was strictly on account of work; otherwise he would have insisted she come as well.

Finally Effie, Brian, Lyn, Eileen and their assorted baggage were put aboard the train and a few minutes later the whistle sounded. Norma and Midge waved the McKenzies on their way.

'Let's get back,' Norma smiled to Midge when the train had

103

gone. She had an argument ready for him should he have suggested they do something else. But he didn't.

'Come upstairs with me, I've got an engagement present for you,' she said when they reached Midge's door.

His face lit up. 'A present? What?'

'Wait and see,' she laughed, and led the way up to the next landing.

She took him into the kitchen. 'Stay here, I won't be long,' she said, and left him standing in front of the fireplace.

She returned a few minutes later wearing a dressing gown and an enigmatic smile. She wasn't carrying or holding anything.

Puzzled, Midge frowned. What was going on? And where was his present?

Her heart was pounding at her own daring and audacity. If she wasn't absolutely certain there was still time for her to change her mind she told herself. But she *was* absolutely certain. She shivered in anticipation.

'Your engagement present,' she said throatily, and dropped her dressing gown to the floor to stand stark naked before him.

Midge gawped at her.

'I've been waiting for a suitable opportunity. Today, and the next four days are it.'

She took him by the hand, and he followed her through to her bedroom where the curtains were already closed, a bedside lamp switched on, and the bed turned down.

'Do I understand correctly?' he asked, finding his tongue again.

'Yes.'

'You want me to ... I mean you and I to ...' He trailed off.

'Yes.'

He swallowed hard. As the saying went, you could have knocked him over with a feather.

'But you told me ... you told me that you'd go to your husband a virgin?'

'And so I am.'

'But I'm not your husband!'

'Not yet. But you're going to be. That's precisely what engaged means, engaged to be married. You're going to be my husband, I your wife. And I have a very expensive diamond ring to prove it,' she replied.

He stared hungrily at her. Taking in her full, well-rounded breasts. The satin sheen of her skin. The blonde tangle at the apex of two perfect legs.

'You're beautiful. Even more beautiful than I'd imagined,' he croaked.

She got into bed, waiting with the bedclothes pulled up to her chin while he undressed. Then he was beside her, his body cold against hers. The pair of them clutched each other for warmth.

His hands began to move. Touching, feeling, exploring, while she did the same. She whispered into his ear that he'd find the necessary under the pillow. She didn't want any 'accidents' happening.

As she'd known it would, the same magic that happened when they danced together happened now. They fused, to become as one. Completely one.

Later they both cried out. In unison.

Chapter Five

Lyn was passing through the filing department at work when she came across Norma propped up against one of the large cabinets in the department. Norma's eyes were closed, and there was a strange expression on her face. Her complexion had gone all pasty, a sort of greeny colour.

'What is it? What's wrong?' demanded Lyn, putting a supporting arm round Norma's shoulders.

Norma's eyes flickered open. 'One moment I was all right, the next quite lightheaded. As if the inside of my head was trying to float out through the top of my skull.'

'Do you feel sick?'

'Aye, a bit.'

'Then let's get you sat down.'

Lyn helped Norma stumble to a nearby chair. 'Can you manage by yourself for a moment or two? I'll get you a glass of water.'

'Please.'

Lyn didn't like the look of Norma at all, and wondered if she should call a doctor.

When Lyn returned she found her sister slumped forward with her head in her hands. Norma glanced up at her approach, and gave her a wan smile.

Norma sipped the water Lyn had fetched. It was lovely and cold. She already felt better, her lightheadedness starting to recede.

'Do you think it's the flu?' Lyn queried anxiously.

'No. It's just tiredness. I'm sure of it. I was right whacked when I got out of bed this morning, totally drained. I'm certain that's what brought on this dizzy turn.'

Lyn's lips thinned. So that was it. She might have guessed.

106

Effie had been saying only the other week that she didn't know how Norma did it.

Norma drank more water, and her colour began to return. 'I'd like to wash my face. That would help a lot,' she said, her voice still a little weak.

On reaching the nearest ladies' toilet, having passed several concerned employees on the way, Lyn made Norma sit on the WC while she filled the basin. When Norma had washed and dried her face Lyn forced her to sit down again saying that she should stay there until fully recovered.

'This working what amounts to two full-time jobs just isn't on you know,' Lyn chided. 'You're at it from early morning till last thing at night. It can't go on for ever.'

Norma nodded. Lyn was right. She was doing far too much, and the strain was beginning to tell. Her dizzy turn was proof of that.

'Pack it in here, you don't need the money after all,' Lyn suggested.

'You forget I'm newly engaged. The sooner we get something behind us the sooner we can get married. Even if the money I earn here is nowhere what I bring in from Barrowland, it does make a big difference to what I put away each week.'

Lyn saw her sister's point. 'But with you and Midge both coining it surely it won't be that long before you can afford to get wed?'

'The sooner the better as far as I'm concerned. I can't wait to be Mrs Midge Henderson and have a wee house of our own.'

'Well it's up to you what you do, but if you go on like you are doing you'll end up in hospital. And that's a fact.'

Just then there was a knock on the toilet door. It was Norma's boss, a Mr Brown, come to inquire how she was, and was there anything he could do?

It was a thoughtful Norma who returned to work.

Norma and Midge were in Joe Dunlop's office, having requested to see the manager privately. Norma had told Midge to let her do the talking, she was a great deal better at this sort of thing than he was.

Norma stared levelly at Dunlop. Shortly after her dizzy turn at work she'd put the word out that she and Midge might be interested in moving dancehalls, if the fee was right. It hadn't taken long for the pair of them to have a 'bite'.

Norma had almost accepted this offer, and then she'd had a further thought. That was why she and Midge were there to see Dunlop. To find out if that further thought would work.

'So what can I do for you?' Dunlop asked with a smile. He took out one of the cigars he was addicted to, clipped it and lit up. When he'd finished Norma replied.

'The Locarno have offered us twenty pounds a week to go and be their professionals.'

Dunlop's smile vanished. Norma and Midge were a huge attraction at Barrowland. If they went to the Locarno they might take a lot of his clientele with them.

'I thought you liked it here?' he said slowly.

'We do. And we like you. But what's that got to do with it?'

Dunlop sighed, and puffed on his cigar. Truth was he'd rather been expecting something like this for a while. Neither Norma or Midge were fools, they knew the draw they were.

'All right then, I'll match the Locarno's offer. Twenty pounds a week as from Monday first,' he said.

Midge glanced at Norma, knowing what was coming next. Her 'further thought' as she'd put it.

'Let's say I go back to the Locarno and tell them about this conversation. What do you suppose their next move would be?'

Dunlop chewed the end of his cigar, regarding Norma through slitted eyes. 'You're saying that they'll offer more?'

'I think so. They're very keen to have us – they made that clear enough.'

Dunlop grunted. She was right, the Locarno would up the ante. The question now was what was the fee she'd decided on. For she obviously had a figure in mind.

'How much to keep you here?' he asked.

Her heart leapt within her. It had worked! It was amazing what a little bit of manipulation could accomplish.

'Thirty a week,' she stated boldly.

Midge choked. She'd told him she was going to ask for twenty-five.

'That's half again of what the Locarno are now offering,' Dunlop said quietly.

'I'm certain I can get them up to twenty-five. If you want us to stay here you'll have to top that, and top it by a reasonable amount.'

Dunlop stared hard at Norma, a cloud of cigar smoke surrounding his head and shoulders. 'How do I know you won't now go to the Locarno and try to get them to top thirty?'

'You think they might?'

Dunlop grinned. 'We shake hands and that's the end of the matter. Agreed?'

'For a reasonable period of time. Agreed?' she retorted.

Dunlop stood, and extended a hand across his desk. He shook first with Norma, then with Midge. 'Agreed,' he said.

Midge was opening the door for Norma when Dunlop suddenly went on, remembering, 'By the way, an American couple called Don and Zelda Caprice have been touring Europe – very successfully too I might add – and will be visiting Scotland before returning to the States. I've booked them for a fortnight next month. They'll be doing four exhibitions a night, alternating their performances with yours. All right?'

'We don't mind the competition if they don't,' Midge answered, and ushered Norma out of the office, shutting the door firmly behind them.

They looked at each other, both quite stunned. Fifteen pounds a week each – it was more than they'd been getting as a pair when they'd walked into Dunlop's office.

They walked down the corridor, away from the office, and turned a corner. There they fell into one another's arms.

'Tell me I'm dreaming!' Midge husked.

'It's no dream, it's for real.'

'It's a fortune, a King's ransom,' Midge enthused.

Norma gave a low laugh. 'Hardly a King's ransom, but it's an awful lot of money all the same.' She took a deep breath. 'I'm handing in my notice at SCWS tomorrow morning, what about you?'

'Aye. Why knock my pan out at the mills when I don't need to. I can live the life of Riley on fifteen quid a week.'

She gazed into his eyes, hoping he might suggest a date for their wedding there and then, but he didn't. She let it go for the moment. A date *would* be set for their wedding soon. She was determined about that.

'We need the daytimes free so we can practise. It's high time we enlarged our repertoire, and we need more than Saturday afternoons at Father Finn's "Pineapple" for that,' she said.

He nodded his agreement.

'Oh Midge!' she exclaimed, bubbling over with excitement and self-satisfaction at what she'd just pulled off. That, and love for this man now in her arms.

'I nearly died when you asked for thirty and not twenty-five as you'd said.'

'I suddenly thought, why not! And so I did.'

'You're a wee miracle worker Norma. And I adore you.'

When they returned to their table they found old man Gallagher waiting for them, come over for one of his chats. He talked about the dead Morna as he always did.

Midge was just about to pull the toilet chain when he heard the slam of a door followed by the click-clack of footsteps he would have recognised anywhere. He pulled the chain, and snecked open the cludgie door.

When Norma appeared he contrived to look mysterious, and crooked a finger, beckoning her to join him in the toilet.

'What is it?' she asked.

'Come here, inside,' he whispered back, and looked down behind the door as if something was there.

The moment she was inside he pulled her close with one hand and resnecked the door with the other.

'Got you,' he whispered, and gently bit her neck.

'What are you doing!' she exclaimed, struggling.

'Ssshhh!' he commanded. 'If you have to speak do so in a whisper.' He touched her breast. 'It's been so long,' he murmured, his eager mouth fastening onto hers.

So that's what this was all about, she thought as his tongue snaked and coiled round hers.

'No one will know we're both in here even if they try the door,' he said urgently when the kiss was over, dropping a hand to bring it up underneath her dress.

She pushed him back but, because there was so little room, couldn't break away from him completely.

'Are you mad! I'm not going to do it in the bog!' she whispered.

Midge was desperate – it had been weeks. 'But we so rarely

have the opportunity. Even though we're not working through the day now, your Ma is always around the house and so is mine. And we can't do it in the "Pineapple", that's completely out of the question.'

She forced his hand from under her dress. 'Stop that!' she ordered.

'But I want you so much.'

'Well it's your own fault. You could have me every night of the week if you wanted.'

He stared at her. 'How do you mean?'

It was the perfect opportunity and she wasn't going to let it go by. 'If we were married we'd have our own home and bed to go to.'

'But we've only been engaged two and a half months!'

'So where does it say you have to have a long engagement?'

Midge considered that. 'It doesn't I suppose. It's just that six or nine months or even a year is usual.'

'Long engagements are to give the engaged couple time to save up. But with what we're earning now that hardly applies to us, does it?'

She was right. What did they need to save up for! With thirty quid a week between them, and with what he had already put by – and her too no doubt – they could furnish a house as easy as pie. And furnish it damned well to boot.

'Let's set a date now,' she urged, her eyes bright with expectation.

The thought of Norma in his bed night and morning made Midge's blood race even more than it had been, which was saying something.

'As soon as we can arrange it then,' he agreed.

She sighed, and went tingly all over. 'How about directly after the All Scotland Dance Championship? That would be the perfect timing as far as I'm concerned.'

The All Scotland Dance Championship was Scotland's most prestigious championship and one of the few left open to them as pros. They'd been practising for it for months and it was now just a few weeks away.

'Directly after the championship then,' he nodded.

'Leave everything to me. I'll see the factor and arrange the house. And if there isn't a suitable one come available by that time we'll just stay in my room till it does.' Norma had been given her own bedroom when the family had moved into their three-room and kitchen. She paused. 'Oh Midge!' she exclaimed, and buried her mouth on his.

When the kiss was over he gave her a wicked grin. 'But only if ...' His hand slipped back underneath her dress.

'Midge!'

'Please?' he whispered urgently.

At that moment she couldn't have refused him anything. Her lack of reply was his answer.

Thankful that he'd just happened to have 'the necessary' with him he turned her to face the door.

Don and Zelda Caprice got a thundering ovation at the conclusion of their first set of exhibition dances at Barrowland, an ovation Norma felt was well deserved.

Don was a man in his late twenties with cropped blond hair and a lithe, whipcord body. He was also handsome, but Norma didn't consider him as handsome as Midge.

Zelda was a little younger than her husband, and a Titian-haired beauty. She moved with the power-packed grace of a cheetah.

The rapturous applause reached new heights as the Americans left the floor. Again Norma was struck by the gown Zelda was wearing. It was couturier-made, Norma was certain of that. And absolutely gorgeous.

Joe Dunlop had introduced Norma and Midge to the Caprices at the beginning of the evening, but the two couples hadn't spoken since, as the Caprice's table was at the other side of the hall. Dunlop had thought it would look better if one couple came on from one side and then the other from the opposite side, rather than have the two couples concentrated at the same table.

Shortly after that it was time to go, and Norma and Midge met up again with the Caprices in the room where their coats, or wraps as Zelda referred to them, were kept.

'That was tremendous, top class,' Midge said to Don.

'And we were mighty impressed with you kids. We never expected anybody of your calibre up here in Scotland.'

Norma gazed in envy at the mink coat Zelda was shrugging

on. It was the sort of mink every girl dreams of.

Zelda caught her look. 'Want to try it hon?' she smiled.

'Oh no I couldn't!'

'Sure you could. Don bought it for me when we appeared in Ottawa last year. Didn't you Don?'

'I did indeed,' Don agreed.

The coat had a brown silk lining which rustled and whispered as Zelda helped Norma into it. When it was on Norma flipped up the collar so that it stood proud round her neck.

There was a full-length mirror attached to one wall. Norma crossed over to it and studied her reflection.

'How do I look?' she asked Midge.

'Like a filmstar.'

Zelda laughed. 'She does indeed. And Don and I should know, living in Hollywood as we do.'

'You live in Hollywood!' Midge exclaimed.

'We certainly do. And know lots of stars. Don't we Don?'

'Yeah,' Don agreed.

Midge thought that brilliant. Imagine, here he was talking to people who knew filmstars in the flesh! '*Who* do you know?' he asked eagerly.

'How about Alice Faye?' Zelda replied.

'Or Jimmy Cagney,' Don added.

Midge gulped. Those were two of the biggest names in Tinsel Town, a place he'd read a great deal about and would have given his eye-teeth to have visited.

'Or what about Jean Harlow – we know her real well,' Zelda continued.

'I like her,' Norma said, thinking of *Red Dust* that she'd seen Harlow in a few weeks previously.

'How about ... Garbo?' Midge asked.

'Sorry, there you have us,' Don admitted.

'We were once at a party she was at, but didn't get to meet her, I'm afraid,' Zelda said.

Don glanced at his wife; he was enjoying this, so why shouldn't they all continue the conversation back at the hotel? from Zelda's manner he guessed she'd also like that.

'Listen kids, we're staying at the Grand Hotel, which has agreed to lay on a dinner for us when we get back. Why don't you join us?'

'Yes, why don't you?' Zelda urged.

'Norma?' Midge queried, his expression and voice telling her he was mad keen to take up the invitation.

Norma thought of Effie and Brian, 'I'd love to have dinner with you, but if I don't turn up at the usual time my mother and father will worry themselves sick thinking something's happened to me. And I know Midge's parents would feel the same. It wouldn't be fair to either of them.'

Don frowned, he couldn't understand this. 'Why not just call and explain?'

Zelda saw Norma's lack of comprehension. 'He means telephone,' she explained.

Norma couldn't help the blush that stained her neck. What would these Hollywood people have thought if they'd seen Bridgeton? She shuddered to think.

'I'm afraid neither my parents or Midge's have a telephone,' she replied.

Don stared at her as if she'd just stated that her mother and father were a couple of orang-utans. 'No telephone! Well I'll be ...' He trailed off, lost for words.

'Perhaps another night then,' Zelda smiled.

'What about Friday?' Midge suggested, desperate to talk to the Caprices at further length.

Zelda glanced at Don. 'We've nothing special planned for then.'

And so it was agreed.. The four of them would have dinner together that Friday night.

Midge couldn't wait.

They went to the Grand Hotel by taxi, to be greeted at the main entrance by a commissionaire in uniform and top hat. The man saluted, and helped first Zelda, then Norma, onto the pavement.

Norma had passed the Grand Hotel, reputedly Glasgow's finest, but had never been inside. As they headed for the dining-room, she made sure she took everything in – having a right good gander as Effie would have put it. In the dining-room they sat down at the table reserved for them.

A frown creased Midge's forehead as he studied the menu. It was almost incomprehensible to him. He swallowed hard, and

114

his frown deepened as he continued staring blankly at words which, in the main, were French.

'I think I'll have the pâté followed by the *carbonnade de boeuf*,' Norma said.

'The same for me,' Midge told the hovering waiter. Norma smiled inwardly, she'd deliberately spoken when she had so that he could copy her order.

'And how about the wine, what would you recommend?' Don asked Midge, handing Midge the winelist.

Norma saw momentary panic in Midge's eyes. Like most working-class Glaswegians of the time he knew as much about wine as he did about riding a camel. It came either red or white, that was the sum of his knowledge on the subject.

'I wouldn't mind some claret. Or perhaps a Châteauneuf-du-Pape?' Norma said.

Midge blinked in astonishment.

'We have an excellent Châteauneuf-du-Pape,' the wine waiter said.

'Then we'll have a bottle of that. No, make it two bottles,' Don ordered.

Norma saw Midge's shoulders sag with relief. He hadn't foreseen what a posh dinner entailed (what had he expected to be on the menu, egg and chips!), but she had, and was prepared.

Bless Charlie Marshall and the Bridgeton Public Library! She'd explained her problem to Charlie who'd conjured up the appropriate books. It hadn't taken her long to learn the basics of what she'd find on the menu of a quality hotel, or to arm herself with some names and facts about wine. She was damned if she was going to look a fool, either in front of these Yankees or anyone else.

Midge shot Norma a glance that said not only 'thank you' but also 'where on Earth did you learn about Châteuneuf-du-Whatsit?' She smiled inscrutably in reply.

'And so we danced for King Leopold of Belgium,' Zelda was saying a little later – she and Don having been telling Norma and Midge about their European tour.

'A real king!' Midge breathed, his eyes popping out like organ stops.

'The second we've danced for on this tour. The other was King Carol of Rumania,' Don added.

'But when we hit Paris, now that really was spectacular,' Zelda went on.

Midge's meal grew cold in front of him. But that didn't bother him one little bit. All he wanted was to hear about the fabulous places the Caprices had been to.

The tales continued. Places, people, happenings, events. Midge drank in each and every word.

'Wasn't that just fantastic!' Midge said. He and Norma were in a taxi on their way back to Bridgeton. The taxi had been Norma's idea. Zelda had asked how they were getting home, and she'd immediately replied by taxi. It would have been humiliating to have answered otherwise.

After a while Midge fell silent, day-dreaming about the wonderful places the Caprices had been to. Oh how he wished . . .

Norma was thinking about the house they'd been promised in Greenvale Street, a stone's throw from Cubie Street. It was a three-room and kitchen, identical to the one she and her family were now in, and an unheard-of luxury for a childless couple. But as she and Midge could afford it, she hadn't seen any reason why they shouldn't indulge themselves with all that space. Why, they'd be the envy of the neighbourhood. She liked the idea of that. She liked it very much.

It was the following Tuesday afternoon and Norma and Midge were practising at the 'Pineapple'. They'd just broken for a breather and a cup of coffee from the flask that Norma always brought along.

'I've been thinking about the Caprices and that meal they treated us to. Don't you think we should return the gesture?' Midge asked.

'Is that necessary?'

'I feel we should. It's the polite thing to do,' he persisted.

Norma thought about that. She'd enjoyed the Americans' company, although it was Midge who'd gone overboard for them – he'd been talking non-stop about them all weekend.

'Perhaps we should do something . . .' she mused.

'What do you mean, something other than a meal?'

116

'Well, it is their first visit to Scotland. What we should do is take them round and about a bit. Show them the sights.'

'In Glasgow!' Midge laughed. 'And this, Zelda, is a ship-building yard, mind the oil on the deck and mind that low swinging crane doesn't take your head off. Or what about this blast furnace spewing dirt and filth into the air, and all over your nice dress. Maybe you'd like to write home about it?'

'Very funny,' Norma said drily.

'Glasgow's a working city, and a gey poor one at that. Slums and heavy industry, I can't see either Zelda or Don being dragged round any of that.'

Norma had an inspiration. 'Then let's forget about Glasgow and take them elsewhere. The Trossachs for example. It's one of Scotland's most famous beauty spots, and not that far away.'

Midge thought that a terrific idea. 'And we could lunch in a pub or hotel in the area,' he enthused.

'Lunch in a pub and high tea in a hotel.'

Midge nodded; that was even better. 'It would have to be next Sunday. They finish at Barrowland on Saturday and travel through to Edinburgh on the Monday.' Edinburgh was where the Caprices were appearing next.

'Sunday it will have to be then.' her face fell. 'The big drawback is getting there and back. It means taking a red bus.'

'They already know we don't have a car. And anyway, they'd probably love going on a red bus. Don't forget they don't have double-deckers in America.'

'Right then, we'll put it to them this evening,' Norma said.

They finished their coffee and returned to practising for the All Scotland Dance Championship, now only a short while away.

'Yeah sure, I think that would be real neat,' Zelda said, Norma and Midge having just proposed the day trip to the Trossachs.

'And we'll go by double-decker,' Midge added.

Don waved a hand. 'We don't have to bother about no bus. We'll travel in my car. Far more comfortable that way.'

'You have a car?' Norma queried in surprise.

117

'Well it's not really mine, I've rented it for the rest of my stay in Scotland. I'm lost without one you know. We Americans just ain't used to public transport.'

'Now you tell us your address beforehand and we'll stop by and pick you up,' Zelda said.

Alarm flared in Norma. The last thing she wanted was the Caprices coming to Bridgeton. It wasn't that she was pretending to be what she wasn't, rather that it would have caused her acute embarrassment for the Americans to see the district where she lived. And she was certain Midge felt the same way.

'Don't trouble yourself. We'll meet you at your hotel,' Norma replied.

'It's no trouble honey,' Don said.

Joe Dunlop popped his head round the door to ask if everything was all right. And tell them that even though it was a Tuesday, traditionally the slackest night of the week, there was already a fair-sized crowd in.

When Dunlop had gone Norma turned again to Don. 'As you don't know Glasgow you could have quite a bit of difficulty finding where Midge and I live. It would be a bad start to the day if you were to get lost and end up driving round and round looking for us. It'd be simpler if we come to you. And that's an end to it,' she said firmly.

'Okay then, if that's what you want,' Don conceded.

They agreed a time when Norma and Midge would turn up at the Grand Hotel.

Bremner's Warehouse in Glassford Street was where Norma decided to buy her wedding dress, and the bridesmaids' dresses for Lyn and Eileen.

'Isn't it exciting,' Lyn said.

Effie nodded. 'Aye, I must admit it is.' She was thoroughly enjoying the shopping and making the arrangements for the forthcoming wedding which was to take place the Saturday after the All Scotland Championship. The couple would be going away for a week's honeymoon, but only Midge knew where. Then they'd return to Greenvale Street which they were now in the process of redecorating.

'I remember my own dress. It wasn't an expensive one you ken, things being gey tight at the time, but bonny all the same.

Your da said I looked like an angel descending when I walked down the aisle,' Effie reminisced.

'You should have had photographs taken so that we could see now what you were like,' Lyn chided.

'Ah lass, there was no money for the likes of that. But I must admit, photographs would have been nice as a keepsake. Aye, they would've been right enough.'

Norma emerged from the cubicle where she'd been trying on yet another wedding dress.

'That's the one I'd go for. You're gorgeous in it,' Eileen enthused.

'I agree,' Lyn added.

Norma studied herself in a full-length mirror. She particularly liked the head-dress which was rather old-fashioned, with a cloche sitting. It was adorned with artificial orange blossom.

She smoothed down the ivory-coloured satin across her front. Eileen and Lyn were right, this was the dress for her. The dress she'd wear to become Mrs Midge Henderson.

'Ma?' she asked.

Effie nodded, tears of happiness in her eyes.

'I think it needs to be taken in a fraction here,' Norma said.

The assistant produced a measuring tape and some pins and they all fell to discussing the alterations that were going to have to be made.

Norma, Midge and Zelda waited at the front of the Grand Hotel while Don brought the car round. He tooted on the horn as he drew up beside them.

The car was green and called a Jowett Javelin. Norma and Zelda got in the back; Midge and Don in at the front. The car growled away with Midge giving Don directions.

There was a slight drizzle to start with, but they left that behind together with the horrible urban tangle that was Glasgow. They took the Bearsden/Milngavie road that would eventually bring them to Aberfoyle, and the Brig o'Turk beyond that.

This was Norma's first ever ride in a private car – the two taxis they'd taken the night of the meal in the Grand Hotel were her first experience of a motor vehicle at all – and she took to it like the proverbial duck to water. Long before they reached Aberfoyle she knew that she wanted a car for herself, and had made up her mind to take lessons directly she and Midge returned from their honeymoon.

When they stopped for petrol and everyone got out to stretch their legs she asked Don if she could sit in the driving seat. That was even better than being in the rear. Sitting there with the wheel between her hands she felt a tremendous sense of power and freedom. Not being in the least mechanical, she'd never have guessed she'd have fallen for cars this way. But she had. Hook, line and sinker.

At Brig o'Turk they parked, then strolled over to the water's edge. The Trossachs stretched from the shores of Loch Achray, where they were now standing, up through a richly wooded gorge – encompassing mountains, rivers and unparalleled landscapes – to that most beautiful of lochs, Loch Katrine. It was an area made famous by Sir Walter Scott in his poems *Lady of the Lake* and *Rob Roy*.

They walked along the lochside, Norma beside Don, and Zelda and Midge a little in front.

'Is it true there are orange trees in California. That you can just reach up and pluck an orange whenever you want one?' Midge asked Zelda.

'It's true enough, in some places there are orange and lemon trees stretching as far as the eye can see.'

'Gosh!' Midge exclaimed, wide-eyed.

'And you just wouldn't believe the sunshine we have there. Day after day, regular as clockwork. In fact we get so much sunshine there it gets boring.'

Midge shook his head in wonderment. 'After being born and brought up in Glasgow I don't think I'd ever get bored with sunshine.'

Zelda laughed. At times there was a little-boy quality about Midge that appealed to her. When they talked like this he made her think of a kid in a candy store.

'Maybe you'll come over and see those orange and lemon trees for yourself one day?' she suggested.

Midge took a deep breath. His heart was hammering; the blood pounding in his head at the thought. 'I've always wanted to travel, to see the world. That's been my dream for as long as I can remember. But ...' The light died in his eyes, and his shoulders drooped. 'That's not to be I'm afraid.'

'Norma?'

'Travelling doesn't appeal to her.'

'And so you'll settle down and be the good little stay-at-home hubby,' Zelda teased. And immediately wished she hadn't when she saw the expression of wretchedness that came over his face.

'I'm sorry, that was uncalled for,' she apologised.

Midge stooped, picked up a chuckie and threw it out into the loch where it plopped dully into the water.

'To be honest, I envy you and Don so much it hurts,' he said in a voice tight with emotion.

Zelda thought of the letter she'd seen Don furtively reading in their Munich hotel room, and how she'd ferreted it out of his case later when he was off having a massage. Going by Don's furtiveness she'd assumed it was a letter from another woman. She couldn't have been more wrong.

She hadn't been planning to do anything about that revelation until she got back to the States, but perhaps the answer to her problem was here beside her.

She looked at Midge with new interest.

They were all laughing at a joke Don had told as they drew up outside the Covenanters Inn, stopping there so that Don could pop in for some cigarettes.

Zelda finally stopped laughing to peer at the words chalked up on a blackboard just inside the main door.

'What's a dinner-dance?' she asked.

'Just that. You have dinner, and during the dinner, and afterwards, a band is playing which you can get up and dance to,' Norma explained.

A gleam came into Zelda's eyes. Turning, she addressed her companions. 'Listen you guys, today's been such a perfect one, why don't we extend it a while longer? I think this dinner-dance thing sounds just great.'

'It could be fun,' Midge said. He liked the idea.

'Are we dressed okay for it though?' Don queried, knowing how sticky the British could be about such matters.

That was a good point, Norma thought. Both men had

jackets and ties on, while she and Zelda were wearing reasonable skirts and tops. 'We should be acceptable,' she declared.

'Right then, in we go!' Zelda said, the gleam still in her eyes.

The inside of the Covenanters' Inn was done out in Jacobean-style decor. Claymores, two-handed swords, dirks, skean dhus, muskets, pistols and pikes adorned the walls. The carpets and curtains were in McGregor tartan, for this was the heart of McGregor country – that one time notorious outlaw clan whose name for years had been 'expressly abolished', the clan members forbidden the use of it.

They had a drink at the bar, where Don also bought some cigarettes, and then went through to where the dinner-dance was being held.

Norma judged there to be roughly forty people present; the tables they were sitting at grouped round three sides of the dancing area. On the fourth side, standing with their backs to a wall, was a six-piece band.

Zelda was right, Norma thought, it had been a perfect day. And what's more it had been extremely relaxing – just what she and Midge needed with the All Scotland Dance Championship coming up.

On this occasion Midge insisted that Don ordered the wine, looking slyly at Norma. Which Don did.

'We have some excellent wines in California you know,' Zelda said.

'Is that true!' Midge said, and gave a small, wondering shake of the head.

'Most palatable. Not quite up to the standard of the very best French and German wines mind you, but very palatable all the same,' Don added.

They all decided to order steak, and were waiting for these, having had their hors d'oeuvres, when the band started playing 'The Moonlight Saunter'.

'In the States we get T-bones – they're cuts of steak, which can be so huge they'll overhang the platters they're served on ...'

Zelda switched her attention from Don to Midge, who was sitting beside her. She smiled, then glanced over to the dancing area.

Midge got the message. 'Would you care to get up?' he asked.

'Why yes. If you don't mind, that is, Norma?'

'Of course not.'

Midge escorted Zelda onto the floor, leaving Norma listening to Don holding forth about T-bone steaks.

By the end of the dance Zelda had found out what she'd wanted to know – and the reason why she'd suggested they go to the dinner-dance. As partners she and Midge were compatible, very compatible indeed.

From 'The Moonlight Saunter' the band went into 'Destiny Waltz'. Midge asked Zelda if she'd like to stay up, to which she replied she would.

As Midge and Zelda glided round the floor Norma thought how strange it was to see Midge dance with someone other than herself.

Later, when Don asked her to dance, she thought it even odder to be with someone other than Midge.

Brian, Effie, Lyn, Eileen and Charlie Marshall were there, so too were Leslie and Alice Henderson, Katy Henderson, Bob and Beryl Gillespie, Finlay Rankine accompanied by a stunning brunette, the Fullartons including Jacky's wife Sylvia, Joe Dunlop with his wife Margie, and Father Finn.

The All Scotland Dance Championship was being held in the Albert Ballroom, the venue of the first ever championship Norma and Midge had competed in, and the original number of entrants had been reduced to six couples, Norma and Midge among them. Of these, four were professional, two amateur.

Norma didn't normally get the jitters when competing, but she had them that night. If they were to win they'd be acknowledged as *the* best dancers in Scotland.

Before the final eliminations and the top three couples were decided there was to be an exhibition by the Caprices who'd come down from Dundee for the occasion.

'And now ladies and gentlemen, a big hand please for those international artistes who've been making such an impact during their tour of our country, and who are currently delighting audiences at the Dundee Trocadero – Don and Zelda Caprice!'

'How do you feel?' Midge whispered to Norma during the applause which greeted the Americans taking the floor.

'How do *you* feel?'

Midge grinned, but didn't reply. Instead he took her nearest hand and squeezed it.

He was jittery too; she could read it in his face. He was reassuring himself as much as her.

The Caprices were superb, quite outstanding Norma thought as they concluded their exhibition. She led what quickly swelled to an overwhelming clamour of appreciation.

Then it was back to the championship, and the MC called out the first of the six remaining couples onto the floor.

The minutes ticked by. Couple after couple performed, and sat down again. Finally it was their turn.

Their first dance was to be the cha cha cha, the second the lola tango. They acknowledged those watching, took their starting position, and were away.

The old magic that always happened between them was happening again, this time even more strongly than usual – Norma could feel the difference. Technically, everything went precisely as they'd planned and practised. They came over as a couple inspired.

They finished to a round of tumultuous applause – there was no question in Norma's mind that they'd won. It was not arrogance or ego on her part, but a frank appraisal of their performance. They'd left the other five couples standing for dead.

And was it proved. When the winners were announced it was them. They'd carried off the All Scotland Dance Championship, Scotland's most prestigious.

For a while there was pandemonium, with friends and relatives crowding round and hundreds of others offering their congratulations.

Effie was crying and Brian looked fit to burst with pride. Finlay Rankine repeated over and over that he'd known they'd do it, and Joe Dunlop was so ecstatic he was beside himself.

The prize was a crystal decanter and glasses to match, but these paled into insignificance compared to the kudos of winning. Norma would treasure the glory forever.

When the prize was presented Dunlop managed to get a private word with Norma and Midge. 'Listen, this calls for a party. All your people back to my place. And they're not to worry about booze or transport, Barrowland will be paying for those.'

When Norma and Midge were finally able to slip away they were taken to the waiting taxi that Dunlop had organised. They arrived at the Dunlop home to be greeted by Dunlop's wife Margie, and to find that nearly all of those invited had arrived before them. Norma learned that Dunlop hadn't only organised one taxi, but a veritable fleet of Black Cabs.

It was a smashing party, with the booze flowing and everyone enjoying themselves. With the exception of Lyn, that is, who, as usual, only enjoyed herself up to a point and had to seek consolation in the food.

Norma turned away from talking to Beryl Gillespie to glance over to a sofa where Midge had been sitting deep in conversation with Zelda Caprice. The two of them were still there with their heads together.

'You'd better keep an eye on her. She looks the carnivorous type to me,' Eileen said to Norma, having come across to join her.

'Who, Zelda?'

Eileen nodded.

'Don't be daft. She's a friend, and happily married. They'll be chaffing about dancing that's all.'

Eileen looked at her eldest sister. Norma might be nearly three and a half years older than her, but beside her she was naïve at times. Often she felt the age difference between them was reversed, and that she was older than Norma. Not only older, but also more of 'a woman of the world'. 'I'll just say this, if it was my Charlie she had on that sofa I'd be over there like a shot,' Eileen said softly.

Norma had never heard anything so ridiculous. Why she and Midge were getting wed that Saturday!

However, just to be on the safe side, she did join Midge and Zelda after that. And they *were* talking about dancing.

Norma paused in her distempering. It was Tuesday afternoon, the day after the All Scotland Dance Championship, and she and Midge were in the Greenvale Street house working on what would be their bedroom.

Midge was standing with a can of distemper in his hand,

staring into space. There was a peculiar look about him, and his eyes had gone strangely glazed. There were beads of sweat on his brow, despite the fact it was chilly in the room.

'Midge?'

Wrapped in his thoughts, not hearing her, he continued staring into space.

'Midge!'

He blinked, then turned to her slowly.

'Is it last-minute panic? Is it just sinking in that by Saturday night you'll be a married man? That the knot will be tied between us?'

He swallowed. Made as though to reply, then changed his mind, and swallowed a second time.

Coming down off the ladder Norma went over to him and put an arm round his waist.

'I'm told that last-minute panic is quite natural, and that most people get it. I expect I'll get it myself. Come Saturday morning I'll probably be in such a paddy that I'll be wanting to take to the hills.'

He tried to smile, but it came out as a sort of lop-sided grimace.

'That's it. Don't think of it as the end of the world, but as a beginning.'

She buried her face in the crook of his neck. How she loved him.

She knew then what would cheer him up, make him feel better. It always did. Without fail.

Their new bed had just been delivered, and was in one of their spare bedrooms waiting to be brought through once they'd finished here. A spare bedroom with curtains up.

She took the can of distemper from his hand and laid it on the floor. She then led him through to the bed.

Dawn was breaking. Midge stood staring up at the shadowy shapes of the surrounding tenements. How horrible they were, he thought. And how squalid.

Somewhere close by a baby cried. A plaintive sound. And then a cat screeched - a screech to set the nerves on edge.

Midge yawned; he'd been prowling the streets for hours. He hadn't been able to sleep so he'd got up, dressed, and

126

crept from the house. He'd never done such a thing before.

Dawn was now fully broken. Bridgeton revealed in all its splendour. A grey, evil-smelling slum.

A little later, when he walked back into his own close, he'd reached a decision.

It was Friday afternoon, the day before the wedding, and Norma was putting the presents away. The show of presents had been held the previous afternoon and the house had been chock-a-block.

It had been a grand show of presents. Effie had said how lucky she was to get so much – it was far more than she and Brian had received when they'd married.

Norma was placing a box of doilies from Jacky and Sylvia Fullarton in a drawer when there was a knock on the outside door. It would be Midge, at long last, she thought. But she was wrong. It was Don Caprice. He was clearly distraught.

'What's up?' she asked. Then, 'Why are you here and not in Dundee?'

Don stared at Norma. 'Can I come in?' he said, avoiding her question.

'Of course.' She shut the door behind them and led him through to the kitchen.

'Where's Midge?' he asked in a strained voice.

'I don't know. I was expecting him here hours ago, but so far he hasn't turned up. Now what is it Don, what's wrong?'

He lit a cigarette with shaking hands. 'I don't know why I came charging down to Glasgow. I suppose I thought... hoped...' He took a quick, nervous, puff of his cigarette. 'Have you got a drink in the house?'

'Sorry, no.'

He nodded. After which he inhaled deeply. 'I tried the Henderson house but there was no one home. Your mother said I'd find you here.'

Norma was bewildered. Don wasn't making any sense at all. 'Why did you go to the Hendersons?'

'You don't know do you?'

'Know what!'

He glanced away, unable to look her in the eye. 'I'm a dying man, Norma. When we were in Germany I started to see!

unwell – loss of energy, constantly feeling drained, dizzy spells. I thought I'd been overdoing it, and that I just needed to ease off a bit. However, Zelda insisted I see a doctor.

'Well the doctor had his suspicions and said that tests had to be made. In the meantime I told Zelda that I'd been pronounced all right, and that the doctor had put me on an iron tonic —' He broke off laughing bitterly. 'I actually did buy a tonic in a drugstore to keep up appearances.

'When the results of the tests came through they were conclusive. I have leukaemia.'

Norma clapped her hands to her mouth.

'I've written a letter to my doc back home. Not that he'll be able to do anything. I'm literally under sentence of death.'

'How . . . how long?' asked Norma in a subdued voice.

'Three, maybe six months. Nine at the outside.'

How truly awful for him, Norma thought. Such a lovely man, cut off in his prime. 'And you haven't told Zelda?'

He shook his head. 'I wanted the tour to be finished and us back in LA before I did. But somehow she's found out – she's left me. Run off with a new partner.'

A sudden fear blossomed in the pit of Norma's stomach. She remembered the party at Joe Dunlop's, and what Eileen had said.

'No!' she whimpered. Midge wouldn't do that to her. He wouldn't!

'Zelda left me a note. Even though you haven't got it yet, or come across it, I would imagine Midge has done the same.'

Bile rose in her throat, and for a few moments she thought she was going to throw up. Then that passed.

'I'm sorry I had to be the one to tell you,' Don whispered.

'Where . . . Did Zelda say where?'

'London first, then the States.'

It was a nightmare, a horrible nightmare. She told herself she'd soon wake up and realise it was only that. But she didn't wake up; the nightmare was for real.

After a while Don left. Norma stood with her back to the front door, closed her eyes and finally let the tears come. Hot tears that coursed down her cheeks and fell on the linoleum below.

And with the tears, anger. Anger that exploded and roared within her.

Frantically she tugged at her engagement ring, ripping the skin of her finger as she pulled it off. Flying through to the kitchen she jerked open the window and threw the ring out as hard as she was able. With a sob she crashed the window shut again, cracking the glass in the process.

It couldn't be true, it just couldn't! And yet it was. Midge, *her* Midge, had run off with Zelda.

She screamed. A scream so powerful and intense it turned the back of her throat red raw. With tightly-clenched fists she beat her thighs. Again and again, as though her fists were hammers.

Then she remembered her wedding dress, hanging in their bedroom wardrobe. Running to the wardrobe she tore the dress and head-dress down from their hangers and screwed them up into a ball.

Then she spied, amongst a pile of her shoes that had been brought over from Cubie Street, a very old pair of red shoes. The red shoes she'd worn the night she'd met Midge, and which she'd kept ever since. She snatched up the red shoes as well and rushed out of the room.

She'd made up the fire earlier because it had been cold. She now tossed her wedding dress and head-dress onto the burning coals, throwing the red shoes on top of them. Using a poker, she rammed the lot down.

Norma watched with grim satisfaction as the dress and head-dress were set alight. The imitation orange blossom sizzled, and charred to a crisp cinder. The red shoes turned black first in places, then finally black all over.

Sinking to her knees, she gazed into the mini inferno. The anger had gone, its fury replaced by an aching emptiness. Where before she'd had a demon's strength, she was now weak as a kitten.

'Oh Midge!' she whispered.

The remains of the red shoes fell apart as she continued to weep.

Part II

DOUGLAS AND FANY
1940-43

Chapter Six

It was late afternoon, getting on towards five o'clock. September 1940, and Norma was sitting in a car outside a private house in Muswell Hill. From this superb vantage point, high on the hill itself, she was watching a vast formation of German bombers droning past overhead.

It was a terrifying sight. Wave after wave, each wave consisting of a dozen squadrons, each squadron consisting of a dozen aircraft, heading east. It would be the Docks they were after, Norma told herself. And she was right.

The sky was perfect for flying, indeed it had been a perfect autumn so far, as the Battle of Britain continued to rage, and now the Blitz began. Spitfires and Hurricanes buzzed and darted among the *Luftwaffe*'s bombers, but there were so few compared to the numbers they were trying desperately to repel.

A parachute opened, then another. That cheered Norma, till it struck her that they might be British lads. She hadn't seen what plane, or planes, had gone down.

Norma tore her gaze from what was happening overhead to glance at the house into which Major-General Gilchrist had disappeared more than half an hour previously. She had no idea whom he'd gone to see, or indeed even what his business in the army was. He'd never volunteered any information about himself, and of course she'd never asked.

A strange, secretive figure, the Major-General. Another Scot like herself, only he was from the Highlands and spoke with the soft unmistakable lilt of the highlander. But that was all that was soft about Major-General Gilchrist. Although he had an intellectual, almost donnish, air about him, that didn't fool Norma any. She'd spent too long in Glasgow not to recognise a hard man when she saw one.

Norma had been Gilchrist's driver for a fortnight now, and he'd certainly kept her busy. Fourteen, sixteen hours some days, hither and yonning all over London and the Home Counties. They'd also been to Birmingham on several occasions, and once to Exeter.

At the outbreak of the war Norma had joined the First Aid Nursing Yeomanry, known as FANY. Formed in 1907, the FANY's original purpose had been to provide nurses on horseback who could move quickly round the fringes of a traditional battlefield giving on-the-spot first aid.

During the Great War the purpose had been modified. The motorised ambulance had replaced the horse, and other aspects of 'on-the-spot' aid had been introduced, such as providing mobile canteens and mobile bathing facilities.

By the time of the Second World War the duties of FANY had changed still further. They were no longer part of the regular army, but worked in conjunction with it, amongst other things, supplying the army with drivers. Most FANYs worked alongside the Auxiliary Territorial Service, and were known as FANY-ATS, but Norma wasn't one of these. She was a Free FANY, which meant her loyalty was to FANY and FANY alone.

Norma looked again at the sky, where the waves of *Luftwaffe* bombers were still passing by. A Hurricane or Spitfire – she couldn't tell the difference – exploded even as she watched it. A ball of red and orange flame, smoke, then tiny bits of wreckage tumbled to earth. One moment the pilot had been alive; the next he was dead, blown to bits. Norma felt sick at the thought.

From far off came the dull boom of exploding bombs. A sound that rapidly grew louder and louder. The Docks, and surrounding areas, were taking a pasting.

Out the corner of her eye she saw the door to the house opening. It wasn't Major-General Gilchrist who emerged, but a Guards' Captain.

The Captain paused to stare up at the sky, then hurried over to the car. Norma rolled down her window.

'The Major-General wants you to go to this address and pick up several box files that will be ready waiting for you. You've to bring them straight back here,' the Captain said, handing

Norma a slip of paper on which the address had been written in best copperplate.

'I'll be as quick as I can,' Norma replied. She got out her *A to Z* as the Captain dashed back indoors.

She'd been in London for ten months, but the city was so huge she still had to look up every address before she set off.

This particular address was in Somers Town, adjacent to King's Cross. She decided to go down the Archway Road, down Holloway Road and then via Liverpool Road. It wasn't the shortest route, but the easiest as far as she was concerned.

She'd learned to drive after Midge had run off with Zelda, something she'd thrown herself into because it was a help to stop herself thinking, and brooding.

She'd never appeared at Barrowland again, nor had she wanted to, even though Joe Dunlop had suggested she might try and find another partner.

She'd given up the house in Greenvale Street that was to have been hers and Midge's, and stayed at home with the family. Without a job she'd been considering asking the SCWS to take her back, when Finlay Rankine had offered her a position – no strings attached he'd assured her, treating her to that crocodile smile of his – as a female dance instructor at Silver's. She'd grabbed the opportunity, and been happy and successful there, only leaving after the outbreak of war, when she'd come down to London to join the FANY at their headquarters in Lower Grosvenor Place.

Whilst working at Silver's an extraordinary event had taken place. She'd been helping Effie make the tea one evening when a man called Jardine had come chapping, asking to speak with her.

He was a Mr Martin Jardine of Jardine, Jardine, Hepburn and Deans, a firm of solicitors in Renfield Street. And acting on behalf of Mr Thomas Gallagher, recently deceased. A Thomas Gallagher whose son had been killed while serving with Allenby at Megiddo, and whose daughter Morna had died of a brain tumour. A daughter Norma was the spitting image of.

To cut a long story short, alone in the world, Mr Gallagher had left all his money and possessions to Norma. This consisted of a substantial amount of money in the bank, four jeweller's shops and a small flat in Kelvinbridge.

135

When she'd finally got over the shock of this totally unexpected windfall, Norma had instructed Jardine to sell the flat and shops. She knew nothing about the jewellery business, and wasn't interested in learning.

The capital realised from the sale, added to what was already in the bank made Norma a woman of considerable financial standing, financially independent for the rest of her life. Providing she didn't squander the money, that was – which she had no intention of doing.

Although she hadn't needed to go on working she'd elected to do so, and continued on at Silver's.

With this money behind her, Norma had been able to join the FANY, whose members were all unpaid volunteers.

Norma started to think about Midge. She'd never got over him and her heart still ached at the memory of what they'd had together. An ache she believed would be with her always.

The last she'd heard was that he was still in America and doing well. Don had died shortly after returning to Hollywood and Midge and Zelda had married soon afterwards.

After a while Norma had made herself go out with other men. Nor had there been any trouble meeting them since joining FANY. Officers were attracted to FANYs the way bees are to honey. It was said they had a special air about them.

She was going out with someone at the moment, a Major called Jeremy Dereham. But he – like the others – meant nothing to her. Love came once, and in her case that once was Midge Henderson. The rest were just good company – fun, jolly to be with, but no more than that.

She was snapped out of her reverie by a very loud bang fairly close by. That bang was followed by another, and then another.

Bombs, she thought grimly. Islington, where she was now, was well away from the Docks. There must be another target they were after.

She saw the side of a building momentarily bulge, then collapse inwards. Debris and dust whooshed into the air. She'd best get away from this, she told herself, and executed a few sharp turns that brought her into Risinghill Street. From there she could see the spires of St Pancras and King's Cross, which she judged to be about half a mile away.

She heard the bomb coming. Not a screech as she'd imagined

136

it would be, but rather as if coarse sand was raining down on a sheet of corrugated iron. A sound that steadily increased as the bomb hurtled groundwards.

And then the sound stopped, and for a split second there was an eerie silence. Suddenly she was enveloped in red and orange flame, exactly the same as that she'd witnessed in Muswell Hill when the plane had blown up.

The car went spinning through the air in a twisting, rotating motion. This is it, she thought, clinging on frantically as the car turned upside down.

How tinny the car now seemed. Quite the opposite to when its four wheels were on the ground.

Would death be instantaneous? she wondered. She prayed it would.

Finally, after what seemed like an eternity, an eternity during which everything happened in slow motion, the car hit the ground again, bounced, and went smashing into a street lamp.

There was the screech of metal being torn asunder. And for one horrifying instant a fountain of bright red blood. Her own? She was contemplating that when, as if a light had been switched off, she lost consciousness.

Norma came to to find a man's anxious face peering into hers. 'This one's alive,' the man said to someone in the background.

Norma groaned. Her chest was very painful, while her left arm was numb from the shoulder down. Then she remembered the fountain of blood.

Glancing quickly at her left arm she saw with relief that it was still there. She was lying in a pile of rubble – she guessed that she'd been thrown from the car. She touched her face, but there was no blood there. Whatever had happened, she hadn't gone through the windscreen.

A stout woman in the green uniform of the Women's Voluntary Service, the WVS, replaced the man. 'He's gone for a stretcher. We'll soon have you sorted out ducks,' the woman said.

Norma tried to take a deep breath, but couldn't because of the pain in her chest. She looked about her, and was appalled at what she saw.

When she'd turned into Risinghill Street it had been a short street with houses on both sides. Not any more. The houses were gone, completely flattened. There was no sign of her car. She could only assume it had been buried.

There were bodies everywhere. And . . . *bits* of bodies. Rising-hill Street residents who'd been at home when the bomb had struck. She later learned that directly after the bomb a land mine had also hit the street, and it was the latter which had inflicted most of the damage.

She didn't know how she had managed to survive this carnage and awful destruction. But one thing she did know, and that was she was extremely lucky to have done so.

The man reappeared with another man and a stretcher. Together, with the help of the WVS lady, they manoeuvred Norma onto the stretcher.

At that point the pain in Norma's chest became so intense she passed out again.

Clouds, a haze of clouds extending in every direction. A puff of clouds parting to reveal . . . Was it? She couldn't be sure. And then she was. Midge had come back for her.

She ran to him, and threw her arms round his neck. Eagerly she pressed her lips onto his, her tongue into his mouth.

They were still kissing when the clouds rose up to envelop them. And with that oblivion once more.

She opened her eyes to stare at a white ceiling. She was in a bed, a very hard bed, and there was an antiseptic smell in the air.

'Hello,' a female voice said.

The girl was younger than her, and a nurse. 'Where am I?' Norma croaked.

'The Royal Free Hospital, Gray's Inn Road.'

'Am I . . . ' She winced as pain stabbed her chest. 'Badly hurt?'

'Doctor will speak to you shortly. He'll answer all your questions,' the nurse replied with a smile.

The nurse left Norma to go off and fetch some screens, which she positioned round the bed.

Why did the girl keep looking sideways at her and smiling like that? Norma wondered. Was there something funny about her? She noticed for the first time that her left arm was in plaster.

138

That meant she'd been out for quite some time.

She was kept waiting for ages. Then a doctor and the same nurse as before came in through the screens.

'I'm Douglas Ross, the Assistant Surgeon. Sorry I've been so long. I was just about to come to you when they wheeled in an emergency. I had to attend to him first.'

'Will he be all right?' Norma asked.

'He died, I'm afraid.'

'Oh!'

Doctor Ross was a slightly built man with a sallow complexion and raven-black hair. He had liquid brown eyes and a slightly acquiline nose. He looked dead beat, as though he'd been on the go for far too long. Which he had.

'How do you feel?' he asked.

'Like I'd tangled with a road roller, and lost.'

He grinned. 'Any headache?'

'No. A sort of mental muzziness, but I wouldn't describe it as a headache.'

'Good,' he said approvingly.

He picked up her chart from where it was hanging on the bottom of the bed, and wrote on it. While he was writing he said, 'Your arm is broken in two places, the higher-up break a compound one. As you can see that's already been attended to.'

'I have an extremely sharp pain in my chest. As though someone was sticking a knife into me.'

He glanced at her over the top of the chart. 'I'd better have a look then. Staff, will you...'

The nurse was moving before he'd asked her to. She undid the top of the gown Norma had been put into.

'It's Miss McKenzie isn't it? There were some identification papers in what's left of your uniform. The uniform itself is only fit for the scrap bin I'm afraid,' Ross said.

By now Norma was bare to the waist. She felt embarrassed that this strange man could see her partial nakedness, and reminded herself he was a doctor. He no doubt saw breasts and other private parts every day of the week. Nonetheless, her neck still flamed when he came over to sit beside her.

'Where is this pain?' he queried.

She indicated. 'Here, and across here.'

139

His hand was cool, and very gentle. Gentle or not she yelped when he touched her, then yelped again.

'Is it sore when I do that?'

'Like Billy-O.'

'And you say it's as though someone was sticking a knife into you?'

'Sometimes it's as though the knife was being twisted this way and that.'

He regarded her thoughtfully. 'A broken rib, if indeed not broken ribs. But are the pressing bits pressing where they shouldn't? That's the question.'

He flipped first one side of her gown closed, then the other, so that her breasts were covered again. She was grateful for that.

'Tell Sister Roberts that I want Miss McKenzie's chest X-rayed from all angles as soon as possible, and to see those X-rays the moment they're available, Staff,' Ross said to the nurse.

He ran a weary hand through his hair. 'I'll speak to you again after I've viewed the X-rays,' he told Norma.

'Fine.'

What a nice man, she thought after he'd gone.

She was lying on a trolley waiting to be taken into X-ray.

There was a large mirror over to her left, behind a reception desk. Eventually her eyes drifted to it, and there, reflected, was Doctor Ross.

He was standing off to one side of her, in conversation with another doctor. Ross was listening to what the other doctor was saying, but his gaze was fastened onto Norma. He was watching her, but didn't realise she could see him doing so.

When, a few minutes later, a technician appeared to take her into X-ray he was still watching her.

'Darling!' Lynsey Dereham squealed, and ran up the ward to Norma's bed. Lynsey was also a FANY, and Norma's best pal. It was through Lynsey that she'd met Jeremy, her brother.

Jeremy was behind Lynsey, and with him William Trevalyn, and, with William, another officer whom she'd never seen before.

'For God's sake don't try and hug me – I've got four broken

ribs!' Norma said in alarm as Lynsey came round to her bedside. Lynsey was a great hugger.

Lynsey's arms dropped back to her sides. 'You look ghastly,' she declared.

'Oh thank you very much. That's a real confidence booster,' Norma replied.

'But you do darling. Quite, quite . . .'

'Ghastly,' Norma finished for her, and they both laughed. At least Lynsey did; Norma quickly stifled her laughter. It hurt to laugh.

'This is Freddy Harcourt, he was with us so we brought him along to meet the patient,' Jeremy said. Freddy was a major with The Royal Green Jackets, the same regiment as William. Jeremy was with The King's Royal Rifle Corps.

'Jolly rotten luck what happened to you,' Freddy sympathised.

'Rotten luck that I was there at the time. But it was lucky that I survived. The street was blown to smithereens,' Norma replied quietly.

'We saw the street. What a mess,' Lynsey said soberly.

Jeremy pecked Norma on the cheek. 'This'll be you out of action for some while, I should imagine.'

She told them the extent of her injuries. 'When I first came in the doctor was worried that I might have a piece of broken rib touching the lung, which they tell me could have been very nasty indeed. However, that wasn't so, I'm happy to say.'

'I've brought you some chocs,' Jeremy said, plonking a box of Cadbury's best down on the bedside table.

'And I've brought you some of your personal things,' said Lynsey, taking a small case from William and placing it between the table and bed.

'I hope there's a nightie in the case?'

'There are two nighties. One of them's the pink, your favourite,' Lynsey reassured her.

They were a merry – if somewhat loud – crew. From the way Freddy and William carried on she suspected they'd been to a pub beforehand.

Freddy began in on an outrageous joke which had them all – with the exception of Norma who kept pleading 'Don't! Don't!' – falling about. In the middle of this hilarity Ross came

141

striding into the ward. He came up short and frowned at them.

'Sssh! Quieten down, you'll get me into trouble!' Norma beseeched them, to no avail. Freddy was determined to deliver his punchline, which he did to the loudest laugh yet.

Turning on his heel, Ross stalked from the ward.

Norma fully expected Sister Roberts to come charging in to tell them to put a sock in it. But Sister didn't, nor did anyone else.

And then Freddy started in on another joke, this one even more outrageous than the one before.

The following day Doctor Ross was in the corridor leading to Marsden Ward when he ran into Sister Roberts carrying the largest bunch of flowers he'd ever seen. And being a hospital surgeon he'd seen large bunches of flowers in his time.

'I'm surprised you can carry that lot,' he said, gesturing at the flowers.

'Aren't they absolutely magnificent! They're for Miss McKenzie.'

Doctor Ross's heart sank a little on hearing that, which was stupid really. She was nothing to him after all.

'She's certainly popular, but then they say that FANYs always are,' Sister Roberts commented.

She was certainly popular all right, Ross thought sourly. Not a day went past without at least one male uniform by her bedside.

He changed the subject.

Norma got into bed, and lay back with a sigh. Her broken arm was throbbing dreadfully thanks to her having bashed the damned thing in the toilet. It was her own fault for being so clumsy; she should have been more careful of what she'd been doing.

Her head had spun with the pain, and she'd felt sick. If she'd fainted and gone crashing to the floor there would have been no one there to help her.

Despair welled up in her. How she hated all this. And how difficult everything was when one arm was incapacitated and you were strapped up like an Egyptian mummy round the middle.

She'd have given anything for a long hot wallow, but that was forbidden her. She was only allowed three or four inches of water and had to have a nurse in attendance to assist. There was no pleasure or relaxation in such a bath. None at all.

Then there was her hair – a complete mess. It needed a lot more doing to it than merely having a comb run through it, which was all she could manage in her present state. If only she could have gone to the hairdresser's, but of course that was impossible in the circumstances.

And now to top it all, just to add to her wretchedness, her period had started. Her despair turned to self-pity.

A murmuring voice caught her attention. The voice belonged to Sister who was further up the ward with Doctor Ross. And there he was, doing it again, *staring* at her. Why was the damned man forever staring at her, she was beginning to find it downright creepy.

Sister left Ross and went over to a nearby student nurse. Seconds later the student was putting the screens round Norma's bed.

And then Norma remembered her comb, an ivory one with an overlaid silver grip that had been a present from Finlay Rankine when she'd left Glasgow to join the FANY. She'd left the bloody thing in the toilet. She'd have to go back for it straight away otherwise it would take a walk, if it hadn't already. She was about to swing her legs out of bed when Ross came through the screens.

'And how are you today?' he smiled.

'Don't tell me I remind you of someone else too?' she snapped at him.

'I beg your pardon?'

'There was another man I used to know who watched me the way you do. Turned out I was the spit of his dead daughter. So is that it, do I remind you of someone else? Is that why you're always staring at me?'

The smile disappeared. His face froze.

'Well?' she demanded, her voice harsh and grating.

'I didn't realise...' He broke off in confusion.

She wanted to take a deep breath, but couldn't thanks to her strapped-up chest. Another irritation. Today, was just full of them.

143

'I'm sorry. I really am...' He trailed off, gulped, then blundered out through the screens, knocking them skewiff in the process.

'Damn!' she muttered angrily. She hadn't meant to do that, attack him almost. As doctors went he couldn't have been nicer or more attentive to her.

It was just one of those days. And he *was* forever watching her when he thought she wasn't aware.

She'd had a bad night, partly because of the pain in her arm where she'd bashed it, and partly because of her guilty conscience at having said to Ross what she had. She'd been waiting all morning for him to come onto the ward so she could make amends. Her outburst had been most unlike her.

Just before lunch he made an appearance in the company of Sister Hennessy, the junior Sister.

'Could I have a private word please Doctor?' she called out to him when he made to pass by the bottom of her bed.

He stopped, then turned to regard her impassively. 'Certainly Miss McKenzie,' he replied, and came round to stand beside her.

Sister Hennessy continued on down the ward.

Norma cleared her throat. 'I'm sorry for snapping at you yesterday. It was completely uncalled for.'

She'd expected him to unbend, perhaps for a smile to come onto his face. No such smile, or any other indication of forgiveness, was forthcoming.

'I mean it. I am sorry.'

He nodded. 'A few more days and I don't see any reason why we can't discharge you. After being discharged you'll still have to attend hospital as an out patient until your arm and ribs are fully mended. Then there will have to be a period of convalescence before you can take up your duties with FANY again. I shall write to your CO to explain the situation.' He glanced at his watch. 'Now if you'll excuse me I must be getting on.'

He strode up the ward to rejoin Sister Hennessy.

She felt like picking something up, preferably something heavy, and chucking it after him. Arrogant silly man! She'd been in the wrong and admitted she had, why couldn't he accept her apology!

When he went off the ward sometime later he was careful to never once let his gaze stray in her direction.

To give herself something to do she'd been helping Staff hand out the afternoon coffee and biscuits, the same Staff who'd been with her when she'd regained consciousness after Risinghill Street. The pair of them were now in Sister's office tucking into the remains of a cake that had been given by the relative of a departing patient.

'Hmm, delish!' Staff crooned, wiping cream from the corners of her mouth.

Norma had to agree, the cake was delish. She wondered how long they'd continue to enjoy such luxuries – already there was talk of food rationing having to be introduced.

'Tell me about Doctor Ross, Staff. What's he like?'

Staff glanced sideways at Norma. 'You mean in his private life?'

'Yes.'

'Very quiet and shy. He doesn't have a girlfriend if that's what you're asking. In fact the last thing he is is a ladies' man. That's why it was so hysterically funny when you...' Staff broke off abruptly and groped for her packet of Black Cat.

'When I what?' Norma demanded. Was Staff referring to the words she'd had with Ross. And how could they be interpreted as hysterically funny. She was lost.

'Forget me, I'm not supposed to say,' Staff replied, and lit up. Thinking, her and her big mouth.

But Norma wasn't the type to let go. There was a mystery here, she wanted an explanation. 'Come on, don't be mean,' she prompted.

Staff blew a stream of smoke towards the ceiling and didn't reply.

'Has he been saying something about me?' Norma queried.

'No, it's nothing like that,' Staff answered in alarm.

'Then what is it like?'

'Oh buggeration!' Staff thought. When would she ever learn to keep her big yap shut.

'Doctor Ross and I were called down from the ward when you

145

arrived in Casualty. He was examining your broken arm when you suddenly threw your other arm round him and gave him a real passionate kiss.'

'I what!' Norma exclaimed.

'Threw your good arm round his neck and gave him a real passionate kiss. And while you were kissing you were making the sort of sounds... well you know the sort of sounds a girl can make at certain times.'

'Oh my God!' Norma whispered, completely stunned by this revelation. Her face and shoulders all the way down to her breasts turned a bright shade of pink.

She remembered the peculiar smile Staff had given her after she'd regained consciousness, and wondering if there was something funny about herself. No wonder Staff had been amused after witnessing that.

And then it all came flooding back; she'd completely forgotten about it until now.

She remembered her dream. The haze of clouds extending in every direction and a puff of cloud parting to reveal Midge. She'd thought Midge had returned to her, gone rushing up to him and ...

She'd kissed Doctor Ross believing she was kissing Midge. That had to be it. She knew now why the dream had seemed so real. Passionate wasn't the word, she must have stuck her tongue halfway down the poor man's throat. It was clear to her now why Ross had been staring at her the way he had. Only too horribly clear indeed.

'How embarrassing,' she muttered to Staff.

'You should have seen how embarrassed *he* was. We thought he was going to expire on the spot. Particularly when you wouldn't let him go. You may have only one working arm but you certainly used it to good effect. In the end it took four of us to prise him free.'

It got worse and worse, Norma thought. 'Did I mention a name at all?' she asked weakly.

Staff shook her head.

Norma wasn't sure whether that was a relief or not.

'Things happen in hospitals, usually under anaesthetic, that we normally keep to ourselves. That was why I was reluctant to tell you about it.' Staff explained.

Norma gave a brittle laugh. 'It was a dream I had. I thought he was someone else.'

'Your chap?' Staff asked with interest.

'No, my ex.'

'You still care for your ex then?'

Norma sidestepped that one. 'He and I were professional ballroom-dancers. We danced as a couple,' she replied instead.

She then went on to tell Staff about Barrowland and the pinnacle of their achievement when they'd won the All Scotland Dance Championship.

She lied a little as a face-saver. She said Midge had always wanted to see the world and had gone off to do just that. She didn't mention that he'd jilted her the day before the wedding to run away with a cold-hearted bitch called Zelda Caprice.

Should she or shouldn't she? She'd been debating that with herself ever since the bombshell Staff had dropped. Now Doctor Ross was back on the ward she had the opportunity to speak to him if she wanted to.

'Doctor? Could I have another word?'

He stopped, to eye her coldly. 'Is something the matter Miss McKenzie?'

'No I eh ... ' She glanced at the nurse with him who got the message. The nurse moved on to another patient several beds further down the ward. He came over.

'I'm told I ... That when I ...' She trailed off. This was damnably difficult.

'Yes?'

She looked into that cold gaze, and withered inside. He was being so off-putting. She knew then that she'd lost her nerve, That she wouldn't go through with making, or trying to make, another apology.

'Nothing. Nothing at all,' she mumbled.

He picked up her chart and studied it.

'You're Scots aren't you? I didn't twig it for quite some time as you're so well-spoken.'

He glanced up at her, but didn't answer.

'Am I wrong then? Is it the north of England perhaps?'

'I am Scots,' he said slowly.

147

'Thought you were. Where from?' she asked in a friendly manner.

'I don't consider that information relevant to your case Miss McKenzie,' he replied.

It was like being slapped in the face and doused with iced water at the same time. If she could have curled up and vanished she would have done.

'You can be discharged after breakfast tomorrow,' he said, replaced the chart, and walked away.

Fuck you too! she thought, which was hardly a ladylike expression. But nonetheless said exactly what she felt.

Fuck you too!

'Thank you for the flowers, they're gorgeous,' Norma said to Major-General Gilchrist, for it was he who'd sent her the huge bunch of flowers that Doctor Ross had commented upon. The flowers, somewhat past their best now, still took pride of place on the window-sill to the right of Norma's bed.

'I should have been to see you before now, but honestly Norma I haven't had a moment. I shouldn't really be taking this time off, but then I realised I could mix business with pleasure so to speak, and so here I am.'

Business? She waited for him to elaborate.

'When will they let you out?' he queried.

'Lucky you came today, otherwise you'd have missed me. I'm to be discharged tomorrow directly after breakfast. I should have been discharged earlier except that my doctor is a very cautious man.'

'And which doctor is that?'

'Doctor Ross. Douglas Ross. He's the Assistant Surgeon on this ward.'

A strange expression came over Gilchrist's face; an amused glint into his eyes. 'That's extremely interesting to hear,' he replied, but more to himself than Norma.

'Is it?' She couldn't think why on earth that should be of interest to the Major-General.

'What will you do when you leave here?' Gilchrist asked, changing the conversation.

'It'll be another seven to eight weeks till my broken bones mend, and I've to have a spell of convalescence after that. I thought I'd spend the time in Glasgow. I haven't been home since I joined the FANY.

'Good idea.'

They talked for a few minutes longer, then Gilchrist reluctantly excused himself to go back to his work.

After Gilchrist had gone Norma went over to choose a magazine from the collection kept for the patients' use. She was leafing through a copy of *My Weekly* when she happened to glance out of the window. From there, she could see the corridors leading to and from Marsden Ward, and framed in one of the windows she could make out the heads and shoulders of Major-General Gilchrist and Doctor Ross. The pair of them were talking together.

Now what was that all about? Norma wondered. Were they discussing her? And if so why? And what was the business Gilchrist had mentioned but failed to elaborate on?

The two men moved away out of sight.

East West, home's best. The old saying was right, Norma thought to herself standing outside the Central Station at the Gordon Street entrance. That familiar smell stung her nostrils. Soot, dirt, the wind off the Clyde. Glasgow, how she'd missed it while down south, and how good it was to be back.

'Here's a taxi now,' the soldier who was helping her with her luggage said, waving at the Black Cab that had suddenly appeared. She'd had to ask the soldier to help her as there hadn't been any porters around. All called up, she'd presumed. Thank goodness at least one taxi driver wasn't.

But she was wrong about the latter. The taxi driver had been called up and the person now driving the taxi was his wife.

'Cubie Street in Bridgeton, just off the Gallowgate,' Norma instructed. 'I'd be obliged if you'd drive slowly. I've got four broken ribs strapped up underneath my uniform.'

'Oh aye, what happened to you then, hen?' the female taxi driver asked as she set the vehicle in motion.

Norma smiled to herself. Typical Glasgow. Straight to the point. It had slipped her mind just how blunt and abrasive Glaswegians were. Other folk, less kindly disposed towards Mungo's children, might have put that another way.

When the taxi drew up outside the McKenzie close the taxi

driver knew all about Risinghill Street and the Royal Free Hospital. Norma also knew about the woman's husband with the Seaforth Highlanders and the couple's wee son who went to a day nursery.

The taxi driver carried Norma's two cases up the stairs for her, and refused a tip, saying she wouldn't take a tip from someone wounded in the course of duty. Norma hadn't thought of herself as being 'wounded in the course of duty' before. Now that she did it made her feel rather proud of herself.

Effie answered the door. Her face lit up with incredulity and joy. 'Norma! I was just this minute writing to you!' And then the face fell. 'But what's wrong with your arm?'

Norma had deliberately not written home about being blown up as she hadn't wanted to worry the family. 'Let's go in and I'll tell you all about it Ma. And could you lift these cases for me. Besides this broken arm I've got four broken ribs as well.'

'Help ma bob!' Effie exclaimed, a hand going to her mouth.

Effie put Norma's cases in her bedroom, then listened wide-eyed as Norma, for the second time that day, but now in more detail, recounted what had happened to her in Risinghill Street and of her subsequent hospitalisation in the Royal Free.

'Oh lass!' Effie whispered when Norma finally came to the end of her tale. Going to Norma she took her very gently in her arms. For almost a minute they remained like that, standing in complete silence. Then Effie, giving her nose a wipe, broke away.

'I thought it best you didn't know, Ma. You'd only have made yourself ill with worry. Or come down to London which is the last place to be while the Blitz is going on.'

'Is the Blitz as bad as they say?'

'It's bad all right, and from all accounts going to get worse. Gerry is determined to bomb London into submission, which he'll never do of course. And certainly never while Mr Churchill is Prime Minister.'

'Aye, Churchill may be a Tory, but he's the man for this job right enough,' Effie admitted grudgingly.

Now she'd had a chance to look at her Norma thought her ma had lost weight, particularly in the face. 'How's Da?' she asked. Brian had gone into the Pioneer Corps earlier on that year.

'Fine according to him. He's currently in North Queensferry building gun emplacements there.' North Queensferry was on the Firth of Forth at the spot where a splendid railway bridge was sited. The bridge joined North Queenferry on the north bank with South Queensferry on the Edinburgh side. Because of the Firth's narrowness there it was a most strategic point, and the best place to defend the naval base at Rosyth.

Effie pointed over at the table on which writing materials were laid out. 'I've just done a letter to him and was in the middle of one to you to say that Eileen is marrying Charlie Marshall this coming Saturday.'

'Oh that's terrific news!' exclaimed Norma. 'I've come back just at the right time.'

Norma remembered that they had originally intended to get married early on last year, but then Charlie shied off when it became apparent there was a war in the offing, saying that he had no intention of leaving Eileen a teenage widow. Eileen had been terribly upset, having been desperately keen to get wed to Charlie and set up house together.

'When you left for London he hadn't been called up, nor was he for some months after. He thought he'd go into one of the fighting regiments, but the army in its wisdom decided otherwise. They put him on a temporary clerking attachment, working out at Maryhill Barracks where he's been since his basic training. Which has been grand for him and Eileen as it's meant they can get together twice and sometimes three times a week.

'Well, yesterday he got the news that his attachment has been made permanent. He's to see out the war from behind a desk – a very safe desk in Aldershot – and he's being transferred there late next week.

'Of course Eileen was ecstatic to know that he's not going to come to any harm, but she was also most upset to lose him to Aldershot. Anyway, to cut a long story short, she convinced him that his argument about leaving her a widow no longer holds water, and so he's agreed to their marriage this Saturday. They're taking out a special licence for it.'

'I really am happy for them. Those two were made for one another,' Norma replied.

'And now you can get to the wedding as well. Eileen will be very pleased about it.'

'What about Da? Will he manage to come?'

'I shouldn't think so. He'll do his damnest, needless to say. But it's very doubtful indeed. It's a top priority job he's on, the men of the Corps there working flat out to get those gun emplacements finished before Gerry takes the notion to have a sail up the Forth. I just can't see him getting away, even more so when it's at such short notice.'

It would break her da's heart to miss his Eileen's wedding, Norma thought. But there you were, war was war. All sorts of sacrifices had to be made.

'Let's go through and put the kettle on,' suggested Effie.

'I was beginning to think you'd never ask.'

Effie laughed at that, but it was a glum laugh. Her mind was still on Brian.

'And how are Lyn and Eileen getting on in their new jobs?' Norma asked in the kitchen. Lyn had left the SCWS and Eileen the baker's she'd tended counter at and they'd both joined an armaments factory where they now worked as machinists.

'Just fine. They say it's gey hard graft, but they were expecting that. And just wait till you clap eyes on Lyn, you're going to get a shock I can tell you.'

'Why's that?'

Effie gave a mysterious smile. 'Wait and see. I don't want to spoil it for you.'

Norma was intrigued, and couldn't for the life of her think what her mother was referring to.

It wasn't long after that Norma heard the scrape of a key in the outside door, followed by the voices of Lyn and Eileen chaffing to each other. She rose from the chair in the living room where she'd been sitting to greet her two sisters.

Eileen was the same, but her mouth literally dropped at the sight of Lyn. Gone was 'podge' of old, in her place a svelte young lady with a curvaceous figure.

Eileen squealed on realising who it was, and Norma had to quickly warn the pair of them about her ribs as they flew at her.

Kisses were exchanged. 'Congratulations!' Norma said to Eileen. 'Ma's told me about Saturday.'

'And to think you'll be here for it. That's absolutely terrific!' Eileen enthused.

'But what's all this broken arm and ribs bit?' Lyn queried.

Lyn and Eileen listened soberly as Norma went through her story yet again.

'Jings but you were fortunate there right enough,' Eileen said when Norma was done.

'If you could have seen what was left of that street you'd appreciate just how fortunate,' Norma replied, and shuddered. It sometimes gave her the willies to think of the narrowness of her escape.

She turned to Lyn. 'I can't believe this. Look at you, you're beautiful! What the hell happened?'

'I suppose it just all boils down to the fact I got sick to the back teeth of being fat and the eternal wallflower. I decided I was going to diet, and that's exactly what I did. The weight just fell off. Didn't it Ma?'

Effie nodded her agreement.

'And what about boyfriends now?'

'I have to beat them off with a club, and that's a fact,' Lyn grinned in reply.

'Oh I'm so pleased, really I am. I come back to find you looking like a fashion model and Eileen about to be wed. I couldn't have had a better homecoming.'

Eileen swung on Effie. 'How long will tea be Ma? I've got so many things to do and organise if the wedding is going to take place on Saturday.' She glanced at her wristwatch. 'I'm meeting Charlie in less than an hour. We're going round to Dow's pub to discuss the arrangements for the reception.' To Norma she said. 'Dow's is hardly ideal but it's the best we'll manage in the time available.'

Norma had been to functions there before. It was a barn of a place, and not exactly the cheeriest of environments. But as Eileen said, time was against her and Charlie.

'The people will make the occasion, not the venue,' she replied, which bucked Eileen up. For that was true enough.

Effie got on with the tea while Eileen laid the table. Norma and Lyn sat in front of the living-room fire.

'Speaking of chaps, what about you?' Lyn asked.

'I have one. His name is Jeremy Dereham. He's all right.'

Lyn raised a well-plucked eyebrow. 'Just all right?'

Norma shrugged.

'Still Midge eh?'

Norma just gazed into the depths of the fire.

Lyn was full of advice on the subject, but wisely didn't offer it.

'So tell me about all these swells you're with nowadays? They are swells aren't they?' Lyn asked instead.

Norma gave a subdued smile. 'They are that. All FANYs are monied, and usually come from top drawer families – yours truly being one of the few exceptions to the latter.'

Norma then told Lyn of an escapade that she and Lynsey Dereham had got up to that, well before she was finished recounting it, had Lyn reduced to tears of laughter.

She'd been right about folks making the occasion and not the venue. You couldn't have had a better reception than Eileen and Charlie's. It was a cracker.

Eileen was radiant, in that special way only a new bride can be, and Charlie was flushed with a combination of drink, pride and happiness.

Norma watched them dance past. She'd been asked up a number of times but had pleaded in each instance that her broken ribs weren't up to it. That was only partially true, for she could've managed a slow waltz like the one now being played. The truth of the matter was that she didn't want to get up because here, amongst all these dear friends and neighbours, the pain of Midge was worse than it had been for a long, long time. To have gone on the floor would only have made that pain even worse.

She sipped her whisky and thought of the wedding that never was, the one that was supposed to have taken place between her and Midge. Many of those now present would have been there, and it would have been she who would have been the radiant bride; Midge the happy groom.

Emotion clogged her throat. She could just see herself and Midge out there, that old magic sparking between them as they swept and glided round the floor.

Eileen's wedding reception faded, replaced by a collage of other places, other times. Competitions they'd been in, exhibitions they'd given. The pair of them at Barrowland, the Plaza, Locarno; the different gowns she'd worn; the ways she'd done her hair; the routines they'd devised together.

She remembered what it was like to be in Midge's arms, to

have the warmth of his body burning against hers. The way the two of them were as one, both on the dancefloor, and in bed. This time she didn't sip her whisky, but took a large swallow.

Her thoughts were interrupted by a great cry going up from the main doorway into the room. She craned her neck to see what was going on.

The knot of people there parted to reveal her da clad from neck to toe in motorbike leathers, gloves and boots, and carrying a crash helmet. The bottom part of his face was filthy from dirt thrown up by the roads he'd been travelling on.

Effie went hurrying over to him. As did Lyn, Eileen and Charlie. Because she'd been furthest away Norma was the last of them to reach Brian.

Eileen threw her arms round her father. 'You did it. You managed to come,' she choked, quite overcome.

Effie, her eyes shining, was staring at Brian. She took his hand when he reached out to her.

The reception had been a cracker before, Norma thought. With her da here it was now perfect. Just perfect.

'I've only got a few hours as I have to be back on site first thing the morn's morn. But I'm here, that's all that matters,' Brian said.

'All that matters,' Effie agreed.

A large dram was thrust into Brian's grasp. 'To the happy couple. Lang may their lum reek!' he toasted.

He downed the dram in one, kissed Eileen on the cheek, then shook with Charlie. 'Welcome to the family, son,' he said.

Eileen began to cry, but they were tears of joy. Charlie hooked an arm round her waist, and pulled her close.

'I should have known you'd move hell and high water,' Effie said to Brian.

'Aye, well it's no' every day you have a daughter get married. I was determined that if there was a way to get here I'd find it. And I did. I'm just disappointed I couldn't get here for the actual ceremony itself.'

Effie gave him a big hug, thinking to herself there weren't many better than her Brian. She'd have walked over broken glass for him, so she would.

Brian looked at Norma, taking in her plastered arm. He knew

all that had happened to her from Effie's letter. They'd talk in a bit, but not right now. 'Hello lass,' he said.

There were more hugs and kisses, then Brian went off to remove his motorcycle gear and give his face a wash. Effie went with him.

'Trust the old man,' Lyn said to Norma.

'I didn't know he could ride a motorbike.'

'Neither did I. I wouldn't put it past him to have learned just to get here.'

Neither did Norma. Later, when she asked him, that transpired to be the case. He'd had half an hour's tuition before setting off from North Queensferry and had borrowed a motorbike. He'd more or less learned to handle the machine *en route*.

'I want a word with you,' Norma said to Eileen and Charlie, having at last managed to get them in a corner alone. She handed Charlie an envelope she'd prepared earlier.

'What's this then?' he asked.

'I know with all the frantic rush and everything you haven't been able to fix up a proper honeymoon and had intended to just take a few days here and there. Rather than that I'd like you to book into a hotel and have those few days complete with all the trappings at my expense.'

Charlie was dumbfounded. 'We can't . . .' he started to protest, but Norma cut him off.

'Yes you can – and will. I can well afford it. It's my wedding present to you.' To Eileen she added. 'And a *posh* hotel mind, the very best.'

Eileen smiled her gratitude. 'That really will be something. A honeymoon to remember.'

'It's awful good of you,' Charlie said.

'The pleasure's all mine. Just you two enjoy yourselves. That's all I ask.'

Charlie glanced down at the envelope. When he came to open it he would find to his astonishment, and delight, that it contained fifty pounds in used fivers. Norma didn't believe in doing things by halves. 'I never said at the time, but I will now. You're a smashing bird Norma, first class. You never deserved what Henderson did to you. That was criminal so it was.'

She somehow forced a smile onto her face. 'That's history now Charlie. Character-building we would call it in the FANY.'

Eileen's heart went out to her big sister. Sod that Midge Henderson for a selfish pig. He'd gutted Norma, that's what he'd done. Gutted her.

The next morning, some hours after Brian had left to return to North Queensferry, Eileen and Charlie boarded a tram for town where they booked into a suite in the Adelphi Hotel. There they spent four glorious days, and four ecstatic nights. As it turned out, their entire married life together.

Effie and Norma reached their close having just returned from the steamie where they'd been doing the washing and mangling. It was a fortnight since Norma had been given the all clear by the hospital, a fortnight during which she'd remained in Glasgow to convalesce.

As they let themselves into the house they saw that the afternoon post had been. An official-looking, buff-coloured envelope was addressed to Norma. She read its contents standing by the living room window.

Effie didn't have to ask what the letter said. She knew. 'When?' she queried.

Norma glanced up at her mother. 'Tomorrow. I've to report in as soon as possible.'

Effie nodded. 'It's just as well we went to the steamie the day then. Everything will be clean to take back with you.'

Effie helped her pack.

Chapter Seven

The train was still a good many miles from London when a sailor in Norma's carriage suddenly exclaimed, pointing out the window. 'Bloody Norah, look at that!' he said, his tone a combination of amazement and awe.

The rest of the passengers in the carriage crowded round his window. The night sky, in the direction of the capital, might have been the sky over hell itself. At the centre it was a deep bloody crimson shot through with white and yellow streaks, the crimson changing colour to red, and then pink when it finally reached its periphery.

'Listen!' another sailor said.

The sounds were faint but there was no mistaking what they were. The dull crump of bombs exploding. So many bombs it was like a long string of Chinese crackers going off, one after the other. And when the end of the string was reached there was a brief pause, and then another string started.

'She's taking a proper pasting from the looks of it,' an Indian officer said unnecessarily.

There was a huge explosion that momentarily drowned out all other sounds, then the Chinese cracker effect was back.

They'd got something big there, Norma thought to herself, and wondered what. From the magnitude of the explosion it might well have been an armaments factory. Her mouth suddenly went dry with the thought that Lyn and Eileen worked in one of those. Thankfully the *Luftwaffe* had stayed away from Glasgow so far.

They resumed their seats to talk and speculate amongst themselves. The nearer they got to London the louder the explosions became. At one point just past Watford they all held

158

their breath as a plane's engines droned overhead. A large heavy plane that had to be a Gerry bomber.

Norma broke out in a cold sweat. She couldn't stop her mind flashing back to Risinghill Street and her left arm began to ache as though from the memory.

The train stopped twice, but only for a few minutes on each occasion. Then it arrived at Euston Station, where they all hurriedly disembarked.

The white lights Norma had seen from afar were in fact searchlights. Besides the noise of bombs exploding there was also the distinctive boom-boom of anti-aircraft ack-ack guns, a number of these directly surrounding the station, and the other nearby stations of King's Cross and St Pancras. At the end of the platform she discovered a miniature lake of water, the result of a burst main, which she had to paddle through.

There were no taxis to be had for love or money, so it would have to be the Underground. She was pleased she'd only brought one suitcase with her, having left the other one in Glasgow.

If it was hell on the surface it was the Black Hole of Calcutta below. There were so many people huddled together that she could hardly get down the stairs, and out on the platform the story was just the same.

It was a pathetic sight: men and women dossing down uncomfortably for the night, some sitting propped up against a wall, others lying prostrate with blankets or other coverings over their faces in an attempt to block out the light. At one place she passed a baby bedded down in an open suitcase. As for the smell – luckily she was used to the Glasgow slums otherwise it might have turned her stomach. It was clear that the poor blighters all around her had become used to it.

Nor was Euston the only station jam-packed in this way. So was every station her tube came to, including the stop where she got out.

It was 10.34am, so her wristwatch told her, as Norma entered Baker Street. She'd come from 10 Grosvenor Place – FANY HQ had moved there from Wilton Place in October – where she'd had a face-to-face with Commandant Hopewell. The Commandant, after welcoming her back and inquiring about her health, had been mysterious, to say the least. She was to report to an address in Baker Street where a VIP wanted to speak to her. That had been all. No explanation as to who the VIP was, or what he wanted to speak to her about.

She arrived at number 64 where a plate bore the legend Inter-Services Research Bureau, whatever that was.

The woman at reception wasn't wearing a uniform, but had an air of cold efficiency about her. Her gaze fastened onto Norma the moment Norma walked through the door, a gaze Norma likened to an eagle's when it sights its prey. A little shiver ran up her spine.

'Are you McKenzie?' the woman asked in a neutral voice. 'Yes.'

The woman rose. 'You're expected. Come with me.'

They went into a corridor which, within a few yards branched hard left and hard right. They took the left-hand way, which in turn soon branched again, this time into three. The place is a rabbit warren, Norma thought to herself. And she was right.

'Wait in there,' the woman said, pointing to a door painted a bilious shade of green. Then, without waiting for a reply, she left.

Norma went through the green painted door to discover a surprise waiting for her on the other side in the shape of Lynsey Dereham. 'Lynsey!' 'Norma!' they exclaimed simultaneously.

Lynsey was about to hug Norma when she suddenly stopped. 'The ribs?'

Norma grinned. 'Mended. But don't squeeze them too tight, just in case.'

They hugged, then kissed each other on the cheek. 'You look tremendous, fit as a fiddle,' Lynsey said.

Norma couldn't say the same about her friend. If asked to describe Lynsey it would have been as death warmed up.

'When did you get back?' Lynsey demanded.

'Last night. I tried several times to ring you to come and meet me at the station, but you were never there.'

'If I said life's been hectic that would be the understatement of the year. I was in the City when the bombing started. It was a nightmare. I thought a dozen times I wasn't going to survive. But I did, and here I am to tell the tale.'

'I heard that they'd concentrated on the City.'

'That was their target all right, and they certainly succeeded in hitting it. Being Christmas, many of the buildings didn't have any fire-watchers, and then the water failed. They tried to take water from the Thames but it was at a very low ebb.'

'You were driving someone?'

'A brass hat from the War Office. As I said, we were already in the City when the raid started. When he realised the City was the designated target he began organising. Suffice it to say it was well after dawn before I saw my kip.'

No wonder Lynsey looked terrible thought Norma. 'So when were you ordered to report here?'

'Early yesterday. And you?'

'About an hour ago when I spoke to Commandant Hopewell.'

The two women stared at one another, puzzlement reflected in their eyes. 'Any idea what it's all about?' asked Norma.

Lynsey shook her head. 'None at all.'

'It can't be coincidence that you and I are here together.'

'Shouldn't think so,' Lynsey agreed, lighting a cigarette.

'I wonder who this VIP is? The Commandant was most mysterious about him.'

'She was exactly the same with me.'

Norma sat on one of the wooden chairs that had been provided, and Lynsey followed suit. 'How was Glasgow?' Lynsey asked.

Norma gave Lynsey a quick rundown on all that had happened to her at home, including an account of Eileen's wedding to Charlie Marshall. She'd never hidden from any of her fellow FANYs the sort of background she came from. Nor had they ever been the least bit sniffy to her. But then the sort of girl who would have been sniffy wasn't the type to join the FANY.

'Jeremy mentioned he'd written to you.'

'Yes. Twice. In his last letter he told me his regiment was being posted abroad. He didn't say where.'

'They left four days ago. He had been trying to contact me and had not been getting through. A message finally reached me via one of his chums, by which time he'd gone.'

'Did the chum say where the regiment was off to?'

'No. But then it was bound to have been a secret.'

'I'll miss him,' Norma said. Which was true enough. She might not love Jeremy, but he was good fun.

The door opened and a FANY came in. 'They're ready for you now. Please step this way,' the FANY said, a FANY neither Norma or Lynsey had ever encountered before. But then that wasn't too surprising, there were quite a number of Free FANYs (if nowhere near the number of FANY-ATS) after all. Lynsey stubbed out her cigarette; then she and Norma followed the FANY out of the room.

'Who are we going to see?' Lynsey queried as the three of them turned into yet another corridor. Her only reply – she hadn't really expected one but it was worth a try – was an enigmatic smile.

When it did come, the answer astonished Norma. 'Hello. I'm glad we managed to get the pair of you here together. That's what we wanted,' said Major-General Gilchrist, rising from behind his desk. There was another female present, Peggy Boughton, Commandant Hopewell's secretary.

The Major-General introduced himself to Lynsey then said to Norma, 'The hospital you were attending in Glasgow tells me you're fighting fit again. Is that correct.'

'Yes sir,' Norma replied weakly. Gilchrist was the last person she'd expected to see.

'Good. Now would the pair of you like to sit down.'

Norma and Lynsey did as they were bid. The Major-General remained standing. 'At the moment you're both being used as drivers. How would you like the opportunity to do something more, *substantially* more, for the war effort?' he asked.

Norma and Lynsey glanced at one another, intrigued. 'What did you have in mind, sir?' Norma answered for the two of them.

'Before I go any further you must both swear to me that nothing you are told inside this room will go further should either of you decide to decline my offer. It's very important.'

'I swear,' Norma said.

'And I,' Lynsey added.

'Right then.' Gilchrist walked a few steps one way, then retraced them. He chuckled suddenly. 'I imagine you've been wondering what the Inter-Services Research Bureau is?'

'Yes sir, we have,' Lynsey replied.

'Well it's a façade, a front for another organisation – an

162

organisation Peggy and I belong to, and which I was in the process of setting up when you were acting as my driver Norma.'

Norma sat forward in her chair. Gilchrist had her absolute attention.

He went on. 'With the fall of France it became apparent to some of us that we needed to organise movements in enemy-occupied territory comparable to the Sinn Fein movement in Ireland, or the Chinese guerrillas now operating against Japan, or – one might as well admit it – to the organisations the Nazis themselves have developed so remarkably in almost every country in the world.

'Halifax approached Churchill last July and he gave us the go-ahead. Neville Chamberlain arranged the details, the last important act of that man's life as he went into hospital a few days later. And so Special Operations Executive was born. An entirely new formation to co-ordinate all action, by way of subversion and sabotage, against the enemy overseas.'

Gilchrist paused. Norma and Lynsey waited with bated breath for him to continue. This was fascinating.

'Churchill's directive to Hugh Dalton – the Minister in charge of SOE when we came into being – was, "And now set Europe ablaze!" Which is precisely what we intend to do. We are to create and foster the spirit of resistance in Nazi-occupied countries, and try to establish a nucleus of trained operatives – a fifth column you could call them – who will be ready to assist in the liberation of the country concerned when we, the British, are able to invade it.

'We will also, as I have already mentioned, be instigating acts of subversion and sabotage. Suddenness, subterfuge and flexibility are the principle characteristics of such operations. They will be stiletto attacks to harry and confuse the enemy, hurting it in both military and economic areas.'

Gilchrist stopped and took a deep breath. 'I think that gives you a fair idea of what we in SOE are up to. We have discovered that FANYs, partly because they are not in the regular army, and partly for various other reasons, are ideal for our purposes, and we have been recruiting a great many over the past few months.'

He looked directly at Norma. 'I was most impressed with you when you were driving for me, and that day I came to see you in the Royal Free decided to ask you to join us when you were better again. I want you to be a WT, that is, a wireless telegraphy operator for us. You will be based in England with contact into France.'

He turned to Lynsey. 'When I spoke to Peggy about Norma she told me you two were fast friends. I've studied your file and records and would like you also to join us. I want you and Norma to train and work together. That is most important.'

Peggy Boughton spoke for the first time. 'Norma, would you mind waiting outside for a few minutes. This next part of the interview is between Lynsey and ourselves.'

'Yes of course,' Norma replied immediately, and left the room.

Outside in the corridor she tried to collect her thoughts. Exciting, that was her initial reaction. The whole thing sounded so exciting. She wondered if she'd be any good as a wireless operator, and didn't see why not. She resolved there and then what her answer was going to be.

The few minutes stretched to five, then Peggy Boughton opened the door and asked Norma to come back in.

'Lynsey's agreed to join us. What about you Norma?' Gilchrist queried.

'Yes please.'

'That's the ticket.' He smiled, and Peggy Boughton smiled as well.

Papers were produced, and both girls had to sign the Official Secrets Act. 'As far as anyone outside SOE is concerned you're still drivers,' Peggy Boughton said.

Norma and Lynsey nodded.

'Now I want you to go off and pack.' Gilchrist glanced at his wristwatch. 'A car will pick you up between seventeen and eighteen hundred hours this evening and take you to your place of training.'

'As quick as that!' Norma exclaimed.

'Why, is there something in London you wish to settle before leaving?' Gilchrist queried.

Norma shook her head.

'I'll probably be seeing you again then fairly soon,' Gilchrist said.

Although Norma hadn't seen it happen Gilchrist or Peggy

Boughton must have pressed a concealed buzzer, for the door opened and the same FANY who'd brought them to the room came in.

'I'll show you out,' she said.

Norma followed the FANY in somewhat of a daze. Lynsey walked beside her looking even paler than previously.

Norma was curious about that part of Lynsey's interview at which she hadn't been present. But as Lynsey didn't volunteer any information about it she didn't ask.

The car came to collect her at quarter to six. Besides Lynsey there were two other girl passengers, a Pamela Parkinson and a Violette Hart. The latter two were both Free FANYs, both vaguely known to Norma and Lynsey. The driver, a FANY-AT, informed them that Norma was the last one she had to pick up. Violette inquired where they were going, what their destination was? The FANY-AT gave Violette a brief glance in the rear-view mirror, but made no reply.

After a while Lynsey fell asleep. A little later so too did Norma.

Bombardier Gutteridge was regular army, and tiny. The first thing you couldn't help noticing about him were his crossed eyes. He reminded Norma of Ben Turpin, the American film comedian.

'Get fell in ladies!' Gutteridge barked. The four girls lined up with their cases at their feet.

'Riiiight turn! Quick march!' He strode off smartly. The girls hastily snatched up their cases and followed. Just before they reached the building he was taking them to it started to snow. The date was 30th December 1940. The following night would be New Year's Eve.

The barrack room contained a dozen beds and was freezing despite there being a coal-burning stove in the centre of the room. They would very quickly learn that the stove only heated the area directly surrounding it. Six feet away and the temperature plunged.

'Those beds with empty lockers beside them are free. Take your choice. Unpack; there will be someone here shortly to take you to the mess for a meal. Welcome to Fawley Court,'

Bombardier Gutteridge barked out, and abruptly left them.

Norma and Lynsey chose beds that were side by side. Pam and Violette, who were also friends, did the same, but in another part of the room.

The FANY who came to take them to the mess had been at Overthorpe Hall, where all FANYs trained, at the same time as Norma, so there was a reunion. Her name was Helen Rolfe.

Pleasantries were exchanged, and introductions made. Helen said she'd been detailed to settle the four of them in, and first of all how about some food?

'I'm ravenous,' Violette proclaimed, and the other three admitted they were hungry too.

The mess was in the main building, a manor-style house. In the mess, dinner being over, a meal had been set aside for each of them.

'There are sixteen FANYs in residence at the moment, including yourselves. The rest are men, and regular army. Some of them our chaps; some not,' Helen explained as they ate.

'When you say "our chaps" do you mean . . .?' Norma trailed off deliberately, not at all sure it was a name she should mention.

Helen smiled. 'SOE?'

Norma nodded.

'Yes, that's exactly what I mean.'

'And the other?' Pam inquired.

'Training in Morse and WT for use within their own units.'

'And how long will we be here for?' Norma asked.

'Until you're competent in Morse and the use of a WT set. The usual time is about four months.'

'Do you get failures?' Violette asked.

'There haven't been any while I've been here. But there were several just before I arrived. Both were regular army chaps and were returned to the outfits they'd come from. I'm happy to say that so far no FANY has failed.'

The four girls were still eating and talking when another FANY burst into the mess. This newcomer was wild-eyed, her hair awry. It was obvious she'd been crying heavily. For a handful of seconds she stared distraughtly at the girls and

166

Helen. Then whirling round, fled out the same entrance she'd come in.

Helen sighed. 'That's Ineke, a Dutchwoman we recruited. Her fiancé is a "joe" for us, working in N Section. She received a message this afternoon that the SD – that's the Sicherheitsdienst, the Nazi Party Security Service who're every bit as awful as the Gestapo – have picked him up. Poor sod, the best he can hope for is that they kill him quickly. Which is most unlikely knowing them.'

Silence reigned round the table. 'What's N Section?' Pam asked eventually.

'The Section dealing with the Netherlands. T Section is that dealing with Belgium, and F Section that dealing with France. You'll all be in F Section when you graduate from here, I believe.'

'And a "joe"?' This time the questioner was Lynsey.

'Our name for an agent in the field.'

Lynsey lit a cigarette. The others continued chatting, but she was now lost in her own thoughts. Every so often she glanced at the doorway through which Ineke had fled.

Fawley Court was surrounded by fair-sized grounds. After dinner Lynsey announced she was off for a stroll; she wanted some fresh air. Norma said she'd tag along.

The moon was up, and very bright. From a part of the main building came the sound of male and female laughter. In the distance a motorbike engine revved, then quickly faded out of hearing range. Lynsey shivered, and pulled the lapels of her greatcoat up round her neck.

'Last night the Blitz; tonight peace and tranquillity,' she said softly.

'Yes, quite a contrast.'

A few steps further on Norma suddenly exclaimed. 'Look!' And pointed to the sky.

A shooting star burned and blazed its way across the heavens, to be finally consumed by its entry into earth's atmosphere. It died in a shower of golden sparks.

'Did you make a wish?' asked Norma.

'Oh yes.' Lynsey's reply was so quiet Norma had to strain to hear it.

'So did I.' She'd wished for happiness, the same thing she always wished for, be it shooting stars, chicken-bones or whatever.

'This morning, with Major-General Gilchrist and Peggy Boughton, it was only words. Tonight, hearing about that Dutchman and his capture by the Germans it all became horribly real,' Lynsey said, lighting yet another cigarette. She'd been smoking heavily all day.

Norma frowned. 'How do you mean?'

'I don't suppose it matters that I tell you now; you'd find out soon enough anyway. The reason you and I are to train together, work as a twosome, is because I'm going to be your "joe". When I'm finished here there will be further training for me, then it'll be into France.'

Norma came up short. 'You speak French?'

'Like a native. When I was a child I always had French nannies. Besides which, Pa has a villa in the Dordogne, where we spent every summer holiday up until the war. I was already bilingual when I started school.'

'And Gilchrist found this out when he went through your file?'

'That's it.'

Norma didn't know what to say. As Lynsey put it, what had been mere words was now horribly real, for Lynsey anyway.

Lynsey gave a brittle laugh. 'It's all too funny really. Too funny by half.'

They walked a little while longer, then returned to their room where they met, between then and the following morning, all the other girls they'd be sharing that particular barrack room with.

As Norma commented more than once, learning to be a proficient WT operator, to the standard demanded by Bombardier Gutteridge, was damned hard work. The Bombardier had been a WT operator in civilian life, and was a natural teacher. He was also a holy terror if he thought his pupil was giving less than a hundred per cent.

The required speed for the Morse Code was twenty-five words a minute. That meant, as all messages in code were in five-letter groups, one hundred and twenty-five letters a minute – slightly more than two a second.

The tricky part was that when you were writing down one letter you had to be reading three letters ahead. There was a technique to this which, Gutteridge assured them early on, once you'd acquired you'd never ever lose again.

Bombardier Gutteridge was in charge of all their technical training and what he said went. Being an SOE establishment – as opposed to regular army – eccentricities about rank prevailed. Ability counted, not rank. At Fawley Court, lieutenants, captains, majors and even a lieutenant-colonel deferred to Bombardier Gutteridge – something that would never have happened in any other unit. But then, as Norma and Lynsey soon discovered, SOE wasn't like any other unit in the British Army. It was unique.

'I'm looking forward to this,' Norma said to Lieutenant Philip Bodington as the car they'd borrowed from Fawley Court brought them into Henley. Henley was the nearest civilised spot to FC (as the inmates referred to it), there being roughly a mile and a half between the two. FC kept a pool of cars, all ancient but still roadworthy, for general use.

Norma and Philip were in the front seats; Lynsey and another Lieutenant called Simon Rafferty in the back. Philip and Simon had arrived at FC a few weeks previously, and had already been out with Norma and Lynsey several times, the two couples having hit it off together. Norma always paired with Philip; Lynsey with Simon. It was a Saturday night in March and they were *en route* to catch the first house of the new Busby Berkeley that the Kingsway in Henley was showing.

Pathe News was just starting as they entered the auditorium. They watched scenes of the recent British raid on the Lofoten Islands, followed by President Roosevelt signing a Lease and Lend Bill which the commentator said was going to be a huge boost to the British war effort. Then the news was over and it was time for the main picture *Strike Up The Band*.

Philip produced a box of chocolates which was clever of him as sweets were becoming harder and harder to get hold of. They were delicious chocs too.

It was about halfway through the film when a dancing

169

number came up on screen. Norma found herself staring up at Midge. It was as though a hand had taken hold of her insides and was squeezing them. Another her brain. She was suddenly breathless, and there was the foul acid taste of bile at the back of her throat.

Midge, huge up there on the silver screen. And with him Zelda, the pair of them dancing up a storm.

Three little words – Norma saw the step quite clearly. And then they repeated it.

She swallowed, and swallowed again. But the taste of bile wouldn't go away. She wondered why Midge and Zelda had gone hazy at the edges, then realised there were tears in her eyes.

The number finished, and Midge and Zelda were replaced by a host of girls swirling in patterns. She blew her nose, then discreetly wiped her eyes.

'Absolutely spiffing eh?' Philip whispered.

'Absolutely,' she agreed in a voice that was cracked and raw.

Philip glanced at her, a questioning glance which she ignored. She continued staring up at the screen as though totally absorbed in what was happening there. In her mind she was re-running the Midge and Zelda sequence.

They were good together, there was no denying it. In fact they were more than good; they were excellent. But *not better* than she and Midge had been. She derived grim satisfaction from that.

When the picture was over and the credits began rolling she eagerly looked for his name. She'd expected to see Michael Henderson, but he was billed as Mike. Zelda was still Zelda Caprice. So although Midge and Zelda had married she hadn't taken his name, at least not for professional purposes.

When, after the full programme was over, Simon suggested they go for a drink Norma was all for it. A drink might dull the pain a little.

'Excuse me, I'll be right back,' Norma said, rising from the marble-topped table at which they were sitting. She walked the length of the pub, though not past all that many people as business was surprisingly slack, to the door marked Ladies, and went inside.

Discovering she was alone, as she'd hoped she'd be, she let

herself go. She started to tremble, and then shake all over. Going to the sink she splashed cold water over her face, and felt a little better. So she splashed some more.

Lynsey came through the door, her expression one of concern. 'Are you all right? You've been looking ... well, strange to say the least ever since we came out of the picture-hall.'

There was no towel. Norma took out a hanky and dried herself with that. When she was finished she noted the hanky was streaked with what little make-up she'd been wearing. She'd have to repair that before going back through again.

'I've stopped shaking,' she said in surprise. 'I was shaking like a leaf just a few moments ago.'

Lynsey, deeply worried now, took Norma by the arm. 'What is it?' she asked gently.

Lynsey knew that Norma had been a professional dancer in the past, but nothing about Midge or Midge running off with Zelda Caprice the day before he and Norma were due to be married. Norma told Lynsey all about that now, and how they'd just watched Midge and Zelda in *Strike Up The Band*.

'Poor darling,' Lynsey said softly when Norma eventually finished her story.

The tears were back; Norma could feel them stinging her newly washed face. 'I'm sorry I'm making such a fool of myself,' she choked.

'No you're not. You're just getting it off your chest to a friend – that's what friends are for.'

'Oh Lynsey,' Norma said, and hung her head.

Lynsey took her into her arms and held her there, comforting her, till finally the tears stopped and Norma was once more in control of herself.

'Find a spot off the road and let's draw in there for a while,' Norma said. On returning to their table with Lynsey she'd pleaded a headache and so Philip was driving her back to FC. Lynsey and Simon had stayed on at her insistence.

Philip shot Norma a questioning look. What did she mean by that? He liked Norma, but was never quite sure what to make of her. 'Head better then?' he asked.

'Yes.'

He remembered a dirt track turn off that he'd noticed on

another excursion out in a car. It meandered past a pond, and then on up to a farm. He turned into that, to stop by the pond.

'You're in a funny mood tonight,' he said.

'Am I? I wasn't aware of that,' she lied.

'Have I done something?'

'Nothing at all I assure you. You've been your usual sweet self.' Leaning across she kissed him on the cheek. Next moment he'd pulled her to him and his lips were on hers, his tongue deep inside her mouth.

He smelled of old leather, she thought. That and boot polish. An odd combination, but one she didn't find at all offensive. In fact it was rather pleasant. And certainly very masculine.

It hadn't been in her mind to do what she did next, not her conscious mind anyway. He stiffened when she took a hand and guided it to her right breast. She'd never allowed, far less instigated, such intimacy before.

He kneaded and squeezed, cupped and caressed. First one breast, then the other. She didn't protest when he sought and found the outline of her mound.

'Let's go in the back?' he suggested, his voice thick with desire. For he fancied Norma rotten, had done since he'd first clapped eyes on her. But he'd never dared hope what he was daring to hope now. That had never seemed a possibility.

Without replying she removed the hand between her legs, and got out of the car. She was in the back before him.

Her thoughts and emotions were in a turmoil. She hurt so much inside, the old wound had been ripped wide open again. Damn Midge for what he'd done to her. Damn herself for still feeling about him the way she did. And most of all damn Zelda, damn Zelda to roast forever in everlasting hell.

She closed her eyes as Philip entered her. It was the first time since the last occasion she and Midge had made love. Jeremy had often tried, but she'd never let him.

In her mind she pictured Midge watching her and Philip. Yes, she thought, that's what she wanted. Him to watch. To see everything.

Watch! you bastard she shouted at him. *Watch!*

She used the small torch she kept under her pillow to glance at the clock by the side of her bed. Another hour and it would be dawn; she hadn't slept a wink. She was hot and sticky, and there was sweat on her forehead, underarms and thighs. She felt wretched.

She turned over for the umpteenth time since coming to bed. Why had she done what she had, why? The answer was revenge of course. She'd imagined she was somehow getting back at Midge, cocking a snook at him.

She wished now she hadn't done it with Philip. It had solved nothing, made nothing better. If anything it had made things worse. She was filled with regret, and remorse, and ... yes, she had to admit it, even revulsion.

Not that there was anything wrong with Philip. He was a nice enough chap – she'd never have gone out with him in the first place if he hadn't been. But she shouldn't have done it with him because she just didn't have those sort of feelings towards him.

She felt she'd cheapened herself. Cheapened and demeaned herself by doing what she had.

She turned over again, saw a mental picture of herself and Philip in the back of the car, and shuddered. First thing she'd do when she got up was have a bath, she promised herself. A piping hot one. And when in it she'd scrub herself hard with soap and loofah, scour her skin clean again. For she felt dirty all over.

Dawn was rising when, at long last, she finally fell into a fitful sleep. A sleep during which she continued to toss and turn, and from time to time mutter reproachfully to herself.

Next morning Norma and Lynsey, as had become their Sunday habit since coming to Fawley Court, took out horses from a nearby riding stable. Norma had learned to ride at Kilmichael House, and, under FANY tutelage, had greatly extended her experience and expertise while training at Overthorpe Hall. For although FANY no longer used horses in the execution of their duties they were still a very horsey-orientated service.

Norma was exhausted after her terrible night, completely drained. Nor had her bath helped; it had neither revived her nor taken away that sensation of dirtiness. Touching her horse with her heels she urged it into a canter.

Lynsey followed suit.

The ground was rock hard, still frozen in its winter sleep,

perfect for riding. Norma touched her horse again, and the canter changed to a gallop. Lynsey came with her.

Hooves drummed the earth; wind sang in her ears. She touched the horse again urging it to go faster.

The gallop became a mad one; the girls remaining in control, but only just. Neither looked at the other, yet each was aware that the other was there, as their horses further lengthened their stride, stretching themselves to their limit.

Still side by side they jumped a hedge. Norma bit the inside of her mouth as her mount landed with a bone-jarring thump. They continued on without let up.

They plunged into a small wood where low hanging branches brushed and whipped their bodies, one branch ripping open a cut on Lynsey's right cheek. And then they were out of the wood and charging up a hill.

'Faster! Faster!' Norma whispered, this time not touching with her heels but positively digging them in. Her beast snorted as it laboured to obey.

Another hedge reared before them which they successfully cleared. Then it was another hedge, this one taller than the previous ones. They jumped that successfully too, though it was a near thing in Norma's case.

On and on they went, flat out. And then just as suddenly as it had started, the madness that had gripped them both was over. They began reining in.

The horses were blowing heavily when they came to a stop overlooking the very pond that Norma and Philip had parked beside the night before. Lynsey, chest heaving, dabbed with a balled handkerchief at the cut on her cheek. 'I suppose the truth of the matter is you can run as hard and fast as you like, but you can't run away from it,' she said softly.

Norma glanced at her friend, knowing exactly what she was talking about. 'I suppose not,' she replied.

Norma watched a crow wing over the pond, and then fly off in the direction of FC. For some reason she thought it looked extremely sinister, though she couldn't have said why. It was only an ordinary crow.

'What were *you* trying to run away from?' she asked Lynsey.

Lynsey's face sort of twisted and crumpled in on itself to

become the face of a little girl. A little girl scared out of her wits. 'Whatever lies in wait for me over there, in France.'

Norma had guessed it was that. 'You could tell M you've changed your mind.' M was the symbol by which Major-General Gilchrist was known in SOE. As M he was director of operations and training.

'I can't; it would be letting the side down. I agreed to go, and so I must.'

Norma patted her horse's neck. It was a chestnut mare, a fine animal. She didn't know what to say in reply to that, so said nothing.

'I'm twenty-three you know. Not very old is it?'

Norma shook her head.

'Normally I'd have an entire life ahead of me. A husband, babies, that sort of thing.'

'You still can,' Norma protested.

Lynsey gave Norma a sad, knowing smile. As if she was in on some secret Norma wasn't. Wheeling her horse round she started back towards the riding stable, and Norma followed.

Somewhere close by, perched in a tree probably, a crow cawed, and it seemed to Norma that the caw had a mocking quality to it. The same sinister-looking crow she wondered?

The crow cawed mockingly again, causing Norma to break out in gooseflesh.

It was raining, a fine drizzle that would soon turn into something nastier if the colour of the sky was anything to go by. The four of them came out the barrack room together. Norma and Lynsey, Pam and Violette. There were two cars waiting for them, each with a FANY-ATS driver at the wheel. One car for Norma and Pam, the other for Lynsey and Violette. Norma and Pam were off to F Section to begin their duties there; Lynsey and Violette to an establishment where they would receive field training.

Norma stowed her suitcase in the boot, then helped Pam with hers. The moment of parting had arrived. Goodbyes had already been said to Bombardier Gutteridge and others at FC.

Lynsey threw her arms round Norma, hugging her tightly. When the two girls pulled slightly apart, still holding onto each other, they both had tears in their eyes.

'I don't know if I'll see you again before I go "over by". If not, good luck,' Lynsey whispered.

'And you, all the luck in the world.'

Norma kissed Lynsey on the cheek, and Lynsey did the same to her. A few feet away Pam and Violette were entangled in an emotional embrace.

The drizzle had got heavier. Over to the east there was a jagged flash of lightning.

'Take care,' Norma whispered.

Lynsey hugged Norma again, then abruptly released her friend.

Norma got into her car, and a couple of seconds later was joined by Pam. Their car started off with the other car following behind. They stayed like that till they reached the main road where Norma and Pam's car turned left, Lynsey and Violette's right.

Norma and Pam watched the other car through the rear window as it gradually receded into the distance. Finally they went round a bend and the other car was lost to view, and they to it.

Norma closed her eyes and offered a brief prayer asking God to keep Lynsey and Violette safe.

They drew into the grounds of an imposing country house that had a hutted encampment off to one side. They would shortly learn that the house was called Grendon Underwood and that the hutted encampment was the wireless station.

There was a FANY standing on the steps leading up to the house's front door. Norma recognised the figure – it was Helen Rolfe who'd left FC shortly after she and Lynsey had arrived there.

The car stopped, and Norma and Pam got out. Norma went straight to Helen who shook her by the hand.

'I thought you'd like a friendly face to meet you. Welcome to F Section,' Helen said.

The modified twin-engined Whitley bomber belonged to 138 Squadron and had taken off from Newmarket racecourse with two passengers aboard, one of whom was Lynsey Dereham.

Lynsey sat staring in fascination at the aircraft's modification which was a hole that had been fitted to its floor. When she was given the signal she was going to have to jump through that hole. A Whitley had no side-doors; the hole was a parachutist's quick exit point.

The aircraft would be flying at five hundred feet when she left it. Her parachute would be opened automatically by static line, and, providing it was packed properly – and she'd packed it herself earlier – would be opened fully for only a few seconds before she hit the ground. The landing shock would be roughly the same as if she'd jumped from a first-floor window. The entire procedure, from jumping out the hole to picking herself up off the ground would take a quarter of a minute. As quick as that.

She held her breath and counted fifteen seconds. It was no time at all. But time enough to go from being very much alive to very, very dead if something did go wrong, which it occasionally did. They hadn't kept that from her. It occasionally did.

She could have jumped from a greater height of course, but that would only have produced risks of a different nature. It was a case of the devil and the deep blue sea.

She fumbled for her cigarettes, then wondered if it was allowed. No one had said.

'Go ahead, it's permitted,' her companion said in perfect French, the first time he'd spoken.

En route to the plane the pilot had informed her that there would be another 'joe' making the journey with her, but that she'd be jumping before him. His destination was further inland.

She'd already been in the Whitley and selected a spot for herself when a car had driven alongside and he'd got out. The moment he was aboard, the Whitley had started its engines, then began getting ready for take-off. He had remained silent throughout the journey, not even saying hello, so she had thought he had wanted it that way.

She offered the packet to him. 'You?'

He shuffled over and took one. When his lighter blazed she saw that he had sallow skin and liquid brown eyes. 'Thank you', he said, and sat beside her.

He'd spoken again in French. Was he French or English? She couldn't tell. She puffed on her cigarette and noted that her

177

hand was trembling ever so slightly. She was aware that he'd also noticed.

'First time in?' he asked.

'Yes.'

'It's my third. DF took me out last month. And now I'm going back in again.' DF was the SOE escape section which every SOE field operative knew about in case he or she had to use it.

She took another drag of her cigarette, drawing the smoke deep down into her lungs. 'I'm Marie Thérèse,' she said on the exhale.

'I'm Gabriel.'

She wondered what his real name was. Marie Thérèse was her code name, just as Gabriel would be his.

'Fresh from Arisaig?' he asked. Arisaig was on the western coast of Scotland a little to the south of Mallaig. That wild and beautiful countryside of South Morar and neighbouring Moidart was ideal for field training, and had been selected by M himself for that very reason.

'I came down by train last night,' she acknowledged. Her eyes strayed back to the hole in the aircraft floor. How long to go now? Not too long she didn't think. A cold shiver ran up her spine. 'Can I ask you something?' she queried softly.

He knew what it was going to be. 'Go ahead.'

'What's it really like down there?'

'You want the truth?'

'Yes.'

He sighed. 'Pretty scary at times. In fact, pretty scary a lot of the time. But what you mustn't ever do is let fear get the upper hand. To let it do so is inevitably fatal.' He paused, and his eyes took on a faraway look. 'The trick is to keep a cool head and, no matter what, never panic. Fear and panic, those are the enemy just as much as the Germans. Conquer them and you stand a fair chance of keeping out of the hands of the latter.'

'I'll remember what you've just said. Thank you.'

The faraway look faded from his eyes, and he brought his gaze to bear on her. 'Are you being met?'

'Yes, by members of the Circuit I'm joining. I'm a replacement WT operator; they lost their previous one the week before last.'

178

He nodded. 'It's good you're being met, particularly as it's your first time in.'

The co-pilot appeared from up front. 'Three minutes to drop point. You'll get a red on the minute, green for go,' he said to Lynsey. Her answer to that was a weak smile. She waited till the co-pilot had disappeared back up front before turning again to Gabriel.

'Will you do me a favour? Will you stand behind me and give me a push if I freeze?'

She'd gone very pale, the colour of curdled milk. She looked so young and vulnerable, and fragile. How could they ask a girl like this to jump into enemy-occupied territory? And yet they did ask because they had to, and the girls did jump. It was a rotten war. 'I'll stand behind you,' he agreed.

The red light winked on and they both came to their feet. She crossed to the hole, hooked up – her parachute would be activated by static line – then stood on the hole's rim. There was nothing to be seen below, only darkness.

'*Bonne chance*, Marie Thérèse,' he whispered, and a moment later the red light winked out and the green on.

His mouth stretched into a thin slash of a smile when she was gone. He hadn't had to push her; he was glad about that.

Norma glanced at the clock on the wall. Lynsey was now two minutes late in coming through for her first contact with Grendon Underwood.

The room she was in was long and bare. The transmitter-receivers and Morse keys were set on benches, the girls who operated them seated on swivel chairs. The slogan *Remember the Enemy is Listening* dominated one wall.

M was present, talking to Helen Rolfe. Then he walked over to Norma, glancing at the wall-clock. Lynsey was now three minutes overdue. The first contact was always the most nerve-wracking one; for all they knew Lynsey could already be dead and buried, not having survived the parachute jump.

M thought of Frère Jacques, the leader of Penelope Circuit which Lynsey had been sent in to join. Nothing but trouble that man; at times it seemed as though he had every single bad trait of the French race. The only Frenchman he knew who was more overbearing was De Gaulle himself. But despite his faults Frère

Jacques *was* good; he excelled at both organisation and sabotage. But was incredibly overbearing and bumptious with it.

'Would you like a cup of tea? I can have one brought to you,' M said to Norma.

She shook her head. 'After Marie Thérèse comes through, yes, but not till then. To be honest, I don't think I could swallow it.'

He placed a comforting hand on her shoulder, and glanced again at the wall-clock. Lynsey was now five minutes overdue.

If she was dead that still meant Frère Jacques would have the plastic explosive that had gone in with her. It was explosive the Penelope Circuit desperately needed. And he'd have the S-phone he'd requested. The S-phone being a device that enabled a person on the ground to make a verbal contact with an aircraft in the immediate vicinity. It was a fairly new invention, and one that was bound to prove extremely helpful.

The minutes ticked slowly, agonisingly by. Nine, ten, eleven, twelve. M's expression was grim; Norma's was filled with despair.

And then suddenly Norma's earphones were beeping with the incoming signal they'd been waiting for. Marie Thérèse calling, Marie Thérèse calling.

Norma's hand flashed to the sender key. Home base receiving, Home base receiving.

Snatching up a pencil she began hurriedly writing down the message Marie Thérèse was sending on behalf of Penelope Circuit.

When the incoming message was over Norma sent the outgoing one. And then that was it, their first exchange was completed.

Norma took off her earphones to discover that M had already left with the incoming message for the decoding room. She joined him there.

'How did Marie Thérèse seem?' M asked Norma.

'Nervous as all get out. Her sending wasn't a patch on what she's capable of. But then I suppose there's a big difference between doing it in Fawley Court and German-occupied France.'

'Now you know why we trained you and the others as

twosomes. Each knows his or her partner's 'fist' so well it makes life a great deal easier all round.'

He studied the decrypt that the decoder handed him. It was full of sending mistakes, but still intelligible.

'Good,' he said, and walked away.

Norma left the wireless station for the main house where she'd now have that cup of tea. What a fifteen minutes that had been, waiting for Lynsey to come through. Each minute had felt like a year in length.

Before tea though, she'd go and root out Pam, to tell her Lynsey was all right and operational. The following week it was going to be Violette's turn to go 'over by'. She was joining Autogiro Circuit.

Lynsey lay on her bed staring up at the fly-blown ceiling. She'd been with Penelope a fortnight now and already she'd come to loathe and detest that little pipsqueak Frère Jacques. He was a horrible man who stank of unwashed armpits. Just to be near him made her want to throw up. She doubted he'd had a bath that year. Or the previous year come to that.

But it wasn't merely his lack of personal hygiene, it was his manner. His air of superiority. His sheer bloody arrogance. The Germans had a reputation for arrogance but that Frenchman beat them by a mile.

She stopped thinking to listen to the approaching sound of jackboots. Tramp, tramp, tramp, a dozen or so soldiers, she judged.

Her heart leapt into her mouth when, at a barked command, the marching ceased directly beneath her window. *They'd come for her, they'd found out who she was and where she was and come for her!*

Don't let fear get the upper hand, don't panic! she commanded herself, remember Gabriel's advice. She'd almost certainly be shot if she tried to make a bolt for it, and it might just *not* be her they were after.

Her groping hand sought and found the phial she'd been given in Arisaig. She looked back up at the ceiling as she placed it between her teeth. If it was her they were after, and they came breaking into her room, a corpse was all they'd find. Death would have been instantaneous, with no pain. The people in Arisaig had assured her of that.

181

Somewhere nearby a door crashed shut, followed by another barked command from the officer in charge. The detachment was continuing on its way.

Lynsey didn't know why the soldiers had stopped where they had, but it hadn't been for her. There were tears in her eyes as she removed the phial from between her teeth.

Lynsey stared coldly at Frère Jacques, who stood with the inevitable cigarette dangling from his lower lip. With his cigarette, beret and bright red neckerchief he was like something out of a comic opera, except there was nothing comic about the business he and the rest of those present were involved in. She wouldn't have believed it possible, but he stank even worse than usual.

'No, I will not transmit from there again,' she said.

His eyes slitted meanly. 'You will do as I tell you.'

'We've used that house twice running. It would be stupid to do so again.'

His eyes slitted even more. 'I say it is safe. That's all that need concern you.'

'Like hell. It's my neck that's on the line, not yours.'

He drew himself up to his full height, which wasn't saying much. 'I am leader of Penelope, you will do as I command. As *I*, Frère Jacques, command. Is that clear?'

'You know the rules, we're supposed to change the place of transmission every time ...'

'Those are London's rules,' he interjected dismissively. 'In the field I can change them if I see fit.'

Lynsey continued staring coldly at him. To go back a third time to that house would be sheer lunacy. The German directional finders were bound to have at least a general fix on the area, probably a fix on the street itself. Give them another chance and they'd have the house surrounded, with herself inside. A rat in a trap. 'No, and that's final,' she said.

Several of the others present were smirking. Frère Jacques wasn't exactly well loved by them. It was amusing to see the Englishwoman defying him.

Frère Jacques scowled. He would have his way with this, even if it meant using force on the bitch. The Germans in that section had been heavily reinforced and were now everywhere, like summer flies round a pile of *merde*. He was at his wit's end trying to find new safe premises, but wasn't going to explain that to Marie Thérèse. A strong leader didn't need to explain. To explain was a weakness, and he was strong, not weak. He puffed out his chest, and stalked over to her.

He was so quick she never even saw it coming. She yelled in fright and pain as he smacked the side of her face. As she staggered backwards he leapt after her and hit her again.

She went completely still when the knife point pricked her throat. 'You transmit in half an hour. And from where I have said. Understand?'

The stink of him in her nostrils was unbelievably vile. 'If you're so convinced that house is safe to be used again then you come with me.'

He gave a Gallic shrug. 'If you want.'

The knife vanished, and he swaggered across to where a jug of wine stood on a table. He poured himself a large tumblerful which he drank straight off.

'We go now,' he said.

She decided to tell Norma she wanted out, and as soon as possible. The dangers were horrendous enough without having to work for a lunatic such as Frère Jacques. DF would get her away, just as it had done Gabriel.

She followed Frère Jacques out of the room.

Norma was busily writing down the incoming message when the Morse coming through on her earphones suddenly changed to a continuous buzz. Nothing like this had ever happened before. Her hand went to the sender key.

Calling Marie Thérèse, calling Marie Thérèse.

The buzzing ceased abruptly, followed by an eerie silence.

Calling Marie Thérèse, calling Marie Thérèse.

There was no answer.

'Let's take a walk Norma,' M said.

She knew from his face what it was all about. Six days had passed since they'd lost contact with Lynsey, six days during which her set had been manned round the clock, mainly by herself, waiting for contact to be re-established. Praying for it. There had been only silence.

They left the wireless station, and headed out across the grass. It was a beautiful August day, the sun cracking the sky.

'She's dead,' M said simply.

In her heart of hearts Norma had known all along, but it was still a shock to hear it confirmed. 'How?'

'The Gestapo surprised her at her set. They ...' He paused, then added softly. 'Shot her through the back of the head. The buzz you heard was caused by her falling forward onto her Morse key.'

Norma could just picture the scene. Lynsey hunched over her key, and then ... She swallowed hard. 'Was anyone else with her?'

'Frère Jacques. He was killed as well. We finally got word of what had happened from Autogiro Circuit. Josephine's signal came in only fifteen minutes ago.' Josephine was Violette's codename.

'I think you should have some time off, perhaps go home for a few weeks. I can arrange to let you have a car,' M said.

'Yes, I'd like that.'

Norma left for Glasgow early the following morning.

Chapter Eight

Norma chapped the door for the fourth time. Someone was in all right, she could hear whoever it was shuffling about. So why didn't they answer? She didn't have a door key on her, having left it behind when she was last up.

The shuffling was coming slowly nearer. There was a bump, followed by a moan of pain that she recognised as coming from her mother.

'Ma, it's Norma, open up will you!' This time she didn't chap the door but pounded it. What on earth was going on!

Finally the door swung open to reveal Effie swaying weakly. Her hair was down and wet with sweat, as was her forehead, and her eyes had a strange, hard, glassy look about them.

'Oh Ma!' Norma whispered. Then leapt forward to catch her mother as she collapsed to the floor.

'Headache, terrible headache,' Effie croaked feverishly.

Effie was far too heavy for Norma to pick up. She had to drag her through to her parents' bedroom where she put her on the bed.

'Ma it's Norma, can you hear me?'

The glassy eyes tried to focus. 'Norma?'

'Aye, it's me Ma. What's wrong with you?'

'Headache, all last night. Got worse after ... after Lyn and Eileen left for work.'

Norma felt her mother's forehead, it was fiery-hot. Her temperature was clearly way up. She pulled the quilt over Effie, then said she wouldn't be gone more than a minute. She hoped. Well, one of the neighbours in the close had to be in!

As it transpired Alice Henderson, Midge's mum, who lived on the next landing down, was. Hurriedly Norma explained the situation, and asked Alice if she'd telephone the family doctor from the nearest payphone. Alice immediately threw her pinny aside and said she'd run to Bell's the newsagents; they had a phone they'd let her use.

'Mind impress on the doctor that it's an emergency,' Norma shouted after Alice as Alice clattered down the stairs.

She rushed back to Effie who gasped that she wanted water. Effie gulped down a glassful, and asked for another. She gulped that one down too.

Effie was soaked through with perspiration, her clothes ringing. With great difficulty Norma stripped her ma, then got her into a clean nightie. When she'd done that she manoeuvred her between the sheets.

At which point Alice Henderson arrived back to say she'd eventually managed to get through to the doctor, his phone had been continually busy, and that he was on his way. He'd be there shortly.

'Is there anything else I could do to help?' queried Alice.

'Put the kettle on while I sit here with Ma. I could fair use a cup of tea after my drive up from England.'

Norma glanced at her wristwatch, and wondered what time Lyn and Eileen would be home from work. She knew from the correspondence she'd had with Effie that they were putting in longer and longer hours at the armaments factory to help boost production, as was everyone who worked there. As for her da, in her last letter to her Effie had mentioned that he was now in Berwick-upon-Tweed constructing a shore defence system there.

She heard Alice go out of the house, and upstairs. When Alice brought through her cup of tea she also brought several fingers of home-baked shortie. It was good shortie too, but not a patch on Lyn's.

Every few minutes Norma wiped Effie's face down with a towel. Where *was* the doctor she thought, glancing yet again at her watch.

'I'll show him ben,' Alice said when there was a tap on the outside door.

Doctor Dickie was old, out of retirement for the war. He and Norma had never met before.

'Let's see what's what then,' Doctor Dickie said, sitting on the edge of the bed.

'Can you hear me, Mrs McKenzie?' he asked.

Effie's eyes fluttered open. Norma had thought her to be asleep as she hadn't uttered or moaned since being put into the clean nightie.

'Can you speak, woman?'

'Headache, awful headache. Like a vice, you understand? A vice.'

'I understand, Mrs McKenzie.' He put a thermometer into her mouth, and in the meantime took her pulse.

Her temperature was a hundred and three. He put an arm behind her shoulders, then brought her upwards in a semi-sitting position. 'Can you drop your head so that your chin touches your breastbone?' he asked her.

She whimpered when she tried. Her head and chin only moved fractionally. 'Sore, too sore,' she complained. He gently eased her back to the vertical.

His expression was grim; his face lined with concern when he turned to Norma. 'One thing's for certain. I'm not moving your mother in her present condition. She's an extremely ill woman.'

'What's wrong with her, doctor?'

Dickie produced an opthalmascope which he shone first in Effie's right eye, then her left. He snapped the light off again. 'It could be either of several things. I'm not really sure which.'

'Then can you get someone who would know?'

He stared at her in surprise, for this was a slum area and he knew nothing at all about her inheritance. 'You mean a specialist? They cost a great deal of money, Miss McKenzie.'

Effie gave a hollow groan, and her eyes rolled upwards. She'd slipped into unconsciousness.

'It doesn't matter what the specialist costs. Get him,' Norma said with authority.

'With all due respect, Miss McKenzie. Can you afford him? If I ask who I have in mind to come to a tenement in Bridgeton he's going to laugh in my face.'

She'd had a cheque book for some time. It had been Lynsey's idea. 'It's an absolute must, darling!' She took it out now. 'The specialist's name?' she queried.

'Rodney Creighton. He's the top neurologist in Glasgow.'

She wrote out a cheque, then tore it from the book and handed it to Dickie. 'Tell him if it costs more than that, all he has to do is say. But I want him here as soon as it is humanly possible.'

Dickie stared at the cheque in astonishment. A cheque for a hundred pounds written out by a Bridgeton lassie. Wonders never ceased.

'And don't worry about your own time, that'll be amply rewarded,' Norma added.

Dickie slipped the cheque into his wallet. 'I'll get onto Creighton right away. In the meantime continue doing as you have been with that towel.'

'Can I change her again? This nightie is already soaked through.'

'By all means. If she comes round and asks for water give her some, as much as she wants.' He rose. 'I'll be as quick as I can.'

'Expense is no object. If this Creighton needs to bring anything with him, tell him to do so.'

'I will, Miss McKenzie,' Dickie replied, and hurried from the bedroom. Alice Henderson went with him to show him out.

'Would you like me to help you change Effie?' Alice asked on her return.

'Please.' Norma went to look out another nightie.

Rodney Creighton was younger than Norma had expected – in his early forties she judged. He wore a pin-striped suit and black Homburg, and had a very grave manner about him. Those who knew him well said he had no sense of humour whatever.

He handed Norma his Homburg (a bit pompous that, she thought, he could have just laid it down), and sat beside Effie, who hadn't regained consciousness. His examination, using various instruments and testing devices, was thorough.

'You were quite correct not to move her, doctor,' he said to Dickie when the examination was over.

'Is it meningitis?'

'No, encephalitis. The symptoms are very similar.'

Norma had never heard of encephalitis. 'What is it?' she queried.

'Infection of the brain caused by a virus. It was first noted in Vienna in 1916, and there was an epidemic of it in London in 1918. It's relatively uncommon today,' Creighton replied.

'Can you cure it?'

'Mrs McKenzie has a most severe case of encephalitis, a most severe case indeed. In my opinion there's only one thing can pull her through and that's a drug called M&B. It's a drug that's fairly new and, what with the war on, extremely difficult to come by.'

'You're saying it's expensive?'

Creighton's expression never wavered. 'Yes. But also difficult to come by.'

'Can you get some?'

He opened his black bag and extracted a sealed bottle. 'From Doctor Dickie's account of the patient's symptoms I realised that M&B might be needed, and so, being in the fortunate position of already having some on the premises, I took the precaution of bringing it along.'

He talked like a textbook, Norma thought. His words were all neutral, without emphasis. It was a little creepy to hear.

'Could you assist please, doctor,' he said to Dickie, taking a metal container from his black bag. He opened the container to reveal a hypodermic syringe.

Doctor Dickie rolled up Effie's right sleeve as Creighton filled the syringe with a dose of M&B. Dickie held Effie's upper arm as Creighton first swabbed it with cotton wool and spirit, then slid in the needle.

'You said only M&B could pull my mother through. Does that mean without it she'd have died?' Norma asked.

Creighton fixed Norma with an unwavering stare. 'Almost certainly. Encephalitis is, when the infection is as severe as your mother's, a killer. I doubt she'd have lasted the night.'

Norma shuddered to hear that. Thank God she'd come home when she had. 'And now she'll be all right?'

'In medicine nothing can be taken for granted. Let's just say she now has a real fighting chance, and that one can be optimistic about a recovery. I shall return later to administer another injection, by which time we should hopefully have signs of improvement.'

Creighton repacked his black bag, then Norma saw him and Doctor Dickie to the front door. Creighton told Norma to expect him around 10pm.

When the doctor and specialist had disappeared down the stairs, Norma went back to her ma. Alice Henderson had gone upstairs before Dickie and Creighton had arrived, to make Leslie and Katy's tea, but had said that if Norma wanted her again all Norma had to do was knock and she'd come running.

Norma wasn't sure whether it was her imagination or not but Effie seemed less fevered than she had been. Was the injection already taking effect? She certainly hoped so.

It wasn't long after that the outside door opened and Norma heard the voices of Lyn and Eileen, the two of them chaffing away to each other about an incident at work.

'Ma, where are you? I'm starving hungry!' Eileen called out from the kitchen. She gaped when Norma appeared in the hall. 'When did you get back?' she queried, then flew at Norma to give her a big hug.

Lyn appeared from the living room, if anything looking even more attractive and curvaceous than the last time Norma had seen her. 'I should have guessed when I saw that army car parked in the street,' she said. She and Eileen were still in their factory overalls.

'Ma's badly ill. I've had a specialist here,' Norma announced.

'What are you havering about?' Lyn demanded with a frown.

Norma then recounted all that had happened, and the three of them went through to their parents' bedroom.

'She mentioned at breakfast that a headache had kept her awake for most of last night, but I never dreamt it was anything more than just that,' said Eileen.

'Do you think we should contact Da?' Lyn asked Norma. 'Can we?'

'There's a telephone in the house where he's billeted, but he's rarely there before nine or ten in the evening,' Lyn replied.

'We'll wait till later then, and see what we think,' Norma said.

The three of them looked down at Effie who was still sweating profusely, but otherwise seemed peaceful enough.

'You never know the minute till the minute after,' Eileen said. A prophetic statement regarding her own circumstances as she was shortly to discover.

A quarter of an hour later Effie started to scream.

Eileen opened the door to Creighton who hurried past her into Effie's bedroom. Effie was in a terrible state, thrashing this way and that; moaning like a stricken animal one minute, screaming in a demented fashion the next.

Creighton felt her boiling forehead, then took her pulse. Effie wasn't unconscious anymore, neither was she properly awake. She was somewhere in between: half unconscious, half awake.

'Damn!' Creighton swore softly.

'The M&B isn't working?' Norma prompted.

'No, it's not that. I'm afraid she's allergic to the drug. What we're witnessing here is her reaction against it.' He looked Norma straight in the eyes. 'It does happen occasionally, and can't be foreseen. I'm sorry.'

When Norma spoke next her voice was quavering. It was the question she'd been dreading having to ask. 'You're saying she's going to die after all?'

'I'm afraid so. Between the encephalitis and her allergy to M&B death is ...' he broke off, and shrugged.

'Surely there's something can be done? Something else you can give her?' Eileen urged frantically.

'I'm afraid not, Miss McKenzie. M&B was her only hope. All we can do now is wait for the end.'

Lyn sobbed, and stuffed a balled fist into her mouth. She just couldn't imagine Ma dying. Ma, like Da, had been there forever. And should continue to be so.

'She'll pass into a coma very soon and when the time comes she'll just sort of drift off,' said Creighton.

Effie screamed again, the loudest scream. Lyn covered her ears.

'I'll come first thing in the morning ...'

'Why bother if she'll be dead by then,' Eileen interjected tartly.

Creighton looked at Norma. 'I can send Doctor Dickie if you prefer. But a death certificate will have to be signed.'

'You come, Mr Creighton. Despite what's happened I know you did your best. Her being allergic to M&B was ...' Norma trailed off.

'Thank you.'

Effie jerked all over, then jerked again. Her body and limbs seemed to relax.

'That's her starting to go into a coma. Within a few minutes it'll be as though she's just fallen asleep.'

'I must know, could *anyone* have done anything for her?' Eileen asked bluntly.

'No, I assure you. M&B was her only known lifeline. I give you my solemn word on that.'

Eileen gave a reluctant nod; she believed him. He reeked of sincerity.

Norma saw him out.

It was just as Creighton had said, Effie appeared to be in a deep sleep. Even the sweating had stopped. Apart from being pale she looked quite normal. Except that she was at death's door, about to pass through.

Norma glanced at her wristwatch to see that Eileen had been gone more than thirty minutes now. Was she having trouble getting through to Da? Or was Da still not back at his billet and Eileen was hanging on at the phone box?

Lyn came into the bedroom. She'd changed into her pyjamas and a pink candlewick dressing gown. Her face was puffed from crying. 'I hope Da gets here before . . . before . . .' She broke off, unable to say it. The tears started flowing again.

Da was going to take this hard, Norma thought. He and Ma had been a proper couple, as one. They would all take it hard of course, but Da most of all. 'I hope and pray he gets here in time too,' Norma replied.

Norma brought her attention back to bear on Effie. How she was going to miss her ma. It was a terrible blow, particularly coming so soon as it did after Lynsey.

And then Eileen was back with them. 'I finally spoke to Da. He says you're not to bother going for him in your car, Norma. He's going to come on his motorbike, he says he'll make better time if he leaves straightaway on that.'

Norma relaxed a little, she'd been all keyed up ready to drive to Berwick-upon-Tweed to pick up Brian and bring him back here. But he was probably right about making better time on his motorbike.

'He broke down and started to cry. I've never heard Da cry before,' Eileen added.

Neither had Norma. All the years of her life she'd never known her da cry. Effie often, but never her da.

Eileen made a pot of tea which no one drank. Then she too

got changed into pyjamas and dressing gown. Not that any of them intended sleeping, but it was more comfortable like that.

They hadn't intended to sleep, but as the hours passed the long hard day at the armaments factory caught up with Lyn and Eileen. Lyn was the first to drop off. Sitting in the living room staring off into space she was awake one moment, snoring the next. Eileen put a travelling rug over her. A little later she too had dozed off, leaving Norma alone with Ma.

It was that time in the early hours of the morning when everything is hushed and still, Norma was dog tired, and thinking that Brian should be arriving at any time now, when Lynsey appeared in the bedroom to stare sorrowfully at her.

She stared back, not frightened or alarmed in the least. Lynsey had come to help, she somehow knew that to be so.

'I lost you, Lynsey, I don't want to lose Ma too,' Norma whispered. Lynsey's still sorrowful stare transferred itself to Effie.

'A life for a life. Hers for yours. I beg it,' Norma pleaded, again in a whisper.

Lynsey walked closer. There was a faint luminous glow surrounding her. And every so often she sort of shimmered, as if it was only an act of supreme willpower that was keeping her there.

Lynsey looked back at Norma, and the hint of a smile touched the corners of her mouth. 'Your hands,' she mouthed.

Norma held her hands out in front of her. 'What about them?'

Lynsey's smile widened a fraction, and as it did a strange tingling invaded Norma's hands. She later described it as like a pins and needles sensation, only pleasant rather than painful.

'On your mother, lay them on your mother.'

Norma did, placing her hands on the exposed flesh between the neck and breasts. The tingling intensified, and it was as though the energy which was causing the tingling flowed from her into Effie.

And then, as suddenly as she'd appeared, Lynsey was gone. So too was the tingling. Everything was back to normal.

Norma lifted her hands off Effie and stared at them. Had she momentarily nodded off to dream what had happened? What had *seemed* to happen? She shook her head, then took a deep breath. She'd either been dreaming or hallucinating, that had to be the case.

She snapped out of her reverie when she heard the sound of boots on the outside landing, followed by the grate of a key going into the lock.

She met Brian in the hall. 'Is she . . .?'

'Ma's still with us.'

Eileen appeared, wiping the sleep from her eyes. 'What time is it? she asked. Norma told her as Brian brushed passed on into the bedroom. Lyn also appeared, she too had been woken up by her da's arrival.

The three sisters went into their parents' bedroom to find Brian sitting beside Effie gazing down at her. Norma noticed right away that Effie's colour had improved, and that her breathing had deepened.

Effie sighed, and then her eyes opened. 'Hello dear, what are you doing here? This is a pleasant surprise.'

With the exception of Norma everyone else was totally stunned to hear Effie speak as she just had, at the transformation in her. Effie glanced across at Norma. 'I feel awfully weak, but that terrible headache's better. Completely gone.'

Norma didn't need a doctor to tell her that Effie had recovered, was going to live. She looked down at her hands – it hadn't been a dream or hallucination after all. It had actually happened.

When she looked up again her da was embracing her ma. It was a sight that brought a lump to her throat so big it threatened to choke her.

She'd expected Creighton to pooh-pooh her story, but he didn't. He listened intently, occasionally nodding his head in affirmation as she recounted what had happened. When she finished there was a silence between them.

'Can I see your hands?' he asked.

She lifted them up and he took them in his own. 'Has anything like this ever occurred before?'

'No.'

'Perhaps . . . perhaps you have healing hands, the hands of a healer.' He stared her straight in the eyes. 'That's not so fantastic as it might at first seem. It's well-documented that some people have this ability to cure by merely placing their hands on an inflicted or diseased person.'

'You believe that?' she queried.

'Oh yes. We've never been able to pin-point a scientific reason why it should be so, but it is. I myself met just such a person in India, a holy man, who could cure by the laying on of hands. I was a sceptic up until then, but not after I'd witnessed him do what he did.'

'And Lynsey?'

Creighton's brow furrowed into a frown. 'It could be that your healing ability – and there can be no other reason that I can think of why your mother has recovered when by all the laws of medicine she should be dead by now – is latent and Lynsey was a device, or catalyst, used by your subconscious to bring that ability to the surface.'

'I thought myself it was more of a miracle.'

'And what's a miracle? Life, death, healing hands, they're all miracles.'

He rose, and reached for his Homburg. 'I'll tell you this, I'm not an envious man, but if you do have this ability within you – which I'm sure you must – then I envy you it. Very much so.' He gave her a sudden smile, something he did rarely. 'It's good for us physicians to feel humility from time to time. At this moment I feel extremely humble indeed.'

Norma went out onto the landing with him. 'Your mother's illness has taken a lot out of her. See that for a while to come she gets plenty of rest; she's not to over-exert herself in any way,' Creighton said, fumbling in an inside pocket.

'I understand.'

He took out a diary-cum-notebook, from which he extracted a piece of paper. This he gave to her. 'You must have that back. I couldn't possibly accept it in the circumstances.'

It was her cheque for a hundred pounds. 'No I...'

'And I insist,' he said with finality.

He made a small, old-fashioned bow, then placed his Homburg on his head. 'I can't tell you how pleased I am about your mother. And it's an honour to have met you Miss McKenzie.'

She liked him, Norma decided as he went down the stairs. She hadn't up until then, but she did now. Who'd have thought he'd

195

believe in healing hands? She certainly wouldn't. Which only proved the saying that you couldn't always judge a book by its cover.

She held her hands up in front of her, remembering the tingling sensation, and the energy that had caused it flowing from her into her mother.

'Thank you Lynsey,' she whispered. Then, in a reverential tone. 'And thank you God.'

She went back inside, closing the door behind her.

By the beginning of the following week Effie was up and about, though still taking it easy. To aid her recuperation Norma took her for a drive in the car to Largs, and the following day to Helensburgh. The third drive was a surprise; she drove Effie to Berwick-upon-Tweed where they met up with Brian, the three of them managing to have dinner in a fish restaurant there. Effie pronounced the trip to Berwick-upon-Tweed as the best treat of all.

Arriving home from Berwick-upon-Tweed Norma and Effie found that the postie had left a letter addressed to Eileen in his afternoon delivery. Effie recognised the writing as Charlie's and placed the letter on the mantelpiece to await Eileen's return from work.

Norma was preparing tea when her sisters came in from the factory. 'There's a letter from Charlie on the mantelpiece for you Eileen!' Effie cried out from her bedroom where, at Norma's insistence, she was having a wee lie down before tea.

Eileen ran to the mantelpiece and snatched up Charlie's letter. Impatiently she tore it open. A handful of seconds later she squealed with joy.

'What is it?' Lyn demanded.

'Charlie's got some leave. He'll get into the Central Station late tonight!' This was the first leave Charlie had been given since going south.

Lyn beamed, that was good news. 'Och I'm awful pleased,' she said.

Norma came into the living room. 'What's up?' An ecstatic Eileen repeated the news. Effie joined them, knowing something was going on and not wanting to be out of it.

'That's tremendous,' she said when she heard what the commotion was all about.

A fire was hurriedly laid so that Eileen could have a bath, and while the water was heating she ransacked her wardrobe trying to decide what to wear. Finally she selected a dress that she herself wasn't daft about but which was a great favourite of Charlie's. She was dressing for her man after all, not herself.

Lyn contributed a pair of silk stockings she'd been keeping for a special occasion (since the start of the war silk stockings had been murder to come by) and Norma lent Eileen a bottle of perfume given to her by Jeremy Dereham. The perfume was French, and had cost Jeremy a small fortune. It smelled heavenly.

Norma went into the bathroom while Eileen was in the tub. 'This is only a suggestion, but as Charlie is getting in pretty late would you like me to drive you to the station and the pair of you back? If you don't want a third party present I'd quite understand.'

'That's a marvellous idea, Norma. Thanks, I'll take you up on it.'

As Norma left Eileen her sister started to sing.

'Ten minutes late,' said Eileen.

'There's a war on you know, everything doesn't just run like clockwork as it used to,' Norma replied.

Eileen had worked herself up into a lather of impatience. She couldn't wait to see Charlie again. To touch him, to be kissed by him, to be safe and warm in his arms. Several times during the journey from Cubie Street she'd shivered all over in anticipation.

Norma glanced up at the arrivals board, but there was no indication as to how much longer the train was going to be. And then the tannoy crackled into life.

'Due to a derailment at Lockerbie . . .'

Eileen's expression changed to one of panic. She clutched Norma by the arm, squeezing the arm so hard Norma grimaced with pain. They looked at one another when the brief message was over. There had been a derailment at Lockerbie and because of this the line from London was blocked. Further news would be relayed as it came through.

'I must know if Charlie's train was involved. I must, and right away,' Eileen said, her voice tight with fear.

'We'll find someone, come on,' Norma replied.

A sign guided them to the station master's office. They knocked, and a voice bid them enter. They discovered the station master chalking a message on a blackboard – a message about the derailment. Norma explained why they'd come.

The station master looked at them from behind thick pebble glasses. He was about to reply when a phone, one of several, rang. 'Excuse me,' he muttered, picking up the receiver. A man appeared behind Norma and Eileen to make the same inquiries that they had. The station master hung up.

'What train was your husband on again, hen?' he asked Eileen. She told him.

'I'm afraid that is one of those involved in the derailment. That phone call was from Lockerbie naming the trains.'

'Is anyone hurt?' Norma demanded.

'I've no idea. I haven't been informed yet.'

'There's more than one train involved you say?' the man behind Norma and Eileen queried.

'Aye, the other was a goods.'

'When will you know more about what's happened?' Norma asked.

'Haven't the foggiest, hen. But I promise you this, if you hang around then when I know you will.' He returned to the blackboard to finish writing his message.

As Norma, Eileen and the man who'd come in behind them left the station master's office they passed a number of others heading where they'd just been.

Eileen had gone strangely quiet, and seemed to have some-how shrunk in on herself. 'Let's go to the buffet and wait there,' Norma suggested. Eileen didn't reply, but just followed her sister to the opposite side of the station where the buffet was situated.

They found a table no bother. 'What will I get you?' Norma asked. She had to repeat the question when Eileen didn't reply.

'Tea, coffee, whatever, it doesn't matter,' Eileen said.

Norma bought two teas; she would have bought a couple of drams as well as she thought they could both use a drink. But it was after hours and the bar was shut.

'Norma, I'm awful scared. Really I am,' Eileen said when Norma was sat beside her.

'I know, but the chances are he's fine. He might even have joined another train beyond the blockage and could be once more on his way.'

Eileen brightened fractionally. 'Do you really think so?'

'I think we should think positively until we find out otherwise.'

Norma glanced at a wall-clock. It was now twenty-five minutes past the time that Charlie's train had been due to arrive.

Every so often the station master repeated his original message over the tannoy, adding that there was still no further news. At half past midnight he used the tannoy to ask those waiting for word about the derailment to assemble in front of his office. About two dozen anxious folk gathered there.

'I've just had a phone call to say the line will definitely not be cleared tonight, and will probably not be until later on tomorrow morning. I suggest therefore that you all go home and come back again sometime then.'

'So it's a serious derailment,' a woman said.

'Must be if it's going to take them that long to clear it,' the station master conceded.

'Are there any casualties?' a man asked.

'I believe there are a few. But I have no idea as to how many or who they are.'

'Is there nothing more you can tell us?' Norma queried.

'I swear to you hen I've relayed everything that I've been told. I'm not holding anything back.'

'Is Lockerbie?' a middle-aged woman asked.

'I don't think they're deliberately doing so, I just think they're busy.'

That sounded ominous to Norma, but she didn't say so to Eileen.

There were a few more questions which the station master answered; then the crowd broke up to head for home.

As they dispersed the station master went into his office and slumped down in an old dilapidated leather armchair he kept there. He'd been over twenty-five years in the railways and knew only too well that in railway matters of this kind no news was bad news. He feared the worst about the derailment at Lockerbie.

The first thing Eileen did when she got up the next morning was turn on the wireless to see if there was anything about the derailment on the early news. There wasn't. Nor was there anything in the paper when it was delivered.

'Right then, let's be on our way,' Norma said when she judged it was time for them to go. She was driving Eileen back in again to the Central Station having said she would do so the night before.

Eileen opened the outside door to discover a policeman with fist raised just about to chap. Her heart plummeted at the sight of him.

'I'm looking for Mrs Charles Marshall,' he stated.

'You'd better come away through,' Eileen replied, and led him ben.

On reaching the living room the policeman took up a position in front of the fireplace where he stood holding his hat. He coughed, then coughed again. Although he'd done this many times before it never got any easier.

'My Charlie's dead isn't he?' Eileen said, staring straight at the policeman.

'I'm sorry Mrs Marshall, the answer's yes.'

Norma's hand flew to her mouth, Effie made a sort of sighing sound that was really a long release of air.

'I knew, I somehow knew,' said Eileen, her face frozen with shock.

Effie started to rise to go to her youngest. 'It's all right Ma, just sit where you are for the moment,' Eileen said. Effie sat again.

'Do you know anything about this derailment, any of the details?' Eileen asked the policeman, her eyes bright with tears.

'There was a head-on collision between the passenger train carrying your husband and a goods train. The derailment was as a result of the collision.'

'How many died?' asked Eileen.

'Thirty-six that we know of. There are still some bodies feared to be in the wreckage.'

'And other casualties?'

'Over a hundred hospitalised. It was a terrible crash apparently.'

'Was Charlie... Did he...' She bit her lower lip. 'Did he suffer much?'

'According to what I was told he must have died instantly. They all must have in the coach he was in, the coach nearest the engine.'

'He'd have chosen that coach specifically because when the train arrived in at the Central that coach would be nearest the barrier, and me,' Eileen said, the tears now streaming down her cheeks. She whimpered, then turned her back to the policeman. Her shoulders sagged, her body drooped. Up until then her crying had been silent; it wasn't anymore.

Norma got to her first, Effie second. 'Oh my wee lassie,' Effie said, and swept Eileen into her arms. She too was crying.

'Four days, that's all the time we had together as man and wife, four days,' Eileen sobbed.

The policeman let himself out as Effie and Norma were putting Eileen to bed.

The funeral was in Riddrie Park Cemetery within sight of Hogganfield Loch. Eileen hadn't been allowed to see the body – the remains they cried it – as it would have been too distressing for her. She was told it was best she remember Charlie as he'd been and not what was going underground in the coffin.

The minister began in on the final part of the service. Eileen was standing with her parents on one side of her, Norma and Lyn on the other. She was holding Brian's hand as she'd been doing ever since the coffin was lowered into the earth.

Facing the McKenzies across the grave were the Marshalls, Mrs Marshall in a state of collapse and being held upright by her husband who was extremely anguished himself. A knot of relatives stood beside them.

It was a small turn-out, Norma thought. But that was only to be expected with a war on. From what Eileen had told her Charlie had had plenty of pals but there were only a couple of them present. The rest, she assumed, were away with the Armed Forces.

There were a handful of girls from the library where Charlie had worked before going into the army. Several of those were blubbing into hankies.

She glanced sideways at Eileen. How she felt for her sister remembering the sheer purgatory she'd gone through when she'd lost Midge. Midge hadn't died true enough, but the severance had been just as final as if he had. Eileen was now suffering all the agonies she'd suffered then.

She looked further across at Ma. Only the previous week they'd all thought they were going to be burying her. But Effie had recovered and it was Charlie they were burying instead. Poor bugger, poor Eileen.

Effie stared down at the coffin top, thinking of Eileen. At least Eileen was still young. Another lad was bound to come along eventually – not to replace Charlie but rather take the place that had been his. The minister started to sing and she joined in. 'The Lord's my shepherd...'

Eileen didn't sing, she couldn't have sung to save herself. She was recalling the happy times she and Charlie had had together, the days of their courting. And of course those four glorious days and ecstatic nights in the Adelphi Hotel, their honeymoon.

How ironic it was that Charlie had only agreed to marry her believing himself to have a safe billet in Aldershot. Well, the billet might have been safe enough, but the journey home hadn't been. He'd left her a widow after all, if not a teenage one. She was twenty years old.

Charlie was dead, her dear darling Charlie was dead, and as far as she was concerned so too was she. Oh she might be breathing and walking about, but she was stone dead inside where it mattered. If Effie had mentioned her thoughts, and hopes, about there being someone else eventually, she could have told her mother there never would be. Just as Effie and Brian were as one, so too had she and Charlie been. There would never be another man in her life, her heart was forever Charlie's.

Before she'd been a flesh and blood person. Now only a shell remained, an empty hollow shell waiting for her own death when she could rejoin Charlie.

When the singing was over the minister intoned. 'Ashes to ashes...'

Chapter Nine

On her return to Grendon Underwood Norma went straight to the room she shared with Helen Rolfe and Pam Parkinson, something Helen had arranged prior to her and Pam's arrival at F Section, to find Pam, off duty, stretched out on her bed reading a novel.

'So how was Bonnie Scotland?' Pam asked, laying the novel aside and swinging her legs onto the floor.

'I had an eventful time to say the least. My mother nearly died of a brain infection and my brother-in-law did, killed in a train-crash.'

Pam's face fell. 'Oh I am sorry.'

Norma put her suitcase onto her bed, then sat beside it. 'Death seems everywhere these days. It's horrible.'

Pam knew Norma was also thinking of Lynsey. 'Autogiro was penetrated while you were away. We lost three "joes".'

'Violette?' asked Norma in alarm.

'She was lucky. Twigging, literally in the nick of time, that the Gestapo were onto her and about to pick her up, she did a bunk over the Pyrenees. DF took her through the Perpignan and Ceret route. The Spaniards connected with her in their Frontier Zone, taking her from there to Figueras and finally to Barcelona where she is still awaiting transport home to England. We're hoping to take her out by sub at the weekend.'

'If the Gestapo have identified her then she won't, thank God, be sent in again. That's the end of Josephine.'

'You can imagine how relieved she must be, as I am. When she returns she and I will go on leave together. After that it's Fawley Court again and a link-up with a new partner. And I suppose that's what'll be happening to you.'

Norma nodded, that's what she also believed would happen.

'I'm really pleased about Violette. If I don't see her then give her my love when you do.'

'I will,' Pam smiled. 'But listen, I musn't keep you here chatting. You're to get cleaned up and report to DR's office, he wants to see you as soon as possible.'

'And who's DR when he's at home?' This was a new one on Norma.

'There have been changes made while you've been in Glasgow. SOE has been expanding at such a rate of knots that M felt the need to delegate some of his responsibilities. As a result the position of regional controller has been created, to be known by the symbol DR, a position directly below M in the hierarchy. Our DR is called Lieutenant-Colonel Roe and as well as being in charge of F Section he is also in charge of DF, RF, N and T Sections. His office here is the one M used to use.' RF was the Free French, or Gaullist, Section while N and T were Holland and Belgium respectively.

'Does that mean we won't be seeing M around as much as we have been doing?' Norma asked, for she'd become quite fond of Gilchrist, viewing him as a paternal figure.

'I don't expect we'll see that much of him, although I would imagine he will put in an appearance from time to time.'

That disappointed Norma. 'So what's this Roe like?'

'Pleasant enough, and very, very efficient.'

Norma went to have a wash and brush-up. When that was completed she took herself along to what had been M's office.

DR was a medium-sized man with a receding hairline, bushy eyebrows and a thick moustache. He shook Norma by the hand, which surprised her; she hadn't expected that.

'Sit down. Looking forward to getting back to work?' he asked. Waiting to sit himself until she'd done so.

'Yes sir.'

'Bad business about Marie Thérèse, bad business indeed. We recently lost three other agents with Autogiro, but the circuit is still managing to function despite that, though I doubt if for all that much longer.'

'I heard about the three "joes", Pam Parkinson told me. She wanted me to know that Josephine is safe in Spain. Pam and Josephine, Marie Thérèse and myself all trained together at FC.'

At Grendon Underwood it was quite permissable for the

people there to talk 'shop' freely amongst themselves. What was strictly forbidden was to talk about F Section and the SOE in general outside the organisation.

DR came to the point. 'I have a challenge for you. Does that appeal?'

She grinned. 'Yes sir, it does.'

'I want you to work with a new partner. He's a very experienced agent who's already been into France, and out again, a number of times. He's going back there shortly to commit various specialised acts of sabotage for us, after which he'll be setting up a new circuit to replace Autogiro when that inevitably collapses altogether. Have you heard of Arisaig?'

She shook her head. 'No.'

'We have several field training establishments there, one of which will be teaching him the special techniques that will be required for the first part of his mission.'

'May I ask something?'

'Of course.'

'What happened to his original partner, the one he trained with?'

'Cigarette?' DR asked, offering his packet.

'No thanks.'

DR lit up, to give Norma a hard stare through a cloud of blue smoke. 'Did you know Mary Cluff?'

'Only to say hello to in passing.' Mary was another WT operator at Grendon Underwood.

'She was his partner. I say *was* because she suffered a minor heart attack, brought on by the stress of the job two nights ago. She's in hospital now, and going to be perfectly all right. But if she does return to duty it'll be FANY mobile canteens for her from here on – for obvious health reasons she's finished with SOE.'

'And I'm to replace her. So when do I get to meet my other half?'

DR gave a thin smile. 'That's the challenge – you don't. As soon as he's finished at Arisaig we're whipping him back to France. From now until he goes you and he will transmit to each other daily, several times daily if he can manage it. You'll get to know each other's "fists", and develop your transmitting relationship that way.'

It was novel, Norma thought. But a viable proposition. After all there was no reason why they *had* to meet.

'I'll contact Arisaig and organise your first session. Any objections, time being of the essence, if that's later on today?'

'None whatever,' Norma replied.

'Right then, I'll send you word after I've spoken to Arisaig.'

Norma could see she was dismissed. She rose. 'Thank you sir. I'll be waiting to hear from you.'

'His code name's Gabriel. That's all you need know about him,' DR said.

Home base calling, Home base calling.

Gabriel receiving. Gabriel receiving.

Hello.

Prepare to take message.

Abrupt, Norma thought, picking up her pencil. No pleasantries and 'how's your father?' it would seem. The message started to beep at almost unbelievable speed in her earphones. Her pencil flew.

> Now is the winter of our discontent,
> Made glorious Summer by this sun of York
> And all the clouds that lower'd upon our house
> In the deep bosom of the Ocean buried.
> Now are our brows bound with victorious wreaths,
> Our bruised arms hung up for monuments;
> Our stern alarums changed to merry meetings...

Norma lost him there. She doodled round what she'd written down while the rest of the message beeped at bewildering speed in her earphones. She'd never known anyone to transmit so quickly. Bombardier Gutteridge must have loved Gabriel. He must have been a star pupil.

Transmission ceased.

Gulp! – she tapped out slowly.

And then there was a new signal in her ears. One that wasn't Morse and didn't make any sense at all. No sense, but something. What? She listened intently as the jumble continued. Then the penny dropped. Jesus he was clever! If she was right that was.

Are you laughing at me?

Very good. Most wouldn't have understood. It shows you have 'feel'.

206

Right now I feel a bit of a twit. Your message, was it Shakespeare?

Richard the Third.

Was way too fast for me.

How far did you get?

Merry meetings.

Mary would have got all of it.

I'm not Mary. I'm Norma.

I transmitted that quickly because it's something I've had to learn to do in the past due to the conditions I've been transmitting under. It's one of my tricks for continuing survival.

So do I take it you always transmit that quickly when in the field?

No, only when it's necessary. Which it occasionally can be.

I understand.

Hello Norma.

She smiled, there were to be the pleasantries after all. Hello Gabriel.

Shall we try again?

Give me the same message, but slowly. If you start slowly and increase your speed a little day by day then eventually, I hope, I'll be able to cope with you at your fastest.

Right, I'll do that. Are you pretty?

The unexpectedness of his question startled her. Some men think so.

Blonde or brunette?

Why do you want to know?

I want to build up a picture of you in my mind. It'll help with the business in hand.

Baloney! she thought. He was just downright curious. Honey-blonde.

Are you small?

Fairly tall for a woman.

How tall is that?

Six feet six.

She smiled again when the sound of his 'laughter' filled her earphones.

Come on Norma, the truth?

Five nine.

And what colour are your eyes?

Sometimes grey, sometimes green. They change back and forth all the time.

Sounds fascinating. What size bust?

Get lost!

Oh come on?

No! And that's final.

Spoilsport. What are your legs like?

I've got two.

You know what I mean!

Do you want me to stop sending?

(Pause) All right, I'll behave. Are you ready to receive a message?

Ready Gabriel. By the way, what colour are your eyes?

> Now is the winter of our discontent,
> Made glorious Summer by this sun of York ...

Three days later a letter arrived for Norma. When she opened it she discovered it was from Jeremy Dereham. She sat on the edge of her bed to read it.

His regiment was back in England, but only temporarily. He'd been devastated to learn of Lynsey's death from his parents. Did she know what had happened? For his parents certainly didn't. They'd been notified that Lynsey had been killed, and that was all.

He'd tried contacting her at her old address, but she'd gone, nor could (or would) anyone, including FANY HQ give him a forwarding one. All FANY HQ would say was that if he wrote care of them she would get the letter.

If she was in London or in reasonable striking range could they meet? He very much wanted to see her for herself, but also to find out what she knew about Lynsey.

His parents had taken Lynsey's death extremely badly, and this mystery surrounding her death certainly didn't help. If only mater and pater could find out what actually did happen then perhaps that might ease their pain a little. It was terrible for them not knowing how their daughter died after all. If it had been in a car crash – and with her being a driver that seemed the likeliest cause of death – then why the evasion and secrecy?

Damn! Norma swore when she'd finished the letter. The War Office had made a right hash of things. An explanation should have been given of Lynsey's death, even if it wasn't the truth. You just didn't do this sort of thing to people. The fact a war was on was no excuse. Not only was it insensitive in the extreme it was, even worse in her book, downright sloppy.

She would reply to Jeremy, but what to say? She was going to have to talk this over with DR.

She had to wait till the following afternoon to see DR as he'd been away at RF Section. 'Come in!' he called out when she knocked on his office door.

She told him what her problem was, then handed him Jeremy's letter to read for himself.

'So what's Dereham to you?' he asked when he'd finished reading.

'We went out together for a while sir. Then his regiment got posted abroad. That's nearly a year ago now.'

DR shook his head. 'Bad show by the War Office. I'll have a word with M, he'll see to it this doesn't happen again.'

'And what do I tell Jeremy, sir?'

DR had a think about that. 'The car crash is probably the best and most likely tale. Embellish it by saying she was carrying a high-ranking foreign brass hat on hush hush business when the crash occurred, and that it was because of the nature of the man's business that the War Office, being over-diligent and cautious, clammed up on the Derehams. That should do the trick eh?'

'Yes sir.'

'Good. And I . . .' DR stopped in mid-sentence as the thought struck him. Rising, he crossed to a filing cabinet and opened the third drawer down. He extracted a file from inside, returned to his seat, sat again and began leafing through the file.

Norma squinted to make out the name typewritten on the front of the file. The name was Lynsey Dereham. It was her dead friend's file that DR was reading.

'It states here that Miss Dereham spoke perfect French as a result of a succession of French nannies she had as a child and because she spent every summer up until the war at her father's villa in the Dordogne.'

'Yes sir.'

DR looked up at Norma. 'What about the brother?'

209

'You mean what's his French like? I've no idea sir.'

DR's eyes took on a hard, calculating gleam. 'Chances are high that it's as good as his sister's was. After all, they would have shared the nannies and the summers in the Dordogne. What's his physical appearance?'

'Mousy coloured hair, brown eyes...'

DR grunted; that was what he wanted to hear. Jeremy would have been ruled out immediately if he'd been extremely Anglo-Saxon in appearance. 'What's your opinion of him Norma, would he make a good "joe"?'

Her stomach turned over on being asked that. The incidence of mortality amongst "joes" was so incredibly high, and not only in F Section but throughout all the sections. They were said to have a fifty-fifty chance of returning from a mission, but in fact the odds against were now higher than that. And as the war progressed those odds could only increase.

Should she say no? The Derehams had lost a daughter already; it wasn't fair to put their son, and sole remaining off-spring, in jeopardy as well. Then again, being in a fighting regiment he was already in jeopardy. She decided after a few more moments of mind tussling that the only answer she could give was an honest one. 'I think it's possible he might sir. He's a fairly cool person, the sort that's good in an emergency I should imagine.'

That was precisely what DR had been hoping Norma would say. 'Which regiment is he with?'

'The King's Royal Hussars.'

DR made a note of that. He would instigate some inquiries right away. 'Normally I'd get him along to Baker Street but right now we have a bit of a flap there.' DR's expression became grim. 'We suspect a leak, only *suspect* mind you, but until it's either discounted or plugged it would be best for potential agents to stay clear of the place. So I'll tell you what, as he himself suggested that you meet, write and invite him here. Say you'll tell him all you know about his sister's death when you see him.'

'I'll write today sir.'

'Let me know when you have a date for his visit so that I can set up a preliminary testing out session for him.'

'Right sir.'

210

On leaving DR's office Norma went straight to her room where she wrote the letter.

Jeremy Dereham stared at Grendon Underwood, thinking it was a most handsome building. He glanced over at the hutted encampment which was the wireless station to note the various clusters of aerials and antennae pointing skyward. He wondered what went on there. Then Norma was striding towards him, waving a hand in greeting.

'It's marvellous to see you again,' he said, and kissed her lightly on the mouth.

'It's been a long time.'

'A lifetime in Lynsey's case.'

Her smile disappeared. 'We'll talk about that shortly. But how about a little fortification first? I could certainly use a drink.'

'Top-hole idea.'

She forced a smile back onto her face. 'Then I'll take you to the bar.'

'This country living certainly seems to agree with you. You look terrific Norma,' he said as they went inside.

'Thank you.' She couldn't say the same for him. There were bags under his eyes and hollows in his cheeks. His skin seemed somehow stretched, and lifeless.

'How was abroad?'

'Far too hot for my taste. And I had recurring bouts of dysentery which wasn't exactly pleasant.'

'I can imagine.' That could explain why he appeared so tired and generally run-down, she thought. From what she'd heard dysentery could really take it out of you.

There was a man and woman standing at the bar. He was called Monckton, she Renée Dufrenoy and they were both there on DR's instructions. Apart from Norma, Jeremy and the barman they were the only others present.

'I think I'll have a G & T. What about you?' Norma asked Jeremy, taking up a position beside Monckton and Renée where Jeremy naturally enough joined her.

'A G & T sounds fine.'

Norma ordered, for it would go on her mess bill, then asked Jeremy if he'd excuse her for a few moments; she'd just remembered something she urgently had to attend to. As she was leav-

211

ing the room Monckton and Renée started talking in French.

She gave them fifteen minutes, then returned to the bar. 'Sorry about that, took longer than I thought it would,' she apologised to Jeremy who'd been deep in conversation with Monckton and Renée.

Renée was standing behind Jeremy and there, where Norma could see but he couldn't, shook her head several times. For whatever reason – Norma later found out that, unlike his sister, he spoke French with a pronounced English accent – Jeremy had failed the crucial language test.

Norma was filled with relief. Thank God for that! After a while she took him over to a table by a window and there told him the lie DR had concocted about Lynsey's death.

What's wrong?

What makes you think something's wrong?

I can tell by the way you're sending. Your mind isn't fully on what you're doing.

Norma put the end of her pencil in her mouth and chewed it. She hadn't been aware there was any difference in her sending. But Gabriel was right, her mind hadn't been fully on the job.

The brother of the girl I trained with at FC came to see me today. He wanted to know how his sister died. I wasn't allowed to tell him the truth of course. I said that she died in a car crash, as we were both drivers before she and I joined the SOE.

Gabriel had never asked about Norma's previous pairing, nor had she mentioned anything. Up until now he hadn't even known whether the pairing was a man or woman. And why hadn't he asked? Because he saw it as personal. An area you only walked into when invited – I take it she died on a mission?

The Gestapo surprised her at her set while transmitting and shot her through the back of the head.

(Pause) At least it was quick. Many aren't so lucky.

I know.

Did the brother believe what you told him?

Totally. I was very convincing.

Would I have known her?

I shouldn't think so. Her code name was Marie Thérèse.

(Pause) I have to stop transmitting now. I'll come through again at twenty-one hundred hours.

He lifted the hand from his Morse key and ran it over his face. 'Shit!' he swore.

He left the transmitting hut to stride down to the beach. There he lit a cigarette and stared out at the island of Eigg, now only partially visible because of the sea mist.

He recalled that she'd offered him a cigarette which he'd accepted, and thinking how young, vulnerable and fragile she'd looked. It was a rotten war he'd thought at the time – and how right he'd been.

It wasn't just a rotten war. It was rapidly becoming a bastard of one.

Dead on the second of twenty-one hundred hours Norma's earphones began to beep.

Hello Norma.

Hello Gabriel.

Sorry I 'rang off' so abruptly earlier. It was just that, well, you gave me a shock.

I did?

Your pairing, Marie Thérèse. I met her.

(Pause)

Norma?

There were tears in her eyes, pain in her heart. She was looking at her Morse key but it was Lynsey's face she was seeing.

How did you meet her?

We shared the same ride when she went in. She asked me to stand behind her and give her a push should she freeze when it came time for her to jump.

Did she freeze?

No. I was glad about that.

We were friends before FC, in fact she was my best friend. It was because of me that she was asked to join SOE and become a "joe".

And now you feel responsible for her death?

If she hadn't been my friend she'd probably still be a driver, and alive.

You're being too hard on yourself. Man only proposes, God disposes. It was her karma.

What's that?

Her fate.

(Pause) Her real name was Lynsey.

Nice name. She seemed a nice girl. I liked her.

Norma dashed away some tears. She'd been so composed when talking to Jeremy, but then she'd been prepared for that. She hadn't been for this. I'm glad you met and liked Lynsey. She was a smashing person. A real gem, and a good pal to me.

(Pause) I've got some news Norma.

?

I'm going back over in ten days time.

She took a deep breath. Your training's almost finished then?

Almost.

Plane?

So I'm told.

She remembered she had a hanky on her, fumbled for it, and blew into it. She then dabbed at her wet cheeks.

In that case we'd better get cracking on some speed work. I'm still not as fast as Mary was.

You will be in ten days time.

So what have you got for me this evening, Shakespeare again? She knew he liked using Shakespeare because of the difficulty and complexity of the language. It made a first-class exercise to send and receive.

A Midsummer Night's Dream. Do you know the play?

No.

It's a great favourite of mine. I've seen it lots of times. Tell you what, when the war's over why don't we meet up and I'll take you to see a production. (Pause) Well?

Sounds fun.

And if the production is in London I'll take you to the Savoy Grill for supper afterwards. I adore the Savoy Grill. Ever been there?

Never.

If we go you'll enjoy it, everyone does. We shall meet for drinks before the show. I shall carry a rolled-up copy of *The Times* and bring you a single red rose. I shall say hello Norma, and you shall reply hello Gabriel. Savoy Grill or not, it shall be a splendid night out.

I'm looking forward to it.

So am I.

214

It'll give me something to think about when... Ready for message Norma?

Ready to receive message Gabriel.

> I know a bank where the wild thyme blows,
> Where oxlips and the nodding violet grows,
> Quite overcanopied with luscious woodbine,
> With sweet musk roses and with eglantine...

Her pencil flew as he sent at his quickest. She got eighty percent of the message, her best result yet. But she was going to need those ten remaining days – she wished it was longer.

He stood staring out to sea, a sea that was pounding ashore in fury. There was a fierce, cutting wind blowing, while overhead dark clouds were scudding against the moon. He shuddered, a shudder brought on not only by the cutting wind.

Shot through the back of the head Norma had said. He hoped, no he prayed, that when his end came it was as quick and final as that. He had a horror of falling into the hands of the Gestapo or SD, a horror that kept him awake nights and brought cold clammy sweat to his forehead.

He knew only too well what the Gestapo and SD were capable of. The bath of icy water they stuck your head into, keeping it under till you were on the point of drowning. Again and again the ducking till in the end even the toughest lost all will and blabbed.

The torture with the pliers, pulling out your fingernails one by one. And when they ran out of fingernails they started on your toes.

He'd told Marie Thérèse never to let fear get the upper hand, but by God what a monumental effort that could be. When over there fear was always with you, day and night, every waking moment. Fear that could become so intense he'd known an agent die of it, literally scared to death.

He'd have given anything not to go back, to stay on in Britain. But when the time came he'd go, just as he'd gone before. Just as Marie Thérèse and the others had gone.

Bending over he threw up.

It was the same Whitley bomber belonging to 138 Squadron

215

that had taken him and Marie Thérèse the last time he'd gone in, only on this occasion it left from Stapleford Abbots rather than Newmarket racecourse. The pilot and co-pilot were also the same. The only difference was that he wasn't sharing this journey with another 'joe'.

He lit a cigarette, then looked at the duffel bag attached to his right ankle by a length of rope. There were a million francs in that bag which he'd be using to set up Oberon Circuit.

He smiled to himself. He'd asked Norma what he should call the Circuit, and Oberon had been her choice. Oberon was the fairy King in *A Midsummer Night's Dream* which she'd been in the middle of reading. So she'd know the play when they went to see it, she'd said. He'd been flattered by that.

He wondered what she was like? He did have a mental picture of her, but it was probably quite different to how she really looked. She certainly sounded a smasher. And intelligent, far more than Mary had been.

A production of *A Midsummer Night's Dream* and supper at the Savoy Grill afterwards? What a lovely dream that was.

The co-pilot appeared and gave him the thumbs up sign. 'Three minutes to drop point. You know the drill,' he said.

Gabriel gave the thumbs-up sign back, then stood up. As he ground his cigarette out underfoot he wondered what Norma was doing at that moment? She certainly wouldn't be at her set, he wasn't due to transmit till the following night. Maybe she was out with a boyfriend? He'd never asked her if she had one, but if she was a good-looking lassie then probably she did. That thought depressed him, though there was no reason why it should. She was nothing personal to him after all. Why, they'd never even met!

The red light came on and his stomach knotted. The breath caught in his throat. He fought to control the fear that flooded through him. Fear that would be with him till he was either dead or out of France again.

He stepped to the rim of the hole and waited. The red light winked out and the green came on.

He was smiling as he jumped into the darkness.

Norma chewed a thumbnail that was already half bitten. Seventy-two hours had gone by and still no signal from Gabriel.

Where was he? What had happened? Was he . . .? She refused even to think of that dread word.

She glanced up at the clock. Another few minutes and it would be past the agreed time during which she would be standing by her set.

Come on Gabriel, where are you! She didn't so much as think but shouted inside her head.

And then her earphones were beeping. Gabriel calling. Gabriel calling.

Her hand flashed to the Morse key. Home base receiving. Home base receiving.

The message was short, delivered at his quickest. A dozen seconds was all it took her to jot it down. It was in code of course – they'd switched to code during the final days of their sessions together – so she had no idea what it said. She would only find out after it had been decoded.

She took a deep breath. He'd survived the jump, and was alive. Though under pressure it would seem from the quickness of his sending.

Tearing the top leaf from her pad she took the message through to the decoders.

He was trapped. If he turned round and tried to get back on the train he'd just come off, the Gestapo man at the barrier would spot him doing so, come after him and that would be that. As he was carrying the wireless set he'd picked up on arrival, not to mention the duffel bag containing the million francs, he hadn't a hope in hell of getting past them undetected. They were checking everyone, every suitcase and every bag.

Never ever panic! There may just be a solution, a way out. Don't panic, think. *Think.*

It was an absurd idea. Yet was it? He held aloft the suitcase containing his wireless and headed straight for the barrier.

'I have a captured British wireless set here! Make way, I have a captured British wireless set here!' he shouted. When one poor woman didn't move out of his path quickly enough, he thrust her aside, she stumbling and nearly falling, only being saved from measuring her length on the platform by a workman who grabbed her by the shoulder. Someone spat. It was a gesture of contempt towards a collaborator.

He arrived at the barrier with a face filled with triumph and excitement. 'I have a captured British wireless set here. Take me immediately to your superiors,' he said.

The Gestapo men looked at one another. 'Let me see this wireless,' the older of the two said.

Gabriel dropped the duffel bag to the ground, then heaved the suitcase onto the barrier and snapped open its locks. He lifted the top of the suitcase to reveal his set.

'How did you come by this?' the same Gestapo man demanded.

He made a tutting sound of impatience. 'I haven't got time to stand here talking, I must speak to your superiors immediately. Besides this set I have important information for them. Information that must be acted upon right away.'

Would his bluff work? His heart was hammering as he waited to find out.

'*Merde*,' someone muttered, meaning Gabriel. There were about twenty other passengers crowded round the barrier staring hostilely at him.

'I'll take you,' the younger Gestapo man said. 'Come.'

He sagged slightly at the knees, but they didn't see that. Snapping his suitcase shut again, he heaved it down off the barrier, snatched up the duffel bag and strode after the younger Gestapo man. Behind him the older Gestapo man continued to search.

The Gestapo man took Gabriel to a Mercedes, instructing him to slide the suitcase into the back seat, which he did, casually tossing the duffel bag on top of it. Then the pair of them got into the front.

'How far to your headquarters?' Gabriel asked as they drove off.

'About a kilometre and a half.'

He would have to make a move soon. For of course he daren't try to extend his bluff to Gestapo HQ. Once in there he'd never come out again – alive that is.

He slid his hand underneath his coat and jacket to touch the hilt of the stiletto he had strapped below his left armpit. Slowly he pulled the knife free.

His opportunity came as they stopped at a set of traffic lights which had changed just before they'd arrived at them. He'd already gone over in his mind how he would do this, the precise spot he'd strike for.

The steel was painted black so there was no flash or glint. The Gestapo man stiffened, eyes bulging, as the slim knife punched home. He was dead almost the moment the blade went into his side.

Gabriel released his hold of the stiletto, opened the car door and stepped out into the street. Taking his time, giving no appearance of hurry, he closed the door again. He then retrieved the suitcase and duffel bag from the rear seat, shut that door also, turned, and walked off. As he walked he looked neither to the left or right.

Behind him a car horn sounded, then sounded again. A few seconds later another car horn sounded, this one very impatiently. He presumed correctly that the lights had changed to 'go'.

He turned into an intersecting street where he caught an autobus. It didn't matter where the autobus was going, just as long as it was away from the Mercedes and dead Gestapo man.

'A little warmer today,' the woman who took his fare commented.

He nodded his agreement. 'Yes it is. It certainly is.'

This time the message, the third he'd sent, came through at a leisurely pace. She tore the top leaf from her pad when it was finished, and was about to rise from her chair to take it through to the coders when he started sending again. She put her earphones back on.

Hello Norma, how are you?

She blinked in astonishment. Not only was he sending in plain language but appeared to want to chat.

I'm fine. Should you be doing this? It's most irregular. The sound of his laughter filled her ears.

It's teeming down with rain here, and earlier on there was fog. The combination is very depressing.

We've also got rain. Are you sure it's safe for you to do this?

Don't worry. Caution's my middle name. There isn't a direction-finding team in the area, I know that for a fact. And if the krauts *are* listening in, so what? They won't learn anything to their advantage. (Pause) Do you like wine?

What an unusual question she thought.

I enjoy a glass though I'm hardly a connoisseur.

Right now I'm drinking a bottle of Grand Vin de Château Latour that I've personally liberated. Sheer nectar.

It sounds a very grand wine.

It is. Premier Grand Cru Classé.

Do you know much about wine?

A fair bit. My mother taught me. She ...

No, don't!

(Pause) What's wrong?

We've never really divulged personal details about one another, apart from me giving you a physical description of myself that is.

And talking about Marie Thérèse.

Yes.

And you don't want to?

Correct.

(Pause) I think I understand your reasons. And you're right, I'm sure of it. (Pause) But will you still go and see *A Midsummer Night's Dream* with me after the war?

And have supper in the Savoy Grill afterwards if the production is in London. Yes, I said I would, and I will.

(Pause) Goodbye then, for now.

Gabriel?

Yes?

Did you ever do this with Mary? Chat when you were in the field I mean.

(Pause) No.

(Long Pause) Do be careful.

I told you, caution's my middle name.

Enjoy the wine. Goodbye.

Goodbye for now Norma.

She took her earphones off. Wherever he was, whatever he was up to he was lonely. She knew that as surely as her name was Norma McKenzie. Lonely, and probably scared. But she *was* right to keep some distance between them, not to let their relationship become too close and intimate. It had been bad enough losing Lynsey, she didn't want to go through that ever again.

She took his message through to the decoders.

There was a click, and the lock was sprung. Gabriel smiled to

220

himself, it was easy when you knew how, and he knew how thanks to the locksmith who'd taught him in Arisaig. He went through the door he'd just opened and relocked it. He padded forwards.

Further into the factory there was yet another door he had to deal with, this one yielding as easily to his pick as the others had done. A few minutes later he found the safe, which was where he'd been briefed it would be.

It was a new safe made just before the war by Schlage Brothers of Berlin, one of Germany's best safe-makers. The safe he'd practised on in Arisaig had been identical, if a little older. Kneeling before it, he went to work.

He was frowning in concentration when he heard the sound of approaching feet. The armed nightwatchman making his rounds.

Swiftly he switched off his torch, gathered up his bits and pieces and hid behind a filing cabinet. The silken cord he now held between his hands had a single knot at its centre. The nightwatchman would die quietly. He didn't want to be interrupted again.

The nightwatchman didn't put the overhead light on, which made it easier for Gabriel. He was carrying a torch that he shone round the room. The first he was aware of Gabriel's presence was when the cord looped round his neck.

When the man was dead, garrotted, Gabriel laid him on the floor. He switched off the fallen torch, and returned to the safe.

Finally the safe swung open. Inside he found what he'd come for, and what the Admiralty in London were most anxious to get hold of.

He spread the plans on the floor, and shone the thin beam of his torch over them. *Schnorchel* was what the Germans had named the device, an underwater breathing system, still in a state of development, that would allow a U-boat to run continuously at periscope depth.

To Gabriel's eye it appeared that development was nearing completion which was going to give the Admiralty a great deal to think about, and act upon. They would also of course incorporate the system, or their version of it, into His Majesty's submarines.

He gathered up the plans, carefully refolding them one by

one, and slipped them into the briefcase he'd brought along. Then he made his way to the shop floor itself, seeking out the area where the tools and dies were kept, may of which were bound to be originals created especially for *Schnorchel*. Unfortunately the plans weren't originals – those would be in Germany along with various other copies.

He'd brought six pounds of plastic along with him, this particular plastic's distinctive almondy odour strong in his nostrils as he broke the six-pound mass into two of roughly three pounds each. He slid a time pencil, preset for thirty minutes, into the first section, and activated the pencil by pressing it. The now primed bomb he placed amongst the tools and dies.

He did the same with the second section of PE, placing that beside what looked to be the most important piece of machinery on the shop floor. When that was done he stealthily left the factory by the same route he'd entered it.

The time pencils he'd used had been known to act up, and even fail, from time to time, but they did neither on this occasion. The two very satisfactory bangs were within seconds of one another.

There must have been a large amount of inflammables and combustibles in the factory because almost immediately it turned into a raging inferno. It was like some huge Guy Fawkes bonfire as whoosh after whoosh of flames leapt skywards.

Next morning the plans he'd stolen began their journey to London and the Admiralty.

Norma was getting ready to go on duty when Madge Philips, one of the decoders, knocked on her door and said she was to stop by and see DR in his office before she did. He wanted a word.

'Come in!' he called after she'd tapped.

When she saw the bottle of scotch on his desk her smile wavered, then disappeared altogether. When DR asked you to his office and produced a bottle it only meant one thing. 'Do you mind if I sit?' she said, for her legs were suddenly weak and in threat of buckling under her.

'What happened?' she asked as DR poured them both hefty ones.

'Gabriel got picked up by the Gestapo last night, and he didn't have his death phial on him. It seemed he'd lost the damned thing and was waiting for a replacement. The rest of the Circuit, knowing the inevitable results of interrogation and torture by the Gestapo, immediately contacted DF and are even now on their way to Spain.'

She took a deep breath, then swallowed half her whisky. She didn't taste a thing. 'How do they know he was picked up by the Gestapo?'

'Another member of the Circuit actually witnessed it happen.'

'So he finally ran out of luck.'

'I'm afraid so.' DR paused, then added softly. 'He was one of our best. In fact I'd go so far as to say he was *the* best.'

'Six months, he lasted six months and it was his fourth trip in. That was quite an achievement,' she said with a choke in her voice.

'Yes. We should really have brought him out some time back but ... well he was doing such a first-class job.'

She leant forward, bending over slightly so that DR couldn't see her face. It was contorted with all manner of emotions.

'You appreciate there's nothing we can do for him. Now that he's in the Gestapo's clutches he's quite lost to us.'

She sat up again and drank off the remainder of her whisky. This time it burned going down. 'So that's that, the end of the Oberon Circuit.'

'Yes.'

'And the end of Gabriel.'

DR took her glass and refilled it. 'How about a spot of leave, eh? You might like to go home?'

Almost the exact same words M had said to her after Lynsey's death. Only Lynsey's death had been quick, over in a second. It wouldn't be like that for Gabriel. His death would be long, drawn-out and agonising. Those fiends in the Gestapo would make certain of that.

'Yes, I think I would,' she replied.

'You can go on leave starting from now. I'll fill out the necessary bumf to make it official.'

'Thank you sir.'

'I am so dreadfully sorry,' DR said in a voice filled with compassion.

'Yes sir, so am I.'

She left for Glasgow the following morning.

Chapter Ten

Norma was asleep in the cabin she shared with Helen Rolfe and Violette Hart when the torpedo struck. She awoke to find herself in mid-air, catapulted from her bunk. She landed on the floor with a jarring thump, and promptly blacked out.

The *Scythia* heeled, and juddered. There was noise and confusion everywhere. A short distance away their escort, a corvette, whooped as it raced for that area of sea its captain had judged the torpedo had come from. As the corvette knifed through the water the captain wished for the umpteenth time that he had the new asdic aboard; what a difference that must make to the locating and killing of U-boats. He gave a terse command and the first of his depth charges were released. The sea behind him fountained as one after one they went off.

Norma came groggily round to find Helen lying moaning beside her and Violette sitting on the floor looking totally and utterly bewildered. She turned to Helen who, from the sounds she was making, was in considerable pain.

On the *Scythia*'s bridge Captain Howat was being given the initial damage report. It wasn't nearly as serious as he'd at first feared, but serious enough nonetheless. Two seamen were dead, but the hole in the *Scythia*'s side was patchable. Thank the Lord they were so close to Algiers, their destination.

Norma left Helen to crawl over to Violette. A quick examination showed that Violette hadn't been physically injured. 'Violette, are you all right? Come on snap out of it, Helen's hurt.'

Violette made a strange animal-like sound at the back of her throat. Norma slapped her, then slapped her again. Violette cried out at this treatment, but it worked, bringing her back to her senses.

'Helen's hurt you say?'

'There don't appear to be any broken bones so it must be something internal.'

Their cabin door flew open. 'Everyone fine in here?' a very young and fresh-faced seaman demanded. He bit his lip when Norma told him about Helen.

'What happened?' Violette asked.

'Torpedo. Took us aft.'

'Are we going to sink?'

'Not according to the First who's up now telling the old man that.' First was the First Officer, the old man Captain Howat.

Jonty Wrolsen and Pat Tunbridge-Briggs, two more of the ten FANY's who were aboard, and the other two bunking on the port side, crowded round the young seaman. 'Awfully exciting what!' Pat exclaimed enthusiastically.

'Helen's hurt, fairly badly I suspect,' Norma said.

Pat's face fell, and she cursed herself inwardly for being so gung ho! That was just typical of her, saying the wrong damned thing at the wrong damned time.

'I'll report what's happened here to the captain. That's all I can do for the moment,' the young seaman said.

'Anyone else hurt?' asked Norma.

'That's what I'm doing the rounds to find out. This lady is the only one so far, though a couple of our chaps who were standing right at the point of impact were killed.' Having said that, the young seaman turned and hurried off down the passageway.

Norma bent again to Helen who'd gone a dirty yellow colour. She didn't like the look of that at all.

Helen's eyes flickered open. She'd been unconscious all this while. 'Excruciating pain in the small of my back,' she whispered.

Violette came over with a towel and wiped away the blood trickling from the left-hand corner of Helen's mouth. As soon as she wiped the blood away it appeared again.

'Should we try and move her onto one of the lower bunks?' Violette asked Norma. There were four bunks in the cabin, two lower and two higher. Norma and Violette had the lower bunks, Helen one of the higher. The second higher was empty. Helen, like Norma, had been asleep when the torpedo had struck, and she too had come flying off her

225

bunk. Only in her case she'd had further to fall than Norma.

Norma wasn't at all sure about that. It would certainly be more comfortable for Helen. But was it the right thing to do?

More depth charges exploded, rocking the *Scythia*. Norma suddenly had a horrible thought – what if they were torpedoed again? She listened to the corvette whoop-whooping like a mad thing, and prayed that one of those depth charges had found its target. 'Let's try and lift Helen,' she replied.

All four girls lent a hand. Helen gasped in agony as she was raised from the floor, and the trickle of blood became a small river.

Captain Howat, still on the bridge, was also considering the possibility of a second torpedo. The *Scythia*, with its speed reduced to four knots – as opposed to its usual ten – was a sitting duck if the U-boat managed to get another crack at them. He glanced round as his Third Officer appeared on the bridge.

'We've started jettisoning the deck cargo sir. Once the hole is clear of the waterline we'll begin on the patch. The entire operation shouldn't take all that long,' Third reported.

Captain Howat grunted; that was good news. He'd go down to the damaged area himself shortly to see what was what. They were extremely lucky the torpedo had hit them where it had – any lower and a patch would have been impossible. The wireless operator came up onto the bridge.

'Escort says she's convinced the U-boat's done a bunk. She wants to know our situation.'

That was even better news, providing it was correct. He gave the wireless operator the answer, then turned to the young seaman to find out about the casualties.

'No more dead other than the two you already know about sir. But there is one serious injury, a FANY. She's in a bad way according to her mates.'

Captain Howat swore. 'Which FANY is it?' he demanded, for he'd made friends with all of them.

'Ensign Rolfe sir.'

'She's in with Ensigns McKenzie and Hart isn't she?'

'Yes sir.'

'Well, away back to their cabin and tell them I'll be down just as soon as possible.'

Captain Howat looked out over the green sea at the corvette

now astern of him on the starboard side. He hoped the corvette's captain was right about the U-boat. He made some mental calculations, then went over to the blow tube and had a word with the First Engineer. As soon as the hole was patched up they could bring their speed back up to seven, maybe eight, knots. Dawn was half an hour gone – if all went well they should reach Algiers somewhere round about midday. He took his medicine chest with him and went below.

'Come in captain,' Norma said when Howat appeared at the door of their cabin. He went over to where Helen was and stared grim-faced, down at her. He thought she looked extremely ill.

'She came to for a short while to complain of an excruciating pain in the small of her back. Then she passed out again,' Norma said.

Helen twisted one way, then the other. Her low moaning was pitiful to hear.

Captain Howat replied. 'We don't have a doctor aboard, but I can give her a morphine injection to deaden the pain.' Suddenly there was an enormous splash outside the porthole. It was followed by an even bigger one. The Captain explained about the *Scythia* having to jettison its deck cargo, then brought his attention back to Helen. 'I'll radio through to Algiers and tell them to have a doctor standing by. I'll make it clear it's an emergency.'

'I'll give her the injection if you like? I'm quite good at them,' Norma volunteered. Giving injections had been part of her original FANY training.

Captain Howat was only too pleased to agree to that. He hated giving injections almost as much as he hated having them. He put his medicine chest on the bunk above Helen's and rummaged inside. 'Right, carry on,' he said, handing Norma the necessary bits and pieces.

The others watched as Norma loaded the syringe, then slid the needle home. The morphine was quick to take effect and soon Helen stopped moaning and twisting about. By which time Captain Howat was back on his bridge giving the wireless operator the message he wanted radioed ahead.

Norma and Violette were with Helen when the *Scythia* limped into Algiers and gently bumped the quayside where it was to berth. Almost instantly there was the rattle and bang of a gangplank going into place.

Captain Howat personally brought the doctor to their cabin. The doctor, without any preliminaries or introductions, went straight to the still unconscious Helen. Bending over her he prised open one eye. While doing that with his left hand he took her neck pulse with his right.

He was a slightly-built man with sallow skin and very dark hair shot through with grey. He had a neatly clipped beard and a thick moustache, also streaked with grey. He'd seemed vaguely familiar to Norma from the moment he'd appeared in the doorway.

Having peered into her eye and taken her pulse he gently lifted Helen up and over onto her side so that he could feel the small of her back. She moaned, the first time she'd done so since the morphine injection. 'An excruciating pain, she said?' he queried of Norma who was closest to him.

'Yes, those were her precise words.'

The doctor, probing very gently, then laid Helen flat again. 'And how long did the bleeding from the mouth go on for?'

'A good hour, maybe more,' Norma replied.

The doctor frowned. 'Was that continuous bleeding?'

'No, it would stop from time to time. Then she'd vomit and it would start up again.'

'Was there blood in the vomit?'

Norma nodded.

'And when was she given the morphine?'

It was Captain Howat who answered, giving the exact time which he'd had to note for his log. The doctor then produced a syringe and proceeded to give Helen another measure of morphine.

'Any idea what's wrong?' queried Norma.

He looked her directly in the eye, and again she had that nagging feeling there was something familiar about him.

'I think it's pretty certain there's been internal haemorrhaging which may still be going on. I'll have to open her up to find out.

'You suspect something other than internal haemorrhaging then?'

'I can assure you that haemorrhaging is serious enough. But

yes, I do have my suspicions. Though nothing I'm going to commit myself to here and now.'

Prickly character, Norma thought. Prickly to the point of being rude.

'I want this young woman in the hospital right away,' the doctor said. The two orderlies who'd come on board with him and had been lurking outside the cabin appeared in the doorway. 'The patient is going to have to be strapped to your stretcher to get her up the companionway. Strap her securely, but as comfortably as you can. And not over the mid-area,' the doctor told them.

Norma touched the doctor on the arm. 'I'm a great friend of hers. Can I go with her? Please?'

A frown of irritation creased his face. 'Please?' she pleaded a second time. He tried to think of a reason why he should refuse her, and couldn't. The frown relaxed a little. 'Oh all right, if you must.'

'Don't worry about anything here. I'll attend to it,' said Violette.

'And we'll help her if she needs it,' Jonty added.

The tricky part was getting the stretcher up the companionway – the stairs leading from that deck to the next. There was no other way that the stretcher could be taken. But this was eventually accomplished, with one orderly pulling and the other pushing and with the stretcher at an angle of about seventy degrees. After that it was through a hatch onto the outer deck, and the gangplank beyond.

Norma said a hurried goodbye to Captain Howat, whom she, and all the other FANYs had come to think very highly of. Then she was off down the gangplank to where an army ambulance was waiting.

Helen's stretcher was loaded in the rear of the ambulance by the two orderlies, who then got in at the front of the vehicle, one of them doubling as driver. The doctor climbed in the rear with his patient, and Norma followed suit. The driver engaged gear and the ambulance pulled away.

Norma glanced out the window beside her. It was her first visit to a foreign country – apart from England that is – and how different it all was. The smell of the place struck her forcibly. Warm, pungent, definitely exotic and . . . dangerous. Yes that was it, dangerous. But it was bound to feel like that after the heavy fighting that had taken place a few weeks previously when the combined Anglo-American force had landed here to take the town and surrounding countryside as part of the invasion of North Africa.

'Are we going to the local hospital?' she asked the doctor.

He looked at her as though she was daft. 'I wouldn't take my dog to the local hospital to have its claws trimmed,' he replied caustically.

There it was again, that feeling of *déjà vu*. Did she know him, and if so from where? She wracked her memory.

'We're going to an army field hospital that's been established fairly close to where you'll be billeted.'

'And where will we be billeted?'

He gave her a sideways look, his eyes narrowing fractionally as he did. It was a look that had something chilling and deadly about it. It made her shiver. 'I was informed that you and the other FANYs aboard that ship are SOE. Is that correct?'

'Yes'

'Then you'll be billeted at the Club des Pins along with the other members of the SOE already here.'

'Club des Pins? Sounds very grand. Is it in the town itself?'

'No, it's a group of villas roughly fifteen miles west of Algiers. It overlooks the beach where the main assault came in.'

'A group of villas. So it's not an actual club then?'

'More what you might call a tiny holiday resort. It was used by wealthy Algerians before the war. It's a rather pleasant spot, I like it.'

'Are you billeted there as well then?'

'I have a bed there. Also a room in the St George Hotel which is in Algiers. I flit between the two as work demands.' He pointed out her window. 'I don't know if it'll interest you but that shell of a building over there was the famous Al-Hani Mosque till it was hit directly by a bomb during the landings.'

She glanced out the window, remembering the bomb in Risinghill Street which had so nearly done for her. And with that association in her mind it suddenly clicked with her who the doctor was.

'You're Doctor Ross,' she blurted out.

His left eyebrow crawled up his forehead in surprise. It stayed there as he regarded her quizzically.

He hadn't had a beard or moustache then, nor had there been any grey in his hair. And gosh, he did appear so much older now, years older than she recalled him. Was she wrong?

'*Are* you Doctor Ross?' she desperately tried to remember his Christian name. Douglas, that was it. 'Doctor Douglas Ross?'

He was thinking back to the cabin on board *Scythia*. He hadn't mentioned his name there. He rarely did unless it was absolutely necessary, something he did from force of habit.

'How do you know me?' he asked quietly.

'I was your patient once, in the Royal Free Hospital in Gray's Inn Road. I was a FANY driver at the time and my car was blown up in Risinghill Street right at the beginning of the Blitz. I had a broken left arm and four broken ribs which you treated in Marsden Ward.'

Recognition dawned on his face. 'Miss McKenzie, yes I remember you now. You were the one who...' He broke off, and coloured.

Still as shy as ever, she thought. 'I kissed you while I was unconscious, thinking you were my boyfriend.'

'So you found out about that?'

'Yes, Staff told me.'

He glanced down at the floor of the ambulance, clearly embarrassed.

Norma went on. 'I remember I tore a strip off you one day because you were forever staring at me. It quite upset you.'

'Did it?' he said casually, as if he couldn't recall that bit.

'If it's not too late, sorry. It was just a bad day for me, a culmination of things.'

'That's all right, no need to apologise.'

'You were very off with me after that. In fact, not to put too fine a point on it, you were downright uncivil.'

'Now it's my turn to say sorry.'

She laughed. 'It was a long time ago – two years would you believe. A lot of water under the bridge since then.'

'Yes, a lot of water,' he agreed.

She recalled something else. 'If you were at this Club des Pins you must be SOE as well?'

'I am.'

'The day M came to visit me I remember seeing him talking to you afterwards and wondering what it was about. Was that when he recruited you?'

'That was when he first approached me. I saw him in Baker Street after that,' Ross said slowly.

'So what do you do in SOE?' she asked.

'What do you think?'

She nodded. 'I suppose SOE needs doctors like everyone else.'

'We take care of our own whenever possible. That's why it was me who came to see Miss Rolfe and not another army doctor.'

'It's a small world,' Norma mused.

'It is indeed.'

When they arrived at the army field hospital – a vast tent – the two orderlies came running round to the rear of the ambulance and threw open the doors. Ross supervised their taking Helen's stretcher out, and once that had been safely accomplished he and Norma followed. Ross gave an order and the stretcher was taken inside. He turned to Norma. 'What will you do now?'

'Wait if you don't mind.'

'It could be quite some while.'

'I'll wait anyway.'

'Right then.' He turned on his heel and strode into the hospital.

Norma couldn't get over bumping into Ross again, or how much he'd aged. He must have had a hard war, poor thing, she thought.

She glanced around. There were several other tents, smaller than the main one, and buildings beyond, several hundred yards away she judged. She spied a wooden bench with some empty wooden crates beside it. She'd sit and wait there.

She'd been sitting a while when she was approached by a Queen Alexandra nurse. 'Can I help you?' the QA asked.

Norma explained why she was waiting.

The QA smiled. 'How about a cup of tea or coffee?'

'Either would be marvellous.'

The QA left Norma to vanish into one of the nearby tents. She reappeared a few minutes later holding a steaming mug of coffee and, of all things, a jam-filled doughnut. It was the first nourishment Norma had had since dinner the previous night.

She stared at a camel that had appeared in the distance, the first she'd ever seen. A number of what she thought must be Shetland ponies appeared behind the camel, then she realised they were donkeys. They were another first.

Two soldiers walked by wearing uniforms she didn't recognise. A thrill ran through her when it dawned they were Americans. The one who'd started to speak sounded just like Clark Gable!

She glanced at her watch, it was an hour and three quarters now since Helen had been carried inside. She'd been worried all along, now her worry intensified. It seemed an awful long time. She just prayed that everything was all right.

A convoy of four ambulances drew up, and a number of wounded were taken from them to be stretchered into the hospital. One squaddie had half a leg blown away, the grotesque, obscene, blood-soaked bandaged stump sticking up into the air. Norma averted her gaze as he went past – she couldn't help herself.

A gaggle of QAs came out of one of the smaller tents to go dashing into the hospital tent. From somewhere inside came a great shriek of agony. It covered Norma from top to toe in gooseflesh.

She'd been sitting for a fraction over three hours when Ross suddenly re-emerged, glancing about him. Norma hurried over.

'Besides the internal bleeding, which is still going on, Miss Rolfe had a severely damaged kidney. So damaged in fact I had no choice but to remove it,' he reported.

'Will she live?' Norma asked softly.

He took a deep breath, then stared off into the distance. 'The next twenty-four hours will tell. It depends on how strong a fighter your friend is, and of course, it has to be said, conditions round here are hardly ideal. So we'll just have to wait and see.'

'But you have done your best for her?' That was a statement, not a question.

That could have been interpreted as impertinent by some, but not by him. He understood her concern. 'Yes Miss McKenzie, my very best.'

'Then thank you Doctor.'

233

He offered her a cigarette. 'I don't,' she smiled. He put one in his mouth and lit up. He drew smoke deep into his lungs, held it there for the space of a few seconds, then blew it out in a long thin blue stream. 'I have to go to Club des Pins to collect a few items, can I give you a lift?'

'That would be kind of you. Have you finished for the day?'

'Not quite, I'll have to come back. There are several patients who need my attention. My car's this way.'

He led her to a camouflage-painted Standard car and they climbed into the front seats. 'What will you be doing at Massingham?' he asked as they drove away.

'Massingham?'

'Inter-Service Signals Unit 6, codename Massingham. In other words our lot at Club des Pins.'

'Oh I see!' she smiled. 'I'm a WT operator. Three of our party are, the others are coders and decoders.'

'There's a lot hoped for Massingham. I think you'll find it's going to be pretty lively there during the coming months. And it'll be even livelier once we've booted the axis powers out of North Africa.'

'And *will* we be able to do that?'

'Before El Alamein I would have said our chances were sixty-forty against. Now I would put it at seventy-five-twenty-five in our favour.' The British victory at El Alamein had taken place the previous month.

'You believe El Alamein meant that much?'

'Not only me, but Monty and Ike. They believe it.'

'You move amongst such exalted company do you?'

He barked out a laugh. 'You'd be surprised whom you meet in the bar of the St George Hotel. Ike was there just the other day.'

'He was?'

'In the flesh.'

'And Monty?'

'I haven't met him. But I know he believes what I've just told you, Eisenhower told me that.'

'Win or lose, there'll be a lot of casualties,' she said, thinking of the soldier with half his leg blown away and that terrible shriek of agony she'd heard directly afterwards.

'There always are during wars,' he replied darkly. And it

seemed to Norma that his mood changed to become as dark as his tone had been.

They didn't speak again till they arrived at Club des Pins, Inter-Service Signals Unit 6, Massingham. 'Why it's gorgeous!' Norma cried out in delight.

There were more villas than she'd thought there would be, together with other pre-fabricated buildings that had been erected since the invasion. The sea was a beautiful bluey-green washing a bone-white shore. The villas were all white with various coloured roofs.

'Let's find out where they've put you,' Ross said, bringing the Standard to a halt beside one of the villas. He got out and vanished into the villa. When he re-emerged there was a French Lieutenant with him. They both came to Norma's side of the car where the Lieutenant flashed her a beaming smile, then saluted.

'Lieutenant Rene Bonnier de la Chapelle at your service, Mademoiselle McKenzie. You have been billeted at Casa Bon-Bon where your friend Mademoiselle Hart – *très charmante*! – is already installed.'

Norma giggled. 'Is it really called Casa Bon-Bon?'

'*Oui mademoiselle.*'

The sweetie house, was how she translated it. How could she not enjoy living in a place like that. 'Thank you Lieutenant,' she said. In reply to which the Frenchman became ramrod stiff, and bowed. Ross, the ghost of a smile hovering round his lips, walked round to the driver's seat, got in, and they continued down the dirt street.

'Who on earth was that?' Norma demanded.

'One of the instructors.'

'What does he instruct?'

'A number of things – you'll find out.'

Casa Bon-Bon had a pantiled roof and looked like something straight out of a story book or picture postcard. Norma gave a laugh when she compared it to Cubie Street and Bridgeton.

'What's so funny?' Ross queried.

'I was just ...' She broke off. She wasn't going to tell him about Bridgeton. Why should she? 'Nothing,' she said, and got out the car.

The door opened and Violette came flying onto the verandah. 'How's Helen?' she demanded anxiously.

235

Norma asked Ross to repeat to Violette what he'd told her outside the field hospital, which he did. 'And now I must away,' he declared.

'Which villa are you in?' Norma asked.

He hesitated for a moment, then pointed behind her and Casa Bon-Bon. 'Over in that direction. The one with the green roof, it's the only one with a roof that colour.'

'Thank you for what you've done.' She stood watching him drive away, and then he turned a corner and was lost to view. 'Damnest thing, I knew him from before,' she said to Violette.

'Really?'

'Let's go inside and I'll tell you about it.'

Once through the doorway Norma came up short. Her initial impression of the inside of Casa Bon-Bon was that it was bare as Mother Hubbard's cupboard.

'We've got a bedroom each. I've stached your gear in one of them, and Helen's in another. As you can see there isn't exactly a lot in here.'

'Do we have beds?' Norma asked, not at all fancying the idea of sleeping on the floor.

'Three iron-framed canvas ones. Also some blankets, storm lanterns and paraffin.'

'No sheets, pillows or pillowcases?'

Violette shook her head.

Norma went to the closest window and stared out over the sea. It was a tremendous view, and so peaceful! She just couldn't imagine the hell it must have been when the invasion had come storming ashore. She turned again to Violette. 'What about eating?'

Violette's face lit up. 'There's a canteen run by – would you believe – a couple of Kenyan FANYs, so we're going to be just dandy there. The chap who brought me out here said that at night the canteen doubles as a club and bar for those who don't want to go into Algiers or are tied here for some reason.'

Norma knew of the Kenyan branch of the FANYs of course, but had never met any.

'I think I'll go out on the scrounge. I'm the world's best scrounger, did you know that?'

Norma laughed. 'No I didn't.'

'When God doled out the talents, one of the main ones he

236

gave me was the ability to scrounge. Give me a few days and, if it's humanly possible, I'll have this place transformed.'

'What about bathing facilities?' Norma queried.

'No baths, yet, but there are showers.'

Norma suddenly felt extremely tired. It had been a long, not to say, eventful day. 'I think I might just lie down and have a couple of hours shut-eye. I'm deadbeat,' she said.

'I'll show you your room.'

The room was a decent size and alive with light. Norma liked it immediately. There was the scent of flowers in the air, a heavy musklike smell. She had no idea what sort of flowers it came from, and wondered if her da would have known. He probably would have done. He had a tremendous knowledge of flowers and plants, not only of British domestic ones, but foreign plants as well. Gardening hadn't only been his job, it had also been his hobby. And no doubt still was.

When Violette had left her to go out scrounging she closed her eyes and prayed for Helen's recovery. Then she shook out her blankets, spread them over the bed, and lay down. Within seconds she was fast asleep. She dreamt she was back in Barrowland dancing with Midge.

The nine new FANY arrivals met up and went to the canteen for dinner together. There they were given an enthusiastic welcome by the two Kenyan FANYs who were eagerly waiting to say hello. The two Kenyans had already met Violette, who'd spoken to them during her afternoon scrounge, a scrounge which had produced a feather bolster, two cans of paint, some very useful wooden boxes that would double as furniture, together with a decorator's pasting-up table. She hadn't a clue how the latter had come to be where she'd liberated it from, but there it had been.

While they were eating, the French Lieutenant, René Bonnier de la Chapelle, came into the canteen. Before joining the small cluster of other Frenchmen he came over for a few words with Violette and Norma, and was introduced to the rest of the party. He informed them that a Major Fulford would come by shortly to speak to them, so would nobody please leave the canteen until the Major had put in an appearance.

Norma spied Doctor Ross sitting by himself at the far end of the canteen. She thought he might look over and smile, or give her a small wave of recognition. He did neither.

When dinner was finished they lingered over coffee waiting for Major Fulford. There were only the nine of them left in the canteen, and the two Kenyan FANYs who were out in the kitchen doing the washing up.

The Major introduced himself, then said in a soft Dorset burr, 'First thing tomorrow morning, seven hundred hours, assemble here for breakfast, after which I'll take you to where you'll be working. Hopefully the nine of you are the advance guard for many more like yourselves, for although we're starting small at Massingham we have great expectations for it. Great expectations. And you girls are in on the business right from the beginning.'

He paraded round their table, tapping his swagger stick against a leg. 'It's been decided that one of you is to be promoted in rank to be in charge of the others.' He stopped beside Norma. 'Congratulations *Captain* McKenzie.'

Norma's mouth dropped open in astonishment. 'Me?'

'*You*, Captain. You may consider yourself to hold the rank of captain as from now.'

Norma didn't know what to say. She was totally dumbfounded – this was the last thing she'd expected. Why, if anyone should have been put in charge it was Helen. And then she remembered that Helen was in hospital, fighting for her life.

'Three cheers for Captain McKenzie!' Violette said, and led the other FANYs in three rousing cheers, for Norma was popular with all of them. Norma blushed.

Major Fulford took Norma aside. 'All your equipment has been set up, all the equipment you'll need for the moment anyway. Tomorrow you're to establish contact with our wireless station in Tunisia, and F Section in Britain. You're also to establish contact with Gibraltar and Baker Street. You'll find that as the days go by a fair volume of signals will be passing between the five stations.'

'Yes sir,' Norma replied, nodding that she understood.

'Right then, see you at seven hundred hours,' Major Fulford said, and strode off.

'Well,' Norma said to Violette, 'wasn't that a turn up for the book? I'm sure Helen was the one originally earmarked for promotion, only they had to change their minds after what happened to her.'

'It could be, she is the most senior of us. But if it couldn't be her I'm glad it was you.'

'Would you like to speak to Pam tomorrow?'

'You mean Pam Parkinson!'

'We're to establish contact with F Section; if she's on duty during the establishing process the pair of you can have a coded exchange.'

'Let's just hope she is,' Violette beamed.

Next day Norma wasn't able to get to the hospital till early evening. She met Ross on his way out.

'I've got some good news for you. Miss Rolfe is doing absolutely splendidly,' he said before she could speak.

It was as if a huge load had been lifted from Norma's shoulders. 'She is going to be all right then?'

'No doubt about it. In fact I'm so pleased with her progress I'm having her transferred to the wards. She's very weak of course, but quite out of danger. It's simply a matter of rest and recuperation.'

'You've no idea what a relief it is to hear you say that.'

His lips slashed into a thin smile. He felt like teasing her, 'I think I do understand Miss McKenzie. This sort of situation isn't exactly new to me after all.'

'I'm sorry, I didn't mean that literally. It was just ... well a way of expressing myself.'

He nodded, but didn't reply. He thinks I'm an idiot! she thought, and felt a warm stain rise in her neck. She indicated the canvas bag she was carrying. 'I've brought in some of Helen's things that she'll probably want. Can I see her to give them to her? Or is that out of the question for now?'

'On the contrary, I insist you see her. It's the best medicine I can prescribe. Tell Sister Littlejohn, on my instructions, that you're to have a full ten minutes with Miss Rolfe. I can't allow more than that for now as it would tire her too much.

'Thank you doctor.'

He walked away without saying anything else. As she went inside to seek out the Sister she felt she'd made a right fool of herself. Then again, there was no need for him to have picked

239

her up as he had. It should have been obvious she hadn't meant what she'd said literally.

Doctor Ross confused her. He could be so charming and pleasant one moment, a real aggravating sod the next.

The following day Ross entered the room that Helen had been moved to. There were only two female patients in the room, Helen and a QA who'd suffered a burst appendix, and the pair of them were the only female patients the hospital had. The wards were filled with men, ninety-five percent of whom were casualties of the fighting that had taken place at the invasion and was continuing as the Allied forces advanced.

Helen was pale but cheerful. She'd made excellent progress, Ross thought as he examined her.

'How long will I be here?' Helen asked, already anxious to be up and about again.

'Between a month and six weeks, it all depends on how you do. Though I must say with your constitution it's much more likely to be the month than the six weeks.'

It bucked Helen up to hear that. 'Then what?'

'Do you want to return to England? If would be easy for me to arrange if you do.'

She shook her head. 'I would feel I was letting everyone down – myself included – if I went back when it wasn't absolutely necessary. If it's possible I'd prefer to stay on here.'

'Then you shall. After you've been discharged you'll still need a few more weeks of convalescence, but after that you should be able to get on with your duties.'

He glanced across at a photograph in a metal frame standing on her bedside locker. It was a photo of a trio of laughing girls, one of whom was Helen, the other the McKenzie lass, and the third ... He frowned, the face was vaguely familiar.

Helen saw what had caught his attention. 'That came with the other things Norma brought me. It was taken at Fawley Court where the tree of us trained.'

'Norma?'

'McKenzie. Norma McKenzie who's just been promoted to Captain. She came in the ambulance with you when you brought me here.'

'And the third girl?'

240

'Lynsey Dereham. She's dead now. She ...' Helen's voice thickened with emotion. 'She went to France as a "joe" and never came out again. Norma was her WT operator; they were particularly close.'

'May I?' he asked, and picked up the photograph. A strange expression played across his face as he stared at it. Slowly, and very carefully, he replaced it on top of the locker.

He rose to smile down at Helen. 'You're doing very well, I'm extremely pleased.' He left the room without waiting for a reply.

Norma glanced at her wristwatch – twenty minutes till Violette relieved her. With Helen out of action she and Violette, the remaining WT operators, were having to work extra long shifts, but another two FANY operators were *en route* from Grendon Underwood and should be with them during the next day or so, coming out by plane as opposed to ship as they had done.

Jonty Wrolsen handed her a coded signal for Tunisia which she sent. Things in Tunisia weren't going as well as had been hoped. The winter conditions – mainly in the form of a tremendous amount of mud – and the stiff resistance were proving considerable problems.

She glanced at her wristwatch again, thirteen minutes to go now. And then her earphones beeped with an incoming signal. A signal in plain language!

Calling Massingham. Calling Massingham.

Massingham receiving. Massingman receiving.

(Pause) Hello Norma.

Little prickles ran all over her skin. She found she was holding her breath. It couldn't be, it was impossible, and yet 'the fist' was identical.

Who is this?

Who do you think?

She rocked back in her chair. This had to be some sort of practical joke, had to be. Except 'the fist' *was the same*!

Gabriel?

Prepare to receive message.

Her shaking hand picked up a pencil. She could hardly see her pad for the tears blurring her vision.

Ready to receive.

> I know a bank where the wild thyme blows,
> Where oxlips and the nodding violet grows,
> Quite overcanopied with luscious woodbine,
> With sweet musk roses and with eglantine ...

She wrote none of it down, she didn't have to, she knew the words off by heart. To confirm it really was him he'd sent it at his fastest.

(Pause) Norma?

It is you.

Yes.

Laugh for me. He did, the sound of his 'laughter' filled her ears.

How's that?

I was told the Gestapo picked you up?

They did.

So how is it you're still alive?

Meet me for a drink and I'll tell you all about it.

Where?

The bar of the St George Hotel.

In Algiers!

Yes.

You're in Algiers?

Yes. Are you free tonight?

I can be.

Would 8 pm suit?

Where?

The bar of the St George Hotel?

I'll be there. How will I recognise you?

I'm only four feet three.

Fibber! Anyway, that was my joke originally.

So it was! Six feet six didn't you say?

Seriously, how will I recognise you?

I'll know who you are, the honey-blonde with grey-green eyes and the enormous bust.

I never said it was enormous!

Didn't you?

No I did not!

Then you'll be the honey-blonde with grey-green eyes and two legs. Any honey-blondes with grey-green eyes and three legs will be ruled out immediately. (He laughed.)

242

Very droll. Till 8 pm then.

Till 8 pm.

Goodbye Gabriel.

Goodbye Norma.

She took her earphones off and laid them beside her sender key. When she looked up and round Violette was staring quizzically at her.

'You don't half look odd. As though you'd just seen a ghost,' Violette said.

Norma gave a semi-hysterical laugh. 'Not seen, "spoken" to.'

Violette frowned. 'I don't understand.'

'You'll never guess who just signalled me?' Norma said.

'Who?'

'Gabriel.'

Violette's jaw dropped. 'But he's dead!'

'No he's not, he's in Algiers. And I'm going to meet him tonight for a drink.'

And having said that Norma fainted clean away, Violette just managing to catch her before she hit the floor.

She was shaking as she walked into the bar. What on earth would Gabriel be like in the flesh? She was dying to know. And how on earth had he managed to pop up in Algiers? She'd been wondering about that ever since he'd come through to her earlier on.

She glanced about. There were a number of people present including the famous American aviator General Doolittle. She stood for several moments waiting for Gabriel to approach her, when he didn't she went over to the bar itself.

'Let me buy you that,' a voice said, from someone who'd come up behind her. It was Douglas Ross, the doctor.

'Thank you, but I'm meeting someone,' she smiled back.

'He's not here already then?'

'I eh . . .' She didn't know what to say. Was Gabriel here? She certainly didn't want to say that she'd no idea what the person she was meeting looked like, that would have sounded most peculiar.

'He doesn't seem to be,' she said evasively.

'Then I insist on buying you that drink.' Ross beckoned the

barman over and asked Norma what she'd like. She said she'd have a gin sling. He ordered a cold beer for himself.

'Out to paint the town red, eh?' he prompted.

She wished she hadn't run into Ross, the last thing she wanted was to talk about Gabriel. Except to Gabriel himself that was. 'Just a quiet drink that's all.'

'A friend from Massingham?'

'No.'

He nodded as though that held some significance for him. She smiled, and he smiled back. She found that irritating. In fact she was beginning to find him irritating.

The barman laid their drinks in front of them and Ross said to put them on his tab. 'Cheers!' he toasted. 'Cheers!' she responded, and they both took a sip from their respective glasses.

'I saw your Miss Rolfe this morning, a big improvement from yesterday. I've told her I can probably discharge her in about a month.'

'Good.'

'She had a photograph on her bedside locker that caught my eye. You, her and Marie Thérèse.'

'It was taken at Fawley Court where we did our WT and Morse training.'

'Yes, she said that.'

Another customer, a male civilian, entered the bar. He was short, swarthy and extremely fat. Surely that wasn't . . . She turned to stare at Ross in astonishment. 'What did you just say?'

'About what?'

'The photograph I took in to Helen.'

'That it caught my eye.'

'And . . .?'

'And what?'

'You named the three of us. Do it again.'

'Let me have one of your hands,' he said.

'I beg your pardon!'

'Let me have one of your hands.'

She looked into his liquid brown eyes and saw amusement there, that and something else, something she couldn't define. Tentatively she extended her right hand which he took in his. Using the forefinger of his free hand he rapped out in Morse on the back of the hand he was holding. Hello Norma.

She recognised 'the fist' instantly. 'You?' she whispered.

'I see there's a table going free over there. Shall we use it?' he smiled in reply. He lifted both drinks, and led the way. She followed him, dumbstruck by this revelation. Douglas Ross of all people!

He put their drinks down, pulled out a chair for her, and pushed it in again as she sat. He sat facing her. 'I never knew you were Norma till I saw that photograph. I didn't recognise Marie Thérèse at first – well, the only time I saw her she was kitted out for a jump which can make quite a difference to the appearance. And then the penny dropped. Miss Rolfe told me that you'd been her WT operator, and that your Christian name was Norma, which of course made you my Norma also,' he explained.

'How . . .' she cleared her throat. Her mind was still whizzing round and round. 'How did you signal me this afternoon?'

'That wasn't difficult. I borrowed a field set from stores and, having already found out what frequency you were transmitting on, the rest was easy. I contacted you from my villa.'

'Excuse me,' she said, taking a deep breath, 'You must appreciate how big a shock this is for me. I was expecting, well I don't know what I was expecting, but certainly not you. You're a doctor.'

'I was also a "joe".'

'Gabriel,' she said amazed.

He swallowed some beer, and she took a sip of her gin sling. 'You asked about the Gestapo,' he said.

She nodded. The mystery was about to be explained.

'When I went in on that last mission I very nearly got caught at Nantes railway station. I came off the train with my wireless in its suitcase to find two Gestapo men, an older and a younger, at the barrier checking everyone and every piece of luggage. I couldn't turn back, or run, so I bluffed it out. I told them I had a captured British wireless set and important information – information that had to be acted upon right away, and that they were to take me to their headquarters immediately. They bought my story, and the younger Gestapo man said he'd drive me there. I managed to kill him *en route* and made my escape.'

Ross paused to light a cigarette, then went on, 'When I was finally picked up by the Gestapo all those months later it wasn't because they were onto me or the Oberon Circuit, but a piece of damned bad luck. The older of the two Gestapo men from Nantes was driving past, saw and remembered me, and that was that. In the bag.

'They drove me straight to their local headquarters and threw me in a cell. That night Bonzo, as I nicknamed the older man, came to my cell with a couple of his chums. They told me it was going to be a long process, that they intended enjoying themselves, and that this session would only be the start.'

Ross swallowed more beer. His stomach heaved at the memory, and he'd gone chill all over. He could see the look in Bonzo's eyes the first time Bonzo hit him, a combination of sadistic pleasure and malicious glee.

'So they tortured you,' Norma said in a quiet voice.

'Only the once. Before they could indulge themselves any further a message arrived from the big cheese himself, Heinrich Himmler, head of the SS and Gestapo, saying that he personally wanted to "interview" me. I have no idea what about.

'I was bundled into a car with Bonzo, another charmer and a driver, with me in between Bonzo and his pal, and off we set. I don't know what our destination was – I did ask and got a clout round the mouth for my trouble, but it was a helluva long drive.

'Hours passed, and night came. We stopped off for food and our third refill of petrol, then set off again. A little past midnight the one on my right dozed off, and about half an hour later Bonzo, on my left, did the same.

'To be truthful I never dreamt I'd get away with it. What I did intend was being shot in the process of trying, killed, so that it would be over and done with, and there would be no more torture. I threw my full weight against Bonzo, at the same time grabbing the door handle. Bonzo gave a yell of surprise, the door flew open, and we both went tumbling out.'

Ross shook his head in disbelief. 'It's the sort of thing you see in the pictures and which wouldn't work in real life. Except on that occasion it did. Bonzo and I bounced on the road while the driver jammed on his brakes and slewed to a stop. Completely unhurt, I jumped to my feet and sprinted for the trees – we were passing through a forest at the time. A number of shots rang out, but none hit me and I was away.'

'That's incredible,' Norma breathed. 'What happened then?'

'I ran and ran till I was nearly sick. There was a full moon that night. Having shaken off pursuit I continued on walking as fast as I could, wanting to put as much distance between me and my captors as possible. I knew that come the dawn the whole area would be crawling with Germans, and that Bonzo and the other two would do everything they could to recapture me to avoid having to go to Himmler and report my escape.'

He drew on his cigarette, and blew out smoke. 'I walked till the first light, then hid out along a riverbank until the next night when I started walking again.

'I had no idea where I was, except that I must be halfway across France, in some direction, from where I'd been picked up; had to be from the number of hours we'd driven. I wasn't worried about the other members of Oberon. Their identities were safe as I hadn't talked, and once they realised I'd disappeared they'd be onto DF like a shot to be taken out of France.

'That second night, starving hungry, I decided to reconnoitre a farm to see if I could find anything to eat. Well I found more than that, I found the Maquis.'

He paused. 'Do you know about the Maquis?'

'A little, not much.'

'They're young men avoiding the STO, which is the compulsory labour service in Germany. They form into bands, often taking to the extreme high ground where they camp out. The group I had fallen in with belonged to a band seven hundred strong that had an encampment on the Glières plateau near Annecy. That particular group had come down off the plateau to collect some arms and ammunition, which they were desperately short of. When I explained to the group who and what I was, and that the Gestapo had taken my papers and money, they said it was best, for the time being, that I went with them. And so, thinking that it was for the best, I did.'

'Why didn't SOE hear you were still alive?' asked Norma.

Ross pulled a face. 'When the Maquis discovered I was a doctor, they were overjoyed, it solved a great many of their medical problems. Again and again they assured me they were trying to get in touch with DF so that I could be taken out of

France but in reality they were doing no such thing. It suited their purpose to have me stay with them, so I was trapped.

'When I finally twigged that they weren't making any effort to contact DF I argued the toss with them hoping they'd change their mind, but they didn't.

'Did you escape from them in the end?' Norma queried.

'There wasn't a hope of that, I was too closely watched. And so the months passed with me thinking I was going to be there, on that damned plateau, for the duration of the war. Then one day one of their leaders, a man called Henri Delmas, caught a bullet that lodged close to the heart. Only a skilled surgeon could remove that bullet, and if it wasn't taken out soon Delmas would die. I realised that was my opportunity and told them, even if it meant my own life, that I wouldn't operate unless they promised me they would do as they'd said originally and contact DF.

'The leaders gave me that promise, and just to make sure they kept it, for they were all devout Catholics, I made each and every one of them swear it on a statue of the Virgin Mary and Infant Jesus.

'I operated – damned tricky it was too given the conditions – and Delmas survived. This time they did keep their word. A fortnight later I had a rendezvous with a DF agent.'

'When was this?' asked Norma.

'Early on this month, five days before the invasion came ashore here.'

'So DF brought you here then?'

'I thought they'd take me out into Switzerland, the Glières plateau being close to the Swiss border, but no, they took me south to the coast close to St Tropez where I was put aboard a felucca and taken to Algiers. I arrived in Algiers two days after the invasion.'

'Why weren't you taken back to England?'

'Various reasons. Now I'm known to the Gestapo I won't be asked to return to France, so my time in the field is over. M knew that I'd be very useful here as a doctor, particularly while the fighting is going on, which it will do until we recapture all of North Africa. It is also better for the SOE to have their own doctor here, a doctor who's SOE himself. The other part of my brief is that when the fighting in North Africa is over I'm to take up duties as an instructor. I'll be teaching parachuting and unarmed combat.'

'To whom?'

'Not regular SOE agents as that's all done for them at Arisaig, so it can only be irregulars of some sort. But that's just a guess on my part, the hierarchy haven't confided in me yet. Only to say that I will be taking up such duties in the course of time.'

'It was a shock to see the grey in your hair,' she said suddenly, then blushed. It was a rather personal comment to make.

He stroked his beard. 'Life in the field does that to you. At least it did to me,' he replied quietly.

An uneasy silence fell between them. 'Would you like another gin sling?' he asked eventually. 'I'd like another beer myself.'

'Please.'

He left her to go to the bar, while she finished her drink. When he returned there were more silences between them, and what conversation there was had become stilted. She felt he'd put up a mental barrier against her.

After a while he offered to drive her home, and she accepted. She'd cadged a lift to the hotel from someone else at Massingham, there was always to-ing and fro-ing between there and Algiers.

'Goodnight then,' he said rather formally at the door of Casa Bon-Bon.

She wondered if she should ask him in, and decided against it. 'Goodnight,' she answered, and shook the hand he extended to her.

She thought he was going to say something further, but he didn't. Leaving her he returned to his car and drove off.

'Damn!' she swore. She'd been so looking forward to meeting Gabriel, and the whole thing had fallen flat. She shouldn't have made that remark about his greyness, everything had been all right up until then.

Violette, waiting up for her, shrieked when she told her who Gabriel had turned out to be.

Norma was sitting on the beach, staring out to sea, thinking about Jeremy Dereham. She hadn't heard from him since he'd visited Grendon Underwood fourteen months previously. But then she hadn't written to him either. War was strange; it brought some people together, made others drift apart. There had been nothing serious between them anyway. It had been fun to go out with him, that had been all.

'Hello.'

She glanced up to find Ross smiling down at her. 'Hello.'

'I saw you were on your own and thought I'd come and join you. Is that all right?'

'It's a free beach.'

His smile vanished. 'Well, if you'd rather I didn't.'

There she was saying the wrong thing again. She seemed to make a habit of it where he was concerned. 'I'd like it if you would,' she stated firmly, and patted the sand beside her.

He sat, pulled his knees up to his chest, and put his arms round them. The years seemed to drop away to make him look young again, boyish almost. He also looked extremely vulnerable. Norma's instinct was to take him to her breast, cuddle him close, and tell him not to worry about the Bogey Man. He was safe from the Bogey Man while she was there.

'Fancy a jeep?' he asked.

'I beg your pardon?'

'You haven't got your own transport yet, so you're having to rely on lifts when you want to go anywhere. I can get a Yankee jeep for you if you want.'

Doctor Ross was just full of surprises. First he reveals himself as Gabriel, now he was offering her a jeep. 'Where's the catch?'

He gave her one of his sideways looks. 'No catch Norma. I'm only trying to be helpful to a . . . friend.' He paused. 'We are still friends aren't we? Like when I was Gabriel?'

She'd been wondering about that in bed the previous night, and her conclusion had been that they weren't. 'Yes,' she said, and meant it.

'I'll have it round at the Casa Bon-Bon tomorrow sometime.'

'As easy as that?'

'As easy as that,' he confirmed.

'How can you . . .' She broke off when he held a finger to his lips. 'It's not stolen is it?'

'Would I give you a stolen jeep?' he replied, in mock outrage.

'You might. How do I know what you'd do?'

He laughed. 'It isn't stolen, I promise you.' He paused, then added as a throwaway. 'At least not around here it isn't.'

'Doctor Ross!'

He laughed again. 'Nor anywhere else. And please, the name is Douglas.'

'All right, Douglas,' she said, almost shyly.

'Do you swim?'

Now what was this about? 'I can do, though I haven't swum in years. I was born by the sea, and learned to swim in it.'

'Where was that?'

'A little place called Kirn on the Firth of Clyde.'

He looked away. 'How about us getting together for a swim tomorrow? I know it's winter here but the sea is warm. Of course I'll understand if you're busy and it's not on.'

Defensive, she thought. But then the last thing he was was a ladies' man, she remembered the Staff in the Royal Free telling her that. 'That would be nice.'

He looked back at her. 'What time?' he asked slowly.

Norma thought of her schedule, and wished those other two FANY WT operators would hurry up and get there. Life was so difficult with only herself and Violette to man their set.

'3 pm?'

He screwed up his face in thought. He had a ward round then but could rejiggle that. 'Yes, that's fine with me. Will this spot do?'

'It's as good as any other.'

'Then three o'clock here.' He ran a hand through bone-white sand. 'Tell me about Kirn, and yourself. I know nothing about you after all. Or very little anyway. Certainly nothing about your background.'

She amazed herself by telling him everything. About her parents, sisters, Bridgeton, Midge, her dancing, and Midge running off with Zelda Caprice. The only thing she didn't spell out was that she and Midge had been lovers, but then that must have been obvious from the way she spoke about him.

Douglas listened intently.

She glanced at her wristwatch. Ten past three, he was late. She was already wearing the costume she'd borrowed underneath her uniform. All she had to do was take her uniform off and she'd be ready for their dip. She had a huge towel with her, one of Violette's scroungings, and could change underneath that when it was time to get dressed again.

Three fifteen now, and still no sign of him. She ran her hands through her hair. She was really looking forward to this, and had been since he'd proposed it. She kicked off her shoes and scrunched sand up between her stockinged feet. It was a good feeling and reminded her of Kirn and those far off, happy, childhood days.

When it reached the half hour her spirits started to sink. Where was he? Then she had a terrible thought, had he changed his mind? Surely not?

Could it be that he'd gone off her when she'd told him her family lived in the Glasgow slums? After all he was what in Bridgeton they'd always called a 'toff'; well-educated, well-spoken, undoubtedly monied to some degree.

She knew her background was totally different to all the other FANYs – theirs were more or less similar to what Douglas's must be. When he realised she was a slummie had that been it? Anger flared in her, if that was the case he might have broken their arrangement or made some excuse – not just left her standing there.

At quarter to, feeling angry, let down, and a little sick, she began walking back to Casa Bon-Bon.

She opened her eyes, what was that? There it was again, a knocking. Someone was knocking on the outside door. She fumbled for the matches she kept by her bedside and lit one. She saw it was gone midnight. The knocking started again.

She lit the storm lantern by her bed, then slipped into her dressing gown. Violette put her head round the bedroom door.

'Who do you think it is?' Violette asked, wiping the sleep from her eyes.

'Search me. But we'd better answer it. It could be something to do with work.'

'At this hour?'

'Since when did the army consider the time?'

Violette nodded, Norma had a point. 'Wait a mo' though,' she said, and returned to her own bedroom. When she met up with Norma in the sitting room she was carrying a .38 Webley revolver.

'Where did you get that from?' Norma whispered. She hadn't known Violette had a gun.

'It was issued to me when I was a "joe". I just never handed it back again,' Violette explained.

The storm lantern Norma was holding cast weird and grotesque shadows on the ceiling and walls as they walked to the outside door. Just before they reached it the person knocked again.

'Who's there?' Violette demanded.

'Field Marshall Rommel,' a male voice replied.

Violette glanced at Norma. Somebody was playing funny buggers. 'I've got a gun here; if Field Marshall Rommel tries anything he shouldn't the krauts will be looking for a new Field Marshall to replace a very dead one,' Violette said, and gestured to Norma to open the door.

The door swung open to reveal a walking stick with a piece of white material tied to its tip. The person holding the stick was hiding round the side of the door.

'Peace. I come in peace and bearing gifts,' Douglas said, having disguised his voice before. He stepped out and smiled at them. Besides the walking stick he was carrying two bottles of wine.

Violette dropped the gun. 'I think it's for you,' she said to Norma.

'My fullest apologies for standing you up, but there was a very good reason which I've now come to tell you. I thought we might have a drink together,' he said, and brandished the wine bottles.

'I'll leave the pair of you to it. I'm going back to bed,' Violette said diplomatically.

'Not until you've seen Norma's jeep,' Douglas told her.

Norma looked at the street beyond, and sure enough there was an American jeep parked in front of the house. 'I thought that . . .' She stopped herself, deciding she didn't want him to know what she had thought.

'It really is for me?' she said.

'Hold this please,' he replied, and gave her the walking stick. He put a hand in a trousers' pocket and pulled out an ignition key. 'As from this moment it's all yours,' he smiled, and exchanged the key for the walking stick.

'Shall we inspect it?' he proposed.

The three of them went to the jeep which was an almost new one with only five thousand miles on the clock. It was left hand drive of course, something Norma was going to have to get used to. 'I don't know what to say,' Norma told him.

'How about "come on in and let's open that wine you've got there"?'

Norma gave a low laugh. 'All right, come on in and we'll open that wine you've got there.'

He smiled broadly. 'Why Miss McKenzie, I thought you'd never ask.'

They returned to the villa and went inside. Violette left Norma and Douglas, saying she needed her beauty sleep.

Douglas sat on a wooden box while Norma lit a second lantern, then opened the wine. 'We've no glasses I'm afraid, we'll have to make do with mugs.'

'That's fine by me.'

The wine was a local red, the labels on the outside of the bottles written in Arabic and English. As Norma was pouring Douglas said, 'I really am terribly sorry about this afternoon, but it was unavoidable.'

'Oh yes?' She let a hint of coolness creep into her voice.

'I was just about to leave the hospital when suddenly we had a flap on. A Stuka dive bombed a fuel dump and the whole shebang went up. We had umpteen survivors brought in, many with the most frightful burns.'

She handed him his mug of wine. She could see now how tired he was, he reminded her of the first time she'd ever seen him at the Royal Free; he'd looked desperately tired then too.

He went on, 'I only left the hospital half an hour ago and went straight to pick up your jeep which I'd intended bringing along this afternoon.'

She felt terrible, she should have realised it was something to do with the hospital that had kept him away from the beach. She'd been stupid to think what she had.

He drank some wine, and a strange, haunted, expression came onto his face, and into his eyes. 'I had three men die on me, one after the other, in the operating theatre. It's horrible when that sort of thing happens. You feel so ineffectual.' He swallowed what was left in his mug. Without his asking she took the mug from him and refilled it.

When he lit a cigarette she noticed his hands were trembling. It was a complete transformation from the chap who'd knocked the door only a couple of minutes previously.

She sipped her own wine. 'Yesterday I told you all about me. What about telling me something about you now?'

He gave her a sideways look, the haunted expression still on his face and in his eyes. 'What sort of thing would you like to know?'

'Whereabouts you come from in Scotland for a start?'

'Glasgow.'

She blinked in surprise. She wasn't sure where she'd expected him to name, but not there. There was absolutely nothing 'Glasgow' about him. 'Do you really?'

'A place called Burnside. It's out on the road to Rutherglen and Cambuslang.'

'I'm afraid those are only names to me, I don't know the south side very well at all. I don't think I've ever been beyond the Plaza Ballroom in Victoria Road.'

'You danced there when you were a professional?'

'And as an amateur. We danced all the ballrooms in Glasgow as both.'

He puffed on his cigarette. 'My father's an eye specialist in the Victoria Infirmary, not far from your Plaza. He's the leading eye specialist in Scotland.'

'And what about your mother?'

'She's French, from Paris.'

'And you speak the language perfectly which was why M asked you to be a "joe".'

'I'm completely bi-lingual. Because of my mother I grew up speaking French as naturally as I did English. I can even vary my accent if I want to, which was handy at times when I was in the field.'

Similar in a way to Lynsey's background she thought. But then it was bound to have been. 'What's your mother called?'

'Solange.'

That was a lovely name, Norma thought. It had a romantic aura about it, but then so many French names did. 'And your father?'

'Forsyth.'

Forsyth Ross, there was nothing romantic about that. It sounded to her like a brand of whisky, or a district in the Western Highlands. 'Is your mother terribly attractive?' she asked, thinking to herself, like you are.

'She certainly was when younger, in fact she was something of a beauty. She and my father are still as in love as when they first met when he was in Paris studying for a short while after the Great War. He worships the ground she walks on.'

'And you take after your mother in looks?'

He stared at her. 'How did you know that?'

'It wasn't too difficult to work out. Your mother's French, and you don't look at all Scots, which I suppose is why – taking into consideration that you're so well spoken with only a hint of accent – that I always have trouble remembering that you actually are.'

He rubbed a hand across his face. 'It's my sallow complexion that's so un-Scottish. At school they used to call me fish-face.'

Norma laughed. 'And what school was that, Kelvinside Academy?'

'Glasgow Academy actually. There's nothing really to choose between the two. I went where I did because my father had gone there before me. They're both frightfully elitist of course.'

'Frightfully,' she agreed in a mocking tone. She was enjoying this, it was somehow terribly intimate, drawing them closer together. 'I went to a local school myself. It wasn't strange to see a bare bum hanging out of a threadbare pair of breeks there, or for children to have no shoes at all, even in deep mid winter.'

'*Not* elitist,' he smiled.

'Most definitely not.'

'But you were happy? That's the most important thing.'

'Oh yes! I had a wonderful family around me and we never went without proper food, clothes or shoes. Da was always in employment.'

'And now you've got money of your own.'

'Thanks to dear old Mr Gallagher and his daughter Morna.'

Douglas drank more wine. It was cheap, far too sweet, and not at all to his taste, but all he'd been able to lay his hands on at such short notice and so late at night. He wished he'd been able to buy something really nice for Norma, a Pauillac perhaps. Yes, a Pauillac would have been the very dab.

'Will you live with your parents after the war, or buy a place of your own?' he asked.

'I don't know. I could buy a wee place, I might enjoy that. What about you?'

'That all depends on where I get a job. I'd like to return to Glasgow, and if I did it would be silly to buy my own place when the house we've got already is so huge we rattle around in it like a handful of peas in a drum.'

'It's that large is it?'

'Absolutely enormous. We have nine bedrooms, which doesn't include those belonging to the servants.'

Norma was intrigued. 'You have servants?'

'Oh indeed, you need them to run a place that size. We have a butler, cook, three maids and a gardener.'

'Your father must be extremely rich?'

'Stinking. He did inherit a great deal mind, but he's added to that considerably. It's very lucrative being the leading eye specialist in Scotland. Anybody who's anybody comes to him, and pays top whack for the privilege.'

'How about brothers and sisters?'

Douglas shook his head. 'There's just me. I did have an elder brother but he died when he was only eight days old. Although they wanted more of a family mother never got pregnant again after she'd had me. It just wasn't to be.'

'It must have been lonely being an only child,' Norma said, thinking how she'd always had Lyn, and later Eileen, to play and fight with.

'I suppose it's a case of never missing what you've never had. I can't say I remember being particularly lonely, though presumably I must have been at times.'

It struck her then that his having been an only child had a lot to do with how he was as an adult. There was a sense about him of being apart from everyone else, it was even noticeable in company. That would also account for his shyness and general reserve. He hadn't had the physical and mental rough and tumble of brothers and sisters to knock that out of him.

He talked about himself some more, and she learned about Burnside and the house in Blairbeth Road which his grandfather, another eye specialist, had had built when the old Queen was on the throne.

Douglas drained his mug, the last of the wine he'd brought. 'I've really enjoyed our chat, it's quite unwound me. And I apologise again about this afternoon.'

'As you said, it was unavoidable.'

He placed his mug on the floor, and stood up. 'You really have done wonders with this place in such a short while. I've been meaning to mention that ever since I came in.'

Norma laughed. 'Not me, Violette. She's a terrific scrounger – as you can see.'

There were all sorts of items in the sitting room that Violette had come up with, though as yet no proper chairs. She'd promised that those, and a settee, would be forthcoming in the near future, but refused to say from where.

Douglas turned to Norma. 'There's a NAAFI dance on Friday night and I was wondering if you'd care to go with me. Hardly the Plaza mind you, and I'm more of a shuffler than anything else, but it might be fun.'

'I'm working till eight, though the two new girls will be here by then so I could rearrange my duty period if it was necessary.'

'No need. I'll pick you up here around nine which should give you time to get yourself ready, and get us there just as things are beginning to hot up.'

'Right then, it's a date as our American friends say.'

'It's a date.'

'And can we go in my jeep? I'd like that.'

'The jeep it is, with you driving.'

It had turned out to be a smashing day after all, she thought when he'd gone. She sang quietly to herself as she washed and dried their mugs, an old favourite of hers that she'd often danced to in Barrowland.

It was the third time they'd taken the floor together, and he was as stiff and unyielding as on the first. Stiffie the goalkeeper he'd have been cried in Glasgow. She suspected he was a better dancer than he appeared, if only he'd relax and let himself go.

'Can I tell you a secret?' she smiled.

'What?'

'I won't bite.'

258

He smiled painfully back. 'Sorry.'

'Relax.'

'I thought I was.'

'Nonsense, you know full well you're not.'

He unloosened a bit, but only a bit. 'It's funny you know,' he said.

'What is?'

'I'm all right when I "talk" to you on the WT. But like this I sort of clam up.'

'You don't have to be embarrassed because you're the bashful type where women are concerned. Lots of men are. And I'll tell you something else: I'd much rather go out with a man like that, who shows some respect, than with many of the Lotharios around.'

'You would?'

'Without a shadow of a doubt.'

He perked up visibly to hear that, and even unloosened a little bit more.

The band were chronic, Norma thought. Even the worst Glasgow dancehalls would soon have given them the order of the boot. As for the standard of dancing, it was on about a par with the band's playing. Which wasn't saying very much at all.

Despite everything, Douglas never did relax properly, but Norma had a good time and was sad when the last Waltz was played. As they climbed into the jeep she contemplated asking Douglas if he'd like to go for a drive along the seafront, but decided not to. She'd have jumped at the chance if he'd suggested it though.

'You're an excellent driver,' Douglas said as they headed for Massingham.

'I like driving, and I suppose if you like doing something you tend to be good at it. Generally speaking anyway.'

He leant back in his seat and closed his eyes.

'Penny for them?'

'I was just thinking how different all this is to . . .' He trailed off.

'France?'

'Yes,' he said softly.

'At least that's all behind you now. You'll never be asked to go back.

Thank God, he said inwardly. 'If I told you what a relief it was to know that, you'd think me quite a coward.'

Norma looked at him, what a bundle of contrasts he was. And so sensitive – a huge streak of sensitivity ran right through him. 'How could Gabriel be a coward after what he did? DR told me after we learned you'd been picked up by the Gestapo that you were the best agent we had.'

'DR said that?'

'And meant it, I can assure you. He also said he kept you in far longer than he should have done because you were doing such a first-class job. He greatly admired you – as I did.'

'Cowardice and bravery, there's a very thin dividing line between the two. Very thin,' Douglas said, so softly Norma had to strain to hear.

'Then how much more of an achievement for the coward to be brave than for the naturally brave person who fears nothing.'

'The ones who fear nothing soon end up dead, heroes or otherwise.'

Silence fell between them till, coming into Club des Pins, Norma cracked a joke which made them both laugh. Immediately the atmosphere lightened.

She parked in front of Casa Bon-Bon behind Douglas's Standard. He was about to get out when she placed a restraining hand on his arm. 'Thank you very much for tonight.'

'Sorry I'm not much of a dancer.'

'Stop apologising, you do so too often. It was a lovely evening.'

He stared at her in the darkness. 'Would you like to go out again?'

'When?'

He hesitated. 'Is tomorrow night too soon? Or inconvenient?'

'Where to?'

'The bar in the canteen?'

'What time?'

'Nine.'

'Do you want to meet me here or there?'

'Here.'

'Right then, I'll be waiting.'

'If I don't turn up, or am late, it'll be because of the hospital,' he said quickly.

'I understand.'

'If you had a phone I could ring, but you haven't.'

'If you don't turn up or are late I'll know that it's the hospital that's to blame,' she repeated. Perhaps it was because of the darkness, there was only a sliver of moon showing in the sky, but it was almost as though they were 'talking' to each other on WT. The old easiness was suddenly back between them.

'Norma?'

'Yes?'

'I know this probably sounds juvenile and trite, but I like you, I like you very much.'

'I'm glad about that. I like you very much too.'

Come on! she thought. Don't just sit there, take me in your arms and kiss me. Can't you see I'm dying for you to do that!

'Goodnight,' he said huskily.

'Goodnight.'

He reached for the doorhandle. 'Is that all?' she asked quietly. He stopped reaching, and turned to her again.

He placed a hand on her cheek, and slowly drew it down her cheek and the length of her neck. She shivered and her insides flared with a sudden excitement. The same hand went to the nape of her neck, and drew her to him. She went willingly.

He kissed her deeply, for a long time. When it was finally over she found herself limp, drained almost. It had been that kind of kiss.

'Tomorrow night,' he breathed.

'Tomorrow night,' she confirmed, in a high-pitched squeak, and wondered at her voice having come out like that. She certainly hadn't intended it to.

She cleared her throat. 'Tomorrow night,' she repeated in what was more like her normal voice.

She continued sitting in the jeep while he went to his Standard, got in and drove away.

She took a deep breath, then another. She stared up at a sky mainly obscured by low scudding clouds. The sliver of moon was still visible, while over to the northeast a small scattering of stars had appeared.

Closing her eyes, she smiled. She hadn't felt this way in a long time. A long long time. Not since ... Breaking off that line of thought she got out the jeep and went inside.

Norma and Douglas were in Algiers doing some Christmas shopping, when, on coming out of a souk, Norma spotted a man on the opposite side of the street, the sight of whose face brought her up short. The man was the double, an absolute *doppelgänger* of ... 'Da!' she screamed, and dropped the parcels she was carrying.

Arms thrown wide she flew across the road. That was no *doppelgänger*, that was the real thing, her father.

Brian was staring at her in a combination of astonishment and joy. As she crashed into him he picked her up and birled her round again and again.

'It really is you, it really is,' she said through the tears of delight and happiness that were streaming down her face.

Brian put her back on the ground. 'Oh lassie!' he whispered, a glint of wet in his eyes. By now Douglas had joined them.

'Da, I'd like you to meet Douglas Ross. He's a friend of mine. Douglas this is my father.'

'Pleased to meet you sir,' Brian said, having taken note of Douglas's rank.

Douglas would have shaken hands but couldn't because of the parcels he was loaded down with. 'And I'm pleased to meet you Mr McKenzie.'

'But what on earth are you doing in Algiers?' Norma asked Brian.

Brian released her. I'm *en route* to Tunisia with the Pioneers. We're to link up with the Royal Engineers there and build various roads and bridges.'

'So when did you arrive?'

'Three days ago. We've another two days in Algiers I'm told, then it's on to Tunisia. If only I'd known you were here! Your letters home are all censored so we didn't have a clue where you were, only that it was someplace hot. And us just bumping into each other, what a coincidence, eh!'

Norma couldn't believe it. Her da, here in Algiers, standing in front of her beaming at her out of that weather-beaten face of his. It was incredible.

'Wait till your ma hears about this,' Brian said.

Norma glanced at her wristwatch, she was due on duty in forty minutes, and it was too late now to rearrange the duty.

Douglas saw her look at her watch and guessed correctly what was going through her mind. 'May I make a suggestion?'

'What?' she replied.

'As you're due back on duty why don't you make an arrangement to meet up with your father this evening. Are you free then Mr McKenzie?'

'I am indeed.'

'How about if I organise a private room for the pair of you in the St George Hotel. You can eat there together, and can be assured the food won't poison you as it would in many Algerian restaurants.'

'That's a terrific idea!' Norma enthused.

'Leave everything to me then.'

Norma gave him a grateful look. She knew there was more to his suggestion than the fact that Algerian restaurants tended to have a very bad reputation – it was because her da was a private and she an officer. It wouldn't be at all correct for her to socialise in public with someone from Other Ranks, even if it was her father. The British Armed Forces could be very sticky indeed about that sort of thing. (Not that it would have done her any damage, the SOE didn't care a fig about such matters, but if they were seen together and it was reported it could rebound on her da.)

'You'll join us of course,' Norma said to him.

'I wouldn't want to intrude,' Douglas replied.

'You wouldn't be.'

There was something in his daughter's voice that made Brian glance from her to Douglas. So that was how the land lay he thought to himself.

Douglas could see this wasn't merely a gesture on Norma's part, that she really did want him to join them. 'All right then, I'd be delighted to.' To Brian he said, 'Do you know where the St George is?'

'Aye, I've walked past it several times.'

'Let's say nine o'clock then. I'll be waiting in reception.'

Brian, his eyes shining, turned again to Norma. 'Who'd have credited it eh lass?'

'Who'd have credited it,' she echoed.

Brian appeared first in reception to find Douglas waiting for him. Douglas took him to the reserved room where he left him with a bottle of malt whisky while he returned to reception. Norma showed up, breathless with excitement, five minutes later.

'Is he here?' demanded Norma.

Douglas nodded. 'Yes.'

'All through my duty period I kept thinking I'd been day-dreaming and that it was all a figment of my imagination. I'm afraid I made a right hash of several signals. A sender in Gib got quite cross with me at one point.'

Douglas had taken her by the crook of the arm and was leading her to where their room was located. It was a smallish, wood-panelled room and was ideal for their purpose.

On entering the room Norma came up short, a smile blossoming on her face to see her da standing there with a glass of whisky in his hand and that same old battered pipe that she could remember from time out of mind stuck in his mouth.

'First decent dram I've had in months,' he smiled back, waving his glass at her.

'You can thank Douglas for that.'

'And I do,' Brian replied, giving Douglas a nod. He held out his drink in front of him. 'To you Norma, God bless and keep you safe during the rest of this terrible war.' He drained his glass.

Besides the whisky Douglas had laid on brandy and wine. He opted for the wine while Norma joined her father with 'the cratur'. 'Slainthe!' Douglas toasted.

Brian rounded on him in surprise, for the Gaelic pronunciation had been perfect. 'You're Scots? I mean, you're Scots sir? I'd never have guessed.'

'While we're alone like this it's Douglas, and yes I am Scots, from Glasgow.'

'You certainly don't sound it.'

Douglas laughed. 'That's what Norma always says.'

Brian's eyes flickered between the two. 'Is she your driver then?'

With a start Norma remembered her father knew nothing about her being in the SOE – as far as he and the rest of the family knew she was still a FANY driver. It was the same with Douglas's parents, they knew nothing about his involvement with SOE either.

'No, I'm hardly important enough for that. I'm just a doctor,' Douglas replied, appreciating the situation.

'I should think doctors are as important as anyone out here, and more important than many,' said Brian.

'True, but you know what I mean. FANYs drive for VIPs, and doctor or not, I'm certainly not that.'

A waiter appeared with some bits and bobs to munch on, a prelude to their meal which would be appearing shortly. When the waiter had gone Brian asked, 'So how did you two meet then?'

It was Norma who answered. 'Remember when I got blown up in London? Well it was Douglas who attended me at the Royal Free Hospital.'

'And a rotten patient she was too,' Douglas joked.

'Nonsense, I was ideal!' Norma retorted.

The undertones of this little exchange weren't lost on Brian; they told him a lot. Hadn't he and Effie had exactly the same sort of exchanges way back.

'Anyway, the ship Norma came in on was torpedoed and her friend had been hurt. I turned up to help and that's how we met a second time,' Douglas explained.

Brian's eyebrows shot up his forehead. 'Torpedoed? This is the first I've heard of that.'

'Well I did mention it, but my letters home are all censored. However, I came to no harm – as you can see.'

'But your pal did?'

'Helen Rolfe, she's making marvellous progress though. Isn't she Douglas?'

'I hope to discharge her for Christmas. She's come on by leaps and bounds.'

'She lost a kidney,' Norma said to Brian.

'Let's just be thankful it wasn't you,' Brian muttered, taking another swallow of his malt.

'How's Eileen? Ma rarely mentions her in her letters.' Turning to Douglas she explained, 'That's my wee sister who lost her hubby in the train crash.'

Brian shook his head. 'I was home just before I left for here, and to be frank Norma that lassie worries the pants off me. She's lost weight, completely let herself go, and most of the time just sort of wanders around looking lost. It fair broke my heart to see her.'

'She was very much in love with Charlie. It's going to take her a long time to get over him.'

'Let's just hope she does. She's still a young woman with her whole life ahead of her. I'm bitter sorry about Charlie, but she mustn't let it sour her for ayeways.'

'Do you think it might Da?'

He shrugged. 'It could well, and that's a fact. As you say, Charlie Marshall was sun and moon to that girl.'

'And what about Lyn?'

'She's hunky dory. Looking lovelier than ever.'

'What a transformation that was eh?'

Brian nodded. 'Talk about the ugly duckling.'

Norma said to Douglas, 'Lyn's the middle sister. She was a right fatso when young, podge I used to call her when I was being nasty. Then suddenly she went on a diet – while I was in London with the FANY – and wham bam! I hardly recognised her. She'd turned into a real glamour puss with the sort of figure that makes other women turn green with envy. Including yours truly.'

'Maybe I'll get to meet them all one day,' Douglas smiled.

'Maybe,' she smiled back.

They chatted on about Glasgow for a while longer, and then the same waiter returned with a trolley and their food. A circular table with three chairs round it had already been set for them.

There was a seafood dish to start with, followed by fillet steak and a choice of vegetables. The hotel did very well out of the Americans who stayed there, the Americans making sure they and their chums didn't go without.

There were some bottles of Pabst and Blatz American beer to go with the steaks, as the hotel was out of British beer for the time being. Brian tasted a Blatz, screwed up his face in disgust and said thank you very much, but he'd stick with the malt whisky.

Halfway through the main course Douglas excused himself to go to the toilet. When he was gone Brian looked levelly at Norma. 'It seems serious between you two.'

She pushed a piece of sautéd potato round her plate. 'It could be Da. I don't know for certain yet,' she replied evasively.

'Well that's what comes across.'

She pushed the potato some more. 'Do you like him?'

'Oh aye, he's a nice enough chap. But he's a different kind to us Norma.'

'You mean that – despite me being in the FANY and an officer – I'm still working-class and he isn't?'

'It's not just between you and him, there are also his parents and friends to take into account. Can you go up to his and their level? For that's what you'd have to do.'

She laid down her fork and took a swallow of whisky. What her father was saying wasn't new to her; she'd already thought along those lines herself. 'I know this Da, that he's the only man I've felt anything for since Midge.'

Brian lowered his eyes, unable to gaze into the old pain that had suddenly appeared in hers.

After a few seconds silence he changed the subject.

It was Christmas Eve 1942 and Norma and Violette were eagerly awaiting the arrival of Helen from the hospital. Douglas was arranging the details of her discharge and would then bring her on to Casa Bon-Bon, where her room was all ready waiting for her. Violette had even managed to scrounge some proper beds – three of them, so they had one each. A vast improvement on the iron framed canvas jobs which had been sheer torture to sleep on.

Norma and Violette had made multi-coloured paper chains which they had strung across the sitting room. A Christmas bell hung suspended from the ceiling.

The tree was a five foot fir provided by Douglas. They hadn't been able to get hold of fairy lights so the tree was decorated with puff balls of cotton wool and various sparkly bits and pieces that Violette had come up with.

Pride of place in the sitting-room, next to the tree, was a three-piece suite that had made its appearance several days previously. It was an old suite, junkable by any standards, but an awful lot better than the wooden boxes they'd been making do with up until then. Violette had refused to say where it, and the beds, had come from. That was her closely-guarded secret.

Underneath the tree were the presents, while on the decorator's pasting-up table, covered with a local fancy-worked tablecloth bought in Algiers, were a host of festive goodies, including a number of bottles of wine and spirits that Douglas had laid on.

Norma glanced at her watch. 'Shouldn't be long now,' she said.

'Fancy a sherry?'

'Why not!'

Violette did the honours, using two of their 'new' glasses, something else she'd recently scrounged.

'Deck the halls with boughs of holly ...' Norma sang to herself as Violette poured. She was really looking forward to Christmas, mainly because she'd be spending a lot of it with Douglas. The following morning, after breakfast, she, Violette and other FANYs (there were now over fifty at Massingham), were going carol singing at the hospital. She'd enjoy that, even if she didn't have a particularly marvellous singing voice.

Violette handed Norma her drink. 'Absent friends,' Norma toasted. Violette knew that Norma was referring to Lynsey and Pam Parkinson, the latter still in F section.

'Absent friends,' Violette agreed, and they both sipped their sherry.

'They're here!' Norma exclaimed on hearing a car drawing up outside the villa. They both laid down their glasses, rushed to the front door and flung it open.

Douglas helped Helen out of his Standard, and up into the house. Once inside, with Norma and Violette fussing about her, she was taken to the settee and told to rest there. They'd show her round the villa when she'd caught her breath. And meanwhile, how about a celebratory sherry?

'Oh yes please,' Helen replied.

'Just what the doctor ordered.' Douglas said. 'And I'll have a large brandy if you don't mind.'

Norma gave him a sharp look. There was something in his

voice that wasn't natural, something disturbing. 'What's wrong?' she demanded.

He lit a cigarette. 'Admiral Darlan was assassinated a couple of hours ago.' Darlan was a collaborator, deputy to Pétain in Vichy France, who'd been unlucky enough to be in Algiers when it was taken by the Allies. At that stage the French political situation in North Africa was basically a tussle between the Darlanists who advocated non-resistance to the axis powers, and the de Gaullists who were determined to fight.

Norma's face lit up. 'But that's good news!'

'Except for one thing.'

'What's that?'

'It was René Bonnier de la Chapelle who shot him.'

Norma thought of the dashing French Lieutenant whom she and many others at Massingham had become so fond of. 'What will they do to him?' she asked quietly.

'It's a capital offence. But they may commute it to a prison sentence, hopefully a short one.'

Norma had a sudden thought. 'Did SOE set this up?'

'He used an SOE pistol, but apart from that I couldn't say.'

'It's certainly to the Allied advantage that the traitor Darlan is dead. And if SOE organised it, good luck to them, they did the right thing,' Violette said venomously.

'Has René been arrested?' queried Norma.

'Yes.' This time it was Helen who answered.

'There'll be a court martial, though no one knows exactly when,' Douglas said.

That was a dampener right enough, thought Norma. Poor René. Time in prison, no matter how short, what a horrible prospect for him.

Violette poured sherry for Helen, and a hefty brandy for Douglas. Then they all sat and talked quietly about Darlan's death and the effect it was going to have on the Allied cause in North Africa, a cause that was still, in the main, bogged down in the mud of Tunisia. The new offensive would be in the spring when the ground would be hardened again, and when wheeled and tracked vehicles and guns could continue advancing.

It was Boxing Day. There had been a non-stop traffic of signals in and out of Massingham. At 8 pm Norma and the three other WT operators on that shift knocked off, handing over to the caretaker shift – two girls, who'd be working through till midnight. The coders and decoders also changed shift at this time, also handing over to a reduced number.

When Norma got back to Casa Bon-Bon, she found that Violette had gone for a drink in the canteen bar, and Helen was preparing to go to bed. Helen was finding it tiring being out of hospital and was, wisely, having early nights.

It was about an hour later when Norma, in pyjamas and a dressing gown, heard a car drive up and park outside the villa. A minute later there was a tap on the front door.

'Can I come in?' Douglas asked when she opened the door.

He took off his hat and threw it onto the settee. 'Is there any of that brandy left?'

'Plenty. Do you want some?'

'Please.'

He sat on the settee beside his hat, and bent forward to put his face in his hands, his elbows resting on his knees. He didn't look up again till Norma handed him his brandy.

He gulped down half the glass's contents, took a couple of deep breaths, then gulped down what remained. 'They shot René half an hour ago,' he said quietly.

Norma was shocked to hear that. 'But he was pardoned by General Giraud!'

'The Darlanists worked on Giraud till they persuaded him to withdraw the pardon. René was then taken out and executed.'

'Vengeance I suppose,' she said heavily.

'It won't do them any good, de Gaulle's the man for the French in North Africa now. But they had to have their pound of flesh for their Admiral.'

Norma poured herself a brandy, and refilled Douglas's glass. She could see now how wretched he looked. His face was taut and he had dark shadows under his eyes.

He shuddered all over, from head to toe, then slumped in on himself. 'So many people, so many dead, gone since the war started,' he whispered in a voice that was riven and raw.

Norma thought of Lynsey, and Charlie Marshall and all the others who had died, all as a direct result of the conflict. 'Yes,' she whispered.

'I only thank God I don't have to go back into the field again.'

She went and knelt beside him. 'At least with Rene it was quick, soon over with. Not like it would have been with you, and has been for so many others, if you hadn't succeeded in escaping from the Gestapo.'

'Sometimes I wake up at night convinced that Bonzo is in the room with me. It's absolutely terrifying.'

She placed her glass on the floor, and took him into her arms. His body was hard against her softness. Holding him seemed the most natural thing in the world. She felt that she'd known him always, that in her arms was where he belonged. It was at that moment, that they first truly became as one.

'Would you like to stay the night?' she asked.

'With you?'

'With me,' she confirmed. 'In my bed.'

He shuddered again, a long racking shudder that left him limp in her embrace. 'I can think of nothing that I'd like more.'

She released him, picked up her glass, rose and extended a hand to him. 'Luckily it's a three-quarter bed so we won't be too squashed,' she said.

He grasped hold of her hand, and rose. 'Hello Norma.'

'Hello Gabriel.'

She led him through to the bedroom.

They stripped together, each watching the other as they did. He finished first, and went to the bed from where he continued to watch Norma. When she too was completely naked she came to lie beside him.

She ran a palm along his leg, a leg that was firm with muscle. His belly too was firm when she touched, then caressed that.

'I eh ... feel I should say something,' he said in a low voice.

She knew what it was going to be. 'You've never been with a woman before have you?'

His embarrassment gave way to surprise. 'Is it that obvious?'

She kissed him lightly on the lips. 'The only thing that's obvious is how right this is between us.'

'That's how I feel Norma. I never because ... well I suppose because I've always been rather shy where women are concerned. Then the war happened, and even if I'd wanted to there wasn't any time for that sort of thing anymore.'

'I'm glad I'm the first, that you waited for me.' She paused, then added softly. 'I won't try and lie to you and pretend that I too am a virgin. I'm not.'

'The boyfriend in Glasgow, the one you danced with?'

'Yes.' She didn't see the point in mentioning that single encounter with Philip what's-his-name at Fawley Court. 'Midge and I were engaged to be married.'

He nodded, understanding and accepting what she'd told him.

She gathered him into her arms again, as she'd done in the sitting room. And for a while they were both sublimely content to lie there just like that.

Norma lay listening to the sound of his breathing. He was breathing shallowly in sleep, every so often giving a sort of snort.

She felt whole again, complete. It was how she'd used to feel with Midge, and she hadn't felt like that since he'd left her to run off with Zelda Caprice.

It wasn't just sex, though that was part of it. It was emotional as well as physical, a combination of both. It was as though all this long while a piece of her had been missing, a piece she'd now found again.

She realised there were tears in her eyes, and her lips curved into a smile as they started trickling down her face. They were tears of joy.

'How do you feel?' Douglas asked.

'Terrified,' Norma replied.

Douglas grinned, it was the answer he'd expected. They were in a Dakota aircraft along with a number of Loyalist Spaniards whom Douglas had been training in the mechanics of parachuting. This was to be their first jump from a plane, as well as Norma's. At her request he'd been training her also.

The Dakota was flying at twelve hundred feet and would shortly be over an area just to the north of Massingham where the Spaniards, Norma and Douglas would be making the jump. They were going to be watched by a group of personnel from Massingham together with a guest of honour, the head of the British Political office at AFHQ (Allied Forces Headquarters-Mediterranean), Mr Harold Macmillan.

It was the beginning of June 1943, and the previous month

Tunisia had fallen to the Allies. And what a victory it had been! The axis capitulation had been the greatest massed surrender of fully equipped troops in modern history.

If it had been a memorable victory for the Allies it had also cost them dear. Nearly seventy thousand men had been lost – dead, wounded and missing. Thirty-five thousand British, eighteen thousand American and fifteen thousand French.

But for every man the Allies had lost, the enemy had lost five. In the end, fifteen full divisions had laid down their arms, two hundred and sixty-six thousand men, mostly German.

'Right then, hook up!' Douglas called out, for their parachutes would be activated by static line.

He went swiftly along the line of men, checking that everything was in order. Then he returned to Norma, checked her parachute, and hooked himself up behind her. She would be the second last person out, he the last.

Suddenly Norma had an overwhelming urge to go to the toilet to do a 'number one' as she'd used to call it. Well there was no chance of that of course, she could only hope she wouldn't disgrace herself.

The red warning light winked on, and they knew from their briefing on the ground that the drop was now only a minute off. There was no need to open the Dakota's side door, it had been left open at take off.

Douglas whispered in Norma's ear. 'Just remember to do everything I taught you and you'll be as right as Larry.'

Norma was wondering why she'd ever thought this would be a good thing to do. The training itself had been fun, but now she was actually airborne and about to leap into nothingness she considered it sheer madness on her part. She'd thought it a good idea at the time because it meant she'd have even more time with Douglas.

They'd been sleeping together regularly since Boxing Day. Douglas would stay the night at Casa Bon-Bon three or four times a week. Their feelings for each other had continued to grow, with a rolling snowball effect.

The red light winked out and the green went on. 'Go!' yelled Douglas unnecessarily as the leading Spaniard was already away.

'Oh mummy daddy,' Norma muttered as she shuffled

towards the door through which Spaniard after Spaniard was vanishing.

Half of them were gone now, each man following hard on the heels of the one in front. And then it was her turn.

Framed in the doorway, she hesitated. Below her the parachutes were billowing and drifting groundwards. The ground itself, even though she could see the watchers staring up, seemed a million miles away.

Lynsey hadn't frozen, she reminded herself. And anything a gel from the upper classes could do so too could a lassie from Bridgeton. Douglas was raising a hand to push her when she leapt from the aircraft.

There were several heart-stopping seconds during which she plummeted like a stone, and then thump! She was pulled upwards and backwards as her parachute fully unfolded. Her terror disappeared, replaced by elation. It was a sensation unlike any she'd ever experienced before. It was almost as if she'd suddenly learned how to fly.

Above her, Douglas was staring down at Norma in concern. Now that her parachute was safely open, the next point of danger was the landing. If she did that badly she could break an ankle or leg. She could even break her neck, he'd seen that happen before now.

He tore his gaze from her to focus on the Spaniards, many of whom were now down and gathering up their 'chutes. They were a fine bunch and quick learners. They would do well in whatever the powers that be had planned for them.

The ground was rushing at her now. Norma gathered her wits together, and forced herself to think coolly. She was determined not to make a hash of this., As she landed she pitched herself forward into the roll Douglas had taught her.

Douglas hit the ground several seconds later. He was up in a flash to punch his 'chute release. As the 'chute had already collapsed, and there was only a hint of wind, he left it where it was to run to Norma.

'How are you?' he demanded.

Her face was ablaze with excitement. 'Wow! Did I enjoy that! When can I do it again?'

He burst out laughing. He needn't have been anxious for her after all, everything had gone hunky dory for her.

'I've never been so exhilarated before. It was just amazing! When *can* I jump again?' she enthused.

She looked so gorgeous, so utterly delectable. And with that thought the laughter died on his lips, and a lump that seemed the size of an egg filled his throat. If the Spaniards and watchers hadn't been present he'd have swept her to him and kissed her there and then.

'When we're finished here I'll buy you a drink,' he said instead.

'Sounds marvellous.'

The lump was still in his throat when, a few minutes later, he met and shook hands with Mr Harold Macmillan.

'So what is this show you're taking me to see?' queried Norma. She and Douglas were in his Standard heading for Algiers. It was 15th June, her twenty-sixth birthday, and Douglas, having picked her up from Casa Bon-Bon, was taking her out for a celebratory evening.

'I told you in the villa, it's a surprise.'

She gave him a replica of one of his sideways looks. 'You're being very mysterious.'

'I mean to be.'

She had a sudden horrible thought. 'It's not something dirty is it?'

He grinned ambiguously back at her.

'Douglas! I don't like filth.'

'It's not dirty, I promise you.'

'Hmm!' She wasn't sure whether he was telling the truth or not, he could be such a damned clever actor when he wanted to be. It was one of the many reasons he'd made an excellent 'joe'. Well, if it was filth she'd walk out, she couldn't abide smut and dirt. As they said in Glasgow, it gave her a dry boak.

Then again, she reminded herself, Douglas was hardly the sort to take her to something dirty. At least he didn't seem to be the sort. On the other hand, you never really knew with men, did you?

'I don't care for surprises like this,' she stated.

He laughed, infuriating her. Leaning across, she took a tiny bit of khaki-covered thigh flesh between thumb and forefinger, and pinched hard. Something Lyn had used to do to her when they were young. She had the satisfaction of hearing and seeing him give a yelp of pain.

'That was sore,' he protested.

'It was meant to be,' parodying his earlier words.

'You're a sadist, Norma McKenzie.'

'So are you for keeping me dangling like this.'

'I told you, it's a surprise. It would hardly be a surprise if I let on what it was, now would it?'

She sniffed disdainfully.

'You'll enjoy it.' He paused, then added uncertainly. 'I think.'

She couldn't tell whether he meant that, or was acting again.

He patted his left hand side uniform pocket for the umpteenth time to reassure himself that 'it' was still there. 'It' was.

'Why do you keep touching that pocket?' Norma demanded.

'Do I?'

'Yes you do.'

'Bit of an itch. I'm not touching, I'm scratching.'

Well she certainly didn't believe *that!* 'Nonsense,' she retorted.

He treated her to another ambiguous grin, then started humming 'Lilli Marlene'. He was still humming it when they pulled up in front of the St George Hotel. 'We're here,' he announced.

She was disappointed. What sort of surprise was this? Not much of a surprise in her opinion. They'd been here any number of times before. It was quite old hat. Unless ... 'Have they got a new floor show, is that it?'

He shook his head.

'But there *is* a show here?'

He came round and opened the door for her. 'Shall we go in?' he smiled, evading her question.

They went through reception, and to the rear of that floor to a room close to the one where they'd entertained Brian. On entering the room Norma found it to be larger than the other, and a lance-corporal waiting for them with a film projector all set up ready to go. Norma was intrigued.

'Evening sir, evening madam,' said the Lance-Corporal, saluting them.

276

A brace of club chairs had been set at a reasonable distance from the mobile screen that dominated the far wall. 'Shall we?' Douglas said, indicating the nearest chair to Norma.

She sat. 'It's a film then?' she said to Douglas, who nodded. 'But when you said a show I thought you meant a live show?'

'These Americanisms will creep in. Impossible for them not to with so many of our Yankee cousins about the place.'

'You were misleading me deliberately.'

'Are you suggesting I'm *devious* Miss McKenzie?'

'Yes,' she stated bluntly.

'I'll take that as a compliment rather than an insult.'

'Take it as a matter of fact.'

'Shall I start sir?' the Lance-Corporal asked.

'What's the film?' Norma asked him.

The Lance-Corporal looked at Douglas for guidance. 'Wait and see,' Douglas said, and squirmed back in his chair. When he was comfy he gave the Lance-Corporal the nod.

The Lance-Corporal switched the lights out, returned to the film projector and set it in motion.

Norma couldn't think what the film was going to be. She gasped with pleasure when the title revealed all. *A Midsummer Night's Dream* by William Shakespeare.

'I know I said when the war was over, but do you mind?' Douglas whispered.

'I think it's a lovely birthday treat. Thank you.'

It was a cast of stars. Mickey Rooney played Puck, Jimmy Cagney playing Bottom, Dick Powell, Olivia de Havilland, Joe E. Brown . . .

A little later those so familiar words were spoken by Oberon.

> . . . I know a bank where the wild thyme blows,
> Where oxlips and the nodding violet grows . . .

She reached over, took Douglas by the hand, and squeezed it. As the Fairy King spoke that particular piece of verse so did she, mouthing it in unison with him.

> . . . More fond of her than she upon her love:
> And look thou meet me ere the first cock crow.

277

To which the mischievous Puck replied, 'Fear not, my lord, your servant shall do so.'

It was a glorious film; Norma adored every moment of it. Adored it for itself, and the association it had for her and Douglas. Far too soon it was over and the Lance-Corporal was switching the lights back on again.

She blinked after the darkness, and the flickering images on the silver screen. She stared at Douglas adoringly.

'There's more to come,' he announced, springing to his feet, and hauling her, for they were still holding hands, to hers. What now? she wondered, bubbling with anticipation.

He led her from that room to the one where they'd entertained Brian. While they'd been watching the film a painted wooden sign had been fastened temporarily above the door, which said, 'Savoy Grill'. Norma laughed with delight.

As they went into the room the *maître d'hôtel* bowed low and said, 'Welcome to the Savoy Grill, madam.'

The same table as before had been set, this time with a crisp, cream linen tablecloth, silver cutlery, white bone china, and Waterford wine glasses. The menus and winelists, which they were handed as soon as they sat down, were the ordinary hotel ones except with a false front saying 'Savoy Grill'.

'May I recommend a Mâcon-Lugny to start with?' the *maître d'hôtel* suggested.

Norma looked at Douglas; he was the knowledgeable one about wine. 'A white Burgundy,' he explained. Then to the *maître d'hotel*, 'Yes, that'll do nicely thank you.'

The Mâcon-Lugny, already chilled, was produced while they perused the food menu, and its cork deftly removed. With a flourish the *maître d'hôtel* poured a soupçon for Douglas's approval.

He made sure it hadn't been corked, held it up to the light to judge its clarity, then took it into his mouth to swish it from side to side, then finally chew it. While he was going through this rigamarole Norma could hardly hide her amusement. She thought it very funny.

'Most satisfactory,' Douglas pronounced solemnly. The smiling *maître d'hôtel* poured them both a glassful, then left them to further study the menu.

As soon as the man was out of the room Norma burst out

giggling. 'Honestly, I can't take all that wine malarkey seriously, it looks so pretentious!'

'For some it is, for others not,' Douglas replied slowly.

'And for you?'

'Well, let me put it this way. This is an excellent wine which the *maître d'hôtel* is justifiably proud in serving. If I was to treat it with less appreciation than it deserves then I'd be insulting the man. Which is the last thing I want to do when he has gone to such lengths on our behalf.'

She studied him shrewdly. 'You always have an answer, don't you?'

He smiled, and took another sip of wine. It was a *premier cru*, and as excellent as he'd just said. 'Now what are we going to eat?' he asked, side-stepping her question.

It was in the middle of the main course that Norma, thoroughly enjoying the fish she'd chosen, said, 'All this, *A Midsummer Night's Dream*, the Savoy Grill, is just perfect. You couldn't have given me a better birthday, it's one I'll never forget.'

'Oh!' he exclaimed, as though just remembering something. 'I haven't given you your present yet.' He fumbled in his left-hand uniform pocket to produce a small, blue box – the sort rings come in. Her mind shot back to another box, a black box containing an engagement ring.

She laid down her knife and fork, then opened up the box. There was a plain gold band inside.

'I'm asking you to marry me,' Douglas said as she stared at it.

She looked from the ring to him. Their eyes didn't just meet, they fused together. Electricity sparked and flowed between the two of them.

'I love you,' he stated quietly.

'And I love you. I've known for some time now that I do.'

'So will you marry me?'

'Yes, of course. When?'

'Just as soon as it can be arranged.'

He rose, came round to her, and brought her to her feet. Their eyes were still fused together. 'We'll have to ask permission of course.'

'Do you foresee any trouble there?'

'I don't think so.'

279

'We'll just have to keep our fingers crossed then.'

Simultaneously, as though on cue, they collapsed into one another's arms. They hugged, squeezed, cuddled and kissed, neither able to get enough of the other.

Norma woke, and stretched languorously. Douglas was lying sprawled asleep beside her, and outside the birds were singing.

She slipped from the bed, and walked to the spiral iron staircase that twisted to the main floor of the room some twelve feet below. Without bothering to put a dressing gown over her thin nightie, for it was already extremely hot, she went down the staircase and across the flagstoned floor to the heavy wooden and metalled door which led out to the verandah. She pulled the door open and sunlight streamed into the room.

She took a deep breath, then ran her hands through her hair. Over to the right, on the pebbled beach, some fishing boats had been drawn up. They were long and slim in design, similar to a Viking longship, only far, far smaller, and were gaily painted. Further along a group of fishermen were sitting mending nets. It was an idyllic setting for their honeymoon.

Their wedding had taken place the previous afternoon. They had been married by the SOE padre at Massingham. Every FANY not on duty had come, with several hundred other SOE personnel crowding in and round the purpose-built chapel that had been erected since the invasion. The chapel was part of the ever-widening sprawl that Massingham was rapidly becoming, the original Club des Pins now only a nucleus of the far greater whole.

When the ceremony itself was over, there had been a reception in the canteen with food and drink in ample supply. While the celebrations were taking place she and Douglas escaped in his Standard, heading west to the little village of Gouraya and the guest house where they were now lodged.

It was Douglas who'd known the village and guest house and said they should go there; as far as Norma was concerned it had been an inspired choice.

The building, a long and rambling one-storey affair, was Moorish in design - at least Norma thought it was Moorish - as was the interior.

The room was the most unusual Norma had ever been in, far

280

less slept in. The walls were open brick, one of which had been whitewashed. There were exotic rugs scattered over the floor, and several hanging on the walls. Also hanging on the walls were various knives, scimitars and intricately worked pieces of leather. At regular intervals around the walls were metal projections from which terracotta pots filled with sweet-smelling flowers and herbs dangled. The high ceiling was curved, and also open brick. Somehow it contrived to be both soaring and intimate at the same time.

For Norma the *pièce de résistance* was the sleeping platform bolted halfway up one of the side-walls to stick out over the area below. On the platform was a double bed covered with silk sheets and a light multi-coloured quilt. The platform was reached by the spiral iron staircase.

Norma placed her hands on her hips, letting them slide sensuously down the outside of her thighs. A puff of wind blew in off the sea, catching the bottom of her nightdress and making it billow.

'Absolutely gorgeous,' Douglas said behind her.

She turned to find him leaning on one elbow watching her. There was a soft smile on his face, and love in his eyes. Her feelings for him welled within her. 'How about some breakfast?' she asked.

He shook his head – breakfast wasn't at all what he had in mind. 'Not yet. Come back to bed Mrs Ross.'

A thrill of pleasure ran through her to hear that. It was the first time she'd been called *Mrs Ross!* That's who she was from now on, Mrs Ross. Douglas's wife, Gabriel's wife.

'Gladly, Mr Ross,' she replied.

She closed the door again and returned to bed where he was waiting for her with open arms, arms she sank into.

She wouldn't have thought it possible, but it was even better than the night before.

Norma was irritable as she completed her deskwork, it had been a particularly hard and trying day. The FANY contingent at Massingham had expanded during the past few months to reach its present two hundred and fifty. Apart from the work centred on the wireless station they were involved in everything from parachute packing to top-level staff duties, and Norma was in charge, and responsible, for every last one of them. There had been more than one occasion when she'd regretted having been promoted to captain.

She didn't work as a WT operator anymore as all her time was now given over to administration and management. Some of which she enjoyed doing, some of which she didn't.

There was a knock on her office door. 'Come in!' she called out without glancing up.

It was a grave-looking Douglas. 'Nearly finished?'

'I am now,' she replied, snapping the ledger in front of her shut.

'I thought we might go for a stroll?'

Her smile disappeared as she took in his expression and tone of voice. 'Is something wrong?'

'I'll tell you as we walk.'

She got up, put on her cap, and led the way through to the outer office, and from there into the street beyond.

'Let's go down to the beach,' he said.

They used her jeep, for it was a fair hike from there to the beach. She parked by a clump of dunes, and they got out.

'It's bad news, I can tell,' she said as they started over the sand.

'I'm afraid so.'

They walked a short way in silence, Douglas searching for words, Norma dreading asking the question that was whirling round in her mind. She knew from his demeanour that the news wasn't just bad but very serious indeed. 'Have you been posted somewhere else?' she asked at last, her voice thick with fear.

He gave her one of his sideways glances, and shook his head.

'Thank God for that!' she exclaimed in relief, thinking that was the worst news he could break to her. But she was wrong.

It was September, and they'd been married for three months. Accommodation had been found for them in one of the new, prefabricated buildings where they had a self-contained one-room apartment.

Douglas bent down, picked up a stone, and threw it out to sea. It made a dull plopping sound as it entered the water. 'I wish it were only a different posting,' he said.

'So what is it then?'

'I'm going back into the field.'

Aghast, she stopped dead in her tracks. 'But you can't! You're known to the Gestapo. It would be suicide.'

'It's not France.'

'Then where?'

'Corsica. I'm going in with several others to link up with, and lead, partisan forces out there.'

She was stunned. Douglas going back into the field! She'd believed, as had he, that was all over for him, that he'd never again have to risk his life in such a way.

'We were only told an hour ago, the first inkling we had that this was on the cards.'

The inside of her head was spinning, and there was a faint taste of bile in her throat. Her stomach heaved, and heaved again. 'When?' she husked.

'Day after tomorrow.'

'So soon!' she exclaimed in dismay.

'I'm afraid so.'

'Can't you get out of it?' She knew as soon as she'd spoken it was a silly question. Even if he could have done, he wouldn't have. 'Sorry,' she added lamely.

He reached out and took her by the hand. 'Life during wartime certainly is full of surprises, isn't it?' He smiled, trying to lighten the situation.

'It certainly is.'

'Will you come and see me off?'

'Wild horses couldn't keep me away.'

He touched her on the cheek. 'You're the best thing that's ever happened to me. I want you to know that.'

She tried to answer, but couldn't. She was too choked with emotion. Hand in hand they resumed their walk.

The night before he left was the longest Norma had ever known, and also paradoxically the shortest. They made love again and again, far more times than they would have done, or been capable of, ordinarily, as though trying to cram into those few hours all the lovemaking that would have taken place during the period of parting that lay ahead.

Bodies slick with sweat, they clung to one another like two lost souls. At one point she cried, and he comforted her. Later, he too was overcome, and this time she comforted him.

Nor was it all hot passion and despondency, there was laughter as well. Norma literally cackled with mirth when, on reaching for the packet of cigarettes he'd laid on the floor, Douglas fell out of bed, cracking a shin which sent him hopping round the room clutching the offending foot and cursing volubly. They laughed, they cried, they made love, they even sang – a Harry Lauder number they both knew and liked.

And all the while they pretended they weren't hearing the clock tick tick ticking the seconds away. Till finally the alarm went off, and the precious seconds had run out.

Dusk was gathering as Douglas and the other agents bound for Corsica went aboard the waiting Lancaster. He paused to wave a final goodbye, then vanished inside. Norma's hand was still raised in farewell as the Lancaster's door slammed shut.

'Oh my love, come back safely to me, please come back safely to me,' she whispered as the Lancaster's propellers burst into life. Her eyes were bright with tears as the plane took off, its mighty engines thundering as it rapidly gained height.

The Lancaster grew smaller and smaller till finally it vanished from sight altogether. 'Please God,' she whispered. 'Please God.'

She dried her eyes before returning to her jeep, and the unmade bed that still smelled of Douglas, and their previous night's lovemaking.

Part III

LADY'S CHOICE
1945–48

Chapter Eleven

It was a bitter cold November's day as the MV *Star of India* kissed the quayside at Southampton Docks. On board, Norma, one of the thousand-plus Forces personnel returning home to Blighty, stood at a passenger rail anxiously scanning the milling throng below. She was looking for Douglas, who'd promised to be there to meet her.

It was now six months since the end of the war in Europe, and two since victory over Japan. After the German defeat many of those at Massingham had been transferred to the SOE's Force 136 in the Far East which was working in conjunction with General Slim's Fourteenth Army. At the height of Massingham's activities there had been two hundred and fifty FANYs under Norma's command. This number was reduced to fifteen at the time of the Japanese surrender. Helen Rolfe had been amongst the first to leave for Force 136.

'There he is, over there!' exclaimed Violette, who was standing beside Norma, and pointed to their left. 'He's wearing a darkish coat and a trilby.'

Norma followed the direction of Violette's jabbing finger to spot Douglas waving frantically at her. She flailed an arm back at him while hot salt tears of pleasure ran down her face. It was twenty-six months since they'd last seen each other, since she'd seen him disappear into the Lancaster that was to take him over Corsica.

Corsica had been bad for him, very bad indeed. And after Corsica there had been one more field assignment for him which had been the worst of them all, before, finally, he'd been taken back to Britain and a desk job.

To begin with the desk job had been in Baker Street where he'd worked closely with M. Then Lieutenant-Colonel Roe,

287

DR for F, DF, RF, N and T Sections had been moved to pastures new, and Douglas had been made the new DR.

Norma's eyes locked onto Douglas's and, in that instant, it was as though they'd never been apart. Her heart swelled and her shoulders started to shake with emotion. 'Oh Gabriel, dear Gabriel,' she whispered to herself, and the tears became a flood.

'And there's Pam!' Violette screeched excitedly. And sure enough, fairly close to Douglas was Pam Parkinson waving like a mad thing.

The brass band went into, 'It's a Long Way to Tipperary', while folk on a higher deck began throwing toilet rolls, the long white ribbons of paper streaming through the air. Some were held at one end to connect ship and quayside.

'Come on, let's go,' Norma said as a brace of gangplanks were manoeuvred into place. They struggled back to the stateroom to pick up their hand-luggage – their heavier luggage had been put outside their stateroom earlier and had already been collected by the crew – and then made their way to the nearest exit point.

'How do you feel?' Violette asked.

Norma shook her head, words were beyond her. Only minutes now and she and Douglas, her husband, would be reunited. The sunburst of feeling she was experiencing was indescribable. At least for her anyway.

There was a great press to leave the *Star Of India*, but in an orderly fashion. The air was electric with excitement as row upon row of feet shuffled and struggled forward. Then Norma and Violette were on the gangplank itself, over a slash of dirty water, and onto the quayside. They were home. *At long last they were home!*

Norma saw Douglas carving his way towards her, and with a shock realised he'd shaved off his beard and moustache. That and the fact he was a great deal greyer than he'd been before to the point of being quite white in places. And then the sublime, magical moment when he swept her into his arms and pressed his lips to hers.

The tears Norma had managed to fight back now returned, hotter and saltier than before. When the kiss was over Douglas hugged her so hard she was certain he must surely break her ribs.

'Norma,' he husked. 'I can't believe it, I really can't. After all this while we're back together again.'

'I really can't believe it either. But it's true, it's true!' she whispered. This time it was she who kissed him.

After that kiss, she embraced Pam, and Violette, Douglas. 'We'll collect your luggage, the car's nearby,' Douglas said to Norma when that was over.

The four of them went into the quayside shed where the heavy luggage would be brought and there, Norma and Douglas hand in hand, they chatted about the sea voyage and Pam's journey down by train from London.

'As Douglas has a car with him can we offer you two girls a lift?' Norma asked as trolleys of cases and kitbags made an appearance.

'No, we can't!' Douglas exclaimed abruptly.

Norma turned to him for an explanation, and his expression became sheepish. 'It's not that we wouldn't be delighted to of course, but I . . .' He coughed. 'I've booked Norma and me into a little inn at Twyford just outside Winchester. I stayed there last night and arranged that Norma and I would return today.'

'He's gone all red,' Violette said, and laughed. It was true, Douglas was flushed with embarrassment.

Norma smiled; he'd done the right thing as far as she was concerned. It was very thoughtful, not to say romantic of him.

'Don't worry about us, we'll be absolutely fine,' Pam said.

All too soon they'd collected their luggage and it was time for Norma and Douglas to say goodbye to the other two. There was more hugging and kissing, and renewed promises to keep in touch. Norma was deeply saddened to be parted from Violette. They'd shared a great deal and become extremely close. Then she brightened again, remembering that she had Douglas once more.

Douglas led the way out of the mêlée into a car park, to stop beside a green 3-litre Lagonda tourer. 'This is it,' he said, running a hand lovingly over the bonnet.

'It's a beauty,' Norma breathed. And indeed it was a most handsome machine, long and low-slung, with a pair of large headlamps dominating its front.

'I couldn't resist it when I saw it in the Motor Market,' Douglas declared proudly.

The Motor Market! Norma thought with a thrill. A name from another time and place. To hear it again made her realise she really was going home to Glasgow. And then she reminded herself, home to Glasgow but not to Bridgeton and Cubie Street, but Burnside and Blairbeth Road, for she and Douglas would be living with his parents in their huge house with all the servants. A shiver of apprehension ran through her. A whole new life lay ahead of her as Douglas's wife, a life that would be, must be, as different to her days in Cubie Street as the proverbial chalk was from cheese.

'Do you want to drive? I've had you put on the insurance.'

'Can I?' she replied quickly.

He tossed her the keys. 'It's your car as well as mine, you know.'

She threw herself into his arms and kissed him again. 'I love you, Douglas Ross,' she whispered.

'And I love you.'

The Lagonda proved to be as delightful to drive as it was to look at.

The Hare and Hounds was a coaching inn several hundred years old. They were greeted by Mrs Hobbs, the landlord's wife, who told them their room was ready and waiting. Her son Henry, a lad in his early teens, took their luggage up for them.

The room was small but very cosy. A fire blazed in the grate, and there was a large scuttle of coal to refuel it with. There was also a bottle of champagne in an ice-bucket.

'Your idea?' she asked him with a smile, pointing to the bucket.

'Hmm! I thought tonight could be a sort of second honeymoon.'

'I like that idea too. In fact, I like it very much.'

He pulled the champagne from its bucket, and opened it, the cork going off with a bang and bounding across the room. Norma giggled with delight.

He filled two glasses and handed her one. 'To us, and the future,' he toasted quietly.

She sipped. 'Now can I make a toast?'

'Of course.'

'Here's to those who didn't make it. Marie Thérèse and the rest.'

His eyes clouded with pain, and he seemed to shrink a little in on himself. 'Yes, Marie Thérèse and the rest who didn't make it,' he repeated in a whisper. As he drank, face after face flicked through his mind, all of them people now dead.

Douglas roused himself from his reverie. 'I have some things for you,' he said, and crossed to get his suitcase standing by the side of the bed.

Some things for her? She couldn't think what they might be. She gasped when he produced an exquisite nightdress of snow-white satin, trimmed with lace. She'd never seen a nightdress so beautiful. It was simply gorgeous.

'It was made in Paris just before the war started. I thought you'd like it,' he said.

'Like it, I adore it!' she exclaimed, taking it from him and holding it up against herself.

'And there's a dressing-gown and underwear,' he added.

The dressing-gown was another stunner. It was a padded Chinese silk affair, black with crimson flowers. 'Mandarin-style,' Douglas explained.

There was masses of the underwear in white, pink, beige and French blue colours. It was the best quality underwear Norma had ever seen, far less owned.

Douglas laughed to see how pleased she was. 'You won't find anything like this lot in the shops, I can tell you.'

'So how did you come by them?'

'Contacts in France. I had them sent over especially.'

Douglas poured out more champagne. 'It's almost dinner-time, I've booked a table for two, and there's another bottle of this champagne on ice. We'll have to go down.'

She heard the undertones in his voice, and saw the same in his eyes. It was what she wanted also, but he was right, if the table was booked they should go down.

He tapped out on his glass: I love you.

I love you too. she tapped in return.

'Do you want to change?'

'Do you think I need to?'

He shook his head. 'It's hardly a formal place. Your uniform will be just fine.'

There was a jug and bowl of water in the room, which Norma used to wash her hands and face. She then applied some light make-up and powder.

'Oh, I almost forgot,' he said, and handed her a small bottle. It was a bottle of perfume, its smell was heavenly.

'You really are spoiling me,' she said.

'Why not? Today's a very special day after all.'

She dabbed a little of the perfume behind both ears, and in other strategic places. He watched her with a slitted gaze, thinking how much he felt for this woman, and how dreadfully he'd missed her while they'd been parted. There had been one particular night during his last field assignment when, certain he was about to die, he'd been convinced he'd never see her again. But here they both were.

Mr and Mrs Hobbs did them proud. Their table was in a secluded spot and had candles on it. The main course was venison, *poached*, Mrs Hobbs whispered, giving them a wink.

'In your final letter to me you mentioned briefly there was a job in the air?' Norma asked, tucking into the venison – the first time she'd ever eaten that meat, and finding it delicious, not at all too gamey for her taste.

'There's a job for a specialist in orthopaedics at the Victoria Infirmary where my father is,' Douglas explained. 'It's now certain that old McNulty, the present senior orthopaedic specialist will retire early in the new year.'

This was new to Norma. Douglas hadn't mentioned any of the details in his letter, only that there was the possibility of a job. 'Will it make any difference that your father's already at this hospital?' she asked.

Douglas pulled a face. 'He believes that's to my advantage, but I'm not so sure. I think it could just as easily be to my disadvantage.'

'What about the job itself, is it what you want?'

'Oh yes, very much so. However, I'm not convinced that the powers that be would consider me properly qualified for such a position. I'm afraid the war has played havoc with what you might call my going along the proper stepping stones for such an eminent post.'

'Could you do it?'

'No doubt in my mind that I could. The trouble is, will they think so?'

'Even if you don't get it there will always be other jobs, it's only a matter of time.'

'It would be nice to stay in Glasgow though. You see, once I accept a post as specialist it's more or less for life. I could easily end up in Cardiff, Belfast, Manchester or Inverness. At that level it's all the luck of the draw.'

Norma hadn't realised that. She didn't think she wanted to live permanently in any of the places he'd just mentioned, though of course she would if she had to. But, as he said, it *would* be nice to stay in Glasgow. 'We'll just have to keep our fingers crossed then,' she said.

He tapped out a love message on the table, which made her smile. She tapped one back.

As they were waiting for the sweet to arrive she tapped out: I want a bath first.

Like me to scrub your back?

I can manage by myself thank you very much.

Spoilsport!

What if someone should see us coming out of the bathroom together?

So what? We're married.

You know what I mean.

I could scrub not only your back but other parts as well.

What other parts did you have in mind?

Tits.

Douglas!

And ...

She interrupted him. If you're going to be disgusting I don't want to hear.

Why is that disgusting?

It just is.

I love you, have I ever told you that?

Once or twice, but never enough.

I love you. I love you. I love you. I want you.

And I love and want you too.

Do we have to eat the sweet?

Yes, it's on its way.

I'm not hungry anymore. Not for food anyway, only you.

293

Smoothie.

The difference between me and a smoothie is that I mean it.

I know that darling.

'Something wrong?'

Startled, they both glanced up to find Mrs Hobbs staring quizzically at them.

'No, nothing's wrong,' Douglas replied hastily.

'Then, excuse me for asking, but why were you both tapping the table as you were?'

Norma fought back a laugh, and stared at Douglas. Let him answer that.

'You mean like this?' he said, and tapped out: Help!

Norma dropped her gaze, and continued to fight back the laugh that was now bursting to get out. Her sides began to ache.

'That's right,' Mrs Hobbs nodded.

'It's eh … eh …' He cleared his throat. God, what to say! The last thing he wanted to do was launch into a lengthy explanation of the truth. 'It's a game actually.'

Mrs Hobbs frowned. 'A game?'

'We learned it in Algeria where we were both stationed for a while. The Arabs play it.'

Mrs Hobbs eyebrows shot up. 'The Arabs! Fancy that.'

Norma stuffed a balled fist into her mouth. Her chest was heaving, which she did her best to disguise by folding and hunching her arms over herself.

Douglas elaborated. 'Did you ever play that game as a child where paper wraps stone, scissors cuts paper, and stone breaks scissors?'

'I know the one. Yes, I did.'

'It's something similar to that.'

'Well, well, you live and learn don't you?'

'You certainly do,' Douglas beamed.

Mrs Hobbs placed Norma's prunes and custard in front of her. 'Are you all right, Mrs Ross?'

It hadn't really been that funny, but Norma had found it hysterically so. 'Something in my throat,' she spluttered.

'Can I get you a glass of water?'

'Please.'

Mrs Hobbs put Douglas's profiteroles in front of him, then hurried off.

'Game played by Arabs!' Norma whispered, choking with laughter.

'I thought it rather a good explanation.'

'And I thought it showed great ingenuity. Take a gold star and go to the top of the class.'

When Mrs Hobbs returned with the water Norma greeted her with a straight face. She drank some of the water just to be polite, and swore it had done the trick in clearing her throat.

Norma rose from the still steaming bath and reached for the fluffy towel she'd brought from their bedroom, one of the pair provided. Slowly, methodically, she began drying herself.

Douglas had been serious about coming into the bathroom with her, but she'd been adamant he didn't. It wouldn't have seemed right in a hotel somehow, though she certainly wouldn't have had any objections to it if they'd been in their own place.

Not that they were going to have their own place, she reminded herself. They'd be sharing the house in Blairbeth Road with Douglas's parents. She really would have preferred a place of their own, but he'd argued against it, saying it would be daft to spend money on another house when there was room and more for them in Blairbeth Road. She just hoped, and prayed, that everything was going to work out all right, that she'd hit it off with his parents. But then she was sure she would do, Solange sounded a gem of a woman, Forsyth – that silly name! – a bit like her own da.

At least she didn't have to worry about the way she spoke. She'd learned early on in the FANY that she had an excellent ear and had lost a fair amount of her Glasgow accent before meeting Douglas again. After he'd gone off to Corsica, anticipating the sort of people she'd have to rub shoulders with after the war if he survived – which thank God he had – she'd worked on her accent even further till now she spoke almost as well as Douglas himself. Solange and Forsyth would find no fault in that department.

When she was dried she doused herself with Johnson's baby powder and then dabbed on some more of the perfume Douglas had given her.

As she slipped into the nightdress she found that she was suddenly nervous about what lay ahead. It might be their second honeymoon but she felt as if it was their first, and this their first night together. She felt like a virgin going to her husband for the first time.

She combed her hair, considered applying a little make-up, and decided against it. She thought of Douglas lying in bed waiting for her, and butterflies fluttered in her stomach. Twenty-six months, she thought grimly. Such a long time for a husband and wife to be separated, such a long, long time. Putting on the Chinese dressing gown she gathered up her bits and pieces. She was ready.

He stared hungrily at her as she came through the bedroom door. She closed it quietly behind her. The key in the lock squeaked as she turned it.

'I stoked up the fire,' he said throatily.

'Good.' Since she'd gone for her bath he'd become as nervous as she was. That made her feel better. She was aware of his gaze rivetted to her as she tidied away the things she'd brought from the bathroom. When that was done she turned to him, and smiled.

'Come here,' he said.

She went slowly, taking her time. When she reached the bed she removed the Chinese dressing gown. 'How do you like the nightdress on?' she asked, and did a sort of twirl round the way she believed fashion models did.

'It's sensational. On you, that is.'

She sat on the bed beside him, and he reached out to place a hand on her thigh. Gently, and sensuously, he ran his hand backwards and forwards over her satin-covered flesh.

'It's sensational on, but I prefer you with it off,' he husked, the words thick in his throat.

She rose again to her feet, and the nightdress whispered to the floor. Naked, she stood before him.

He pulled back the covers to reveal that he too was completely naked, and ready for her. He drew her down till she was lying stretched alongside him. 'Oh Norma, how I've dreamed of this since leaving Massingham.'

'Me too.'

'I don't ever want to be separated from you again.'

'We won't be.'

He lightly kissed first one breast, then the other.

Her nervousness was gone, as was his. She could tell. A sense of peace descended on her. Peace intermingled with passion. 'Now,' she said.

He came over, and into her. She sighed with the sheer pleasure of their joining. 'Oh yes,' she murmured. 'Oh yes.'

Dracula's castle, that was her initial impression of the house in Blairbeth Road. Tall, gothic, and sinister. An impression that was further enhanced by the thunder and lightning storm raging outside.

'Won't be a mo',' Douglas said. He stepped out of the Lagonda, dashed to the large wrought-iron gates and swung them open.

They'd run into the beginnings of the storm at Crawford, and it had worsened steadily as they'd approached and come into Glasgow. Now the house in Blairbeth Road seemed to be at the centre of the storm. Flashes of lighning, again and again, split the coal-black sky directly overhead.

'My God, what a night!' Douglas said, climbing back into the car.

'Dreadful', she agreed, wincing as a particularly loud bang of thunder made the Lagonda's windows rattle.

Douglas drove in through the gates and parked in front of the main entrance. There was another car in front of them, a Daimler by the shape of it. In fact it was a Vanden Plas.

The door of the house opened and a man emerged carrying a large multi-coloured umbrella. 'Travers, the butler. Did his bit during the war as an ARP warden,' Douglas explained.

Travers came to Norma first, helping her out of the Lagonda and escorting her to the doorway where she went inside. He then returned for Douglas.

Norma found herself in a tiled vestibule. She stood there waiting for Douglas to join her.

'Thank you Travers,' Douglas said as he and the butler entered the hall. Travers closed the door behind himself and Douglas, let down the umbrella and placed it in a corner.

'This is my wife, Travers,' Douglas said.

Travers, a man of about fifty, Norma would have judged, gave her a small bow. 'Pleased to meet you, Mrs Ross.'

Her right hand had moved instinctively to shake his. She

turned this into a vague gesture of touching her coat lapels. 'And I'm pleased to meet you, Travers.'

'Welcome home, Master Douglas. And may I say on behalf of the entire staff how pleased we are to have you back again, and relieved that you came through the recent conflict unscathed.'

'Why thank you Travers, most kind.'

There was a tone in Douglas's voice that Norma had never heard before – she was soon to learn that it was the tone he employed when addressing servants. There was nothing patronising or condescending about it, but it stated clearly that a servant was a servant, and – no matter how highly thought-of or even treasured he was – a hired employee.

Travers assisted Norma out of her coat, then Douglas out of his. 'The master and mistress are in the large sitting-room taking sherry,' he said.

Douglas grasped Norma by the arm, giving her a warm smile as he did. 'Shall we?' She gave him a weak smile in return.

'I'll fetch your luggage from the car and take it up to your room,' Travers said.

'Which room is that?'

'Your old one, Master Douglas. The mistress instructed me to put you and Mrs Ross there.'

'Fine.'

Leaving the hall, they entered a circular reception area, the floor of which was green marble. There was old wood everywhere, mahogany and oak, and hanging from the wood-panelled walls were a number of pictures of highland scenes. Two complete suits of armour – one holding a sword, the other what looked like a pike – guarded a staircase sweeping upwards. Norma shivered.

'Cold? The house is always chilly in winter. Because of its size it would cost a fortune to heat properly,' Douglas said.

Although it was cold Norma didn't tell him it wasn't that which had made her shiver. The house, at least what she'd seen of it so far, was gloomy and forbidding, not at all as cheery and hospitable as she'd have wished it.

They went to a room that was exactly as Travers had called it, a large sitting-room. Some thirty to thirty-five feet long, Norma thought, and roughly half that in width.

The curtains on the windows were brocade, and gave the

impression of being extremely ancient. Everything in the room was old and the furniture positively antediluvian. The wallpaper was so faded it could well have been there since the turn of the century.

There was a wooden baronial-style fireplace in which a log fire was burning. Standing by the fireplace was Forsyth, while Solange was sitting smiling.

Norma took all this in as she and Douglas walked towards the fireplace, and his waiting parents. As they came closer Solange rose and surprised Norma by how tiny she was. Norma would later learn that Solange was only four feet ten inches tall.

Forsyth was fractionally taller than his son, broad shouldered, with a florid face. His thin, sandy-coloured hair was swept straight back from his forehead, and he had a distinct paunch.

Solange had the same sallow skin as Douglas, a pronounced aquiline nose – Douglas's was only slightly so – and dark, birdlike eyes. She couldn't have been anything else but French.

Solange said something very fast in her native tongue, which Douglas answered in the same language; then he had left Norma's side and enveloped his mother in his arms. Forsyth beamed on.

Finally Douglas disentangled himself. 'Mother, Father, I'd like you to meet Norma, my wife.'

Solange turned a penetrating gaze onto Norma. 'Welcome,' she said.

'Welcome,' Forsyth repeated.

Norma stared about her in dismay. She and Douglas were in their bedroom and it was simply ghastly. The carpet was threadbare; the wallpaper as faded as that in the large sitting-room; the curtains not only on their last legs but hideously patterned; the whitewashed ceiling now yellow with age. There was a huge oak wardrobe that was scarred and chipped all over, an oak chest-of-drawers in even worse condition, and an oak headboard – with inset mirror – over the bed. The bed itself was as hard as stone.

Norma laid out the two dresses she'd managed to acquire in London. They'd stopped off there so that she could personally hand in a report on the final days of Massingham to FANY HQ, and her letter of resignation from the Service. Being an officer, she'd felt it the proper thing to do to personally hand in the letter rather than merely sending it.

'Which one?' she asked Douglas.

They were dressing for dinner; he was in the process of knotting a black tie. It had shaken her that mealtimes were so formal, and that she was expected to dress for dinner every night. She was going to have to expand her stock of civvy clothes, and fast, if she was to do that. Which wasn't going to be easy as clothing was rationed.

'The blue I think,' he smiled.

There was a paraffin heater in the room which took the chill off the air. It would have been really cold, and damp, without it.

She hated the room! Well, things in *here* were certainly going to change, she was utterly determined about that. Even if she had to use her own money to bring it about. What amazed her was that Douglas seemed to find it quite acceptable – she would have thought he'd have considered it as awful as she did.

She was applying the final touches of her make-up when a gong sounded, announcing that dinner was served. She went downstairs on Douglas's arm, forcing herself to smile.

'And how exactly did you two meet? Douglas has told us hardly anything at all about you in his letters,' Forsyth queried.

Norma glanced at Douglas sitting facing her across the width of the long dining-table. Forsyth and Solange sat at its head and bottom, and so far apart they almost had to shout when speaking to one another. The dining-room was like all the other rooms she'd been in so far, horrendous in her view.

'We first met when I was at the Royal Free,' Douglas explained, taking a sip of claret.

'I was his patient,' Norma expanded. Then Douglas told the story of how she'd been blown up in Risinghill Street.

'Marvellous body of women, the FANY, I have tremendous respect for them,' Forsyth commented – a little pompously Norma thought – when Douglas had finished.

'You say you met at the hospital for the first time. When did you meet again?' Solange probed. She spoke perfect English, but with a pronounced French accent.

Douglas drank more wine, and wondered how to answer that.

300

He finally decided that as the war was now over there was no reason why his parents shouldn't know about the SOE, and his and Norma's involvement with it. 'She was my partner in England while I was in France, but because I was operating under a codename she didn't know it was me, the doctor who'd treated her at the Royal Free. Nor did I appreciate that the Norma I communicated with by wireless was my ex-patient. We met up later, in the flesh that is, in Algeria where we were both stationed with SOE. That was where and when we learned that we'd been partners.'

Solange and Forsyth had stopped eating to stare at their son. 'You were in France? You mean before the liberation?' Solange queried.

'Yes. I was an agent, a spy and saboteur if you like, for an organisation called Special Operations Executive. When I transmitted into homebase, F Section it was called, it was Norma on the other end.'

'A spy? But you're a doctor!' Forsyth exclaimed, flabbergasted.

'I can also speak French like a native and can easily pass as a born and bred Frenchman. SOE capitalised on that.'

Forsyth shook his head. 'I can hardly believe this. We had no idea. Not even an inkling.'

'Neither do my parents. Everything to do with SOE was a secret. My people all think I was a FANY driver and nothing else,' Norma said.

'Did you also go into France?' Solange asked with a frown.

'I have no French at all so that was out of the question. I had a good and close girlfriend who did go in however.'

'And didn't return,' Douglas added quietly.

Norma dropped her eyes. Remembering Lynsey and that last interrupted transmission always brought a lump to her throat.

'A spy and saboteur, it's incredible!' Forsyth muttered.

And assassin, Douglas thought darkly. But that was something not even Norma knew about. 'A lot of what SOE did was just that, incredible,' he answered.

'Your son is a very brave man,' Norma told the older Rosses.

Douglas made a gesture of dismissal. 'I was no more brave than thousands, if not millions of others.'

'There's brave and brave, and you were the latter,' Norma retorted.

He glowered at her.

'You *were*.'

'No more than any of the others who went into France as agents, or into Holland or Belgium or Yugoslavia or any of the other places that SOE sent "joes" into.'

'"Joes"?' Forsyth queried.

'SOE name for an agent,' explained Norma.

Douglas's glower intensified, he was acutely embarrassed.

'You were,' she repeated.

'Well, I don't agree, and that's an end of this conversation for now if you don't mind,' Douglas said, and turned to his plate.

Solange's birdlike eyes shone with fierce pride. Norma wouldn't have been at all surprised if her mother-in-law had suddenly burst into 'La Marseillaise'.

Douglas pointedly changed the subject and asked his father about a very tricky eye operation that Forsyth had listed for the following morning.

They retired into the larger sitting room for coffee and liqueurs. Once they were all settled round the log fire, and with rain lashing the windows, Solange said 'Douglas did mention in one of his infrequent letters that you were an officer. Is that correct, *chérie*?'

'Yes, I was a Captain.'

'With two hundred and fifty FANYs under her command when we were in Algeria,' Douglas said.

'An enormous amount of responsibility,' Forsyth acknowledged, nodding his approval.

'It was. I thoroughly enjoyed the experience, even if it was extremely difficult at times.'

'There were many French where we were, Mama. We both met de Gaulle.'

'You did!' Solange exclaimed.

'A great Frenchman,' Forsyth declared.

Norma couldn't help teasing. 'He was part Irish you know.'

Solange rounded on her. 'Never!'

'Oh yes. His mother's mother was a MacCartan, descendant

302

of one of the mercenaries who fought for Louis the Fourteenth against Marlborough.'

'You're storytelling,' Solange accused, shocked to think that such a famous French hero should in fact have foreign blood in him, and Irish blood at that.

'Not all that many people know about it, but it's true, nonetheless.'

'Well, I'll be jiggered!' muttered Forsyth. 'It's almost like hearing Montgomery was a Frenchman.'

'But he was,' Norma smiled.

'Eh? Now you are storytelling.'

Norma shook her head. 'Not so. The Montgomery family came to England from Normandy. I think, though I'm not a hundred percent certain, that they arrived with the Conqueror. What I am sure of is that Monty's ancestors were Norman-French.'

'How did you learn all this?' Douglas laughed.

'About de Gaulle, at Massingham where I had to read through various, non-secret, papers about him and his followers. It was Helen Rolfe who told me about Montgomery. Her family had the same history, and they *did* come over with the Conqueror.'

Forsyth put another log on the fire which had begun to die away. As he dusted off his hands there was a vivid flash of lightning outside, followed almost instantly by a loud crash of thunder.

'Speaking of families, we know absolutely nothing about yours, Norma *chérie*. Other than the fact they live in Glasgow, that is,' Solange said to Norma, smiling.

'You were very sparing with details in your letters,' Forsyth chided.

'Perhaps the outskirts of Glasgow? We couldn't think of any McKenzies with a daughter in Glasgow itself,' Solange went on.

'There is McKenzie the advocate, but he's got a son not a daughter,' Forsyth said.

Norma glanced at Douglas. She'd presumed he'd told his parents about her background, but apparently not. Nor was it something she'd thought to ask him during their journey up from Southampton. 'I come from Bridgeton,' she repied levelly.

Forsyth blinked. 'Bridgeton?'

'Before the war my father was a gardener with the Corporation Parks Department. During the war he was with the Pioneer Corps, and now the war's over he's returned to his old job at Glasgow Green. I had a letter from my mother just before I left Massingham telling me that.'

'I see,' Forsyth said slowly.

Solange's face had become set, giving nothing away. With a sinking feeling Norma realised they were bitterly disappointed in her. They'd presumed that Douglas had married someone of equal social standing.

'And you yourself, Norma *chérie*, what did you work at before the war? I take it you did work?'

Caustic undertones, Norma thought grimly. 'Yes, I was a professional ballroom-dancer.'

'Professional dancer!' Forsyth exclaimed, seeming to choke on the words.

'Professional *ballroom*-dancer,' Norma emphasised.

'She and her partner were the All Scotland Champions. Isn't that right Norma?' Douglas said.

She could have slaughtered him for putting her in this position. It was so humiliating. 'Yes.'

'How interesting,' Solange murmured, her face still set and closed.

Norma sipped her liqueur. It was Drambuie and should have tasted sweet. But it tasted sour to her. Why hadn't Douglas told them about her, prepared them for her! she raged inwardly. It was quite unlike his normal sensitive self. 'I have money of my own you know, a legacy,' she said. She knew fine well it was considered bad manners to talk about money amongst people like these, but she wanted them to appreciate she'd married Douglas for himself and not what he, or they, might have in the bank.

'Is that so?' Forsyth replied, raising an eyebrow as if to say, what are you talking about, twenty pounds, thirty?

'Enough to keep me in comfort, *considerable* comfort, for the rest of my days should that ever be necessary,' Norma spelled out.

'A relative who went abroad and made his fortune perhaps?' Solange inquired casually, thinking that money of that scale could never have come out of Bridgeton. Why, they were all peasants there!

'No, it was a man, a stranger, whose dead daughter I was the spitting image of. He died leaving me everything.'

'How extraordinary,' Forsyth said.

'It was rather. His name was Thomas Gallagher; his daughter's name was Morna. He used to come and watch me dance.' She paused, then added, 'Being financially independent was how I was able to join FANY.'

'I understand now,' Forsyth said slowly.

A pregnant silence descended on the room. Norma was acutely aware that her mother- and father-in-law were both staring at her. She took another sip of her drink and stared right back.

'Why didn't you tell them about me?' Norma demanded. She and Douglas were back in their bedroom, having just said goodnight to Solange and Forsyth, whose bedroom was further along the passageway.

Douglas lit a cigarette. 'I love you, that's enough for me. I don't care whether you come from Kelvinside, Bridgeton or bloody Mars.'

That mollified her somewhat. 'Nonetheless, you could see how disappointed they were. They quite clearly had higher hopes for you.'

He gave a light laugh. 'And her name is Catherine Stark. No doubt you'll meet her before long. She and Mama get along like the proverbial house on fire and visit each other regularly.'

This was new to Norma. 'And who is Catherine Stark?'

'Her father is Sir John Stark. He owns a number of companies and is on the boards of others. They figure prominently amongst what you might call the cream of Scottish society.'

'And what is Catherine to you?'

'A friend, a very old friend. But there was never anything more to it than that. At least not on my side.'

'And hers?'

'Oh definitely so, she made that plain to me years ago.'

'But you didn't fancy her?'

'Not in the least. As a friend, yes. Anything else, no.'

305

'But she's always held out hope?'

Douglas nodded. 'That's partially Mama's doing. It was her fondest wish that I marry Catherine. The family's wealthy and terribly well-connected. From Mama's point of view it would have been the ideal match.'

'No wonder she's so disappointed that you've married me instead.'

'She'll just have to get used to the idea – they both will in time, I promise you.' He took off his jacket and threw it across a chair. His tie quickly followed. Outside it was quiet as the grave, the storm having petered out and the rain having stopped. 'Will you do something for me, Norma?'

She was at the paraffin heater warming her hands. She noticed there were two bulges in the bed that told her hot water bottles had been put in. Thank God for that! 'If I can.'

'Please don't say to anyone else that I was brave.'

'But you were!'

'Think that if you will, but please don't say it to anyone else.'

'Your parents are hardly anyone else. It's only right that they should know such a thing about their son.'

'I've said to you before, I never felt brave. In fact, to put it crudely, I was shit-scared most of the time.'

'But it was because you felt like that and still went on to do all the things you did, that you are particularly brave.'

He shook his head. 'Well, I don't see it that way. So promise me, no more chat about me being brave? Please?'

Her anger with him had quite disappeared. She placed a now warm palm on his left cheek. 'If that's what you want.'

'It is.'

'Then you have my promise.'

He took her into his arms, loving the pressure of her body against his. He nibbled her neck, which made her giggle, then kissed her, which promptly stopped her giggling.

She squirmed as his tongue probed the recesses of her mouth. She felt him stir, felt his maleness nudging her thigh.

'Did you ever kiss Catherine Stark like that?' she asked when the kiss was over.

'I've only ever kissed Catherine on the cheek. Why, would you be jealous if I had?'

'Pea-green with it. If I met her, instead of saying hello, I'd scratch her eyes out.'

'Hardly the actions of a lady.'

'I'm no lady. I'm from Bridgeton.'

He laughed at that. 'I'll tell you this. You're more of a lady than many so called ladies I know.'

'Let's get into bed.'

'Are you propositioning me?'

'Unashamedly.'

He touched, then gently squeezed her right breast, which made her sigh. She caressed him in return, smiling to see the way his eyes narrowed.

'Oh Norma!'

'Oh Douglas!'

'Bed,' she repeated, and broke away from him to turn off the paraffin heater.

Despite the hot water bottles, the bed was freezing. They cuddled each other for warmth, and as they cuddled their fingers were busy feeling, kneading, caressing. Finally the bed was warm and both of them more than ready. She groaned with pleasure as he entered her.

'Bloody hell!' he swore, stopping in mid-action. The bed-springs were squeaking, making a tremendous racket. At least it seemed a tremendous racket to him.

'Didn't you know they squeaked?'

'How would I? I've never had a woman in here before. I was a virgin until I met you, remember?'

'Do you think they can hear?'

'It is frightfully loud.'

'That's the understatement of the year.'

He continued on, to stop again almost immediately. Norma began laughing at the ludicrousness of it, at the sheer, down-right silliness of it. And he began laughing as well.

'Do you know something?' she said, still laughing.

'What?'

'I don't care whether they hear or not.'

'Well I do. They're my parents.'

She had an idea then, which would stop the squeaking – a

new bed, a *non-squeaking* new bed, that was the first item on the agenda for their room, she decided.

Norma woke and stretched languorously. She felt absolutely marvellous, refreshed and very relaxed. She reached out for Douglas to discover she was alone in the bed. Opening her eyes she glanced around. She wasn't only alone in the bed, she was alone in the room.

Slipping out from underneath the covers she put on the Chinese dressing gown, and went over to the window to look at the view.

The window overlooked an extensive garden containing lots of flower beds, shrubs and trees, the latter mainly fruit trees. The garden disappeared round either side of the house.

After the night's storm it was a beautiful day. The light was extremely bright, while a touch of frost lent a sparkle to almost everything. A beautiful day, but a cold one. She'd have to wrap up well, she told herself.

She was about to turn away from the window when Douglas and Solange came into view. They were walking side by side, he with his head bent as he listened intently to what his mother was saying.

Now what was that all about? Norma wondered. From their physical attitudes, and expressions – which Norma could make out quite clearly – it appeared to be a very serious discussion. Now Douglas was speaking, waving his arms around in a most Gallic manner.

Norma frowned as a sudden thought struck her. Was she the subject of conversation? Was Solange complaining to Douglas about how bitterly disappointed she and Forsyth were that he'd married someone from Bridgeton, a social inferior?

Biting her lip she went over to the oak chest of drawers and started to get dressed. Her things had been unpacked and put away for her the previous evening, while she'd been at dinner.

She was running a comb through her hair, and speculating further about that conversation in the garden, when the gong sounded, announcing that breakfast was served.

Douglas and Forsyth rose to their feet as Norma entered the

dining room. 'You came down then, we thought you might want to sleep on,' Douglas smiled.

'No, I've had enough sleep thank you,' she replied, addressing all three of them, Solange also being present.

A long sideboard had been laid out with food. It was obviously a case of helping yourself, which Norma did now. There might be food rationing in force, but that didn't seem to affect the Rosses, she noted. There was a choice of boiled or fried eggs (not a sign of powdered scrambled which the *hoi polloi* had to endure), kedgeree, Loch Fyne kippers, toast, butter (she could tell it was butter and not marg by the colour), marmalade and jam. There was also tea or coffee. She opted for tea, toast, butter and jam.

'If you had lain in, Mama suggested I bring you a tray up after we'd finished here,' Douglas said as she sat down. Somehow Norma found this irritating. Perhaps it had something to do with having seen Douglas and Solange talking together, discussing her in the garden?

Forsyth glanced at them. 'Have to dash in a moment. Busy day ahead of me.'

'Any idea what time you'll be home?' Solange enquired.

He shook his head. 'I'll telephone late afternoon. Might know by then.'

Solange smiled at Norma, who smiled back. Had Solange been complaining to Douglas earlier on, she wondered again? If she had been, it certainly didn't show in her manner. Solange appeared pleasantness itself.

'And what about you two, what will you do today?' Solange asked, directing the question at Norma and Douglas.

Douglas looked apologetically at Norma. 'I have a pile of back *Lancets* and other papers I must plough through. An awful lot has happened in the field of orthopaedics during the war that I must catch up on, and be *au fait* with, if I'm to stand a chance of landing that job at the Victoria when it comes up.'

'Fine, you do that,' Norma answered. 'But I must go and visit my folks later on, round about teatime say. I was hoping you'd come with me – my mother and sisters are dying to meet you.'

'Of course I'll come with you.'

'Right, that's settled then. I'll give you a call when it's time to leave.'

309

Forsyth wiped his mouth with a napkin, and stood up. 'That's me,' he announced, and came round to kiss Solange on the cheek. Solange said something in French, which he responded to in the same language. Douglas laughed.

Norma found that irritating. She considered it rude for people to speak another language in front of her, which she didn't understand, when all the others did. Then again, she reminded herself, it was probably a long-standing habit of theirs to switch backwards and forwards between the two languages. They might not even realise they were doing it. She was just going to have to learn French so that she wouldn't be excluded. That seemed the answer to the problem.

When Forsyth was gone, Solange said to Norma, 'You mentioned sisters?'

'I have two, Lyn and Eileen. They're both younger than me.'

'And are they married?'

'Eileen was, but her husband was killed in a collision between the passenger train he was on and a goods train. She was twenty years old when it happened.'

Solange pulled a long face. 'How sad.'

'Lyn's been going out with someone for a while now, according to my mother. She expects them to get engaged soon.'

'Someone who was in the Armed Forces?'

'No, he was exempt.' Norma waited for Solange to ask what the chap did, but Solange didn't. Which was probably just as well, the chap was an engine fireman on the railways. She doubted Solange would have appreciated that.

'And your mother, what's her name?'

'Euphemia, but she's always been called Effie.'

'Euphemia, how pretty! I much prefer it to Effie. And your father?'

'Brian.'

'We must have the McKenzies over soon,' said Forsyth.

Solange dropped her gaze to stare at her plate. Picking up her side knife she buttered a small rectangle of toast. 'Yes, we must,' she answered vaguely.

Hell would freeze over first, before her folks were invited to Blairbeth Road, Norma thought grimly. For it was clearly evident that her mother-in-law, and perhaps her father-in-law as well, was a dyed-in-the-wool snob.

310

'After breakfast I'll show you round the house if you like,' Solange said, glancing up at Norma.

'That's kind of you. I'd like that.'

'Good.'

'You'll find me in the study when you get that far,' said Douglas.

Norma went over to the sideboard and poured herself another cup of tea.

'And this is the ninth, and final, bedroom,' Solange declared, opening a door. This bedroom was situated on a between floor in an out-of-the-way corner of the house. It was by far the smallest.

There was a musty smell inside the bedroom which suggested it hadn't been aired for quite some time. It had the same broad decor that all the others had, indeed that the entire house had – worn-out Victorian drear.

'I must say I'm surprised you haven't . . . well, done the house up before now,' Norma smiled.

'Oh no, we prefer it as it is,' Solange replied quickly. 'I don't think any of us would change a thing. Gives a sense of continuity, which is very important to us.'

Norma could see Solange was deadly serious, her mother-in-law genuinely did prefer the house the ways it was. There was bound to be conflict when she let it be known she wanted her and Douglas's bedroom redecorated and refurnished. What should she do, state her intentions here and now? Or should she speak to Douglas first and let him deal with the problem? The latter was the wisest course, she decided. The last thing she wanted was a row during her first day at Blairbeth Road. She was already regretting that she'd agreed to come and stay here – she should have insisted she and Douglas get a place of their own. But it had been so difficult to argue by letter, and his reasons for choosing Blairbeth Road had been so plausible.

'And now we'll go below stairs and I'll introduce you formally to the servants,' Solange announced.

Imperious, yes, that was the word to describe Solange, Norma thought to herself as they left the bedroom, imperious.

'What were you and your mother talking about in the garden

this morning?' Norma asked. She and Douglas were in the Lagonda, having just left Blairbeth Road for Bridgeton.

'You saw us then?'

'From our bedroom window. You appeared to be having a very serious conversation.'

'She wanted to know more about my work as a "joe", where exactly I went, what I did, that kind of thing. She was deeply shocked at some of the details I gave her.'

'I can imagine.'

'She said it was just as well she hadn't been aware of what I was up to, the worry would probably have given her a nervous breakdown. She's very highly strung, you know.'

'I hadn't realised.'

'Yes, very much so.'

'And was that all you talked about?'

He gave her one of his sideways looks. 'What do you mean?'

'Come on, you know fine well what I mean. They're obviously disappointed that you've married me. I thought perhaps she was taking the opportunity to register that disappointment with you.'

He changed gear, then drove for a few seconds in silence. 'Well?' Norma prompted.

'Your name did come up.'

'I was sure it had.'

'Of course she's not exactly thrilled that I've married a girl from the other side of the tracks, so to speak. But she thinks you're charming and intelligent and . . .' He suddenly exploded. 'And they're just bloody well going to have to get used to the idea. You're the woman I love, I've married you and that's all there is to it.'

'You said that to her?'

'I did.'

Norma smiled. 'When I was watching you, you became very Gallic, waving your arms about as if you were shooting off semaphore.'

He smiled too. 'When I'm with French people that half of me tends to be uppermost. Just as when I'm with the British the other side comes to the fore.'

'I want our bedroom redecorated and refurnished,' Norma stated bluntly.

His smile disappeared. 'What's wrong with it? I like it the way it is. It's how it's always been.'

'It's terrible, Douglas. I want to re-do it completely.' When he didn't reply she went on. 'I have to have some part of the house which is mine, which is *ours*. Otherwise I'm living completely in someone else's home, and that's hardly a good way to start our marriage.'

'Mama will be upset.'

'We can still get our own place, you know. I've never asked about your financial situation, but if you can't stretch to it, I most certainly can.'

'No, I much prefer to stay on in Blairbeth Road. It would be such a waste not to.'

'Then that room has to be gutted. I'll put up with the rest of the house if I have to, but not our bedroom.'

'You really find it that offensive?'

'Yes, I do. And I'm surprised you don't.'

'Perhaps . . . Well I don't know. I have such happy childhood memories of it. Maybe you see it differently to the way I do.'

He fumbled for a cigarette, put one in his mouth, and lit it. 'I'll ask Mama's permission when I get the chance.'

'Don't ask her, Douglas, *tell* her,' Norma replied softly.

He gave her another of his sideways looks. He found her very sexy when she was being determined. 'How about stopping outside the Victoria Infirmary so you can have a gander at it? After all, if I get that job it could be my place of employment for the next thirty odd years.'

'I'd love to see it. That's a terrific idea. And Douglas?'

'Yes?'

'About the bedroom, the first thing to go is that bed. Last night was all right, but I don't want to do it that way every night.'

'I'll see to it.'

'No darling, I will. Leave everything concerning the bedroom to me. And one other thing.'

'What's that?'

'I'm going to get myself a car.'

'But we've got this Lagonda!' he protested.

'When you start work you'll monopolise it all day long. Well, no thank you to that. I'm used to having my own transport, and want to continue to have it.'

'I'll buy you a car then.'

'Can you afford to?'

'I do have some money, but it's a tiny amount compared to what I'll inherit from my parents. Of course once I become a specialist I'll start to earn quite a bit, just as my father's been doing all these years.'

'I'll tell you what, in that case I'll buy this car myself. You can buy the next one for me.'

'Are you sure? I feel that being your husband I should pick up all the bills.'

'That's a very old-fashioned, and honourable, way of looking at marriage. I think the war has changed a lot of those old notions though, don't you? An awful lot of women have got used to being more independent than we were, and we're not about to toss that independence out the window just because the war's over.'

He regarded her quizzically. 'I'm not altogether certain I know what you're talking about?'

'It means I'll pay for the car, and you're not to worry about it. At least, for the time being that's what it means anyway.'

He was still thinking about that, and the best way to approach his mother about their bedroom when the Victoria Infirmary – the Vicky to those who worked there and lived round about – hove into view.

The Victoria Infirmary was an imposing grey edifice situated in the district of Battlefield, the latter named after the Battle of Langside which Mary Queen of Scots fought, and lost. 'It's a big hospital,' Norma commented as they parked opposite. And indeed it was. There was the urgent clang of an ambulance which went charging past them, and into an entranceway that would take it to Casualty.

'Big, busy and a fine hospital to work in,' Douglas said as the rear of the ambulance disappeared.

They had a good look at the Vicky, and were about to drive on when Norma spotted what seemed a familiar face. She frowned, trying to place the man. And then she had it. 'Mr Creighton!' she exclaimed, pointing at Creighton, who'd stopped to talk to another man.

314

Douglas turned to her in surprise. 'You know him? Creighton's the top neurologist in Glasgow. He's as big in his field as my father is in his. He's also, incidentally, a great friend of my father.'

Creighton was wearing the same black Homburg hat that she remembered so well – if it wasn't the same it was an identical twin. 'We called him to Cubie Street when my ma had encephalitis,' she exclaimed.

'And he cured your mother.'

She could remember it all as if it was only yesterday. Coming home on leave after Lynsey's death to find her mother alone, and suffering from a horrendous headache; asking Alice Henderson from downstairs to ring Doctor Dickie who'd told her Effie needed Creighton. The M&B Creighton had given Effie which it had turned out Effie was allergic to, and everyone thinking Effie was a goner. Then Lynsey appearing to her – she still didn't know whether that had been a dream or not – and the tingling sensation in her hands. Lynsey instructing her to lay her hands on Effie, and Effie's subsequent recovery. A miracle? She still thought of it as such.

Norma roused herself from her reverie. 'No, Creighton didn't cure Ma, I did.'

Douglas's eyebrows shot up his forehead. '*You* did?'

She recounted to him exactly what had happened, while he listened to her tale in obvious astonishment.

'Healing hands?' he said, and shook his head in disbelief.

'It's true, I assure you.'

'And have you had occasion to use this healing ability since?'

'No. That was the one and only time. Then again, I haven't tried to use it.'

'It's eh ...' He coughed. 'Excuse me for saying so but the whole thing sounds a bit far-fetched.'

'Mr Creighton didn't think so. My mother was in a coma and dying; neither he nor the rest of the medical profession could do anything to save her. And yet, within the space of a few seconds, her condition completely changed. She came out of the coma and lived.'

'And Creighton had no rational, medical explanation for what occurred? This turnaround in her condition?'

'None at all. He said my healing ability is probably latent and

315

that Lynsey was a device, or catalyst, used by my subconscious, to bring the ability to the surface.'

Douglas looked over at Rodney Creighton, whom he held in great respect. He was amazed that the dour and humourless Creighton of all people should believe in something as airy fairy as healing hands. Why, that sort of thing was complete stuff and nonsense. There were certain psychosomatic instances where a bit of hocus pocus might do some good, but hardly in the situation that Norma had just described. There had to be a rational explanation for Mrs McKenzie's recovery. Even if Creighton hadn't come up with one there just had to be. As for healing hands and miracles, they belonged strictly to the Bible.

'I can see you're sceptical to say the least,' Norma smiled.

'I'm a man of science. I'd have to actually witness such an event before I believed it. I'm sorry.'

She dismissed the subject as not worth wrangling over. Effie was alive and well, that was all that mattered. 'Let's get on to Cubie Street. I can't wait to see them all again.'

Smiling cynically, Douglas put the car into gear and they continued their journey to Bridgeton.

Lyn opened the door. 'Return of the prodigal, with husband,' Norma said.

Lyn squealed with delight, and threw herself at Norma. The sisters embraced, the pair of them squeezing one another like mad. 'You're back! We've been expecting you at any time, but didn't know exactly when. Oh, let me have a dekko at you!' Lyn said, and thrust her older sister to arms' length. 'You look just terrific.'

'You too Lyn. By the way, this is Douglas.'

'You look terrific as well,' Lyn said, and roared with laughter while Douglas blushed bright red. 'Ma! Da! Eileen! It's Norma!' Lyn yelled into the house.

There was a terrific commotion. Effie was the first to appear, with Brian right behind her and Eileen behind him. They all rushed out onto the landing where Effie fell upon Norma. 'Oh lassie,' she cried, tears streaming down her face.

Norma hugged her ma, then Eileen joined in. Brian stood slightly apart, his expression one of deep love and fierce pride.

Douglas might have been there, but for the moment he only had eyes for Norma, his firstborn.

'Da!'

'Girl,' Brian whispered. She put her arms round him, and her head on his shoulder. 'Welcome home, girl. Welcome home,' he said, a choke in his voice.

Norma dashed away a tear, for she was crying too. 'Ma, Eileen, I'd like you to meet Douglas,' she said, standing up straight again.

'Hello Mrs McKenzie,' Douglas smiled, feeling somewhat selfconscious.

'Och away with you, call me Ma.'

'Then, hello *Ma*.'

Effie beamed. 'That's more like it.' She and Douglas shook. On a sudden impulse he kissed her on the cheek, which pleased her hugely.

'Eileen.' They shook. 'Pleased to meet you, Douglas.'

'Now let's away ben,' Effie said, and shooed eveyone through the door. She went into the kitchen to make some fresh tea, while the rest of them went into the living-room.

Norma was shocked by Eileen's appearance. She was thin as a stick, pasty-faced, her hair dull, lifeless, and scraped back into an untidy bun. This was as different to the vibrant, vital, ever-bubbling wee sister she'd watched grow up as could be. Charlie's death had put Eileen through the mill, and apparently was continuing to do so, right enough.

'So when did you get into Glasgow?' Lyn demanded of Norma. Brian and Douglas were renewing their acquaintance, as Brian ushered Douglas to what was normally his chair, the best chair in the house.

'Last night.'

'Wasn't that a humdinger of a storm? Fair gave me the willies listening to it,' Eileen said.

'It was pretty bad.'

'And the pair of you are staying with your parents, is that right?' Brian asked Douglas.

'In Burnside. It's a big house so there's plenty of space.'

'That's handy.' He reached for his pipe and tobacco tin which were sitting on the mantelpiece. 'And the army sent you back to Blighty some time ago, I understand?'

317

Douglas glanced over at Norma to see if she wanted him to spill the beans about the SOE, something they'd failed to discuss during their drive there. Her reply was a slight shake of the head; she wasn't sure yet whether she'd tell her family about SOE, but if she did it certainly wasn't going to be here and now.

'I got posted to London for a while. And then I was shunted round the place after that,' Douglas confirmed.

'He came down to Southampton in the car and met me off the ship,' Norma said.

'Am I right in assuming you've been discharged early like me then?' Brian asked Douglas.

'Yes, I was lucky. It's going to take quite some time before everyone's back in civvy street.'

'Da's got some news!' Eileen exclaimed suddenly.

Brian began packing his pipe. 'I was only told on Friday. I'm to be made foreman of Bellahouston Park. It means more money of course.'

'Oh Da, I am pleased!' Norma enthused.

'So's your ma. Me home and promoted into the bargain. She's thrilled to bits.'

'How many men under you?' asked Norma.

'Fifteen, when we have a full complement again.'

'Twelve more than Kilmichael House, and you were head gardener there.'

'Aye, that's a fact,' Brian acknowledged. It filled him with quiet satisfaction to think that was so.

'Now I want to hear about your time in Algeria. Da says Algiers where you were stationed was a marvellous place,' Lyn chipped in.

'We were stationed a little outside Algiers, fifteen miles to the west to be exact. I originally shared a villa at Club des Pins overlooking the beach.'

'Club des Pins! Sounds dead romantic,' Lyn sighed.

'It was, for some,' Norma smiled, glancing at Douglas. He smiled back.

'Did you drive many big wigs?' Eileen queried.

'Lots and lots.'

Effie came bustling in with tea and home-made scones, and for the next half hour Norma and Douglas talked about Algiers, the surrounding countryside, Club des Pins, the field hospital

318

where he'd worked after the Allied landings, but never mentioning the names of Massingham, SOE, or any business connected with either.

'Now enough about us, tell me about this new boyfriend of yours?' Norma demanded of Lyn.

Lyn went all coy. 'His name is Iain and he's an engine fireman with LMS. He and I are like that,' she replied, and held out two crossed fingers.

'So is it really a walk down the aisle job?'

'I'm just waiting for him to pop the question, which I'm hoping he'll be doing any week now.'

'That's tremendous, Lyn. I'm happy as Larry for you.'

'I met him at a party and it was a click right away. I knew the first time he got me up to dance that he was going to be my fate. He lives in the Calton, so we get to see quite a bit of one another.'

'Does that mean he doesn't do all that many long distance runs?'

'He's mainly on the Cathcart Circle, but occasionally does part of the London run, sleeping the night at Crewe and coming up again the following day. But he doesn't do that all that often.'

The women gassed on, till finally Brian, fed up with all the female blether, said to Douglas, 'Do you fancy escaping down the road for a pint?'

Douglas was instantly on his feet. 'That sounds a smashing idea. I'm your man.' A few minutes later the pair of them were going out the front door together, with Effie shouting after them to make sure it was only the one pint mind!

'He's a dish, I'm fair impressed,' Lyn said to Norma the moment the outside door had banged shut. For now Douglas was gone they could talk about him.

'He suits me all right.'

'And he's half French?' But before Norma could reply she said to Eileen, giving Eileen a lecherous wink, 'And you know what they say about Frenchmen?' She shook her right hand as though it was burning hot.

'Don't be crude lass,' Effie admonished.

Norma couldn't help herself. She waved her right hand just as Lyn had done. 'He is! He is!' Which caused them all to burst out laughing, even Effie. Norma went on, 'The mother, Solange, is French, the father, Forsyth, Scots.'

'And what are they like?' Effie queried.

'She's toaty wee with kind of birdlike eyes, and *very very* French. He's pleasant enough, if a bit pompous at times.'

'You don't care for them,' Effie commented shrewdly.

'It's early days to be that definite. Let's just say I'm not as taken with them as I'd hoped,' Norma prevaricated.

Eileen started putting more coal on the fire from the scuttle standing beside it. 'And what about the house? What do you think of that?'

Norma screwed up her face. 'Dracula's castle, that was my first impression. If there had been bats flying round the chimney stacks I wouldn't have been at all surprised.'

'Sounds spooky,' Lyn commented.

'Well, it certainly was from the outside in last night's storm, I can tell you.'

'And inside?' Effie probed.

'Very gloomy. As for our bedroom, I took a complete scunner to it the instant I saw it. It's hateful, though amazingly, Douglas likes it. But he admits that his opinion is probably clouded by happy childhood memories of the place. It's the bedroom he's been in since he was old enough to have a bedroom of his own.' She went on to describe in detail every room in the house.

'Sounds very creepy,' Eileen commented.

'It is a bit. But I'm going to have our bedroom gutted and totally re-done, I'm determined about that. There will be nothing spooky, creepy or antediluvian about it when I'm finished.'

'That's it,' Effie said, nodding her approval, 'you start as you mean to go on.'

'Are the Rosses snobby? Noses in the air?' Lyn queried.

'Very much so, the parents that is. Not Douglas, he isn't in the least.'

Effie sat back in her chair, her lips thinning, her eyes becoming partially hooded. 'So how does this... Solange did you cry her?' Norma nodded. 'How do this Solange and Forsyth feel about you then?'

'To be frank Ma, I'm a big disappointment to them. But Douglas is certain they'll get over that before long.'

'Let's just hope they do. Otherwise it may be you've done the wrong thing in agreeing to live in Blairbeth Road.'

Norma sighed. 'That could be the case. But I'll give it a go anyway, if nothing else to show willing.'

'And they've got proper servants?' Eileen asked, fascinated by that idea.

'Oh aye, the full works. A butler called Travers...' Lyn sniggered, imagining herself ordering a fancy butler by the name of Travers around, 'a cook called Mrs Knight who's married to the gardener, and three maids,' Norma replied.

'*Only* three?' mocked Lyn. 'And does one of them wipe your arse for you after you've been to the bog?'

'Lyn!' Effie exclaimed, shocked. Honestly, what was the girl going to come out with next!

While Norma was smiling, thinking her sister's remark quite funny, Eileen stared into space, seeing another time and place. 'I can vaguely remember the servants at Kilmichael House, but only vaguely,' she muttered.

'A fine lot of people they were, I mind them all well,' Effie said, remembering faces and personalities.

'So tell us more about Blairbeth Road?' urged Lyn.

'I'm expected to dress for dinner every night.'

Tongue in cheek, Lyn replied. 'You always dressed for meals here. I've never seen anybody at our table in his or her bare scuddy. Have you Eileen?'

'Oh ha ha!' Norma retorted sarcastically. 'But that brings me to something else. I only have a couple of suitable frocks that I managed to pick up in London when Douglas and I stopped off there.'

'Coupons,' Effie cut in, catching on right away.

'You've hit the nail on the head Ma. I've spent all my coupons and need more, quite a few more actually. Can any of you help?'

'Extra coupons are no bother, if you've got the cash to pay for them that is,' Effie replied.

Eileen said. 'There are several black marketeers round here who'd sell you anything, including their granny, for the right price.'

'Good. I can't give you money right now as I haven't had the chance to go to the bank yet, but I will go tomorrow. When I've been I'll call back here and give you what you think you'll need,

321

then you can send me the coupons on in the post. Would that be all right?'

'You'll have as many coupons as you want,' promised Effie.

'And there's something else. We desperately, and I mean desperately, need a new bed. So I'll need additional coupons for that.'

'Why a new bed?' Eileen queried with a frown.

'It's a bit embarrassing but . . . eh . . . the one we're in at the minute squeaks like Billy-O.'

Lyn guffawed, a rich fruity sound that reverberated round the room. 'And you can be overheard "at it". Is that what you're saying?'

Norma, blushing slightly, nodded. 'You'd hardly credit the racket the present bed makes, quite unbelievable. And the thing is that Douglas's parents are just along the passageway from us.'

'Dear me,' muttered Effie. She knew she'd have been mortified to find herself in that situation. She would hardly have dared move all night long, far less anything else. She could only sympathise with Norma and Douglas, and them having been separated for so long too.

'A new bed is a must, and as soon as possible,' Norma went on.

Eileen was gazing into the fire, remembering those four glorious, ecstatic nights she and Charlie had spent in the Adelphi Hotel, and thinking there would never be such nights, and pleasures, for her ever again.

'Right then, additional coupons for a new bed it is pet,' said Effie.

'So if the bed squeaked as badly as you say what did you do?' Lyn asked eagerly, dying to know the answer. Before Effie could tell Lyn off Norma changed the subject, nor would she return to it despite all Lyn's repeated attempts.

'Can I ask you something please Ma'am?' Phyl Casden asked. Phyl was the maid who, in addition to her many other duties, cleaned and tidied Norma and Douglas's bedroom. She was a horsey-faced woman with a drainpipe build of about Norma's age. Norma later found out that Phyl was a year younger than her, which is to say that Phyl was twenty-seven.

'Certainly. What is it?'

'You are the Norma McKenzie who used to give exhibitions at Barrowland aren't you?'

Norma smiled. 'Yes, I am.'

Phyl clapped her hands together. 'I knew it was you, I recognised you right off. A Mr Henderson used to be your partner.'

'That's correct. Michael Henderson, though he was always known to his friends as Midge.'

'You were a terrific couple, a real pair of bobby dazzlers. When the two of you took the floor it was like magic happening. Me and my china of that time used to go whenever we could to watch you.'

'You did?'

'We did indeed Ma'am. We were devoted fans. It broke our hearts when you and Mr Henderson stopped dancing.'

Norma turned away so that Phyl couldn't see her expression. 'Mr Henderson decided to go to America. He believed there to be more opportunities for him there.'

'And were there?'

'So I understand. We never kept in touch.'

Phyl tucked a stray wisp of hair behind an ear. 'You and he were in a class of your own. For my money, and a lot like me, there was no one else in Glasgow could touch you.'

'We won the All Scotland Dance Championship just before we ... we retired.'

'I wanted to go and spectate at that, but couldn't because of the flu. I knew you'd win mind, it was a foregone conclusion as far as I was concerned.'

Norma laughed. 'We didn't see it at all like that. There was some very stiff competition. I didn't normally get the jitters when competing, but I did that night. I can remember that quite clearly.'

Phyl's eyes were shining with heroine worship when she said, 'I hope you don't mind me speaking out like this, but I've been dying to ever since you arrived and I recognised who you were.'

'Who I *used* to be,' corrected Norma.

'Well ... you know what I mean Ma'am. Now I'd better get on with my work or I'll be in trouble with Mr Travers.' She went to move, then stopped again. 'And Ma'am, whether I'm on duty or not, if there's ever anything you want, or need, anything whatever, you've only got to say. It's my great honour to look after you Ma'am. Great honour.'

'Why thank you Phyl. I appreciate that.'

Norma left Phyl and joined Douglas in the study where he was poring over medical papers and back copies of the Lancet. The conversation with Phyl Casden had cheered her enormously. She felt she had a friend in the house – apart from Douglas that is – which made a big difference. A very big difference. She was humming gaily when she entered the study.

Norma couldn't wait to show Douglas the canary yellow MG she'd bought. It was a real cracker, and a snip at the price. She halted the MG, nipped out of the car and opened the large wrought-iron gates, then drove the MG to the main entrance where she parked it behind the Lagonda. She caressed the wooden rim of the steering wheel. The MG was a beauty, a proper stotter as they would have said in Cubie Street.

She was walking through the reception area, heading for the study where she presumed Douglas would be, when Solange appeared and beckoned to her. She stopped, waiting impatiently as Solange came over, for she was dying to drag Douglas outside and show him the car.

Solange came up and smiled. 'Don't bother Douglas just now *chérie*. He has one of Forsyth's colleagues from the Southern General with him. Mr Riach has kindly agreed to help Douglas catch up on the recent advances in orthopaedics.' The Southern General was another major Glasgow hospital situated in Govan.

'Oh!'

Solange hooked an arm round one of Norma's. 'Best he's left undisturbed for the moment. Don't you think?'

'I eh... yes, I suppose so.'

Solange's smile widened. 'Good.' And with that she drew Norma away from the study towards the small sitting-room which was only a quarter the size of the large sitting-room, and ideal for cosy chit-chats. 'In the meantime you and I can have a little talk together, no?'

'If you like.'

Once in the small sitting room Solange closed the door behind them. 'Mr Riach is an extremely clever man, so Forsyth says, and he knows about such things. However, that aside, Douglas tells me you wish to make changes in your bedroom?'

Norma felt herself tense. She hadn't expected Solange to approach her directly about the bedroom.

'Yes,' she replied.

Solange made a very Gallic gesture. 'I understand perfectly, of course I do. The room is your nest and you wish to feather it according to your own taste.'

'That's it exactly,' Norma replied. Was this going to be easy after all?

'You wish a new carpet perhaps? And curtains?'

'I want the room *completely* re-done,' Norma answered.

'I see.'

'Wallpaper, paint, carpet, curtains, furniture, the lot – top to bottom. And a new bed, the one we have now is . . . well, past its best, and most uncomfortable.'

Solange averted her gaze, she knew precisely what Norma was getting at about the latter. She had heard the squeaking, and very disturbing she'd found it too. 'I'm sure you'll do marvels with the room, a total transformation eh?'

'I hope so.'

Both women were now seated, staring at one another from either side of the fireplace. Solange nodded her head several times, then said slowly, 'All this will be expensive *chérie*.'

'I'll pay myself if need be,' Norma interjected.

Solange held up a hand. 'No need for that. But it strikes me it would be a waste of money should you and Douglas not end up using that room on a permanent basis.' She paused to let that sink in, then went on softly. 'We have to remember we have no guarantee he *will* get the job at the Victoria. I know Forsyth is positive he will, but what is it you British say? Many a slip twixt cup and lip?' Norma experienced a sinking feeling when Solange said that. She knew what was coming next. Solange continued. 'So I would suggest we leave the redecoration until, hopefully, it is confirmed that Douglas has landed that job, or if not that, another in Glasgow. Otherwise it would be a great deal of expense for nothing. Or very little anyway. Don't you agree?'

Reluctantly Norma replied. 'I suppose I do.' It did make perfect sense after all. Her own mother would probably have said the same thing.

'I know it's a myth that you Scots are mean, but why throw money away? That would be silly, eh *chérie*?'

Again reluctantly. 'Waste not want not, my father used to say when we were wee.'

'A man with his head screwed on the right way obviously. So we will leave all further discussion about your bedroom until after we know where we are.'

Norma had been looking forward so much to ripping that damned dreary wallpaper off and getting stuck in, for she planned to do the redecoration herself. 'With the exception of the bed,' she said emphatically. 'Even if we are only here for a short while I still want the new bed. We can always take it with us if we have to go anyway.'

That suited Solange who didn't want to hear any more of that squeaking, subdued though it was. She bowed her head, conceding the point. 'Do you want me to...'

'I already have everything in hand thank you,' Norma cut in.

'Then shall I ring for tea? And you can tell me all about this new car you've bought,' Solange suggested, reaching for the bell-pull that would summon Travers.

It wasn't till later that it dawned on Norma that Solange must have been watching her drive up to the house and must have known that she had been *en route* to tell Douglas about it. Which set her wondering again.

Chapter Twelve

She found Douglas sitting on a bench in the garden staring at the falling snow. His shoulders were hunched, his expression morose and vacant. 'Hello,' she said. Then, louder, when she got no reply. 'Hello husband mine.'

He blinked, came back from wherever he'd been, and gave her a wan smile. 'Hello Norma.'

'You looked as though you were away with the fairies – ?'

'Something like that.'

She sat beside him. 'It's a lovely garden. It must be quite beautiful in the summer.'

'Knight has always done a good job on it. And yes, it is beautiful. I found myself often thinking about it when...' He trailed off, groped for his cigarettes, and lit up. 'I'm glad it's snowing for Christmas. It should always snow for then, though it rarely does.'

'When you were in France, were you going to say?'

He gave her one of his sideways looks. 'Don't you find it odd now that the war's over?'

'You mean anti-climactic?'

'That's it exactly.'

'In a way.'

He wiped snow from his face, leaving wet marks which made it seem as though he'd been crying. His liquid brown eyes were even more liquid than usual. They might have been endless brown pools into which you could sink forever. 'I feel like a bow that had been kept taut for a long, long time and then released. It's a very strange sensation.'

'Are you saying you wish the war was still going on?'

'Good Heavens no! God forbid! I can't tell you how many times I prayed for it to end, with us, the Allies, as victors of course. But now that it is over, and after all that training, and what I went through in the field, and the life and death responsibility that was mine as DR, it now all seems —'

'Anti-climactic,' she interjected.

He drew deeply on his cigarette, then blew smoke at the swirling gusts of snow.

'It's a huge transition for you, and others like you, to make. There's no denying that,' Norma said.

'Time, I suppose that's the answer.'

'I'm sure it is.'

'To readjust, to become... normal again I suppose.'

'Douglas?' He turned to face her. 'You've never told me anything about that very last field assignment you were on. Is that part of all this?' She watched his sallow complexion change to a distinct greenish colour.

'I don't want to talk about that. I can't,' he replied, his voice tight and raw.

'But is that to do with these moods you've been getting? For today's isn't the first you know, although it's the first time I've tried to speak to you while you were in one.'

'I didn't realise they were so obvious.'

'They are to me darling.'

'I'm sorry.'

She placed a hand on his thigh. 'There's no need to apologise, I understand.' She then tapped out.

I understand Gabriel. And I'm here whenever you need me.

'I know.'

He flicked his half-finished cigarette away. It hissed where it hit the snow. 'Speaking about this garden, I always wanted a pond in it when I was a lad.'

'A pond?'

'I adored frogs you see, and toads. I wanted a pond with lilies in it, and frogspawn and toadspawn. And newts, I rather fancied newts as well. They get gorgeous bellies on them you know. I remember seeing one that was salmon-pink underneath, quite spectacular.'

Norma wrinkled her nose. 'I don't like slimies, never have.'

'They're not slimy.'

'Of course they are!'

'People just *think* they are. Same with snakes, people think they're slimy also, whereas in fact it can be like touching parchment.'

'I wouldn't touch a snake for all the tea in China. Yuuch!' she said, the last an exclamation, and shuddered all over.

He laughed. 'They really aren't that bad. Honestly!'

'I have no intention of finding out one way or the other. The moment I see a snake I'm off. You won't see me for dust.'

'What about frogs and toads?'

'Loathsome creatures.'

'And newts?'

She shuddered again.

'You're just like Mama, she hates those animals as well. That's why I never had a pond as a lad, she wouldn't allow it.'

'Well that's one thing your mother and I are in agreement about. Anyway, I'm glad to see I've managed to cheer you up. You actually laughed a second or two ago.'

He put a hand on top of the one of hers that was still on his thigh.

Hello Norma.

She tapped on his thigh.

Hello Gabriel.

Thanks.

I don't like it when you're all mizzy. Makes me depressed for you.

Sorry.

Once you get this job the war will begin to fade into the past.

If I get this particular one.

I have every confidence you will.

His eyes flicked over her shoulder.

Mama's signalling from the conservatory.

Norma glanced round at the rear of the house, and sure enough there was Solange in the conservatory waving at them.

Who's that with her?

You mean the scrumptious redhead with the enormous...

Douglas! You have a fixation about enormous whatsits.

He waved back at Solange, acknowledging that they'd seen her, and were coming in.

You mean tits?

Breasts is the proper word.

329

Breasts, tits, knockers, bazooms, what's wrong with a bit of honest vulgarity? The redhead is Catherine Stark.

She stopped sending. 'Is it really?'

'I'm only surprised she hasn't been before now.'

Norma put a hand to her hair, and wished now she hadn't come out in the snow. Even though she was wearing a scarf her hair would be bedraggled as the snow had soaked through. And she didn't have any make-up on. Blast! Well she was damned if she was going to meet this Stark female looking like something the cat had dragged in. She'd pay her bedroom a lightning visit to sort herself out before saying hello.

As they rose from where they'd been sitting she told Douglas what she had in mind. 'I'll only be a jiffy and then I'll join you,' she said as they made for a rear door.

In her bedroom she launched into feverish activity. Less than five minutes after leaving Douglas she was entering the small sitting room, where she'd heard voices coming from, to discover Solange, Douglas and Catherine Stark standing round the fireplace holding drinks.

'Darling, I'd like you to meet Catherine, an old friend of mine and the family. Catherine, this is Norma,' Douglas introduced.

She wasn't a redhead, but ginger, Norma thought to herself. Ginger, the colour of marmalade, and cats. The nervousness that had been fluttering in her stomach vanished abruptly when she saw that, rather than Catherine having enormous breasts as Douglas had said, Catherine was flat as a board. That cheered her enormously.

'How do you do, Norma,' Catherine smiled, holding out a limp hand.

She's a bitch, Norma thought. A bitch through and through. And hard with it. 'I'm pleased to meet you at long last. Douglas has told me so much about you,' Norma smiled back.

The hint of a frown clouded Catherine's forehead, and her gaze flicked to Douglas as she and Norma shook hands, Norma making her grip as limp and unenthusiastic as Catherine's.

'We're having gin and tonics, what about you love?' Douglas asked Norma.

'Sounds absolutely marvellous,' she replied. Flat as a board! She felt so good she could have burst out laughing.

*   *   *

330

Norma was in her bedroom chatting to Phyl Casden while Phyl dusted, when she heard the commotion. Leaving the bedroom she hurried along the passageway to the top of the main staircase, when Douglas and Solange appeared from the large sitting room, Douglas with an arm round his mother.

'It came just now in the afternoon post,' he cried to Norma, waggling a sheet of paper. 'I've got the job at the Victoria. I'm to be their new junior orthopaedic specialist.' He'd had several interviews, the last of which had been the previous week.

Elation leapt in Norma. This was wonderful news. It was what she and Douglas had both been praying for.

'I start the first of April, April Fool's Day!' he said, and laughed.

Norma was about to run down the stairs and throw herself at him when Solange said, and was it her imagination or was there a hint of triumph in her mother-in-law's voice? 'He came directly to me so that I should be the first to know. Didn't you *mon ange?*'

Norma went very cold inside to hear that. And then annoyance flared. Why had he gone straight to his mother? It was *she*, his wife, whom he should have told first.

'Well, aren't you going to say anything?' Douglas asked.

'Congratulations.'

'We have decided to hold a party to celebrate Douglas's appointment,' Solange announced.

We! Norma thought. Solange and Douglas. *Not* Solange, Douglas and Norma, but Solange and Douglas, as if she didn't even exist. Her annoyance deepened.

'Don't you think that's a terrific idea?' Douglas said.

'Terrific,' she echoed, and started down the stairs.

'Forsyth insisted you'd get the post, and of course he was right, as usual. We are both very proud of you my son. Very proud.' Solange disentangled herself from Douglas. 'We will have the party this Saturday, so there is lots to do. I will ring for Travers in the study, and give him his orders. You join me there in half an hour Douglas and we will make up the invitation list together.'

Norma was seething now. There it was again, her being excluded. Why couldn't she have been asked to join in making up the invitation list? Even if she wasn't expected to make any

331

suggestions Solange could have at least, for common courtesy if nothing else, made a pretence of allowing her to be part and parcel of the business.

'We will have music, and wine, and it will be a night to remember!' Solange enthused, her birdlike eyes shining with anticipation. 'Now kiss me again.' He did, on the cheek. 'Half an hour Douglas, half an hour!' And with that Solange swept away to the study.

Douglas went over to where Norma was standing at the foot of the stairs. 'You don't seem all that ecstatic. I was expecting more of a reaction from you.'

Should she say something? Or not? What amazed her was that someone normally so sensitive could also be so bloody insensitive. 'I am ecstatic I assure you. Perhaps I'll have more of a reaction later when the news has had time to sink in.' She gave him a sudden smile. 'Now I can get started on our bedroom.'

'You do approve of the party idea don't you?'

'Of course.'

'You'll enjoy yourself. I'll make sure of that.'

'I just wish...' That you'd come and given me your news first, she wanted to say. But didn't.

'Wish what Norma?'

'Nothing. And don't forget, half an hour in the study. It wouldn't do to keep your mama waiting.'

She left him to go back up the stairs. When she reached the top she glanced down again, and there he was, a puzzled expression on his face, still standing where she'd left him. She gave him a little wave before moving on out of sight.

She'd known the moment she'd clapped eyes on the dress that it was made for her. It was black, plain, and a knockout when on. It had cost her a small fortune, not to mention a number of the coupons that Effie and her sisters had been able to supply her with. But the money had been worth it. The dress was pure quality, and in excellent taste. She couldn't have asked for anything better to wear to Douglas's party.

A glance at the bedside clock told her that the party had been underway for just over twenty minutes now. She'd give it another fifteen before going down. As she hadn't been involved in any of the details of the thing she didn't see why she should be there to greet people, or help get the ball rolling. She would take her own sweet time, and go down when she was ready, and not before.

There was a tap on the door. 'Come in!'

It was Phyl Casden with a flushed face. 'Master Douglas has sent me up to see what's keeping you?'

Norma continued buffing a nail she'd discovered to have a slightly jagged edge. 'Do you think you could get me a dram?'

'Oh aye. And bring it here you mean?'

Norma nodded. 'What's it like below?'

'Murder polis. We told Travers he should lay on extra staff, but he wouldn't have it. Now we're all running around like chickens with their heads cut off.'

'Has Miss Stark arrived yet?'

'She was talking to Master Douglas when I left him.'

'What's she wearing?'

Norma listened to a description of Catherine's dress. It didn't sound a patch on hers. 'See if you can get me that drink then. But forget it if it's too much trouble.'

'I'll do my best.'

'A little bit of Dutch courage. It'll be the first time I've faced the family friends,' Norma explained.

Phyl was no fool. Aware that Norma was working-class by birth, she knew fine well what Norma was referring to. 'I'll make sure you get that dram, a big one too. And Master Douglas?'

'Tell him I'll be there directly.'

When Phyl was gone Norma listened to the music wafting up from downstairs. She wasn't sure whether it was classical or not, but whatever, it was stodgy as old porage. She thought of some of the bands she'd danced to in her time, and smiled at the memory. Now that was her kind of music, the sort to make your feet twitch and the blood race.

When another fifteen minutes were up, and with a large malt whisky under her belt, she rose and hoisted a smile onto her face. Then she went downstairs.

She spied Douglas right off deep in conversation with a most distinguished looking elderly gentleman and a woman whom she took, correctly, to be the gentleman's wife. She saw Solange glance over and give her what Effie would have called a sinker.

Pretending not to have taken the look on board, she made for Douglas.

She sipped at her fourth wine of the evening and told herself this glass was her final one. The last thing she wanted was to get tipsy. She was listening to a Sir Ranulf Fordyce wittle on about farming – apparently he owned a great deal of acreage in Perthshire, and deadly dull he was being about it too. All the man seemed to know about were crop yields, drainage and fertilisers. 'How interesting,' she murmured. Then, a few seconds later. 'How *very* interesting.'

'Why Norma, I've been trying to get to you all evening to compliment you. You look absolutely ravishing.'

Norma turned to Catherine Stark who'd come over with two other women, cronies of Catherine's she supposed. 'Thank you. How kind.'

'I'd like you to meet Henrietta Lockhart.' Norma shook hands with Henrietta. 'And Elsie Buchan.' Norma shook with Elsie.

Henrietta and Elsie were smiling as Norma was, but behind their smiles they were staring at her as if she was something nasty that had crawled out from underneath a stone.

'Do you know Sir Ranulf?' Norma queried.

Catherine gave a tinkling laugh. 'I hope so, he's my God-father.'

The other two women and Sir Ranulf also laughed, thinking that a fine joke. Norma's smile never wavered.

Catherine and Sir Ranulf chatted briefly, then he excused himself and moved on.

'We were wondering . . .' Catherine started to say to Norma, and as she did a glance passed between Henrietta and Elsie that set the alarm bells ringing for Norma. Hello, she thought. They're up to something, 'if you'd care to join us this Wednesday for a ride? Pater owns stables at Eaglesham and the three of us meet up there every Wednesday morning at about ten and go for a canter. Would that appeal?'

Norma had another sip of wine while she considered the invitation. 'You *can* ride I take it?' Elsie asked, a sneer in her voice.

So that was it. They presume that because I'm working-class

I've never been on a horse, Norma thought. This was a little ploy to make her feel inferior, to underline that she was an outsider and not 'one of the chaps'. She'd been dead right in placing Catherine as a bitch. The other two clearly were as well. 'Sounds a jolly good suggestion. I'd love to come along,' she replied.

Three faces fell fractionally. 'Oh marvellous!' Catherine answered with difficulty.

'Ten o'clock on Wednesday? I'll be there. Douglas can give me the precise directions.'

'We'll look forward to that then,' Catherine said.

'So will I.'

At which point Douglas joined them with a Mrs Hills-Carmichael whom he wanted Norma to meet, and the three harpies moved off. One up for the home team! Norma congratulated herself.

'I thought it went very well. Didn't you?' Douglas said as he struggled into the bottom of his striped flannelette pyjamas.

Norma looked at him from their bed where she was already tucked up. 'I felt like a goldfish in a bowl. All eyes on me.'

'Well, people were bound to be curious. You were completely new to them after all.'

'I got the distinct impression they were waiting for me to hawk on the floor and pick my nose.'

He laughed. 'You're exaggerating.'

'Like hell I am!'

He slowly tied his waist cord. 'You were a success. They liked you.'

'Who said?'

'No one had to. I could tell.' He came over to sit beside her. 'I was proud of you tonight Mrs Ross.'

'Were you really?'

'Very much so.'

'No regrets?'

He frowned. 'About what?'

'Marrying me.'

'Not in a million years. Nor will I ever have any.'

She sighed. 'My da warned me that night at the St George

Hotel that I'd have to fit in at your and your friends' level. Tonight was my first big test.'

'And you passed with flying colours. I promise you.' He pulled the bedclothes back a bit and began stroking her. A gorgeous sensation that made her feel all warm and watery inside. 'I hear Catherine asked you out riding.'

'On Wednesday, yes.'

'Well there you are then. Even she's accepted you.'

He'd missed the whole point of Catherine's invitation, she thought to herself. He didn't realise it had been made out of malice to put her in her place, and to give Catherine and the other two a giggle at her expense. Which made her wonder about his judgement where the other guests were concerned. She squirmed as a hand came under the clothes to seek out, and find, her softest part. 'Switch the light off,' she whispered.

What they did next made her forget all about the party and watching eyes. For the time being, that was.

The hunter went over the dry stane dyke to land with a pile-driving crunch that sent an instant wave of nausea shooting through Norma. As the hunter galloped on, cold sweat broke on her forehead, and wave after wave of even more intense nausea followed the original.

Norma gritted her teeth, and clung on tightly. The sensible thing to do of course was rein in till she was feeling better again, but she was damned if she was going to do that.

Henrietta Lockhart came alongside on a grey. 'Smashing ride eh?' Norma grinned. Her reply was a curt nod, and then Henrietta's mount spurted ahead.

There were five of them. Herself, Catherine, Henrietta, Elsie and a female called Vivienne Gregory who seemed, on their short acquaintance anyway, to be a far nicer person than Catherine and co.

A hedge loomed ahead, this one taller than the dry stane dyke. A taste of bile came into her mouth as the hunter left the ground, a taste that became reality when the animal landed on the other side.

Norma groaned, and forced herself to swallow the foulness. What was the matter with her? She'd jumped on horses many times before and it had never previously had this effect. Then the world started to spin.

She wouldn't come off, *she wouldn't!* She refused to give the harpies that satisfaction. It would have made their day to see her go sprawling, and no doubt their month should she be unfortunate enough to break a bone or two. Grimly she hung on, and prayed that the ride would soon be over and they'd be back at the stables.

It began to rain, which was a godsend. The rain splashed against her face, helping to steady her and even banish the nausea somewhat.

The onset of flu? Norma wondered. For the moment she couldn't think of any other reason for her feeling as she did. But how extraordinary for it to hit her the way it had. Right out of the blue in the middle of a ride.

They were trotting back into the stables when the full force of the nausea returned with a vengeance. And once more the world started to spin.

Gratefully, and with her stomach heaving, Norma slid from the saddle. She patted the neck of the hunter before it was led away by a stablelad.

'You're not a bad rider,' Catherine admitted reluctantly to Norma.

Norma desperately wanted away from there as quickly as possible. 'I thoroughly enjoyed myself,' she lied. 'I hope you'll ask me again sometime.'

'We usually have a noggin of sherry before calling it a day,' Catherine said.

'It wouldn't be the first time we've all ended up legless after a ride out,' Vivienne Gregory smiled.

'Not today thanks.' Norma glanced at her wristwatch. 'I have an important appointment in town which I really must fly to keep.'

Henrietta and Elsie brightened on hearing that, something Norma, despite her condition, didn't fail to notice. She'd disliked those two before, but she disliked them even more now.

Norma took her leave of them all. How she managed to keep up the bright and cheerful presence she didn't know. 'Must dash, and thanks again!' she said, and sprinted for the MG parked close by.

She got in the car, slammed the door, and fumbled for the key. As the engine roared into life she gagged. She had to get out of here, and fast! Her rear wheels spun, and then the MG was tearing towards the main road leading back to Glasgow.

As soon as she was out of sight of the stables she wheeled the MG onto the grass verge, and shot from the car. Opening her mouth she let it all come out, a fountain of hideous vomit that spattered in all directions when it landed. Again and again, till finally her stomach was empty. But it wasn't finished yet, she had to endure several convulsive dry retches before at long last it was over, and the world stopped spinning. Using a clean handkerchief she wiped the sheen of perspiration from her face and throat.

'Christ!' she croaked, what a nightmare. At least she hadn't been ill in front of the others. She would have hated that. Nor had she come off the hunter, the humiliation of which would have been absolutely awful.

The beginnings of flu she told herself as she climbed back into the MG. Then she had another thought, perhaps she'd eaten something that had disagreed with her? It could be either.

Halfway home she felt top notch again, quite her usual self. Which made her think it must have been something 'off' she had eaten rather than flu.

And then she had a sudden idea. Why not? For old times' sake? When she came to the turn-off for Burnside she passed on, continuing towards the town itself.

She parked across the road from Barrowland and stared at it. The outside was in a fairly rundown state, but that was only to be expected. With materials and labour in such short supply during the war there were very few buildings that hadn't suffered as a result.

It was a long shot that she'd find Joe Dunlop there, for although middle-aged he was bound to have been conscripted at some point in the war, but it was just possible that he might now be back at his old job again. He wasn't. There was a manageress in charge of the dancehall who knew nothing of Joe's present situation, all she could do was confirm that Joe had indeed gone into the Forces, though which branch she couldn't say.

338

Before leaving Barrowland, with the manageress's permission, Norma went onto the dancefloor and gazed about.

How long ago it all seemed. With a jolt she realised it was nine years since Midge had walked out on her. Nine years! A lifetime. An eternity. Nine years during which there had been a world war, and she'd got married.

She recalled burning the wedding dress the night Don Caprice had come to break the news to her in Greenvale Street that Midge and Zelda had run off together. And burning the red shoes she'd been wearing the first ever time she and Midge had danced together.

There were tears in her eyes, which she wiped away with the side of a hand. Old times, good times, never-to-be-forgotten times. Who would ever have thought she'd end up in Burnside married to a junior orthopaedic specialist who was half French and an ex-spy? Life was strange right enough. Who could foresee the quarter of it? Certainly not her.

On leaving Barrowland she pointed the MG in the direction of the Gorbals, probably Glasgow's best-known, and certainly its most notorious, district. It was also where Silver's was located. As she'd gone to Barrowland with the vague hope of finding Joe Dunlop there, so too would she go to Silver's in the hope of finding Finlay Rankine.

On entering the studios she was confronted by a smiling woman at a reception desk. 'Can I help you?' the woman asked.

Norma was about to open her mouth to reply when a well-kent male voice exclaimed. 'I don't believe it! Is it really you Norma?'

She whirled to discover Finlay staring at her, out of one eye. The other had a black patch across it, the patch part of, and held in place by, a black band that circled his head. With a squeal she ran to him, and he wrapped her in his arms. 'Oh Finlay, it's so good to see you again!' she husked.

'You look tremendous Norma. Obviously being a FANY agreed with you.'

'It did. But you... the...?'

'Eye?' he finished for her.

She nodded.

'Flak over Germany. But listen, I'm expecting a client at any moment for a half hour's lesson. Can you wait, or come back?'

'I'll wait.'

'Do you remember the "greasy spoon" round the corner? I'll meet you there as soon as I can.'

She minded the café he was referring to well. She'd gone there often when working at Silver's after leaving Barrowland. 'I'll be there,' she replied.

A fat woman bustled into the studios, Finlay's client. 'Half an hour,' he whispered releasing Norma. Then, with a beaming smile. 'Why hello Mrs Clark, prompt as usual.'

Thirty-two minutes later by Norma's watch Finlay came striding into the café. He ordered a tea for himself, and another for Norma, then joined her at a wooden table. He took her right hand in his, and squeezed it.

'You look like a buccaneer with that patch on,' she said.

He treated her to one of his crocodile smiles. 'Does that mean at long last you fancy me?'

She held up her left hand and waggled her wedding ring at him. 'Too late for that Finlay. I'm a married woman.'

He exclaimed in delight. 'That's smashing. Who is the lucky blighter?'

She didn't tell him anything about SOE, completely missing out that part of the story, but explained about being blown up in Risinghill Street, and then meeting up again with the doctor who'd treated her at the Royal Free Hospital in Algiers where they'd fallen in love and wed.

'And you're happy?'

She nodded. 'Yes.'

'Then I'm happy for *you*.'

'When did you get back to Glasgow?' she queried.

'Early February. I'd managed to keep my flat on all the while, so there was no problem there. I reported in to Silver's who said I could start right away, which I did. It seems the ladies had been missing me.' He and Norma both laughed at the latter.

'And what's this about flak over Germany?'

'Shortly after you went down south to join the FANY I decided, what the hell! it was only a matter of time anyway, so why not volunteer rather than wait to be conscripted. So I went into the RAF where they, in their wisdom, made me a navigator. I flew Wellingtons for a while, then Lancasters. I lost the eye over Hamburg when the Lanc I was in took a direct flak hit. We were very lucky to get the Lanc home again, but we did. And that was the end of my flying war. It was hospital for a few months, a spot of leave, and then a desk.' He took a deep breath. 'And that's it.'

'You're still not married I take it?'

'No, there have been lots of ladies since I last saw you of course...' 'Of course,' she interjected, which made him smile before continuing. 'But nothing that was even remotely serious.'

He's changed, she thought. He wasn't the same Finlay Rankine she remembered. There was a sadness in him there hadn't been before. And... she groped for it. Yes, despite the old bravado, a sense of humility that was new. But then the war had changed an awful lot of people. Herself too no doubt.

They chatted at length about the pre-war days. The first time she'd come to Silver's inquiring about lessons, his proposition-ing her – they had a good giggle over that – all the way through to when she'd worked at Silver's before going south to join the FANY. It was a great chin-wag which they both thoroughly enjoyed.

Finally Finlay reluctantly said. 'I hate to break this reunion up but I have to get back for another booking.'

'We must keep in touch. See each other regularly?' she suggested.

'There's nothing I'd like better.'

She took a small notepad from her handbag and wrote out her address and telephone number, which she handed to Finlay. He wrote down his details for her.

'And I'd like you to meet my husband.'

He stared into those marvellous grey-green eyes, wondering about Midge. She hadn't mentioned Midge during their chat, so neither had he. 'Does your husband dance?'

'When it comes to that his middle name's Stiffie the goal-keeper.'

Finlay laughed. 'And do you still?'

'If you mean properly, how can I with a husband like that?'

'First chance we get, a turn round the floor eh?'

'First chance we get,' she promised.

Outside the café she kissed him lightly, and affectionately, on the cheek. 'Goodbye for now buccaneer.'

'Goodbye for now Norma.'

It pleased her that she'd made contact with Finlay Rankine again. It pleased her enormously. He was a true friend.

'Douglas?'

He mumbled something indistinct in reply, and pulled his share of the bedclothes up higher.

'Douglas, I'm going to be sick.' She'd woken a moment or two before to find herself in the same state she'd been in the previous Wednesday when she'd gone riding at Eaglesham. It was now the very early hours of the following Monday. 'Douglas please ...' She clamped a hand over her mouth.

'What is it?' he asked groggily, having finally come awake.

'Sick ... I'm going to be sick,' she said, her words muffled from behind her hand.

He snapped on the bedside light, to blink at her. On registering the sheen of perspiration covering her face and neck he came wide awake. 'Can you make it to the toilet if I help you?' he queried.

She wasn't sure, but nodded anyway. He swiftly got out of bed, came round to her side, and assisted her to her feet. There was no time for the niceties of slippers and dressing-gowns – he just hurried her from the room, supporting her all the way to the toilet. There she sank to her knees before the WC, and spewed into it.

When she was finished he wiped her face and neck with a towel, gave her a glass of water to rinse out her mouth with, flushed the WC and took her back to bed. She explained how this was the second time it had happened to her.

He took her temperature and pulse, and made some checks. Well it certainly wasn't flu, nor was it food poisoning. He was positive about the former, fairly certain about the latter. 'Pull up your nightie,' he instructed her.

'How far?'

'To your breasts.'

'But it's cold in here,' she protested.

He rubbed his hands to warm them. 'I'll be as quick as I can.'

'Yes *doctor*,' she replied, taking the mickey.

He felt her tummy. 'Aren't you putting on weight?'

'Just a little,' she conceded. 'Well, I'm not working anymore,

342

that's bound to make a difference. And your parents do keep an excellent table.'

His hands moved upwards. 'Is that tender?'

'Yes,' she answered, surprised. Wondering why she hadn't noted that herself.

'When was your last period?'

'You should know. You're my husband after all,' she teased.

He smiled at her. 'I suppose like most men I only notice when it happens. I don't put a date on it, or even know what time of the month it comes.'

'I'm due one shortly. Next few days or so.'

'You had a last period then?'

'Yes,' she said, again surprised. And then the penny dropped. 'Do you think I'm pregnant?'

'Was your last period normal?'

'No it wasn't,' she replied slowly, thinking back. 'It was a lot lighter than usual. A great deal lighter actually, only traces.'

'And the period before that?'

She frowned. 'You know that too was a bit odd. Not as light as the last one, but definitely on the light side.'

He tugged her nightgown back into place, then covered her with the bedclothes. 'I'd say you're in the pudding club!' he announced, and took a deep breath.

That rocked her. 'You're not a hundred percent sure though?'

'All the signs point that way. If you'd like we can go into the Vicky tomorrow and have some tests done?'

'I . . . Yes, let's have the tests done. Oh Douglas, if it's true are you pleased?'

'Pleased! If it's true I'll be walking on air. And how do you feel about it?'

'A baby, a ba-ba,' she whispered, her face lighting up in a huge grin. 'That would be marvellous. Absolutely marvellous.'

'Absolutely,' he agreed.

Flu and food poisoning! she thought. How dense could she be. The real reason should have been obvious to her.

He got back into bed. 'We'll drive to the Vicky first thing after breakfast.'

'Right.' Then, almost coyly. 'What would you prefer, a boy or a girl?'

'I honestly don't care. Just as long as it's healthy.'

'That's how I feel too. Oh Douglas, I'm so excited.'

'That's fine. But let's just not count our chickens until it's confirmed eh?'

Norma sniggered. 'It's not a chicken I'll be expecting to produce.'

'Idiot.'

It took them ages to get to sleep again, but when they finally did so they did holding hands. And with both of them smiling.

'A baby!' Solange cried, clapping her hands together in glee. She and Forsyth were in the small sitting-room at Douglas and Norma's request. Douglas had just broken the news – tests conducted at the Victoria Infirmary during the day had confirmed that Norma was indeed pregnant.

Forsyth was pleased as Punch, this was tremendous news. 'We must have champagne, nothing less, to celebrate,' he said, and crossed to the bell pull to summon Travers.

Solange took Douglas in her arms, and hugged him. She said something in French to him which he replied to in the same language.

Still embracing Douglas, Solange looked over at Norma. 'Congratulations *chérie*.'

'Thank you.' There wasn't going to be a hug for her, Norma thought. And she was right. She did get a peck on the cheek from Forsyth however, who'd gone quite puce from a combination of excitement and elation.

When Douglas told his parents about Norma being sick after riding with Catherine they both immediately showed concern. 'Nothing strenuous from here on in. Mustn't take risks,' Forsyth counselled.

'I wouldn't have gone riding if I'd *known* I was pregnant,' Norma replied.

'Of course not. Your head's screwed on the right way.'

'And she was sick early this morning. I was surprised you didn't hear us up,' Douglas said.

'I suffered a great deal of sickness with you Douglas,' Solange told him, and pulled a face. 'It was awful.' To Norma she added. 'You have my sympathy, *chérie*.'

Travers appeared, and Forsyth instructed him to go to the

cellar and pick out the best bottle of champagne. When he explained why they were celebrating, the butler was effusive in his congratulations to Douglas and Norma.

'It'll be a boy, I feel sure of it,' Solange said directly. Travers had left the room.

'You can't possibly know that!' Douglas laughed.

'I feel it here, in my water.'

Nonsense, Norma wanted to say. But restrained herself.

'Do you have a name in mind?' Solange inquired of Douglas.

'Give us a chance Mama.'

'Then we shall have to start thinking of a suitable one right away.' She really was convinced it was going to be a boy.

We! Norma thought. If Solange believed she was going to choose the baby's name she was wrong.

Solange turned to Norma. 'What a pity about your bedroom though.'

Norma frowned. 'I'm not following you?'

'You can't redecorate it now, not when you're pregnant. That would be dangerous. Don't you agree Forsyth?'

'Quite out of the question.'

'We could get decorators in,' Douglas suggested.

'But Norma has insisted she does your bedroom herself, to give it her personal touch. Such a good idea I think. So decorators are totally unacceptable to her. It just means she'll have to wait a while longer, have a little more patience, before setting to work and doing what she wants. Till after the baby is born,' Solange said silkily.

Norma was flabbergasted by this turn of events. She was, as the saying went, hoisted by her own petard. For she had, it was quite true, made a song and dance about doing the bedroom herself. Something she'd been so looking forward to, and for which, since Douglas had landed the job at Victoria, she'd begun gathering materials.

'I'm sure I'd be all right,' she said slowly.

'No no! You mustn't.' Solange paused, then added dramatically, 'What if you lost the baby *chérie*? How would you live with yourself?'

Norma felt the colour drain from her face. Such a thing would be... Well, it was just unthinkable.

'It's not for long really. Then, when the baby is here, you can

345

roll up your sleeves and get down to it,' Solange smiled.

You cow! Norma thought, looking straight into those birdlike eyes. And when the baby was born it would be something else, another excuse for postponement. And another excuse after that, and another, till in the end hopefully, from Solange's point of view, the whole matter would just fade away and be forgotten. And then it dawned on Norma that there was more to it than that. What this was really all about was a battle of wills, Solange's against hers, as to who was going to be the dominant female in the house. And further still, yet another dimension, could it be that Solange was also trying to drive a wedge between her and Douglas? 'Even if I can't redecorate I can refurnish in the meantime.'

'A mistake. A bad mistake,' Solange said emphatically.

'How so?'

'To get it absolutely right these things must be done in sequence. First the decorating, then the carpet and curtains, then the furnishings. That way you can be certain everything fits as a piece, an ensemble. Do it any other way and you risk catastrophe. In fact you are courting it.'

What Solange said made sense, that was the damnable thing! Norma raged inwardly.

'I agree,' Forsyth nodded.

Norma forced a smile, and by God it was an effort, onto her face. 'What do you think Douglas?'

'What Mama says is logical.'

He rarely ever disagreed with his mother, Norma thought. He may have done all manner of fantastically brave deeds in France and Corsica, but at home he was a mummy's boy. Well Solange might have dominated Douglas long since, but she wasn't going to dominate her. Pigs would fly first! 'I've changed my mind,' she declared softly, and watched triumph creep over Solange's face.

'Good,' Forsyth agreed.

'You're all quite right. I mustn't try and decorate myself. It would be foolhardy.'

'Utterly,' Forsyth agreed.

'Nor will I call the professionals in. As I've said emphatically all along when the room is done I want it to have that personal touch.'

'After the baby is born,' Solange repeated.

'No, *before*.'

Solange's face froze. 'I thought you just said ...'

'That I wouldn't do it myself? That's so. Nor would I think to ask Douglas when he's just about to start a new job. My father will do it in the evenings and at weekends, and I will supervise every single brushstroke he makes.'

'How clever of you love,' Douglas said to her, his expression one of admiration.

'But —'

'No buts Solange,' Norma interjected. 'That's how it's going to be.'

'Are you sure your father will agree?' Forsyth queried.

'He will. No doubt about it. Once he understands how important this is to me he'll be here like a shot. Wild horses wouldn't keep him away.'

There was a tap on the door, and Travers re-entered the room carrying the champagne and glasses. 'Would you care to pop the cork Master Douglas?' he asked.

Douglas laughed. 'Precisely what I should do. Thank you for suggesting it Travers.'

'Not at all sir.'

As Douglas was squeezing the cork with his thumbs Norma and Solange were staring at one another. Both of them were very still, both faces now completely expressionless.

The cork gave a most satisfactory bang and went shooting off across the room. She'd drive over and speak to Brian that night Norma decided. She'd have him start work on the bedroom just as soon as it was possible.

When the glasses were filled they all toasted the baby.

Norma's eyes fluttered, then opened as she came out of a deep sleep. She'd been having an afternoon nap, as she had every afternoon at Douglas's insistence. It was now May and she was six months gone. It wasn't proving to be a particularly easy pregnancy. She was suffering terribly from recurring bouts of sickness, swollen legs and chronic indigestion, and was never sure which distressed her the most. They were all bad, but in different ways.

She glanced about the bedroom, and smiled. Her da had

347

done a wonderful job on it. A better job than she would have done herself. Everything in the room was just perfect, exactly as she had envisioned it.

The walls, ceiling and woodwork were cream. There was a new fitted cornflower blue carpet and rust-coloured curtains that complemented the carpet. She'd been extremely lucky about the wardrobe, tallboy and dressing table – Brian knew someone who worked on the Docks and the furniture had come through him. It was Canadian-made, and very modern in design. Norma loved it the moment she'd seen it. And the lovely thing was she hadn't had to pay all that much over the odds for it either.

She glanced at the bedside clock. She'd be up in a minute or two and start getting ready to go to Cubie Street. As Douglas was working late – when wasn't he? – she'd agreed to have tea there and discuss the preparations for Lyn's forthcoming wedding.

Iain McElheney had proposed to Lyn in March, and told her he didn't fancy a long engagement. And so they were to be married next month, in June. Lyn had particularly chosen June because she thought being a June bride sounded ever so romantic.

Norma had a sudden idea which made her smile. The last time she'd been over to talk about the preparations Lyn had been worried about a lack of single men going to the reception. Nearly all Iain's pals worked on the railway with him, and were already married, the latter a result of being in a reserved occupation during the war – and they'd all been available when other men were away in the Armed Forces. Iain hadn't fallen till he'd met Lyn, and then, according to Lyn anyway, he'd fallen head over heels. Something Norma could well understand considering how gorgeous 'podge' was. If there was still a shortage of single chaps she'd suggest Finlay Rankine. An old smoothie like him was bound to be a huge success with the lassies going on their tod. Of which there were quite a number, Lyn's workmates from the SCWS in Morrison Street where Lyn was back working.

Norma got up, dressed, and freshened her make-up. On leaving the bedroom she ran into one of the maids and asked where Solange was. She wanted to say goodbye as she always did when going out for a while. She was informed that Solange was in the nearest bedroom to the stairs on the floor above.

Norma went upstairs wondering what her mother-in-law was up to. None of the bedrooms on the next floor were in use. She found Solange with Knight the gardener, who also doubled as handyman, Knight in the process of reassembling a baby's cot, the cot evidently having been dismantled in the past. 'What on earth's going on?' she queried.

Solange's face was glistening from exertion. 'I'm having Knight bring a lot of the stuff down from the loft where it's been stored these past years. What do you think of this crib, isn't it beautiful?'

The crib was wicker, and if not exactly beautiful certainly very pretty. At least it would be when washed down – it was covered in dust and even had a spider's web in it – and made up. 'Yes it is,' she replied diplomatically.

'I had it sent over from Paris you know.'

That tickled Norma's fancy. 'You mean it was Douglas's?'

'Everything Knight is bringing down was his. I kept it all.'

Besides the cot and crib there was a multitude of toys, baby clothes – including a christening gown – games, rattles and other noisemakers, and the *pièce de résistance*, an ancient pram.

'This room gets plenty of sun. It will make an excellent nursery,' Solange smiled.

Norma took a deep breath, Solange was at it again. The damned woman would never let up. 'For whom?' she asked coldly.

'The baby.'

'You mean my baby?'

'Yours and Douglas's, *oui*.'

Norma glanced again at the crib and partially reassembled cot. 'Are you suggesting our baby sleep here?'

'Of course.'

'But I don't want the baby to sleep in a bedroom other than ours, at least not for quite some time. To begin with I intend the baby to sleep in our bedroom where I can hear and see it.'

Solange shook her head. 'I can assure you that is entirely the wrong thing to do. Once the baby is used to sleeping in your room you will have the devil's own job breaking him of the habit.'

Norma was really irritated now. 'He, as you insist on calling the baby, might be a she. And he or she will sleep in our room for the first six to nine months of his or her life. I am quite determined about that.'

Knight continued reassembling the cot, pretending to be totally engrossed in what he was doing. His face might have been impassive, but inwardly he was laughing, enjoying every moment of this, and couldn't wait to tell Mrs Knight. It was time someone stood up to Her High and Mightiness as he and Mrs Knight called Solange. Good for the young one.

'You'll spoil the child,' Solange said, an edge to her voice.

'I disagree with you.'

'I'll speak to Douglas about this.'

Norma's eyes slitted factionally. Her stomach was afire with indigestion that this contretemps had brought on. 'You may be Douglas's mother, but I'm his wife.'

'He'll listen to reason.'

'He'll listen to me.'

Solange glared at Norma. 'The baby should have a nursery. We con... con...' She snapped her fingers in annoyance as for once her usually excellent English failed her.

'Converted?' Norma offered.

'We converted a bedroom to one for Douglas when he was a baby.'

'What you did then was your affair. What I do now is mine. When I consider the time to be right, between six and nine months as I have already said, I will put the baby in a bedroom of its own. But *not* one on another floor. I don't just consider that dangerous, I consider it downright cruel.'

Solange muttered something in French which of course Norma didn't understand. And probably just as well too, Norma thought.

'You don't wish a nursery then?' Solange said, reverting to English.

'A room for the baby to play in would be nice. If this is to be the nursery then that's all the baby will be doing in it. There is however the third bedroom in our passageway, the one separating yours and ours. That would be better still don't you think? And certainly I would be happy for the baby to sleep there when the time comes.'

Solange fumed silently.

Norma went on slowly, her voice now not only cold but filled with steel. 'And you're not hoisting that pram on me either. It's so old and decrepit Methuselah might have used it.'

Knight had to fight to keep his face impassive. Oh he was fair loving this. It was a proper treat.

'What about the crib and cot?'

Norma looked over at them again, considering them. 'The crib will be fine after a good scrub, the cot also providing it has a new coat of paint. Can you attend to those things Knight?'

'Yes Ma'am.'

It was on the tip of Solange's tongue to say she gave the orders in this house, but she bit back the rebuke. 'And the rest of the stuff?'

'I'm going out now and won't be back in till later. I'll go through it tomorrow and see what I can use.' She and Solange stared at one another, and you could have cut the atmosphere between them.

'Let me know what you decide about the bedroom downstairs, the one between yours and ours,' Norma said, and left the room.

She was just starting down the stairs when she heard a crash, which brought a wicked smile to her lips. Unless she was very much mistaken Solange had just thrown something in fury. She liked the idea of that, she liked it very much indeed.

She turned the MG into Cubie Street to come to a halt before her parents' close. She was struggling out of the car, her damned bump made manoeuvres like this one so difficult! when a well-dressed man appeared in the close mouth. She had a quick look at him, registering that his face was vaguely familiar, then continued with her struggle. At last puffing and peching, she made it to her feet. She slammed the car door and locked it.

The man was still in the closemouth, and staring at her. With an actual physical jolt, as if she'd been punched hard right between the breasts, she realised who he was.

'Hi!' said Midge.

He'd aged, but that was only to be expected. It was nine years after all. His face was thinner, and there were lines where none had been previously. His hair was blonder than she

351

remembered, but his eyes were the same. Gorgeous blue peepers, Lyn had once called them, with a brightness to them that could dazzle and bewitch a girl where she stood. As indeed they'd once dazzled and bewitched her. Staring back at him she noted, amongst other things, that his neck was stained with embarrassment. Should she speak to him, or ignore him? Just walk on past. 'Hi yourself,' she replied after a good dozen seconds had ticked by. The Yankee form of address wasn't totally alien to her, she'd used it before – and been addressed by it countless times – at Massingham where, particularly towards the end of the war, there had been many Americans.

'I expected, hoped, I'd run into you. But hardly thought it would happen so soon.'

'Why, when did you arrive back?'

He attempted a smile that came out all sort of twisted and lopsided. 'I got into the house just two hours ago, would you believe.'

She didn't reply to that, just continued staring at him. As she did the stain on his neck began creeping upwards into his face. Her own face was devoid of expression, but at the same time hard.

'I'm away for a walk about. A stroll down memory lane you could say.'

'Oh aye?'

'You're looking good.'

'Am I? I don't feel it.

He coughed nervously. 'I heard from my folks that you were married, but not that you were . . .' He trailed off.

'Pregnant?' she finished for him as he seemed reluctant, or unable, to say the word.

'Congratulations. When are you due?'

'End of August.'

He nodded.

Her legs were murdering her, and her indigestion had started up again. Suddenly she felt fat and ugly and . . . just plain bloody awful. 'See you then,' she said, and made to brush by him, only to be stopped when he grasped her by the upper arm.

'We have to talk Norma.'

'I thought that's what we've just been doing?'

'You know what I mean.'

'You mean about you jilting me the day before our wedding to go hightailing off with someone else?'

The stain shot right up to the roots of his scalp. 'About everything,' he mumbled.

Some of the rage and anguish she'd felt that night in Greenvale Street when she'd burned her wedding dress and the red shoes surged again within her. What she did next she did without thinking. Her right hand flashed through the air to crack against his cheek. With an exclamation of surprise and pain Midge went reeling backwards and went crashing into the closemouth wall.

He shook his head, for he was literally seeing stars. That had been some smack, powerful enough to have come from a man. 'I can't deny I deserved that.'

She fought down her emotions, bringing them under control. 'And more.'

The stars faded into oblivion. When he looked again at Norma there were two of her. But already the double vision was readjusting, her twin images coming together. 'We should still talk.'

She was about to tell him to stick his talk up his bahookie, then abruptly changed her mind. Why not? He might think she was carrying a torch for him if she avoided a proper, arranged meeting, and that was the last thing she wanted. What she did want was him to know how happy and fulfilled she was. 'How long are you home for?'

'A fortnight.'

She needed a breathing space to prepare herself, physically as well as mentally. 'I'll meet you the day after tomorrow if that's suitable?'

'Where?'

She frowned as she thought about that. 'There's a City Bakeries tearoom this end of Sauchiehall Street. I'll see you there at four in the afternoon?'

'Four it is,' he agreed.

Leaving him still clutching his face she went further into the close, and up the stairs.

Norma was in the small living-room enjoying the whisky and water that Phyl Casden had fetched for her when Douglas came in. A glance at her wristwatch told her it was almost 10 pm.

'I'm bushed,' he said. He came over and kissed her lightly on the lips. 'May I?' he asked, indicating her drink.

'Help yourself.'

He reminded her of the first time she'd met him in the Royal Free Hospital, done in, almost out on his feet. She watched him drain her glass, then give a deep sigh of satisfaction.

'I was needing that. I'll ring for two more.'

'You're working far too hard Douglas, you really must ease off a little,' she said as he tugged the bell pull.

He ran a weary hand across his face. 'I've explained to you, I have to make my name, a reputation. I've got to get *established*.'

'Are you certain that's what it is?'

He glanced at her, his expression one of puzzlement. 'What do you mean?'

She opened her mouth to tell him, then decided not to. 'If you're not careful you'll end up as one of the patients in the Victoria rather than one of the doctors.'

He made a dismissive gesture, which annoyed her. 'Don't exaggerate.'

'I'm not.'

He crossed to the fireplace, gazed moodily into the fire burning there, and drummed his fingers on the mantelpiece. 'I met Mama on the way in. She mentioned about the pair of you having a real old ding-dong.'

She would have bet money that hadn't been an accidental meeting. Solange would have been waiting in ambush. 'It wasn't my fault.'

He gave her one of his sideways glances. 'Mama was only trying to help. I wish the pair of you would get along better.'

There was a tap on the door, and Travers came in. Norma stared grimly at Douglas as he ordered their drinks. She had no doubt that if she and he had met in Glasgow they would never have got married, Solange would have made sure of that. Solange had him wrapped round her little finger, as she had Forsyth.

'The baby is going to sleep in our room until I decide otherwise,' she stated firmly after Travers had gone again.

'I'm sorry, but I can't help thinking Mama's right about this.

That you're creating a rod for your own back. For both our backs.'

'Well of course I expect you to side with her,' Norma snapped.

'It's not a case of taking sides, it's a case of saying what I believe to be right.'

'You mean what your mother believes to be right.'

He picked up the poker and jabbed crossly at the fire. 'This is all I need after a day like I've had.'

She went to him, took the poker and replaced it in its stand, then put her hands on his arms. 'I've asked before, and I'll ask again. Can't we move house, get one of our own?'

His lips thinned into a stubborn line. 'Even if I wanted to, which I don't, now is hardly the time with me working all hours and you shortly about to produce.'

'After the baby's born then?' she pleaded.

'But you don't seem to understand, I like it here.'

'And you don't seem to understand I don't.'

'Why? That's what I fail to understand, why?'

She spelt it out for him. 'Your mother and I are incompatible. She wants to rule the roost and I'm just not having that.'

He gave a soft, and to Norma infuriating, laugh. 'You're exaggerating again. She's only trying to be helpful and kind.'

He was blind as far as Solange was concerned, but then she'd known that for some while now. He just couldn't imagine that his mother may be other than the angel he perceived her to be.

He went on. 'You're being over-emotional because you're pregnant, it affects many women that way. Everything will settle down after the baby arrives, you wait and see if it doesn't.'

She broke away from him when the door opened and Travers came in with their drinks. Douglas changed the subject, and refused point blank to have any further discussion about a change of house.

She reached out in the darkness to place a hand on his left shoulder. He was lying on his right, facing away from her. 'Douglas? Are you still awake?' He grunted in reply, but made no move to turn to her.

She removed the hand from his shoulder, squirmed as close to him as she was able and, using the other hand which was under the bedclothes, sent it snaking over the hill of his hip to plunge into the fly of his pyjama bottoms. Finding the mole in its hole she called it.

'Norma I'm absolutely whacked. It would take me all my time to raise a smile far less anything else.'

Slowly she withdrew her hand, and stared at his back. A back that seemed like a wall between them. This was the fifth night running they hadn't made love, which in the past would have been unheard of for him.

Was he really working all these long hours because he was trying to get established? Or was there more to it than that? Was he working as he was to keep out of *her* way? Could it be that he'd gone right off her because she'd put on so much weight she now resembled Two Ton Tessie? When she needed his love and reassurance most, he was denying her, in this particular instance literally giving her the cold shoulder.

It wasn't just lovemaking she wanted, the actual sex that is, but for him to put his arms round her, to cuddle her close and tell her he didn't mind in the least that she was the size of a barrage balloon, or that her legs were so swollen they resembled a couple of ginormous white puddings, with veins.

Tears bloomed in her eyes, to go rolling down her cheeks. She was still crying silently when he began to snore.

She was damned if she was going to be there first, so she arrived at the City Bakeries fifteen minutes late. Midge rose as she approached.

'I was beginning to think you'd given me a dissy,' he said, using the old Glasgow expression, meaning to be stood up.

She gave him an icy smile. 'When *I* make an appointment I keep it. I don't let the other person down.'

He winced, and went to help her into her chair. 'Let's order first,' he said, beckoning a waitress over. He asked for a pot of tea. She chose a cookie to go with the tea; he a scone.

When the waitress had gone Midge closed his eyes, massaged his forehead, then reached into a jacket pocket to produce a small brown bottle. He took two pills from the bottle, poured himself a glass of water from the jug on the table, and swallowed the pills with the help of the water.

'What are those for?' she queried, curious.

'Aspirins. I've had a blinder of a headache ever since I got up this morning.'

'You're looking pale,' she acknowledged, something she'd already noticed and put down to apprehension of their meeting.

He shivered. 'I think I've got a cold coming on. Not surprising really, the weather here is a bit of a shock to the system after California.'

She watched him shiver again. 'If I was you I'd take myself home to bed directly you leave here.'

'I'll see how I go, but I might well just do that.'

Silence fell between them during which he scraped a thumbnail with the nail of his other thumb. 'You said we had to talk?' she prompted.

'It's where to begin, what words to use.' He paused, then went on in a small, tight voice. 'In the letter I wrote to you at the time I said I was sorry for what had happened. I meant that, very much so.'

'You weren't sorry enough to stop you going through with it though, were you?' she replied tartly, which made him flinch.

'I did a right dirty on you Norma, I want you to know it's been heavy on my conscience ever since.'

'Good,' she said, giving him a thin smile.

'I'm not asking for forgiveness —'

'That's just as well,' she cut in, 'for you certainly wouldn't get any.'

There was another silence between them, during which he gazed at, as though mesmerised by, the tablecloth. 'God, I really hurt you didn't I?'

She just stared glacially at him.

'It was the lure of seeing the world Norma. I couldn't resist it. Not even for you. When Zelda dangled that carrot in front of me the temptation was just too great.'

She relented a little. 'I know,' she said softly. 'The wanderlust was always strong in you. One of the first things you ever told me was that your greatest desire in life was to travel and see the world.'

An inner glow came into his eyes. 'I've been to so many places I'd dreamed of and never thought I ever actually would see. LA, 'Frisco, Houston, Tampa, Baton Rouge, Kalamazoo, Kansas City, Chicago, Milwaukee, St Louis, Atlanta, New York – and

357

that's in the States alone. I've also been to Canada, Hawaii, Alaska, Mexico, Panama, Bermuda, Puerto Rico, Jamaica, Haiti, and when I leave here I'm going to Cuba to meet up with Zelda. We're vacationing there, then when we return to Hollywood we're going to make a movie with the great man himself, Astaire. The movie is to be called *The Ziegfield Follies*.'

'Astaire? That is something.' She couldn't help showing enthusiasm at the name of Astaire. He was the best after all.

'Do you remember we saw him in *Dancing Lady* at Green's Playhouse? I said that dancing alongside him would be the ultimate, and you said —'

She remembered as though it was yesterday. 'That to be as *good* as him would be the ultimate,' she interjected.

Midge barked out a laugh. 'You do remember!'

'How could I forget? We were both dancing daft, and he was a dancing god.'

'And now I'm not only going to be dancing alongside him, but Zelda and I will have second billing.'

Second billing to Astaire, she was impressed. 'The pair of you have become that big then?'

He nodded. 'In the States. Not so much overseas, but in the States yes.'

She relented even more. His dreams had come true, even if they were at her expense. 'I'm pleased for you... Mike isn't it nowadays?'

'That doesn't sound right coming from you somehow. I'd prefer if you continued to call me Midge.'

The waitress arrived with their tea and a plate on which were their cookie and scone. 'I'll pour,' Norma told the waitress. Norma filled his cup, and handed it to him. 'And how is Zelda?'

Midge dropped his gaze. 'Fine, never better.'

'Didn't she want to come here with you?'

'When I decided to go home for a visit she decided to do the same. She's gone to Corvallis, Oregon, where she was born, and where her family still live.'

Norma filled her cup. 'Have you had children?'

'No, children don't fit into our plans. It's career first and foremost with us.' He reached up and massaged his temples. 'I swear this headache is getting worse.'

'Do you want to leave?'

'Not yet,' he answered quickly. He continued massaging his forehead. 'I suppose I've said what I wanted to, about the carrot being too big a temptation. I felt it was important, for both of us if that's not too presumptuous, that I face you like this. As I should have faced you that day I ran off, but didn't have the guts to do so. I wish I'd never taken the coward's way out and sent a letter instead.'

Norma took a bite of cookie, and slowly chewed on it. She may have suffered when he absconded with Zelda, but he had also. She derived a great deal of satisfaction from the confirmation of that. 'Are you happy? With Zelda I mean?'

'We have a good marriage, I can't complain,' he replied in a neutral voice. 'But what about you? You've married a doctor, I'm told.'

It hadn't been in her mind to do so, but all this talk of Hollywood, films, Fred Astaire and exotic places made everything seem very one-sided in Midge's favour. She thought she'd redress the balance. 'I married a spy who also happened to be doctor.'

Midge gaped at her in astonishment. 'A spy! You're having me one?'

'Not in the least.' She then went on to tell him about FANY, Douglas, SOE and Massingham.

'Well I'll be jiggered!' he exclaimed softly when she eventually came to the end of her tale. He regarded her with new eyes, who would have believed his Norma would have done all that! Then he corrected himself, she wasn't *his* Norma anymore. She was this chap called Douglas's Norma.

The article was on page two of the Express which Norma read every morning over breakfast. She was raising a cup of coffee to her mouth when the name leapt out at her. *Mike Henderson*, underneath that it proclaimed, *Stricken in Sauchiehall Street*. Slowly she replaced the cup on its saucer, and read the article through.

Midge had collapsed in Sauchiehall Street and been rushed by taxi to the Western Infirmary. From there he'd been almost immediately transferred to Ruchill Hospital. A diagnosis was yet to be made, but whatever the illness, Mr Henderson's condition was serious. This was followed by a potted history of

Midge's career, including the information he was shortly to star in a picture with Fred Astaire to be called *The Ziegfield Follies*.

Ruchill Hospital, Norma thought grimly. That was a fever hospital. She recalled how pale he'd been in the tea-room where they'd talked, and the headache he'd complained of. A headache that had come on, he'd said, just that morning. Whatever was wrong with him that must have been the start of it.

She read the article through again.

It had been a lovely wedding, Lyn in white and looking so beautiful that Norma had shaken her head in wonderment to remember 'podge' as she'd once been. The reception, where they now all were, was being held in the local Cooperative Hall, and was well under way.

Norma was sitting beside Eileen, Douglas standing beside her. The band, a three-piece affair, were giving it big licks, and Brian and Effie were up on the floor doing their stuff. As the dancers swirled by, Finlay Rankine gave Norma a wink, he being up with one of the single lassies from the SCWS. The lassie was giggling, her expression coy. Finlay was clearly a hit with her. But then wasn't Finlay nearly always with the women?

Norma glanced across to where Jim Fullarton was standing with his wife, the pair of them chaffing to the Reids. Jacky Fullarton had been one of those not to come back from the war. He'd joined the Merchant Navy and gone down with his ship during the Battle of the Atlantic. Jacky had left a widow, Sylvia, and a wean.

She turned to Eileen. 'I hope you're going to get up tonight and not just sit there like a right misery puss.'

'No one's asked me,' Eileen replied. 'And yes, I probably will sit here like a misery puss as you put it. My dancing days are over.'

'Don't talk rot!'

'Would you ladies care for another drink?' Douglas asked them. He was gasping for another beer himself; it was very hot inside the hall.

'A shandy would be nice,' Norma answered. 'And you Eileen?'

'Ach, why the hell not! I'll have a dram. But with lemmy loo mind.'

Norma saw Douglas's mystifield expression. 'Lemonade,' she interpreted for him.

'Lyn's got herself a good chap. They make a fine couple,' Eileen said after Douglas had left them.

Norma glanced over at Lyn and Iain, the pair of them having momentarily paused in their dancing to chat to the best man and his girlfriend who were also on the floor. She had to agree, they were a fine couple together. She and Eileen clapped as the music ended.

'You could grow bananas in here so you could,' Eileen complained.

Norma laughed, that was true enough. She watched Finlay escort the lassie he'd been up with off the floor, have a quick word with her, then, to her obvious disappointment, leave her to walk over to the band. On reaching the band he fell into conversation with their leader.

Two children went racing by playing cops and robbers, they belonged to someone on Iain McElheney's side. A cousin of his Norma thought. She smiled to herself. If she had a boy how long till he was running about just like that? She patted her tummy – the end of August wasn't far away. She wondered if Douglas was enjoying himself? The people here were hardly his sort after all, he was far more at home with the Catherine Starks, and that ilk, of this world. Still, if he wasn't enjoying himself it wasn't apparent.

Somebody let out a great wheech which caused a group of folk to burst out laughing. The Laidlaws and Mathers from Cubie Street were among them Norma noted.

The band leader tapped his microphone for attention. 'Ladies and gentlemen, some of you will know, others not, that we have amongst us here tonight a former winner of the All Scotland Dance Championship...' Whistling and cheering broke out. Norma glared at Finlay, he'd put the bandleader up to this. 'Norma McKenzie, now Mrs Ross. Can you give her a big hand please.'

It wasn't a big hand Norma got, it was an enormous one. The McElheney contingent, not to be outdone, clapping as hard and loud as the McKenzie one.

'You'll have to stand up and acknowledge it,' Eileen whispered.

She would too, Norma thought. It was only polite. Sod that Finlay Rankine! She stood and gave an inclination of the head to first one end of the hall, then the other.

Eventually the bandleader was able to go on. 'And not only was Norma a former winner of the All Scotland Dance Championship, she was also a professional at Barrowland where I myself remember seeing her before the war. You used to give exhibitions at Barrowland Norma, will you give us one now?'

Norma pulled a face, and pointed to her tummy which got a huge laugh. Finlay Rankine came striding up. 'You're not getting out of it that easily Norma. Will you partner me for the anniversary waltz? That shouldn't do you any harm.'

She hesitated, not sure. She hadn't intended dancing for obvious reasons, but then again, the anniversary waltz was so slow she would hardly have to exert herself at all. That was the reason Finlay had chosen it of course.

He treated her to one of his crocodile smiles. 'You did promise me a turn round the floor first chance we got,' he reminded her. 'And this is the first chance there's been.'

She looked for Douglas, wanting him to give her a nod of approval, but couldn't see him. 'Go on Norma!' someone shouted. 'Aye, go on,' Eileen urged.

She made up her mind, she'd do it. Another cheer rang out when she extended a hand for Finlay to take. 'You're a conniving bugger,' she whispered.

'I am, I am,' he agreed as he led her onto the floor.

When they reached the centre of the floor they stopped and Finlay took her into his arms. The band struck up, and they were away.

As they danced, gliding and seemingly floating round the floor, a thousand memories were tumbling through Norma's mind, all of them of her and Midge. Poor Midge, he'd transpired to have infantile paralysis, which the Americans call polio, and was still in Ruchill where he was fighting for his life. Zelda had come over to be with him and was staying in a hotel.

Norma had been shocked to the core to learn what was wrong with Midge. Infantile paralysis! That was a nightmare right enough. The terrible thing was that if he did survive, and please God that he did, it was almost a certainty

362

that he'd be left with a physical disability of some sort.

What was really awful was that there were times in the past, many many times if she was truthful, when she'd wished all manner of horrible revenges on him for what he'd done to her. But now this had befallen him she wished with all her heart that it hadn't. There was no sweetness in the knowledge he could end up a cripple. No sweetness whatever. Somehow, and this was a source of wonder to her, his tragedy only added to what remained of her own hurt.

'You're as good as you ever were,' Finlay said.

Heartsore, she came out of her reverie. 'Flattery will get you everywhere.'

'Promise?' he teased, giving her a salacious leer.

She didn't reply to that. But he had succeeded in making her smile.

Douglas stood watching Norma and Finlay Rankine. What a marvellous and talented dancer she was, he thought, appreciating that fact for the first time. How she must hate to dance with him considering how he clumped round the floor. So graceful, even with that bump of hers, and the swollen legs she was forever grumbling about.

The band stopped, and Douglas led the applause. And thunderous applause it was too. Holding hands, Norma and Finlay took several bows, very small bows on her part, then he walked her back to her seat.

'You were terrific,' Eileen enthused to Norma as Norma sat down again. 'You too Mr Rankine.'

Brian and Effie came over to enthuse as Eileen had just done. As also did Douglas when he rejoined them with the drinks he'd gone to get.

'May I have the pleasure?' Finlay asked Eileen.

She blushed. 'No, I'm not getting up Mr Rankine. Thank you very much though.'

'You told me to go on, go on yourself,' Norma cajoled.

'Aye, a wee birl will do you the world of good,' Brian told his youngest daughter.

'No, but thanks all the same,' Eileen said to Finlay.

His face dropped in a comical fashion. 'I take your refusal personally Miss McKenzie.' Then, with the most disarming of smiles. 'And please call me Finlay.'

Her blush had become a full-blown reddie. 'It isn't personal I assure you.'

'How else can I interpret it?' he replied haughtily. Abruptly he changed his tone once more to become the beseeching plaintiff. 'And may I call you Eileen?'

She was totally thrown by this play acting. 'Yes, I eh...'

'I'll cry if you refuse me,' he said seriously.

'Ach away and don't be daft!'

'I will. I'm a most sensitive plant. Isn't that so Norma?'

'Oh *most*,' she replied sarcastically.

Brian and Effie were both grinning, enjoying this. They thought Finlay a right old hoot.

'So will you do me the great honour, please missus?' Finlay pleaded.

Eileen just had to laugh at that, missus indeed! She capitulated. 'Well the one dance then. I'd hate to see a grown man cry after all.'

Quick as a wink Finlay had Eileen by the arm, and was helping her to her feet. As he was doing so the bandleader announced another waltz. 'Will you lead or shall I?' Finlay asked Eileen, which got him a sharp punch in the chest from her, and a guffaw from Brian.

'Lord help us from comic singers, chantie wraslers and dance instructors,' Eileen muttered as they took the floor.

'Don't you like my patter?' Finlay asked in broad Glasgow.

'Your patter's like watter,' Eileen riposted in an accent as broad.

'Oh see you!' said Finlay.

'And see you *too*!' They were both laughing as the band struck up.

'Awfy man,' Brian commented to Effie, shaking his head.

Finlay Rankine was surprised, though now he came to think of it he should have foreseen the possibility. Eileen was Norma's sister. 'You've got it,' he said.

Eileen frowned, what was he havering on about now? 'Got what?'

'You're a natural mover, like Norma. I recognised it in her the first time I danced with her, just as I've recognised it in you.'

She wasn't sure whether he was pulling her leg or not. 'Is that more patter?'

'No, I'm serious.'

She was chuffed, pleased indeed to have been told that by a dancer of his calibre. She knew all about Finlay Rankine from Norma who'd often talked about him in the past before the war. 'Well thank you very much.'

'There's nothing to thank me for, I'm only stating what's fact. Some people are born with music inside them; others with the talent to paint, or act. Then there are those like myself, and Norma, and you with movement inside them. I think I can safely say you'd have been a first-class dancer if you'd ever seriously taken it up.'

'My husband...' she started to say, then trailed off.

'I met your husband at the All Scotland Dance Championship which Norma and Midge won, you'll recall we all went back to Joe Dunlop's to celebrate after, and Charlie and I had a bit of a blether there. We talked about the books he'd arranged from the library which had helped Norma and Midge so much earlier on. Norma told me what happened to him. I was very sorry to hear it, I thought him a nice man.'

Eileen glanced sideways at Finlay. There was no play acting about him now, his voice rang with sincerity. 'Nearly everyone liked Charlie, he was that sort of person.' She paused, then went on softly, 'What I was going to say was that Charlie always maintained I was a good dancer, but I just put it down to a little verbal syrup from a loving husband.'

'Verbal syrup or not, he was right.'

They danced on in silence, and then it was the end of the waltz. After the clapping had subsided Eileen was about to start from the floor when Finlay said, 'I know you only promised one, but how about another?'

She bit her lip, uncertain. She *had* enjoyed that mind you. In fact she'd enjoyed it a lot.

Norma took another sip of her shandy, it really was boiling inside the hall and she swore it was getting hotter. Not that the heat and discomfort were stopping people from having a rare old tear, it wasn't in the least. Nonetheless, maybe there were some windows somewhere that could be opened. She was about to mention it to Douglas when it suddenly caught her attention that Eileen had stayed up with Finlay Rankine. That pleased her, trust Finlay to take Eileen out of herself. He could charm the birds off the trees that man. Or, as someone had once crudely put it, a nun out of her knickers.

Norma was in the same 'greasy spoon' round the corner from Silver's where she'd previously rendezvoused with Finlay Rankine, and now she was back having arranged to do the same again. Masked by the table she rubbed the lower part of her tummy. The baby was moving, and she had chronic indigestion. There was only a fortnight to go till the big event, scheduled to take place at the Victoria Infirmary where Mr Wright, the senior obstetrician, would be delivering her.

Finlay came bustling in through the café door, gave her a cheery wave and asked, by means of mime, if she wanted another cup of tea. She nodded that she did.

'So what's this all about Norma? You sounded quite mysterious on the telephone,' he demanded when he joined her.

Norma put sugar in her fresh cup of tea, and slowly stirred it. This was going to be awkward, and the chances were high she was going to lose a pal. 'You're my friend Finlay, but Eileen is my sister.' She paused, then added softly. 'I'm worried.'

'Because we've been going out together?'

'Charlie's death gutted her. She suffered dreadfully because of it, and has continued to suffer. I'll do anything to stop her being hurt further.'

'Which you think I'll do?'

Norma raised an eyebrow. 'Look at your track record Finlay. You're strictly a love-them-and-leave-them chap, and that's the last thing Eileen needs.' Several seconds ticked by before she went on. 'I must admit I was surprised to say the least when she told me that not only had you asked her out, surprise number one, but that she'd accepted, surprise number two.'

'We are an odd couple, there's no denying that,' Finlay replied. 'I suppose you might call it an attraction of opposites. And perhaps that's why we get on so well together, which we really do.'

'But for how long? Eileen doesn't need a fly-by-night as I said.'

Finlay drank some tea, and thought about Eileen. 'I find your sister different to my women in the past – we actually talk to one another. We're relaxed in each other's company, I certainly

366

am in hers and she says she is in mine. And if we talk there are other occasions when we say nothing, nothing at all, and neither of us minds. Just being together is a pleasure in itself.' He shook his head. 'No one is more amazed than me that this has happened, but it has.'

'Are you telling me the pair of you are in love?' Norma asked incredulously.

'Love is a word that has many shades of meaning. Eileen desperately loved Charlie, that's undeniable. As it's also undeniable that she's still in love with his memory. But she's come to care for me, which in itself is surely a form of love?'

'And how do you feel about her?'

'As you know only too well I had my flings before the war, but they were based on lust rather than love. Maybe I'm getting old, maybe the war changed me, but now I'd much rather sit and talk to Eileen than be in bed with one of those sexpots I knew previously.' He gazed at his cup, shifting it round in its saucer. 'I swear this to you though Norma, whatever happens I'll never knowingly hurt Eileen. As you've pointed out she's had more than her fair share of that already.' He glanced up to stare Norma straight in the eyes. 'You have my solemn oath on that.'

She believed him, and it made her happy for him, and enormously happy for Eileen. It also gave her a huge sense of relief for she'd been worried sick for Eileen.

'Incongruous, but there you are,' Finlay added, giving Norma one of his crocodile smiles which had become even more crocodiley since he'd acquired an eye patch.

'Eileen tells me you take her dancing quite a bit?'

'I'm gradually teaching her steps and techniques, which she enjoys learning. Who knows? He paused, and added eagerly, 'And she's started looking after herself better, hasn't she? I put my foot down about that. Insisted she have her hair done, wear make-up and generally spruce herself up. Nor did I get any argument on the subject. She just said right Finlay, and began doing it.

There had been a noticeable difference in Eileen of late. The entire family had commented on it, and were delighted by it. It wasn't an overnight transformation, but gradually Eileen was getting back to looking like her old self. 'I hope it works out for the pair of you,' Norma said, and patted him affectionately on the hand.

They chatted a while longer, then left the café. Norma's indigestion had been bad before, but it was positively raging now. She shouldn't have drunk that second cup of tea she chided herself. That had only made matters even worse.

'I'll walk you to your car,' Finlay volunteered.

'It's over there,' she replied, pointing to where the Lagonda was parked. She and Douglas had done a swap for the duration the previous week because she'd grown so large it had become too difficult for her to get in and out of the MG.

They had just reached the Lagonda when it hit her. Gasping in agony, and clutching her stomach, she sagged against the side of the vehicle.

'What is it Norma? What's wrong?' Finlay asked in alarm.

She tried to speak, but couldn't. The pain was too intense. She gritted her teeth instead, and waited for it to pass, which it soon did. 'It would seem the baby is coming early,' she said at last.

'What!' Finlay's face was a picture.

'Must get to the Victoria Infirmary.'

'Leave everything to me, I'll . . .' He broke off when, with a moan, she doubled over.

'Shit!' he swore.

Douglas paced up and down outside the delivery theatre. A glance at his watch told him it was now forty minutes since Norma had come in as an emergency admittance, and thirty minutes since he'd been informed.

He stopped abruptly in his pacing when Norma shrieked, a shriek that brought memories of the field hospital he'd been working in when Norma arrived at Massingham. He fumbled for his cigarettes and lighter, taking in the fact as he lit up that his hands were shaking like Billy-O.

He'd just resumed pacing when Norma shrieked again, this time even more loudly.

There was the sound of a smack, hand against bottom, followed by a lusty, protesting wail. 'What is it?' she croaked.

Mr Wright's face swam into vision, and he was smiling.

'Congratulations Mrs Ross, you have a lovely baby boy.'

A boy! So Solange had been right after all. 'Is he... Is everything there, as it should be?'

'He's absolutely perfect.'

'Ah!' she sighed. That had been her secret fear, as it probably was of most expectant mothers. That something would be found to be wrong with the baby when it was born.

Shortly after that the baby, wrapped in a length of white cotton, was placed in her arms. And then a beaming Douglas was by her side, bending over to kiss her on the cheek.

'It's a boy and he's perfect,' she croaked.

'I know.'

Douglas reached down and very gently placed a hand over the baby's front. 'Hello Lindsay.'

There had been quite a to do over what they called the child when it arrived. Solange had wanted a boy to be called Forsyth, but Norma, hating the silly name, had been vehemently against that. In the end the question of names had been resolved when Norma had come up with the perfect solution. If it was a girl she would be called Lynsey after Lynsey Dereham, if a boy Lindsay, a male version of the name. When she and Douglas explained who Lynsey had been, and that Lynsey had died working for the SOE in France, and by implication also for France and therefore a French heroine, Solange, being the patriot she was, had been forced to accept this compromise.

'How do you feel?' Douglas asked Norma.

Her eyelids were leaden, and she was physically drained. She was also extremely sore. 'Very tired,' she mumbled in reply.

'You've given me a fine son and heir. Thank you,' Douglas said, and kissed her again, this time lightly on the lips.

Norma smiled at him, then turned her head to smile at the baby.

When Douglas spoke to her again he got no reply. Still smiling, she'd fallen asleep.

Chapter Thirteen

Norma glanced up from her soup plate, and over at Douglas who was sitting opposite her across the width of the dining table. He looked ghastly she thought, like a limp dishrag Effie would have said. There were coal black bags under his eyes.

It was April the following year, 1947, and Lindsay was now eight months old. And what a wee darling he was. It was rare for Norma to pick him up but her heart didn't turn over inside her.

He was in his cot now, with Phyl Casden keeping an eye on him. He still slept in their bedroom, but would shortly be moving into his own nursery, next door to theirs which she herself had redecorated from top to bottom.

Shortly after she'd returned from hospital with the baby, Solange had suggested she and Douglas employ a nanny. Initially she'd resisted the idea, not at all happy at the thought of a stranger looking after her child. And then one day, while Phyl was helping her bathe the baby, the answer had come to her. Phyl adored Lindsay and Lindsay adored Phyl. She'd put it to Phyl who'd agreed there and then. The following week Phyl had officially become Lyndsay's nanny, and a new girl had started, taking over Phyl's duties as maid.

Forsyth had been speaking down the length of the table to Solange, and now stopped to get on with his soup. Douglas finished his, leaned back in his chair, closed his eyes and gave a deep sigh.

'You look shattered,' Norma said quietly.

His eyes flickered open again. 'I feel it.'

'You really are working far too hard, Douglas. Do you realise it has been eight days since you last sat down to dinner with us. You were even absent on Saturday and Sunday night.'

'I have to get established, make a name for myself. I've explained that to you countless times,' he replied, a trace of annoyance in his voice.

'And I've told you countless times that you'll end up as one of the patients if you're not careful. You must stop driving yourself the way you are.' She appealed to Forsyth. 'What do you say? Don't you agree?'

Forsyth paused in his eating. His eyes flicked to Douglas, then to Norma. 'Douglas is making a big impression at the hospital, I can tell you that. People are coming to speak very highly of him.'

Douglas shot Norma a look that said, see!

'What he's doing is rapidly becoming detrimental to his health, and I don't need to be a doctor to diagnose that,' Norma stated bluntly.

Solange said something to Douglas in French, which he replied to in the same language. God how it irritated Norma when the other members of the family did that! She was trying to learn the language, but not getting on very well at all. It was rapidly becoming more and more obvious that learning foreign languages just wasn't her forte. Nonetheless she would persevere, she was determined about that.

'I beg your pardon?' Norma said after there had been another interchange between mother and son, making the point that she didn't understand.

'Mama says there is nothing wrong in being ambitious, that it is an excellent quality to have.' Norma had to stop herself from glaring at Solange. 'But that perhaps I have been overdoing it a bit.'

'More than a bit,' Norma said quietly, surprised that Solange had even partially agreed with her.

'What you should have is a hobby, I find mine most relaxing and recuperative,' Forsyth chipped in, having now finished his soup. He collected matchboxes and books of matches, of which he had thousands from all over the world. Seeing they were now all finished, he rang the handbell for Travers.

'I don't have time for a hobby,' Douglas muttered dismissively.

'Then perhaps you should make time,' Norma snapped.

They fell silent when Travers entered the room to remove

their plates and stack them on a trolley. Before leaving the room again to fetch the next course he refilled their wineglasses.

Douglas lit a cigarette between courses in the French manner, and looked thoughtful. As soon as Travers was gone he said, 'There is one hobby that appeals. In fact it appeals a great deal.'

'What's that?' Norma inquired.

He gave her a sideways glance. 'I'd love to build and maintain that pond I once told you about. You know, frogs, toads, newts . . .'

'Eech!' Norma burst out, which caused him to laugh. 'Horrible, slimy things!' she added.

'He always wanted a pond as a boy,' Solange said.

'And you forbade it.'

Solange shrugged her shoulders. 'I don't exactly appreciate those animals either.' Her eyes darted to Norma, then quickly away again. 'But maybe not so much now as I once did.'

Douglas seized on this. 'Does that mean you wouldn't now object to me building a pond?'

Solange lifted her wineglass, sipped its contents, and didn't reply.

'I'm against it,' Norma said levelly to Douglas.

He puffed on his cigarette, and studied her through the smoke. 'I can appreciate you don't like frogs, toads, etc, but think how educational they will be for Lindsay when he's old enough to appreciate such things.'

'A pond could be dangerous with a young child about,' she riposted.

Douglas chuckled, infuriating her. 'There will be no danger I promise you. And a pond would give me a great deal of enjoyment. A great deal.'

'I loathe slimies, they give me the creeps. I can just imagine me staying out of the garden altogether because it's crawling with them.'

'Aren't you being just a little selfish *chérie*?' Solange smiled. 'As Douglas has pointed out, a pond would be most educational for Lindsay when he's older.'

Norma stared hard at her mother-in-law. The cow was doing this just to spite and annoy her. She didn't believe for one instant that Solange had changed her mind about slimies. As for Solange accusing her of being selfish – how hypocritical of

Solange who, ignoring the educational benefits at the time, had forbidden the young Douglas to have a pond.

Solange turned her attention to Douglas. 'Where will you build this pond?'

Norma knew then that she'd been outflanked by her mother-in-law, and her lips thinned in anger. If she'd been in favour of this pond that damned woman wouldn't have entertained the idea.

Travers and the new maid came in with the next course.

The young woman's face filled with stark, and total, terror when he pointed his pistol at it. 'No please ... please ... there's been a mistake,' she pleaded, sinking to her knees, her hands outspread in a gesture of entreaty.

But there had been no mistake, his orders were clear. His finger tightened on the trigger.

'No,' she whispered, her last word on earth.

The pistol fired, and everything seemed to happen in slow motion. He imagined he saw the bullet fly from the pistol's muzzle to home in on that spot where the bridge of her nose emerged from the bottom of her forehead.

Slowly, oh so slowly, her face exploded into a million gory, bloody bits. Blood sprayed, while pieces of bone, brain, skin, hair and other tissue flew, everywhere. The most gruesome, awful sight he had ever seen. And he had made it happen.

Douglas came awake with a start to find his body had gone rigid as it always did when he had *the* nightmare. He was lathed in sweat, his mouth desert-dry, his throat constricted. He was breathing very quickly, his chest pumping out and in like some hard-worked bellows.

He turned in the darkness to look at the outline that was Norma. He hadn't woken her, she was still sleeping soundly.

He took a deep breath, then another, forcing his breathing to normalise, which it did after a few seconds.

Of all the things he'd done in the war that was the one that had affected him most. It haunted him, and he knew it was going to keep on haunting him till his own dying day.

Slowly, oh so slowly, her face exploding into ... Making a

373

small animal-like sound he jammed a fist into his mouth. It would be hours before he got back to sleep, if indeed he did at all. Hours of torment, remembering, reliving . . .

Norma plucked the teat of the now empty bottle from Lindsay's mouth and handed it to Phyl Casden. She then put Lindsay over her left shoulder and gently patted his back. She was rewarded by a long burp, followed by another. When she judged he was properly winded she gave him to Phyl who would now change him.

She gazed lovingly at her wee son as Phyl laid him out and began stripping off his nappy. It had been a great disappointment to her that she hadn't been able to feed him herself, but in the event that had proved impossible. And so a bottle it had had to be. At eight months old he was now on a combination of milk and solids.

'I thought I'd put him in his pram and take him for a walk in the King's Park,' Phyl said.

'Fine. Just make sure he's well wrapped up as there's still a nip in the air.'

'Phyl will make sure of that. We don't want you catching a chill, do we bonnie baby?' Phyl said, and chucked Lindsay under the chin, which made him smile and blow bubbles at her.

Norma kissed him on the forehead, then took her leave of the pair of them as she was off out. She'd say goodbye to Douglas before she went, and knew where to find him.

She put on her coat and scarf, then made her way to the rear garden. And there he was, just as he'd said he'd be, digging the hole that would become the pond.

It was the morning following his decision to build the pond, and the first Saturday he'd stayed at home since starting at the Victoria Infirmary. If building the pond meant she was going to see more of him at weekends then that at least was something in its favour.

He spied her at last, stopped what he was doing, and waved. She continued on over to him.

'You're off then,' he said.

She viewed the already sizeable hole with distaste. 'I'm still worried that a pond will be dangerous.'

He sighed. 'It'll be safe as houses once I've put some netting over it, which I will personally fix in place just as soon as Lindsay becomes mobile. All right?'

'Hmm,' she answered reluctantly. 'How deep is it going to be?'

'Two feet. Twelve long, eight wide and two deep. Any other questions?'

His tone was sarcastic. And not only sarcastic, but patronising also. 'No.'

'Then I'll see you later. Give my regards to your family.'

'I will.' She was off to Cubie Street to have lunch. He was impatient to return to his digging, nor was he doing anything to disguise his impatience. 'Cheerio for now then,' she said, and gave him a quick kiss on the lips.

She hadn't even completed turning away from him when his spade thunked back into the earth.

'And where is it tonight?' Norma asked Eileen, whose relationship with Finlay Rankine was continuing from strength to strength. And what a change for the better that relationship had wrought in her sister Norma thought. For quite some time now Eileen had been back to her old self, as she'd been before Charlie's death.

'We're going jigging, though I don't know where.'

Lyn wasn't present, having moved into her own house when she married Iain McElheney. The two of them now lived in a single end in Parkhead. Nor was Brian there. He'd gone in to do some work, and was going straight from there to a football match.

'Speaking of jigging,' Effie said as she laid a plate of margarined slices of cut pan loaf on the table, 'Midge Henderson is home. An ambulance brought him back from Ruchill Hospital earlier on in the week.'

Norma thought of the last time she'd seen Midge Henderson, that day in the City Bakeries when he'd told her he was going to make a film with Fred Astaire. Well he'd be making no more films, or not as a dancer anyway. He'd survived the infantile paralysis, but what an horrendous price he'd had to pay for that survival. He was now paralysed from the waist down. 'Have you spoken to him?' she asked her mother.

'No, but I have to Alice. She says he's very depressed. But that's only to be expected, I suppose.'

'Who would have thought it, Midge Henderson ending up in a wheelchair,' Eileen said, shaking her head in disbelief.

'Aye,' Norma mused, who would have thought it. What agony and sheer torture his new state must be for him. Midge, who used to dance like a dream, now unable to walk, not even put one foot in front of the other. And that's how he was going to be for the rest of his life.

When the meal was over Norma said, 'I think I'll away down and say hello to Midge. I feel I should.'

'You owe that man nothing after what he did to you. Not even the time of day,' Effie said bitterly, beginning to gather up the dirty dishes. She'd never forgiven Midge for what he'd done to Norma.

'I wouldn't wish what's happened to him on my worst enemy,' Norma stated quietly.

Effie shot her daughter a dark look. 'I know I shouldn't say this, that it's not right. But maybe he's only, at long last, got what was coming to him.'

'Ma!'

'I know, lass, but that's how I feel.'

Norma left the house as Effie and Eileen were starting on the washing up, to chap on the Hendersons' door. It was Leslie, Midge's Da, who answered.

'Well hello!' he exclaimed, pleased to see her. For he'd aye been fond of Norma. Midge might be his only son, and a son he dearly loved, but he too had never forgiven Midge for what he'd done to Norma. He'd understood *why* Midge had acted as he had, but had never forgiven Midge for the manner in which it had been done. As far as he was concerned, and he'd told Midge by letter, Midge had brought shame on the entire Henderson household.

'Ma mentioned Midge was back. I thought I'd pay him a visit.'

'Come away in Norma, you'll find him in his old bedroom.' Leslie closed the front door behind the pair of them, then called out. 'Midge, there's someone here to see you!'

She didn't have to be shown where his old bedroom was, she knew. She found him sitting by the window in his wheelchair with a tartan travelling rug draped over his now useless legs. He didn't appear at all pleased that she'd come.

Her heart went out to him. How pale and frail he looked, a shadow of his former self. He'd lost a great deal of weight, and his shoulders were bowed in a combination of resignation and defeat. A lump that felt the size of an egg came into Norma's throat. How the once mighty were fallen indeed. 'Hello,' she said, not smiling in case he misinterpreted that.

He scowled at her. 'Come to gloat have you?'

'Don't talk stupid,' she snapped back.

He seemed to relax a little on hearing that. 'I saw you arrive from the window. That's my chief occupation nowadays, staring out the window like some nosey wifey with nothing better to do.'

He was bitter all right, that stood out a mile. 'I am sorry for what's happened to you Midge. And I mean that.'

His mouth twisted cynically. 'Are you?'

'Yes, I am.'

Their eyes locked, and he read in hers that she was telling the truth. He also read pity there, which made him writhe inside. 'Did you hear that Zelda left me? Once she knew it was definite my dancing days were over she hopped it back to the States.'

'Yes, I had heard that.'

'What you won't have heard is that she's divorced me. One of those Mexican jobs. I got notification of it the day before I left Ruchill.

Had he expected any different? Norma wondered. Zelda had shown her colours all those years ago when she'd dumped the dying Don to run off with him. 'Has she found another partner?'

He barked out a laugh that was more self-mocking than anything else, and answered her wondering if he'd expected anything different. 'Oh I would imagine so. And if she hasn't already, I'm sure she soon will have.'

Norma was tempted to say what she thought of Zelda, how she both despised and detested the woman. But decided, thinking that might turn the knife in Midge, not to. 'So what are your plans now? Will you return to America?'

He glanced away from her, and on out the window. She couldn't be certain, but she imagined she could see a glint of tears in his eyes. 'No, I won't return to America,' he replied in a voice so soft it was almost a whisper.

'You'll stay here then, in Cubie Street?'

'That's it. I've no alternative, other than go into a home that is. And I certainly don't want to do that.'

'No,' she agreed.

He ran a hand through hair that was lank and lifeless, then brought his attention back onto her. 'And what about you? How are things with you?'

'Can't complain. I'm pregnant again.'

'So soon!' he exclaimed.

Norma was surprised too, but not because of the relative shortness of time involved. Douglas so rarely approached her nowadays it had frankly amazed her that she'd been able to get pregnant. Weeks could pass, sometimes a month or more, without him showing any interest in that direction. Nor was there any point in her making the advances – when she tried that all she got was how tired he was after a long and arduous day at the hospital. And yet, one of the very few occasions they had made love since Lindsay's birth had resulted in her becoming pregnant again. 'Douglas says I must be just naturally fecund.'

Midge frowned, he didn't know the word. 'Fecund?'

'Easily put in the club,' she laughed, thinking to herself Midge wouldn't, couldn't, appreciate the irony of that statement. Just how true it actually was.

Midge was about to laugh with Norma when he chillingly recalled that he would never make a female pregnant now, nor ever again have one. The ability to do that, like his legs, was forever lost to him. 'I'm happy for you,' he said in a strangled voice. 'Very happy, Norma.'

With a flash of insight she realised what his tone, and his anguished expression, really meant. He glanced away from her, and on out the window again, and this time there was no doubt whatever, there was a glint of tears in his eyes.

'I'd better be going,' she mumbled.

'Aye. Well it was thoughtful of you to drop by,' he replied, continuing to look on out the window.

'Goodbye for now then Midge.'

'Goodbye for now Norma.'

Alice was waiting for her in the hall to show her out. The two of them spoke briefly at the front door, then Norma left Alice to away upstairs again. Before going in she stopped and had a weep, knowing that in his bedroom Midge was doing the same.

When she left the closemouth half an hour later she glanced up at Midge's bedroom window before getting into the MG, and there he was, a pale face partially hidden by net curtain, staring down at her.

She swithered whether to wave, and decided not to. Climbing into the MG she drove off.

Midge watched the MG till it turned into Gallowgate, and was lost to view. Then he went back to just watching the street.

Sir John and Lady Stark, Catherine's parents, were throwing a Summer Ball in the St Enoch Hotel, and naturally enough the Rosses had all been invited. It was a glittering affair with the *crème de la crème* of lowland Scottish society there. All the titled, nobs, and high heid bummers was how Norma thought of it to herself.

Catherine had an escort for the evening, a young chap – far younger than Catherine – who'd come over to Norma as a right pain in the backside. With his poppy eyes, thinning hair, and receding chin, Archibald Paterson certainly wasn't a looker.

Catherine's two cronies were also in attendance, Henrietta Lockhart with an Irish fellow – now he was a dish – and Elsie Buchan on her lonesome. Vivienne Gregory too was there, though Norma hadn't spoken to her yet. Vivienne had been part of the party that had gone riding out at Eaglesham the day Norma had been invited, and the one member of the party that Norma had quite liked. A little earlier Norma had been told by Douglas that Vivienne was married to the tall, bearded man she was with.

'And how are you getting along with this pregnancy? Solange tells me you had a great deal of trouble with the last one,' Catherine inquired of Norma, her voice loud and sharp, and with no sympathy whatever in it.

'This one isn't nearly so bad,' Norma replied.

'No indigestion? Solange said you had an awful time with that.'

'Some, but nothing like so severe as it was with Lindsay.'

'And what about . . .' Catherine's gaze slowly dropped to the lower part of Norma's gown, then just as slowly was raised again till she was once more staring straight into Norma's eyes. 'What about your legs? They got all horribly swollen before I believe.'

Oh she was a bitch Norma thought, smiling. If she ever got pregnant Norma hoped she went through all the agonies of hell with it. 'A little puffiness round the ankles, that's all on this occasion.'

'Oh good!' Catherine exclaimed mildly, matching Norma's smile.

'I think we're having a girl as Norma's symptoms are so different from when she was expecting Lindsay,' Douglas said.

Archibald Paterson stopped a passing waiter and they all exchanged their empty champagne glasses for full ones. 'Jolly tiptop ball, thoroughly enjoying,' Archibald said to Catherine.

'I think we're all enjoying ourselves,' Douglas said, making smalltalk.

'I don't suppose you know many people here,' Elsie Buchan smiled at Norma, her tone silky on the outside.

Norma sipped her champagne. 'No. Not many.'

Solange and Forsyth joined them. 'We were just commenting that poor Norma doesn't know many people here,' Catherine said to Solange, the faintest tinge of malice in her voice. 'I simply must take her round and introduce her.'

Solange, registering the tinge of malice, caught on right away. Her gaze flicked to Norma, then back again to Catherine. 'What an excellent idea,' she enthused.

Oh God! Norma thought. Here it was again, another device to try and show her up. She glanced at Douglas, was he blind as well as deaf? Didn't he realise the claws were out and doing their best to rake? Oblivious, that's what he was, quite oblivious to what was really going on. Not for the first time since returning to Glasgow she wondered what had happened to the sensitivity she'd once credited him with having.

She could just imagine what Catherine's introductions would be like. The sneer in the voice, the smirk. The combined condescending and patronising tone. Nothing would be said outright of course, but it would be all there nonetheless. She'd be made to feel like Cinderella of the fairystory, somebody masquerading as what she was not. 'Douglas can introduce me to who he thinks I should meet.'

'And I shall help. I insist!' Catherine said emphatically.

'Yes, you must,' Henrietta Lockhart told Catherine, her eyes flashing with amusement.

Norma looked at Forsyth for help, but he didn't appreciate what was going on either.

'Catherine?'

They all turned to Sir John Stark who'd approached them unseen. With him was a man Norma, with a sudden jolt, her mind flying back over the years, recognised right away. He was a lot older looking of course, but unmistakable nevertheless. 'Catherine, I'd like you to meet a longstanding, and very dear, friend of mine whom I don't see nearly enough of nowadays. Catherine, this is the Earl of Arran and Clydesdale.'

The Earl took Catherine's proffered hand and kissed the back of it. 'Delighted,' he murmured.

'Father has often talked of you. I'm just surprised we haven't met before now.'

'The Earl has become something of a recluse, haven't you Biffie?'

The Earl nodded. 'I used to be far more gregarious...' He shrugged his shoulders. 'There we are.'

'Now let me introduce you to everyone here,' Catherine said, and proceeded to do just that. When she came to Norma, whom she'd purposely left to last, the Earl frowned.

'Mrs Ross? Mrs Ross?' he muttered, and shook his head. Norma's face struck a terribly familiar chord in his memory, but he was unable to place her. Should she remind him, should she not? Norma wondered. And then he had it. 'Norma McKenzie! Of course!' he exclaimed. 'By all that's wonderful!'

Norma was on tenterhooks. Was this going to be embarrassing or what?

'You *know* Norma?' Catherine frowned.

'Of course I know her. How could I forget her! Many's the time I dangled her on my knee when she was a child.'

Which was true enough, Norma thought. She could recall him doing so.

'Good gracious!' said Forsyth, that was the last thing he'd expected the Earl to say.

'And how are your dear parents and sisters?' the Earl demanded eagerly of Norma.

'Fine Earl.'

'Dearie me, what memories you bring back Norma. What marvellous memories. I lost touch with your father you know. One thing and another, the war.'

'Yes,' she nodded.

'And this is your husband.'

'I have that pleasure,' Douglas answered, totally mystified, as were the others, as to how Norma knew the Earl of Arran and Clydesdale, and the Earl her.

'You must let me steal Norma from you for a short while. I have so much I'd love to talk over with her.'

'Please do.'

The Earl turned to Sir John whom Norma had met on arrival at the Ball, the host and hostess having personally welcomed every guest as they entered the Grand Hall where the ball was taking place. 'Will you excuse us?'

'Of course Biffie.'

The Earl extended an arm to Norma. 'Shall we find a seat my dear? Or we could dance if you prefer?'

Norma gestured to her bump which, in the past few weeks, had started to become quite noticeable. 'I'd prefer to sit.'

'Then sit we shall!' the Earl said. And, with Norma's arm crooked in his, he led her away.

Catherine, Solange, Henrietta and Elsie Buchan stared after Norma in astonishment. Then Catherine swung on Douglas to ask how Norma knew the Earl.

'I really have no idea,' he replied. It wasn't till a little later that he recalled Norma mentioning the Earl's name to him shortly after he'd revealed to her that he was Gabriel. Then the jigsaw fell into place, Norma's father had been employed by the Earl when the Earl had owned a house in Kirn. And it was the Earl who'd originally found Brian a job with the Glasgow Parks Department.

As Norma walked away with the Earl she was filled with a huge sense of relief. Thank God the Earl had appeared to save her from a potentially extremely embarrassing situation. And what a smack in the eye for Catherine and co. The incident quite made her night.

It was about an hour later that Norma went to the toilet where she ran into Vivienne Gregory. 'Oh hello. I was hoping to have a word with you,' Vivienne said.

Norma couldn't think about what. 'Oh?'

'I only learned recently that you were in the FANY during the war. Is that correct?'

'Yes.'

'Then perhaps you'd care to meet two of my chums who are coming to tea on Tuesday afternoon. They were also in FANY.'

'Really!' exclaimed Norma, immediately interested. 'What are their names?'

'Heather Innes and Madeleine Pallin. They both ran canteens, Heather for the Polish Forces that were stationed in Scotland.'

'Did they join through the Scottish Headquarters?' Norma queried. A Scottish HQ having been established some while after she had joined FANY.

'In Perth, yes.'

'As they were purely on the Scottish side I wouldn't know them, but I'd be delighted to meet them. We probably know some folk in common, FANY wasn't that vast an organisation after all.'

'So you'll come Tuesday?'

'I'd like to very much.'

Vivienne opened a tiny clutchbag to produce a card which she handed to Norma. 'Shall we say three?'

'Eh . . .' Norma hesitated. She could be on dicey ground here, but did want to find out just what was what. 'How well do you know Catherine Stark and her friends?'

'I know them, but we're not exactly close. My husband Jim is a business associate of Sir John's, and I keep my horse at the stables in Eaglesham. We have a town house ourselves, so it's convenient for me to keep my horse there. Why do you ask?'

'Just curiosity,' Norma lied.

But Vivienne was no fool. Catherine had been sweet on Douglas Ross for years, everyone knew that. And Douglas had married this girl Norma whom Catherine had hinted to her that day in Eaglesham wasn't exactly out of the top drawer. Further-more, Catherine could be a proper bitch when she wanted to be. Vivienne put two and two together. She took Norma by the hand, and squeezed it warmly. 'Till Tuesday then. I'll look forward to it.'

There was that in Vivienne's eyes and expression which told Norma she'd be most welcome in Vivienne's home, and that this was no trap to have another dig at her and her background. 'And so shall I,' she answered with enthusiasm.

Vivienne's invitation made Norma feel chuffed in the ex-treme. She felt she was on the verge of making a friend amongst this new circle she now moved in.

It was a glorious July day with the sun cracking a clear blue sky that was devoid of even a wisp of cloud. Norma hummed happily to herself as she drove in the direction of Blairbeth Road. She'd just had a smashing afternoon with Vivienne Gregory, the pair of them having gone to an art exhibition and then taking coffee afterwards. She'd thought the night of the Summer Ball when Vivienne had invited her to tea that Vivienne might turn into a friend, and so it was proving to be. She and Vivienne got on like the proverbial house on fire.

Norma was still humming as she drove in through the wrought-iron gates and parked behind Douglas's Lagonda. He was at home, as he was to be at home all that week, though not on holiday. He was writing a paper, which he was very excited about, and which he'd told her was something of an honour to have been asked to do.

It was a struggle getting out of the MG and she made a mental note to tell Douglas they were going to have to swop cars again soon as they'd done before Lindsay arrived.

Once inside she went straight to the study expecting to find Douglas there beavering away, but the study was empty. Wondering where he was she went upstairs to Lindsay's nur-sery, only to discover that too was empty.

She met Nettie Simpson, one of the maids, in the passageway. 'Do you know where Miss Casden and Lindsay are?' she asked.

'While you were out Miss Casden took a sudden raging toothache, and your husband packed her off to see a dentist. He said he would look after Master Lindsay until she got back.'

Well that explained that, Norma thought. Phyl had mentioned having several tooth twinges of late, though had done nothing about it. 'And where is my husband and Master Lindsay?'

'I believe they're in the garden Ma'am.'

'And my mother-in-law?'

'She's having a nap Ma'am.'

Good, Norma thought, she'd have Douglas and Lindsay to herself. Forsyth was at the hospital of course.

Norma resumed humming as she tripped down the staircase. It really was a beautiful day, so beautiful and sunny in fact it had even contrived to do the impossible, namely make the inside of Castle Dracula appear almost a pleasant place to be.

There was a letter for Norma on the silver tray in the reception area which she had missed on the way in. She exclaimed with delight to recognise Helen Rolfe's handwriting. She popped the letter into one of her two pockets, she would read it later when she could take her time over it.

She was thinking about Helen as she went out into the garden, stopping to smile when Douglas and the pram came into view. He was slumped in a deckchair with a straw hat pulled over his eyes. There was an open folder on his lap which he'd either been reading or writing in before dozing off. The pram was beside him, at the edge of the pond.

He'd made an excellent job of his pond, she had to give him that. There were various lilies in it and all manner of weeds, the latter which, he'd explained to her, oxygenated the water. As of yet there were no slimies as he'd completed the pond well past spawning time, but there would be the following year when Douglas would stock it with spawn from some marshy land he knew over at Muirend. The pond wasn't empty though, he had put half a dozen goldfish in.

Norma took a deep breath, and closed her eyes. What a fabulous day it was! She listened to the steady drone of bees, a sophorific sound that would soon have sent her off had she allowed it to. Opening her eyes again she watched a red admiral flit by. And then a pair of cabbage whites caught her attention, one of them seemingly chasing the other as though they were having a game together.

She continued on to Douglas and the pram, and as she neared

them she noticed something on the netting which covered the pond at water level. Lindsay's big teddy that Eileen had given him she thought. Phyl was forever dressing it up for him as though it was a doll and the wee monkey must have thrown it out of his pram.

She glanced up as a plane passed overhead. An RAF plane she saw. It was most unusual for either a military or commercial aircraft to fly over Burnside. She could only remember it happening once before since she'd come to live in Blairbeth Road.

'Douglas?' she called out. 'Douglas, I'm back.' He mumbled something but didn't waken. She turned to the pram, and the instant she looked into it an icy-cold hand gripped her heart. The pram was empty.

With a whimper she whirled to stare with horror at what she'd thought from a distance was Lindsay's big teddy. But it wasn't the teddy at all, it was Lindsay, face down, arms and legs enmeshed in the netting. He was quite still.

She galvanised into action. Throwing herself forward she went down onto her knees by the verge of the pond, grabbed hold of Lindsay, and pulled him to her, at the same time grasping hold of the netting with her other hand. The netting ripped away with the frenzied force of her action.

Lindsay's face was tinged blue, his eyes open and staring. There were bits of weed clinging to his cheeks and in his mouth. He wasn't breathing.

'Oh my God! Oh my God!' she whispered, her hands all thumbs as she tried to free him from the netting entangling his arms and legs. Swearing loudly she took hold of the netting and hauled on it so that what had still been secured to its fixings now broke away.

Douglas came out of his sound sleep. What was going on? What was happening? He blinked, still disorientated, trying to focus. What was Norma doing with Lindsay? And why was the pond netting all . . . The sight of Lindsay's blue-tinged face went through him like an electric shock. He erupted from his deck-chair to swiftly kneel beside Norma and the boy.

'Do something! Do something!' Norma urged him as she tried to massage Lindsay's front. She'd learned how to do this in FANY, but her mind had gone blank, she couldn't remember the details of what she'd been taught.

'What happened?' Douglas demanded.

'Pond, he was face down in the pond.' Sick bubbled into her throat and out over her lips. It was something she was only dimly aware of.

Douglas fought to control the panic that was threatening to engulf him. He thrust Norma aside and started to massage the child's heart. 'Get the weed out of his mouth,' he ordered Norma, who did so. Feeling as far back as she could with a finger to find out if there was any lodged at the rear of the throat, which there wasn't.

She began crying, hot scalding tears that flowed down to mix with the streaks of sick on her chin. She began to shake violently all over.

She didn't know how long Douglas massaged. A few minutes? Ten? It seemed like all eternity. Finally, he stopped, and bowed his head. 'It's no use, the wee fella's gone,' he said, then he too started to weep.

She stared at the body of her bonnie boy whose arms and legs were still enmeshed in the netting. He'd come out the pram, fallen onto the netting face down, become entangled, and because his face was downwards hadn't been able to cry out. And like that, a fish in a net, he'd drowned. Throwing back her head she screamed out her agony. She screamed and screamed and screamed, and as she did it was as though something snapped inside her.

Travers emerged from the house at a run, and behind him two of the maids. Solange appeared in an upstairs window.

'Norma! Norma!' Douglas shouted, trying to take hold of her to shake her, but she pushed him away.

The pain brought Norma out of her hysteria, an explosion of it that caused her to gasp and bend over. Then, in rapid succession, the pain hit again and again. 'No! Please God no!' she pleaded, realising what was occurring.

Douglas and Travers both caught her when she lapsed into unconsciousness.

She came to, to find her eyes were gummy and that there was a terrible metallic taste in her mouth. The unmistakable smell of a hospital filled her nostrils.

387

'Mrs Ross? I'm Mr Imlach who's looking after you.'

And then she remembered. 'Oh my wee boy...' she whispered, and fresh tears started to flow. Mr Imlach looked grimly on. There were times he considered being a doctor the most awful job in the world. This was one of them. 'And...?'

'I'm sorry Mrs Ross. It was a stillborn birth. There was absolutely nothing we or anyone else could have done.'

She turned her head away from Imlach to stare at a blank wall. Her mind, her body – her oh so empty body – were numb. She might have been dead, as dead as the baby she'd lost, as dead as the wee son she'd dragged from the pond.

She pictured Lindsay as she'd last seen him. The bluish tinge to his face, his eyes open and staring, his body limp. Bits of weed still clinging to his cheeks, though gone from his mouth. But Imlach was speaking again. She tried to concentrate, to make sense of his words.

'I said your husband is outside. Shall I send him in to you?'

'No, I don't want to see him.' There was a long pause, then she added. 'Not yet. No, not yet.'

'I'll tell him that then.'

Her tears were blinding her, but she didn't care. She felt she'd never care about anything ever again.

She saw Douglas the following day. He came into her room carrying a bunch of flowers and a small case containing some clean nighties and other things from Blairbeth Road. She ignored the flowers when he laid them on her bedside table. There was a wooden chair which he placed beside the bed, and sat on. She waited for him to speak. It was ages before he did.

'I thought... I honestly believed I'd reined Lindsay properly in,' he mumbled eventually.

'Are you saying you hadn't?' She kept her voice neutral, though it was an effort to do so.

He swallowed hard. 'It's not clear. There's the possibility that I only half did the buckle up. If so either the strap worked its way loose, or else Lindsay somehow managed to open it himself.'

'They can't tell?'

Douglas shook his head. 'I have to say that I might not have buckled him in at all, that I forgot about it. I just... well I can't believe that of myself, that I'd be so careless.'

'You mean you don't want to believe it?'

He was unable to hold her gaze and looked away. 'My mind was full of the paper, and I was so damned tired. I had a dreadful night the night before. I was awake for hours before we got up.'

'You never said.'

'I'm often troubled with insomnia, far more than you've realised. I've never let on not wanting to bother or distress you.' He paused, then continued. 'I've wracked my memory trying to recall exactly what I did do, and I can't.' There was another silence between them. 'Aren't you going to say "I told you so" about the pond?'

'No,' she answered in a whisper.

'Thank you. I — ' He broke down, dissolving into tears.

Norma watched him impassively.

She took a deep breath, and closed her eyes. What a fabulous day it was! She listened to the steady drone of bees, a sophorific sound that would soon have sent her off if she'd allowed it. Opening her eyes again she watched a red admiral flit by. And then a pair of cabbage whites caught her attention, one of them seemingly chasing the other as though they were having a game together.

She looked back to Douglas and the pram, and there was Lindsay, standing up in the pram, staring down into the pond. He began to topple, ever so slowly, like some tiny tree that had just been felled.

She screamed a warning to Douglas, but he didn't hear. Hair streaming out behind her she raced for the pond, only for some reason she was moving as slowly as Lindsay was falling. He hit the netting to send a great splash of water drops arching high into the air. Face down he struggled, but the more he did the more enmeshed he became. She could see it all quite clearly even though she was yet some distance away.

Finally, at long last she reached the pondside where she dropped to her knees. He was still alive, she could tell from the bubbles streaming to the surface. She reached down to grab hold of him, to pull him free. *And her hands went straight through him.*

Frantically, again and again she tried, but her hands

wouldn't connect. They criss-crossed through his body, as if she was a ghost, unreal. Screaming again, she came back to her feet – everything continuing in that strange slow motion – to go to Douglas asleep in his deckchair.

Once more it happened. When she tried to grasp hold of Douglas her hands went straight through him, just as they'd done with Lindsay.

Her screaming turned to a shouted plea. 'Douglas! Douglas wake up! *Wake up!*' He continued asleep, unhearing.

She returned to the spot she'd just come from to find that the bubbles had stopped. And with that she resumed screaming. Why couldn't she get hold of Lindsay? Why couldn't she save him? Why couldn't Douglas hear her? Why couldn't...

'There, there Mrs Ross, it's all right. You're only having a nightmare,' a soothing female voice whispered from afar.

'My boy, my little boy...' Norma mumbled.

'Yes, I know. I understand.'

'Can't... can't seem to...' There was a sharp prick in her right arm. 'I can't seem to... Oh Lindsay, Lindsay, mummy's here, but I can't seem to... can't seem to...'

Blackness, as though she was in some deep dark cellar whose only door had just been clanged shut, closed in on her. And she knew no more.

Norma stared at herself in the mirror above the washbasin. Her cheeks were sunken and she was hollow-eyed. Her complexion was muddy, unhealthy looking. She placed the black hat on her head, and pinned it so that it would stay in position. She carefully tucked several stray wisps of hair out of sight, then dropped the veil down over her face.

She was dressed entirely in black, in clothes she'd had Effie buy and bring into the hospital.

It was the day of the funeral, and the day Norma was to leave the hospital. She'd insisted that the latter coincide with the former, and had a reason for that insistence which she hadn't confided to anyone.

The Procurator Fiscal, as was his duty in such cases, had held an inquiry into Lindsay's death, his judgement being that death had been by misadventure. The PF had called personally, along with a WPC, at the hospital to take her statement.

Douglas came into the room. His hair had gone snow-white since Lindsay's death. 'Are you ready?' he asked in a quiet voice.

'Yes,' she replied, her tone firm and unemotional. He picked up her case and they went out into the corridor where Sister McLeish was waiting to say goodbye.

'Can I have the case,' Norma said to Douglas, which took him by surprise. He gave it to her, she in turn passing it on to Sister McLeish. 'If you can use any of the contents on the ward, please do. Otherwise I'd be obliged if you'd get rid of them for me.'

'Right Mrs Ross.' Sister McLeish held out a hand which Norma shook. 'Goodbye, good luck.' Only three words, but they had a wealth of meaning and understanding in them. Norma nodded her appreciation.

'Let's go,' Norma said to Douglas, and strode off down the corridor. There was only one item she'd kept from those Douglas had brought into the hospital for her, that was the ivory comb with overlaid silver grip Finlay Rankine had given her when she'd left Glasgow to join the FANY. She wouldn't have parted with that for all the tea in China.

Outside the Victoria, Douglas led the way to where their car was parked. 'The Vanden Plas, I didn't think either the Lagonda or MG was suitable. I was going to hire but Father and Mama thought we should use the Daimler. They're hiring instead.'

Norma remained silent, just waiting by the front passenger door until Douglas unlocked it for her. She slid inside, her first ever time in the Vanden Plas.

Douglas got into the driver's seat, and glanced at his watch. They were on schedule. Engaging the gears he started off for Rutherglen where the funeral parlour they were using was, and where the funeral would be departing from. He'd wanted it to leave from Blairbeth Road, but Norma had vetoed that, saying *she* wanted it to leave from the funeral parlour. He hadn't argued, but had capitulated instantly.

They drove some way in silence. 'I don't understand, why did you leave those bits and pieces with Sister McLeish?' Douglas asked eventually. Norma continued staring out the window and didn't reply.

'Norma?' He got no answer to that either. Holding the wheel

391

with one hand he groped for his cigarettes, and lit up. 'I'm going to have to live with this for the rest of my life you know,' he said in a strained, tight, voice.

She glanced at him, her eyes cold and hard as diamonds. 'So am I.'

Outside the funeral parlour the hearse and three cars were parked waiting for them. Forsyth and Solange were in the leading car; Effie and Brian in the second; Lyn, Iain, Eileen and Finlay in the third. Norma had insisted that only the immediate family attend the funeral. With the exception of Brian it was the first time the two families had met.

Douglas drew up beside Forsyth and Solange, and the hearse slowly moved off. He followed on behind, the other three behind him.

When they arrived at Rutherglen Cemetery Douglas came round to help Norma from the Vanden Plas and she told him curtly she could manage. Douglas and Brian carried Lindsay's small coffin down to the graveside; Forsyth and Finlay the coffin of the stillborn female baby.

The minister, Bible in hand, was already by the graveside. He had a few brief words with Norma and Douglas, then the service got under way.

Most of it was a jumble of words as far as Norma was concerned. When everyone else sang, she didn't. When the two coffins, under the guidance of the cemetery people, were lowered into the grave, she was the only female present not weeping. She was cried out; she had no more tears to shed.

Finally it was all over, and they began drifting back to where the cars were. Solange had offered to lay on a meal for the mourners, Norma had said no.

When they reached the cars Norma called out quietly to Brian. 'Da, could you come here please.' When Brian had joined her and Douglas she turned to her husband, stared him straight in the face, and said, 'I'm not going back to that house in Blairbeth Road. I'll never step inside it again. I'm leaving you.'

That pole-axed Douglas. He was completely lost for words.

'There is one thing, and one thing only, that I want from Blairbeth Road, the rest you can do with as you please. And that's the photograph of Lindsay in the brass frame.'

392

Douglas, still unable to speak, nodded. He was shocked, bewildered, his mind frozen like a block of ice.

'Take me home to Cubie Street Da.' Brian grasped her by the elbow and led her to his hired car where Effie was waiting.

Forsyth, sensing something was wrong, crossed over to Douglas. Brian assisted Norma into the car, then gestured to the rest of the family not to query anything for the moment, but to get into their cars and follow on.

A stricken Douglas watched Norma drive away. She didn't even glance once in his direction.

Brian answered the knock on the outside door. 'I brought the photograph Norma asked for,' Douglas said, looking even more awful and wretched than he had at the funeral three days previously.

Brian held out a hand. 'Thank you.'

'Can I...' Douglas nervously licked his lips. 'Can I see her? Please?'

Brian wasn't at all sure he agreed with what Norma had done in leaving Douglas. But she'd made her decision and, right or wrong, he'd stand by her, and it. 'I'm sorry, but she doesn't want to see you.'

'If only I could —'

'She was adamant about that,' Brian interjected.

Douglas realised there was no point in arguing. He gave Brian the photograph in its brass frame, a frame Norma had herself chosen. 'Wait!' he exclaimed when Brian went to close the door on him. Brian hesitated.

'I know she said she didn't want anything else from Blairbeth Road, but I brought her MG over anyway. It's outside the close mouth.' He handed the car keys to Brian. 'Tell her...' He took a deep breath. 'Tell her ...' He changed his mind, and shook his head. Turning away from the door and, with head bowed, shoulders slumped, made his way back down the stairs again.

Brian shut the door, leaned against it, and closed his eyes. 'Shit!' he swore softly. Then he went through to the bedroom where Norma was.

She was sitting in the rocking chair they'd brought from Kirn, and which had aye been a great favourite of his. He told

393

her who had been at the front door, and what had been said. He gave her the photograph and car keys.

'Thank you Da.'

'There's a fresh pot of tea just making, do you want to come ben?'

'No.'

'Will I bring you a cup in here?'

'No thanks.'

'Is there anything you want?'

'Only to be left alone Da.'

When Brian was gone from the bedroom she held the photograph out in front of her and gazed at it. After a while she clasped the photo to her bosom, and slowly began to rock back and forth.

Chapter Fourteen

'Come away in,' Eileen said to Alice Henderson who'd just chapped.

'It's yourself I want a wee word with, Eileen.'

'Well you're not standing on the landing while you do so, it's perishing,' Eileen replied. It was mid October and freezing outside. The weather forecast was that there might be snow.

Entering the living room Alice discovered Brian sitting smoking his pipe on one side of a blazing fire, Effie knitting on the other. Norma was at the table polishing the brasses, a job she enjoyed doing, and found relaxing.

Brian rose out of politeness. 'No no, sit where you are,' Alice said. Brian sank back into his comfy chair, and Alice sat on a wooden chair that Eileen brought over from the table.

'I've come to thank you for your invitation, it was most kind of you to ask us,' Alice said to Eileen. The invitation referred to was to Eileen and Finlay's wedding reception which was to take place in a fortnight's time. 'Leslie and myself will be delighted to attend.'

'Good,' Eileen nodded.

Alice coughed, and looked uncomfortable. 'I hope you won't be offended, but Midge won't be going.'

Eileen glanced at Effie. Effie hadn't wanted Midge to be included in the invitation, but she had said it wouldn't be right if he wasn't. They could hardly leave out Midge and invite his parents who, despite the fact their son had jilted Norma, had been the best of neighbours down through the years. And it would have been a terrible insult to the Hendersons not to ask them when the rest of the close was being invited.

'I'm sorry to hear that,' Eileen replied.

'And why can't he go?' Effie asked bluntly, but politely.

Alice started to rub her hands together as if she was washing them. 'It's not a case of can't, but won't,' she answered truthfully. Then, seeing Effie's expression. 'Oh it's nothing personal, I can assure you, which is why I came up to explain the situation to Eileen. It's just that, well I don't know if you've realised it or not, but Midge hasn't been over the door since he came back from Ruchill, not once. Leslie and I have argued with him and badgered him till we were both blue in the face, to no avail. He refuses to leave the house.'

'But why?'

'He doesn't want folk to see him in his wheelchair. He feels...' She groped for the words, 'just so much less than he was I suppose.'

Norma laid aside the soft cloth she'd been using to shine up a candlestick. Now that she came to think of it, she hadn't seen Midge out and about since she'd returned to live in Cubie Street. She'd been caught up so much in her own grief the fact hadn't registered. Nor had it registered with anyone else in the family as no one had commented.

Alice, becoming more distressed with every passing second, went on. 'He just sits in that room of his staring out the window and brooding. He doesn't even read, we get books from the library for him, but they lie there untouched. It's a real worry.'

'He can't go on like that,' Norma said.

'You try telling him that.'

'It must have been particularly hard for him having been a professional dancer, his legs and feet being the tools of his trade so to speak,' Brian commiserated.

Alice nodded.

'You can tell him that Finlay and I understand, and that no offence has been taken,' Eileen said softly.

'That's why I wanted to explain it myself.'

'Here, I'm not being sociable. I'll put the kettle on,' Effie said, rising.

'Och don't bother for me. And I'd better get back, I've left Midge alone in the house. Leslie has gone to visit a crony of his who's down with the bronchitis.'

'You bide and chaff a wee while,' Norma said to Alice. 'If you don't mind I'll go and have a talk with Midge. Maybe I can persuade him to go.'

396

'Oh if only you could! It would do him the world of good to get out.'

'Then you put that kettle on Ma,' Norma said, getting up. She went with Effie through to the kitchen where she washed her hands, after which she returned to the living room for Alice's front door key, intending to let herself into the Henderson house. When she had the key, she went away downstairs.

Midge glanced over from where he was sitting by the window, his face creasing with surprise to see it was her framed in his doorway. 'Hello,' she said.

'Hello,'

'Do you always sit in the dark?' For although the hallway light was on, his bedroom was in darkness.

'There's nothing wrong with being in the dark. I like it,' he replied aggressively. Then he remembered he hadn't spoken to her since she'd come back to Cubie Street. In a far softer voice he said, 'I was shocked to hear what happened. That must have been dreadful for you.'

'Aye, it was.'

'Words are so inadequate at times. So all I'll say is I'm sorry, and have you know I mean that from the very bottom of my heart.'

She appreciated his simplicity, it was the way all condolences should be given. She went over to him and kissed him on the forehead, which seemed the right thing to do. 'Thank you.'

The wheels of his chair whispered away from her. There was a click, and light from a tablelamp flooded the room. 'I can't have you here in the darkness with me, what would folk think?' he said, and laughed, a laugh that was sharp-edged and bitter.

'I've come to talk to you Midge.'

He gestured to a chair. 'Park your bum and tell me what about.'

He didn't speak like an American anymore, she noted. That had disappeared. 'Your ma says you won't go to Eileen and Finlay's wedding reception?'

He dropped his gaze and began picking imaginary bits of fluff from the tartan travelling rug draped over his legs. 'No.'

'Can we talk frankly? I am an old friend after all.' When he didn't answer she went on. 'You can't stay cooped up in this room and this house for the rest of your days. That's absurd.'

'Not to me it's not,' he replied defensively.

'What are you scared of?'

'I don't wish to go on with this...'

'I asked you what you're scared of Midge?' she interrupted.

He coloured slightly. 'Thanks for coming in Norma. I did want to see you, and would have come up before now except I have this little trouble getting up and down stairs.'

'You could have come up if you'd really wanted to. Your da would have helped you.'

He put his left thumb in his mouth, and started to chew its nail.

Norma decided to change tack, and tone. Very gently she said, 'You're going to have to start learning to come to terms with things, as I'm having to learn. God knows it isn't easy, but it has to be done.'

He stopped chewing his nail, his expression now a combination of anguish and despair. Slowly, reluctantly, as if he was divulging some awful secret, he replied. 'It's the pity I can't stand. The pity in people's eyes when they look at me and see what I've become, what I've been reduced to.'

'That's natural, for you and them. But no reason for you to hide yourself away like a hermit.' She paused, then added, 'If you don't want people to feel pity for you then you've got to stop feeling pity for yourself. That's the key.'

'And how can I *not* feel pity for myself? I've lost the use of my legs for fucksake!' he erupted.

'Yes you have, and that's something you're going to have to accept. Just as I'm having to accept that my little son is drowned, and that my baby daughter will never now be born.'

'Jesus!' he breathed, and ran a hand though his lank and listless hair.

She went over to him, and knelt beside his chair. 'So will you go to Eileen and Finlay's reception after all? It's as good a time and place as any to break out of this self-imposed isolation. To get out once more to face the world.'

A shudder ran through his upper torso. 'It's not really as good a time and place Norma. You're wrong about that.'

She frowned, failing to understand what he was getting at. 'I'm not with you?'

'I couldn't... I couldn't bear to sit in a wheelchair and watch

398

you dance with someone else. That would just tear me apart inside,' he admitted in a choked whisper.

She nodded. She should have realised that would be sheer torture for him. But she had a solution. 'If I promise you that I won't dance with anyone, anyone at all, will you promise me to go?'

He went back to chewing the same nail as before.

'Do you want to be stuck away in this room for the rest of your natural? Is that what you really want?'

'No, of course not.'

'Then I ask you again. If I promise not to dance with anyone will you promise me to go?'

There was a long pause during which it was clear that a mental tussle was going on. Finally, he made his decision. 'I promise,' he said quietly.

'That's settled then,' she said, and rose to her feet. She stared at him, and he stared back. 'If I don't see you before I'll see you there. We'll sit together, all right?'

He gave her a weak smile. 'All right.'

As the front door clicked shut behind Norma, Midge was reaching out to switch off the table lamp so that he'd once more be in darkness. He hesitated, thought about it for a few moments, and then withdrew his hand. He'd leave the light on.

Norma turned away from the makeshift bar in the big rear room of Dow's pub where Eileen and Finlay's wedding reception was being held. She'd been to the bar to get drinks for her and Midge, and was now about to take them back to where she'd left him.

'Norma, wait up!'

Norma looked round to see Eileen making towards her. The wedding ceremony itself had been in a registry office a little over an hour and a half previously, and had gone just dandy. Eileen had been positively radiant as Finlay had slipped the ring onto her finger. A Finlay, it must be said, who was self-conscious for once in his life, which had amused Norma no end.

'How are you doing? Enjoying yourself?' Eileen asked as she joined her oldest sister.

'I am. It's a great reception.'

'Everyone appears to be having a fine old time.' She paused, then added. 'I never said at home but I was doubtful about coming back here to Dow's rear room, it being a bit of a barn. But in my heart of hearts it really was where I wanted the reception to take place, and so we settled on it.'

'I never asked, not wanting to appear nosy, but I take it Finlay knows this is where you and Charlie had your reception?'

'Oh aye.'

'And it doesn't bother him?'

'Not in the least. There's no jealousy on his part about me and Charlie, none at all. In fact, we often talk together about him. At times it's almost as if . . . I hope this doesn't sound perverted, but it's almost as if Charlie was still here in a way and that we were a threesome, Charlie, Finlay and me.' She laughed. 'It does sound perverted doesn't it? But it isn't at all.'

'Well I certainly don't have to ask if you're happy. You're fair bursting with it.'

'That's true Norma. I thought it was all finished for me when Charlie died. And then Finlay came along and I got a second chance.'

'I'm so pleased, for the pair of you.'

'We're an odd couple, as Finlay puts it. Like two strangely shaped pieces of carving that don't look like they'd fit together to form a whole, but surprisingly do.'

Norma pecked Eileen on the cheek. 'If I don't get a chance in the hubbub of your going away, have a smashing honeymoon. Any idea where you're off to?'

Eileen shook her head. 'Finlay's keeping that to himself. But wherever I'll tell you where it won't be, and that's the Adelphi Hotel. Dow's pub is one thing, the Adelphi Hotel quite another. That would have been quite wrong, in bad taste even.'

One of the neighbours from Cubie Street shouted Eileen's name and she waved she'd be right over. 'I'll away back to Midge then,' Norma said.

'Before you do.' Eileen placed a hand on the top of her sister's right arm, and drew Norma fractionally closer to her. 'After Charlie died I thought that was the end of it for me, as you know. But it wasn't. I want you to remember that.' And having said what she'd waylaid Norma to say, Eileen moved off, crossing to the neighbour who'd shouted to her. Norma stared after Eileen for four or five seconds, then began weaving a path through tables and chairs back to where Midge was waiting.

'Here you are,' she said, handing him the dram he'd asked for.

'I'd better not have too many of these,' he replied, waggling the glass at her. 'I don't want to be drunk in charge of a wheelchair.'

Norma laughed, and he laughed too.

'It's good you can make jokes about yourself,' she told him when they'd stopped laughing.

'You know something?'

'What?'

'That's the first time I have since,' he tapped his legs, 'this happened.'

'Then tonight's a breakthrough.'

'So it would seem.' He paused, then added softly, 'Thank you for persuading me to come.'

A few minutes later Finlay joined them, and gave Norma an exaggerated bow. 'May I have the pleasure Miss McKenzie?' he asked, using her maiden name.

'I'm not dancing tonight Finlay. But thanks for asking.'

'Och come on, you wouldn't refuse me on my wedding night surely?'

Midge started to look uncomfortable, thinking Norma was going to have to break her promise to him. And with Finlay too, by far and away the best male dancer in the hall.

But Norma was adamant she wasn't going to break her promise. 'Finlay, I'm not dancing this evening, not with you or anybody. Now please, as we are friends, don't press me.'

Finlay treated her to one of his crocodile smiles, thinking she was just having him on. He was about to do precisely what she'd asked him not to, when she reached over and took Midge by the hand. There was that in the gesture made him realise, as Norma had wished it to convey, why she didn't want to dance. And a quick glance into Midge's face told him he was right.

Norma saw that Finlay had got the message, that he understood. 'Why don't you get Mrs Rankine up?' Norma suggested. 'She's the one you should be tripping the light fantastic with.'

'Mrs Rankine?' Finlay repeated, and barked out a laugh. 'That's the first time I've heard her called that. And yes, I'll do just that.' He gave Norma another exaggerated bow, and

Midge a wink. Then left them to go off and seek out Eileen.

Norma raised her glass to Midge. 'Slainthe!' she toasted.

'Slainthe!' Midge repeated, his eyes shining with gratitude.

Norma, Midge, Alice and Leslie Henderson left the reception together. Effie and Brian were staying on for a wee while longer to continue chaffing with an aunt and uncle of Finlay's who they'd hit it off with.

'I'll push,' Norma said when they were outside Dow's pub. Then to Midge. 'If you don't mind that is?'

'I don't mind at all.'

Their glances held, and she read in his that he meant what he said. He *didn't* mind, which pleased her. In fact it pleased her a great deal.

They started off for Cubie Street, Alice and Leslie, arm in arm, in the lead with Norma and Midge following directly behind.

'So you enjoyed yourself after all?' Norma teased Midge.

'You know I did.'

'And I enjoyed myself too.'

'You didn't feel you'd missed out by not dancing?'

She shrugged. 'I get nowhere near the kick out of dancing as I used to, so not doing so wasn't that much of an imposition. Do you know "Lily of Laguna"?'

Her so abruptly changing the subject momentarily threw him. 'Eh?'

'I said do you know "Lily of Laguna"?'

'Aye, of course I do.'

'Right then. One two three go!'

From there they sang all the way back to the closemouth, Alice and Leslie readily joining in. They sang 'Lily of Laguna', 'Pedro the Fisherman', 'Red Sails in the Sunset', 'She'll be Coming Round the Mountains When She Comes' – as many of the old favourites as they could cram in in the distance.

It was rare.

A week that Sunday Midge was in the middle of reading the *Sunday Post*. He might not read anything else but he never missed The Broons and Oor Wullie, when the door to his bedroom opened and his father came striding in.

'Right lad, you're for out,' Leslie announced.

'No I'm not.'

'Yes, you are! Those are orders,' Alice said from the doorway where she'd appeared holding one of Midge's warm winter coats. She marched over to Midge and, with the help of Leslie, started getting Midge into it.

'What is all this?' Midge protested.

'We told you, you're going out.'

'But I don't want to go out. I want to stay here.'

'Hard cheese!' Alice answered, struggling to get an arm into a sleeve.

'You're going and that's an end of it,' Leslie informed him. 'And you should be so lucky to have a young woman, no I should say young lady, offer to take you out for the day.'

'What young lady?'

'The pair of you are having a picnic. Spam and jam sannies with a flask of good strong tea to wash it down with,' Alice added.

'What bloody young lady!'

'Language!' Alice admonished, waving a right forefinger under her son's nose.

'*What* young lady?' Midge pleaded as Alice did up his front coat buttons.

'Norma. She's taking you for a run in her car,' Leslie replied.

Norma! That cheered him, and a small smile curled the corners of his mouth upwards. He'd only seen her from the window to wave to since the reception.

'She says you need a breath of fresh air, and I can only say I heartily agree with her. Why just look at you, you're as peely wally as anything,' Alice said vehemently.

Midge rubbed a hand over his face. He couldn't argue there, he was peely wally. Suddenly he was excited at the prospect of going somewhere, anywhere. Particularly as it was with Norma. *Because* it was with Norma, he corrected himself.

When Midge was ready - well wrapped up, for despite the sun shining outside it was still very cold - Leslie pushed his chair out of the house, and bumped it down the stairs. Outside on the street they found Norma and Brian waiting.

Brian opened the MG's passenger door, then turned to Midge who'd been brought alongside. 'Right,' he said. He and Leslie

403

bodily lifted Midge out of the wheelchair and manoeuvred Midge into the car seat. When they'd done this Norma got into the other side. 'Ready?' she asked.

'Aye.'

'Then let's be off.'

Brian and Leslie waved to them from the pavement; Alice and Effie from respective windows as they drove down Cubie Street and into Gallowgate.

'I feel like I've been kidnapped,' Midge said.

'Is that a complaint?'

'Would it make any difference if it was?'

She laughed. 'Not in the least.'

'Then it isn't. It's an observation.'

How easy it was between them again, she thought. Just as it had been in the old days when they'd been together. Before he'd . . . She put that memory forcibly from her mind.

'Where are we going then?'

'Where do you fancy?'

He gestured at her. 'It's your car. You choose.'

'What would you think of a trip down the coast to the Cloch Lighthouse?'

'I'd think it was a good idea, just the ticket.'

She grinned. 'The Cloch Lighthouse it is then.'

He watched her drive, noting how expertly she handled the car. The machine transformed into an extension of herself. 'You drive well.'

'Thank you. I did a lot of it earlier on in the war with FANY, fourteen and sixteen hours a day sometimes.'

'Did they teach you?'

'No, I eh . . . learned in Glasgow before the war and FANY.' She wasn't going to tell him she'd taken up driving shortly after he'd run off with Zelda as a device to stop herself thinking and brooding.

'Ma mentioned in one of her letters that you'd come into money.'

'From old man Gallagher who used to come into Barrowland to watch me because I was the spit of his dead daughter Morna. Remember?'

'How could I forget!' Midge laughed. 'And he popped off leaving you a pile?'

'I don't know if I'd call it a pile exactly, but certainly enough to keep me comfortably off for the rest of my days.'

'Well, good for you Norma. I suppose that means you didn't have to worry about money when you walked out on your husband.'

Norma shifted uneasily in her seat. She wasn't too keen on Midge talking about Douglas. 'Yes,' she replied quietly.

'Can I ask you something about him? Something I've been wondering about. I mentioned it to my father but he didn't know the answer, and he said it wouldn't be polite to ask your folks about it.'

God, what on earth was he going to come out with? She dreaded to think. 'What do you want to know?'

'It's a real Glasgow question. His mother is French, right?'

'Yes.'

'So is she a Catholic?'

Now Norma knew what he was driving at. And he was right, it was a real Glasgow question, Glaswegians being almost paranoic where religion is concerned. Or to be more specific, where Catholicism and Protestantism were concerned. 'She is.'

'Does that make him one then? And if it does did you turn when the two of you married?'

Norma smiled. 'I thought you were broad-minded? I thought you'd travelled?'

'I am broad-minded, and I certainly have travelled. But I'm still curious.'

'Once Glasgow always Glasgow,' she riposted.

'Particularly when other Glaswegians are involved,' he acknowledged, and they both laughed.

'Douglas is a Protestant so I didn't have to turn,' she explained. 'It was my father-in-law's wish that as Douglas was to be brought up in Scotland and as he himself was a Protestant, then Douglas was to be one too. I doubt my mother-in-law was very happy about that, but she agreed, and so Douglas was baptised into the Church of Scotland. Curiosity satisfied?'

He nodded.

'Good.'

They swung into the Great Western Road which would quickly take them out of Glasgow. 'I can smell the sea already,' Midge said, closing his eyes and letting his head drop back.

'You can smell the sea in Sauchiehall Street sometimes. You don't have to leave the city for that,' she jibed.

'You know what I mean!'

She glanced at him. 'You're looking better already. You're beginning to get some roses in your cheeks.'

'And I feel better already. As if I were undergoing a spring-clean.'

'And not before time. How long is it since you came out of Ruchill?'

'Nearly seven months.'

'Well now I've winkled you from the house a second time I'm going to make sure you get out more often. And there's no use saying you won't want to go, I'll drag you down the stairs screaming if I have to.'

'Why Norma?' he asked, suddenly very serious.

'Why what?'

'Why are you doing this for me?'

She considered that for a few seconds, then replied softly. 'Because I hate to see what you're doing to yourself. And also ...' She hesitated, then added in an even softer voice. 'Also maybe it's good for me to be concerned about somebody else's problems rather than just my own.'

He nodded. 'I understand.'

They went via Port Glasgow, Greenock and then Gourock. When they reached Cloch Point, Norma drew the car off the road and onto the grass verge from where they had a splendid view of the Firth of Clyde.

'I could murder a cup of that tea I was promised,' Midge said.

Norma got the picnic things out and soon they were delving into the sandwiches and being thawed out by the steaming tea.

'If you look just over there, to the right, that's Dunoon,' Norma said, pointing. 'Kirn, where I was born and where we lived before coming to Cubie Street, is to the right of that.'

'I'd forgotten about Kirn. You left there, when?'

She had to think, work it out. 'Let me see, I was fourteen, no fifteen at the time. And I'm thirty now. So it was fifteen years ago.'

He shook his head in amazement. 'As long as that!'

'Fifteen years we've known one another,' she mused.

'Murray Muir's engagement to Jenny Elder, it was during

their party in the street that I first clapped eyes on you.'

'No, that was when we first spoke and you asked me to dance. The first time we saw each other was in Gilmour's shop when I went in with my sister Lyn to get a few messages. You were in front of the counter chaffing to Chic Gilmour who was serving.'

'Oh aye, you're right,' Midge said, remembering.

'That was the day we arrived in Glasgow.' She screwed up her forehead in memory. 'It's coming back to me now. I was still fourteen when we came to Glasgow, and we saw each other in Gilmour's shop, and I was fifteen on the day of the engagement party when we danced together for the first time. And you annoyed me by calling me a bairn!'

'Well I was very ancient myself – I would have been seventeen then.'

'Most venerable,' Norma agreed, and they both laughed.

They reminisced right through the picnic, and most of the way back to Glasgow, Norma taking them the alternative route which was through Largs and Johnstone. She had a reason for this other than just a change of scenery to their outward journey.

When they reached Paisley she said. 'I brought us back this way because it takes us into the south side, and not all that far from Rutherglen. I'd like to stop off at the cemetery and pay a visit, which I do every Sunday. do you mind?'

'Not at all,' he replied, sobering up.

She parked outside the cemetery. 'I won't be long.'

'You take as long as you want. I only wish I could go in with you.'

She nodded, then got out the car and went through the gates into the cemetery. When she finally returned her face was stony, and there was a cold look about her that had nothing whatever to do with the weather.

'Okay?' he queried gently.

'Yes.' She started the engine, engaged the gears and drove slowly away.

Going down Mill Street he placed a hand on her thigh nearest him. There was nothing sexual about the gesture. Rather it was one of understanding, comfort and sympathy. He kept his hand there for quite some time before removing it again.

*　　*　　*

'Not fair!' Midge exclaimed as Norma threw yet another six to win her third successive game of Snakes and Ladders. 'I think you're cheating.'

'I am not!'

'No one can be that lucky without some kind of humphery mumphery going on.'

'Humphery mumphery yourself. You're just a bad loser, that's all.'

'I'm nothing of the sort.'

She stuck her tongue out at him. 'You are sought.'

His reply to that was to cross his eyes at her, and blow a loud raspberry.

'Disgusting,' she said. 'Want a cup of coffee?'

'Please.'

She left him to gather up the bits and pieces and put them away in their box while she went through to the kitchen. When she'd put the kettle on, she returned to the living room where she stoked up the fire. It was a Wednesday night in December and she'd come down to keep Midge company while his parents were out at the pictures. His sister Katy wasn't at home anymore, having married an Irishman towards the end of the war and moved to a place called Portadown. Since their run down the coast the previous month Norma had been seeing quite a bit of Midge, taking him out in the car when she could get the petrol and staying in with him, sometimes when his folks were there, other times when they weren't, to talk and play various card and board games which she'd discovered they both enjoyed.

When the kettle started to sing she went back again to the kitchen and made the coffee. While she was doing this she swithered whether to bring the subject up or not. The last thing she wanted to do was raise false hopes.

'There's a terrific heat off that fire. Best coal we've had in ages,' Midge commented when Norma rejoined him, and handed him his coffee.

'Midge, I want to talk to you.'

'Oh aye?'

'The truth is I don't really know whether I should do this or not. However, for better or worse, I've decided I'm going to.'

He was both mystified and intrigued. 'Do what?'

'Tell you a story.'

He gave a short laugh. 'Is that all?'

She sat in one of the armchairs by the fire, from where she regarded him steadily. 'It's a story about my mother and me, and what happened in '41.' She began to tell him of the time when she'd come home on leave to find Effie seriously ill, and what had occurred after that. As she spoke Midge's expression grew more and more intent and he became more and more entranced by what she was telling him.

Finally the story was over. She sipped at her coffee to find it had gone completely cold.

'Healing hands? Is such a thing really possible?'

'According to Mr Creighton it is. He says it's a well-documented fact that some people have this ability to cure by merely placing their hands on an inflicted or diseased person. Mr Creighton told me he was a sceptic until he witnessed a holy man in India cure by this method, after which he became a firm believer in the phenomenon.'

'And you have it, this ability?'

She gave him a rueful smile. 'I did that time with Ma. There was no other explanation for what took place. She was dying through a combination of encephalitis and her allergy to M & B, and then suddenly she wasn't dying anymore, but had recovered.' Norma paused, then went on hesitantly. 'But I must emphasise that this is the only time this miracle, what else could you call it? has worked for me.'

'Have you *tried* to make it work? Have you tried it on anyone else?'

'No.'

Midge couldn't help the excitement from creeping into his voice. 'So you don't really know if you could make it work again or not?'

In a tremulous whisper she replied. 'No, I don't.'

He licked lips that had suddenly gone dry. It was ridiculous, too far-fetched. And yet. And yet it had worked on Mrs McKenzie. Norma said it had. 'Do you think it might –'

'I don't want to raise false hopes Midge, that's the last thing I want to do,' she interrupted. 'But on the other hand it seems to me to be worth a try. After all, what have you got to lose?'

He glanced down at his useless legs. 'Nothing at all,' he replied quietly.

'And there is something else. Remember when I wanted to improve our dancing I went to the library and Eileen's Charlie got me books on the subject? Well, thinking about this, and your infantile paralysis, I decided I'd do the same again, that I'd read up on what was wrong with you. And that's where I learned of the coincidence.'

'What coincidence?' he demanded harshly.

'I discovered that infantile paralysis is caused by a virus infection which specifically attacks the anterior, motor, horn cells in the spinal cord. It may also, however, affect the brain, especially the mid-brain, producing encephalitis.'

'You mean what your mother had?'

'Her encephalitis was probably caused by a different virus. But nonetheless you see the tie-in?'

'And you think that if you can cure your mother you can cure me?'

'No no, I'm saying I'm willing to try if you are.'

Midge took a deep breath. The excitement that had come into his voice was now hammering inside him. 'You're damn right I am!'

'You sure?'

'Of course I'm sure!' he exploded. 'As you said, what have I got to lose?'

'Right then.' She rose from the chair, took Midge's cup and saucer from him and laid those with her own on the table. Then she returned to stand in front of him.

She looked thoughtful for a few moments. 'The lights I think,' she muttered. She went and switched off the overhead light, then the standard lamp that was in a corner. After which she returned to Midge.

He was covered in gooseflesh, and had prickles all over the tops of his shoulders. His stomach had tightened into a knot.

Norma stood in the darkness, the only illumination coming from the fire, and wondered what to do next. She decided to go down on her knees in front of Midge.

When she was so positioned she removed the tartan travelling rug covering his legs, dropped it aside, and placed her palms and outspread fingers on his thighs.

Midge swallowed hard as he watched Norma close her eyes, then bow her head in concentration. Oh to be able to walk again, to leave this bloody chair behind forever, to ... A cold sheen of perspiration burst on his forehead.

In her mind Norma conjured up a picture of Lynsey as Lynsey had appeared to her in her mother's bedroom. Lynsey stared sorrowfully at her.

Please Lynsey, help Midge as you did my mother, she pleaded silently.

Norma made Lynsey come closer. As before, there was a faint luminous glow surrounding Lynsey. And every so often she sort of shimmered as if it was an act of supreme willpower that was keeping her there.

Please Lynsey, help Midge as you did my mother, Norma pleaded a second time.

Lynsey's sorrowful stare transferred itself to Midge. Then she glanced back at Norma, and the hint of a smile touched the corner of her mouth. Your hands, she said.

Norma, with her hands still on Midge's thighs, visualised herself holding them out to Lynsey, and waited for Lynsey to make them tingle as they had done with Effie.

Lynsey's smile widened a fraction, and as it did ... Norma waited expectantly for the strange tingling to invade her hands. She waited in vain.

She tried again, starting at the beginning where Lynsey appeared to her. And again nothing happened, no tingling, no sense of energy flowing into Midge.

She opened her eyes and looked up at Midge. 'I'm sorry,' she said, removing her hands.

'What do you mean?'

She sat back on her heels. 'Nothing, nothing at all.'

'Maybe ...'

'No maybes Midge, there was nothing. Nothing happened. I did my best but it just didn't happen.'

He bit back bitter disappointment. He felt like cursing, but didn't.

She shook her head. 'Perhaps the power was only given to me as a one-off thing.'

'Do you think that?'

'I honestly don't know, Midge. I'm just as in the dark,' she smiled thinly, thinking at the moment that was literally true, 'about this as you are. Mr Creighton said that my healing ability could be latent and that Lynsey Dereham was a device, or catalyst, used by my subconscious to bring that ability to the surface. That's why I've been thinking of Lynsey, recreating events as they occurred in Ma's bedroom, trying to get that device or catalyst activated again.' She pulled a long face. 'But as I just said, I failed to do so.'

This time he did swear. 'Fuck!'

She knew she'd done precisely what she hadn't wanted to, raise his hopes only to dash them again. 'I'm sorry,' she repeated.

'Just because it didn't work this time doesn't mean it won't,' he said doggedly. 'Let's have another attempt?'

'I don't ...'

'Please Norma?' Then, throwing her own words back at her. 'After all, what have we got to lose?'

How could she refuse? She couldn't. 'All right then.' She decided that on this occasion she would keep her hands free so she could physically extend them when entreating Lynsey.

Coming back to her knees, she closed her eyes and bowed her head.

'What you're talking about isn't medicine as I know it,' Rodney Creighton said. Norma had made an appointment to see him, and was now facing him across his desk. She'd just finished telling him about her sessions with Midge, and how each of them had ended in total failure. 'I can't even begin to advise you how to turn on this talent of yours which was so successful with your mother.'

'I thought ... Well it seemed the natural thing to consult you for advice. You do believe in healing hands after all, and you are a doctor.'

Creighton frowned. 'How many times did you say you'd tried with Mr Henderson?'

'Half a dozen occasions in all.'

'Hmmh!' Creighton mused, and leaned back in his chair. This was a real poser.

'If you can't suggest anything then I'll give up. I've already told Mr Henderson that.'

'And what did he say?'

'What could he say. I just feel rotten about the whole business now and wish I'd never brought it up with him.'

'It was a gamble that didn't come off Miss McKenzie. You mustn't reproach yourself.' He paused to turn something over in his mind. When he spoke again it was in the same neutral tone that he normally employed. 'May I ask, Miss McKenzie, are you a religious woman?'

That surprised her. 'I don't exactly go to church every Sunday. But yes, I am.'

'Then why don't you try the power of prayer to unlock the door to your gift. That might possibly be the answer.'

She stared at the specialist. 'What an odd recommendation for a doctor to make,' she said slowly.

'Is it really? Love and prayer, Miss McKenzie, aren't they the two strongest forces in the universe?'

'But I don't love Mr Henderson,' she blurted out.

'Excuse me for presuming, but you spoke about him as though you did.'

'Well I used to, but that was a long time ago.'

'Oh, I see!'

Of course she didn't still love Midge. Or did she? Had she ever fallen out of love with him? One thing was certain, she had been in love with Douglas when she'd married him. But at that time Midge had been out of her life, and unlikely ever to return into it. Could you love two men simultaneously? Of course you could, an old love and a new. Certainly she hadn't thought of herself still to be in love with Midge. Or to put that another way, she hadn't thought about it at all. Was she?

She brought her attention back to Creighton.

'What do you think?' Norma asked having just pulled the MG into the kerb and parked.

'About what?' Midge queried, mystified.

She pointed over to their right. 'That house.'

Whatever was she on about? Was it some sort of game? 'It's a very nice house. Why?'

'It's a bungalow actually, which means there are no stairs to go up and down. It has a lovely garden out at the back, and a small one in the front as you can see.' She sucked in a breath.

413

'And savour that air, country fresh! A far cry from the pong you get in Bridgeton eh?'

'A far cry,' he agreed. 'Norma, what is this all about?'

'Have you ever been to Nitshill before? I hadn't until a couple of days ago. It not only smells like the country round here, it is the country. The village is surrounded by fields which at other times of the year,' it was mid-February, 'are filled with cows, sheep, horses and, I don't know! all sorts of animals. And there are several woods. One over there,' she said, indicating. 'And a smaller one down that way.' She indicated in a different direction.

'The area is new to me,' he confessed. 'And yes it is very countrified.'

'You like it here then?'

He wished she would get to the point, this was becoming aggravating. 'Indeed, it's most pleasant.'

'And the bungalow?'

He glanced again at the bungalow in question. 'Looks very solidly built.'

'How would you care to live in it? With me.'

He turned to stare at her. 'Say that again?'

'I'm not joking Midge, I mean it. How would you like to live in that bungalow with me? It's up for sale and I could easily afford the price.'

He was dumbstruck. This was completely out of the blue.

'Staying up flights of stairs in a tenement is a terrible drawback when you're in a wheelchair. You're utterly reliant on others, which in your case means your father as you're too heavy for either your Ma or I to get up and down. It would be totally different in a bungalow, we can put in a couple of small ramps at the front and rear and you can come and go as you please. Think of the freedom that would give you?'

It would indeed. He couldn't argue with that.

'And here there would be the gardens for you to sit out in during good weather, and then there's the pub just along the road if you fancied a pint. It would be a whole new way of life for you.'

He swallowed hard. 'You and I, *together*?'

'That's right.'

He glanced away, and an expression of anguish came over his

414

face. 'I thought you understood. It's not only my legs that don't function, it's everything down there. I'm not a man anymore, not in that sense of the word.'

'That won't matter, Midge,' she told him softly.

He shot her a look which clearly said *liar*!

'It won't, I assure you. Lindsay's death and losing the baby has left me . . . Well, let's say I'll be content to settle for a cuddle.'

'You would?'

She nodded.

He wasn't the only cripple, he thought. But the damage inflicted on Norma was in her mind, not her body. 'I know a shop where we can buy those ramps,' he said.

'We'll go there now.' And they did.

Norma was walking up Sauchiehall Street. She'd come into the town for a rendezvous, had arrived early, and so was doing a wee bit of window shopping to pass the time.

The typewriter was in a pawnbroker's window, and the moment she set eyes on it, it gave her an idea. She and Midge had been living in the bungalow for four months now, and were both well settled in. Locally they were known as Mr and Mrs Henderson, something that had been assumed, and which they'd agreed not to deny.

Midge had changed for the better. Gone was the moroseness and listlessness of Cubie Street, replaced by a restless energy that was forever sending him prowling round the house and village in his wheelchair. Quite simply he needed something to occupy his mind and for a while now Norma had been trying to think of an activity or project to fill the bill. The typewriter she was staring at just could be the solution.

Going into the pawnbroker's she bought the machine, then had the man load it into the boot of her Austin 12 which she brought round to the front of the shop. The Austin 12 had swiftly replaced the MG after they'd moved to Nitshill because it was far easier, being a larger vehicle and a saloon, to get Midge in and out of.

Norma reparked the Austin 12 where it had been before, then hurried into Treron's tearoom where she found Vivienne Gregory waiting for her. It was the first time she'd seen Vivienne since that nightmarish day the previous July when she'd left

Vivienne to return to Blairbeth Road, and find Lindsay dead in the pond.

Vivienne rose as Norma approached the table at which she'd already been sitting. 'Hello,' she said, not quite sure whether a handshake or kiss was in order.

'Hello Vivienne,' Norma replied somewhat shyly. She made to kiss Vivienne on the cheek, just as Vivienne stuck out a hand. That caused them to laugh, and broke the ice. She kissed Vivienne on the cheek, and Vivienne did the same to her.

'It's good to see you again.'

'And you,' Vivienne smiled.

They sat. 'You've been on my conscience,' Norma said. 'You were the only friend I had amongst the circle I moved in when at Blairbeth Road. There was no need for me to stop seeing you because I'd walked out on Douglas.' She hesitated. 'Or don't you agree?'

'If I didn't I wouldn't be here.'

A waitress came over, and they ordered tea and crumpets. When the waitress had left Vivienne said, 'On a number of occasions I nearly asked Douglas for your address so I could look you up. In the event I never did. After what happened I wasn't sure you'd want to see anyone who might remind you.' She paused, then asked tenderly, 'So how has it been for you?'

'To begin with it didn't bother me whether I lived or died. Let's just say I now prefer to live.'

Vivienne reached across and squeezed Norma's hand. 'Good.'

'You've seen Douglas then?'

'Jim and I had him to dinner a fortnight ago.'

'I suppose I should ask how he is?'

'A man demented is how I'd describe him. He's going through absolute hell. I heard on the grapevine that if it wasn't for his father he'd have lost his job at the hospital. Apparently the standard of his work has fallen right away.'

Norma stared grimly at Vivienne. 'I can't say I feel any sympathy for him. I don't.'

'When he was at dinner he spoke about you. He misses you dreadfully. He blames himself totally for what happened.' Norma didn't reply to that, and silence fell between them. Eventually Vivienne said, 'Did you know he's left home?'

'What! I don't believe it!' That really rocked her.

'It's true.'

'I couldn't get him out of that mausoleum, and away from his damned mother. I pleaded with him but he wouldn't budge.'

'Well he's left now, shortly before Christmas. I'm not clear on the details, he was vague about those, but there was an unholy row that involved Catherine Stark.'

'Catherine Stark?'

'I think, reading between the lines, that his mother must have been trying to do a bit of stage-managing to which he strongly objected.'

Norma nodded, that made sense. 'Trying to replace me with her I'd imagine. A liaison Solange has long favoured.'

'But not Douglas?'

'No. He likes Catherine as a friend, but that's as far as it goes. Something Solange has always refused to accept, as has Catherine herself.'

'And so Douglas decamped. He's renting a flat in University Avenue. A one-bedroom affair which he says is liveable in, if only just.'

'Well, well, well,' mused Norma. Douglas had moved out of Blairbeth Road! That really was a turn up for the book.

Their tea and crumpets arrived, and Vivienne played mother. 'Do you mind if I make an observation concerning your marriage – you might not appreciate it?' Vivienne asked slowly.

'Go ahead.'

'I know you lost Lindsay, and the child you were carrying. But because it was Douglas's fault doesn't mean he feels it any less than you do. In fact, with the guilt he's riven by, surely it's fair to say he feels it even more? And on top of losing Lindsay and the baby you were carrying he also lost you.' She paused for emphasis. 'You got rid of him – he lost you.'

'Are you suggesting I forgive him?'

Vivienne shook her head. 'It's not my place or business to suggest any such thing. But I would like you to consider that your children had two parents, and it's not only you that's grieving for them. And that, no matter how you might feel towards him, Douglas is still in love with you.'

'He said that?'

'When he came to dinner, yes.'

'You don't think I should have left him?' Norma accused.

'I can tell you this, I've thought about it and if I had been in your position, and Jim had been in Douglas's, I wouldn't have left Jim. Mistakes were made that had tragic results, but I wouldn't have left Jim because of those results. But then again, what's right for me isn't necessarily right for you.'

Norma stared into her cup as she stirred her tea. It wasn't tea she was seeing, but a pond with Lindsay lying face down in the netting covering the pond. Then the vision changed to Massingham and happier times. How good it had been between her and Douglas then. She came out of her reverie as Vivienne asked her a question.

'How are you getting on staying again with your parents? Everything going smoothly there?'

Norma lifted her cup, and sipped its contents. While she was doing this she regarded Vivienne over the cup's rim. Should she tell Vivienne about Midge and their bungalow, or not? It was something she'd been debating with herself since telephoning Vivienne to arrange this meeting. 'Can you keep something to yourself? Not that it's a secret, I would just prefer it didn't go any further for the time being.'

'My lips are sealed,' Vivienne promised.

Norma believed her. Vivienne was the type who kept her word. She started at that day sixteen years previously when she and Lyn had walked into Gilmour's shop.

Norma kneaded Midge's left calf as she'd learned to do. She began at the buttocks, worked her way down the left leg, and then the right. It was a ritual she performed every day, as had Alice Henderson before her. The people at Ruchill had said it was necessary to maintain proper circulation, and keep the flesh and muscles as healthy as was possible in the circumstances.

Midge grunted. 'Ouch! That was sore,' he complained.

'Sorry,' she smiled in reply. A smile that froze on her face as the import of what he'd just said sunk home. His back suddenly stiffened as it sunk home on him also.

'Oh my God!' he breathed, and twisted round to stare at her in wonderment.

Heart thumping, she took a small piece of flesh between thumb and forefinger, and nipped.

He grimaced.

'You felt that?'

He swallowed hard, and nodded. At the back of his mind he was noting that there was a feeling of unreality about the moment, as if he'd somehow slipped into a dream situation.

Norma was feeling exactly the same way. 'You're certain? You're not just imagining it?'

Had he imagined it? Was it just wishful thinking? 'Pinch me again.' She did, and this time he laughed, a laugh that died and choked in his throat. A hint of tears gleamed in his eyes. 'That was quite, gloriously painful.'

She lightly tickled the same spot. 'How about that?'

'Yes.' Nodding vigorously. 'Yes, yes!'

She moved further down his left calf. 'And there?'

'Yes ... no ... I'm not sure.'

The nip she now gave him was the most vicious yet, it left an angry red weal on his skin.

'Definitely. But nowhere near as much sensation as further up.'

She quickly went over his entire lower torso, but there was only one small section that registered feeling. The section was roughly circular, and about four to five inches in diameter.

Midge reached behind him and touched the area for himself. 'Do you think this might be the start ...?' He trailed off.

'I honestly don't know. What I do know is that when I rubbed you there yesterday you felt nothing.'

He tickled himself, and what had been a gleam of wet became actual tears which welled in his eyes, spilling over to trickle down his cheeks. 'I must go back to Ruchill right away and report this to the doctors there,' he husked.

'Yes, right away,' she agreed.

'Oh Norma!'

She took the hand he held out to her, and clasped it tightly to her bosom. Bending over she kissed a tear-stained cheek.

Half an hour later, Midge bubbling over with excitement, they pulled up in front of the hospital's main entrance.

Norma let herself in through the cemetery gates as she did every Sunday, and started down the path that would lead, via a side path, to the grave. She was several rows behind the one the grave was located on when she spotted him. She hadn't seen the

419

Lagonda out on the street so he must have parked it round a corner. Or perhaps he'd changed his car as she herself had.

She stopped, and stared at him. He was standing sort of hunched up with his hair, longish and unkempt, flapping in the stiff breeze. His shoulders were shaking.

She walked a little closer and saw that he'd brought a bunch of flowers which he'd laid on the grave. Then she got a good look at his face and understood what Vivienne had meant by him being a man demented.

A man demented and riven with guilt, Vivienne had said, both plainly obvious to Norma. His contorted, agonised expression showed only too clearly the depth and agony of his emotions. Douglas Ross, her husband, was living in hell.

She had the urge to go to him, to speak. But couldn't bring herself to do so. Turning, she walked silently back up the path. She'd drive round for a bit, then return later.

The party was Norma's idea, and had come to her during one of the daily visits to Ruchill that had followed the localised return of sensation to Midge's left calf. Sensation that had swiftly begun to spread out from the original area, and then appeared also in the right leg.

When it was eventually confirmed that he would be able to walk again – and what a joyous never-to-be-forgotten day that had been! – Midge had declared to Norma that he was going to continue to keep his new progress secret from his parents until such time as he was able to give them the surprise of their lives by going to Cubie Street and walking in on them.

Norma's idea was, rather than surprise the Hendersons, then surprise all their friends and relatives piecemeal, why not surprise the entire kit and caboodle at once? Midge had thought that a terrific suggestion and so, with his legs technically fully operational again, Norma had gone ahead and arranged the party they were now at. And the venue? Where else but the big rear room of Dow's pub.

Norma smiled to herself. *Was* it her healing hands that had brought life back to Midge's lower torso? Or was that something which would have happened anyway? Only God had the answer to that and, as the saying went, he wasn't telling. Her smile widened a fraction. As far as she was concerned the whys and wherefores were irrelevant, the important thing was that Midge was back on his pins again.

Norma brought herself out of her reverie to gaze about her. Alice and Leslie Henderson were chaffing with their daughter Katy who'd come over with her husband from Northern Ireland for the occasion. And beside them Beryl and Bob Gillespie who'd helped her and Midge with their dancing all those years ago when she and Midge were first starting out.

And there were the Fullartons and Reids. While across on the far side talking to Granda McNaughton from number 22 was Rodney Creighton. She had rung Creighton personally to invite him to the party, and had hinted heavily that, in the light of the last conversation they'd had, he might find it more than interesting. He was the only person at the party who had any inkling what the celebration was all about.

Eileen and Finlay, looking radiantly happy, went gliding by, dancing to a foxtrot the small band was playing. If an odd match, it was certainly proving a successful one Norma thought. And now there was talk of Finlay opening his own dance studio with Eileen as a partner. She might invest some money in that, she contemplated. And decided there and then she would.

She glanced at her watch. The party had been going for an hour and forty minutes, long enough for it to get warmed up and for those who drank to have something of a bucket. She judged the time was ripe.

'Now?' she asked Midge who was beside her in his wheelchair.

He looked round the hall, came back to her and nodded. 'Now,' he agreed.

She went up to the band, and had a word with them when they'd finished the foxtrot. She then returned to Midge and pushed his wheelchair out into the centre of the room. 'Ladies and gentleman can I have your attention please!' Norma called out. As the chatter and general hubbub died away she noted that Creighton was staring at her very expectantly indeed.

When she had silence she went on. 'Many of you are wondering why Midge and I are holding this party. We told you when we invited you that the reason for it was an extremely important one, but didn't say what that reason was. Friends, relatives, neighbours, we'd now like to show you that reason.'

Whispering broke out, folk speculating amongst themselves.

Norma again appealed for silence, which she got. 'As most of you will know Midge and I were professional dancers in the thirties, the last occasion we danced together being the night we won the All Scotland Dance Championship.' She paused for effect. 'Until tonight that is.'

She signalled the band who struck up, as she'd instructed them, an old-fashioned waltz. She then held out a hand to Midge who accepted it, and rose from his wheelchair.

Somebody screamed. For the most part people just stood and sat there, goggling at what was taking place, looking stunned.

'It's been a long time, Midge.'

'A long long time,' he agreed, taking her into his arms. And with that they moved off round the floor.

As they danced Norma began to cry. The first time she'd done so since Lindsay's death, and losing the baby.

Midge was driving them home; since getting the power of his legs back he drove at every opportunity. Like walking, it was something he'd come to believe he'd never do again.

'Creighton was right, we were lucky we never gave anyone a heart attack,' he said.

'I should have thought of that you know. Wouldn't it have been awful if that had happened? Thank God it didn't.'

'Thank God for more than that,' he stated quietly.

'Yes,' she agreed in the same hushed, almost reverential, tone of voice.

Midge took a deep breath. 'I want to return to the States, Norma, that's the place for me. My legs are getting stronger all the time, and their movement improving. If they go on as they are there's every hope that I can dance professionally again. But if it turns out I can't I can always develop my writing and earn a living from that. In fact I wouldn't mind being a screenwriter at all. A screenwriter of musicals say.' He glanced at her in the darkness. Since she'd given him the typewriter he'd written and sold a number of stories to various magazines. The response from the magazines and public alike was that there was no doubt he had a career ahead of him as a writer if he so chose. 'You're going to enjoy it in California, I know you will. And just as soon as you're divorced we'll get married.'

She'd known he was going to ask her this, but until she'd got

422

to dance with him in the big rear room of Dow's pub hadn't known what her answer would be. When she'd started to cry it was as though a purging was taking place, a purging that had sorted all manner of things out for her, and left her seeing clearly, aware of where her path lay. 'I won't be coming with you, Midge, nor will I be getting divorced. I'm returning to Douglas.'

Midge was shocked to hear that. He'd thought it was all finished between Norma and Douglas. 'But I love you,' he protested, 'and always have done. And although you haven't said, I'd come to believe you still loved me.'

'I do love you Midge, and always have done just as you have me. But now you're better I know our futures aren't together. Mine is with Douglas, my husband, whom I also love.' She paused, then added, 'You and I came together a second time because we both needed each other. Now you can walk again and I . . . well I'm healed as well. What I must do now is go to Douglas and help him, give him all the understanding, support and forgiveness that I'm able.'

'Will he want you back?' Midge asked desperately.

'Oh yes, I'm certain of that.'

'Perhaps if you and I were to talk further. There's also the possibility of us resuming our partnership. I haven't even touched on that yet.'

'No Midge. You have your way to go, and I mine,' she said firmly, and with finality.

They drove for about a mile during which neither of them spoke. Then Midge said, his voice crackling at the edges, 'I want you to remember this. If ever you need anything, if there's anything you ever want me to do, you only have to write or phone.'

'Thank you.'

'If only bloody Zelda had never come to Glasgow!' he suddenly exploded vehemently.

With tenderness and affection she replied. 'Thinking about it, maybe what happened with Zelda was for the best. You longed to travel, see the world, whereas at the time that didn't appeal to me at all. If we had married then the odds are that you would have come to resent me after a while, resent me for tying you down. We may have loved one another, but with hindsight, I doubt very much the marriage would have lasted.' She smiled softly, and in a voice that matched her smile added, 'Let's face it Midge, you and I just weren't to be. Not then, not now.'

Douglas must have been standing behind the door for she'd no sooner knocked it than it swung open. 'Hello Norma,' he said.

'Hello.'

'Come in, come in. It's not much I'm afraid, but it suits me for the time being.' She glimpsed a tiny kitchen, then she was in the living-room.

'Students usually live in these flats so they're fairly plainly done out,' he explained.

It wasn't that bad actually, she thought, gazing about. A woman's hand would soon work wonders.

'I must admit I was surprised when you telephoned me at the hospital.'

She took off her coat and hat, and gave them to him. He looked absolutely appalling, quite ghastly. 'If you want me, I'd like to come back to you.'

His body jerked all over, as if he'd been given a jolt of electricity. 'Eh?'

'I said, if you wish I'll come back to you. We'll be man and wife again.'

He stared at her, hardly daring to believe his ears. 'Yes,' he answered simply.

'Are you sure? Things weren't all that good between us before the ... before the accident. They'd deteriorated considerably.'

He sat facing her, and ran a hand through his snow-white hair. 'That was all my fault. Working too hard, finding it difficult to fit back into civvy street. And then there were the nightmares you see, I never really spoke to you about those. Nightmares, or the same nightmare over and over again that has haunted me ever since the last field assignment I went on. That day in the garden with Lindsay I fell asleep because I was so tired, so terribly tired. I'd had the nightmare the night before and been awake for hours before getting up.' He stopped and sighed. A lost, lonely sound that seemed to come from the very depths of his being.

'I've asked you to tell me about that last field assignment in the past, but you never have. Do you want to now?'.

He lit a cigarette with trembling hands. Took a deep drag, and blew the smoke savagely away. 'After Corsica, and even though I was known to the Gestapo, I agreed to return to France. It was something directly connected with Oberon Circuit, and my responsibility.' He recounted the story, quietly, but clearly, reliving it all yet again. Finally he finished.

'That, then Lindsay and the miscarriage to live with. Poor Gabriel,' she whispered.

He looked at her through tortured eyes. 'I've wanted you back more than anything Norma. You coming here today and saying what you have has been a dream come true.'

'There's something you must know though, something I have to tell you.' Now he listened while she recounted about her and Midge.

'And Midge has gone?' Douglas asked after he'd digested her story.

'He flew out of Prestwick this morning. I saw him off.' She gazed deep into those tortured eyes. 'Do you still want us to get back together?'

'Yes,' he repeated.

'A new start Douglas. As from this moment, a new start.'

'Do you wish me to come and stay in this house of yours?'

She shook her head. 'That wouldn't be right. I'll sell it. You and I will stay here in your flat until I can find,' she corrected, 'until *we* can find a house of our own. Just one condition though, I would prefer it to be on the north side, in a completely opposite direction to Burnside and Blairbeth Road.'

'In the opposite direction,' he agreed. 'We'll go as far out on the north side as you like.'

There was a little pause, then she said softly. 'That's it then.'

'That's that.'

They both rose. 'I brought a case with me. It's in the boot of the Austin 12 that's parked outside. Would you care to go and get it for me?'

He crossed to her, reached up and tapped on her jawline.

I love you Norma.

'And I love you too.'

'Give me your keys and I'll get that case.'

She kissed him, a shy tentative kiss as though they were kissing for the first time. 'Have you eaten?' she asked suddenly.

Then, when he shook his head, 'Would you like me to make us some supper?'

'I've only got eggs in.'

'Milk?'

'There are two full pints.'

'So how about an omelette?'

He grinned. 'Sounds marvellous. And I have a bottle of wine. A rather special St Emilion.'

'Omelette and St Emilion it is.'

Now he kissed her, a darting peck on the lips. 'Do you want me to show you where things are?'

'You get my case. I'll find what I need.'

When he was gone from the flat she went into the kitchen, which was so tiny you couldn't have swung the proverbial cat in it, and sure enough quickly found what she was after.

She cracked a couple of eggs into a bowl, added milk and salt, and as she beat the mixture began to sing. A happy song.